Paula Gu... ...enior editor ... the annua... ...ar's ...est Dark Fant... ...or... ...ology series. H... ...revious anthologies include *Embraces; Best New Paranor... Romance; Zombies: The Recent Dead; Vampires: The Recent Undead; New Cthulhu: The Recent Weird, Halloween, Brave New Love, Witches: Wicked, Wild and Wonderful, Obsession, Extreme Zombies, Rock On: The Greatest Hits of Science Fiction and Fantasy, Ghosts: Recent Hauntings, Season of Wonder, Future Games* and *Weird Detectives: Recent Investigations*. She edited the Juno Books fantasy imprint for six years from its incarnation in small press and then for Simon & Schuster's Pocket Books. Guran has been honoured with two Bram Stoker Awards and two World Fantasy Award nominations.

THE MAMMOTH BOOK OF
ANGELS
and
DEMONS

Edited by
PAULA GURAN

ROBINSON

RUNNING PRESS
PHILADELPHIA · LONDON

Constable & Robinson Ltd.
55–56 Russell Square
London WC1B 4HP
www.constablerobinson.com

First published in the UK by Robinson,
an imprint of Constable & Robinson Ltd., 2013

A copy of the British Library Cataloguing in Publication
Data is available from the British Library

UK ISBN: 978-1-78033-799-9 (paperback)
UK ISBN: 978-1-78033-800-2 (ebook)

1 3 5 7 9 10 8 6 4 2

First published in the United States in 2013 by Running Press Book Publishers,
A Member of the Perseus Books Group

Books published by Running Press are available at special discounts for bulk purchases
in the United States by corporations, institutions, and other organizations. For
more information, please contact the Special Markets Department at the Perseus
Books Group, 2300 Chestnut Street, Suite 200, Philadelphia, PA 19103, or call
(800) 810-4145, ext. 5000, or e-mail special.markets@perseusbooks.com.

US ISBN: 978-0-7624-4937-8
US Library of Congress Control Number: 2012944621

9 8 7 6 5 4 3 2 1
Digit on the right indicates the number of this printing

Running Press Book Publishers
2300 Chestnut Street
Philadelphia, PA 19103-4371

Visit us on the web!
www.runningpress.com

Printed and bound in the UK

For John Shirley,
a man who knows both angels and demons.

Contents

Introduction: Things Are Complicated

Paula Guran

> Those who consider the Devil to be a partisan of Evil and angels to be warriors for Good accept the demagogy of the angels. Things are clearly more complicated.
> – Milan Kundera, *The Book of Laughter and Forgetting*

The combination of the angelic with the demonic is not a pairing of opposites: angels fall and demons sometimes seek redemption. Despite Western religion's tendency to define the one as purely "good" and the other as completely "evil", other religions, mythologies, traditions and folklore do not always hold fast to that dichotomy. Today, humankind's fascination – even *belief*, as numerous polls substantiate – in these supernatural entities remains as strong or stronger than ever. Of course, modern ideations of what angels and demons are may be totally secular, indifferent to established religion, or vaguely based on past traditions and embroidered with more recent notions.

Storytellers, like the imaginative and talented ones assembled here, often provide us with new ways of looking at old concepts or devise entirely new visions of demons and angels. Their ideas are sometimes spurred by the concept of good versus evil, but they often find the gray area between the two even more inspiring.

This is an anthology of speculative fiction, not an exploration of angelology or demonology. The stories will delight and provoke without any editorializing, but the more I discovered about angels and demons, the more I felt inclined to include at least a very basic overview here and provide additional tidbits of trivia in story introductions. Please feel free to ignore my non-fictional tangents and simply enjoy these fine tales of fantasy and science fiction solely without editorial intrusion.

Popular interest in both angels and demons – and related beings that dwell between Heaven and Hell – borders on the obsessive.

Current (*Supernatural, Grimm, Once Upon a Time*) and recent television series (the British series *Demons, Buffy the Vampire Slayer, Angel, Touched By an Angel, Charmed*, etc.) bring the angelic and the demonic right into one's home. "Real" demons are encountered on paranormal investigation "reality" shows. CMT, a cable channel, presented *Angels Among Us*, with episodes featuring folks who felt they had been saved by an angel.

Demons are a mainstay of film (*Possession, The Rite*, M. Night Shyamalan's *Devil, Paranormal Activity, To the Devil a Daughter, The Exorcist, Rosemary's Baby, The Omen, The Witches of Eastwick, Hellraiser, Wishmaster, The Devil's Advocate, The Ninth Gate, End of Days, Hellboy*, etc.), gaming (*Diablo, Doom, World of Warcraft*, others) and comics.

Angels have entertained us on the silver screen from the 1940s (*Here Comes Mr Jordan, It's a Wonderful Life, Stairway to Heaven, Heaven Only Knows*, etc.) through the eighties and nineties (*Date With an Angel, Ghost, Angels in the Outfield, The Prophecy, City of Angels, What Dreams May Come, Michael, Wide Awake, Dogma*, etc.) and into the current century (*Down to Earth, Constantine, Legion*). Angels appear on television (*Touched by an Angel, Teen Angel, Fallen, Saving Grace, Highway to Heaven*, and more), fly through video games (*Sacred 2, Fallen Lords, Aion, Heaven*, others) and comics as well.

Writers from Dante to C. S. Lewis to Stephen King have dealt fictionally with the devil or demons. This figure of many guises – adversary, trickster, rebel, tempter – has appeared in countless tales. Demons, like vampires before them, have even become romantic heroes and heroines, seductive enemies, and fascinating supporting characters in bestselling fantasy series from Kim Harrison, Richelle Mead, Kelley Armstrong and others.

In modern entertainment, demons and devils may be portrayed as forces of great supernatural evil: incorporeal, or taking benign human visage, or hideous form. They can be fallen angels . . . or not. They may torture the damned in the fires of Hell or connive to lead humans to sell their souls. Demons might be cute little red tricksters with horns and pitchforks. Or they are God's foes who Jesus will defeat in the Battle of Armageddon. Some see the Devil and his demons as a path to power and magic. For others, demons are just difficult monsters to be defeated in role-playing and video games.

Angels – messengers, guardians, warriors; fearsome or friendly, sexy or innocent; godly or fallen – have ascended of late in bestselling fantasy literature: Anne Rice had a series of novels concerning angels. Danielle Trussoni's *Angelology* was a *New York Times* bestseller in 2010 and a sequel is expected. Paranormal and urban fantasy series with angels in major and supporting roles include those by Cassandra Clare, Sharon Shinn, Faith Hunter, Nalini Singh and more.

Otherworldy aliens, fluffy-winged babies with haloes, spiritual guides, protectors, the foci of meditation – whether obvious or disguised as mere humans, many find comfort in a belief in angels that has no direct connect with traditional religion.

But whatever we believe or imagine demons and angels are, ancient myth and religion probably supplied at least part of our ideas.

Angels and demons – or their close equivalents – exist in many cultures and religions. These spiritual beings mediate between humans and the domain of the transcendent and holy or the realm of that which brings misfortune or opposes the holy. In Western religions, angels are seen as benevolent and demons as malevolent. But the roles of these intermediaries are not so clear-cut in Eastern religions and more ancient belief systems. They often can be both righteous and wicked and can switch roles as needed.

The ancient Greeks considered a *daemon*[1] to be a spirit or demigod. Depending on the source and era, they played a number of roles – including that of a guardian spirit – but they could be either good or evil. Although we derive the English word *demon* from this Greek word, it came to mean a supernatural being that troubles, tempts, or brings woe (including illness and bad luck) to humankind. Sometimes the demon's power could then be harnessed by a magician or summoned and controlled by sorcery.

The Jews were influenced by Egyptian, Chaldean and Persian beliefs in good and evil spirits. In the Hebrew Bible, there are two types of demons, the *se'irim* ("hairy beings") and the *shedim*. The *se'irim* resembled goatish satyrs and were described as dancing in the wilderness. Sacrifices were offered to both and they seem to be more akin to the pre-Islamic jinn – a supernatural being that could be either good or bad – rather than evil demons. In popular lore, the early Hebrews may have seen demons as ungodly creatures from a netherworld, which either acted on their own or were ruled by a particular devil.

That demons or unclean spirits were thought to exist in Judea 2,000 years ago is borne out in the New Testament. According to the gospels, Jesus cast out many demons causing various afflictions. Some of the disciples cast out demons by uttering the Messiah's name.

By the time the last books of the New Testament were written, demons were associated by Christians with "fallen angels" – followers of Satan/the Devil, an angel who rebelled against God and was cast out from heaven. (The Devil was also the serpent that convinced Eve to disobey God, and the tempter

---

1   Or *daimon*, another spelling.

of Job and Jesus.) Satan's intent was to lead mortals away from God; demons (or lowercase "devils") assisted him in his goal.

Using the few references to demons and Satan in the New Testament, especially the Book of Revelation – in which the ultimate battles between God and the Devil were envisioned – Christian theologians began postulating more complicated beliefs about the demonic.

Similarly, although not truly a part of Judaic theology, rabbis, Talmudists, and later medieval scholars – with the exception of Maimonides (1135–1204) and Abraham ibn Ezra (1089–1164) – accepted them as real. Rabbis eventually developed a classification of demons.

The Kabbalah – a mystical school of thought not taken seriously by most Jews but integral to Chasidic Judaism – has a vast demonology of its own. Under the influence of Kabbalah, popular belief in demons became widespread and even influenced Christian scholars constructing their own demonologies.

Although other mythologies and religions posit helpful guardian spirits and supernatural messengers from the gods, angels are specific to the three Abrahamic religions. Angels were mentioned in the Hebrew Bible, but angelic mythology was greatly expanded between 530 BCE and 70 CE in non-biblical Judaic literature, particularly the Book of Enoch[2] which includes an angel hierarchy, describes different types of angels and provides several with names. As with demons, the mystic Kabbalah also developed an influential angelology.

Islam views angels as beings who have no free will and only obey God. They praise God and ask forgiveness for humans. Angels act as messengers for God and perform other tasks. In Islamic tradition, Muslims have two recording angels – *kirman katiban* ("honourable scribes") – named Raqib and Atid that note all of a person's good or bad deeds.

---

2   The Book of Enoch is sometimes referred to as 1 Enoch, as there are actually three books of Enoch.

Belief in angels is an article of Islamic faith, but Muslims don't have demons per se. According to the Qu'ran, God created three sentient species: angels, jinns and humans. Jinn, like humans, have free will and can choose between good and evil. One early jinn, Iblis, disobeyed God and was condemned to Hell. But God also granted Iblis respite until the final day of judgement. Jinns who chose evil become *shayatin* and Iblis – or Shaytan – rules them. Shaytan and his minions tempt those who are not sincere believers into sin.

The closest mainstream Judaism comes to belief in *the* Devil is a being whose role as accuser and adversary has been assigned to him by God. Demons and dybbuks (dead spirits that possess the living), however, are mentioned in both biblical and rabbinic literature, and are often found in Jewish folk tales and fiction.

Early Christian theologians wrestled with what to believe about angels for several centuries, always fearing adherents would worship them rather than Christ. Eventually deemed acceptable, there was much scholarly discussion of roles, classifications and hierarchies. Much of that tradition is still kept by the Roman Catholic Church.

Martin Luther (1483–1563) was more concerned with the corruption Satan and his demons could bring to humans than dealing with angels. He acknowledged angels as providential agents of God, but nixed praying to them (or the saints) or regarding them as "helpers in time of need" or as assigned to individual functions. John Calvin (1509–1564), even more concerned with the demonic, kept strictly to scripture and further downplayed the angelic. Later Protestant theologians continued in this vein.

The division continues to this day. Catholic doctrine affirms that prayers can be made to angels asking for intercession. Protestants only pray directly to God.

Although there is now a great diversity among Protestant denominations, Protestant belief can be discussed in a general manner. Both Protestants and Catholics agree there are angels, and both accept what is written of angels in the Bible, but they have different Bibles. The Catholic Bible includes the Book of Tobit, which mentions the archangel Raphael; for Protestants the only named angels are Michael, Gabriel and Lucifer. The Catholic Church also accepts traditional teachings about angels not included in the Bible, including other named angels and the role of guardian angels assigned at conception. The recognition of the presence of angels in daily life is also part of the Catholic faith; Protestants differ on the ministry of angels, but few denominations emphasize them. Protestants do not accept the nine choirs of angel hierarchy, while Catholics have a long, if unofficial, tradition recognizing seraphim, cherubim, thrones, dominions, virtues, powers, principalities, archangels and angels. In worship services, Protestants mention angels primarily at Christmas and Easter while Catholics are reminded they worship with the angels, archangels and hosts of heaven. The Roman Church also observes two angelic feasts: the Feast of the Archangels (29 September) and the Feast of Guardian Angels (2 October).

Christian fundamentalist Billy Graham's 1975 book, *Angels: God's Secret Agents,* spurred new angelic interest among many Protestants, but Graham's lessons stayed strictly within the confines of his interpretation of the (Protestant) Bible.

The Catholic Church noted a rise in angelic popularity during the twentieth century. Given in a series of six General Audiences from 9 July to 20 August 1996, the Catechesis on the Holy Angels by Pope John Paul II reaffirmed the existence, mission and role of the angels, including the Church's faith in the guardian angels, their veneration in liturgy and feast, and "recommending recourse to their protection by frequent prayer".

As for demons, the Pope also reminded the faithful of the reality and presence of Satan and "that in certain cases the evil spirit goes so far as to exercise his influence not only on material things, but even *on man's body* so that one can speak of 'diabolical possession'." In 2004, Pope John Paul II asked Cardinal Ratzinger (now Pope Benedict XVI) to direct bishops to appoint and train more exorcists in their dioceses.

Whether you abide by mainstream faith or seek your own path, there's far more to know about angels and demons than my limited space can convey. For me, they are both equally fascinating . . . but then, maybe the devil made me write that . . . or an unseen angel guided my thoughts . . .

Paula Guran
9 September 2012

Now I Lay Me Down to Sleep

Suzy McKee Charnas

In this entertaining and thoughtful story, Rose Baum, an atheist suicide, meets her guardian angel. The angel also serves as a psychopomp (from the Greek word for "guide of souls"). Although not always portrayed as angels, psychopomps act as non-judgemental guides for the recently dead. In Rose's case, her angel-guide provides her with a way to delay what she thinks awaits her in the afterlife . . . and we learn an interesting explanation for both ghosts and vampires.

After Rose died, she floated around in a nerve-wracking fog for a time looking for the tunnel, the lights, and other aspects of the near-death experience as detailed in mass-media reports of such events.

She was very anxious to encounter these manifestations since apparently something loomed in the offing, in place of the happy surcease of consciousness her father had insisted on as the sequel to death. The older she had grown, the more inclined Rose had been to opt for Papa Sol's opinion. Maybe he would show up now trying to explain how he was right even though he was wrong, a bewildered figure of light along with Mom and Nana and everybody?

It would be nice to see a familiar face. Rose felt twinges of panic laced with a vague resentment. Here she was with the gratifyingly easy first step taken, and nothing was going on. Since she was still conscious, shouldn't there be something to exercise that consciousness on?

A siren wailed distantly. Suddenly she found herself walking on – or almost on, for her feet made only the memory of contact – the roof of her apartment building with its expensive view eastward across Central Park. She hadn't been to the park in years, nor even outside her own apartment. Her minute terrace had provided quite enough contact with the streets below. As far as Rose was concerned, these streets were not the streets she had grown up in. She preferred the comfortable security of her own apartment.

Being on the roof felt very odd, particularly since it seemed to be broad daylight and cold out. Far below in the street she could see one of the doormen waving down a cab; he wore his overcoat with the golden epaulets on the shoulders. Rose could have sworn she had taken her carefully hoarded pills late at night, in the comfortable warmth of 14C. Why else would she be wearing her blue flannel nightgown?

Turning to go back to the refuge of her own place, she found an Angel standing close behind her. She knew him – it? – at once by its beautifully modeled, long-toed feet, the feet of a Bernini Angel she had seen in an Italian church on a tour with Fred. Indeed, the entire form was exactly that of the stone Angel she remembered, except that the exposed skin was, well, skin-toned, which she found unsettling. Like colorizing poor old Humphrey Bogart.

"Leave me alone," she said. "I don't want to go."

"You'll go," the Angel said in a drifting, chiming voice that made her ears itch. "Eventually. Everyone does. Are you sure you want to stand out there like that? I wouldn't say anything, but you're not really used to it yet."

Rose looked down and discovered that she had unwittingly backed off or through or over the parapet and now hovered nineteen stories above the street. She gasped and flailed about, for though she had no body to fall – nor for that matter arms to flail or breath to gasp with – sensory flashes still shot along her shadowy, habitual nerve pathways.

Thus the Angel's fingers closed, cool and palpable, on hers and lifted her lightly back onto the roof. She snatched her hand back at once. No one had touched her in years except her doctor, and that didn't count.

But it was not really the Angel's touch she feared.

"I don't want to go anywhere," she said, unable to bring herself to mention by name the anywhere she did not wish to go. "I'm a suicide. I killed myself."

"Yes," the Angel said, clasping its hands in front of its chest the way Dr Simkin always used to do when he was about to say something truly outrageous. But it said nothing more.

"Well, how does—how do you, um, all feel about that, about people who kill themselves?" She knew the traditional answer, but dared to hope for a different one.

The Angel pursed its perfect lips. "Grouchy," it replied judiciously.

Unwillingly Rose recalled instances from the Old Testament of God's grouchiness. Actually there had been no Bible in her parents' house. She had read instead a book of bible stories slipped to her one birthday by Nana and kept hidden from Papa Sol. Even watered down for kids, the stories had been frightening. Rose trembled.

"I was brought up an atheist," she said faintly.

The Angel answered, "What about the time you and Mary Hogan were going to run away and enter a convent together?"

"We were kids, we didn't know anything," Rose objected. "Let me stay here. I'm not ready."

"You can't stay," the Angel said. Its blank eyes contrasted oddly with its earnest tone of voice. "Your soul without its body is light, and as memories of the body's life fade, the spirit grows lighter, until you'll just naturally rise and drift. "Drift? Drift where?" Rose asked.

"Up," the Angel said. Rose followed the languid gesture of one slender hand and saw what might to living eyes seem just a cloud bank. She knew it was nothing of the kind. It was a vast, angry, looming presence of unmistakable portent.

She scuttled around trying to put the Angel between herself and the towering form. At least the face of cloud was not looking at her. For the moment. Luckily there was lots else to look down disapprovingly at in New York City, most of it a good deal more entertaining than Rose Blum.

She whispered urgently to the Angel, "I changed my mind, I want to go back. I can see now, there are worse things than having your cats die and your kids plan to put you away someplace for your own good. Let them, I'll go, they can have my money, I don't care."

"I'm sorry," the Angel said, and Rose suddenly saw herself from above, not her spirit self but her body, lying down there in the big white tub. The leaky old faucets still dribbled in a desultory way, she noted with an exasperated sigh. Her "luxury" building had high ceilings and the rooms were sizable, but the plumbing was ancient.

Her pale form lay half submerged in what looked like rust-stained water. Funny, she had forgotten entirely that after the pills she had taken the further step of cutting her wrists in the bath. The blue nightgown was an illusion of habit.

Not a bad body for her age, she reflected, though it was essentially an Old World model, chunky flesh on a short-boned frame. The next generation grew tall and sleek, a different species made for playing tennis and wearing the clothes the models in the magazines wore. Though her granddaughter Stephanie, now that she thought of it, was little, like Rose herself; petite, but not so wide-hipped, an improved version of the original import with a flavor of central Europe and probably an inclination to run to fat if allowed.

Good heavens, somebody was in there, also looking at her – two men, Bill the super and Mr Lum the day concierge! Rose recoiled, burning with shame. Her vacated body couldn't even make the gestures of modesty.

They were talking, the two of them. She had given them generous holiday tips for years to repay them for helping her organize a life that had never required her to leave her apartment after Fred's death and the consequent money squabbles in the family.

Bill said, "Two mil at least, maybe more on account of the terrace."

Mr Lum nodded. "Forgot the terrace," he said.

She wished she hadn't tipped them at all. She wished her body didn't look so – well – dead. Definitively dead.

"Okay, I can't go back," she admitted to the Angel, relieved to find herself alone with it on the roof again. "But there must be something I can do besides go – you know." She shuddered, thinking of the monstrous shape lowering above her – a wrathful, a terrible, a vengeful God. She needed time to get used to the idea, after Papa Sol and a lifetime of living in the world had convinced her otherwise. Why hadn't somebody told her?

Well, somebody besides Mary Hogan, who had been a Catholic, for crying out loud.

"Well," the Angel said, "you can postpone."

"Postpone," Rose repeated eagerly. "That's right, that's exactly what I had in mind. How do I postpone?"

The Angel said, "You make yourself a body out of astral material: this." Its slim hand waved and a blur of pale filaments gathered at the tapered fingertips.

"Where did that stuff come from?" Rose said nervously. Was the Angel going to change form or disintegrate or do something nasty like something in a horror movie?

"It's all around everybody all the time," the Angel said, "because the physical world and the non-physical world and everything in between interpenetrate and occupy the same space and time interminably."

"I don't understand physics," Rose said.

"You don't need to," the Angel said. "Astral sculpting is easy, you'll get the hang of it. With a body made of this, you can approach living people and ask them to help you stay. At night, anyway – that's when they'll be able to see you."

Rose thought of Bill and Mr Lum standing there talking about the value of her apartment. Then she thought of her kids whom she hadn't liked for quite a while and who didn't seem to like her either. Not much use asking them for anything. Maybe Frank, the elevator man? He had always struck her as decent.

"Help, how?" she asked.

"By letting you drink their blood," said the Angel.

Appalled, Rose said nothing for a moment. Down below, a taxi pulled in at the awning and disgorged a comically fore-shortened figure. Rose watched this person waddle into the building. "Drink their blood," she said finally. "I'm supposed to go around drinking blood, like Dracula?"

The Angel said, "You need the blood to keep you connected with the physical world. But you can't take it against a person's will, you have to ask. That's the meaning of the business about having to be invited into the donor's house. The house is a metaphor for the physical shell—"

"I'm a vampire?" Rose cried, visions of Christopher Lee and Vampirella and the rest from late-night TV flashing through her stunned mind.

"You are if you want to put off going up," the Angel said with a significant glance skyward. "Most suicides do."

Rose didn't dare look up and see if the mighty cheek of cloud had turned her way.

"That's why suicides were buried at crossroads," the Angel went on, "to prevent their return as vampires."

"Nobody gets buried at a crossroad!"

"Not now," the Angel agreed, "and cremation is so common; but ashes don't count. It's no wonder there's a vampire craze in books and movies. People sense their presence in large numbers in the modern world."

"This is ridiculous," Rose burst out. "I want to see some-body senior to you, I want to talk to the person in—"

She stopped. The Person in charge was not likely to be sympathetic.

The Angel said, "I'm just trying to acquaint you with the rules."

"I'm dead," Rose wailed. "I shouldn't have rules!"

"It's not all bad," the Angel said hastily. "You can make your astral body as young as you like, for instance. But sunlight is a problem. Living people have trouble seeing astral material in sunlight."

For the first time in years she wished Fred were around, that con man. He could have found a way out of this for her if he'd felt like showing off.

"It's not fair!" Rose said. "My G— Listen, what about crosses? Am I supposed to be afraid of crosses?"

"Well," the Angel said, "in itself the cross is just a cross, but there's the weight of the dominant culture to consider, and all its symbols. When Western people see a cross, what are they most likely to think of, whether they're personally Christians or not?"

Rose caught herself in time to avoid glancing upward at the shadow giant in the sky. Little charges of terror ran through her so that she felt herself ripple like a shower curtain in a draft. No poor scared dead person would be able to hold her astral self together under that kind of stress.

The Angel began to move away from her, pacing solemnly on the air over the street where a cab trapped by a double-parked delivery truck was honking dementedly.

"Wait, wait," Rose cried, ransacking her memory of *Dracula*, which she and her sister had read to each other at night by flashlight one winter. "What about crossing water? Is it true that a vampire can't cross water?"

"Running water can disorient you very severely," the Angel said over its exquisite shoulder. "You could find yourself visiting places you never meant to go to instead of the ones you did."

Water flows downhill, Rose thought. Down. Hell was down, according to Mary Hogan, anyway. She made a shaky mental note: Don't cross running water.

"How am I supposed to remember all this?" she wailed.

The Angel rose straight into the air without any movement of the translucent wings she now saw spreading from its back. "Just think of the movies," it said. "Film is the record of the secret knowledge of the cultural unconscious."

"You sound like Dr Simkin, that terrible shrink my daughter sent me to," Rose accused the floating figure.

"I was Harry Simkin," the Angel replied. "That's why I'm doing your intake work." It folded its aristocratic hands and receded rapidly toward the high, rolling clouds.

"My God, you were a young man," Rose called after it. "Nobody told me you died."

The door onto the roof burst open with a crash and two boys lugging heavily weighted plastic bags tumbled out, shouting. Ignoring Rose, they rushed to the parapet. Each one took a spoiled grapefruit out of one of the bags and leaned out into space, giggling and pointing, choosing a passing car roof to aim for.

Rose sidled up to the smaller one and cleared her throat. As loudly as she could she said, "Young man, how would you like to meet a real vampire?"

He lobbed a grapefruit and ducked behind the parapet, howling in triumph at the meaty sound of impact from below but apparently deaf to Rose's voice. Revolting child. Rose bent over and tried to bite his neck. He didn't seem to notice. But she couldn't unwrap the scarf he wore, her fingers slipped through the fabric. So she aimed for a very small patch of exposed skin, but she had no fangs that she could discover and made no impression on his grimy neck.

The whole thing was a ludicrous failure. Worse, she couldn't imagine how it could work, which did not augur well for her future as a vampire. Maybe the Angel had lied. Maybe it was really a devil in disguise. She had never trusted that Simkin anyway.

Worst of all, she was continually aware of the looming, ever-darkening presence, distant but palpable to her spirit, of Him whom Papa Sol had scoffed at with good socialist scorn. It was all so unfair! Since He was up there after all, why didn't He do something about these horrible boys instead of harassing a poor dead old woman?

Rose didn't want Him witnessing her ineptitude, which might inspire Him to drag her up there to face Him right now. She gave up on the grapefruit-hurling boys and drifted back down to 14C.

It gave her some satisfaction to sift under the sealed apartment door in the form of an astral mist. She floated around admiring the handsomely appointed rooms; she had always had excellent taste.

In the bathroom the tub was empty and reeked of pine-scented disinfectant. Someone had already made off with her silver-backed hairbrush, she noted. But what did that matter, given that her strides were unusually long and slightly bounding, as if she were an astronaut walking on the moon? This could only mean that she was lightening up, just as the Angel had warned.

Frantically she clawed astral material out of the air and patted it into place as best she could, praying that in the absence of blood this astral gunk itself might help to hold her down until somebody came and consented to be a – donor. Her children would come, if only to calculate the considerable value of her things. She was determined to greet them as herself, or as near to that as she could get, to cushion the shock of her request for their donations.

She couldn't see herself in the mirror to check the likeness or to inspect her mouth for fangs. Astral material had a number of limitations, it seemed, among them inability to cast a reflection. She couldn't even turn on the television; her astral fingers wouldn't grip the switch. She couldn't pick up things, the Chinese figurines and fine French clocks that she had brought back from travel and had converted into lamps. Very nice lamps, too. Fred had done his import deals or whatever had been really going on – half the time she had thought him a secret arms trader – but Rose was the one who had had the eye.

My God, she'd been a shopper!

How light she was, how near to drifting – up. No wonder vampires were so urgent about their hunger. By the time Bill the super showed up with two yuppies in tow, Rose felt that for the first time she understood what her daughter Roberta used to mean by that awful phrase "strung out".

Bill was saying, "—first refusal on the lease, that's the law, but if nobody in the old lady's family wants to take it up, then—"

He saw her – the windowpanes, Rose noted, were now dark – and turned red. "I don't know how you got in here, lady, but you'll have to leave."

He didn't seem to recognize her. Of course he wasn't expecting her. Maybe she hadn't done such a hot job with the astral stuff?

She said firmly, "Bill, I have every right to be here, and if these are prospective new tenants you've sneaked in for bribe money, they ought to know that I'm staying."

The young woman said, "Excuse me, but who is this?"

The color drained from Bill's face. He said hoarsely, "What are you doing here, Mrs Blum? You were dead in the tub, I found you." He waved his arms. "You can't stay here!"

"Let's cut the crap, all right?" the young man said. He thrust money at Rose. Several fifties and three of his fingers went through her forearm.

"Ted, she's a ghost," the woman said, clutching at his coat. "She must be the ghost of the woman who died here."

"Well," Ted said, letting his extended hand float slowly back down to his side. "Tiffany, honey, I think you're right. So, uh, what would you think about living in a haunted, I mean, co-occupying with, um? I'm sure we could work something out, a sort of timeshare arrangement? I mean, look at the height of these ceilings."

Rose said, "Sure, we can fix it. All I need is for you to let me drink a little blood now and then. You could take turns."

"Ah, Jesus," sobbed Bill.

Tiffany's eyes bulged. "It's not a ghost," she gasped. "It's a vampire."

"How much blood, exactly?" Ted said, pale but still game.

"I don't exactly know," Rose said. "We'd have to experiment a little at first—"

They fled.

"That's a ten-thousand-dollar finder's fee you cost me!" howled Bill the super, lunging at her.

His breath reached her before he did, and Rose felt her careful astral assemblage fly apart. He had been eating garlic, and the fumes acted on her new body like acid. Her consciousness bounced around like a beach ball in the slipstream of a speeding truck as her body dissolved.

Bill jammed his fist into his mouth and ran, slamming the door so hard behind him that a very nice French Empire miniature fell off the wall.

"Garlic," said a familiar voice. "It's a remarkable food. Completely dissolves the cohesibility of astral material."

Grabbing for errant parts of her body, Rose grumbled, "Why didn't you tell me?"

"I tried to cover everything," the Angel said.

"Listen, Dr Simkin," Rose said. "I can't do this. I'm no vampire. I'm a nice Jewish girl."

"A nice Jewish radical girl, not religious at all," the Angel reminded her. "You named your first cat Emma Goldman."

"We were all freethinkers in those days, but so what? A Jew is a Jew, and Jews don't have vampires. I can't do this blood-drinking thing. It's not natural."

The Angel sighed. "It's your choice, of course, but you'll have to go up. Your life review is overdue as it is."

Rose thought of God reviewing her life. "What about you?" she said desperately. "You must be drinking blood yourself, to be sticking around driving me crazy like this. You could spare me some."

"Oh, no," the Angel said, "I do all my work strictly on the astral, nothing physical at all. I don't need weight."

"Why do you look like that?" Rose said. "Harry Simkin didn't look like that, don't think I don't remember."

"Well, I like it," the Angel answered rather shyly. "And I thought it would reassure you. You always had a good eye for art, Mrs Blum."

"A lot of good it does me now," she said. "Listen, I want to talk to Fred. You know Fred, my husband?"

The Angel cocked its head to one side and rolled its blank eyes. Then it said, "Sorry, he's not available. He's finished his processing and moved on to another stage."

"What stage?" Rose said, feeling a surprising twinge of

apprehension for Fred. She remembered all those *New Yorker* cartoons showing fat-bellied businessmen making glum quips to each other in hell, with pitchfork-toting devils leering in the background.

"Don't you think you have enough to deal with as it is?" the Angel countered. "You're bobbing, you know, and your head isn't on straight. It won't be long at this rate."

"I'll find somebody," Rose said quickly. "I need more time to get used to the idea."

"Don't take too long," the Angel said. "Isn't it interesting? This is the first time you've asked me about anybody who's come before you."

"What?" said Rose. "Anybody, who? Who should I ask about? I've been on my own for twenty years. Who cares for an old woman, so who should I care for?"

The Angel, inspecting its fingernails again, drifted silently out through the pane of the closed window.

It was very quiet in the apartment. The walls in these old buildings were very thick, with real plaster. Rose had peace and quiet in which to reassemble herself. It wasn't much fun – no point in making yourself look like, say, Marilyn Monroe, if you couldn't see yourself in the mirror – and it wasn't easy, either. At one point she looked down and realized she had formed up the shape of her most recent cat, Mimsy, on a giant scale.

She was losing contact with her physical life, and nobody was likely to come around and help her re-establish it again for a while. Maybe never, if Bill the super went gibbering about what he'd seen in the apartment.

She hovered in front of the family photographs on the wall over the living-room mantel. The light was hard to see by, odd and watery – was it day or night? – but she knew who was who by memory: Papa Sol and Mama; Auntie Lil with that crazed little dog of hers, Popcorn was its name (God, she missed Mimsy, and the others); the two Kleinfeldt cousins who had gone to California and become big shots in television produc-tion; Nana in her old-fashioned bathing suit at Coney Island;

Uncle Herb; more cousins. She had completely lost track of the cousins.

There was one picture of Fred, and several of the two cute babies who had turned into Mark and Roberta. I should have stuck to shopping and skipped the kids, she thought.

Two pictures showed Rose herself, once amid the cousins now scattered to their separate marriages and fates, and once with two school friends, girls whose names now escaped her. As everything seemed bent on escaping her. She sat in the big wing chair and crossed her astral arms and rocked herself, whispering, "Who cares for an old woman?"

There was no help, and no safe place. She had to hold on to the arms of her chair to keep from floating several inches off the seat. If she didn't get some blood to drink soon, she would float up before that huge, angry face in the sky and be cast into hell on a bolt of black thunder . . .

The door opened cautiously and a man walked into the apartment. It was her lawyer, Willard.

"Oh, my God," he murmured, looking straight at her. "They told me the place was haunted. Mrs Blum, is that you?"

"Yes," she said. "What time is it, Willard?"

"Seven thirty," he said, still staring. "I stayed late at the office."

Seven thirty on a November evening; of course he could see her. She hoped her head was on straight and that it was her own head and not Mimsy's.

"Oh, Willard," she said, "I've been having the most terrible time." She stopped. She had never talked to anyone like that, or at least not for a very long time.

"No doubt, no doubt," he said, steadying himself against the hall table and putting his briefcase down carefully on the floor. "Do you still keep Scotch in the breakfront?"

She did, for the occasional visitor, of which scant number Willard had been one. He poured himself a drink with shaking hands and gulped it, his eyes still fixed on Rose. He poured himself another. "I think I'd better tell you," he said in a high, creaky tone very unlike him, "this haunting business could have serious repercussions on the disposition of your estate."

"It's not haunting, exactly," Rose said, gliding toward him. She told him what it was, exactly.

"Ha, ha, you're kidding, Mrs Blum," Willard said, smiling wildly and turning a peculiar shade of yellow. He staggered backward against the edge of the couch, turned, and fell head-long. His glass rolled across the carpet and clinked against the baseboard. Rose saw a pale mist drift out of the top of Willard's head as his body thrashed briefly in the throes of what she immediately recognized as a heart attack like the one that had killed Fred.

"Willard, wait," she cried, seeing that his foggy spirit stuff was rapidly escaping upward into the ceiling. "Don't leave me!"

But he did.

Rose knelt by the body, unable to even attempt to draw its still and cooling blood. The Angel didn't show. Willard Carn-aby must have gone directly wherever he was headed. She felt abandoned and she cried, or something like it, not for Willard, who had known, as usual, where to go and how to get there with a minimum of fuss, but for herself, Rose the vampire.

After they took the body away nobody came for days. Rose didn't dare to go out. She was afraid she would get lost in the uncertain light; she was afraid she would run into the outwash from some restaurant kitchen and be blasted to such smither-eens by garlic fumes that she would never be able to get herself together again; she was afraid of water running in the gutters and crosses on churches. She was afraid of the eyes of God.

She was bumping helplessly against the bedroom ceiling in doomed panic when someone did arrive. Not Roberta (as she at first thought because of the honey-gold hair) but Stephanie, from the next generation; her granddaughter, who wanted to be – what? An actress. She was certainly pretty enough, and so young. Rose blinked hungrily at her.

Someone was with her, a boy. Stephanie pulled back the curtains and daylight streamed in. She would not be able to see Rose, maybe not even hear her.

Rose noticed something new – a shimmer of color and motion around Stephanie, and another around this boy. If she concentrated hard, while floating after them as they strolled through the place giggling and chatting with their heads together, Rose could see little scenes like bits of color TV taking place within the aura of each of the young people: quick little loops of the two of them tangled in each other's arms in his, and a rapid wheel of scenes in Stephanie's aura involving this boy dancing with her, applauding from an excited audience, showing her off to important people.

Their hopes and dreams were visible to Rose, like sit-com scenes without sound. The walking-on-the-beach scene, a comfortable winter beach with gray skies and green sea and no sand fleas Rose recognized at once. She had had the same fantasy about Fred.

While he was having, no doubt, fantasies like this boy's, of sex, sex and more sex; and sex with another girl, some friend of Stephanie's . . .

"Dump him, Stephanie, he's nothing but a wolf," she said indignantly, out loud.

The boy was too rapt in his hormones to hear. Stephanie frowned and glanced sharply around the room.

"Come on," the boy said. "Who'd know? It would be exciting." Good grief, he was proposing that the two of them make love right here – on the floor, on Rose's antique Chinese carpet! Rose saw the little scene clearly in his aura.

Stephanie hesitated. Then she tossed her honey hair and called him an idiot and tugged him out of the place by the hand. But she came back. She came back alone after dark and without turning on the lights she sat down quietly in the big wing chair by the window.

"I heard you, Gramma Rose," she said softly, looking wide-eyed around the room. "I heard what you said to me about Jeff, and you're right, too. I know you're here. The stuff about the apartment being haunted is true, isn't it? I know you're here, and I'm not scared of you. You can come out, you can talk to me. Really. I'd like it."

Rose hung back, timid and confused now that her moment had come. After all, did she really want her grandchild's presumably fond memories of Gramma Rose replaced with the memory of Rose the vampire?

Stephanie said, "I won't go until you come talk to, me, Gramma Rose."

She curled up on Rose's empty bed and went to sleep.

Rose watched her dreams winking and wiggling in her aura. Such an appealing mixture of cynicism and naivety, so unlike her mother. Fascinated, Rose observed from the ceiling where she floated.

Involuntarily reacting to one of the little scenes, she murmured, "It's not worth fighting with your mother; just say yes and go do what you want."

Stephanie opened her eyes and looked directly up. Her jaw dropped. "Gramma Rose," she squeaked. "I see you! What are you doing up there?"

"Stephanie darling," Rose said in the weak, rusty voice that was all she could produce now, "you can help me. Will you help me?"

"Sure," Stephanie said, sitting up. "Didn't you stop me from making an utter idiot of myself with Jeff Stanhope, which isn't his real name of course, and he has a gossip drive on him that just won't quit. I don't know what I was thinking of, bringing him up here, except that he's cute of course, but actors are mostly cute. It's his voice, I think, it's sort of hypnotic. But you woke me up, just like they say, a still, small voice. So what can I do for you?"

"This will sound a little funny," Rose said anxiously – to have hope again was almost more than she could bear – "but could you stand up in the bed and let me try to drink a little blood from your neck?"

"Ew." Stephanie stared up at her. "You're kidding."

Rose said, "It's either that or I'm gone, darling. I'm nearly gone as it is."

"But why would it help to, ugh, suck a person's blood?"

"I need it to weigh me down, Stephanie. You can see how high I'm drifting. If I don't get some blood to anchor me, I'll float away."

"How much do you need?" Stephanie said cautiously.

"From you, darling, just a little," Rose assured her. "You have a rehearsal in the morning, I don't want to wear you out. But if you let me take a little, I can stay, I can talk to you."

"You could tell me all about Uncle Herb and whether he was gay or not," Stephanie said, "and whether Great-Grandpa really left Hungary because of a quarrel with a hussar or was he just dodging the draft like everybody else – all the family secrets."

Rose wasn't sure she remembered those things, but she could make up something appropriate. "Yes, sure."

"Is this going to hurt?" Stephanie said, getting up on her knees in the middle of the mattress.

"It doesn't when they do it in the movies," Rose said. "But, Stephanie, even if there's a little pinprick, wouldn't that be all right? Otherwise I have to go, and . . . and I don't want to."

"Don't cry, Gramma Rose," Stephanie said. "Can you reach?" She leaned to one side and shut her eyes.

Rose put her wavery astral lips to the girl's pale skin, thinking, FANGS. As she gathered her strength to bite down, a warm sweetness flowed into her mouth like rich broth pouring from a bowl. She stopped almost at once for fear of overdoing it.

"That's nice," Stephanie murmured. "Like a toke of really good grass."

Rose, flooded with weight and substance that made her feel positively bloated after her recent starvation, put her arm around Stephanie's shoulders and hugged her. "Just grass," she said, "right? You don't want to poison your poor old dead gramma."

Stephanie giggled and snuggled down in the bed. Rose lay beside her, holding her lightly in her astral arms and whispering stories and advice into Stephanie's ear. From time to time she sipped a little blood, just for the thrill of feeling it sink through her newly solid form, anchoring it firmly to her own familiar bed.

Stephanie left in the morning, but she returned the next day with good news. While the lawyers and the building owners and the relatives quarreled over the fate of the apartment and everything in it (including the ghost that Bill the super wouldn't shut up about), Stephanie would be allowed to move in and act as caretaker.

She brought little with her (an actress has to learn to travel light, she told Rose), except her friends. She would show them around the apartment while she told them how the family was fighting over it, and how it was haunted, which made everything more complicated and more interesting, of course. Rose herself was never required to put in a corroborating appearance. Stephanie's delicacy about this surprised and pleased Rose.

Still, she preferred the times when Stephanie stayed home alone studying her current script, which she would declaim before the full-length mirror in the bedroom. She was a terrible show-off, but Rose supposed you had to be like that to be on the stage.

Rose's comments were always solicited, whether she was visible or not. And she always had a sip of blood at bedtime.

Of course this couldn't go on forever, Rose understood that. For one thing, at the outer edges of Stephanie's aura of thoughts and dreams she could see images of a different life, somewhere cool and foggy and hemmed in with dark trees, or city streets with a vaguely foreign look to them. She became aware that these outer images were of likely futures that Stephanie's life was moving toward. They didn't seem to involve staying at Rose's.

She knew she should be going out to cultivate alternative sources for the future – vampires could "live" forever, couldn't they – but she didn't like to leave in case she couldn't get back for some reason, like running water, crosses, or garlic.

Besides, her greatest pleasure was coming to be that of floating invisibly in the air, whispering advice to Stephanie based on foresight drawn from the flickering images she saw around the girl:

"It's not a good part for you, too screechy and wild. You'd hate it."

"That one is really ambitious, not just looking for thrills with pretty actresses."

"No, darling, she's trying to make you look bad – you know you look terrible in yellow."

Rose became fascinated by the spectacle of her granddaughter's life shaping itself, decision by decision, before her astral eyes. So that was how a life was made, so that was how it happened! Each decision altered the whole mantle of possibilities and created new chains of potentialities, scenes and sequences that flickered and fluttered in and out of probability until they died or were drawn in to the center to become the past.

There was a young man, another one, who came home with Stephanie one night, and then another night. Rose, who drowsed through the days now because there was nothing interesting going on, attended eagerly, and invisibly, on events. The third night Rose whispered, "Go ahead, darling, it wouldn't be bad. Try the Chinese rug."

They tumbled into the bed after all; too bad. The under rug should be used for something significant, it had cost her almost as much per yard as the carpet itself.

Other people's loving looked odd. Rose was at first embarrassed and then fascinated and then bored: bump bump bump, squeeze, sigh, had she really done that with Fred? Well, yes, but it seemed very long ago and sadly meaningless. The person with whom it had been worth all the fuss had been – whatshisname, it hovered just beyond memory.

Fretful, she drifted up onto the roof. The clouds were there, the massive form turned toward her now. She cringed but held her ground. No sign from above one way or the other, which was fine with her.

The Angel chimed, "How are you, Rose?"

Rose said, "So what's the story, Simkin? Have you come to reel me in once and for all?"

"Would you mind very much if I did?"

Rose laughed at the Angel's transparent feet, its high, delicate arches. She was keenly aware of the waiting form of the cloud-giant, but something had changed.

"Yes," she said, "but not so much. Stephanie has to learn to judge things for herself. Also, if she's making love with a boy in the bedroom knowing I'm around, maybe she's taking me a little for granted. Maybe she's even bored by the whole thing."

"Or maybe you are," the Angel said.

"Well, it's her life," Rose said, feeling as if she were breaking the surface of the water after a deep dive, "not mine."

The Angel said, "I'm glad to hear you say that. This was never intended to be a permanent solution."

As it spoke, a great throb of anxiety and anger reached Rose from Stephanie.

"Excuse me," she said, and she dropped like a plummet back to her apartment.

The two young people were sitting up in bed facing each other with the table lamp on. The air vibrated with an anguish connected with the telephone on the bed table. In the images dancing in Stephanie's aura Rose read the immediate past: There had been a call for the boy, a screaming voice raw with someone else's fury. He had just explained to Stephanie, with great effort and in terror that she would turn away from him. The girl was indeed filled with dismay and resentment. She couldn't accept this dark aspect of his life because it had all looked so bright to her before, for both of them.

Avoiding her eyes, he said bitterly, "I know it's a mess. You have every right to kick me out before you get any more involved."

Rose saw the pictures in his aura, some of them concerned with his young sister who went in and out of institutions and, calamitously, in and out of his life. But many showed this boy holding Stephanie's hand, holding Stephanie, applauding Stephanie from an audience, sitting with Stephanie on the porch of a wooden house amid dark, tall trees somewhere . . .

Rose looked at Stephanie's aura. This boy was all over it. Invisible, Rose whispered in Stephanie's ear, "Stick with him, darling, he loves you and it looks like you love him too."

At the same moment she heard a faint echo of very similar

words in Stephanie's mind. The girl looked startled, as if she had heard this too.

"What?" the boy said, gazing at her with anxious intensity.

Stephanie said, "Stay in my life. I'll try to stay in yours."

They hugged each other. The boy murmured into her neck, where Rose was accustomed to take her nourishment, "I was so afraid you'd say no, go away and take your problems with you . . ."

Seeing the shine of tears in the boy's eyes, Rose felt the remembered sensation of tears in her own. As she watched, their auras slowly wove together, flickering and bleeding colors into each other. This seemed so much more intimate than sex that Rose felt she really ought to leave the two of them alone.

The Angel was still on the roof, or almost on it, hovering above the parapet.

Rose said, "She doesn't need me anymore; she can tell herself what to do as well as I can, probably better."

"If she'll listen," the Angel said.

Rose looked down at the moving lights of cars on the street below. "All right," she said. "I'm ready. How do I get rid of the blood I got from Stephanie this morning?"

"You mean this?" The Angel's finger touched Rose's chest, where a warm red glow beat in the place where her heart would have been. "I can get rid of it for you, but I warn you, it'll hurt."

"Do it," Rose said, powered by a surging impatience to get on with something of her own for a change, having been so immersed in Stephanie's raw young life – however long it was now. Time was much harder to divide intelligibly than it had been.

The Angel's finger tapped once, harder, and stabbed itself burningly into her breast. There came a swift sensation of what it must feel like to have all the marrow drawn at once from your bones. Rose screamed.

She opened her eyes and looked down, gasping, at the Angel. Already she was rising like some light, vaned seed on the wind. She saw the Angel point downward at the roof with one glowing, crimson finger. One flick and a stream of bright fire shot down through the shadowy outline of the building and landed – she saw it happen, the borders of her vision were rushing away from her in all directions – in the kitchen sink and ran away down the drain

Stephanie turned her head slightly and murmured, "What was that? I heard something."

The boy kissed her temple. "Nothing." He gathered her closer and rolled himself on top of her, nuzzling her. What an appetite they had, how exhausting!

Other voices wove in and out of their murmuring voices. Rose could see and hear the whole city as it slowly sank away below her, a net of lights slung over the dark earth.

But above her – and she no longer needed to direct her vision to see what was there but saw directly with her mind's eye – the sky was thick with a massed and threatening darkness that she knew to be God: still waiting, scowling, implacable, for His delayed confrontation with Rose.

Despite the panic pulsating through her as the inevitable approached, she couldn't help noticing that there was something funny about God. The closer she got, the more His form blurred and changed, so that she caught glimpses of tiny figures moving, colors surging, skeins of ceaseless activity going on all at once and overlapping inside the enormous cloudy bulk of God.

She recognized the moving figures: Papa Sol, teasing her at the breakfast table by telling her to look, quick, at the horse on the windowsill, and grabbing one of the strawberries from her cereal while she looked with eager, little-girl credulity; Roberta, crying and crying in her crib while grown-up Rose hovered in the hallway torn between exhaustion and rage and love and fear of doing the wrong thing no matter what she did; Fred, sparkling with lying promises he'd never meant to keep, but pleased to entertain her with them; Stephanie, with crooked braids and scabby knees, counting the pennies from the penny jar that Rose had once kept for her. And that was the guy, there, Aleck Mills, one of Fred's associates, with whom love had felt like love.

If she looked beyond these images, Rose realized that she could see, deeper in the maze, the next phase of each little scene, and the next, the whole spreading tangle of consequences that she was here to witness, to comprehend, and to judge.

The web of her awareness trembled as it soared, curling in on itself as if caught in a draught of roasting air.

"Simkin, where are you?" she cried.

"Here," the Angel answered, bobbing up alongside of her and looking, for once, a bit flustered with the effort of keeping up. "And you don't need me anymore. Guardian angels don't need guardian angels."

"Now I lay me down to sleep," Rose said, remembering that saccharine Humperdinck opera she had taken Stephanie to once at Christmas time, years ago, because it was supposed to be for kids. "A bunch of vampires watch do keep?"

"You could put it that way," the Angel said.

"What about Dracula?" Rose said. "Could I have done that instead?"

"Sure," the Angel said. "There's always a choice. Who do you think it is who goes around making deals for the illusion of immortal life? And the price isn't anything as romantic as your soul. It's just a little blood, for as long as you're willing."

"And when you stop being willing?"

The Angel flashed its blank eyes upward. "Your life will wait as long as it has to."

"I'm scared of my life," Rose confessed. "I'm scared there's nothing worthwhile in it, nothing but furniture, and statuettes made into lamps."

"Kid," the Angel said, "you should have seen mine."

"Yours?"

"Full of people I tried to make into furniture, all safe and comfortable, with lots of dust cuzzies stuck underneath."

"What's in mine?" Rose said.

"Go and see," the Angel said gently.

"I am, I'm going," Rose said. In her heart she moaned, This will be hard, this is going to be so hard.

But she was heartened by a little scene flickering high up where God's eye would have been if there had been a god instead of this mountain of Rose's own life, and in that scene Stephanie and the boy did walk together on a winter beach. By the way they hugged and turned up their collars and hurried along, it was cold and windy there; but they kept close together and made blue-lipped jokes about the cold.

Beyond them, beyond the edges of the cloud-mountain itself, Rose could make out nothing yet. Perhaps there was nothing, just as Papa Sol had promised. On the other hand, she thought, whirling aloft, so far Papa Sol had been 100 per cent dead wrong.

Stackalee

Norman Partridge

Stagger Lee – or "Stackalee", "Stackolee", "Stagolee", and other versions – was a real man, Lee Shelton, who murdered William "Billy" Williams on Christmas night, 1895, in St Louis, Missouri. Versions of a song about the incident were sung by African-Americans long before folklorist John Lomax first published one in 1911. Stag Lee became a legend – either bargaining with the Devil before execution or hanged for the murder, but still so powerfully bad he kicks the Devil out and takes over Hell itself. The real Shelton Lee went to prison. Pardoned in 1909, in 1911 he killed another man while robbing his house. Again imprisoned, he was pardoned a second time, but died of tuberculosis in the prison hospital before he could be released. His fictional counterpart lives on, celebrated in song and literature hundreds of times. In Norman Partridge's story, Lee pays a demonic visit to a modern musician who has sung "his" song.

Billy Lyons stared at the painted message above the fireplace. The red letters dripped, still wet, trickling down the grass cloth wallpaper and over the white Fender Stratocaster that hung above the oak mantelpiece. He dropped his car keys, took down the guitar, and wiped its polished body with his shirt-sleeve. The red paint came off too easily, soaking Billy's forearm. The few droplets that remained beaded like water on the instrument's glassy pickguard, trapped beneath the strings.

The Fender slipped from Billy's grip; a gunshot crack sounded as it struck the hardwood floor. Red droplets spit through the strings and spattered Billy's tennis shoes as the instrument bounced once, twice, and then collapsed. He backed away, trembling, not thinking about how much the guitar was worth, not worrying about damage.

Blood, he thought, and for a long moment that was the only word in his vocabulary. *Blood . . . not paint!*

Billy wiped his hands on his jeans and stared at the message. Part of it had been written on the guitar, and now without the instrument mounted on the wall the red letters looked like a puzzle from some twisted game show. But Billy was a winner; he'd been clued in ahead of time and recognized the message well enough. It was the same garbage that had been eating at him for weeks, ever since his recording of "Stackalee" had hit number one.

Where's my magic Stetson? That's what the message had said, just like the postcards he'd been receiving. But this was one hell of a lot worse than a postcard – this had rattled Billy to the bone. Without thinking, he'd smeared the bloody writing and touched things he should have left alone, like the guitar, and the cops would be highly pissed about that. He'd probably screwed the whole crime scene. And with his fingerprints all over everything and blood splattered on his clothes and shoes, he might be accused of setting up the scene himself, for publicity.

The phone rang and Billy snatched it up, expecting to hear the song again, figuring that his tormentors would have their cues planned perfectly. Instead, he was greeted by his agent's voice: "Billy, where are you? You were supposed to be here an hour ago for the costume fitting. We're shooting the 'Stackalee' video tomorrow, remember, and—"

"They've been here, Alan," Billy interrupted. "They've been inside my house. This time they stole a page from Charlie

Manson's playbook and painted a message on the wall. It's about the song again . . . Jesus, I don't care if it is a hit, I wish I would have listened to those old bluesmen and left the damn tune alone."

"Calm down. What'd they write?"

Billy looked at the wall. The blood was dripping over the mantel, dribbling down the stone hearth. The words that had stared at him from the grass cloth were nearly illegible now, just pinkish shadows. "Doesn't matter what they wrote. It was written in blood, that's what matters, and it just dripped away." Billy sighed. "But it was about the hat again. Just some silly shit about magic."

"I want you to call the cops. I'll be there as fast as I can."

"I don't know, Alan. I touched a lot of stuff. I got blood all over my clothes. The cops might think—"

A sharp series of clicks rippled over the line. Billy heard laughter, then the sound of a needle skating across a record.

"Alan? What's going on?"

The answer came in Billy's own voice, singing softly:

At midnight on that stormy night there came an awful wail –
Billy Lyons and a graveyard ghost outside the city jail.
"Jailer, jailer," says Stack. "I can't sleep.
For around my bedside poor Billy Lyons still creeps.
He comes in the shape of a lion with a blue steel in his hand.
For he knows I'll stand and fight if he comes in shape of man.

"Alan, don't pull this shit."

"It's not coming from my end, Billy."

Floorboards complained in an upstairs bedroom. The receiver squawked like a wounded bird and then went quiet. A single thought hit Billy, something he should have realized long before now: if the blood on the wall was fresh enough to drip down the fireplace, the painter couldn't be far away.

"Alan, I think someone's in the house."

"Get out of there. Get the hell out. If you won't go to the cops, come over here . . ."

Billy dropped the receiver and ran for the door. He twisted the knob as his own voice roared at him from somewhere upstairs:

> *Red devil was sayin', "You better hunt your hole;*
> *I've hurried here from hell just to get your soul."*

Billy hit the brakes and the Testarossa screeched to a stop just inches away from a Pinto's rusty bumper. Music slammed at him from six speakers, and he stared at the red light and tried to stop thinking about the blood on his Fender Stratocaster. He popped the clutch when the light turned green and the Testarossa peeled out, whipped up an on-ramp, and roared onto the freeway.

> *Yes, Stackalee, the gambler, everybody knowed his name:*
> *Made his livin' hollerin' high, low, jack and the game.*

Once more, Billy slapped at the tape deck controls, but his effort was useless. In the short time that he'd been in the house, someone had screwed with the deck. The knobs wouldn't turn. The eject button wouldn't work. The deck was caked with some kind of superglue, and the only song that Billy was going to hear tonight was his newest hit, his own version of "Stackalee" cranked up to full volume, over and over—

A horn blared from the right. Billy jerked the wheel and brought the Testarossa back into the fast lane. He glanced at the rear-view mirror and spotted the car he'd nearly side-swiped. A big lemon-yellow Cadillac. The Caddy flipped its brights and pulled behind him.

Shit. Billy eyed the pimpmobile's smoked windows and angry lights, and then he eyed himself in the Testarossa's rear-view mirror. His long blond hair was stringy with sweat (the same hair that *Tiger Beat* always referred to as "Lyons' mane"), and his eyes were swimming with fear.

Billy looked away. He rolled down the window and gulped a

deep breath of winter air as he hit the gas, leaving the Caddy behind.

> *It was on one cold and frosty night*
> *When Stackalee and Billy Lyons had one awful fight.*
> *All about an old Stetson hat.*

Billy stared at the tape deck, his lips curling in disgust. "It'll be a great record, Billy," he said, his voice a lisping imitation of his agent's. "Folk music's in. Ethnic music too. We can hire these Delta blues boys for next to nothing. It worked for Paul Simon, didn't it? He gave those African singers a hit record, and you can do the same thing for these old boys."

Billy gripped the wheel and thought about that. The Delta bluesmen hadn't even cared about having a hit. They'd only wanted the money. All through the session they'd treated Billy like a plantation overseer who was pushing for an extra bag of cotton. Oh, they'd been polite about it, but they'd never gone out of their way to influence the project. Until Alan said that they should record "Stackalee", that is.

The old men wouldn't touch it. "You shouldn't ought to sing that one," said a guitar player called Iron Box Jack.

"Why not?" Alan asked. "It's too perfect to pass up. It's got a guy called Billy Lyons in it, just like our Billy."

Iron Box shook his head. "That's 'xactly why. Boy name of Billy Lyons shouldn't even be thinkin' 'bout Stackalee, let alone singing 'bout him. Man, don't you know about Stack? Don't you know that old Scratch give him a magic oxblood Stetson that allow him to do all kind of devilment? Don't you know how he shot Billy Lyons on account of he thought Billy stole his magic hat?" The old man looked straight at Billy. "You don't want to sing that one. Stack's a trickster, Billy. He might use you to worm his way out of hell."

Billy laughed. Alan shook his head.

"Iron Box, they don't believe you," a wizened bass player said. "Why, just look at 'em. They ain't got no knowledge of that stuff."

"Guys, guys, it's just a song," Alan began, but the

conciliatory coaxing routine didn't work with this crew. The bluesmen flat-out refused to record "Stackalee" with a singer named Billy Lyons, contract or no. So Billy did the only thing possible to please Alan – he strapped on an old acoustic and went into the studio alone, where he made a hit record that put anything Springsteen did on *Nebraska* to shame.

Thinking about that, Billy smiled in spite of himself, and in spite of the damn song blaring in his ears. He'd shown those old bastards, even with all the shit he was taking about it now. He'd shown them. He'd recorded the song on his own, without their help, and the fact that it was an unexpected hit was just icing on the fucking—

Billy's head snapped back, slamming against the crown of the driver's seat. Sharp pain bloomed at the tip of his spinal column. The Testarossa shuddered, Billy managed to pull out of a skid, and then his head snapped back once more. Black spots of agony danced before his eyes; he squinted around them and focused on the rear-view mirror.

The Caddy sat on his tail, its angry headlights blinking like wild strobes.

> *Stackalee got his gun. Boy, he got it fast!*
> *He shot poor Billy through and through: the bullet broke a*
>   *lookin' glass.*

A bullet exploded the Testarossa's back window, ricocheted, and shattered the rear-view mirror before its power was spent. Billy ducked low, his neck muscles twitching spasmodically. The Caddy rammed the Testarossa a third time. Billy lost control of the car, skidded across three lanes and raced along the dirt shoulder, the Testarossa's thick wheels kicking up beer cans and garbage. He screamed, braking just short of a chain-link fence that separated the freeway from a shadowy embankment.

The Caddy roared through a cloud of dust, its wheels spitting gravel that pelted the Testarossa, then pulled back onto the blacktop and sped away into the night.

★　★　★

The dust died down. Traffic whispered past Billy, the drivers unaware that the nation's number one singing sensation sat locked in his fancy car at the side of the road, shivering, fearful of losing his dinner.

The worst part was not knowing who was after him. So many people had made threats. A headline-grabbing Muslim minister had called him a white devil, and a rap group from Chicago had threatened to kill him. It had been in all the papers. The rappers had called him "Massa Billy" and used his album for target practice. And they weren't the only ones calling for his head; the critics were after him too. *Rolling Stone* had done an article claiming, not too subtly, that Billy Lyons had climbed to the top of the charts on the backs of a bunch of poor, old black men.

Okay, maybe he had, but who hadn't? Had the critics forgotten about the Rolling Stones? Had they forgotten about Elvis?

> *He says Billy. "I always treated you like a man.*
> *'Tain't nothin' to that old Stetson but the greasy band."*

Billy shifted into first gear and pulled onto the freeway. He was going to make it through this. He'd just recorded a song, that was all. He hadn't done anything wrong or broken any laws. He listened to his singing, heard the pain and energy there. "I'm not Salman Rushdie," he whispered, "and I'm not Pat fucking Boone, either."

> *"Have mercy," Billy groaned. "Oh, please spare my life;*
> *I've got two little babies and an innocent wife."*

Billy entered Alan's house through the unlocked front door. After spending an hour at the mercy of the Testarossa's blaring speakers, his ears rang as if he had two enormous seashells jammed against his head. The whispering sound was worse than any shellshock he'd ever suffered after performing in front of the towering speakers he used at stadium shows. It didn't hurt as much, but it was twice as haunting.

Billy flipped on lights as he moved from room to room. He covered the downstairs – all clear – and then started toward the stairway that led to Alan's bedroom.

Billy paused at the foot of the staircase. Quiet. No music upstairs. No voices. He climbed into the shadows and found a light switch at the top of the stairs.

And then, standing alone in the dark, he noticed a knocking sound. Not anything with a solid beat, but measured, insistent. Definitely there.

Billy turned on the lights and almost fell backward. A man stood ramrod straight at the far end of the hallway. Big shoulders and an ankle-length black leather duster. An oxblood Stetson hat. No face.

A mannequin. Jesus. Suddenly Billy remembered the costume fitting for the "Stackalee" video. This was his outfit. Had to be.

"Alan," Billy said, "this isn't funny."

Billy moved down the hallway, following the knocking sound that seemed to be coming from Alan's bedroom. He pushed against the bedroom door, but it wouldn't give. He pushed harder, the knocking stopped for a moment, and he managed to squeeze into the room.

The door fell closed immediately, pushed by Alan's weight. The agent was still alive, but Billy could tell that there wasn't anything left of him. There was a small black hole on one side of his forehead and a bigger hole on the other, and his white sideburns were sticky with blood. Part of his brain lay in a glob on the carpet, but there was enough left in his skull to control his right hand, which tapped a measured beat on the bedroom door.

The costume designer was on the bed. He had a similar wound, but he wasn't moving. On the wall above the bed, four words were scrawled in blood: WHERE'S MY MAGIC STETSON?

Billy pulled the bedcovers over the designer's corpse. A silver-plated Colt .45 tumbled out of the tangled blankets and landed at his feet. He scooped up the weapon and checked for ammunition. Four bullets remained. Billy clicked the cylinder closed.

And then he realized that the whispering ringing in his ears was gone.

Alan's meaningless Morse code suddenly took on a steady beat, like one of the old bluesmen pounding a guitar to keep the rhythm. A gold bracelet on the agent's wrist made a shivery sound like a tiny cymbal. Billy cocked the pistol. Involuntarily, his foot began to tap.

Billy licked his lips. He stared at Alan's wrist, at the gold bracelet. And then he sang, his voice quavering with horror as the words spilled out of his mouth, unbidden.

> *The White Elephant Barrel House was wrecked that night;*
> *Gutters full of beer and whiskey; it was an awful sight.*
> *Jewelry and rings of the purest solid gold*
> *Scattered over the dance and gamblin' hall.*

Billy slipped through the doorway, holding the pistol before him. The house was quiet now. He'd moved Alan to the center of the bedroom, where the only thing to tap was the lush, soft carpet.

The silence felt good. No seashell echo. No singing. Billy took a deep breath. He'd get into the car and drive to a police station, or anyplace where he could find people. He'd find safety in numbers.

At the top of the staircase, Billy turned abruptly and stared down the hallway.

The mannequin was gone.

A blast of heat boiled up the staircase; the smell of hot slag and brimstone burned Billy's nostrils. He whirled and pointed the gun at the looming figure who stood in the shadows below. A smoky red glow enveloped the man, and Billy stepped back from the power of his evil smile.

"Thanks for the return trip ticket, Billy Boy. I've been too long in old Scratch's Jailhouse." The man grinned. "I'd surely rather spend my time in one of these here Cadillacs than in a little ol' brimstone cell." He spread his big hands, weaponless, and the song rumbled from his gut and boiled over his lips.

> *Stackalee shot Billy once; his body fell to the floor.*
> *He cried out, "Oh, please, Stack, please don't shoot me no*
> *   more."*

"Not this time, you son of a bitch," Billy said.

Stackalee threw open his coat and went for his gun, but Billy was already firing. The first shot pierced the Stetson. Blood and brain matter splattered the wall behind the black man, sticking there like gory pudding, but the Stetson stayed on Stackalee and he barely rocked back on his heels. The second and third bullets slammed into the big man's chest, and the last hit him in the mouth.

Stackalee spit teeth, laughing. Blood pumped from the holes in his chest and dripped down his shiny black coat, pooling in his pockets and around the pointy tips of his boots. Again, he sang.

> *And brass-buttoned policemen all dressed in blue*
> *Came down the sidewalk marchin' two by two.*
> *Sent for the wagon and it hurried and come*
> *Loaded with pistols and a big Gatling gun.*

Billy dropped the gun and wiped his bloodstained hands on his jeans; Alan's blood mixed with the blood from the Fender Stratocaster. His eyes went from the stains to the gun to Stackalee.

Stack's a trickster, Billy. He might use you to worm his way out of hell.

"No," Billy whispered. "No!"

Stack nodded. "Fingerprints, Billy Boy. All yours. Powder burns on your gun hand, too." Growling laughter, he pointed a long index finger at Billy and cocked the imaginary weapon with his thumb. "Bang bang, Billy Boy."

Outside, sirens wailed.

Stackalee tipped his Stetson and disappeared into the shadows. His footsteps echoed through the house, keeping time for the lyrics that spilled over his bloody lips.

Now late at night you can hear him in his cell,
Arguin' with the devil to keep from goin' to hell.
And the other convicts whisper, "Watcha know about that?
Gonna burn in hell forever over an old Stetson hat!"

Billy Lyons closed his eyes and whispered, "Everybody's talking 'bout Stackalee."

Bed and Breakfast

Gene Wolfe

Gene Wolfe's wonderful "Bed and Breakfast" takes place at a homey place located on the road to Hell where weary wanderers can spend the night. Some of the "regulars" are demons, of course, others aren't. Just because you are on the road to Hell doesn't necessarily mean you are planning a visit, although literature is full of those who have – fictionally or faithfully – visited Hell and returned to write of it. Dante Alighieri (c. 1265–1321) may not actually have gone to Hell, but he wrote convincingly of a journey there with the Roman poet Virgil (70 BCE–19 BCE) as his guide in his Divina commedia. Virgil himself penned the Aenid, a Latin epic in which Aeneas travels down to Dis, the underworld, and visits his father. Emanuel Swedenborg (1688–1772) claimed to visit both Heaven and Hell and converse with angels and demons. His book Heaven and Hell (1758) provided details. In 1868, Saint John Bosco (1815–1888), founder of the Society of St Francis de Sales visited Hell in his dreams, a trip he later vividly described.

I know an old couple who live near Hell. They have a small farm, and, to supplement the meager income it provides (and to use up its bounty of chickens, ducks and geese, of beefsteak tomatoes, bull-nose peppers and roastin' ears), open their spare bedrooms to paying guests. From time to time, I am one of those guests.

Dinner comes with the room if one arrives before five; and leftovers, of which there are generally enough to feed two or three more persons, will be cheerfully warmed up afterward – provided that one gets there before nine, at which hour the old woman goes to bed. After nine (and I arrived long after nine last week) guests are free to forage in the kitchen and prepare whatever they choose for themselves.

My own choices were modest: coleslaw, cold chicken, fresh bread, country butter and buttermilk. I was just sitting down to this light repast when I heard the doorbell ring. I got up, thinking to answer it and save the old man the trouble, and heard his limping gait in the hallway. There was a murmur of voices, the old man's and someone else's; the second sounded like a deep-voiced woman's, so I remained standing.

Their conversation lasted longer than I had expected; and although I could not distinguish a single word, it seemed to me that the old man was saying no, no, no, and the woman proposing various alternatives.

At length he showed her into the kitchen; tall and tawny-haired, with a figure rather too voluptuous to be categorized as athletic, and one of those interesting faces that one calls beautiful only after at least half an hour of study; I guessed her age near thirty. The old man introduced us with rustic courtesy, told her to make herself at home, and went back to his book.

"He's very kind, isn't he?" she said. Her name was Eira something.

I concurred, calling him a very good soul indeed.

"Are you going to eat all that?" She was looking hungrily at the chicken. I assured her I would have only a piece or two. (I never sleep well after a heavy meal.) She opened the refrigerator, found the milk, and poured herself a glass that she pressed against her cheek. "I haven't any money. I might as well tell you."

That was not my affair, and I said so.

"I don't. I saw the sign, and I thought there must be a lot of work to do around such a big house, washing windows and making beds, and I'd offer to do it for food and a place to sleep."

"He agreed?" I was rather surprised.

"No." She sat down and drank half her milk, seeming to pour it down her throat with no need of swallowing. "He said I could eat and stay in the empty room – they've got an empty room tonight – if nobody else comes. But if somebody does, I'll have to leave." She found a drumstick and nipped it with strong white teeth. "I'll pay them when I get the money, but naturally he didn't believe me. I don't blame him. How much is it?"

I told her, and she said it was very cheap.

"Yes," I said, "but you have to consider the situation. They're off the highway, with no way of letting people know they're here. They get a few people on their way to Hell, and a few demons going out on assignments or returning. Regulars, as they call them. Other than that—" I shrugged "—eccentrics like me and passers-by like you."

"Did you say Hell?" She put down her chicken leg.

"Yes. Certainly."

"Is there a town around here called Hell?"

I shook my head. "It has been called a city, but it's a region, actually. The infernal Empire. Hades. Gehenna, where the worm dieth not, and the fire is not quenched. You know."

She laughed, the delighted crow of a large, bored child who has been entertained at last.

I buttered a second slice of bread. The bread is always very good, but this seemed better than usual.

"Abandon hope, you who enter here. Isn't that supposed to be the sign over the door?"

"More or less," I said. "Over the gate Dante used at any rate. It wasn't this one, so the inscription here may be quite different, if there's an inscription at all."

"You haven't been there?"

I shook my head. "Not yet."

"But you're going—" she laughed again, a deep, throaty, very feminine chuckle this time "—and it's not very far."

"Three miles, I'm told, by the old country road. A little less, two perhaps, if you were to cut across the fields, which almost no one does."

"I'm not going," she said.

"Oh, but you are. So am I. Do you know what they do in Heaven?"

"Fly around playing harps?"

"There's the Celestial Choir, which sings the praises of God throughout all eternity. Everyone else beholds His face."

"That's it?" She was skeptical but amused.

"That's it. It's fine for contemplative saints. They go there, and they love it. They're the only people suited to it, and it suits them. The unbaptized go to Limbo. All the rest of us go to Hell; and for a few, this is the last stop before they arrive."

I waited for her reply, but she had a mouthful of chicken. "There are quite a number of entrances, as the ancients knew: Dodona, Ephyra, Acheron, Averno, and so forth. Dante went in through the crater of Vesuvius, or so rumor had it; to the best of my memory, he never specified the place in his poem."

"You said demons stay here."

I nodded. "If it weren't for them, the old people would have to close, I imagine."

"But you're not a demon and neither am I. Isn't it pretty dangerous for us? You certainly don't look – I don't mean to be offensive—"

"I don't look courageous." I sighed. "Nor am I. Let me concede that at once, because we need to establish it from the very beginning. I'm innately cautious, and have been accused of cowardice more than once. But don't you understand that courage has nothing to do with appearances? You must watch a great deal of television; no one would say what you did who did not. Haven't you ever seen a real hero on the news? Someone who had done something extraordinarily brave? The last one I saw looked very much like the black woman on the pancake mix used to, yet she'd run into a burning tenement to rescue three children. Not her own children, I should add."

Eira got up and poured herself a second glass of milk. "I

said I didn't want to hurt your feelings, and I meant it. Just to start with, I can't afford to tick off anybody just now – I need help. I'm sorry. I really am."

"I'm not offended. I'm simply telling you the truth, that you cannot judge by appearances. One of the bravest men I've known was short and plump and inclined to be careless, not to say slovenly, about clothes and shaving and so on. A friend said that you couldn't imagine anyone less military, and he was right. Yet that fat little man had served in combat with the Navy and the Marines, and with the Israeli Army."

"But isn't it dangerous? You said you weren't brave to come here."

"In the first place, one keeps one's guard up here. There are precautions, and I take them. In the second, they're not on duty, so to speak. If they were to commit murder or set the house on fire, the old people would realize immediately who had done it and shut down; so while they are here, they're on their good behavior."

"I see." She picked up another piece of chicken. "Nice demons."

"Not really. But the old man tells me that they usually overpay and are, well, businesslike in their dealings. Those are the best things about evil. It generally has ready money, and doesn't expect to be trusted. There's a third reason, as well. Do you want to hear it?"

"Sure."

"Here one can discern them, and rather easily for the most part. When you've identified a demon, his ability to harm you is vastly reduced. But past this farm, identification is far more difficult; the demons vanish in the surging tide of mortal humanity that we have been taught by them to call life, and one tends to relax somewhat. Yet scarcely a week goes by in which one does not encounter a demon unaware."

"All right, what about the people on their way to Hell? They're dead, aren't they?"

"Some are, and some aren't."

"What do you mean by that?"

"Exactly what I said. Some are and some are not. It can be difficult to tell. They aren't ghosts in the conventional sense, you understand, any more than they are corpses, but the person who has left the corpse and the ghost behind."

"Would you mind if I warmed up a couple of pieces of this, and toasted some of that bread? We could share it."

I shook my head. "Not in the least, but I'm practically finished."

She rose, and I wondered whether she realized just how graceful she was. "I've got a dead brother, my brother Eric."

I said that I was sorry to hear it.

"It was a long time ago, when I was a kid. He was four, I think, and he fell off the balcony. Mother always said he was an angel now, an angel up in heaven. Do dead people really get to be angels if they're good?"

"I don't know; it's an interesting question. There's a suggestion in the book of Tobit that the Archangel Raphael is actually an ancestor of Tobit's. Angel means 'messenger', as you probably know; so if God were to employ one of the blessed as a messenger, he or she could be regarded as an angel, I'd think."

"Devils are fallen angels, aren't they? I mean, if they exist." She dropped three pieces of chicken into a frying pan, hesitated, and added a fourth. "So if good people really get recycled as angels, shouldn't the bad ones get to be devils or demons?"

I admitted that it seemed plausible.

She lit the stove with a kitchen match, turning the burner higher than I would have. "You sound like you come here pretty often. You must talk to them at breakfast, or whenever. You ought to know."

"Since you don't believe me, wouldn't it be logical for you to believe my admissions of ignorance?"

"No way!" She turned to face me, a forefinger upraised. "You've got to be consistent, and coming here and talking to lots of demons, you'd know."

I protested that information provided by demons could not be relied upon.

"But what do you think? What's your best guess? See, I want to find out if there's any hope for us. You said we're going to Hell, both of us, and that dude – the Italian—"

"Dante," I supplied.

"Dante says the sign over the door says don't hope. I went to a school like that for a couple years, come to think of it."

"Were they merely strict, or actually sadistic?"

"Mean. But the teachers lived better than we did – a lot better. If there's a chance of getting to be one yourself, we could always hope for that."

At that moment, we heard a knock at the front door, and her shoulders sagged. "There goes my free room. I guess I've got to be going. It was fun talking to you, it really was."

I suggested she finish her chicken first.

"Probably I should. I'll have to find another place to stay, though, and I'd like to get going before they throw me out. It's pretty late already." She hesitated. "Would you buy my wedding ring? I've got it right here." Her thumb and forefinger groped the watch pocket of her blue jeans.

I took a final bite of coleslaw and pushed back my plate. "It doesn't matter, actually, whether I want to buy your ring or not. I can't afford to. Someone in town might, perhaps."

A booming voice in the hallway drowned out the old man's; I knew that the new guest was a demon before I saw him or heard a single intelligible word.

She held up her ring, a white gold band set with two small diamonds. "I had a job, but he never let me keep anything from it and I finally caught on – if I kept waiting till I had some money or someplace to go, I'd never get away. So I split, just walked away with nothing but the clothes I had on."

"Today?" I enquired.

"Yesterday. Last night I slept in a wrecked truck in a ditch. You probably don't believe that, but it's the truth. All night I was afraid somebody'd come to tow it away. There were furniture pads in the back, and I lay on a couple and pulled three more on top of me, and they were pretty warm."

"If you can sell your ring," I said, "there's a Holiday Inn in town. I should warn you that a great many demons stay there, just as you would expect."

The kitchen door opened. Following the old man was one of the largest I have ever seen, swag-bellied and broad-hipped; he must have stood at least six foot six.

"This's our kitchen," the old man told him.

"I know," the demon boomed. "I stopped off last year. Naturally you don't remember, Mr Hopsack. But I remembered you and this wonderful place of yours. I'll scrounge around and make out all right."

The old man gave Eira a significant look and jerked his head toward the door, at which she nodded almost imperceptibly. I said, "She's going to stay with me, Len. There's plenty of room in the bed. You don't object, I trust?"

He did, of course, though he was much too diffident to say so; at last he managed, "Double's six dollars more."

I said, "Certainly," and handed him the money, at which the demon snickered.

"Just don't you let Ma find out."

When the old man had gone, the demon fished business cards from his vest pocket; I did not trouble to read the one that he handed me, knowing that nothing on it would be true. Eira read hers aloud, however, with a good simulation of admiration. "J. Gunderson Foulweather, Broker, Commodities Sales."

The demon picked up her skillet and tossed her chicken a foot into the air, catching all four pieces with remarkable dexterity. "Soap, dope, rope, or hope. If it's sold in bulk I'll buy it, and give you the best price anywhere. If it's bought in bulk, I sell it cheaper than anybody in the nation. Pleasure to meet you."

I introduced myself, pretending not to see his hand, and added, "This is Eira Mumble."

"On your way to St Louis? Lovely city! I know it well."

I shook my head.

She said, "But you're going somewhere – home to some city – in the morning, aren't you? And you've got a car. There are cars parked outside. The black Plymouth?"

My vehicle is a gray Honda Civic, and I told her so.

"If I . . . you know."

"Stay in my room tonight."

"Will you give me a ride in the morning? Just a ride? Let me off downtown, that's all I ask."

I do not live in St Louis and had not intended to go there, but I said I would.

She turned to the demon. "He says this's close to Hell, and the souls of people going there stop off here sometimes. Is that where you're going?"

His booming laugh shook the kitchen. "Not me! Davenport. Going to do a little business in feed corn if I can."

Eira looked at me as if to say, *There, you see?*

The demon popped the largest piece of chicken into his mouth like a hors d'oeuvre; I have never met one who did not prefer his food smoking hot. "He's giving you the straight scoop though, Eira. It is."

"How'd you do that?"

"Do what?"

"Talk around that chicken like that."

He grinned, which made him look like a portly crocodile. "Swallowed it, that's all. I'm hungry. I haven't eaten since lunch."

"Do you mind if I take the others? I was warming them up for myself, and there's more in the refrigerator."

He stood aside with a mock bow.

"You're in this together – this thing about Hell. You and him." Eira indicated me as she took the frying pan from the stove.

"We met before?" he boomed at me. I said that we had not, to the best of my memory.

"Devils – demons, are what he calls them. He says there are probably demons sleeping here right now, up on the second floor."

I put in, "I implied that, I suppose. I did not state it."

"Very likely true," the demon boomed, adding, "I'm going to make coffee, if anybody wants some."

"And the damned, they're going to Hell, but they stop off here."

He gave me a searching glance. "I've been wondering about you to tell the truth. You seem like the type."

I declared that I was alive for the time being.

"That's the best anybody can say."

"But the cars—" Eira began.

"Some drive, some fly." He had discovered slices of ham in the refrigerator, and he slapped them into the frying pan as though he were dealing blackjack. "I used to wonder what they did with all the cars down there."

"But you don't any more." Eira was going along now, once more willing to play what she thought (or wished me to believe she thought) a rather silly game. "So you found out. What is it?"

"Nope." He pulled out one of the wooden, yellow-enameled kitchen chairs and sat down with such force I was surprised it did not break. "I quit wondering, that's all. I'll find out soon enough, or I won't. But in places this close – I guess there's others – you get four kinds of folks." He displayed thick fingers, each with a ring that looked as if it had cost a great deal more than Eira's. "There's guys that's still alive, like our friend here." He clenched one finger. "Then there's staff. You know what I mean?"

Eira looked puzzled. "Devils?"

"J. Gunderson Foulweather—" the demon jerked his thumb at his vest "—doesn't call anybody racial names unless they hurt him or his, especially when there's liable to be a few eating breakfast in the morning. Staff, okay? Free angels. Some of them are business contacts of mine. They told me about this place, that's why I came the first time."

He clenched a second finger and touched third with the index finger of his free hand. "Then there's future inmates. You used a word J. Gunderson Foulweather himself wouldn't say in the presence of a lady, but since you're the only lady here, no harm done. Colonists, okay?"

"Wait a minute." Eira looked from him to me. "You both claim they stop off here."

We nodded.

"On their way to Hell. So why do they go? Why don't they just go off—" she hesitated, searching for the right word, and finished weakly "—back home or something?"

The demon boomed, "You want to field this one?"

I shook my head. "Your information is superior to mine, I feel certain."

"Okay, a friend of mine was born and raised in Newark, New Jersey. You ever been to Newark?"

"No," Eira said.

"Some parts are pretty nice, but it's not, like, the hub of Creation, see? He went to France when he was twenty-two and stayed twenty years, doing jobs for American magazines around Paris. Learned to speak the language better than the natives. He's a photographer, a good one."

The demon's coffee had begun to perc. He glanced around at it, sniffed appreciatively, and turned back to us, still holding up his ring and little fingers. "Twenty years, then he goes back to Newark. J. Gunderson Foulweather doesn't stick his nose into other people's business, but I asked him the same thing you did me, how come? He said he felt he belonged there."

Eira nodded slowly.

I said, "The staff, as you call them, might hasten the process, I imagine."

The demon appeared thoughtful. "Could be. Sometimes, anyhow." He touched the fourth and final finger. "All the first three's pretty common from what I hear. Only there's another kind you don't hardly ever see. The runaways."

Eira chewed and swallowed. "You mean people escape?"

"That's what I hear. Down at the bottom, Hell's pretty rough, you know? Higher up it's not so bad."

I put in, "That's what Dante reported, too."

"You know him? Nice guy. I never been there myself, but that's what they say. Up at the top it's not so bad, sort of like one of those country-club jails for politicians. The guys up there could jump the fence and walk out. Only they don't, because they know they'd get caught and sent down where things aren't so nice. Only every so often somebody does. So you got them, too, headed out. Anybody want coffee? I made plenty."

Long before he had reached his point, I had realized what it was; I found it difficult to speak, but managed to say that I was going up to bed and coffee would keep me awake.

"You, Eira?"

She shook her head. It was at that moment that I at last concluded that she was truly beautiful, not merely attractive in an unconventional way. "I've had all I want, really. You can have my toast for your ham."

I confess that I heaved a sigh of relief when the kitchen door swung shut behind us. As we mounted the steep, carpeted stair, the house seemed so silent that I supposed for a moment that the demon had dematerialized, or whatever it is they do. He began to whistle a hymn in the kitchen, and I looked around sharply.

She said, "He scares you, doesn't he? He scares me too. I don't know why."

I did, or believed I did, though I forbore.

"You probably thought I was going to switch – spend the night with him instead of you, but I'd rather sleep outside in your car."

I said, "Thank you," or something of the kind, and Eira took my hand; it was the first physical intimacy of any sort between us.

When we reached the top of the stair, she said, "Maybe you'd like it if I waited out here in the hall till you get undressed? I won't run away."

I shook my head. "I told you I take precautions. As long as you're in my company, those precautions protect you as well to a considerable extent. Out here alone, you'd be completely vulnerable."

I unlocked the door of my room, opened it, and switched on the light. "Come in, please. There are things in here, enough protection to keep us both safe tonight, I believe. Just don't touch them. Don't touch anything you don't understand."

"You're keeping out demons?" She was no longer laughing, I noticed.

"Unwanted guests of every sort." I endeavored to sound confident, though I have had little proof of the effectiveness of those old spells. I shut and relocked the door behind us.

"I'm going to have to go out to wash up. I'd like to take a bath."

"The Hopsacks have only two rooms with private baths, but this is one of them." I pointed. "We're old friends, you see; their son and I went to Dartmouth together, and I reserved this room in advance."

"There's one other thing. Oh, God! I don't know how to say this without sounding like a jerk."

"Your period has begun."

"I'm on the pill. It's just that I'd like to rinse out my under-wear and hang it up to dry overnight, and I don't have a nightie. Would you turn off the lights in here when I'm ready to come out of the bathroom?"

"Certainly."

"If you want to look you can, but I'd rather you didn't. Maybe just that little lamp on the vanity?"

"No lights at all," I told her. "You divined very quickly that I am a man of no great courage. I wish that you exhibited equal penetration with respect to my probity. I lie only when forced to, and badly as a rule; and my word is as good as any man's. I will keep any agreement we make, whether expressed or implied, as long as you do."

"You probably want to use the bathroom too."

I told her that I would wait, and that I would undress in the bedroom while she bathed, and take my own bath afterward.

Of the many things, memories as well as speculations, that passed through my mind as I waited in our darkened bedroom for her to complete her ablutions, I shall say little here; perhaps I should say nothing. I shot the nightbolt, switched off the light and undressed. Reflecting that she might readily make away with my wallet and my watch while I bathed, I considered hiding them; but I felt certain that she would not, and to tell the truth my watch is of no great value and there was less than a hundred dollars in my wallet. Under these circumstances, it seemed wise to show I trusted her, and I resolved to do so.

In the morning I would drive her to the town in which I live or to St Louis, as she preferred. I would give her my address and telephone number, with twenty dollars, perhaps, or even thirty. And I would tell her in a friendly fashion that if she could find no better place to stay she could stay with me whenever she chose, on tonight's terms. I speculated upon a relationship (causal and even promiscuous, if you like) that would not so much spring into being as grow by the accretion of familiarity and small kindnesses. At no time have I been the sort of man women prefer, and I am whole decades past the time in life in which love is found if it is found at all, overcautious and over-intellectual, little known to the world and certainly not rich.

Yet I dreamt, alone in that dark, high-ceilinged bedroom. In men such as I, the foolish fancies of boyhood are superseded only by those of manhood, unsought visions less gaudy, perhaps, but more foolish still.

Even in these the demon's shadow fell between us; I felt certain then that she had escaped, and that he had come to take her back. I heard the flushing of the toilet, heard water run in the tub, and compelled myself to listen no more.

Though it was a cold night, the room we would share was warm. I went to the window most remote from the bathroom door, raised the shade, and stood for a time staring up at the frosty stars, then stretched myself quite naked upon the bed, thinking of many things.

I started when the bathroom door opened; I must have been half asleep.

"I'm finished," Eira said, "you can go in now." Then, "Where are you?"

My own eyes were accommodated to the darkness, as hers were not. I could make her out, white and ghostly, in the starlight; and I thrilled at the sight. "I'm here," I told her, "on the bed. It's over this way." As I left the bed and she slipped beneath its sheets and quilt, our hands touched. I recall that moment more clearly than any of the rest.

Instructed by her lack of night vision (whether real or feigned), I pulled the dangling cord of the bathroom light before I toweled myself dry. When I opened the door, half expecting to find her gone, I could see her almost as well as I had when she had emerged from the bathroom, lying upon her back, her hair a damp-darkened aureole about her head and her arms above the quilt. I circled the bed and slid in.

"Nice bath?" Then, "How do you want to do it?"

"Slowly," I said.

At which she giggled like a schoolgirl. "You're fun. You're not like him at all, are you?"

I hoped that I was not, as I told her.

"I know – do that again – who you are! You're Larry."

I was happy to hear it; I had tired of being myself a good many years ago.

"He was the smartest boy in school – in the high school that my husband and I graduated from. He was Valedictorian, and president of the chess club and the debating team and all that. Oh, my!"

"Did you go out with him?" I was curious, I confess.

"Once or twice. No, three times. Times when there was something I wanted to go to – a dance or a game – and my husband couldn't take me, or wouldn't. So I went with Larry, dropping hints, you know that I'd like to go, then saying okay when he asked. I never did this with him, though. Just with my husband, except that he wasn't my husband then. Could you sorta run your fingers inside my knees and down the backs of my legs?"

I complied. "It might be less awkward if you employed your husband's name. Use a false one if you like. Tom, Dick, or Harry would do, or even Mortimer."

"That wouldn't be him, and I don't want to say it. Aren't you going to ask if he beat me? I went to the battered women's shelter once, and they kept coming back to that. I think they wanted me to lie."

"You said that you left home yesterday, and I've seen your face. It isn't bruised."

"Now up here. He didn't. Oh, he knocked me down a couple times, but not lately. They're supposed to get drunk and beat you up."

I said that I had heard that before, though I had never understood it.

"You don't get mean when you're drunk."

"I talk too much and too loudly," I told her, "and I can't remember names, or the word I want to use. Eventually I grow ashamed and stop talking completely, and drinking as well."

"My husband used to be happy and rowdy – that was before we got married. After, it was sort of funny, because you could see him starting to get mad before he got the top off the first bottle. Isn't that funny?"

"No one can bottle emotions," I said. "We must bring them to the bottles ourselves."

"Kiss me."

We kissed. I had always thought it absurd to speak of someone enraptured by a kiss, yet I knew a happiness that I had not thought myself capable of.

"Larry was really smart, like you. Did I say that?"

I managed to nod.

"I want to lie on top of you. Just for a minute or so. Is that all right?"

I told her truthfully that I would adore it.

"You can put your hands anyplace you want, but hold me. That's good. That's nice. He was really smart, but he wasn't good at talking to people. Socially, you know? The stuff he cared about didn't matter to us, and the stuff we wanted to talk about didn't matter to him. But I let him kiss me in his dad's car, and I always danced the first and last numbers with him. Nobody cares about that now, but then they did, where we came from. Larry and my husband and I. I think if he'd kept on drinking – he'd have maybe four or five beers every night, at first – he'd have beaten me to death, and that was why he stopped. But he used to threaten. Do you know what I mean?"

I said that I might guess, but with no great confidence.

"Like he'd pick up my big knife in the kitchen, and he'd say, I could stick this right through you – in half a minute it would all be over. Or he'd talk about how you could choke somebody with a wire till she died, and while he did he'd be running the lamp cord through his fingers, back and forth. Do you like this?"

"Don't!" I said.

"I'm sorry, I thought you'd like it."

"I like it too much. Please don't. Not now."

"He'd talk about other men, how I was playing up to them. Sometimes it was men I hadn't even noticed. Like we'd go down to the pizza place, and when we got back he'd say, the big guy in the leather jacket – I saw you. He was eating it up, and you couldn't give him enough, could you? You just couldn't give him enough.

"And I wouldn't have seen anybody in a leather jacket. I'd be trying to remember who this was. But when we were in school he was never jealous of Larry, because he knew Larry was just a handy man to me. I kind of liked him the way I kind of liked the little kid next door."

"You got him to help you with your homework," I said.

"Yes, I did. How'd you know?"

" A flash of insight. I have them occasionally."

"I'd get him to help before a big quiz, too. When we were finishing up the semester, in Social Studies or whatever, I wouldn't have a clue about what she was going to ask on the test, but Larry always knew. He'd tell me half a dozen things, maybe, and five would be right there on the final. A flash of insight, like you said."

"Similar, perhaps."

"But the thing was – it was – was—"

She gulped and gasped so loudly that even I realized she was about to cry. I hugged her, perhaps the most percipient thing I have ever done.

"I wasn't going to tell you that, and I guess I'd better not or I'll bawl. I just wanted to say you're Larry, because my husband never minded him, not really, or anyhow not very much, and he'd kid around with him in those days, and sometimes Larry'd help him with his homework too."

"You're right," I told her, "I am Larry; and your name is Martha Williamson, although she was never half so beautiful as you are, and I had nearly forgotten her."

"Have you cooled down enough?"

"No. Another five minutes, possibly."

"I hope you don't get the aches. Do you really think I'm beautiful?"

I said I did, and that I could not tell her properly how lovely she was, because she would be sure I lied.

"My face is too square."

"Absolutely not! Besides, you mean rectangular, surely. It's not too rectangular, either. Any face less rectangular than yours is too square or too round."

"See? You are Larry."

"I know."

"This is what I was going to tell, if I hadn't gotten all weepy. Let me do it, and after that we'll . . . You know. Get together."

I nodded, and she must have sensed my nod in the movement of my shoulder, or perhaps a slight motion of the mattress. She was silent for what seemed to me half a minute, if not longer. "Kiss me, then I'll tell it."

I did.

"You remember what you said in the kitchen?"

"I said far too many things in the kitchen. I'm afraid. I tend to talk too much even when I'm sober. I'm sure I couldn't recall them all."

"It was before that awful man came in and took my room. I said the people going to Hell were dead, and you said some were and some weren't. That didn't make any sense to me till later when I thought about my husband. He was alive, but it was like something was getting a tighter hold on him all the time. Like Hell was reaching right out and grabbing him. He went on so about me looking at other men that I started really doing it. I'd see who was there, trying to figure out which one he'd say when we got home. Then he started bringing up ones that hadn't been there, people from school – this was after we were out of school and married, and I hadn't seen a lot of them in years."

I said, "I understand."

"He'd been on the football team and the softball team and run track and all that, and mostly it was those boys he'd talk about, but one time it was the shop teacher. I never even took shop."

I nodded again, I think.

"But never Larry, so Larry got to be special to me. Most of those boys, well, maybe they looked, but I never looked at them. But I'd really dated Larry, and he'd had his arms around me and even kissed me a couple of times, and I danced with him. I could remember the cologne he used to wear, and that checkered wool blazer he had. After graduation most of the boys from our school got jobs with the coal company or in the tractor plant, but Larry won a scholarship to some big school, and after that I never saw him. It was like he'd gone there and died."

"It's better now," I said, and I took her hand, just as she had taken mine going upstairs.

She misunderstood, which may have been fortunate. "It is. It really is. Having you here like this makes it better." She used my name, but I am determined not to reveal it.

"Then after we'd been married about four years, I went into the drugstore, and Larry was there waiting for a prescription for his mother. We said hi, and shook hands, and talked about old times and how it was with us, and I got the stuff I'd come for and started to leave. When I got to the door, I thought Larry wouldn't be looking any more, so I stopped and looked at him."

"He was still looking at me." She gulped. "You're smart. I bet you guessed, didn't you?"

"I would have been," I said. I doubt that she heard me.

"I'll never, ever, forget that look. He wanted me so bad, just so bad it was tearing him up. My husband starved a dog to death once. His name was Ranger, and he was a blue-tick hound. They said he was good coon dog, and I guess he was. My husband had helped this man with some work, so he gave him Ranger. But my husband used to pull on Ranger's ears till he'd yelp, and finally Ranger bit his hand. He just locked Ranger up after that and wouldn't feed him any more. He'd go out in the yard and Ranger'd be in that cage hoping for him to feed him and knowing he wouldn't, and that was the way Larry looked at me in the drugstore. It brought it all back, about the dog two years before, and Larry, and lots of other things. But the thing was . . . thing was . . ."

I stroked her hand.

"He looked at me like that, and I saw it, and when I did I knew I was looking at him that very same way. That was when I decided, except that I thought I'd save up money, and write to Larry when I had enough, and see if he'd help me. Are you all right now?"

"No," I said, because at that moment I could have cut my own throat or thrown myself through the window.

"He never answered my letters, though. I talked to his mother, and he's married with two children. I like you better anyway."

Her fingers had resumed explorations. I said, "Now, if you're ready."

And we did. I felt heavy and clumsy, and it was over far too quickly; yet if I were given what no man actually is, the opportunity to experience a bit of his life a second time, I think I might well choose those moments.

"Did you like that?"

"Yes, very much indeed. Thank you."

"You're pretty old for another one, aren't you?"

"I don't know. Wait a few minutes, and we'll see."

"We could try some other way. I like you better than Larry. Have I said that?"

I said she had not, and that she had made me wonderfully happy by saying it.

"He's married, but I never wrote him. I won't lie to you much more."

"In that case, may I ask you a question?"

"Sure."

"Or two? Perhaps three?"

"Go ahead."

"You indicated that you had gone to a school, a boarding school apparently, where you were treated badly. Was it near here?"

"I don't remember about that – I don't think I said it."

"We were talking about the inscription Dante reported. I believe it ended '*Lasciate ogni speranza, voi ch'entrate!*' Leave all hope, you that enter!"

"I said I wouldn't lie. It's not very far, but I can't give you the name of a town you'd know, or anything like that."

"My second—"

"Don't ask anything else about the school. I won't tell you."

"All right, I won't. Someone gave your husband a hunting dog. Did your husband hunt deer? Or quail, perhaps?"

"Sometimes. I think you're right. He'd rather have had a bird dog, but the man he helped didn't raise them."

I kissed her. "You're in danger, and I think that you must know how much. I'll help you all I can. I realize how very trite this will sound, but I would give my life to save you from going back to that school, if need be."

"Kiss me again." There was a new note in her voice, I thought, and it seemed to me that it was hope.

When we parted, she asked, "Are you going to drive me to St Louis in the morning?"

"I'll gladly take you further. To New York or Boston or even to San Francisco. It means Saint Francis, you know."

"You think you could again?"

At her touch, I knew the answer was yes; so did she.

Afterward she asked, "What was your last question?" and I told her I had no last question.

"You said one question then it was two, then three. So what was the last one?"

"You needn't answer."

"All right, I won't. What was it?"

"I was going to ask you in what year you and your husband graduated from high school."

"You don't mind?"

I sighed. "A hundred wise men have said in various ways that love transcends the power of death; and millions of fools have supposed that they meant nothing by it. At this late hour in my life I have learned what they meant. They meant that love transcends death. They are correct."

"Did you think that salesman was really a cop? I think you did. I did, too, almost."

"No or yes, depending upon what you mean by 'cop'. But we've already talked too much about these things."

"Would you rather I'd do this?"

"Yes," I said, and meant it with every fiber of my being. "I would a thousand times rather have you do that."

After some gentle teasing about my age and inadequacies (the sort of thing that women always do, in my experience, as antic- ipatory vengeance for the contempt with which they expect to be treated when the sexual act is complete), we slept. In the morning, Eira wore her wedding band to breakfast, where I introduced her to the old woman as my wife, to the old man's obvious relief. The demon sat opposite me at the table, wolfing down scrambled eggs, biscuits and home-made sausage he did not require, and from time to time winking at me in an offen- sive manner that I did my best to tolerate.

Outside I spoke to him in private while Eira was upstairs searching our room for the hairbrush that I had been careful to leave behind.

"If you are here to reclaim her," I told him, "I am your debtor. Thank you for waiting until morning."

He grinned like the trap he was. "Have a nice night?"

"Very.

"Swell. You folks think we don't want you to have any fun. That's not the way it is at all." He strove to stifle his native malignancy as he said this, with the result that it showed so clearly I found it difficult not to cringe. "I do you a favor, maybe you'll do me one sometime. Right?"

"Perhaps," I hedged.

He laughed. I have heard many actors try to reproduce the hollowness and cruelty of that laugh, but not one has come close. "Isn't that what keeps you coming back here? Wanting favors? You know we don't give anything away."

"I hope to learn, and to make myself a better man."

"Touching. You and Doctor Frankenstein."

I forced myself to smile. "I owed you thanks, as I said, and I do thank you. Now I'll impose upon your good nature if I may. Two weeks. You spoke of favors, of the possibility of accommodation. I would be greatly in your debt. I am already, as I acknowledge."

Grinning, he shook his head.

"One week then. Today is Thursday. Let us have – let me have her until next Thursday."

"Afraid not, pal."

"Three days then. I recognize that she belongs to you, but you'll have her for eternity, and she can't be an important prisoner."

"Inmate. Inmate sounds better." The demon laid his hand upon my shoulder, and I was horribly conscious of its weight and bone-crushing strength. "You think I let you jump her last night because I'm such a nice guy? You really believe that?"

"I was hoping that was the case, yes."

"Bright. Real bright. Just because I got here a little after she did, you think I was trailing her like that flea-bitten dog, and I followed her here." He sniffed, and it was precisely the sniff of a hound on the scent. The hand that held my shoulder drew me to him until I stood with the almost insuperable weight of his entire arm on my shoulders. "Listen here. I don't have to track anybody. Wherever they are, I am. See?"

"I understand."

"If I'd been after her, I'd have had her away from you as soon as I saw her. Only she's not why I came here, she's not why I'm leaving, and if I was to grab her all it would do is get me in the soup with the big boys downstairs. I don't want you either."

"I'm gratified to hear it."

"Swell. If I was to give you a promise, my solemn word of dishonor, you wouldn't think that was worth shit-paper, would you?"

"To the contrary." Although I was lying in his teeth, I persevered. "I know an angel's word is sacred, to him at least."

"Okay then. I don't want her. You wanted a couple of weeks, and I said no deal because I'm letting you have her forever, and vice versa. You don't know what forever means, whatever you think. But I do."

"Thank you, sir," I said; and I meant it from the bottom of my soul. "Thank you very, very much."

The demon grinned and took his arm from my shoulders. "I wouldn't mess around with you or her or a single thing the two of you are going to do together, see? Word of dishonor. The boys downstairs would skin me, because you're her assignment. So be happy." He slapped me on the back so hard that he nearly knocked me down.

Still grinning, he walked around the corner of someone's camper van. I followed as quickly as I could, but he had disappeared.

Little remains to tell. I drove Eira to St Louis, as I had promised, and she left me with a quick kiss in the parking area of the Gateway Arch; we had stopped at a McDonald's for lunch on the way, and I had scribbled my address and telephone number on a paper napkin there and watched her tuck it into a pocket of the denim shirt she wore. Since then I have had a week in which to consider my adventure, as I said on the first page of this account.

In the beginning (especially Friday night), I hoped for a telephone call or a midnight summons from my doorbell. Neither came.

On Monday I went to the library, where I perused the back issues of newspapers; and this evening, thanks to a nephew at an advertising agency, I researched the matter further, viewing twenty-five and thirty-year-old tapes of news broadcasts. The woman's name was not Eira, a name that means "snow", and the name of the husband she had slain with his own shotgun was not Tom, Dick, Harry, or even Mortimer; but I was sure I had found her. (Fairly sure, at least.) She took her own life in jail, awaiting trail.

She had been in Hell. That, I feel, is the single solid fact, the one thing on which I can rely. But did she escape? Or was she vomited forth?

All this has been brought to a head by the card I received today in the mail. It was posted on Monday from St Louis, and has taken a disgraceful four days to make a journey that the most cautious driver can complete in a few hours. On its front, a tall, beautiful, and astonishingly busty woman is crowding a fearful little man. The caption reads, *I want to impress one thing on you*.

Inside the card: *My body*.

Beneath that is the scrawled name *Eira*, and a telephone number. Should I call her? Dare I?

Bear in mind (as I must constantly remind myself to) that nothing the demon said can be trusted. Neither can anything that she herself said. She would have had me take her for a living woman if she could.

Has the demon devised an excruciating torment for us both?

Or for me alone?

The telephone number is at my elbow as I write. Her card is on my desk. If I dial the number, will I be blundering into the snare, or will I have torn the snare to pieces?

Should I call her?

A final possibility remains, although I find it almost impossible to write of it.

What if I am mad?

What if Foulweather the salesman merely played up to what he assumed was an elaborate joke? What if my last conversation with him (that is to say, with the demon) was a delusion?

What if Eira is in fact the living woman that almost every man in the world would take her for, save I?

She cannot have much money and may well be staying for a few days with some chance acquaintance.

Am I insane? Deluded?

Tomorrow she may be gone. One dash three one four . . .

Should I call?

Perhaps I may be a man of courage after all, a man who has never truly understood his own character.

Will I call her? Do I dare?

Frumpy Little Beat Girl

Peter Atkins

One theory of angels is that they are archetypes representing the positive/negative polarity of the universe: light and dark, good and evil, yin and yang. But, really, is the universe . . . or the multiverse . . . always so neatly divided? Has your own – most likely infinitesimally insignificant – life always reflected such distinct divisions? Does our world, or at least our consensus reality, always retain a tidy equilibrium? Anomalies happen. Someone has to set things back in balance. Peter Atkins's delightfully quirky story offers an original take on the angelic.

"They don't make hats like that anymore," says Mr Slater.

Jesus. Five minutes in and first thing out of his mouth. Bethany looks up from her book and through the windshield to see what the hell he's talking about.

There's a pedestrian, a Hispanic guy, crossing in front of the Lexus. He's in no particular hurry about it, and he doesn't need to be. The light they're stuck at, the one at San Fernando and Brand, can take three minutes even in a good mood and, at eight thirty in the morning, you can usually count on it being pissy.

"Sure they do," Bethany says, meaning the hat.

"No," Mr Slater says, his head moving to watch the man reach the sidewalk and turn to wait, like them, for the northbound green. Bethany hears the pleasure, the admiration, in his voice. "They make things that *look* like it, maybe," he says. "But that's *period*."

He has a point. It's not only the gray fedora. The pedestrian – elderly but vigorous, his body lean and compact, face like leather but like, you know, *good* leather – is dressed in a subtly pinstriped black suit that could be new or that could have been really well looked after for decades. There's a tight quarter-inch of white handkerchief showing above the suit's breast pocket, and the man wears opinionated shoes.

"Cool," Bethany says. "*Buena Vista Social Club*."

"You think he's Cuban?" Mr Slater asks, as if she was being literal. "I mean, like, not Mexican?"

Bethany, no idea, shrugs and smiles. The light changes and Mr Slater – *you know, you really can start calling me David*, he's said more than once but she's been babysitting for him and his wife since she was fourteen and just can't get her head around it – moves through the intersection and takes one last look back at the guy. "Check him out," he says, happy and impressed. "It's 1958. And it's never not going to be."

Gay Michael's on with a customer when Bethany comes into the bookstore but he takes the time to cover the phone's mouthpiece and stare pointedly out the plate-glass window as Mr Slater's Lexus pulls away into the Glendale traffic. He gives her an eyebrow. "Bethany Lake," he says, delighted. "You appalling little slut."

"My neighbor," she starts to tell him, ready to add that she'd needed a ride because her piece-of-shit Dodge is in the shop again but he's already back on the phone giving directions.

"Yes, ma'am," he's saying, "Michael & Michael. On Brand. Between Wilson and California." Listens for a moment. "Of course. Consider it held. And it really is in lovely condition. The website pictures don't do it justice." Bethany watches him run his hand over the tooled leather binding of the book on the counter in front of him as if he can send the seductive feel of it down the line. It's an 1827 *Paradise Lost*, the famous one with the John Martin mezzotints. Bethany catches his eye, points to the curtained annex at the rear of the store, mimes a coffee cup at her mouth.

She'd figured she'd have to brew a fresh pot but Fat Michael's already on it; three mugs waiting, OCD'd into a handle-matching line atop a napkin that's folded in geometric precision. On a shelf above the coffee-maker, his iPod is nestled in its cradle-and-mini-speakers set-up and its random shuffle – which Bethany pretends is a radio station with the call-sign K-FMO, for *Fat Michael's Oddities* – is playing "Jack the Ripper" by Screaming Lord Sutch. "Is your name Mary Blood?" his Lordship is currently screaming, albeit at low volume; Fat Michael would like to pipe K-FMO through to the store, but Gay Michael's foot is firmly down on that one. "What are we, fucking Wal-Mart?" is about as far as the conversation ever gets.

"He's really got a bite on that Milton?" Bethany says, knowing the guys have been asking high four figures. The coffee-maker pings.

"Some sitcom star's trophy wife," Fat Michael says, filling Bethany's mug first and handing it to her, no milk no sugar, just right. "She's shopping for his birthday. You know, like he can read."

"None of your customers read, Michael," she says. "They *collect*."

"Hmph," he says, because he doesn't like to be reminded, and then, as the next selection comes up on K-FMO, "Oh, listen. It's your song."

It so is *not* her song. It's a bad novelty record called "Kinky Boots" about how everybody's wearing, you know, kinky boots. The only boots Bethany owns are a pair of Doc Martens but it wasn't footwear that had made the boys declare it her song. Couple of months earlier, Gay Michael, bored on a customer-less afternoon, had treated her to an appraising look as she was leaning on the counter reading.

"Look at you," he'd said. "With your jean jacket and your ironic T-shirts." The one she'd been wearing that day had read

"Talk Nerdy to Me". "With your Aimee Bender paperbacks and your rah-rah skirts and leggings. You know what you are, Bethany? You're a frumpy little beat girl."

Fat Michael had clapped his hands in delight. Sometimes Bethany wondered which of the partners was actually the gay one. "'Sweet girls, Street girls, Frumpy little beat girls'," he'd recited, just in case Bethany had missed the reference to the stupid song's lyrics. She couldn't be mad at either of them – it was all so obviously coming from a place of affection – but, you know, Jesus Christ. Frumpy little beat girl.

She takes a sip of her coffee. "Not my song," she reminds Fat Michael, even though she knows it's like trying to lose a high school nickname.

Gay Michael pulls the annex curtain aside. "I have to drive it over at lunchtime," he says, meaning the Milton.

"She won't come here?" says Fat Michael.

"What, and leave the 'two-one-oh?" Gay Michael says. "She'd melt like Margaret Hamilton." He raises a pre-emptive hand before Fat Michael can object further. "I am not risking losing this sale, Michael," he says. "It's two months' rent."

"It's just that I have that, you know, that thing," says Fat Michael.

"I'll mind the store," Bethany says. She knows that "that thing" means a lunch date with a woman from whatever dating service he's currently using. She also knows it won't work out, they never do, but Fat Michael is a trier and Bethany sort of loves him for it.

She's never been left alone in charge of the store because the Michaels always stagger their lunch hours, so her offer to tend it for a couple of hours without adult supervision prompts – big surprise – a discussion. But they do their best not to make a drama out of it – which Bethany appreciates 'cause God knows it's an effort for both of them – and it boils down to her receiving several overcautious instructions, all of which pretty much translate as *don't do anything stupid*. After she promises that she'll do her best not to, they take her up on it and Gay Michael's gone by 11.45 to beat traffic and Fat Michael's out of there by noon.

Which is how Bethany comes to be alone when the man in the Chinese laundry initiates the Apocalypse.

Bethany's lost in her Kelly Link collection when the old-school bell tinkles on the entrance door. She looks up to see the door swinging shut behind a new customer as he walks in, holding a hardcover book in one gloved hand.

Huh, Bethany thinks. Gloves.

They're tight-fitting gray leather and, given that it's spring in California, would look even odder than they do were it not that the man's pretty overdressed anyway. His suit is a three-piece and its vest sports a chain that dangles in a generous curve from a button and leads, Bethany presumes, to a pocket watch that is currently, well, pocketed.

He's not in *costume* exactly, Bethany realizes – the suit is of modern cut and fit – but he's hardly inconspicuous. She flashes on the elderly Hispanic guy she and Mr Slater had seen at the light earlier and wonders if she somehow missed the memo about this being Sharp-Dressed-Man Day in Glendale. ZZ Top start riffing in her head but the accompanying mind-video is a spontaneous mash-up with Robert Palmer and his fuck-me mascarenes and Bethany makes a note to self that she needs to start spending a little less time watching *I Love the 80s*.

"I wonder if you can help me?" the customer says, coming to the counter. Cute accent. Like the guy from *House* when he's not being the guy from *House*.

"Almost certainly not," she says. "But I'll be real nice about it."

"Ah," he says, not put out at all. Far from it. "I take it, then, that you are neither Michael nor, indeed, Michael?" Now he's doing the other Hugh – Grant, not Laurie – and Bethany thinks he's laying it on a bit thick but decides to gives him the benefit of the doubt.

"Just Bethany," she says.

"Exactly who I was looking for," he says, laying the book he's carrying onto the counter. "I wanted to ask you about this."

There's no such thing as a book you never see again, Fat Michael had told her, a little booksellers' secret, shortly after she started working here. *Sooner or later, no matter how rare it is, another copy comes across the counter.* He'd been trying to make her feel better because she'd fallen in love with a UK first of Kenneth Grahame's *The Golden Age* and had been heartbroken when it left the store with somebody who could afford it. He'd been right, too; in her time with the Michaels, Bethany had seen many a mourned book wander back to their inventory, including the Grahame; one of the store's freelance scouts had scored another copy at an estate sale just a few weeks ago.

And now here comes this customer with another book, another blast from Bethany's past, from long before she worked here, but just as she remembers it; rich green cloth boards with a stylized Nouveau orchid on the front panel, its petals cupping the blood-red letters of the title.

"You do recognize it, don't you?" the man says.

"Sure," Bethany says, because she does. "*The Memory Pool.* Nineteen seventeen. First and only edition."

When she looks up from the book she sees that the customer is staring at her with an expression that she finds confusing, one of well intentioned but distant sympathy, the kind of expression you might give to a recently bereaved stranger. He touches the book's front panel lightly and briefly. "Mm," he says. "And quite rare, wouldn't you say?"

"Extremely rare," Bethany says, and immediately wants to slap her stupid mouth. Curse me for a novice, she thinks, a mantra of Gay Michael's whenever he's made a rare misstep in a negotiation. She's only been at the store a year, really *is* a novice still, but tipping a customer off that they've got something of real value is like entry-level dumb.

"Oh, don't worry. I'm not actually looking to sell it," he says, as if reading her dismay. "Just wanted to see if you knew it."

"Huh," says Bethany because, you know, *huh.*

The customer looks at her again, cocking his head as if intrigued. He extends his gloved hand across the counter.

"James Arcadia," he says, as Bethany shakes it. "I think, Just Bethany, we'd best have lunch."

"Why?" she asks, and she's smiling. Not too much, though; he's cute and all but, c'mon, he has to be forty at least. Still, she's flattered. Feels like she should conference-text the Michaels. *Not so frumpy*.

Arcadia returns the smile and she's glad that his eyes are kind because it softens the blow of his reply. "We need to discuss exactly how we're going to save the world," he says.

Well, Bethany thinks, that was dramatic, and, as if on cue, a woman screams from somewhere beyond the store. By the time a man's voice, equally horrified, hollers "My God, look at that!" Bethany and Arcadia have already turned to look through the window.

On the street outside, a man is melting.

He'd presumably been walking, but he's not walking anymore. He's rooted to the sidewalk, his legs already a fused and formless mass, his flesh and his clothes running in multi-colored ripples of dissolution down what used to be his body as if he was some life-size religious candle burning in fast-forward.

Other people on Brand Boulevard are screaming now, some running away, some gathering to see, one idiot on his cell-phone like he could actually fetch help, another using hers to snap a little souvenir of the atrocity. A group forms around the vanishing man, circling him but not going near, as if instinctively establishing a perimeter from which to bear witness but to keep themselves safe.

From what's left of the man's face – now liquidly elongated into a vile burlesque that puts Bethany briefly and horribly in mind of Munch's screamer – he appears to be, have been, a middle-aged white guy. He has a life, Bethany thinks, he has a story, has people who love him. But he's featureless in little more than a second. One of his arms has already disappeared into the oozing chaos of the meltdown but the other is waving grotesquely free, fingers twitching either in agony or, as Bethany wonders with a devastating stab of pity, as if he just wants someone to hold his hand in farewell as he slides helplessly from life.

When there's finally nothing about it to suggest it had ever been human, the roiling mass begins to shrink in on itself, disappearing into a vanishing center as if hungry for its own destruction, growing smaller and smaller until, at last, it shivers itself into nothingness. There's not even a stain on the sidewalk. It's taken maybe seven seconds.

"Oh my God," says Bethany.

Arcadia is keeping his eyes on the window. "Watch what happens next," he says. And when Bethany does, she decides that it's even more appalling than what came before.

Everybody walks away.

There's a blink or two from one or more of them, and one older woman in a blue pantsuit looks to her left as if she thought her peripheral vision may have just registered something, but there's no screaming, no outrage, no appeals to heaven or cries of *What-just-happened?* Everybody on the street quietly moves on about their day, neither their manner nor their expressions suggesting that anything out of the ordinary had occurred.

"What's *wrong* with them?" says Bethany. "They're all acting like it never happened."

"Don't be cross with them," Arcadia tells her. "It sort of *didn't* happen."

"But it did."

"I don't want to get too abstract about it," he says, "but it's a sort of tree falling in the forest question, isn't it? Can something actually be said to have happened if it's something nobody in the world remembers?"

"*I* remember," Bethany says.

Arcadia holds her gaze for a second or two, his face expressionless. "Aha," he says quietly.

Bethany's still trying to think about that when he pulls his watch from his vest pocket and checks it. "Hmm," he says. "Only eleven minutes in and already a serious anomaly. That's a bit worrying."

"What?" says Bethany, horrified as much at his calmness as at the idea that this nightmare is on some kind of a schedule.

"Clock's a-ticking," he says. "Lunch will have to wait. Come on."

Bethany's surprised to see that she's following him as he moves to the door and opens it. Perhaps it's the tinkling of the bell, perhaps just a desire to remember what she was doing the last time the world made sense, but something makes her look back at the counter.

"Wait," she says. "What about your book?"

Arcadia throws it an unconcerned glance. "Do you know what a McGuffin is, Bethany?" he says.

"Yes," she says, because she does. She watches her fair share of Turner Classic Movies and she briefly dated a guy who once had an actual name but whom she's long decided will be known to her memoirs only as the Boy Who Loved Hitchcock.

"Well, the book's a McGuffin," Arcadia says. "It's not *irrelevant* – I mean, it never existed and yet you remember it, which is good for a gasp or two and certainly pertains to the matter at hand – but it's real function is this: to propel us headlong into a thrilling and probably life-threatening adventure. You good to go?"

He waves her through the door with a hurrying motion and they're on the street and walking south before Bethany can get her question out.

"What do you mean, 'it never existed'?" she says.

"Well, not in this particular strand of the multiverse. It's a crossover, like the unfortunate gentleman outside your shop. Do you have a car, by the way?"

"No," she says. "I mean, not here."

"Oh," he says, stopping in front of a green Mercedes. "Let's take this one then." He opens the passenger door for her, apparently without needing a key. Bethany doesn't ask. Nor does she look too closely at how he starts it up before making an illegal U-turn and heading down Brand towards Atwater Village.

"What are we *doing*?" she asks, because she figures it's about time.

"Well, we're fixing a hole—"

"Where the rain gets in?" she says, flashing absurdly on the Beatles vinyl she'd rescued from her dad's stuff.

"Would that it were merely rain," he says. He nods toward the sidewalk they're speeding past, and Bethany looks to see a small boy turning to green smoke while pedestrians stare open-mouthed and his screaming mother tries to grab him, her desperate fingers clawing only at his absence. By the time Bethany has swung in her seat to look out the rear window, the smoke has vanished and the crowd, including the mother, has forgotten it was ever there.

Bethany's eyes are wet with pity as she turns back to Arcadia. "Tell me what's happening!" she almost shouts.

Arcadia swings the car into the right lane as they pass under the railroad bridge. "I'll try to make this as quick as I can," he says, and takes a preparatory breath. "The spaces between the worlds have been breached. Realities are bleeding through to each other. People who took one step in their own dimension took their next in another. What you've witnessed is the multiverse trying to correct itself by erasing the anomalies. Problem is it's happening in each reality and the incidents will increase exponentially until there's nothing left in any of them." He turns to look at her. "With me so far?"

Bethany unfortunately *is* with him so far, though she wishes she'd heeded those schoolyard theories that comic books weren't really for girls. "Collapse of the space-time continuum," she says in a surprisingly steady voice.

"Precisely," says Arcadia, pleased that this is going so well. "A return to a timeless shining singularity without form, thought, or feeling."

"But how?" she says. "And why?"

Arcadia has started to slow the car down now, scanning the storefronts of Atwater Village's main drag. "Because about seventeen minutes ago, something that's lived all its life as a man remembered what it really is and spoke certain words of power."

Bethany doesn't like the sound of that at all and, as Arcadia pulls up outside one of the few remaining un-gentrified stores on a strip that is mostly hipper new businesses and milk-it-quick franchises, she stays silent, feeling the sadness and fear tightening in her stomach like cancer, thinking of people vanishing from the world like a billion lights blinking out one by one.

"Is this where we're going?" she finally says, nodding at the store as they get out of the car.

"Yes," Arcadia says. "Have you seen it before?"

Bethany nods, because she has. It could have been here since 1933, she's always thought; peeling red paint on aged wood; plate-glass window whitewashed from the inside to keep its secrets; and a single hanging sign with the hand-painted phrase, CHINESE LAUNDRY. She doesn't think she's ever seen it open for business. "I always figured it was a front for the Tongs," she says as if she was kidding, but realizes as she says it that that actually *is* what she's always thought.

"You're such a romantic," Arcadia says, and he sounds delighted with her. He opens the door to the laundry and leads her inside.

Its interior is as weathered and as free of decoration as the outside. A hardwood floor that hasn't seen varnish for decades and utterly plain walls painted long ago in the kind of institutionally vile colors usually reserved for state hospitals in the poorest neighborhoods. Bethany is surprised, though, to smell the heavy detergent and feel the clammy humidity of what is clearly a working laundry. There's even the slow hissing, from behind the screen space-divider, of a heavy-duty steam press. The place isn't menacing, merely nondescript. The fifty-year-old man behind the bare wood counter would be nondescript too were it not for the subtle phosphorescent glow of his flesh.

Arcadia makes the introductions. "Bethany Lake," he says – and Bethany registers the use of the surname she hadn't told him – "meet the entity formerly known as Jerry Harrington."

Bethany gasps a little as the man fixes his eyes on her because they are the almost solid black of a tweaker on an overdose about to kill him.

Not Chinese at all, a part of her brain wastes its time

thinking, and wonders if it's entirely PC of him not to have changed the name, however generic, of the business he bought.

"What do you want?" Harrington says. His tone is hardly gracious, but at least it still sounds human, for which Bethany is grateful.

"What *do* we want?" she says to Arcadia.

"Well, *I* want him to stop destroying reality," Arcadia says. "Don't you?"

"Yes," Bethany says. "Of course."

Arcadia turns back to Harrington. "There you go," he says. "Two votes to one. Majority rules. What do you say?"

Harrington laughs, but there's little humor in it.

"What *is* he?" Bethany asks Arcadia quietly. She's turned her head away from Harrington because his face seems to be constantly coming in and out of focus in a way that she finds not just frightening but physically disturbing.

"A being from a time outside time," Arcadia says. "There's several of them around, hidden in the flesh since the Fall. Most of them don't remember themselves, but occasionally there's a problem."

The Fall? Bethany hesitates to ask, because she doesn't want to say something that sounds so ridiculous, but she supposes she has to. "Are you talking about angels?" she says. "Fallen angels?"

"Well, you needn't be so Judeo-Christian specific about it," he says, a little sniffily. "But, yes."

"What do you want?" Harrington says again, exactly as he'd said it before. So exactly that it creeps Bethany out. Less like a person repeating themselves and more like someone just rewound the tape.

"We're here to make you reconsider," Arcadia says. "We can do it the hard way, if you want, but I'd prefer to talk you out of it."

Again, the laugh. But there's little human in it.

Arcadia moves closer to the counter, which Bethany finds almost indescribably brave. "Look, I get it," he says. "You're home-sick. You want a return to the *tabula rasa*, the blank page, the white light, the glorious absence. You yearn for it like a sailor for the sea or a child for its mother. You're disgusted by all this . . . this . . ." He waves his hands, searching for the words. "All this multiplicity, this variousness, this detail and color and noise and *stuff*."

"You talk too much," Harrington says, and Bethany, though shocked at her treachery, thinks he's got a point.

"But isn't there another way to look at it?" Arcadia says. "We're all going back to the white light eventually, so what does it matter? Couldn't we imagine looking at these people amongst whom your kind has fallen not with contempt but with delight? Isn't it possible that an angel could embrace the flesh rather than loathe it? Could choose to be humanity's protector rather than its scourge?"

"You can imagine whatever you like if it makes you feel better," Harrington says, and his voice is confident and contemptuous. "But you won't imagine it for very long. Because that's not the path I've chosen."

Arcadia smiles, like there's been some misunderstanding. "Oh, I wasn't talking about you," he says.

Bethany is wondering just who the hell he *is* talking about when the pores of her flesh erupt and the light starts to stream from her body. The rush of release almost drowns out the beating of her terrible wings and the sweet music of Harrington's scream.

Arcadia picks up the small-pitted cinder-like object from the laundry counter with a pair of tweezers. It's still smoking slightly and he blows on it to cool it before dropping it into a thin test tube which he slips back into an inside pocket of his suit.

"I'll put it with the others," he says to Bethany. She wonders where the *if that's all right with you* tone has come from, like he's her Beautiful Assistant rather than vice versa, but she nods anyway. She and he are the only people in the place and she's sort of grateful that she has no memory of the last few minutes. She feels quite tired and is glad of Arcadia's arm when he walks her to the car.

★   ★   ★

Bethany's relieved that she's back in the store before either of the Michaels. As ever, there are several out-of-shelf books lying around here and there and she decides to do a little housekeeping to assuage her guilt for playing hooky. She shelves most of them in the regular stacks, some in the high-end display cases, and one in the spaces between the worlds, though she doesn't really notice that because she's thinking about her crappy Dodge and how much the shop is going to charge her to fix it this time.

Gay Michael gets back first. Maybe Fat Michael's date is going better than expected. Bethany hopes so.

"Anything happen?" Gay Michael says.

"Not so you'd notice," Bethany tells him.

The Night of White Bhairab

Lucius Shepard

*Commissioned in 1769 by King Rana Bahadur Shah (1775–
1805), the "White Bhairab" is a portrayal of a fierce
manifestation of Lord Shiva associated with annihilation. It
was intended to ward off evil influences and protect a palace.
About ten feet high, it sports a golden crown made of serpents,
skulls and jewels. A huge open mouth shows terrifying white
teeth and fangs. Angry red-pupiled eyes are set in a golden face
detailed with red, black, blue and white paint. Usually mostly
hidden behind a carved wooden screen, during the days of Indra
Jatra and the coinciding festival of the Living Goddess, it is
open to public view. Lucius Shepard sets his exotic and exciting
story during the festival, but the evil that visits Katmandu is
imported from the West: a demonically possessed spirit that
takes more than human effort to fight.*

Whenever Mr Chatterji went to Delhi on business, twice
yearly, he would leave Eliot Blackford in charge of his
Katmandu home and, prior to each trip, the transfer of keys
and instructions would be made at the Hotel Anapurna. Eliot
– an angular, sharp-featured man in his mid-thirties, with thinning blond hair and a perpetually ardent expression – knew
Mr Chatterji for a subtle soul and he suspected that this
subtlety had dictated the choice of meeting place. The

Anapurna was the Nepalese equivalent of a Hilton, its bar equipped in vinyl and plastic, with a choirlike arrangement of bottles fronting the mirror. Lights were muted, napkins mono- grammed. Mr Chatterji, plump and prosperous in a business suit, would consider it an elegant refutation of Kipling's famous couplet ("East is East", etc.) that he was at home here, whereas Eliot, wearing a scruffy robe and sandals, was not; he would argue that not only the twain met, they had actually exchanged places. It was Eliot's own measure of subtlety that restrained him from pointing out what Mr Chatterji could not perceive: that the Anapurna was a skewed version of the American Dream. The carpeting was indoor-outdoor runner; the menu was rife with ludicrous misprints (*Skotch Miss, Screwdiver*), and the lounge act – two turbaned, tuxedoed Indi- ans on electric guitar and traps – was managing to turn "Evergreen" into a doleful raga.

"There will be one important delivery." Mr Chatterji hailed the waiter and nudged Eliot's shot glass forward. "It should have been here days ago, but you know these custom people." He gave an effeminate shudder to express his distaste for the bureaucracy, and cast an expectant eye on Eliot, who did not disappoint.

"What is it?" he asked, certain that it would be an addition to Mr Chatterji's collection: he enjoyed discussing the collec- tion with Americans; it proved that he had an overview of their culture.

"Something delicious!" said Mr Chatterji. He took the tequila bottle from the waiter and – with a fond look – passed it to Eliot. "Are you familiar with the Carversville Terror?"

"Yeah, sure." Eliot knocked back another shot. "There was a book about it."

"Indeed," said Mr Chatterji. "A bestseller. The Cousineau mansion was once the most notorious haunted house of your New England. It was torn down several months ago, and I've succeeded in acquiring the fireplace, which—" he sipped his drink "—was the locus of power. I'm very fortunate to have obtained it." He fitted his glass into the circle of moisture on the bar and waxed scholarly. "Aimée Cousineau, was a most unusual spirit, capable of a variety of . . ."

Eliot concentrated on his tequila. These recitals never failed to annoy him, as did – for different reasons – the sleek Western disguise. When Eliot had arrived in Katmandu as a member of the Peace Corps, Mr Chatterji had presented a far less pompous image: a scrawny kid dressed in Levi's that he had wheedled from a tourist. He'd been one of the hangers-on – mostly young Tibetans – who frequented the grubby tea rooms on Freak Street, watching the American hippies giggle over their hash yogurt, lusting after their clothes, their women, their entire culture. The hippies had respected the Tibetans, they were a people of legend, symbols of the occultism then in vogue, and the fact that they liked James Bond movies, fast cars and Jimi Hendrix had increased the hippies' self-esteem. But they had found laughable the fact that Ranjeesh Chatterji – another Westernized Indian – had liked these same things, and they had treated him with mean condescension. Now, thirteen years later, the roles had been reversed; it was Eliot who had become the hanger-on.

He had settled in Katmandu after his tour was up, his idea being to practice meditation, to achieve enlightenment. But it had not gone well. There was an impediment in his mind – he pictured it as a dark stone, a stone compounded of worldly attachments – that no amount of practice could wear down, and his life had fallen into a futile pattern. He would spend ten months of the year living in a small room near the temple of Swayambhunath, meditating, rubbing away at the stone; and then, during March and September, he would occupy Mr Chatterji's house and debauch himself with liquor and sex and drugs. He was aware that Mr Chatterji considered him a burnout, that the position of caretaker was in effect a form of revenge, a means by which his employer could exercise his own brand of condescension; but Eliot minded neither the label nor the attitude. There were worse things to be than a burnout in Nepal. It was beautiful country, it was inexpensive, it was far from Minnesota (Eliot's home). And the concept of personal failure was meaningless here. You lived, died, and were reborn over and over until at last you attained the ultimate success of non-being: a terrific consolation for failure.

". . . yet in your country," Mr Chatterji was saying, "evil has a sultry character. Sexy! It's as if the spirits were adopting vibrant personalities in order to contend with pop groups and movie stars."

Eliot thought of a comment, but the tequila backed up on him and he belched instead. Everything about Mr Chatterji – teeth, eyes, hair, gold rings – seemed to be gleaming with extraordinary brilliance. He looked as unstable as a soap bubble, a fat little Hindu illusion . . .

Mr Chatterji clapped a hand, to his forehead. "I nearly forgot. There will be another American staying at the house. A girl. Very shapely!" He shaped an hourglass in the air. "I'm quite mad for her, but I don't know if she's trustworthy. Please see she doesn't bring in any strays."

"Right," said Eliot. "No problem."

"I believe I will gamble now," said Mr Chatterji, standing and gazing toward the lobby. "Will you join me?"

"No, I think I'll get drunk. I guess I'll see you in October."

"You' re drunk already, Eliot." Mr Chatterji patted him on the shoulder. "Hadn't you noticed?

Early the next morning, hungover, tongue cleaving to the roof of his mouth, Eliot sat himself down for a final bout of trying to visualize the Avalokitesvara Buddha. All the sounds outside – the buzzing of a motor scooter, birdsong, a girl's laughter – seemed to be repeating the mantra, and the gray stone walls of his room looked at once intensely real and yet incredibly fragile, papery, a painted backdrop he could rip with his hands. He began to feel the same fragility, as if he were being immersed in a liquid that was turning him opaque, filling him with clarity. A breath of wind could float him out the window, drift him across the fields, and he would pass through the trees and mountains, all the phantoms of the material world . . . but then a trickle of panic welled up from the bottom of his soul, from that dark stone. It was beginning to smolder, to give off poison fumes: a little briquette of anger and lust and fear. Cracks were spreading across the clear substance he had become, and if he didn't move soon, if he didn't break off the meditation, he would shatter.

He toppled out of the lotus position and lay propped on his elbows. His heart raced, his chest heaved, and he felt very much like screaming his frustration. Yeah, that was a temptation. To just say the hell with it and scream, to achieve through chaos what he could not through clarity: to empty himself into the scream. He was trembling, his emotions flowing between self-hate and self-pity. Finally, he struggled up and put on jeans and a cotton shirt. He knew he was close to a breakdown, and he realized that he usually reached this point just before taking up residence at Mr Chatterji's. His life was a frayed thread stretched tight between those two poles of debauchery. One day it would snap.

"The hell with it," he said. He stuffed the remainder of his clothes into a duffel bag and headed into town.

Walking through Durbar Square – which wasn't really a square but a huge temple complex interspersed with open areas and wound through by cobbled path – always put Eliot in mind of his brief stint as a tour guide, a career cut short when the agency received complaints about his eccentricity. ("... As you pick your way among the piles of human waste and fruit rinds, I caution you not to breathe too deeply of the divine afflatus; otherwise, it may forever numb you to the scent of Prairie Cove or Petitpoint Gulch or whatever citadel of gracious living it is that you call home ...") It had irked him to have to lecture on the carvings and history of the square, especially to the just-plain-folks who only wanted a Polaroid of Edna or Uncle Jimmy standing next to that weird monkey god on the pedestal. The square was a unique place and, in Eliot's opinion, such unenlightened tourism demeaned it.

Pagoda-style temples of red brick and dark wood towered on all sides, their finials rising into brass lightning bolts. They

were alien-looking – you half expected the sky above them to
be of an otherworldly color, and figured by several moons.
Their eaves and window screens were ornately carved into the
images of gods and demons, and behind a large window screen
on the temple of White Bhairab lay the mask of that god. It was
almost ten feet high, brass, with a fanciful headdress and long-
lobed ears and a mouth full of white fangs; its eyebrows were
enameled red, fiercely arched, but the eyes had the goofy quality common to Newari gods – no matter how wrathful they
were, there was something essentially friendly about them, and
they reminded Eliot of cartoon germs. Once a year – in fact, a
little more than a week from now – the screens would be
opened, a pipe would be inserted into the god's mouth, and
rice beer would jet out into the mouths of the milling crowds;
at some point a fish would be slipped into the pipe, and
whoever caught it would be deemed the luckiest soul in the
Katmandu Valley for the next year. It was one of Eliot's traditions to make a try for the fish, though he knew that it wasn't
luck he needed.

Beyond the square, the streets were narrow, running
between long brick buildings three and four stories tall, each
divided into dozens of separate dwellings. The strip of sky
between the roofs was bright, burning blue – a void color – and
in the shade the bricks looked purplish. People hung out the
windows of the upper stories, talking back and forth: an exotic
tenement life. Small shrines – wooden enclosures containing
statuary of stucco or brass – were tucked into wall niches and
the mouths of alleys. The gods were everywhere in Katmandu,
and there was hardly a corner to which their gaze did not
penetrate.

On reaching Mr Chatterji's, which occupied half a block-
long building, Eliot made for the first of the interior
courtyards; a stair led up from it to Mr Chatterji's apartment,
and he thought he would check on what had been left to
drink. But as he entered the courtyard – a phalanx of ugly
plants arranged around a lozenge of cement – he saw the girl
and stopped short. She was sitting in a lawn chair, reading,

and she was indeed very shapely. She wore loose cotton trousers, a T-shirt and a long white scarf shot through with golden threads. The scarf and the trousers were the uniform of the young travelers who generally stayed in the expatriate enclave of Temal: it seemed that they all bought them immediately upon arrival in order to identify themselves to each other. Edging closer, peering between the leaves of a rubber plant, Eliot saw that the girl was doe-eyed, with honey-colored skin and shoulder-length brown hair interwoven by lighter strands. Her wide mouth had relaxed into a glum expression. Sensing him, she glanced up, startled; then she waved and set down her book.

"I'm Eliot," he said, walking over.

"I know. Ranjeesh told me." She stared at him incuriously.

"And you?" He squatted beside her.

"Michaela." She fingered the book, as if she were eager to get back to it.

"I can see you're new in town."

"How's that?"

He told her about the clothes, and she shrugged. "That's what I am," she said. "I'll probably always wear them." She folded her hands on her stomach; it was a nicely rounded stomach, and Eliot – a connoisseur of women's stomachs – felt the beginnings of arousal.

"Always?" he said. "You plan on being here that long?"

"I don't know." She ran a finger along the spine of the book. "Ranjeesh asked me to marry him, and I said maybe."

Eliot's infant plan of seduction collapsed beneath this wrecking ball of a statement, and he failed to hide his incredulity. "You're in love with Ranjeesh?"

"What's that got to do with it?" A wrinkle creased her brow; it was the perfect symptom of her mood, the line a cartoonist might have chosen to express petulant anger.

"Nothing. Not if it doesn't have anything to do with it." He tried a grin, but to no effect. "Well," he said after a pause. "How do you like Katmandu?"

"I don't get out much," she said flatly.

She obviously did not want conversation, but Eliot wasn't ready to give up. "You ought to," he said. "The festival of Indra Jatra's about to start. It's pretty wild. Especially on the night of White Bhairab. Buffalo sacrifices, torchlight . . ."

"I don't like crowds," she said.

Strike two.

Eliot strained to think of an enticing topic, but he had the idea it was a lost cause. There was something inert about her, a veneer of listlessness redolent of Thorazine, of hospital routine. "Have you seen the Khaa?" he asked.

"The what?"

"The Khaa. It's a spirit . . . though some people will tell you it's partly animal, because over here the animal and spirit worlds overlap. But whatever it is, all the old houses have one, and those that don't are considered unlucky. There's one here."

"What's it look like?"

"Vaguely anthropomorphic. Black, featureless. Kind of a living shadow. They can stand upright, but they roll instead of walk."

She laughed. "No, I haven't seen it. Have you?"

"Maybe," said Eliot. "I thought I saw it a couple of times, but I was pretty stoned."

She sat up straighter and crossed her legs; her breasts jiggled and Eliot fought to keep his eyes centered on her face. "Ranjeesh tells me you're a little cracked," she said.

Good ol' Ranjeesh! He might have known that the son of a bitch would have sandbagged him with his new lady. "I guess I am," he said, preparing for the brush-off. "I do a lot of meditation, and sometimes I teeter on the edge."

But she appeared more intrigued by this admission than by anything else he had told her; a smile melted up from her carefully composed features. "Tell me some more about the Khaa," she said.

Eliot congratulated himself. "They're quirky sorts," he said. "Neither good nor evil. They hide in dark corners, though now and then they're seen in the streets or in the fields out near Jyapu. And the oldest ones, the most powerful ones, live in the temples in Durbar Square. There's a story about the one here that's descriptive of how they operate . . . if you're interested."

"Sure." Another smile.

"Before Ranjeesh bought this place, it was a guest house, and one night a woman with three goiters on her neck came to spend the night. She had two loaves of bread that she was taking home to her family, and she stuck them under her pillow before going to sleep. Around midnight the Khaa rolled into her room and was struck by the sight of her goiters rising and falling as she breathed. He thought they'd make a beautiful necklace, so he took them and put them on his own neck. Then he spotted the loaves sticking out from her pillow. They looked good, so he took them as well and replaced them with two loaves of gold. When the woman woke, she was delighted. She hurried back to her village to tell her family, and on the way, she met a friend, a woman, who was going to market. This woman had four goiters. The first woman told her what had happened, and that night the second woman went to the guest house and did exactly the same things. Around midnight the Khaa rolled into her room. He'd grown bored with the necklace, and he gave it to the woman. He'd also decided that bread didn't taste very good, but he still had a loaf and he figured he'd give it another chance. So in exchange for the necklace, he took the woman's appetite for bread. When she woke, she had seven goiters, no gold, and she could never eat bread again the rest of her life."

Eliot had expected a response of mild amusement, and had hoped that the story would be the opening gambit in a game with a foregone and pleasurable conclusion; but he had not expected her to stand, to become walled off from him again.

"I've got to go," she said and, with a distracted wave, she made for the front door. She walked with her head down, hands thrust into her pockets, as if counting the steps.

"Where are you going?" called Eliot, taken aback.

"I don't know. Freak Street, maybe."

"Want some company?"

She turned back at the door. "It's not your fault," she said, "but I don't really enjoy your company."

Shot down!

Trailing smoke, spinning, smacking into the hillside, and blowing up into a fireball.

Eliot didn't understand why it had hit him so bad. It had happened before, and it would again. Ordinarily, he would have headed for Temal and found himself another long white scarf and pair of cotton trousers, one less morbidly self-involved (that, in retrospect, was how he characterized Michaela), one who would help him refuel for another bout of trying to visualize Avalokitesvara Buddha. He did, in fact, go to Temal; but he merely sat and drank tea and smoked hashish in a restaurant, and watched the young travelers pairing up for the night. Once he caught the bus to Patan and visited a friend, an old hippie pal named Sam Chipley who ran a medical clinic; once he walked out to Swayambhunath, close enough to see the white dome of the stupa, and atop it, the gilt structure on which the all-seeing eyes of Buddha were painted: they seemed squinty and mean-looking, as if taking unfavorable notice of his approach. But mostly over the next week he wandered through Mr Chatterji's house, carrying a bottle, maintaining a buzz, and keeping an eye on Michaela.

The majority of the rooms were unfurnished, but many bore signs of recent habitation: broken hash pipes, ripped sleeping bags, empty packets of incense. Mr Chatterji let travelers – those he fancied sexually, male and female – use the rooms for up to months at a time, and to walk through them was to take a historical tour of the American counterculture. The graffiti spoke of concerns as various as Vietnam, the Sex Pistols, women's lib and the housing shortage in Great Britain, and also conveyed personal messages: "Ken Finkel please get in touch with me at Am. Ex. in Bangkok . . . love, Ruth." In one of the rooms was a complicated mural depicting Farrah Fawcett sitting on the lap of a Tibetan demon, throttling his barbed phallus with her fingers. It all conjured up the image of a moldering, deranged milieu. Eliot's milieu. At first the tour amused him, but eventually it began to sour him on himself, and he took to spending more and more time on a balcony overlooking the courtyard that was shared with the connecting house, listening to the Newari women sing at their chores and reading books from Mr Chatterji's library. One of the books was titled *The Carversville Terror*.

"... bloodcurdling, chilling ..." said the *New York Times* on the front flap. "... the Terror is, unrelenting ..." commented Stephen King. "... riveting, gut-wrenching, mind-bending horror ..." gushed *People* magazine. In neat letters, Eliot appended his own blurb: "... piece of crap ..." The text – written to be read by the marginally literate – was a fictionalized treatment of purportedly real events, dealing with the experiences of the Whitcomb family, who had attempted to renovate the Cousineau mansion during the sixties. Following the usual build-up of apparitions, cold spots and noisome odors, the family – Papa David, Mama Elaine, young sons Tim and Randy, and teenage Ginny – had met to discuss the situation.

... even the kids, thought David, had been aged by the house. Gathered around the dining-room table, they looked like a company of the damned, haggard shadows under their eyes, grim-faced. Even with the windows open and the light streaming in, it seemed there was a pall in the air that no light could dispel. Thank God the damned thing was dormant during the day!

"Well," he said, "I guess the floor's open for arguments."

"I wanna go home!" Tears sprang from Randy's eyes and, on cue, Tim started crying, too.

"It's not that simple," said David. "This *is* home, and I don't know how we'll make it if we do leave. The savings account is just about flat."

"I suppose I could get a job," said Elaine unenthusiastically.

"I'm not leaving!" Ginny jumped to her feet, knocking over her chair. "Every time I start to make friends, we have to move!"

"But Ginny!" Elaine reached out a hand to calm her. "You were the one ..."

"I've changed my mind!" She backed away, as if she had just recognized them all to be mortal enemies. "You can do what you want, but I'm staying!" And she ran from the room.

"Oh, God," said Elaine wearily. "What's gotten into her?"

What had gotten into Ginny, what was in the process of getting into her and was the only interesting part of the book, was the spirit of Aimée Cousineau. Concerned with his daughter's behavior, David Whitcomb had researched the house and learned a great deal about the spirit. Aimée Cousineau, née Vuillemont, had been a native of St Berenice, a Swiss village at the foot of the mountain known as the Eiger (its photograph, as well as one of Aimée – a coldly beautiful woman with black hair and cameo features – was included in the central section of the book). Until the age of fifteen, she had been a sweet, unexceptional child; however, in the summer of 1889, while hiking on the slopes of the Eiger, she had become lost in a cave.

The family had all but given up hope, when, to their delight – three weeks later – she had turned up on the steps of her father's store. Their delight was short-lived. This Aimée was far different from the one who had entered the cave. Violent, calculating, slatternly.

Over the next two years, she succeeded in seducing half the men of the village, including the local priest. According to his testimony, he had been admonishing her that sin was not the path to happiness when she began to undress. "I'm wed to Happiness," she told him. "I've entwined my limbs with the God of Bliss and kissed the scaly thighs of Joy." Throughout the ensuing affair, she made cryptic comments concerning "the God below the mountain", whose soul was now forever joined to hers.

At this point the book reverted to the gruesome adventures of the Whitcomb family, and Eliot, bored, realizing it was noon and that Michaela would be sunbathing, climbed to Mr Chatterji's apartment on the fourth floor. He tossed the book

onto a shelf and went out onto the balcony. His continued
interest in Michaela puzzled him. It occurred to him that he
might be falling in love, and he thought that would be nice.
Though it would probably lead nowhere, love would be a
good kind of energy to have. But he doubted this was the case.
Most likely his interest was founded on some fuming product
of the dark stone inside him. Simple lust. He looked over the
edge of the balcony. She was lying on a blanket – her bikini
top beside her at the bottom of a well of sunlight: thin, pure
sunlight like a refinement of honey spreading down and
congealing into the mold of a little gold woman. It seemed her
heat that was in the air.

That night Eliot broke one of Mr Chatterji's rules and slept in
the master bedroom. It was roofed by a large skylight, mounted
in a ceiling painted midnight blue. The normal display of stars
had not been sufficient for Mr Chatterji, and so he'd had the
skylight constructed of faceted glass that multiplied the stars,
making it appear that you were at the heart of a galaxy, gazing
out between the interstices of its blazing core. The walls
consisted of a photomural of the Khumbu Glacier and
Chomolungma; and, bathed in the starlight, the mural had
acquired the illusion of depth and chill mountain silence.
Lying there, Eliot could hear the faith sounds of Indra Jatra:
shouts and cymbals, oboes and drums. He was drawn to the
sounds; he wanted to run out into the streets, become an
element of the drunken crowds, be whirled through torchlight
and delirium to the feet of an idol stained with sacrificial blood.
But he felt bound to the house, to Michaela. Marooned in the
glow of Mr Chatterji's starlight, floating above Chomolungma
and listening to the din of the world below, he could almost
believe he was a bodhisattva awaiting a call to action, that his
watchfulness had some purpose.

The shipment arrived late in the afternoon of the eighth day.
Five enormous crates, each requiring the combined energies
of Eliot and three Newari workmen to wrangle up to the

third-floor room that housed Mr Chatterji's collection. After
tipping the men, Eliot sat down against the wall to catch his
hot, sweaty, panting breath. The room was about twenty-five
feet by fifteen, but looked smaller because of the dozens of
curious objects standing around the floor and mounted one
above the other on the walls. A brass doorknob, a shattered
door, a straight-backed chair whose arms were bound with a
velvet rope to prevent anyone from sitting, a discolored sink, a
mirror streaked by a brown stain, a slashed lampshade. They
were all relics of some haunting or possession, some grotesque
violence, and there were cards affixed to them testifying to the
details and referring those who were interested to materials in
Mr Chatterji's library. Sitting surrounded by these relics, the
crates looked innocuous, bolted shut, chest-high, branded with
customs stamps.

When he had recovered, Eliot strolled around the room,
amused by the care that Mr Chatterji had squandered on his
hobby; the most amusing thing was that no one except Mr
Chatterji was impressed by it: it provided travelers with a foot-
note for their journals. Nothing more.

A wave of dizziness swept over him – he had stood too soon
– and he leaned against one of the crates for support. Jesus, he
was in lousy shape! And then, as he blinked away the tangles of
opaque cells drifting across his field of vision, the crate shifted.
Just a little shift, as if something inside had twitched in its sleep.
But palpable, real. He flung himself toward the door, backing
away. A chill mapped every knob and articulation of his spine,
and his sweat had evaporated, leaving clammy patches on his
skin. The crate was motionless. But he was afraid to take his eyes
off it, certain that if he did, it would release its pent-up fury.

"Hi," said Michaela from the doorway.

Her voice electrified Eliot. He let out a squawk and wheeled
around, his hands out held to ward off attack.

"I didn't mean to startle you," she said. "I'm sorry."

"Goddamn!" he said. "Don't sneak up like that!" He remembered the crate and glanced back at it. "Listen, I was just
locking . . ."

"I'm sorry," she repeated, and walked past him into the room. "Ranjeesh is such an idiot about all this," she said, running her hand over the top of the crate. "Don't you think?"

Her familiarity with the crate eased Eliot's apprehension. Maybe he had been the one who had twitched: a spasm of overstrained muscles. "Yeah, I guess."

She walked over to the straight-backed chair, slipped off the velvet rope and sat down. She was wearing a pale brown skirt and a plaid blouse that made her look schoolgirl-ish. "I want to apologize about the other day," she said; she bowed her head, and the fall of her hair swung forward to obscure her face. "I've been having a bad time lately. I have trouble relating to people. To anything. But since we're living here together, I'd like to be friends." She stood and spread the folds of her skirt. "See? I even put on different clothes. I could tell the others offended you."

The innocent sexuality of the pose caused Eliot to have a rush of desire. "Looks nice," he said with forced casualness. "Why've you been having a bad time?"

She wandered to the door and gazed out. "Do you really want to hear about it?"

"Not if it's painful for you."

"It doesn't matter," she said, leaning against the doorframe. "I was in a band back in the States, and we were doing okay. Cutting an album, talking to record labels. I was living with the guitarist, in love with him. But then I had an affair. Not even an affair. It was stupid. Meaningless. I still don't know why I did it. The heat of the moment, I guess. That's what rock 'n' roll's all about, and maybe I was just acting out the myth. One of the other musicians told my boyfriend. That's the way bands are – you're friends with everyone, but at the same time . . . See, I told this guy about the affair. We'd always confided. But one day he got mad at me over something. Something else stupid and meaningless." Her chin was struggling to stay firm; the breeze from the courtyard drifted fine strands of hair across her face. "My boyfriend went crazy and beat up my . . ." She gave a dismal laugh. "I don't know what to call him. My lover.

Whatever. My boyfriend killed him. It was an accident, but he tried to run, and the police shot him."

Eliot wanted to stop her; she was obviously seeing it all again, seeing blood and police flashers and cold white morgue lights. But she was riding a wave of memory, borne along by its energy, and he knew that she had to crest with it, crash with it.

"I was out of it for a while. Dreamy. Nothing touched me. Not the funerals, the angry parents. I went away for months, to the mountains, and I started to feel better. But when I came home, I found that the musician who'd told my boyfriend had written a song about it. The affair, the killings. He'd cut a record. People were buying it, singing the hook when they walked down the street or took a shower. Dancing to it! They were dancing on blood and bones, humming grief, shelling out $5.98 for a jingle about suffering. Looking back, I realize I was crazy, but at the time everything I did seemed normal. More than normal. Directed, inspired. I bought a gun. A ladies' model, the salesman said. I remember thinking how strange it was that there were male and female guns, just like with electric razors. I felt enormous carrying it. I had to be meek and polite or else I was sure people would notice how large and purposeful I was. It wasn't hard to track down Ronnie – that's the guy who wrote the song. He was in Germany cutting a second album. I couldn't believe it; I wasn't going to be able to kill him! I was so frustrated that one night I went down to a park and started shooting. I missed everything. Out of all the bums and joggers and squirrels, I hit leaves and air. They locked me up after that. A hospital. I think it helped, but . . ." She blinked, waking from a trance. "But I still feel so disconnected, you know?"

Eliot carefully lifted away the strands of hair that had blown across her face and laid them back in place. Her smile flickered. "I know," he said. "I feel that way sometimes."

She nodded thoughtfully, as if to verify that she had recognized this quality in him.

*   *   *

They ate dinner in a Tibetan place in Temal; it had no name and was a dump with flyspecked tables and rickety chairs, specializing in water buffalo and barley soup. But it was away from the city center, which meant they could avoid the worst of the festival crowds. The waiter was a young Tibetan wearing jeans and a T-shirt that bore the legend MAGIC IS THE ANSWER, earphones of a personal stereo dangled about his neck. The walls – visible through a haze of smoke – were covered with snapshots, most featuring the waiter in the company of various tourists, but a few showing an older Tibetan in blue robes and turquoise jewelry, carrying an automatic rifle; this was the owner, one of the Khampa tribesmen who had fought a guerrilla war against the Chinese. He rarely put in an appearance at the restaurant, and when he did, his glowering presence tended to dampen conversation.

Over dinner, Eliot tried to steer clear of topics that might unsettle Michaela. He told her about Sam Chipley's clinic, the time the Dalai Lama had come to Katmandu, the musicians at Swayambhunath. Cheerful, exotic topics. Her listlessness was such an inessential part of her that Eliot was led to chip away at it, curious to learn what lay beneath; and the more he chipped away, the more animated her gestures, the more luminous her smile became. This was a different sort of smile than she had displayed on their first meeting. It came so suddenly over her face, it seemed an autonomic reaction, like the opening of a sunflower, as if she were facing not you but the principle of light upon which you were grounded. It was aware of you, of course, but it chose to see past the imperfections of the flesh and know the perfected thing you truly were. It boosted your sense of worth to realize that you were its target, and Eliot – whose sense of worth was at low ebb – would have done pratfalls to sustain it. Even when he told his own story, he told it as a joke, a metaphor for American misconceptions of oriental pursuits.

"Why don't you quit it?" she asked. "The meditation, I mean. If it's not working out, why keep on with it?"

"My life's in perfect suspension," he said. "I'm afraid that if I quit practicing, if I change anything, I'll either sink to the bottom or fly off." He tapped his spoon against his cup, signaling for more tea. "You're not really going to marry Ranjeesh, are you?" he asked, and was surprised at the concern he felt that she actually might.

"Probably not." The waiter poured their tea, whispery drumbeats issuing from his earphones. "I was just feeling lost. You see, my parents sued Ronnie over the song, and I ended up with a lot of money – which made me feel even worse . . ."

"Let's not talk about it," he said.

"It's all right." She touched his wrist, reassuring, and the skin remained warm after her fingers had withdrawn. "Anyway," she went on, "I decided to travel, and all the strangeness . . . I don't know. I was starting to slip away. Ranjeesh was a kind of sanctuary."

Eliot was vastly relieved.

Outside, the streets were thronged with festival-goers, and Michaela took Eliot's arm and let him guide her through the crowds. Newari wearing Nehru hats and white trousers that bagged at the hips and wrapped tightly around the calves; groups of tourists, shouting and waving bottles of rice beer; Indians in white robes and saris. The air was spiced with incense, and the strip of empurpled sky above was so regularly patterned with stars that it looked like a banner draped between the roofs. Near the house, a wild-eyed man in a blue satin robe rushed past, bumping into them, and he was followed by two boys dragging a goat, its forehead smeared with crimson powder: a sacrifice.

"This is, crazy!" Michaela laughed.

"It's nothing. Wait till tomorrow night."

"What happens then?"

"The night of White Bhairab." Eliot put on a grimace. "You'll have to watch yourself. Bhairab's a lusty, wrathful sort."

She laughed again and gave his arm an affectionate squeeze.

Inside the house, the moon – past full, blank and golden – floated dead center of the square of night sky admitted by the roof. They stood close together in the courtyard, silent, suddenly awkward.

"I enjoyed tonight," said Michaela; she leaned forward and brushed his cheek with her lips. "Thank you," she whispered.

Eliot caught her as she drew back, tipped her chin and kissed her mouth. Her lips parted, her tongue darted out. Then she pushed him away. "I'm tired," she said, her face tightened with anxiety. She walked off a few steps, but stopped and turned back. "If you want to . . . to be with me, maybe it'll be all right. We could try."

Eliot went to her and took her hands. "I want to make love with you," he said, no longer trying to hide his urgency. And that was what he wanted: to make love. Not to ball or bang or screw or any other inelegant version of the act.

But it was not love they made.

Under the starlit blaze of Mr Chatterji's ceiling, she was very beautiful, and at first she was very loving, moving with a genuine involvement; then abruptly, she quit moving altogether and turned her face to the pillow. Her eyes were glistening. Left alone atop her, listening to the animal sound of his breathing, the impact of his flesh against hers, Eliot knew he should stop and comfort her. But the months of abstinence, the eight days of wanting her, all this fused into a bright flare in the small of his back, a reactor core of lust that irradiated his conscience, and he continued to plunge into her, hurrying to completion. She let out a gasp when he withdrew, and curled up, facing away from him.

"God, I'm so sorry," she said, her voice cracked.

Eliot shut his eyes. He felt sickened, reduced to the bestial. It had been like two mental patients doing nasty on the sly, two fragments of people who together didn't form a whole. He understood now why Mr Chatterji wanted to marry her: he planned to add her to his collection, to enshrine her with the other splinters of violence. And each night he would complete his revenge, substantiate his cultural overview, by making something less than love with this sad inert girl, this American ghost. Her shoulders shook with muffled sobs. She needed someone to console her, to help her find her own strength and capacity for love. Eliot reached out to her, willing to do his best. But he knew it shouldn't be him.

Several hours later, after she had fallen asleep, inconsolable, Eliot sat in the courtyard, thoughtless, dejected, staring at a rubber plant. It was mired in shadow, its leaves hanging limp. He had been staring for a couple of minutes when he noticed that a shadow behind the plant was swaying ever so slightly; he tried to make it out, and the swaying subsided. He stood. The chair scraped on the concrete, sounding unnaturally loud. His neck prickled, and he glanced behind him. Nothing. Ye Olde Mental Fatigue, he thought. Ye Olde Emotional Strain. He laughed, and the clarity of the laugh – echoing up through the empty well alarmed him; it seemed to stir little flickers of motion everywhere in the darkness. What he needed was a drink! The problem was how to get into the bedroom without waking Michaela. Hell, maybe he should wake her. Maybe, they should talk more before what had happened hardened into a set of unbreakable attitudes.

He turned toward the stairs . . . and then, yelling out in panic, entangling his feet with the lawn chairs as he leaped backward midstep, he fell onto his side. A shadow – roughly man-shaped and man-sized – was standing a yard away; it was undulating the way a strand of kelp undulates in a gentle tide. The patch of air around it was rippling, as if the entire image had been badly edited into reality. Eliot scrambled away, coming to his knees. The shadow melted downward, puddling on the cement; it bunched in the middle like a caterpillar, folded over itself, and flowed after him: a rolling sort of motion. Then it reared up, again assuming its manlike shape, looming over him.

Eliot got to his feet, still frightened, but less so. If he had previously been asked to testify as to the existence of the Khaa, he would have rejected the evidence of his bleared senses and come down on the side of hallucination, folk tale. But now, though he was tempted to draw that same conclusion, there was too much evidence to the contrary. Staring at the featureless black cowl of the Khaa's head, he had a sense of something staring back. More than a sense. A distinct impression of personality. It was as if the Khaa's undulations were producing a breeze that bore its psychic odor through the air. Eliot began to picture it as a loony, shy old uncle who liked to sit under the basement steps and eat flies and cackle to himself, but who could tell when the first frost was due and knew how to fix the tail on your kite. Weird, yet harmless. The Khaa stretched out an arm: the arm just peeled away from its torso, its hand a thumbless black mitten. Eliot edged back. He wasn't quite prepared to believe it was harmless. But the arm stretched further than he had thought possible and enveloped his wrist. It was soft, ticklish, a river of furry moths crawling over his skin.

In the instant before he jumped away, Eliot heard a whining note inside his skull, and that whining – seeming to flow through his brain with the same suppleness that the Khaa's arm had displayed – was translated into a wordless plea. From it he understood that the Khaa was afraid. Terribly afraid. Suddenly it melted downward and went rolling, bunching, flowing up the stairs; it stopped on the first landing, rolled halfway down, then up again, repeating the process over and over. It came clear to Eliot (*Oh, Jesus! This is nuts!*) that it was trying to convince him to follow. Just like Lassie or some other ridiculous TV animal, it was trying to tell him something, to lead him to where the wounded forest ranger had fallen, where the nest of baby ducks was being threatened by the brush fire. He should walk over, rumple its head, and say, "What's the matter, girl? Those squirrels been teasing you?" This time his laughter had a sobering effect, acting to settle his thoughts. One likelihood was that his experience with Michaela had been sufficient to snap his frayed connection with consensus reality; but there was no point in buying that. Even if that were the case, he might as well go with it. He crossed to the stairs and climbed toward the rippling shadow on the landing.

"Okay, Bongo," he said. "Let's see what's got you so excited."

*   *   *

On the third floor, the Khaa turned down a hallway, moving fast, and Eliot didn't see it again until he was approaching the room that housed Mr Chatterji's collection. It was standing beside the door, flapping its arms, apparently indicating that he should enter. Eliot remembered the crate.

"No, thanks," he said. A drop of sweat slid down his ribcage, and he realized that it was unusually warm next to the door.

The Khaa's hand flowed over the doorknob, enveloping it, and when the hand pulled back, it was bulging, oddly deformed, and there was a hole through the wood where the lock mechanism had been. The door swung open a couple of inches. Darkness leaked out of the room, adding an oily essence to the air. Eliot took a backward step. The Khaa dropped the lock mechanism – it materialized from beneath the black, formless hand and clattered to the floor – and latched onto Eliot's arm. Once again he heard the whining, the plea for help, and since he did not jump away, he had a clearer understanding of the process of translation. He could feel the whining as a cold fluid coursing through his brain, and as the whining died, the message simply appeared the way an image might appear in a crystal ball. There was an undertone of reassurance to the Khaa's fear, and though Eliot knew this was the mistake people in horror movies were always making, he reached inside the room and fumbled for the wall switch, half expecting to be snatched up and savaged. He flicked on the light and pushed the door open with his foot.

And wished that he hadn't.

The crates had exploded. Splinters and shards of wood were scattered everywhere, and the bricks had been heaped at the center of the room. They were dark red, friable bricks like crumbling cakes of dried blood, and each was marked with black letters and numbers that signified its original position in the fireplace. But none were in their proper position now, though they were quite artfully arranged. They had been piled into the shape of a mountain, one that – despite the crudity of its building blocks – duplicated the sheer faces and chimneys and gentle slopes of a real mountain. Eliot recognized it from

its photograph. The Eiger. It towered to the ceiling and, under
the glare of the lights, it gave off a radiation of ugliness and
barbarity. It seemed alive, a fang of dark red meat, and the
charred smell of the bricks was like a hum in Eliot's nostrils.

Ignoring the Khaa, who was again flapping its arms, Eliot
broke for the landing; there he paused and, after a brief struggle between fear and conscience, he sprinted up the stairs to
the bedroom, taking them three at a time. Michaela was gone!
He stared at the starlit billows of the sheets. Where the
hell . . . her room! He hurtled down the stairs and fell sprawling on the second-floor landing. Pain lanced through his
kneecap, but he came to his feet running, certain that something was behind him.

A seam of reddish, orange light – not lamplight – edged the
bottom of Michaela's door, and he heard a crispy chuckling in
the hearth. The wood was warm to the touch. Eliot's hand
hovered over the doorknob. His heart seemed to have swelled
to the size of a basketball and was doing a fancy dribble against
his chest wall. The sensible thing to do would be to get out
quick, because whatever lay beyond the door was bound to be
too much for him to handle. But instead he did the stupid
thing and burst into the room.

His first impression was that the room was burning, but
then he saw that though the fire looked real, it did not spread;
the flames clung to the outlines of things that were themselves
unreal, that had no substance of their own and were made of
the ghostly fire: belted drapes, an overstuffed chair and sofa, a
carved mantelpiece, all of antique design. The actual furniture
– production-line junk – was undamaged. Intense reddish-
orange light glowed around the bed, and at its heart lay
Michaela. Naked, her back arched. Lengths of her hair lifted
into the air and tangled, floating in an invisible current; the
muscles of her legs and abdomen were coiling, bunching, as if
she were shedding her skin. The crackling grew louder, and
the light began to rise from the bed to form into a column of
even brighter light; it narrowed at the mid-point, bulged in an
approximation of hips and breasts, gradually assuming the

shape of a burning woman. She was faceless, a fiery silhouette. Her flickering gown shifted as with the movements of walking, and flames leaped out behind her head like windblown hair.

Eliot was pumped full of terror, too afraid to scream or run. Her aura of heat and power wrapped around him. Though she was within arm's length, she seemed a long way off, inset into a great distance and walking toward him down a tunnel that conformed exactly to her shape. She stretched out a hand, brushing his cheek with a finger. The touch brought more pain than he had ever known. It was luminous, lighting every circuit of his body. He could feel his skin crisping, cracking, fluids leaking forth and sizzling. He heard himself moan: a gush of rotten sound like something trapped in a drain.

Then she jerked back her hand, as if *he* had burned her.

Dazed, his nerves screaming, Eliot slumped to the floor and – through blurred eyes – caught sight of a blackness rippling by the door. The Khaa. The burning woman stood facing it a few feet away. It was such an uncanny scene, this confrontation of fire and darkness, of two supernatural systems, that Eliot was shocked to alertness. He had the idea that neither of them knew what to do. Surrounded by its patch of disturbed air, the Khaa undulated; the burning woman crackled and flickered, embedded in her eerie distance. Tentatively, she lifted her hand, but before she could complete the gesture, the Khaa reached with blinding swiftness and its hand enveloped hers.

A shriek like tortured metal issued from them, as if some ironclad principle had been breached. Dark tendrils wound through the burning woman's arms, seams of fire striped the Khaa, and there was a high-pitched humming, a vibration that jarred Eliot's teeth. For a moment he was afraid that spiritual versions of antimatter and matter had been brought into conjunction, that the room would explode. But the hum was sheared off as the Khaa snatched back its hand: a scrap of reddish orange flame glimmered within it. The Khaa melted downward and went rolling out the door. The burning woman – and every bit of flame in the room – shrank to an incandescent point and vanished.

Still dazed, Eliot touched his face. It felt burned, but there was no apparent damage. He hauled himself to his feet, staggered to the bed and collapsed next to Michaela. She was breathing but deeply unconscious. "Michaela!" He shook her. She moaned, her head rolled from side to side. He heaved her over his shoulder in a fireman's lift and crept out into the hall. Moving stealthily, he eased along the hall to the balcony overlooking the courtyard and peered over the edge . . . and bit his lip to stifle a cry. Clearly visible in the electric blue air of the predawn darkness, standing in the middle of the courtyard, was a tall, pale woman wearing a white nightgown. Her black hair fanned across her back. She snapped her head around to stare at him, her cameo features twisted by a gloating smile, and that smile told Eliot everything he had wanted to know about the possibility of escape. Just try to leave, Aimée Cousineau was saying. Go ahead and try. I'd like that. A shadow sprang erect about a dozen feet away from her, and she turned to it. Suddenly there was a wind in the courtyard: a violent, whirling wind of which she was the calm center. Plants went flapping up into the well like leathery birds; pots shattered, and the shards flew toward the Khaa. Slowed by Michaela's weight, wanting to get as far as he could from the battle, Eliot headed up the stairs toward Mr Chatterji's bedroom

It was an hour later, an hour of peeking down into the courtyard, watching the game of hide-and-seek that the Khaa was playing with Aimée Cousineau, realizing that the Khaa was protecting them by keeping her busy . . . it was then that Eliot remembered the book. He retrieved it from the shelf and began to skim through it, hoping to learn something helpful. There was nothing else to do. He picked up at the point of Aimée's rap about her marriage to Happiness, passed over the transformation of Ginny Whitcomb into a teenage monster, and found a second section dealing with Aimée.

In 1895, a wealthy Swiss-American named Armand Cousineau had returned to St Berenice – his birthplace – for a visit. He was smitten with Aimée Vuillemont, and her family, seizing the opportunity to be rid of her, allowed Cousineau to marry Aimée and sail her off to his home in Carversville, New Hampshire. Aimée's taste for seduction had not been curbed by the move. Lawyers, deacons, merchants, farmers: they were all grist for her mill. But in the winter of 1905, she fell in love – obsessively, passionately in love – with a young schoolmaster. She believed that the schoolmaster had saved her from her unholy marriage, and her gratitude knew no bounds. Unfortunately, when the schoolmaster fell in love with another woman, neither did her fury. One night while passing the Cousineau mansion, the town doctor spotted a woman walking the grounds, "a woman of flame, not burning but composed of flame, her every particular a fiery construct . . ." Smoke was curling from a window; the doctor rushed inside and discovered the schoolmaster wrapped in chains, burning like a log in the vast fireplace. He put out the small blaze spreading from the hearth and, on going back into the grounds, he stumbled over Aimée's charred corpse.

It was not clear whether Aimée's death had been accidental, a stray spark catching on her nightgown, or the result of suicide, but it was clear that thereafter the mansion had been haunted by a spirit who delighted in possessing women and driving them to kill their men. The spirit's supernatural powers were limited by the flesh, but were augmented by immense physical strength. Ginny Whitcomb, for example, had killed her brother Tim by twisting off his arm, and then had gone after her other brother and her father, a harrowing chase that had lasted a day and a night: while in possession of a body the spirit was not limited to nocturnal activity . . .

Christ!

The light coming through the skylight was gray.

They were safe!

Eliot went to the bed and began shaking Michaela. She moaned, her eyes blinked open. "Wake up!" he said. "We've got to get out!"

"What?" She batted at his hands. "What are you talking about?"

"Don't you remember?"

"Remember what?" She swung her legs onto the floor, sitting with her head down, stunned by wakefulness; she stood, swayed, and said, "God, what did you do to me? I feel . . ." A dull, suspicious expression washed over her face.

"We have to leave." He walked around the bed to her. "Ranjeesh hit the jackpot. Those crates of his had an honest-to-God spirit packed in with the bricks. Last night it tried to possess you." He saw her disbelief. "You must have blanked out. Here." He offered the book. "This'll explain . . ."

"Oh, God!" she shouted. "What did you do? I'm all raw inside!" She backed away, eyes wide with fright.

"I didn't do anything." He held out his palms as if to prove he had no weapons.

"You raped me! While I was asleep!" She looked left, right, in a panic.

"That's ridiculous!"

"You must have drugged me or something! Oh, God! Go away!"

"I won't argue," he said. "We have to get out. After that you can turn me in for rape or whatever. But we're leaving, even if I have to drag you."

Some of her desperation evaporated, her shoulders sagged.

"Look," he said, moving closer. "I didn't rape you. What you're feeling is something that goddamn spirit did to you. It was . . ."

She brought her knee up into his groin.

As he writhed on the floor, curled up around the pain, Eliot heard the door open and her footsteps receding. He caught at the edge of the bed, hauled himself to his knees and vomited all over the sheets. He fell back and lay there for several minutes, until the pain had dwindled to a powerful throbbing, a throbbing that jolted his heart into the same rhythm; then, gingerly, he stood and shuffled out into the hall. Leaning on the railing, he eased down the stairs to Michaela's room and lowered himself into a sitting position. He let out a shuddering sigh. Actinic flashes burst in front of his eyes.

"Michaela," he said. "Listen to me." His voice sounded feeble: the voice of an old, old man.

"I've got a knife," she said from just behind the door. "I'll use it if you try to break in."

"I wouldn't worry about that," he said. "And I sure as hell wouldn't worry about being raped. Now will you listen?"

No response.

He told her everything and, when he was done, she said, "You're insane. You raped me."

"I wouldn't hurt you. I . . ." He had been on the verge of telling her he loved her, but decided it probably wasn't true. He probably just wished that he had a good, clean truth like love. The pain was making him nauseated again, as if the blackish, purple stain of his bruises were seeping up into his stomach and filling him with bad gases. He struggled to his feet and leaned against the wall. There was no point in arguing, and there was not much hope that she would leave the house on her own, not if she reacted to Aimée like Ginny Whitcomb. The only solution was to go to the police, accuse her of some crime. Assault. She would accuse him of rape, but with luck they would both be held overnight. And he would have time to wire Mr Chatterji . . . who would believe him. Mr Chatterji was by nature a believer; it simply hadn't fit his notion of sophistication to give credence to his native spirits. He'd be on the first flight from Delhi, eager to document the Terror.

Himself eager to get it over, Eliot negotiated the stairs and hobbled across the courtyard; but the Khaa was waiting, flapping its arms in the shadowed alcove that led to the street. Whether it was an effect of the light or of its battle with Aimée, or, specifically, of the pale scrap of fire visible within its hand, the Khaa looked less substantial. Its blackness was somewhat opaque, and the air around it was blurred, smeary, like waves over a lens; it was as if the Khaa were being submerged more deeply in its own medium. Eliot felt no compunction about allowing it to touch him; he was grateful to it, and his relaxed attitude seemed to intensify the communication. He began to see images in his mind's eye: Michaela's face, Aimée's, and then the two faces were superimposed. He was shown this over and over, and he understood from it that the Khaa wanted the possession to take place. But he didn't understand why. More images. Himself running, Michaela running. Durbar Square, the mask of White Bhairab, the Khaa. Lots of Khaa. Little black hieroglyphs. These images were repeated, too, and after each sequence the Khaa would hold its hand up to his face and display the glimmering scrap of Aimée's fire. Eliot thought he understood, but whenever he tried to convey that he wasn't sure, the Khaa merely repeated the images.

At last, realizing that the Khaa had reached the limits of its ability to communicate, Eliot headed for the street. The Khaa melted down, reared up in the doorway to block his path and flapped its arms desperately. Once again Eliot had a sense of its weird-old-man-ness. It went against logic to put his trust in such an erratic creature, especially in such a dangerous plan; but logic had little hold on him, and this was a permanent solution. If it worked. If he hadn't misread it. He laughed. The hell with it!

"Take it easy, Bongo," he said, "I'll be back as soon as I get my shootin' iron fixed."

The waiting room of Sam Chipley's clinic was crowded with Newari mothers and children, who giggled as Eliot did a bow-legged shuffle through their midst. Sam's wife led him into the examination room, where Sam – a burly, bearded man, his long hair tied in a ponytail – helped him onto a surgical table.

"Holy shit!" he said after inspecting the injury. "What you been into, man?" He began rubbing ointment into the bruises.

"Accident," gritted Eliot, trying not to cry out.

"Yeah, I bet," said Sam. "Maybe a sexy little accident who had a change of heart when it came down to strokes. You know, not gettin' it steady might tend to make you a tad intense for some ladies, man. Ever think about that?"

"That's not how it was. Am I all right?"

"Yeah, but you ain't gonna be superstud for a while." Sam went to the sink and washed his hands. "Don't gimme that innocent bullshit. You were trying to slip it to Chatterji's new squeeze, right?"

"You know her?"

"He brought her over one day, showin' her off. She's a headcase, man. You should know better."

"Will I be able to run?"

Sam laughed. "Not hardly."

"Listen, Sam." Eliot sat up, winced. "Chatterji's lady. She's in bad trouble, and I'm the only one who can help her. I have to be able to run, and I need something to keep me awake. I haven't slept for a couple of days."

"I ain't givin' you pills, Eliot. You can stagger through your doper phase without my help." Sam finished drying his hands and went to sit on a stool beside the window; beyond the window was a brick wall, and atop it a string of prayer flags snapped in the breeze.

"I'm not after a supply, damn it! Just enough to keep me going tonight. This is important, Sam!"

Sam scratched his neck. "What kind of trouble she in?"

"I can't tell you now," said Eliot, knowing that Sam would laugh at the idea of something as metaphysically suspect as the Khaa. "But I will tomorrow. It's not illegal. Come on, man! There's got to be something you can give me."

"Oh, I can fix you up. I can make you feel like King Shit on Coronation Day." Sam mulled it over. "Okay, Eliot. But you get your ass back here tomorrow and tell me what's happenin'." He gave a snort of amusement. "All I can say is it must be some strange damn trouble for you to be the only one who can save her."

After wiring Mr Chatterji, urging him to come home at once, Eliot returned to the house and unscrewed the hinges of the front door. He was not certain that Aimée would be able to control the house, to slam doors and make windows stick as she had with her house in New Hampshire, but he didn't want to take any chances. As he lifted the door, and set it against the wall of the alcove, he was amazed by its lightness; he felt possessed of a giddy strength, capable of heaving the door up through the well of the courtyard and over the roofs. The cocktail of painkillers and speed was working wonders. His groin ached, but the ache was distant, far removed from the center of his consciousness, which was a fount of well-being. When he had finished with the door, he grabbed some fruit juice from the kitchen and went back to the alcove to wait.

In mid-afternoon Michaela came downstairs. Eliot tried to talk to her, to convince her to leave, but she warned him to keep away and scuttled back to her room. Then, around five o'clock, the burning woman appeared, floating a few feet above the courtyard floor. The sun had withdrawn to the upper third of the well, and her fiery silhouette was inset into slate-blue shadow, the flames of her hair dancing about her head. Eliot, who had been hitting the painkillers heavily, was dazzled by her: had she been a hallucination, she would have made his All-Time Top Ten. But, even realizing that she was not, he was too drugged to relate to her as a threat. He snickered and shied a piece of broken pot at her. She shrank to an incandescent point, vanished, and that brought home to him his foolhardiness. He took more speed to counteract his euphoria, and did stretching exercises to loosen the kinks and to rid himself of the cramped sensation in his chest.

Twilight blended the shadows in the courtyard, celebrants passed in the street, and he could hear distant drums and cymbals. He felt cut off from the city, the festival. Afraid. Not even the presence of the Khaa, half merged with the shadows along the wall, served to comfort him. Near dusk, Aimée Cousineau walked into the courtyard and stopped about twenty feet away, staring at him. He had no desire to laugh or throw things. At this distance he could see that her eyes had no whites or pupils or irises. They were dead black. One moment they seemed to be the bulging head of black screws threaded into her skull; the next they seemed to recede into blackness, into a cave beneath a mountain where something waited to teach the joys of hell to whoever wandered in. Eliot sidled closer to the door. But she turned, climbed the stairs to the second landing, and walked down Michaela's hallway.

Eliot's waiting began in earnest.

An hour passed. He paced between the door and the courtyard. His mouth was cottony; his joints felt brittle, held together by frail wires of speed and adrenaline. This was insane! All he had done was to put them in worse danger. Finally, he heard a door close upstairs. He backed into the street, bumping into two Newari girls who giggled and skipped away. Crowds of people were moving toward Durbar Square.

"Eliot!"

Michaela's voice. He'd expected a hoarse demon voice, and when she walked into the alcove, her white scarf glowing palely against the dark air, he was surprised to see that she was unchanged. Her features held no trace of anything other than her usual listlessness.

"I'm sorry I hurt you," she said, walking toward him. "I know you didn't do anything. I was just upset about last night."

Eliot continued to back away.

"What's wrong?" She stopped in the doorway.

It might have been his imagination, the drugs, but Eliot could have sworn that her eyes were much darker than normal. He trotted off a dozen yards or so and stood looking at her.

"Eliot!"

It was a scream of rage and frustration, and he could scarcely believe the speed with which she darted toward him. He ran full tilt at first, leaping sideways to avoid collisions, veering past alarmed, dark-skinned faces, but after a couple of blocks, he found a more efficient rhythm and began to anticipate obstacles, to glide in and out of the crowd. Angry shouts were raised behind him. He glanced back. Michaela was closing the distance, beelining for him, knocking people sprawling with what seemed effortless blows. He ran harder. The crowd grew thicker, and he kept near the walls of the houses, where it was thinnest; but even there it was hard to maintain a good pace. Torches were waved in his face; young men – singing, their arms linked – posed barriers that slowed him further. He could no longer see Michaela, but he could see the wake of her passage. Fists shaking, heads jerking. The entire scene was starting to lose cohesiveness to Eliot. There were screams of torchlight, bright shards of deranged shouts, jostling waves of incense and ordure. He felt like the only solid chunk in a glittering soup that was being poured through a stone trough.

At the edge of Durbar Square, he had a brief glimpse of a shadow standing by the massive gilt doors of Degutale Temple It was larger and a more anthracitic black than Mr Chatterji's Khaa: one of the old ones, the powerful ones. The sight buoyed his confidence and restored his equilibrium. He had not misread the plan. But he knew that this was the most dangerous part. He had lost track of Michaela, and the crowd was sweeping him along; if she caught up to him now, he would not be able to run. Fighting for elbow room, struggling to keep his feet, he was borne into the temple complex. The pagoda roofs sloped up into darkness like strangely carved mountains, their peaks hidden by a moonless night; the cobbled paths were narrow, barely ten feet across, and the crowd was being squeezed along them, a lava flow of humanity. Torches bobbed everywhere, sending wild licks up the walls revealing scowling faces on the eaves. Atop its pedestal, the gilt statue of Hanuman – the monkey god – looked to be swaying. Clashing cymbals and arrhythmic drumming scattered Eliot's heartbeat; the sinewy wail of oboes seemed to be graphing the fluctuations of his nerves.

As he swept past Hanuman Dhoka Temple, he caught sight of the brass mask of White Bhairab shining over the heads of the crowd like the face of an evil clown. It was less than a hundred feet away, set in a huge niche in the temple wall and illuminated by light bulbs that hung down among strings of prayer flags. The crowd surged faster, knocking him this way and that, but he managed to spot two more Khaa in the doorway of Hanuman Dhoka. Both melted downward, vanishing, and Eliot's hopes soared. They must have located Michaela, they must be attacking! By the time he had been carried to within a few yards of the mask, he was sure that he was safe.

They must have finished her exorcism by now. The only problem left was to find her. That, he realized, had been the weak link in the plan. He'd been an idiot not to have foreseen it. Who knows what might happen if she were to fall in the midst of the crowd. Suddenly he was beneath the pipe that stuck out of the god's mouth; the stream of rice beer arching from it looked translucent under the lights, and as it splashed his face (no fish), its coldness acted to wash away his veneer of chemical strength. He was dizzy, his groin throbbed. The great face, with its fierce fangs and goofy, startled eyes, appeared to be swelling and rocking back and forth. He took a deep breath. The thing to do would be to find a place next to a wall where he could wedge himself against the flow of the crowd, wait until it had thinned, and then search for her. He was about to do that very thing when two powerful hands gripped his elbows from behind.

Unable to turn, he craned his neck and peered over his shoulder. Michaela smiled at him: a gloating "got-cha!" smile. Her eyes were dead-black ovals. She shaped his name with her mouth, her voice inaudible above the music and shouting, and she began to push him ahead of her, using him as a battering ram to forge a path through the crowd. To anyone watching, it might have appeared that he was running interference for her, but his feet were dangling just off the ground. Angry Newari yelled at him as he knocked them aside. He yelled too. No one noticed. Within seconds they had got clear into a side street, threading between groups of drunkards. People laughed at Eliot's cries for help, and one guy imitated the funny loose-limbed way he was running.

Michaela turned into a doorway, carried him down a dirt-floored corridor whose walls were carved into ornate screens; the dusky orange lamplight shining through the screens cast a lacework of shadow on the dirt. The corridor widened to a small courtyard, the age-darkened wood of its walls and doors inlaid with intricate mosaics of ivory. Michaela stopped and slammed him against a wall. He was stunned, but he recognized the place to be one of the old Buddhist temples that surrounded the square. Except for a life-sized statue of a golden cow, the courtyard was empty.

"Eliot." The way she said it, it was more of a curse than a name.

He opened his mouth to scream, but she drew him into an embrace; her grip on his right elbow tightened, and her other hand squeezed the back of his neck, pinching off the scream.

"Don't be afraid," she said. "I only want to kiss you."

Her breasts crushed into his chest, her pelvis ground against him in a mockery of passion, and inch by inch she forced his face down to hers. Her lips parted, and – *oh, Christ Jesus!* – Eliot writhed in her grasp, enlivened by a new horror. The inside of her mouth was as black as her eyes. She wanted him to kiss that blackness, the same she had kissed beneath the Eiger. He kicked and clawed with his free hand, but she was irresistible, her hands like iron. His elbow cracked, and brilliant pain shot through his arm. Something else was cracking in his neck. Yet none of that compared to what he felt as her tongue – a burning black poker – pushed between his lips. His chest was bursting with the need to scream, and everything was going dark. Thinking this was death, he experienced a peevish resentment that death was not – as he'd been led to believe – an end to pain, that it merely added a tickling sensation to all his other pain. Then the searing heat in his mouth diminished, and he thought that death must just have been a bit slower than usual.

Several seconds passed before he realized that he was lying on the ground, several more before he noticed Michaela lying beside him, and – because darkness was tattering the edges of his vision – it was considerably longer before he distinguished the six undulating darknesses that had ringed Aimée Cousineau. They towered over her; their blackness gleamed like thick fur, and the air around them was awash with vibration. In her fluted white nightgown, her cameo face composed in an expression of calm, Aimée looked the antithesis of the vaguely male giants that were menacing her, delicate and finely worked in contrast to their crudity. Her eyes appeared to mirror their

negative color. After a moment, a little wind kicked up, swirling about her. The undulations of the Khaa increased,
becoming rhythmic, the movements of boneless dancers, and
the wind subsided. Puzzled, she darted between two of them
and took a defensive stance next to the golden cow; she lowered
her head and stared up through her brows at the Khaa. They
melted downward, rolled forward, sprang erect and hemmed
her in against the statue. But the stare was doing its damage.
Pieces of ivory and wood were splintering, flying off the walls
toward the Khaa, and one of them was fading, a mist of black
particles accumulating around its body; then, with a shrill
noise that reminded Eliot of a jet passing overhead, it misted
away.

Five Khaa remained in the courtyard. Aimée smiled and
turned her stare on another. Before the stare could take effect,
however, the Khaa moved close, blocking Eliot's view of her;
and when they pulled back, it was Aimée who showed signs of
damage. Rills of blackness were leading from her eyes, webbing
her cheeks, making it look as if her face were cracking. Her
nightgown caught fire, her hair began to leap. Flames danced
on her fingertips, spread to her arms, her breast, and she
assumed the form of the burning woman.

As soon as the transformation was complete, she tried to
shrink, to dwindle to her vanishing point, but, acting in unison,
the Khaa extended their hands and touched her. There was
that shriek of tortured metal, lapsing to a high-pitched hum,
and to Eliot's amazement, the Khaa were sucked inside her. It
was a rapid process. The Khaa faded to a haze, to nothing, and
veins of black marbled the burning woman's fire; the blackness
coalesced, forming into five tiny stick figures, a hieroglyphic
design patterning her gown. With a fuming sound, she
expanded again, regaining her normal dimensions, and the
Khaa flowed back out, surrounding her. For an instant she
stood motionless, dwarfed: a schoolgirl helpless amidst a circle
of bullies. Then she clawed at the nearest of them. Though she
had no features with which to express emotion, it seemed to
Eliot there was desperation in her gesture, in the agitated

leaping of her fiery hair. Unperturbed, the Khaa stretched out their enormous mitten hands, hands that spread like oil and enveloped her.

The destruction of the burning woman, of Aimée Cousineau, lasted only a matter of seconds, but to Eliot it occurred within a bubble of slow time, a time during which he achieved a speculative distance. He wondered if – as the Khaa stole portions of her fire and secreted it within their bodies – they were removing disparate elements of her soul, if she consisted of psychologically distinct fragments: the girl who had wandered into the cave, the girl who had returned from it, the betrayed lover. Did she embody gradations of innocence and sinfulness, or was she a contaminated essence, an unfractionated evil? While still involved in this speculation – half a reaction to pain, half to the metallic shriek of her losing battle – he lost consciousness, and when he reopened his eyes, the courtyard was deserted. He could hear music and shouting from Durbar Square. The golden cow stared contentedly into nowhere.

He had the idea that if he moved, he would further break all the broken things inside him, but he inched his left hand across the dirt and rested it on Michaela's breast. It was rising and falling with a steady rhythm. That made him happy, and he kept his hand there, exulting in the hits of her life against his palm. Something shadowy above him. He strained to see it. One of the Khaa . . . No! It was Mr Chatterji's Khaa. Opaquely black, scrap of fire glimmering in its hand. Compared to its big brothers, it had the look of a skinny, sorry mutt. Eliot felt camaraderie toward it.

"Hey, Bongo," he said weakly. "We won."

A tickling at the top of his head, a whining note, and he had an impression not of gratitude – as he might have expected – but of intense curiosity. The tickling stopped, and Eliot suddenly felt clear in his mind. Strange. He was passing out once again, his consciousness whirling, darkening, and yet he was calm and unafraid. A roar came from the direction of the square. Somebody – the luckiest somebody in the Katmandu

Valley – had caught the fish. But as Eliot's eyelids fluttered shut, as he had a last glimpse of the Khaa looming above them and felt the warm measure of Michaela's heartbeat, he thought maybe that the crowd was cheering the wrong man.

Three weeks after the night of White Bhairab, Ranjeesh Chatterji divested himself of all worldly possessions (including the gift of a year's free rent at his house to Eliot) and took up residence at Swayambhunath, where – according to Sam Chipley, who visited Eliot in the hospital – he was attempting to visualize the Avalokitesvara Buddha. It was then that Eliot understood the nature of his newfound clarity. Just as it had done long ago with the woman's goiters, the Khaa had tried his habituation to meditation on for size, had not cared for it, and had sloughed it off in a handy repository: Ranjeesh Chatterji.

It was such a delicious irony that Eliot had to restrain himself from telling Michaela when she visited that same afternoon; she had no memory of the Khaa, and news of it tended to unsettle her. But otherwise she had been healing right along with Eliot. All her listlessness had eroded over the weeks, her capacity for love was returning and was focused solely on Eliot. "I guess I needed someone to show me that I was worth an effort," she told him. "I can't stop trying to repay you." She kissed him. "I can hardly wait till you come home." She brought him books and candy and flowers; she sat with him each day until the nurse shooed her away. Yet being the center of her devotion disturbed him. He was still uncertain whether or not he loved her. Clarity, it seemed, made a man dangerously versatile, his conscience flexible and instituted a cautious approach to commitment. At least this was the substance of Eliot's clarity. He didn't want to rush into anything.

When at last he did come home, he and Michaela made love beneath the starlit glory of Mr Chatterji's skylight. Because of Eliot's neck brace and cast, they had to manage the act with extreme care, but despite that, despite the ambivalence of his feelings, this time it *was* love they made. Afterward, lying with his good arm around her, he edged nearer to commitment.

Whether or not he loved her, there was no way this part of things could be improved by any increment of emotion. Maybe he'd give it a try with her. If it didn't work out, well, he was not going to be responsible for her mental health. She would have to learn to live without him.

"Happy?" he asked, caressing her shoulder.

She nodded and cuddled closer and whispered something that was partially drowned out by the crinkling of the pillow. He was sure he had misheard her, but the mere thought that he hadn't was enough to lodge a nugget of chill between his shoulder blades.

"What did you say?" he asked.

She turned to him and propped herself on an elbow, silhouetted by the starlight, her features obscured. But when she spoke, he realized that Mr Chatterji's Khaa had been true to its erratic traditions on the night of White Bhairab; and he knew that if she were to tip back her head ever so slightly and let the light shine into her eyes, he would be able to resolve all his speculation about the composition of Aimée Cousineau's soul.

"I'm wed to Happiness," she said.

. . . And the Angel With Television Eyes

John Shirley

*In Judeo-Christian culture, the concept of the warrior angel is
personified in the Archangel Michael. For the Hebrews, he was
a "great prince who protects your people" and "captain of the
host of the Lord". In the Christian New Testament, Michael led
the angels in a war against Satan and defeated him. Michael
– Mikhail in Arabic – is mentioned along with Gabriel (Jibreel)
only once in the Qu'ran (Sura 2.98), but it has a warlike
connotation: "Whoever is an enemy to God, and His angels
and His messengers, and Jibreel and Mikhail! Then, lo! God is
an enemy to the disbelievers." Artists often depict Michael as
armed and battle-ready or actually fighting. The warrior-angel
of John Shirley's enthralling science fictional story is a new,
unique and indelible image of an ancient icon.*

On a gray morning, 11 April, the year 2030, Max Whitman
woke in his midtown Manhattan apartment to find a living,
breathing griffin perched on the right-hand post at the foot of
his antique four-poster bed.

Max watched with sleep-fuzzed pleasure as the griffin – a
griffin made of shining metal – began to preen its mirror-
bright feathers with a hooked beak of polished cadmium. It
creaked a little as it moved.

Max assumed at first that he was still dreaming; he'd had a

series of oddly related Technicolor-vivid dreams recently. Apparently one of these dreams had spilled over onto his waking reality. He remembered the griffin from a dream of the night previous. It had been a dream bristling with sharp contrasts: of hard-edged shafts of white light – a light that never warms – breaking through clouds the color of suicidal melancholy. And weaving in and out of those shafts of light, the griffin came flying toward him ablaze with silvery glints. And then the clouds coming together, closing out the light and letting go sheets of rain. Red rain. Thick, glutinous rain. A rain of blood. Blood running down the sheer wall of a high-towered, gargoyle-studded castle carved of transparent glass. Supported by nothing at all: a crystalline castle still and steady as Mount Everest, hanging in mid-air. And laying siege to the sky-castle was a flying army of wretched things led by a man with a barbed-wire head . . .

Just a bad dream.

Now, Max gazed at the griffin and shivered, hoping the rest of the dream wouldn't come along with the griffin. He hadn't liked the rain of blood at all.

Max blinked, expecting the griffin to vanish. It remained, gleaming. Fulsome. Something hungry . . .

The griffin noticed Max watching. It straightened, fluttered its two-meter wingspread, wingtips flashing in the morning light slanting through the broad picture window, and said, "Well, what do you want of me?" It had a strangely musical, male voice.

"Whuh?" said Max blearily. "Me? Want with you?" Was it a holograph? But it looked so solid . . . and he could hear its claws rasping the bedpost.

"I heard your call," the griffin went on. "It was too loud, and then it was too soft. You really haven't got the hang of mind-sending yet. But I heard and I came. Who are you and why did you call me?"

"Look, I didn't . . ." He stopped, and smiled. "Sandra. Sandra Klein in Special Effects, right? This is her little cute-ness." He yawned and sat up. "She outdid herself with you, I must admit. You're a marvel of engineering. Damn." The griffin was about a meter high. It gripped the bedpost with metallic eagle's claws; it sat on its haunches, and its lion's forepaws – from a lion of some polished argent alloy – rested on its pin-feathered knees. The pin feathers looked like sweepings from a machine shop. The griffin had a lion's head, but an eagle's beak replaced a muzzle. Its feathered chest rose and fell.

"A machine that breathes . . ." Max murmured.

"Machine?" The griffin's opalescent eyes glittered warningly. Its wire-tufted lion's tail swished. "It's true my semblance is all alloys and plastics and circuitry. But I assure you I am not an example of what you people presume to call 'artificial intelligence'."

"Ah." Max felt cold, and pulled the bedclothes up to cover his goose-pimpled shoulders. "Sorry." *Don't make it mad.* "Sandra didn't send you?"

It snorted. "Sandra! Good Lord, no."

"I . . ." Max's throat was dry. "I saw you in a dream." He felt odd. Like he'd taken a drug that couldn't make up its mind if it were a tranquilizer or a psychedelic.

"You saw me in a dream?" The griffin cocked its head attentively. "Who else was in this dream?"

"Oh there were – *things*. A rain of blood. A castle that was there and wasn't there. A man – it looked like he was made of . . . of hot metal. And his head was all of wire. I had a series of dreams that were . . . Well, things like that."

"If you dreamed those things, then my coming here is ordained. You act as if you honestly don't know *why* I'm here." It blinked, tiny metal shutters closing with a faint *clink*. "But you're not much *surprised* by me. Most humans would have run shrieking from the room by now. You accept me.

Max shrugged. "Maybe. But you haven't told me why you're here. You said it was – ordained?"

"*Planned* might be a better word. I can tell you that I am Flare, and I am a Conservative Protectionist, a High Functionary in the Fiefdom of Lord Viridian. And you – if you're human – must be wild talent. At least. You transmitted the mindsend in your sleep, unknown to your conscious mind. I should have guessed from the confused signal. Well, well, well. Such things are outside the realm of my expertise. You might be one of the Concealed. We'll see, at the meeting. First, I've got to have something to eat. You people keep food in 'the kitchen', I think. That would be through that hallway . . ."

The griffin of shining metal fluttered from the bedpost, alighted on the floor with a light clattering, and hopped into the kitchen, out of sight.

Max got out of bed, thinking: He's right. I should be at least disoriented. But I'm not. I *have* been expecting him.

Especially since the dreams started. And the dreams began a week after he'd taken on the role of Prince Red Mark. He'd named the character himself – there'd been last moment misgivings about the original name chosen by the scripters, and he'd blurted, "How about 'Prince Red Mark'?" And the producer went for it, one of the whims that shape show business. Four tapings for the first two episodes, and then the dreams commenced. Sometimes he'd dream he was Prince Red Mark; other times a flash of heat lightning; or a ripple of wind, a breeze that could think and feel, swishing through unseeable gardens of invisible blooms . . . And then the dreams became darker, fiercer, so that he awoke with his fists balled, his eyes wild, sweat cold on his chin. Dreams about griffins and rains of blood and sieges by wretched things. The things that flew, the things with claws.

He'd played Prince Red Mark for seven episodes now. He'd been picked for his athletic build, his thick black hair and his air of what the PR people called "aristocratic detachment". Other people called it arrogance.

Max Whitman had found, to his surprise, he hadn't had to act the role. When he played Prince Red Mark, he *was* Prince Red Mark. Pure and simple . . . The set-hands would make fun of him, when they thought he couldn't hear, because he'd forget to step out of the character between shootings. He'd swagger about the set with his hand on the pommel of his sword, emanating Royal Authority.

This morning he didn't feel much like Prince Red Mark. He felt sleepy and confused and mildly threatened. He stretched, then turned toward the kitchen, worried by certain sinister noises: claws on glass. Splashings. Wet, slapping sounds. He burst out, "Damn, it got into my aquarium!" He hurried to the kitchen. "Hey – oh, hell. My fish." The griffin was perched beside the ten-gallon aquarium on the breakfast bar. Three palm-sized damselfish were gasping, dying on the wet blue-tile floor. The griffin fluttered to the floor, snipped the fish neatly into sections with its beak, and gobbled them just as an eagle would have. The blue tile puddled with red. Max turned away, saddened but not really angry. "Was that necessary?"

"It's my nature. I was hungry. When we're bodied, we have to eat. I can't eat those dead things in your refrigerator. And after some consideration I decided it would be best if I didn't eat *you* . . . Now, let's go to the meeting. And don't say, 'What meeting?'"

"Okay. I won't."

"Just take a fast cab to 862 Haven, apartment 17. I'll meet you on their balcony . . . wait. Wait. I'm getting a send. They're telling me – it's a message for *you*." It cocked its head to one side as if listening. "They tell me I must apologize for eating your fish. Apparently you have some unusual level of respect in their circle." It bent its head. "I apologize. And they say you are to read a letter from 'Carstairs'. It's been in your computer's mail sorter for two weeks under 'Personal' and you keep neglecting to retrieve it. Read it. That's the send . . . Well, then . . ." The griffin, fluttering its wings, hopped into the living room. The French doors opened for it as if slid back by some ghostly hand. It went to the balcony, crouched, then sprang into the air and soared away. He thought he heard it shout something over its shoulder at him: something about Prince Red Mark.

It was a breezy morning, feeling like spring. The sun came and went.

Max stood under the rain shelter in the gridcab station on the roof of his apartment building. The grid was a webwork of

metal slats and signal contacts, braced by girders and upheld
by the buildings that jutted through the finely woven net like
mountaintops through a cloud field. Thousands of wedge-
shaped cabs and private gridcars hummed along the grid in as
many different directions.

Impatiently, Max once more thumbed the green call button
on the signal stanchion. An empty cab, cruising by on automatic pilot, was dispatched by the Uptown area's traffic
computer; it detached from the feverishly interlacing main
traffic swarm and arced neatly into the pick-up bay under the
rain shelter. Max climbed inside and inserted his Unicard into
the cab's creditor. The small terminal's screen acknowledged
his bank account and asked, "Where to?" Max tapped his
destination into the keyboard: the cab's computer, through the
data-feed contacts threaded into the grid, gave the destination
to the main computer, which maneuvered the cab from the
bay and out onto the grid. *You are to read a letter from Carstairs*,
the griffin had said.

He'd met Carstairs at a convention of fantasy fans. Carstairs
had hinted he was doing "some rather esoteric research" for
Duke University's parapsychology lab. Carstairs had made
Max nervous – he could feel the man following him, watching
him, wherever he went in the convention hotel. So he'd deliberately ignored the message. But he hadn't gotten around to
deleting it.

As the cab flashed across the city, weaving in and out of the
peaks of skyscrapers, over the narrow parks that had taken the
place of the Avenue, Max punched a request to connect to his
home computer. The cab charged his bank account again, tied
him in, and he asked his system to print out a copy of the email
from Carstairs. He scanned the message, focusing first on:
". . . when I saw you at the convention I knew the Hidden Race
had chosen to favor you. They were there, standing at your
elbow, invisible to you – invisible to me too, except in certain
lights, and when I concentrate all my training on looking . . ."
Max shivered, and thought: A maniac. But – the griffin had
been real.

He skipped ahead to: ". . . You'll remember, perhaps, back in the last century, people were talking about a 'plasma body' that existed within our own physiological bodies, an independently organized but interrelated skein of subatomic particles; this constituted, it was supposed, the so-called soul. It occurred to some of us that if this plasma body could exist in so cohesive a form within an organism, and could survive for transmigration after the death of that organism, then perhaps a race of creatures, creatures who seem to us to be 'bodiless', could exist alongside the embodied creatures without humanity's knowing it. This race does exist, Max. It accounts for those well-documented cases of 'demonic' possession and poltergeists. And for much in mythology. My organization has been studying the Hidden Race – some call them plasmagnomes – for fifteen years. We kept our research secret for a good reason . . ."

Max was distracted by a peculiar noise. A scratching sound from the roof of the cab. He glanced out the window, saw nothing and shrugged. Probably a news sheet blown by the wind onto the car's roof. He looked again at the letter. ". . . for a good reason. Some of the plasmagnomes are hostile . . . The Hidden Race is very orderly. It consists of about ten thousand plasmagnomes, who live for the most part in the world's 'barren' places. Such places are not barren to them. The bulk of the plasmagnomes are a well-cared-for serf class, who labor in creating base plasma fields, packets of non-sentient energy to be consumed or used in etheric constructions. The upper classes govern, study the various universes and, most of all, concern themselves with the designing and elaboration of their Ritual. But this monarchist hierarchy is factioned into two distinct opposition parties, the Protectionists and the Exploitationists: they gave us those terms as being the closest English equivalent. The Protectionists are sanctioned by the High Crown and the Tetrarchy of Lords. Lately the Exploitationists have increased their numbers, and they've become harder to police. They have gotten out of hand. For the first time since a Protectionist walked the Earth centuries ago as 'Merlin' and an

Exploitationist as 'Mordred', certain members of the Hidden Race have taken bodied form among us . . ."

Max glanced up again.

The scratching sound from the roof. Louder this time. He tried to ignore it; he wondered why his heart was pounding. He looked doggedly at the letter. ". . . The Exploitationists maintain that humanity is small-minded, destructive of the biosphere, too numerous, and in general suitable only for slavery and as sustenance. If they knew my organization studied them, they would kill me and my associates. Till recently, the Protectionists have prevented the opposition party from taking physical form. It's more difficult for them to affect us when they're unbodied, because our biologic magnetic fields keep them at a distance . . . Centuries ago, they appeared to us as dragons, sorcerers, fairies, harpies, winged horses, griffins, angels, demons . . ."

Max leaned back in his seat and slowly shook his head. Griffins. He took a deep breath. This could still be a hoax. The griffin *could* have been a machine.

But he knew better. He'd known since he was a boy, really. Even then, certain Technicolor-vivid dreams—

He tensed: the phantom scrabbling had come again from overhead. He glimpsed a dark fluttering from the corner of one eye; he turned, thought he saw a leathery wingtip withdraw from the upper edge of the window frame.

"Oh God." He decided it might be a good idea to read the rest of the letter. Now. Quickly. Best he learn all he could about them. Because the scratching on the roof was becoming a grating, scraping sound. Louder and harsher.

He forced himself to read the last paragraph of the letter. ". . . in the old days they manifested as such creatures because their appearance is affected by our expectation of them. They enter the visible plane only after filtering through our cultural psyche, the society's collective electromagnetic mental field. And their shapes apparently have something to do with their inner psychological make-up – each one has a different self-image. When they become bodied, they manipulate the atoms of the atomic-physical world with plasma-field telekinesis, and shape it into what at least seem to be actually functioning organisms, or machines. Lately they take the form of machines – collaged with more ancient imagery – because ours is a machine-minded society. They're myth robots, perhaps. They're not magical creatures. They're real, with their own subtle metabolism – and physical needs and ecological niche. They have a method of keeping records – in 'Closed-system Plasma Fields' – and even constructing housing. Their castles are vast and complex and invisible to us, untouchable and all but undetectable. We can pass through them and not disturb them. The Hidden Race has a radically different relationship to matter, energy – and death. That special relationship is what makes them seem magical to us . . . Well, Mr Whitman, we're getting in touch with you to ask you to attend a meeting of those directly involved in plans for defense against the Exploitationists' campaign to—"

He got no further in his reading. He was distracted. Naked terror is a distracting thing.

A squealing sound of ripped metal from just over his head made him cringe in his seat, look up to see claws of polished titanium, claws long as a man's fingers and wickedly curved, slashing the cab's thin roof. The claws peeled the metal back.

Frantically, Max punched a message into the cab's terminal: *Change direction for nearest police station. Emergency priority. I take responsibility for traffic disruption.*

The cab swerved, the traffic parting for it, and took an exit from the grid to spiral down the off-ramp. It pulled up in the concrete cab stop at street level, across from a cop just getting out of a patrol car at a police station. Wide-eyed, the cop drew his gun and ran toward the cab.

Claws snatched at Max's shoulders. He opened the cab door, and flung himself out of the car, bolting for shelter.

Something struck him between the shoulder blades. He staggered. There was an icy digging at his shoulders – he howled. Steel claws sank into his flesh and lifted him off his feet – he could feel the muscles of his shoulders straining, threatening to tear. The claws opened, released him and he fell face down; he lay for a moment, gasping on his belly. He had a choppy impression of something blue-black flapping above and behind. He felt a tugging at his belt, and then he was lifted into the air, the clawed things carrying him by the belt as if it were a luggage handle.

He was two, three, five meters above the concrete, and spiraling upward. He heard a gunshot, thought he glimpsed the cop fallen, a winged darkness descending on him.

The city whirled into a gray blur. Max heard the regular beat of powerful wings just above. He thought: I'm too heavy. It's not aerodynamically possible.

But he was carried higher still, the flying things making creaking, whipping sounds with their pinions. Otherwise, they were unnervingly silent. Max stopped struggling to free himself. If he broke loose now, he'd fall ten stories to the street. He was slumped like a rabbit in a hawk's claws, hanging limply, humiliated.

He saw two of the flying things below, now, just climbing into his line of sight. They carried the policeman – a big bald man with a paunchy middle. They carried him between them; one had him by the ankles, the other by the throat. He looked lifeless. Judging by the loll of his head, his neck was broken.

Except for the rush of wind past his face, the pain at his hips where the belt was cutting into him, Max felt numb, once more in a dream. He was afraid, deeply afraid, but the fear had somehow become one with the world, a background noise that one grows used to, like the constant banging from a neighborhood construction site. But when he looked at the things carrying him, he had a chilling sense of déjà vu. He remembered them from the dreams. Two mornings before, he'd awakened, mumbling, "The things that flew, the things with claws . . ."

They were made of vinyl. Blue-black vinyl stretched over, he guessed, aluminum frames. They were bony, almost skeletal women, with little hard knobs for breasts, their arms merging into broad, scalloped imitation leather wings. They had the heads of women – with DayGlo wigs of green, stiff-plastic bristles – but instead of eyes there were the lenses of cameras, one in each socket; and when they opened their mouths he saw, instead of teeth, the blue-gray curves of razors following the line of the narrow jaws. Max thought: It's a harpy. A vinyl harpy.

One of the harpies, three meters away and a little below, turned its vinyl head, its camera lenses glittering, to look Max in the face; it opened its mouth and threw back its head like a dog about to howl and out came the sound of an air-raid warning: "GO TO THE SHELTERS. GO IMMEDIATELY TO THE SHELTERS. DO NOT STOP TO GATHER POSSESSIONS. TAKE FAMILY TO THE SHELTERS. BRING NOTHING. FOOD AND WATER WILL BE PROVIDED. GO IMMEDIATELY . . ."

And two others took it up. "GO IMMEDIATELY . . ." in a sexless, emotionless tone of authority. "TAKE FAMILY TO THE SHELTERS . . ."

And Max could tell that, for the harpies, the words had no meaning. It was their way of animal cawing, the territorial declaration of their kind.

They couldn't have been in the air more than ten minutes – flapping unevenly over rooftops, bits and pieces of the city churning by below – when they began to descend. They were going down beyond the automated zone. They entered Edgetown, what used to be the South Bronx. People still sometimes drove combustion cars here, on the potholed, cracked streets, when they could get contraband gasoline; here policemen were rarely seen; here the corner security cameras were always smashed, the sidewalks crusted with trash and two-thirds of the buildings deserted.

Max was carried down toward an old-fashioned tar rooftop; it was the roof of a five-story building, wedged in between three taller ones. All four looked derelict and empty; the building across the street showed a few signs of occupation: laundry in the airshaft, one small child on the roof. The child, a little black girl, watched without any sign of surprise. Max felt a little better, seeing her.

Where the shadows of the three buildings intersected on the fourth, in the deepest pocket of darkness, there was a small outbuilding; it was the rooftop doorway into the building. The door hung brokenly to one side. A cherry-red light pulsed just inside the doorway, like hate in a nighted soul.

Max lost sight of the red glow as the vinyl harpies turned, circling for a landing. The rooftop rushed up at him. There was a sickening moment of freefall when they let go. He fell three meters to the rooftop, struck on the balls of his feet, plunged forward, shoulder-rolled to a stop. He gasped, trying to get his breath back. His ankles and the soles of his feet ached.

He took a deep breath and stood, swaying, blinking. He found he was staring into the open doorway. Within, framed by the dusty, dark entrance to the stairway, was a man made of red-hot steel. The heat-glow was concentrated in his torso and arms. He touched the wooden frame of the doorway – and it burst into flame. The harpies capered about the tar rooftop, leaping atop chimneys and down again, stretching their wings to flap, cawing, booming, "GO IMMEDIATELY TO THE SHELTERS, GO IMMEDIATELY, GO GO GO . . ."

The man made of hot metal stepped onto the roof. The harpies quieted, cowed. They huddled together behind him, cocking their heads and scratching under their wings with pointed chins. To one side lay the lifeless body of the policeman, its back toward Max; the corpse's head had been twisted entirely around on its neck; one blue eye was open, staring lifelessly; the man's tongue was caught between clamped teeth, half severed.

For a moment all was quiet, but for the rustling of wings and crackling of the small fire on the outbuilding.

The man of hot chrome wore no clothes at all. He was immense, nearly two-and-a-half meters tall, and smooth as the outer hull of a factory-new fighter jet. He was seamless – except for the square gate on his chest, with the little metal turn-handle on it. The gate was precisely like the door of an old-fashioned incinerator; in the center of the gate was a small, thick pane of smoke-darkened glass, through which blue-white fires could be seen burning restlessly. Except for their bright metal finish, his arms and legs and stylized genitals looked quite human. His head was formed of barbed wire – a densely woven wire sculpture of a man's head, cunningly formed to show grim, aristocratic features. There were simply holes for eyes, behind which red fires flickered in his hollow head; now and then flames darted from the eyeholes to play about his temples and then recede; his scalp was a crest of barbs; eyebrows and ears were shaped of barbs. Gray smoke gusted from his mouth when he spoke to the harpies: "Feed me." The wire lips moved like a man's; the wire jaw seemed to work smoothly. "Feed me, while I speak to this one." He stepped closer Max, who cringed back from the heat. "I am Lord Thanatos." A voice like metal rending.

Max knew him.

One of the harpies moved to the corpse of the policeman; it took hold of the arm, put one stunted foot on the cop's back, and began to wrench and twist. It tore the corpse's arm from its shoulder and dragged it to Thanatos, leaving a trail of red blood on black tar. The harpy reached out with its free hand and turned the handle on its lord's chest. The door swung open; an unbearable brightness flared in the opening; ducking its head, turning its eyes from the rapacious light, the vinyl harpy stuffed the cop's arm, replete with wrist-com and blue coat-sleeve, into the inferno, the bosom of Thanatos. Sizzlings and poppings and black smoke unfurling. And the smell of roasting flesh. Max's stomach recoiled; he took another step backward. He watched, feeling half paralysed, as the harpies scuttled back and forth between the corpse and Thanatos, slowly dismembering and disemboweling the dead policeman, feeding the pieces into the furnace that was their lord.

And his fire burned more furiously; his glow increased.

"This is how it will be," said Thanatos. "You will serve me. You can look on me, Max Whitman, and upon my servants, and you do not go mad. You do not run howling away. Because you are one of those who has always known about us in some way. We met on the dream-plane once, you and I, and I knew you for what you were then. You can serve me, and still live among men. You will be my emissary. You will be shielded from the cowards who would prevent my entry into your world. You will go to certain men, the few who control the many. The wealthy ones. You will tell them about a great source of power, Lord Thanatos. I will send fiends and visitations to beset their enemies. Their power will grow, and they will feed me, and my power will grow. This is how it will be."

As he finished speaking, another harpy flapped down from the sky, dropping a fresh corpse into the shadows. It was a young Hispanic man in a smudged white suit. Thanatos opened the wiry mouth of his hollow head and sighed; blue smoke smelling of munitions factories dirtied the air. "They always kill them, somehow, as they bring them to me. I cannot break them of it. They always kill the humans. Men are more pleasurable to consume when there is life left in them. My curse is this: I'm served by half-minds."

Max thought: Why didn't the harpies kill me, then?

The vinyl harpies tore an arm from the sprawled dead man, and fed it into their master's fire. Their camera-lens eyes caught the shine of the fire. Thanatos looked at Max. "You have not yet spoken."

And Max thought: Say anything. Anything to get the hell away. "I'll do just what you ask. Let me go and I'll bring you lives. I'll be your, uh, your emissary."

Another long, smoky sigh. "You're lying. I was afraid you'd be loyal. Instinct of some sort, I suppose."

"Loyal to who?"

"I can read you. You see only the semblance I've chosen. But I see past your semblance. You cannot lie to one of us. I see the lie in you unfolding like the blossoming of a poisonous purple orchid. You cannot lie to a lord."

He licked barbed-wire lips with a tongue of flame.

So they will kill me, Max thought. They'll feed me into this monstrosity! Is that a strange death? An absurd death? No stranger than dying by nerve gas on some foreign battlefield; no more absurd than my Uncle Danny's death: he drowned in a big vat of fluorescent pink paint.

"You're not going to die," said Thanatos. "We'll keep you in stasis, forever imprisoned, unpleasantly alive."

What happened next made Max think of a slogan stenciled on the snout of one of the old B-112 bombers from World War II: "Death From Above". Because something silvery flashed down from above and struck the two harpies bending over the body of the man in the smudged white suit . . . both harpies were struck with a terrible impact, sent broken and lifeless over the edge of the roof.

The griffin pulled up from its dive, raking the tar roof, and soared over the burning outbuilding and up for another pass. The remaining harpies rose to meet it.

Other figures were converging on the roof, coming in a group from the north. One was a man who hovered without wings; he seemed to levitate. His body was angelic, his skin dazzling white; he wore a loincloth made of what looked like aluminum foil. His head was a man's, haloed with blond curls, but where his eyes and forehead should have been was a small television screen, projecting from the bone of his skull. On the screen was an image of human eyes, looking about; it was as if he saw from the TV screen. Two more griffins arrived, one electroplated gold, another of nickel, and just behind them came a woman who drifted like a bit of cotton blown on the breeze. She resembled Mother Mary, but nude: a plastic Madonna made of the stuff of which inflatable beach toys are made; glossy and striped in wide bands of primary colors. She seemed insubstantial as a soap bubble, but when she struck at a vinyl harpy it reeled back, turning end over end to fall senseless to the rooftop. Flanking her were two miniature helicopters – helicopters no bigger than horses. The lower section of each helicopter resembled a medieval dragon attired in armored metal, complete with clawed arms in place of landing runners. Each copter's cab was conventionally shaped, but no pilot sat behind the windows; and just below those sinister windows was a set of chrome teeth in a mouth opening to let loose great peals of electronically amplified laughter. The dragon copters dived to attack the remaining harpies, angling their whirring blades to shred the vinyl wings.

Thanatos grated a command, and from the burning

doorway behind him came seven bats as big as vultures, with camera-lens eyes and sawing electric knives for teeth and wings of paper-thin aluminum.

Max threw himself to the roof, coughing in the smoke of the growing fire; the bats whipped close over his head and climbed, keening, to attack Our Lady of the Plastics.

Two dog-sized spiders made of high-tension rubbery synthetics, their clashing mandibles forged of the best Solingen steel, raced on whirring copper legs across the roof to intercept the angel with television eyes. The angel alighted and turned to gesture urgently to Max. The spiders clutched at the angel's legs and dragged him down, slashed bloody hunks from his ivory arms.

Max saw Lord Thanatos catch a passing griffin by the tail and slam it onto the roof; he clamped the griffin in his white-hot hands. It shrieked and began to melt.

Two metal bats collided head-on with a copter dragon and all three disintegrated in a shower of blue sparks. Our Lady of the Plastics struck dents into the aluminum ribs of the vinyl harpies who darted at her, slashed and boomed, "GO IMME-DIATELY," bellowing it in triumph as she burst open – but they recoiled in dismay, flapping clumsily out of reach, when she re-formed, gathering her fragments together, making herself anew in mid-air.

Max sensed that the real battle was fought in some other dimension of subatomic physicality, with a subtler weaponry; he was seeing only the distorted visual echoes of the actual struggle.

The spiders were wrapping the angel's legs with cords of optical fiber. He gave a mighty wrench and threw them off, levitating out of their reach, shouting at Max: "Take your life! You—"

"SILENCE HIM!" Thanatos bellowed, stabbing a hot finger at the angel. And instantly two of the harpies plummeted to sink their talons in the throat of the angel with television eyes. They tore at him, made a gouting, ragged wreckage of his white throat – and Max blinked, seeing a phosphorescent mist, the color of translucent turquoise, issuing from the angel's slack mouth as he fell to the ground.

I'm seeing his plasma body escape, Max thought. I'm realizing my talent.

He saw the blue phosphorescence, vaguely man-shaped, drift to hang in the air over the body of the dead Hispanic. It settled, enfolding the corpse. Possessing it.

Sans its right arm, half its face clawed away, the corpse stood. It swayed, shuddered, spoke with shredded lips. "Max, kill yourself and lib—"

Thanatos lunged at the wavering corpse, closed hot metal fingers around its throat, burned its voice box into char. The body slumped.

But Max stood. His dreams were coming back to him, or was someone sending them back? Someone mindsending. *You were of the Concealed.*

Thanatos turned from the battle, scowling, commanding: "Take him! Bind him, carry him to safety!" The spiders, gnawing on the corpse of the angel with television eyes, moved reluctantly away from their feeding and crept toward Max. A thrill of revulsion went through him. He forced himself forward. He knelt, within the spiders' reach. "Don't hurt him!" Thanatos bellowed. "Take care that he does not—"

But he did. He embraced a spider, clasping it to him as if it were something dear, and used its razor-sharp mandibles to slash his own throat. He fell, spasming, and knew inexpressible pain and numbness, and grayness. And a shattering white light.

He was dead. He was alive. He was standing over his own body, liberated. He reached out and, with his plasma-field, extinguished the fire on the outbuilding. Instantly.

The battle noises softened, then muted – the combatants drew apart. They stood or crouched or hovered silently, watching him and waiting. They knew him for Prince Red Mark, a sleeping Lord of the Plasmagnomes, one of seven Concealed among humanity years before, awaiting the day of awakening, the hour when they must emerge to protect those the kin of Thanatos would slaughter for the eating.

He was arisen, the first of the Concealed. He would awaken

the others, those hidden, sleeping in the hearts of the humble and the unknown. In old women and tired, middle-aged soldiers and . . . and there was one, hidden in a young sepia-skinned girl, not far away.

Thanatos shuddered and squared himself for the battle of wills.

Max, Lord Red Mark, scanned the other figures on the rooftop.

Now he could see past their semblances, recognize them as interlacing networks of rippling wavelength, motion that is thought, energy equal to will. He reached out, reached past the semblance of Lord Thanatos.

A small girl, one Hazel Johnson, watched the battle from a rooftop across the street. She was the only one who saw it; she had the only suitable vantage.

Hazel Johnson was just eight years old, but she was old enough to know that the scene should have surprised her, should have sent her yelling for Momma. But she had seen it in a dream, and she'd always believed that dreams were real.

And now she saw that the man who'd thrown himself on the spider had died, and his body had given off a kind of blue glow; and the blue cloud had formed into something solid, a gigantic shape that towered over the nasty-looking wire-head of hot metal. All the flying things had stopped flying. They were watching the newcomer.

The newcomer looked, to Hazel, like one of the astronauts you saw on TV coming home from the space station; he wore one of those spacesuits they wore, and he even had the US flag stitched on one of his sleeves. But he was a whole lot bigger than any astronaut, or any man she'd ever seen. He must have been four meters tall. And now she saw that he didn't have a helmet like a regular astronaut had. He had one of those helmets that the Knights of the Round Table wore, like she saw in the movie on TV. The knight in the spacesuit was reaching out to the man of hot metal . . .

*   *   *

Lord Red Mark was distantly aware that one of his own was watching from the rooftop across the street. Possibly Lady Day asleep in the body of a small human being; a small person who didn't know, yet, that she wasn't really human after all.

Now he reached out and closed one of his gloved hands around Lord Thanatos's barbed-wire neck (that's how it looked to the little girl watching from across the street) and held him fast, though the metal of that glove began to melt in the heat. Red Mark held him, and with the other hand opened the incinerator door, and reached his hand into the fire that burned in the bosom of his enemy . . .

And snuffed out the flame, like a man snuffing a candle with his thumb and forefinger.

The metal body remained standing, cooling, forever inert. The minions of Lord Thanatos fled squalling into the sky, pursued by the Protectionists, abandoning their visible physicality, becoming once more unseeable. And so the battle was carried into another realm of being.

Soon the rooftop was empty of all but the two corpses, and a few broken harpies, and the shell of Thanatos, and Lord Red Mark.

Red Mark turned to look directly at the little girl on the opposite roof. He levitated, rose evenly into the air, and drifted to her. He alighted beside her and took off his helmet. Beneath was a light that smiled. He was beautiful. He said, "Let's go find the others."

She nodded, slowly, beginning to wake. But the little-girl part of her, the human shell, said, "Do I have to die too? Like you did?"

"No. That was for an emergency. There are other ways."

"I don't have to die now?"

"Not now and . . ." The light that was a smile grew brighter. "Not ever. You'll never die, my Lady Day."

Lost Souls

Clive Barker

Clive Barker wrote of his occult detective Harry D'Amour in one other short story ("The Last Illusion") and two novels, The Great and Secret Show *and* Everville. *He's also the protagonist of film* The Lords of Illusion. *According to his creator, D'Amour is a reluctant demon hunter, not someone "defiantly facing off against some implacable evil with faith and holy water. His antecedents are the troubled, weary and often lovelorn heroes of film noir . . ." Similar hunters now abound in fantasy, but exorcists are the more traditional foes of demons. Roman Catholicism, Hinduism, Islam and Judaism have religious rituals of exorcism. Some Protestant denominations use prayer to get rid of demons; Buddhists use prayer and meditation to persuade an evil spirit to leave. Taoists employ chanting, prayer and physical movements to combat possession. Many New Age religions employ exorcism. Self-appointed exorcists abound.*

Everything the blind woman had told Harry she'd seen was undeniably real. Whatever inner eye Norma Paine possessed – that extraordinary skill that allowed her to scan the island of Manhattan from the Broadway Bridge to Battery Park and yet not move an inch from her tiny room on Seventy-fifth – that eye was as sharp as any knife juggler's. Here was the derelict house on Ridge Street, with the smoke stains besmirching the brick. Here was the dead dog that she'd described, lying on the sidewalk as though asleep, but that it lacked half its head. Here too, if Norma was to be believed, was the demon that Harry had come in search of: the shy and sublimely malignant Cha'Chat.

The house was not, Harry thought, a likely place for a desperado of Cha'Chat's elevation to be in residence. Though the infernal brethren could be a loutish lot, to be certain, it was Christian propaganda that sold them as dwellers in excrement and ice. The escaped demon was more likely to be downing fly eggs and vodka at the Waldorf-Astoria than concealing itself amongst such wretchedness.

But Harry had gone to the blind clairvoyant in desperation, having failed to locate Cha'Chat by any means conventionally available to a private eye such as himself. He was, he had admitted to her, responsible for the fact that the demon was loose at all. It seemed he'd never learned, in his all too frequent encounters with the Gulf and its progeny, that Hell possessed a genius for deceit. Why else had he believed in the child that had tottered into view just as he'd leveled his gun at Cha'Chat? – a child, of course, which had evaporated into a cloud of tainted air as soon as the diversion was redundant and the demon had made its escape.

Now, after almost three weeks of vain pursuit, it was almost Christmas in New York; season of goodwill and suicide. Streets thronged; the air like salt in wounds; Mammon in glory. A more perfect playground for Cha'Chat's despite could scarcely be imagined. Harry had to find the demon quickly, before it did serious damage; find it and return it to the pit from which it had come. In extremis he would even use the binding syllables which the late Father Hesse had vouchsafed to him once, accompanying them with such dire warnings that Harry had never even written them down. Whatever it took. Just as long as Cha'Chat didn't see Christmas Day this side of the Schism.

It seemed to be colder inside the house on Ridge Street than out. Harry could feel the chill creep through both pairs of

socks and start to numb his feet. He was making his way along
the second landing when he heard the sigh. He turned, fully
expecting to see Cha'Chat standing there, its eye cluster looking a dozen ways at once, its cropped fur rippling. But no.
Instead, a young woman stood at the end of the corridor. Her
undernourished features suggested Puerto Rican extraction,
but that – and the fact that she was heavily pregnant – was all
Harry had time to grasp before she hurried away down the
stairs.

Listening to the girl descend, Harry knew that Norma had
been wrong. If Cha'Chat had been here, such a perfect victim
would not have been allowed to escape with her eyes in her
head. The demon wasn't here.

Which left the rest of Manhattan to search.

The night before, something very peculiar had happened to
Eddie Axel. It had begun with his staggering out of his favorite
bar, which was six blocks from the grocery store he owned on
Third Avenue. He was drunk, and happy, and with reason.
Today he had reached the age of fifty-five. He had married
three times in those years; he had sired four legitimate children
and a handful of bastards; and – perhaps most significantly –
he'd made Axel's Superette a highly lucrative business. All was
well with the world.

But Jesus, it was chilly! No chance, on a night threatening a
second Ice Age, of finding a cab. He would have to walk home.

He'd got maybe half a block, however, when – miracle of
miracles – a cab did indeed cruise by. He'd flagged it down,
eased himself in, and the weird times had begun.

For one, the driver knew his name.

"Home, Mr Axel?" he'd said. Eddie hadn't questioned the
godsend. Merely mumbled, "Yes," and assumed this was a
birthday treat, courtesy of someone back at the bar. Perhaps
his eyes had flickered closed; perhaps he'd even slept. Whatever, the next thing he knew the cab was driving at some speed
through streets he didn't recognize. He stirred himself from
his doze. This was the Village, surely; an area Eddie kept clear

of. His neighborhood was the high Nineties, close to the store. Not for him the decadence of the Village, where a shop sign offered EAR PIERCING. WITH OR WITHOUT PAIN and young men with suspicious hips lingered in doorways.

"This isn't the right direction," he said, rapping on the Perspex between him and the driver. There was no word of apology or explanation forthcoming, however, until the cab made a turn toward the river, drawing up in a street of warehouses, and the ride was over.

"This is your stop," said the chauffeur. Eddie didn't need a more explicit invitation to disembark.

As he hauled himself out the cabbie pointed to the murk of an empty lot between two benighted warehouses. "She's been waiting for you," he said, and drove away. Eddie was left alone on the sidewalk.

Common sense counseled a swift retreat, but what now caught his eye glued him to the spot. There she stood – the woman of whom the cabbie had spoken – and she was the most obese creature Eddie had ever set his sight upon. She had more chins than fingers, and her fat, which threatened at every place to spill from the light summer dress she wore, gleamed with either oil or sweat.

"*Eddie*," she said. Everybody seemed to know his name tonight. As she moved toward him, tides moved in the fat of her torso and along her limbs.

"Who are you?" Eddie was about to enquire, but the words died when he realized the obesity's feet weren't touching the ground. *She was floating.*

Had Eddie been sober he might well have taken his cue then and fled, but the drink in his system mellowed his trepidation. He stayed put.

"Eddie," she said. "Dear Eddie. I have some good news and some bad news. Which would you like first?"

Eddie pondered this one for a moment. "The good," he concluded.

"You're going to die tomorrow," came the reply, accompanied by the tiniest of smiles.

"*That's good?*" he said.

"Paradise awaits your immortal soul . . ." she murmured. "Isn't that a joy?"

"So what's the bad news?"

She plunged her stubby-fingered hand into the crevasse between her gleaming tits. There came a little squeal of complaint, and she drew something out of hiding. It was a cross between a runty gecko and a sick rat, possessing the least fetching qualities of both. Its pitiful limbs pedaled at the air as she held it up for Eddie's perusal. "This," she said, "is your immortal soul."

She was right, thought Eddie: the news was not good.

"Yes," she said. "It's a pathetic sight, isn't it?" The soul drooled and squirmed as she went on. "It's undernourished. It's weak to the point of expiring altogether. And *why*?" She didn't give Eddie a chance to reply. "A paucity of good works . . ."

Eddie's teeth had begun to chatter. "What am I supposed to do about it?" he asked.

"You've got a little breath left. You must compensate for a lifetime of rampant profiteering—"

"I don't follow."

"Tomorrow, turn Axel's Superette into a Temple of Charity, and you may yet put some meat on your soul's bones."

She had begun to ascend, Eddie noticed. In the darkness above her, there was sad, sad music, which now wrapped her up in minor chords until she was entirely eclipsed.

The girl had gone by the time Harry reached the street. So had the dead dog. At a loss for options, he trudged back to Norma Paine's apartment, more for the company than the satisfaction of telling her she had been wrong.

"I'm never wrong," she told him over the din of the five televisions and as many radios that she played perpetually. The cacophony was, she claimed, the only sure way to keep those of the spirit world from incessantly intruding upon her privacy: the babble distressed them. "I saw power in that house on Ridge Street," she told Harry, "sure as shit."

Harry was about to argue when an image on one of the screens caught his eye. An outside news broadcast pictured a reporter standing on a sidewalk across the street from a store (AXEL'S SUPERETTE, the sign read) from which bodies were being removed.

"What is it?" Norma demanded.

"Looks like a bomb went off," Harry replied, trying to trace the reporter's voice through the din of the various stations.

"Turn up the sound," said Norma. "I like a disaster."

It was not a bomb that had wrought such destruction, it emerged, but a riot. In the middle of the morning a fight had begun in the packed grocery store; nobody quite knew why. It had rapidly escalated into a bloodbath. A conservative estimate put the death toll at thirty, with twice as many injured. The report, with its talk of a spontaneous eruption of violence, gave fuel to a terrible suspicion in Harry.

"Cha'Chat . . ." he murmured.

Despite the noise in the little room, Norma heard him speak. "What makes you so sure?" she said.

Harry didn't reply. He was listening to the reporter's recapitulation of the events, hoping to catch the location of Axel's Superette. And there it was. Third Avenue, between Ninety-fourth and Ninety-fifth.

"Keep smiling," he said to Norma, and left her to her brandy and the dead gossiping in the bathroom.

Linda had gone back to the house on Ridge Street as a last resort, hoping against hope that she'd find Bolo there. He was, she vaguely calculated, the likeliest candidate for father of the child she carried, but there'd been some strange men in her life at that time; men with eyes that seemed golden in certain lights; men with sudden, joyless smiles. Anyway, Bolo hadn't been at the house, and here she was – as she'd known she'd be all along – alone. All she could hope to do was lie down and die.

But there was death and death. There was that extinction she prayed for nightly, to fall asleep and have the cold claim her by degrees; and there was that other death, the one she saw

whenever fatigue drew her lids down. A death that had neither
dignity in the going nor hope of a Hereafter; a death brought
by a man in a grey suit whose face sometimes resembled a
half-familiar saint, and sometimes a wall of rotting plaster.

Begging as she went, she made her way uptown toward
Times Square. Here, amongst the traffic of consumers, she felt
safe for a while. Finding a little deli, she ordered eggs and
coffee, calculating the meal so that it just fell within the begged
sum. The food stirred the baby. She felt it turn in its slumber,
close now to waking. Maybe she should fight on a while longer,
she thought. If not for her sake, for that of the child.

She lingered at the table, turning the problem over, until the
mutterings of the proprietor shamed her out onto the street
again.

It was late afternoon, and the weather was worsening. A
woman was singing nearby, in Italian, some tragic aria. Tears
close, Linda turned from the pain the song carried, and set off
again in no particular direction.

As the crowd consumed her, a man in a grey suit slipped
away from the audience that had gathered around the street-
corner diva, sending the youth he was with ahead through the
throng to be certain they didn't lose their quarry.

Marchetti regretted having to forsake the show. The singing much amused him. Her voice, long ago drowned in
alcohol, was repeatedly that vital semitone shy of its intended
target – a perfect testament to imperfectability – rendering
Verdi's high art laughable even as it came within sight of
transcendence. He would have to come back here when the
beast had been dispatched. Listening to that spoiled ecstasy
brought him closer to tears that he'd been for months; and he
liked to weep.

Harry stood across Third Avenue from Axel's Superette and
watched the watchers. They had gathered in their hundreds in
the chill of the deepening night, to see what could be seen; nor
were they disappointed. The bodies kept coming out: in bags,
in bundles; there was even something in a bucket.

"Does anybody know exactly what happened?" Harry asked his fellow spectators.

A man turned, his face ruddy with the cold.

"The guy who ran the place decided to give the stuff away," he said, grinning at this absurdity. "And the store was fuckin' swamped. Someone got killed in the crush—"

"I heard the trouble started over a can of meat," another offered. "Somebody got beaten to death with a can of meat."

This rumor was contested by a number of others; all had versions of events.

Harry was about to try and sort fact from fiction when an exchange to his right diverted him.

A boy of nine or ten had buttonholed a companion. "Did you smell her?" he wanted to know. The other nodded vigorously. "Gross, huh?" the first ventured. "Smelled better shit," came the reply, and the two dissolved into conspiratorial laughter.

Harry looked across at the object of their mirth. A huge overweight woman, underdressed for the season, stood on the periphery of the crowd and watched the disaster scene with tiny, glittering eyes.

Harry had forgotten the questions he was going to ask the watchers. What he remembered, clear as yesterday, was the way his dreams conjured the infernal brethren. It wasn't their curses he recalled, nor even the deformities they paraded: it was the smell of them. Of burning hair and halitosis; of veal left to rot in the sun. Ignoring the debate around him, he started in the direction of the woman.

She saw him coming, the rolls of fat at her neck furrowing as she glanced across at him.

It was Cha'Chat, of that Harry had no doubt. And to prove the point, the demon took off at a run, the limbs and prodigious buttocks stirred to a fandango with every step. By the time Harry had cleared his way through the crowd the demon was already turning the corner into Ninety-fifth Street, but its stolen body was not designed for speed, and Harry rapidly made up the distance between them. The lamps were out in several places along the street, and when he finally snatched at the demon, and heard the sound of tearing, the gloom disguised the vile truth for fully five seconds until he realized that Cha'Chat had somehow sloughed off its usurped flesh, leaving Harry holding a great coat of ectoplasm, which was already melting like overripe cheese. The demon, its burden shed, was away; slim as hope and twice as slippery. Harry dropped the coat of filth and gave chase, shouting Hesse's syllables as he did so.

Surprisingly, Cha'Chat stopped in its tracks, and turned to Harry. The eyes looked all ways but Heavenward; the mouth was wide and attempting laughter. It sounded like someone vomiting down an elevator shaft.

"*Words*, D'Amour?" it said, mocking Hesse's syllables. "You think I can be stopped with words?"

"No," said Harry, and blew a hole in Cha'Chat's abdomen before the demon's many eyes had even found the gun.

"*Bastard!*" it wailed. "*Cocksucker!*" and fell to the ground, blood the color of piss throbbing from the hole. Harry sauntered down the street to where it lay. It was almost impossible to slay a demon of Cha'Chat's elevation with bullets, but a scar was shame enough amongst their clan. Two, almost unbearable.

"Don't," it begged when he pointed the gun at its head. "Not the face."

"Give me one good reason why not."

"You'll need the bullets," came the reply.

Harry had expected bargains and threats. This answer silenced him. "There's something going to get loose tonight, D'Amour," Cha'Chat said. The blood that was pooling around it had begun to thicken and grow milky, like melted wax. "Something wilder than me."

"Name it," said Harry. The demon grinned. "Who knows?" it said. "It's a strange season, isn't it? Long nights. Clear skies. Things get born on nights like this, don't you find?"

"*Where?*" said Harry, pressing the gun to Cha'Chat's nose.

"You're a bully, D'Amour," it said reprovingly. "You know that?"

"*Tell me . . .*"

The thing's eyes grew darker; its face seemed to blur.

"South of here, I'd say . . ." it replied. "A hotel . . ." The tone of its voice was changing subtly; the features losing their solidity. Harry's trigger finger itched to give the damned thing a wound that would keep it from a mirror for life, but it was still talking, and he couldn't afford to interrupt its flow. ". . . on Forty-fourth," it said. "Between Sixth . . . Sixth and Broadway." The voice was indisputably feminine now. "Blue blinds," it murmured. "I can see blue blinds . . ."

As it spoke the last vestiges of its true features fled, and suddenly it was Norma who was bleeding on the sidewalk at Harry's feet.

"You wouldn't shoot an old lady, would you?" she piped up.

The trick lasted seconds only, but Harry's hesitation was all that Cha'Chat needed to fold itself between one plane and the next, and flit. He'd lost the creature, for the second time in a month.

And to add discomfort to distress, it had begun to snow.

The small hotel that Cha'Chat had described had seen better years; even the light that burned in the lobby seemed to tremble on the brink of expiring. There was nobody at the desk. Harry was about to start up the stairs when a young man whose pate was shaved as bald as an egg, but for a single kiss curl that was oiled to his scalp, stepped out of the gloom and took hold of his arm.

"There's nobody here," he informed Harry.

In better days Harry might have cracked the egg open with his bare fists, and enjoyed doing so. Tonight he guessed he would come off the worse. So he simply said, "Well, I'll find another hotel then, eh?"

Kiss Curl seemed placated; the grip relaxed. In the next instant Harry's hand found his gun, and the gun found Kiss Curl's chin. An expression of bewilderment crossed the boy's face as he fell back against the wall, spitting blood.

As Harry started up the stairs, he heard the youth yell, "Darrieux!" from below.

Neither the shout nor the sound of the struggle had roused any response from the rooms. The place was empty. It had been elected, Harry began to comprehend, for some purpose other than hostelry.

As he started along the landing a woman's cry, begun but never finished, came to meet him. He stopped dead. Kiss Curl was coming up the stairs behind him two or three at a time; ahead, someone was dying. This couldn't end well, Harry suspected.

Then the door at the end of the corridor opened, and suspicion became plain fact. A man in a grey suit was standing on the threshold, skinning off a pair of bloodied surgical gloves. Harry knew him vaguely; indeed had begun to sense a terrible pattern in all of this from the moment he'd heard Kiss Curl call his employer's name. This was Darrieux Marchetti, also called the Cankerist; one of the whispered order of theological assassins whose directives came from Rome, or Hell, or both.

"D'Amour," he said.

Harry had to fight the urge to be flattered that he had been remembered.

"What happened here?" he demanded to know, taking a step toward the open door.

"Private business," the Cankerist insisted. "Please, no closer."

Candles burned in the little room and, by their generous light, Harry could see the bodies laid out on the bare bed. The woman from the house on Ridge Street, and her child. Both had been dispatched with Roman efficiency.

"She protested," said Marchetti, not overly concerned that Harry was viewing the results of his handiwork. "All I needed was the child."

"What was it?" Harry demanded. "A demon?"

Marchetti shrugged. "We'll never know," he said. "But at this time of year there's usually something that tries to get in under the wire. We like to be safe rather than sorry. Besides, there are those – I number myself amongst them – who believe there is such a thing as a surfeit of Messiahs."

"Messiahs?" said Harry. He looked again at the tiny body.

"There was power there, I suspect," said Marchetti. "But it could have gone either way. Be thankful, D'Amour. Your world isn't ready for revelation." He looked past Harry to the youth, who was at the top of the stairs. "Patrice. Be an angel, will you, bring the car over? I'm late for Mass."

He threw the gloves back onto the bed.

"You're not above the law," said Harry.

"Oh *please*," the Cankerist protested, "let's have no nonsense. It's too late at night."

Harry felt a sharp pain at the base of his skull, and a trace of heat where blood was running.

"Patrice thinks you should go home, D'Amour. And so do I."

The knifepoint was pressed a little deeper.

"Yes?" said Marchetti.

"Yes," said Harry.

"He was here," said Norma, when Harry called back at the house.

"Who?"

"Eddie Axel; of Axel's Superette. He came through, clear as daylight."

"Dead?"

"Of course dead. He killed himself in his cell. Asked me if I'd seen his soul."

"And what did you say?"

"I'm a telephonist, Harry; I just make the connections. I don't pretend to understand the metaphysics." She picked up the bottle of brandy Harry had set on the table beside her chair. "How sweet of you," she said. "Sit down. Drink."

"Another time, Norma. When I'm not so tired." He went to the door. "By the way," he said. "You were right. There was something on Ridge Street . . ."

"Where is it now?"

"Gone . . . home."

"And Cha'Chat?"

"Still out there somewhere. In a foul temper . . ."

"Manhattan's seen worse, Harry."

It was little consolation, but Harry muttered his agreement as he closed the door.

The snow was coming on more heavily all the time.

He stood on the step and watched the way the flakes spiraled in the lamplight. No two, he had read somewhere, were ever alike. When such variety was available to the humble snowflake, could he be surprised that events had such unpredictable faces?

Each moment was its own master, he mused, as he put his head between the blizzard's teeth, and he would have to take whatever comfort he could find in the knowledge that between this chilly hour and dawn there were innumerable such moments – blind maybe, and wild and hungry, but all at least eager to be born.

Uncle Chaim and Aunt Rifke and the Angel

Peter S. Beagle

Unlike Uncle Chaim in Peter S. Beagle's delightful story, artists have never had angels pose for them. And, if they did, they'd be difficult to portray: in Judeo-Christian tradition they are incorporeal beings who occasionally assume human form. The history of how angels came to be depicted in art – and firmly instated in Western and other cultures – is a long and fascinating one. Suffice to say the concept of a winged human figure dates back to ancient Assyro-Babylonian art and representations of the Egyptian goddess Isis, whose worship began more than six thousand years ago. Adapted by the Greeks, portrayed in other religions and literature, the image of a powerful, beautiful winged being still inspires, evokes awe and creates wonder.

My Uncle Chaim, who was a painter, was working in his studio – as he did on every day except Shabbos – when the blue angel showed up. I was there.

I was usually there most afternoons, dropping in on my way home from Fiorello LaGuardia Elementary School. I was what they call a "latchkey kid" these days. My parents both worked and traveled full-time, and Uncle Chaim's studio had been my home base and my real playground since I was small. I was shy and uncomfortable with other children. Uncle Chaim didn't have any kids, and didn't know much about them, so he talked to me like an adult when he talked at all, which suited me perfectly. I looked through his paintings and drawings, tried some of my own, and ate Chinese food with him in silent companionship, when he remembered that we should probably eat. Sometimes I fell asleep on the cot. And when his friends – who were mostly painters like himself – dropped in to visit, I withdrew into my favorite corner and listened to their talk, and understood what I understood. Until the blue angel came.

It was very sudden: one moment I was looking through a couple of the comic books Uncle Chaim kept around for me, while he was trying to catch the highlight on the tendons under his model's chin, and the next moment there was this angel standing before him, actually posing, with her arms spread out and her great wings taking up almost half the studio. She was not blue herself – a light beige would be closer – but she wore a blue robe that managed to look at once graceful and grand, with a white undergarment glimmering beneath. Her face, half shadowed by a loose hood, looked disapproving.

I dropped the comic book and stared. No, I *gaped*, there's a difference. Uncle Chaim said to her, "I can't see my model. If you wouldn't mind moving just a bit?" He was grumpy when he was working, but never rude.

"*I* am your model," the angel said. "From this day forth, you will paint no one but me."

"I don't work on commission," Uncle Chaim answered. "I used to, but you have to put up with too many aggravating rich people. Now I just paint what I paint, take it to the gallery. Easier on my stomach, you know?"

His model, the wife of a fellow painter, said, "Chaim, who are you talking to?"

"Nobody, nobody, Ruthie. Just myself, same way your Jules does when he's working. Old guys get like that." To the angel, in a lower voice, he said, "Also, whatever you're doing to the light, could you not? I got some great shadows going right now." For a celestial brightness was swelling in the grubby little warehouse district studio, illuminating the warped floorboards, the wrinkled tubes of colors scattered everywhere, the canvases stacked and propped in the corners, along with several ancient rickety easels. It scared me, but not Uncle Chaim. He said. "So you're an angel, fine, that's terrific. Now give me back my shadows."

The room darkened obediently. "*Thank* you. Now about *moving* . . ." He made a brushing-away gesture with the hand holding the little glass of Scotch.

The model said, "Chaim, you're worrying me."

"What, I'm seventy-six years old, I'm not entitled to a hallucination now and then? I'm seeing an angel, you're not – this is no big deal. I just want it should move out of the way, let me work." The angel, in response, spread her wings even wider, and Uncle Chaim snapped, "Oh, for God's sake, shoo!"

"It is for God's sake that I am here," the angel announced majestically. "The Lord – Yahweh – I Am That I Am – has sent me down to be your muse." She inclined her head a trifle, by way of accepting the worship and wonder she expected.

From Uncle Chaim, she didn't get it, unless very nearly dropping his glass of Scotch counts as a compliment. "A muse?" he snorted. "I don't need a muse – I got models!"

"That's it," Ruthie said. "I'm calling Jules, I'll make him come over and sit with you." She put on her coat, picked up her purse, and headed for the door, saying over her shoulder, "Same time Thursday? If you're still here?"

"I got more models than I know what to do with," Uncle Chaim told the blue angel. "Men, women, old, young – even a cat, there's one lady always brings her cat, what am I going to do?" He heard the door slam, realized that Ruthie was gone, and sighed irritably, taking a larger swallow of whisky than he usually allowed himself. "Now she's upset, she thinks she's my mother anyway, she'll send Jules with chicken soup and an enema." He narrowed his eyes at the angel. "And what's this, how I'm only going to be painting you from now on? Like Velázquez stuck painting royal Hapsburg imbeciles over and over? Some hope you've got! Listen, you go back and tell—" he hesitated just a trifle "—tell whoever sent you that Chaim Malakoff is too old not to paint what he likes, when he likes and for who he likes. You got all that? We're clear?"

It was surely no way to speak to an angel, but as Uncle Chaim used to warn me about everyone from neighborhood bullies to my fourth-grade teacher who hit people, "You give the bastards an inch, they'll walk all over you. From me they get *bupkes*, *nichevo*, nothing. Not an inch." I got beaten up more than once in those days saying that to the wrong people.

And the blue angel was definitely one of them. The entire room suddenly filled with her: with the wings spreading higher than the ceiling, wider than the walls, yet somehow not touching so much as a stick of charcoal; with the aroma almost too impossibly haunting to be borne; with the vast, unutterable beauty that a thousand medieval and Renaissance artists had somehow not gone mad (for the most part) trying to ambush on canvas or trap in stone. In that moment, Uncle Chaim confided later, he didn't know whether to pity or envy Muslims their ancient ban on depictions of the human body.

"I thought maybe I should kneel, what would it hurt? But then I thought, What would it hurt? It'd hurt my left knee, the one had the arthritis twenty years, that's what it would hurt." So he only shrugged a little and told her, "I could manage a sitting on Monday. Somebody cancelled, I got the whole morning free."

"Now," the angel said. Her air of distinct disapproval had become one of authority. The difference was slight but notable.

"Now," Uncle Chaim mimicked her. "All right, already – Ruthie left early, so why not?" He moved the unfinished portrait over to another easel, and carefully selected a blank canvas from several propped against a wall. "I got to clean off a couple of brushes here, we'll start. You want to take off that thing, whatever, on your head?" Even I knew perfectly well that it was a halo, but Uncle Chaim always told me that you had to start with people as you meant to go on.

"You will require a larger surface," the angel instructed him. "I am not to be represented in miniature."

Uncle Chaim raised one eyebrow (an ability I envied him to the point of practicing – futilely – in the bathroom mirror for hours, until my parents banged on the door, certain I was up to the worst kind of no good). "No, huh? Good enough for the Persians, good enough for Holbein and Hilliard and Sam Cooper, but not for you? So okay, so we'll try this one ..." Rummaging in a corner, he fetched out his biggest canvas, dusted it off, eyed it critically – "Don't even remember what I'm doing with anything this size, must have been saving it for you" – and finally set it up on the empty easel, turning it away from the angel. "Okay, Malakoff's rules. Nobody – *nobody* – looks at my painting till I'm done. Not angels, not Adonai, not my nephew over there in the corner, that's David, Duvidl – not even my wife. Nobody. Understood?"

The angel nodded, almost imperceptibly. With surprising meekness, she asked, "Where shall I sit?"

"Not a lot of choices," Uncle Chaim grunted, lifting a brush from a jar of turpentine. "Over there's okay, where Ruthie was sitting, or maybe by the big window. The window would be good, we've lost the shadows already. Take the red chair, I'll fix the color later."

But sitting down is not a natural act for an angel: they stand or they fly; check any Renaissance painting. The great wings inevitably get crumpled, the halo always winds up distinctly askew; and there is simply no way, even for Uncle Chaim, to ask an angel to cross her legs or to hook one over the arm of the chair. In the end they compromised, and the blue angel rose up to pose in the window, holding herself there effortlessly, with her wings not stirring at all. Uncle Chaim, settling in to work – brushes cleaned and Scotch replenished – could not refrain from remarking, "I always imagined you guys sort of hovered. Like hummingbirds."

"We fly only by the Will of God," the angel replied. "If Yahweh, praised be His name—" I could actually *hear* the capital letters "—withdrew that mighty Will from us, we would fall from the sky on the instant, every single one."

"Doesn't bear thinking about," Uncle Chaim muttered. "Raining angels all over everywhere – falling on people's heads, tying up traffic ..."

The angel looked first startled and then notably shocked. "I was speaking of *our* sky," she explained haughtily, "the sky of Paradise, which compares to yours as gold to lead, tapestry to tissue, heavenly choirs to the bellowing of feeding hogs . . ."

"All *right* already, I get the picture." Uncle Chaim cocked an eye at her, poised up there in the window with no visible means of support, and then back at his canvas. "I was going to ask you about being an angel, what it's like, but if you're going to talk about us like that – bad-mouthing the sky, for God's sake, the whole *planet*."

The angel did not answer him immediately and, when she did, she appeared considerably abashed and spoke very quietly, almost like a scolded schoolgirl. "You are right. It is His sky, His world, and I shame my Lord, my fellows and my breeding by speaking slightingly of any part of it." In a lower voice, she added, as though speaking only to herself, "Perhaps that is why I am here."

Uncle Chaim was covering the canvas with a thin layer of very light blue, to give the painting an undertone. Without looking up, he said, "What, you got sent down here like a punishment? You talked back, you didn't take out the garbage? I could believe it. Your boy Yahweh, he always did have a short fuse."

"I was told only that I was to come to you and be your model and your muse," the angel answered. She pushed her hood back from her face, revealing hair that was not bright gold, as so often painted, but of a color resembling the night sky when it pales into dawn. "Angels do not ask questions."

"Mmm." Uncle Chaim sipped thoughtfully at his Scotch. "Well, one did, anyway, you believe the story."

The angel did not reply, but she looked at him as though he had uttered some unimaginable obscenity. Uncle Chaim shrugged and continued preparing the ground for the portrait. Neither one said anything for some time, and it was the angel who spoke first. She said, a trifle hesitantly, "I have never been a muse before."

"Never had one," Uncle Chaim replied sourly. "Did just fine."

"I do not know what the duties of a muse would be," the angel confessed. "You will need to advise me."

"What?" Uncle Chaim put down his brush. "Okay now, wait a minute. *I* got to tell you how to get into my hair, order me around, probably tell me how I'm not painting you right? Forget it, lady – you figure it out for yourself, I'm working here."

But the blue angel looked confused and unhappy, which is no more natural for an angel than sitting down. Uncle Chaim scratched his head and said, more gently, "What do I know? I guess you're supposed to stimulate my creativity, something like that. Give me ideas, visions, make me see things, think about things I've never thought about." After a pause, he added, "Frankly, Goya pretty much has that effect on me already. Goya and Matisse. So that's covered, the stimulation—maybe you could just tell them, *him*, about that . . ."

Seeing the expression on the angel's marble-smooth face, he let the sentence trail away. Rabbi Shulevitz, who cut his blond hair close and wore shorts when he watered his lawn, once told me that angels are supposed to express God's emotions and desires, without being troubled by any of their own. "Like a number of other heavenly dictates," he murmured when my mother was out of the room, "that one has never quite functioned as I'm sure it was intended."

They were still working in the studio when my mother called and ordered me home. The angel had required no rest or food at all, while Uncle Chaim had actually been drinking his Scotch instead of sipping it (I never once saw him drunk, but I'm not sure that I ever saw him entirely sober), and needed more bathroom breaks than usual. Daylight gone, and his precarious array of sixty-watt bulbs proving increasingly unsatisfactory, he looked briefly at the portrait, covered it, and said to the angel, "Well, *that* stinks, but we'll do better tomorrow. What time you want to start?"

The angel floated down from the window to stand before him. Uncle Chaim was a small man, dark and balding, but he already knew that the angel altered her height when they faced each other, so as not to overwhelm him completely. She said, "I will be here when you are."

Uncle Chaim misunderstood. He assured her that if she had no other place to sleep but the studio, it wouldn't be the first time a model or a friend had spent the night on that trundle bed in the far corner. "Only no peeking at the picture, okay? On your honor as a muse."

The blue angel looked for a moment as though she were going to smile, but she didn't. "I will not sleep here, or anywhere on this Earth," she said. "But you will find me waiting when you come."

"Oh," Uncle Chaim said. "Right. Of course. Fine. But don't change your clothes, okay? Absolutely no changing." The angel nodded.

When Uncle Chaim got home that night, my Aunt Rifke told my mother on the phone at some length, he was in a state that simply did not register on her long-practiced seismograph of her husband's moods. "He comes in, he's telling jokes, he eats up everything on the table, we snuggle up, watch a little TV, I can figure the work went well today. He doesn't talk, he's not hungry, he goes to bed early, tosses and tumbles around all night . . . okay, not so good. Thirty-seven years with a person, wait, you'll find out." Aunt Rifke had been Uncle Chaim's model until they married, and his agent, accountant and road manager ever since.

But the night he returned from beginning his portrait of the angel brought Aunt Rifke a husband she barely recognized. "Not up, not down, not happy, not *not* happy, just . . . *dazed*, I guess that's the best word. He'd start to eat something, then he'd forget about it, wander around the apartment – couldn't sit still, couldn't keep his mind on anything, had trouble even finishing a sentence. One sentence. I tell you, it scared me. I couldn't keep from wondering, Is this how it begins? A man starts acting strange, one day to the next, you think about things like that, you know?" Talking about it, even long past the moment's terror, tears still started in her eyes.

Uncle Chaim did tell her that he had been visited by an angel who demanded that he paint her portrait. *That* Aunt Rifke had no trouble believing, thirty-seven years of marriage to an artist having inured her to certain revelations. Her main concern was how painting an angel might affect Uncle Chaim's working hours, and his daily conduct. "Like actors, you know, Duvidl? They become the people they're doing, I've seen it over and over." Also, blasphemous as it might sound, she wondered how much the angel would be paying, and in what currency. "And saying we'll get a big credit in the next world is not funny, Chaim. Not funny."

Uncle Chaim urged Rifke to come to the studio the very next day to meet his new model for herself. Strangely, that lady, whom I'd known all my life as a legendary repository of other people's lives, stories and secrets, flatly refused to take him up on the offer. "I got nothing to wear, not for meeting an angel in. Besides, what would we talk about? No, you just give her my best, I'll make some *rugelach*." And she never wavered from that position, except once.

The blue angel was indeed waiting when Uncle Chaim arrived in the studio early the next morning. She had even made coffee in his ancient glass percolator, and was offended when he informed her that it was as thin as rain and tasted like used dishwater. "Where I come from, no one ever *makes* coffee," she returned fire. "We command it."

"That's what's wrong with this crap," Uncle Chaim answered her. "Coffee's like art, you don't order coffee around." He waved the angel aside and set about a second pot, which came out strong enough to widen the angel's eyes when she sipped it. Uncle Chaim teased her – "Don't get stuff like *that* in the Green Pastures, huh?" – and confided that he made much better coffee than Aunt Rifke. "Not her fault. Woman was raised on decaf, what can you expect? Cooks like an angel, though."

The angel either missed the joke or ignored it. She began to resume her pose in the window, but Uncle Chaim stopped her. "Later, later, the sun's not right. Just stand where you are, I want to do some work on the head." As I remember, he never used the personal possessive in referring to his models' bodies: it was invariably "turn the face a little", "relax the shoulder", "move the foot to the left". Amateurs often resented it; professionals tended to find it liberating. Uncle Chaim didn't much care either way.

For himself, he was grateful that the angel proved capable of holding a pose indefinitely, without complaining, asking for a break, or needing the toilet. What he found distracting was her steadily emerging interest in talking and asking questions. As requested, her expression never changed and her lips hardly moved; indeed, there were times when he would have sworn he was hearing her only in his mind. Enough of her queries had to do with his work, with how he did what he was doing, that he finally demanded point-blank, "All those angels, seraphs, cherubim, centuries of them – all those Virgins and Assumptions and whatnot – and you've never once been painted? Not one time?"

"I have never set foot on Earth before," the angel confessed. "Not until I was sent to you."

"Sent to me. Directly. Special Delivery, Chaim Shlomovitch Malakoff – one angel, totally inexperienced at modeling. Or anything else got anything to do with human life." The angel nodded, somewhat shyly. Uncle Chaim spoke only one word. "*Why?*"

"I am only eleven thousand, seven hundred and twenty-two years old," the angel said, with a slight but distinct suggestion of resentment in her voice. "No one tells me a *thing.*"

Uncle Chaim was silent for some time, squinting at her face from different angles and distances, even closing one eye from time to time. Finally he grumbled, more than half to himself, "I got a very bad feeling that we're both supposed to learn something from this. Bad, bad feeling." He filled the little glass for the first time that day, and went back to work.

But if there was to be any learning involved in their near-daily meetings in the studio, it appeared to be entirely on her part. She was ravenously curious about human life on the blue-green ball of damp dirt that she had observed so distantly for so long, and her constant questioning reminded a weary Uncle Chaim – as he informed me more than once – of me at the age of four. Except that an angel cannot be bought off, even temporarily, with strawberry ice cream, or threatened with loss of a bedtime story if she can't learn to take "I don't *know!*" for an answer. At times he pretended not to hear her; on other occasions, he would make up some patently ridiculous explanation that a grandchild would have laughed to scorn, but that the angel took so seriously that he was guiltily certain he was bound to be struck by lightning. Only the lightning never came, and the tactic usually did buy him a few moments' peace – until the next question.

Once he said to her, in some desperation, "You're an angel, you're supposed to know everything about human beings. Listen, I'll take you out to Bleecker, MacDougal, Washington Square, you can look at the books, magazines, TV, the classes, the beads and crystals . . . it's all about how to get in touch with angels. Real ones, real angels, never mind that stuff about the angel inside you. Everybody wants some of that angel wisdom, and they want it bad, and they want it right now. We'll take an afternoon off, I'll show you."

The blue angel said simply, "The streets and the shops have nothing to show me, nothing to teach. You do."

"No," Uncle Chaim said. "No, no, no, no no. I'm a painter – that's all, that's it, that's what I know. Painting. But you, you sit at the right hand of God—"

"He doesn't have hands," the angel interrupted. "And nobody exactly *sits*."

"The point I'm making, you're the one who ought to be answering questions. About the universe, and about Darwin, and how everything really happened, and what is it with God and shellfish, and the whole business with the milk and the meat – *those* kinds of questions. I mean, I should be asking them, I know that, only I'm working right now."

It was almost impossible to judge the angel's emotions from the expressions of her chillingly beautiful porcelain face, but as far as Uncle Chaim could tell, she looked sad. She said, "I also am what I am. We angels – as you call us – we are messengers, minions, lackeys, knowing only what we are told, what we are ordered to do. A few of the Oldest, the ones who were there at the Beginning – Michael, Gabriel, Raphael – *they* have names, thoughts, histories, choices, powers. The rest of us, we tremble, we *hide* when we see them passing by. We think, if those are angels, we must be something else altogether, but we can never find a better word for ourselves."

She looked straight at Uncle Chaim – he noticed in some surprise that in a certain light her eyes were not nearly as blue as he had been painting them, but closer to a dark sea-green – and he looked away from an anguish that he had never seen before, and did not know how to paint. He said, "So okay, you're a low-class angel, a heavenly grunt, like they say now. So how come they picked you to be my muse? Got to *mean* something, no? Right?"

The angel did not answer his question, nor did she speak much for the rest of the day. Uncle Chaim posed her in several positions, but the unwonted sadness in her eyes depressed him past even Laphroaig's ability to ameliorate. He quit work early, allowing the angel – as he would never have permitted Aunt Rifke or me – to potter around the studio, putting it to rights according to her inexpert notions, organizing brushes, oils, watercolors, pastels and pencils, fixatives, rolls of canvas, bottles of tempera and turpentine, even dusty chunks of rabbit skin glue, according to size. As he told his friend Jules Sidelsky, meeting for their traditional weekly lunch at a Ukrainian restaurant on Second Avenue, where the two of them spoke only Russian, "Maybe God could figure where things are anymore. Me, I just shut my eyes and pray."

Jules was large and fat, like Diego Rivera, and I thought of him as a sort of uncle too, because he and Ruthie always remembered my birthday, just like Uncle Chaim and Aunt Rifke. Jules did not believe in angels, but he knew that Uncle Chaim didn't necessarily believe in them either, just because he had one in his studio every day. He asked seriously, "That helps? The praying?" Uncle Chaim gave him a look, and Jules dropped the subject. "So what's she like? I mean, as a model? You like painting her?"

Uncle Chaim held his hand out, palm down, and wobbled it gently from side to side. "What's not to like? She'll hold any pose absolutely forever – you could leave her all night, morning I guarantee she wouldn't have moved a muscle. No whining, no bellyaching – listen, she'd make Cinderella look like the witch in that movie, the green one. In my life I never worked with anybody gave me less *tsuris.*"

"So what's with—?" Jules mimicked his fluttering hand. "I'm waiting for the *but*, Chaim."

Uncle Chaim was still for a while, neither answering nor appearing to notice the steaming *varyniki* that the waitress had just set down before him. Finally he grumbled, "She's an angel, what can I tell you? Go reason with an angel." He found himself vaguely angry with Jules, for no reason that made any sense. He went on, "She's got it in her head she's supposed to be my muse. It's not the most comfortable thing sometimes, all right?"

Perhaps due to their shared childhood on Tenth Avenue, Jules did not laugh, but it was plainly a near thing. He said, mildly enough, "Matisse had muses. Rodin, up to here with muses. Picasso about had to give them serial numbers – I think he married them just to keep them straight in his head. You, me . . . I don't see it, Chaim. We're not muse types, you know? Never were, not in all our lives. Also, Rifke would kill you dead. Deader."

"What, I don't know that? Anyway, it's not what you're thinking." He grinned suddenly, in spite of himself. "She's not that kind of girl, you ought to be ashamed. It's just she wants to help, to inspire, that's what muses do. I don't mind her messing around with my mess in the studio – I mean, yeah, I mind it, but I can live with it. But the other day—" he paused briefly, taking a long breath "—the other day she wanted to give me a haircut. A haircut. It's all right, go ahead."

For Jules was definitely laughing this time, spluttering tea through his nose, so that he turned a bright cerise as other diners stared at them. "A haircut," he managed to get out, when he could speak at all clearly. "An angel gave you a haircut."

"No, she didn't give me a haircut," Uncle Chaim snapped back crossly. "She wanted to, she offered – and then, when I said *no, thanks*, after a while she said she could play music for me while I worked. I usually have the news on, and she doesn't like it, I can tell. Well, it wouldn't make much sense to her, would it? Hardly does to me anymore."

"So she's going to be posing *and* playing music? What, on her harp? That's true, the harp business?"

"No, she just said she could command the music. The way they do with coffee." Jules stared at him. "Well, I don't know – I guess it's like some heavenly Muzak or something. Anyway, I told her no, and I'm sorry I told you anything. Eat, forget it, okay?"

But Jules was not to be put off so easily. He dug down into his *galushki poltavski* for a little time, and then looked up and said with his mouth full, "Tell me one thing, then I'll drop it. Would you say she was beautiful?"

"She's an angel," Uncle Chaim said.

"That's not what I asked. Angels are all supposed to be beautiful, right? Beyond words, beyond description, the works. So?" He smiled serenely at Uncle Chaim over his folded hands.

Uncle Chaim took so long to answer him that Jules actually waved a hand directly in front of his eyes. "Hello? Earth to Malakoff – this is your wake-up call. You in there, Chaim?"

"I'm there, I'm there, stop with the kid stuff." Uncle Chaim flicked his own fingers dismissively at his friend's hand. "Jules, all I can tell you, I never saw anyone looked like her before. Maybe that's beauty all by itself, maybe it's just novelty. Some days she looks eleven thousand years old, like she says – some days . . . some days she could be younger than Duvidl, she could be the first child in the world, first one ever." He shook his head helplessly. "I don't *know*, Jules. I wish I could ask Rembrandt or somebody. Vermeer. Vermeer would know."

Strangely, of the small corps of visitors to the studio – old painters like himself and Jules, gallery owners, art brokers, friends from the neighborhood – I seemed to be the only one who ever saw the blue angel as anything other than one of his unsought acolytes, perfectly happy to stretch canvases, make sandwiches and occasionally pose, all for the gift of a growled thanks and the privilege of covertly studying him at work. My memory is that I regarded her as a nice-looking older lady with wings, but not my type at all, I having just discovered Alice Faye. Lauren Bacall, Lizabeth Scott and Lena Horne came a bit later in my development.

I knew she was an angel. I also knew better than to tell any of my own friends about her: we were a cynical lot, who regularly got thrown out of movie theaters for cheering on the Wolf Man and booing Shirley Temple and Bobby Breen. But I was shy with the angel, and – I guess – she with me, so I can't honestly say I remember much either in the way of conversation or revelation. Though I am still haunted by one particular moment when I asked her, straight out, "Up there, in heaven, do you ever see Jesus? Jesus Christ, I mean." We were hardly an observant family, any of us, but it still felt strange and a bit dangerous to say the name.

The blue angel turned from cleaning off a palette knife and looked directly at me, really for the first time since we had been introduced. I noticed that the color of her wings seemed to change from moment to moment, rippling constantly through a supple spectrum different from any I knew; and that I had no words either for her hair color, or for her smell. She said, "No, I have never seen him."

"Oh," I said, vaguely disappointed, Jewish or not. "Well – uh – what about his mother? The . . . the Virgin?" Funny, I remember that *that* seemed more daringly wicked than saying the other name out loud. I wonder why that should have been.

"No," the angel answered. "Nor—" heading me off "—have I ever seen God. You are closer to God now, as you stand there, than I have ever been."

"That doesn't make any sense," I said. She kept looking at me, but did not reply. I said, "I mean, you're an angel. Angels live with God, don't they?"

She shook her head. In that moment – and just for that moment – her richly empty face showed me a sadness that I don't think a human face could ever have contained. "Angels live alone. If we were with God, we would not be angels." She turned away, and I thought she had finished speaking. But then she looked back quite suddenly to say, in a voice that did not sound like her voice at all, being lower than the sound I knew, and almost masculine in texture, "*Dark and dark and dark . . . so empty . . . so dark . . .*"

It frightened me deeply, that one broken sentence, though I couldn't have said why: it was just so dislocating, so completely out of place – even the rhythm of those few words sounded more like the hesitant English of our old Latvian rabbi than that of Uncle Chaim's muse. He didn't hear it, and I didn't tell him about it, because I thought it must be me, that I was making it up, or I'd heard it wrong. I was accustomed to thinking like that when I was a boy.

"She's got like a dimmer switch," Uncle Chaim explained to Aunt Rifke; they were putting freshly washed sheets on the guest bed at the time, because I was staying the night to interview them for my Immigrant Experience class project. "Dial it one way, you wouldn't notice her if she were running naked down Madison Avenue at high noon, flapping her wings and waving a gun. Two guns. Turn that dial back the other way, all the way . . . well, thank God she wouldn't ever do that, because she'd likely set the studio on fire. You think I'm joking. I'm not joking."

"No, Chaim, I know you're not joking." Rifke silently undid and remade both of his attempts at hospital corners, as she always did. She said, "What I want to know is, just where's that dial set when you're painting her? And I'd think a bit about that answer, if I were you." Rifke's favorite cousin Harvey, a career social worker, had recently abandoned wife and children to run off with a beautiful young dope dealer, and Rifke was feeling more than slightly edgy.

Uncle Chaim did think about it, and replied, "About a third, I'd say. Maybe half, once or twice, no more. I remember, I had to ask her a couple times, turn it down, please – go work when somebody's glowing six feet away from you. I mean, the moon takes up a lot of space, a little studio like mine. Bad enough with the wings."

Rifke tucked in the last corner, smoothed the sheet tight, faced him across the bed and said, "You're never going to finish this one, are you? Thirty-seven years, I know all the signs. You'll do it over and over, you'll frame it, you'll hang it, you'll say, 'Okay, that's it, I'm done,' but you won't be done, you'll just start the whole thing again, only maybe a different style, a brighter palette, a bigger canvas, a smaller canvas. But you'll never get it the way it's in your head, not for you." She smacked the pillows fluffy and tossed them back on the bed. "Don't even bother arguing with me, Malakoff. Not when I'm right."

"So am I arguing? Does it look like I'm arguing?" Uncle Chaim rarely drank at home, but on this occasion he walked into the kitchen, filled a glass from the dusty bottle of *grappa*, and turned back to his wife. He said very quietly, "Crazy to think I could get an angel right. Who could paint an angel?"

Aunt Rifke came to him then and put her hands on his shoulders. "My crazy old man, that's who," she answered him. "Nobody else. God would know."

And my Uncle Chaim blushed for the first time in many years. I didn't see this, but Aunt Rifke told me.

Of course, she was quite right about that painting, or any of the many, many others he made of the blue angel. He was never satisfied with any of them, not a one. There was always *something* wrong, something missing, something there but not there, glimpsed but gone. "Like that Chinese monkey trying to grab the moon in the water," Uncle Chaim said to me once. "That's me, a Chinese monkey."

Not that you could say he suffered financially from working with only one model, as the angel had commanded. The failed portraits that he lugged down to the gallery handling his paintings sold almost instantly to museums, private collectors and corporations decorating their lobbies and meeting rooms, under such generic titles as *Angel in the Window*, *Blue Wings*, *Angel with Wineglass* and *Midnight Angel*. Aunt Rifke banked the money, and Uncle Chaim endured the unveilings and the receptions as best he could – without ever looking at the paintings themselves – and then shuffled back to his studio to start over. The angel was always waiting.

I was doing my homework in the studio when Jules Sidelsky visited at last, lured there by other reasons than art, beauty, or deity. The blue angel hadn't given up the notion of acting as Uncle Chaim's muse, but never seemed able to take it much beyond making a tuna salad sandwich, or a pot of coffee (at which, to be fair, she had become quite skilled), summoning music, or reciting the lost works of legendary or forgotten poets while he worked. He tried to discourage this habit; but he did learn a number of Shakespeare's unpublished sonnets, and was able to write down for Jules three poems that drowned with Shelley off the Livorno coast. "Also, your boy Pushkin, his wife destroyed a mess of his stuff right after his death. My girl's got it all by heart, you believe that?"

Pushkin did it. If the great Russian had been declared a saint, Jules would have reported for instruction to the Patriarch of Moscow on the following day. As it was, he came down to Uncle Chaim's studio instead, and was at last introduced to the blue angel, who was as gracious as Jules did his bewildered best to be. She spent the afternoon declaiming Pushkin's vanished verse to him in the original, while hovering tirelessly upside down, just above the crossbar of a second easel. Uncle Chaim thought he might be entering a surrealist phase.

Leaving, Jules caught Uncle Chaim's arm and dragged him out his door into the hot, bustling Village streets, once his dearest subject before the coming of the blue angel. Uncle Chaim, knowing his purpose, said, "So now you see? Now you see?"

"I see." Jules's voice was dark and flat, and almost without expression. "I see you got an angel there, all right. No question in the world about that." The grip on Uncle Chaim's arm tightened. Jules said, "You have to get rid of her."

"*What*? What are you *talking* about? Just finally doing the most important work of my life, and you want me . . . ?" Uncle Chaim's eyes narrowed, and he pulled forcefully away from his friend. "What is it with you and my models? You got like this once before, when I was painting that Puerto Rican guy, the teacher, with the big nose, and you just couldn't stand it, you remember? Said I'd stolen him, wouldn't speak to me for weeks, weeks, you remember?"

"Chaim, that's not true—"

"And so now I've got this angel, it's the same thing – worse, with the Pushkin and all—"

"Chaim, damn it, I wouldn't care if she were Pushkin's sister, they played Monopoly together—"

Uncle Chaim's voice abruptly grew calmer; the top of his head stopped sweating and lost its crimson tinge. "I'm sorry, I'm sorry, Jules. It's not I don't understand, I've been the same way about other people's models." He patted the other's shoulder awkwardly. "Look, I tell you what, anytime you want, you come on over, we'll work together. How about that?"

Poor Jules must have been completely staggered by all this. On the one hand he knew – I mean, even I knew – that Uncle Chaim never invited other artists to share space with him, let alone a model; on the other, the sudden change can only have sharpened his anxiety about his old friend's state of mind. He said, "Chaim, I'm just trying to tell you, whatever's going on, it isn't good for you. Not her fault, not your fault. People and angels aren't supposed to hang out together – we aren't built for it, and neither are they. She really needs to go back where she belongs."

"She can't. Absolutely not." Uncle Chaim was shaking his head, and kept on shaking it. "She got *sent* here, Jules, she got sent to *me*—"

"By whom? You ever ask yourself that?" They stared at each other. Jules said, very carefully, "No, not by the Devil. I don't believe in the Devil any more than I believe in God, although he always gets the good lines. But it's a free country, and I *can* believe in angels without swallowing all the rest of it, if I want to." He paused, and took a gentler hold on Uncle Chaim's arm. "And I can also imagine that angels might not be exactly what we think they are. That an angel might lie, and still be an angel. That an angel might be selfish – jealous, even. That an angel might just be a little bit out of her head."

In a very pale and quiet voice, Uncle Chaim said, "You're talking about a fallen angel, aren't you?"

"I don't know what I'm talking about," Jules answered. "That's the God's truth." Both of them smiled wearily, but neither one laughed. Jules said, "I'm dead serious, Chaim. For your sake, your sanity, she needs to go."

"And for my sake, she can't." Uncle Chaim was plainly too exhausted for either pretense or bluster, but there was no give in him. He said, "*Landsmann*, it doesn't matter. You could be right, you could be wrong, I'm telling you, it doesn't matter. There's no one else I want to paint anymore – there's no one else I can paint, Jules, that's just how it is. Go home now." He refused to say another word.

In the months that followed, Uncle Chaim became steadily more silent, more reclusive, more closed off from everything that did not directly involve the current portrait of the blue angel. By autumn, he was no longer meeting Jules for lunch at the Ukrainian restaurant; he could rarely be induced to appear at his own openings, or anyone else's; he frequently spent the night at his studio, sleeping briefly in his chair, when he slept at all. It had been understood between Uncle Chaim and me since I was three that I had the run of the place at any time; and while it was still true, I felt far less comfortable there than I was accustomed, and left it more and more to him and the strange lady with the wings.

When an exasperated – and increasingly frightened – Aunt Rifke would challenge him, "You've turned into Red Skelton, painting nothing but clowns on velvet – Margaret Keane, all those big-eyed war orphans," he only shrugged and replied, when he even bothered to respond, "You were the one who told me I could paint an angel. Change your mind?"

Whatever she truly thought, it was not in Aunt Rifke to say such a thing to him directly. Her only recourse was to mumble something like, "Even Leonardo gave up on drawing cats," or "You've done the best anybody could ever do – let it go now, let *her* go." Her own theory, differing somewhat from Jules's, was that it was as much Uncle Chaim's obsession as his model's possible madness that was holding the angel to Earth. "Like Ella and Sam," she said to me, referring to the perpetually quarrelling parents of my favorite cousin Arthur. "Locked together, like some kind of punishment machine. Thirty years they hate each other, cats and dogs, but they're so scared of being alone, if one of them died—" she snapped her fingers "—the other one would be gone in a week. Like that. Okay, so not exactly like that, but like that." Aunt Rifke wasn't getting a lot of sleep either just then.

She confessed to me – it astonishes me to this day – that she prayed more than once herself, during the worst times. Even in my family, which still runs to atheists, agnostics and cranky anarchists, Aunt Rifke's unbelief was regarded as the standard by which all other blasphemy had to be judged, and set against which it invariably paled. The idea of a prayer from her lips was, on the one hand, fascinating – how would Aunt Rifke conceivably address a Supreme Being? – and more than a little alarming as well. Supplication was not in her vocabulary, let alone her repertoire. Command was.

I didn't ask her what she had prayed for. I did ask, trying to make her laugh, if she had commenced by saying, "To whom it may concern . . ." She slapped my hand lightly. "Don't talk fresh, just because you're in fifth grade, sixth grade, whatever. Of course I didn't say that, an old Socialist Worker like me. I started off like you'd talk to some kid's mother on the phone, I said, 'It's time for your little girl to go home, we're going to be having dinner. You better call her in now, it's getting dark.' Like that, polite. But not fancy."

"And you got an answer?" Her face clouded, but she made no reply. "You didn't get an answer? Bad connection?" I honestly wasn't being fresh: this was my story too, somehow, all the way back, from the beginning, and I had to know where we were in it. "Come on, Aunt Rifke."

"I got an answer." The words came slowly, and cut off abruptly, though she seemed to want to say something more. Instead, she got up and went to the stove, all my aunts' traditional *querencia* in times of emotional stress. Without turning her head, she said in a curiously dull tone, "*You* go home now. Your mother'll yell at me."

My mother worried about my grades and my taste in friends, not about me; but I had never seen Aunt Rifke quite like this, and I knew better than to push her any further. So I went on home.

From that day, however, I made a new point of stopping by the studio literally every day – except Shabbos, naturally – even if only for a few minutes, just to let Uncle Chaim know that someone besides Aunt Rifke was concerned about him. Of course, obviously, a whole lot of other people would have been, from family to gallery owners to friends like Jules and Ruthie, but I was ten years old, and feeling like my uncle's only guardian, and a private detective to boot. A guardian against what? An angel? Detecting what? A portrait? I couldn't have said for a minute, but a ten-year-old boy with a sense of mission definitely qualifies as a dangerous flying object.

Uncle Chaim didn't talk to me anymore while he was working, and I really missed that. To this day, almost everything I know about painting – about *being* a painter, every day, all day – I learned from him, grumbled out of the side of his mouth as he sized a canvas, touched up a troublesome corner, or stood back, scratching his head, to reconsider a composition or a subject's expression, or simply to study the stoop of a shadow. Now he worked in bleak near-total silence; and since the blue angel never spoke unless addressed directly, the studio had become a far less inviting place than my three-year-old self had found it. Yet I felt that Uncle Chaim still liked having me there, even if he didn't say anything, so I kept going, but it was an effort some days, mission or no mission.

His only conversation was with the angel – Uncle Chaim always chatted with his models; paradoxically, he felt that it helped them to concentrate – and while I honestly wasn't trying to eavesdrop (except sometimes), I couldn't help overhearing their talk. Uncle Chaim would ask the angel to lift a wing slightly, or to alter her stance somewhat: as I've said, sitting remained uncomfortable and unnatural for her, but she had finally been able to manage a sort of semi-recumbent posture, which made her look curiously vulnerable, almost like a tired child after an adult party, playing at being her mother, with the grown-ups all asleep upstairs. I can close my eyes today and see her so.

One winter afternoon, having come tired, and stayed late, I was half asleep on a padded rocker in a far corner when I heard Uncle Chaim saying, "You ever think that maybe we might both be dead, you and me?"

"We angels do not die," the blue angel responded. "It is not in us to die."

"I told you, lift the chin," Uncle Chaim grunted. "Well, it's built into us, believe me, it's mostly what we do from day one." He looked up at her from the easel. "But I'm trying to get you into a painting, and I'll never be able to do it, but it doesn't matter, got to keep trying. The head a *little* bit to the left – no, that's too much, I said a *little*." He put down his brush and walked over to the angel, taking her chin in his hand. He said, "And you ... whatever you're after, you're not going to get that right, either, are you? So it's like we're stuck here together – and if we were dead, maybe this is hell. Would we know? You ever think about things like that?"

"No." The angel said nothing further for a long time, and I was dozing off again when I heard her speak. "You would not speak so lightly of hell if you had seen it. I have seen it. It is not what you think."

"*Nu?*" Uncle Chaim's voice could raise an eyebrow itself. "So what's it like?"

"*Cold.*" The words were almost inaudible. "So cold ... so lonely ... so *empty*. God is not there ... no one is there. No one, no one, no one ... no one ..."

It was that voice, that other voice that I had heard once before, and I have never again been as frightened as I was by the murmuring terror in her words. I actually grabbed my books and got up to leave, already framing some sort of gotta-go to Uncle Chaim, but just then Aunt Rifke walked into the studio for the first time, with Rabbi Shulevitz trailing behind her, so I stayed where I was. I don't know a thing about ten-year-olds today, but in those times one of the major functions of adults was to supply drama and mystery to our lives, and we took such things where we found them.

Rabbi Stuart Shulevitz was the nearest thing my family had to an actual regular rabbi. He was Reform, of course, which meant that he had no beard, played the guitar, performed bar mitzvahs and interfaith marriages, invited local priests and imams to lead the Passover ritual, and put up perpetually with all the jokes told, even by his own congregation, about young, beardless, terminally tolerant Reform rabbis. Uncle Chaim, who allowed Aunt Rifke to drag him to *shul* twice a year, on the High Holidays, regarded him as being somewhere between a mild head cold and mouse droppings in the pantry. But Aunt Rifke always defended Rabbi Shulevitz, saying, "He's smarter than he looks, and anyway he can't help being blond. Also, he smells good."

Uncle Chaim and I had to concede the point. Rabbi Shulevitz's immediate predecessor, a huge, hairy, bespectacled man from Riga, had smelled mainly of rancid hair oil and cheap peach schnapps. And he couldn't sing "Red River Valley", either.

Aunt Rifke was generally a placid-appearing, *hamishe* sort of woman, but now her plump face was set in lines that would have told even an angel that she meant business. The blue angel froze in position in a different way than she usually held still as required by the pose. Her strange eyes seemed almost to change their shape, widening in the center and somehow *lifting* at the corners, as though to echo her wings. She stood at near-attention, silently regarding Aunt Rifke and the rabbi.

Uncle Chaim never stopped painting. Over his shoulder he said, "Rifke, what do you want? I'll be home when I'm home."

"So who's rushing you?" Aunt Rifke snapped back. "We didn't come about you. We came so the rabbi should take a look at your *model* here." The word burst from her mouth trailing blue smoke.

"What look? I'm working, I'm going to lose the light in ten, fifteen minutes. Sorry, Rabbi, I got no time. Come back next week, you could say a *barucha* for the whole studio. Goodbye, Rifke."

But my eyes were on the rabbi, and on the angel, as he slowly approached her, paying no heed to the quarreling voices of Uncle Chaim and Aunt Rifke. Blond or not, "Red River Valley" or not, he was still magic in my sight, the official representative of a power as real as my disbelief. On the other hand, the angel could fly. The Chasidic wonder-*rebbes* of my parents' Eastern Europe could fly up to heaven and share the Shabbos meal with God, when they chose. Reform rabbis couldn't fly.

As Rabbi Shulevitz neared her, the blue angel became larger and more stately, and there was now a certain menacing aspect to her divine radiance, which set me shrinking into a corner, half concealed by a dusty drape. But the rabbi came on.

"Come no closer," the angel warned him. Her voice sounded deeper, and slightly distorted, like a phonograph record when the Victrola hasn't been wound tight enough. "It is not for mortals to lay hands on the Lord's servant and messenger."

"I'm not touching you," Rabbi Shulevitz answered mildly. "I just want to look in your eyes. An angel can't object to that, surely."

"The full blaze of an angel's eyes would leave you ashes, impudent man." Even I could hear the undertone of anxiety in her voice.

"That is foolishness." The rabbi's tone continued gentle, almost playful. "My friend Chaim paints your eyes full of compassion, of sorrow for the world and all its creatures, every one. Only turn those eyes to me for a minute, for a very little minute, where's the harm?"

Obediently, he stayed where he was, taking off his hat to reveal the black yarmulke underneath. Behind him, Aunt Rifke made as though to take Uncle Chaim's arm, but he shrugged her away, never taking his own eyes from Rabbi Shulevitz and the blue angel. His face was very pale. The glass of Scotch in his left hand, plainly as forgotten as the brush in his right, was beginning to slosh over the rim with his trembling, and I was distracted with fascination, waiting for him to drop it. So I

wasn't quite present, you might say, when the rabbi's eyes
looked into the eyes of the blue angel.

But I heard the rabbi gasp, and I saw him stagger backwards
a couple of steps, with his arm up in front of his eyes. And I
saw the angel turning away, instantly; the whole encounter
couldn't have lasted more than five seconds, if that much. And
if Rabbi Shulevitz looked stunned and frightened – which he
did – there is no word that I know to describe the expression
on the angel's face. No words.

Rabbi Shulevitz spoke to Aunt Rifke in Hebrew, which I
didn't know, and she answered him in swift, fierce Yiddish,
which I did, but only insofar as it pertained to things my
parents felt were best kept hidden from me, such as money
problems, family gossip and sex. So I missed most of her
words, but I caught anyway three of them. One was *shofar*,
which is the ram's horn blown at sundown on the High Holidays, and about which I already knew two good dirty jokes.
The second was *minyan*, the number of adult Jews needed to
form a prayer circle on special occasions. Reform *minyanim*
include women, which Aunt Rifke always told me I'd come to
appreciate in a couple of years. She was right.

The third word was *dybbuk*.

I knew the word, and I didn't know it. If you'd asked me its
meaning, I would have answered that it meant some kind of
bogey, like the Invisible Man, or just maybe the Mummy. But
I learned the real meaning fast, because Rabbi Shulevitz had
taken off his glasses and was wiping his forehead, and whispering, "No. No. *Ich vershtaye nicht* . . ."

Uncle Chaim was complaining, "What the hell is this? See
now, we've lost the light already, I *told* you." No one – me
included – was paying any attention.

Aunt Rifke – who was never entirely sure that Rabbi
Shulevitz *really* understood Yiddish – burst into English. "It's a
dybbuk, what's not to understand? There's a *golem* in that
woman, you've got to get rid of it! You get a *minyan* together,
right now, you get rid of it! Exorcise!"

Why on earth did she want the rabbi to start doing

push-ups or jumping jacks in this moment? I was still puzzling over that when he said, "That woman, as you call her, is an angel. You cannot . . . Rifke, you do not exorcise an angel." He was trembling – I could see that – but his voice was steady and firm.

"You do when it's possessed!" Aunt Rifke looked utterly exasperated with everybody. "I don't know how it could happen, but Chaim's angel's got a *dybbuk* in her—" she whirled on her husband "—which is why she makes you just keep painting her and painting her, day and night. You finish – really finish, it's done, over – she might have to go back out where it's not so nice for a *dybbuk*, you know about that? Look at her!" She pointed an orange-nailed finger straight in the blue angel's face. "She hears me, she knows what I'm talking about. You know what I'm talking, don't you, Miss Angel? Or I should say, Mister Dybbuk? You tell me, okay?"

I had never seen Aunt Rifke like this; she might have been possessed herself. Rabbi Shulevitz was trying to calm her, while Uncle Chaim fumed at the intruders disturbing his model. To my eyes, the angel looked more than disturbed – she looked as terrified as a cat I'd seen backed against a railing by a couple of dogs, strays, with no one to call them away from tearing her to pieces. I was anxious for her, but much more so for my aunt and uncle, truly expecting them to be struck by lightning, or turned to salt, or something on that order. I was scared for the rabbi as well, but I figured he could take care of himself. Maybe even with Aunt Rifke.

"A *dybbuk* cannot possibly possess an angel," the rabbi was saying. "Believe me, I majored in Ashkenazic folklore – wrote my thesis on Lilith, as a matter of fact – and there are no accounts, no legends, not so much as a single *bubbemeise* of such a thing. *Dybbuks* are wandering spirits, some of them good, some malicious, but all houseless in the universe. They cannot enter heaven, and Gehenna won't have them, so they take refuge within the first human being they can reach, like any parasite. But an angel? Inconceivable, take my word. Inconceivable."

"In the mind of God," the blue angel said, "nothing is inconceivable."

Strangely, we hardly heard her; she had almost been forgotten in the dispute over her possession. But her voice was that other voice – I could see Uncle Chaim's eyes widen as he caught the difference. That voice said now, "She is right. I am a *dybbuk*."

In the sudden absolute silence, Aunt Rifke, serenely complacent, said, "Told you."

I heard myself say, "Is she bad? I thought she was an angel."

Uncle Chaim said impatiently, "What? She's a model."

Rabbi Shulevitz put his glasses back on, his eyes soft with pity behind the heavy lenses. I expected him to point at the angel, like Aunt Rifke, and thunder out stern and stately Hebrew maledictions, but he only said, "Poor thing, poor thing. Poor creature."

Through the angel's mouth, the *dybbuk* said, "Rabbi, go away. Let me alone, let me be. I am warning you."

I could not take my eyes off her. I don't know whether I was more fascinated by what she was saying, and the adults having to deal with its mystery, or by the fact that all the time I had known her as Uncle Chaim's winged and haloed model, someone else was using her the way I played with my little puppet theater at home – moving her, making up things for her to say, perhaps even putting her away at night when the studio was empty. Already it was as though I had never heard her strange, shy voice asking a child's endless questions about the world, but only this grown-up voice, speaking to Rabbi Shulevitz. "You cannot force me to leave her."

"I don't want to force you to do anything," the rabbi said gently. "I want to help you."

I wish I had never heard the laughter that answered him. I was too young to hear something like that, if anyone could ever be old enough. I cried out and doubled up around myself, hugging my stomach, although what I felt was worse than the worst bellyache I had ever wakened with in the night. Aunt Rifke came and put her arms around me, trying to soothe me, murmuring, half in English, half in Yiddish, "Shh, shh, it's all right, *der rebbe* will make it all right. He's helping the angel, he's getting rid of that thing inside her, like a doctor. Wait, wait, you'll see, it'll be all right." But I went on crying, because I had been visited by a monstrous grief not my own, and I was only ten.

The *dybbuk* said, "If you wish to help me, Rabbi, leave me alone. I will not go into the dark again."

Rabbi Shulevitz wiped his forehead. He asked, his tone still gentle and wondering, "What did you do to become . . . what you are? Do you remember?"

The *dybbuk* did not answer him for a long time. Nobody spoke, except for Uncle Chaim muttering unhappily to himself, "Who needs this? Try to get your work done, it turns into a *ferkockte* party. Who needs it?" Aunt Rifke shushed him, but she reached for his arm, and this time he let her take it.

The rabbi said, "You are a Jew."

"I was. Now I am nothing."

"No, you are still a Jew. You must know that we do not practice exorcism, not as others do. We heal, we try to heal both the person possessed and the one possessing. But you must tell me what you have done. Why you cannot find peace."

The change in Rabbi Shulevitz astonished me as much as the difference between Uncle Chaim's blue angel and the spirit that inhabited her and spoke through her. He didn't even look like the crew-cut, blue-eyed, guitar-playing, basketball-playing (well, he tried), college-student-dressing young man whose idea of a good time was getting people to sit in a circle and sing "So Long, It's Been Good to Know You" or "Dreidel, Dreidel, Dreidel" together. There was a power of his own inhabiting him, and clearly the *dybbuk* recognized it. It said slowly, "You cannot help me. You cannot heal."

"Well, we don't know that, do we?" Rabbi Shulevitz said brightly. "So, a bargain. You tell me what holds you here, and I will tell you, honestly, what I can do for you. *Honestly.*"

Again the *dybbuk* was slow to reply. Aunt Rifke said hotly, "What is this? What *help*? We're here to expel, to get rid of a demon that's taken over one of God's angels, if that's what she really is, and enchanted my husband so it's all he can paint, all he can think about painting. Who's talking about *helping* a demon?"

"The rabbi is," I said, and they all turned as though they'd forgotten I was there. I gulped and stumbled along, feeling like I might throw up. I said, "I don't think it's a demon, but even if it is, it's given Uncle Chaim a chance to paint a real angel, and everybody loves the paintings, and they buy them, which we wouldn't have had them to sell if the – the *thing* – hadn't made her stay in Uncle Chaim's studio." I ran out of breath, gas and show-business ambitions all at pretty much the same time, and sat down, grateful that I had neither puked nor started to cry. I was still grandly capable of both back then.

Aunt Rifke looked at me in a way I didn't recall her ever doing before. She didn't say anything, but her arm tightened around me. Rabbi Shulevitz said quietly, "Thank you, David." He turned back to face the angel. In the same voice, he said, "Please. Tell me."

When the *dybbuk* spoke again, the words came one by one – two by two, at most. "A girl . . . There was a girl . . . a young woman . . ."

"*Ai*, how not?" Aunt Rifke's sigh was resigned, but not angry or mocking, just as Uncle Chaim's "*Shah*, Rifkela," was neither a dismissal nor an order. The rabbi, in turn, gestured them to silence.

"She wanted us to marry," the *dybbuk* said. "I did too. But there was time. There was a world . . . there was my work . . . there were things to see . . . to taste and smell and do and be . . . It could wait a little. She could wait . . ."

"Uh-huh. Of course. You could die waiting around for some damn man!"

"*Shah*, Rifkela!"

"But this one did not wait around," Rabbi Shulevitz said to the *dybbuk*. "She did not wait for you, am I right?"

"She married another man," came the reply, and it seemed to my ten-year-old imagination that every tortured syllable came away tinged with blood. "They had been married for two years when he beat her to death."

It was my Uncle Chaim who gasped in shock. I don't think anyone else made a sound.

The *dybbuk* said, "She sent me a message. I came as fast as I could. I *did* come," though no one had challenged his statement. "But it was too late."

This time we were the ones who did not speak for a long time. Rabbi Shulevitz finally asked, "What did you do?"

"I looked for him. I meant to kill him, but he killed himself before I found him. So I was too late again."

"What happened then?" That was me, once more to my own surprise. "When you didn't get to kill him?"

"I lived. I wanted to die, but I lived."

From Aunt Rifke – how not? "You ever got married?"

"No. I lived alone, and I grew old and died. That is all."

"Excuse me, but that is *not* all." The rabbi's voice had suddenly, startlingly, turned probing, almost harsh. "That is only the beginning." Everyone looked at him. The rabbi said, "So, after you died, what did happen? Where did you go?"

There was no answer. Rabbi Shulevitz repeated the question. The *dybbuk* responded finally, "You have said it yourself. Houseless in the universe I am, and how should it be otherwise? The woman I loved died because I did not love her enough – what greater sin is there than that? Even her murderer had the courage to atone, but I dared not offer my own life in payment for hers. I chose to live, and living on has been my punishment, in death as well as in life. To wander back and forth in a cold you cannot know, shunned by heaven, scorned by purgatory . . . do you wonder that I sought shelter where I could, even in an angel? God himself would have to come and cast me out again, Rabbi – you never can."

I became aware that my aunt and uncle had drawn close around me, as though expecting something dangerous and possibly explosive to happen. Rabbi Shulevitz took off his glasses again, ran his hand through his crew cut, stared at the glasses as though he had never seen them before, and put them back on.

"You are right," he said to the *dybbuk*. "I'm a rabbi, not a *rebbe* – no Solomonic wisdom, no magical powers, just a degree from a second-class seminary in Metuchen, New Jersey. You wouldn't know it." He drew a deep breath and moved a few steps closer to the blue angel. He said, "But this *gornisht* rabbi knows anyway that you would never have been allowed this refuge if God had not taken pity on you. You must know this, surely?" The *dybbuk* did not answer. Rabbi Shulevitz said, "And if God pities you, might you not have a little pity on yourself? A little forgiveness?"

"Forgiveness . . ." Now it was the *dybbuk* who whispered. "Forgiveness may be God's business. It is not mine."

"Forgiveness is everyone's business. Even the dead. On this earth or under it, there is no peace without forgiveness." The rabbi reached out then, to touch the blue angel comfortingly. She did not react, but he winced and drew his hand back instantly, blowing hard on his fingers, hitting them against his leg. Even I could see that they had turned white with cold.

"You need not fear for her," the *dybbuk* said. "Angels feel neither cold nor heat. You have touched where I have been."

Rabbi Shulevitz shook his head. He said, "I touched you. I touched your shame and your grief – as raw today, I know, as on the day your love died. But the cold . . . the cold is yours. The loneliness, the endless guilt over what you should have done, the endless turning to and fro in empty darkness . . . none of that comes from God. You must believe me, my friend." He paused, still flexing his frozen fingers. "And you must come forth from God's angel now. For her sake and your own."

The *dybbuk* did not respond. Aunt Rifke said, far more sympathetically than she had before, "You need a *minyan*. I could make some calls. We'd be careful, we wouldn't hurt it."

Uncle Chaim looked from her to the rabbi, then back to the blue angel. He opened his mouth to say something, but didn't.

The rabbi said, "You have suffered enough at your own hands. It is time for you to surrender your pain." When there was still no reply, he asked, "Are you afraid to be without it? Is that your real fear?"

"It has been my only friend!" the *dybbuk* answered at last. "Even God cannot understand what I have done so well as my pain does. Without the pain, there is only me."

"There is heaven," Rabbi Shulevitz said. "Heaven is waiting for you. Heaven has been waiting a long, long time."

"*I am waiting for me!*" It burst out of the *dybbuk* in a long wail of purest terror, the kind you only hear from small children trapped in a nightmare. "You want me to abandon the one sanctuary I have ever found, where I can huddle warm in the consciousness of an angel and sometimes – for a little – even forget the thing I am. You want me to be naked to myself again, and I am telling you *no, not ever, not ever, not ever.* Do what you must, Rabbi, and I will do the only thing I can." It paused, and then added, somewhat stiffly, "Thank you for your efforts. You are a good man."

Rabbi Shulevitz looked genuinely embarrassed. He also looked weary, frustrated and older than he had been when he first recognized the possession of Uncle Chaim's angel. Looking vaguely around at us, he said, "I don't know – maybe it *will* take a *minyan.* I don't want to, but we can't just . . ." His voice trailed away sadly, too defeated even to finish the sentence.

Or maybe he didn't finish because that was when I stepped forward, pulling away from my aunt and uncle, and said, "He can come with me, if he wants. He can come and live in me. Like with the angel."

Uncle Chaim said, "*What?*" and Aunt Rifke said, "*No!*" and Rabbi Shulevitz said, "*David!*" He turned and grabbed me by the shoulders, and I could feel him wanting to shake me, but he didn't. He seemed to be having trouble breathing. He said, "David, you don't know what you're saying."

"Yes, I do," I said. "He's scared, he's so scared. I know about scared."

Aunt Rifke crouched down beside me, peering hard into my face. "David, you're ten years old, you're a little boy. This one, he could be a thousand years, he's been hiding from God in an angel's body. How could you know what he's feeling?"

I said, "Aunt Rifke, I go to school. I wake up every morning, and right away I think about the boys waiting to beat me up because I'm small, or because I'm Jewish, or because they just don't like my face, the way I look at them. Every day I want to stay home and read, and listen to the radio, and play my All-Star Baseball game, but I get dressed and I eat breakfast, and I walk to school. And every day I have to think how I'm going to get through recess, get through gym class, get home without running into Jay Taffer, George DiLucca. Billy Kronish. I know all about not wanting to go outside."

Nobody said anything. The rabbi tried several times, but it was Uncle Chaim who finally said loudly, "I got to teach you to box. A little Archie Moore, a little Willie Pep, we'll take care of those *mamzers*." He looked ready to give me my first lesson right there.

When the *dybbuk* spoke again, its voice was somehow different: quiet, slow, wondering. It said, "Boy, you would do that?" I didn't speak, but I nodded.

Aunt Rifke said, "Your mother would *kill* me! She's hated me since I married Chaim."

The *dybbuk* said, "Boy, if I come . . . outside, I cannot go back. Do you understand that?"

"Yes," I said. "I understand."

But I was shaking. I tried to imagine what it would be like to have someone living inside me, like a baby, or a tapeworm. I was fascinated by tapeworms that year. Only this would be a spirit, not an actual physical thing – that wouldn't be so bad, would it? It might even be company, in a way, almost like being a comic-book superhero and having a secret identity. I wondered whether the angel had even known the *dybbuk* was in her, as quiet as he had been until he spoke to Rabbi Shulevitz. Who, at the moment, was repeating over and over, "No, I can't permit this. This is wrong, this can't be allowed. No." He began to mutter prayers in Hebrew.

Aunt Rifke was saying, "I don't care, I'm calling some

people from the *shul*, I'm getting some people down here right away!" Uncle Chaim was gripping my shoulder so hard it hurt, but he didn't say anything. But there was really no one in the room except the *dybbuk* and me. When I think about it, when I remember, that's all I see.

I remember being thirsty, terribly thirsty, because my throat and my mouth were so dry. I pulled away from Uncle Chaim and Aunt Rifke, and I moved past Rabbi Shulevitz, and I croaked out to the *dybbuk*, "Come on then. You can come out of the angel, it's safe, it's okay." I remember thinking that it was like trying to talk a cat down out of a tree, and I almost giggled.

I never saw him actually leave the blue angel. I don't think anyone did. He was simply standing right in front of me, tall enough that I had to look up to meet his eyes. Maybe he wasn't a thousand years old, but Aunt Rifke hadn't missed by much. It wasn't his clothes that told me – he wore a white turban that looked almost square, a dark red vest sort of thing and white trousers, under a gray robe that came all the way to the ground – it was the eyes. If blackness is the absence of light, then those were the blackest eyes I'll ever see, because there was no light in those eyes, and no smallest possibility of light ever. You couldn't call them sad: *sad* at least knows what joy is, and grieves at being exiled from *joy*. However old he really was, those eyes were a thousand years past sad.

"Sephardi," Rabbi Shulevitz murmured. "Of course he'd be Sephardi."

Aunt Rifke said, "You can see through him. Right through."

In fact he seemed to come and go: near-solid one moment, cobweb and smoke the next. His face was lean and dark, and must have been a proud face once. Now it was just weary, unspeakably weary – even a ten-year-old could see that. The lines down his cheeks and around the eyes and mouth made me think of desert pictures I'd seen, where the earth gets so dry that it pulls apart, cracks and pulls away from itself. He looked like that.

But he smiled at me. No, he smiled *into* me, and just as I've never seen eyes like his again, I've never seen a smile as beautiful. Maybe it couldn't reach his eyes, but it must have reached mine, because I can still see it. He said softly, "Thank you. You are a kind boy. I promise you, I will not take up much room."

I braced myself. The only invasive procedures I'd had any experience with then were my twice-monthly allergy shots and the time our doctor had to lance an infected finger that had swollen to twice its size. Would possession be anything like that? Would it make a difference if you were sort of inviting the possession, not being ambushed and taken over, like in *Invasion of the Body Snatchers*? I didn't mean to close my eyes, but I did.

Then I heard the voice of the blue angel.

"There is no need." It sounded like the voice I knew, but the *breath* in it was different – I don't know how else to put it. I could say it sounded stronger, or clearer, or maybe more musical; but it was the breath, the free breath. Or maybe that isn't right either, I can't tell you – I'm not even certain whether angels breathe, and I knew an angel once. There it is.

"Manassa, there is no need," she said again. I turned to look at her then, when she called the *dybbuk* by his name, and she was smiling herself, for the first time. It wasn't like his; it was a faraway smile at something I couldn't see, but it was real, and I heard Uncle Chaim catch his breath. To no one in particular, he said, "*Now* she smiles. Never once, I could never once get her to smile."

"Listen," the blue angel said. I didn't hear anything but my uncle grumbling, and Rabbi Shulevitz's continued Hebrew prayers. But the *dybbuk* – Manassa – lifted his head, and the endlessly black eyes widened, just a little.

The angel said again, "Listen," and this time I did hear something, and so did everyone else. It was music, definitely music, but too faint with distance for me to make anything out of it. But Aunt Rifke, who loved more kinds of music than you'd think, put her hand to her mouth and whispered, "*Oh.*"

"Manassa, listen," the angel said for the third time, and the two of them looked at each other as the music grew stronger and clearer. I can't describe it properly: it wasn't harps and psalteries – whatever a psaltery is, maybe you use it singing psalms – and it wasn't a choir of soaring heavenly voices, either. It was almost a little scary, the way you feel when you hear the wild geese passing over in the autumn night. It made me think of that poem of Tennyson's, with that line about "the horns of Elfland faintly blowing". We'd been studying it in school.

"It is your welcome, Manassa," the blue angel said. "The gates are open for you. They were always open."

But the *dybbuk* backed away, suddenly whimpering. "I cannot! I am afraid! They will see!"

The angel took his hand. "They see now, as they saw you then. Come with me, I will take you there."

The *dybbuk* looked around, just this side of panicking. He even tugged a bit at the blue angel's hand, but she would not let him go. Finally he sighed very deeply – Lord, you could feel the dust of the tombs in that sigh, and the wind between the stars – and nodded to her. He said, "I will go with you."

The blue angel turned to look at all of us, but mostly at Uncle Chaim. She said to him, "You are a better painter than I was a muse. And you taught me a great deal about other things than painting. I will tell Rembrandt."

Aunt Rifke said, a little hesitantly, "I was maybe rude. I'm sorry." The angel smiled at her.

Rabbi Shulevitz said, "Only when I saw you did I realize that I had never believed in angels."

"Continue not to," the angel replied. "We rather prefer it, to tell you the truth. We work better that way."

Then she and the *dybbuk* both looked at me, and I didn't feel even ten years old; more like four or so. I threw my arms around Aunt Rifke and buried my face in her skirt. She patted my head – at least I guess it was her, I didn't actually see her. I heard the blue angel say in Yiddish, "*Sei gesund*, Chaim's Duvidl. You were always courteous to me. Be well."

I looked up in time to meet the old, old eyes of the *dybbuk*. He said, "In a thousand years, no one has ever offered me freely what you did." He said something else, too, but it wasn't in either Hebrew or Yiddish, and I didn't understand.

The blue angel spread her splendid, shimmering wings one last time, filling the studio, as, for a moment, the mean winter sky outside seemed to flare with a sunset hope that could not have been. Then she and Manassa, the *dybbuk*, were gone, vanished instantly, which makes me think that the wings aren't really for flying. I don't know what other purpose they could serve, except they did seem somehow to enfold us all and hold us close. But maybe they're just really decorative. I'll never know now.

Uncle Chaim blew out his breath in one long, exasperated sigh. He said to Aunt Rifke, "I never did get her right. You know that."

I was trying to hear the music, but Aunt Rifke was busy hugging me, and kissing me all over my face, and telling me not ever, ever to do such a thing again, what was I thinking? But she smiled up at Uncle Chaim and answered him, "Well, she got you right, that's what matters." Uncle Chaim blinked at her. Aunt Rifke said, "She's probably telling Rembrandt about you right now. Maybe Vermeer, too."

"You think so?" Uncle Chaim looked doubtful at first, but then he shrugged and began to smile himself. "Could be."

I asked Rabbi Shulevitz, "He said something to me, the *dybbuk*, just at the end. I didn't understand."

The rabbi put his arm around me. "He was speaking in old Ladino, the language of the Sephardim. He said, 'I will not forget you.'" His smile was a little shaky, and I could feel him trembling himself, with everything over. "I think you have a friend in heaven, David. Extraordinary Duvidl."

The music was gone. We stood together in the studio, and although there were four of us, it felt as empty as the winter street beyond the window where the blue angel had posed so often. A taxi took the corner too fast, and almost hit a truck; a cloud bank was pearly with the moon's muffled light. A group of young women crossed the street, singing. I could feel everyone wanting to move away, but nobody did, and nobody spoke, until Uncle Chaim finally said, "Rabbi, you got time for a sitting tomorrow? Don't wear that suit."

Demon

Joyce Carol Oates

The spawn of evil were once just that: the offspring of demons. The twentieth century brought variations on the theme: alien-sired kiddies like those of the film The Village of the Damned *(1961) or the sociopathic child exemplified in* The Bad Seed *(1955). Pundits claimed such representations reflected the societal fear that post-war parents were losing control of both their children and their culture. Ira Levin's novel* Rosemary's Baby *(1967) and, more emphatically, the film (1968) based on it, brought back the old-fashioned Satan-impregnated heroine in updated gothic trappings.* The Omen *(1976, remade in 2003) and its sequels reintroduced modern audiences to a variation: the changeling child with Devil daddy. Joyce Carol Oates gives us a riveting, if ambiguous, tale that may or may not involve supernatural sperm.*

Demon-child. Kicked in the womb so his mother doubled over in pain. Nursing tugged and tore at her young breasts. Wailed through the night. Puked, shat. Refused to eat. *No he was loving, mad with love.* Of Mama. (Though fearful of Da.) Curling burrowing pushing his head into Mama's arms, against Mama's warm fleshy body. Starving for love, food. Starving for what he could not know yet to name: *God's grace, salvation.*

Sign of Satan: flamey-red ugly-pimply birthmark snake-shaped. On his underjaw, coiled below his ear. Almost you can't see it. A little boy he's teased by neighbor girls, hulking, big girls with titties and laughing-wet eyes. *Demon! demon! Look it, sign of the demon!*

Those years passing in a fever-dream. Or maybe never passed. Mama prayed over him, hugged and slapped. Shook his skinny shoulders so his head flew. The minister prayed over him. *Deliver us from evil* and he was good, he *was* delivered from evil. Except at school his eyes misting over, couldn't see the blackboard. Sullen and nasty-mouthed the teacher called him. Not like the other children.

If not like *the other children*, then like *who? what?*

Those years. As in a stalled city bus, exhaust pouring out the rear. The stink of it everywhere. Your hair, eyes. Clothes. Same view through the same flyspecked windows. Year after year the battered-tin diner, the vacant lot high with weeds and rubble and the path worn through it slantwise where children ran shouting above the river. Broken pavement littered like confetti from a parade long past.

Or maybe it was the edge of something vast, infinite. You could never come to the end of. Wavering and blinding in blasts of light. *Desert*, maybe. *Red Desert* where demons dance, swirl in the hot winds. Never seen a *desert* except pictures, a name on a map. And in his head.

Demon-child they whispered of him. But no, he was loving, mad with love. Too small, too short. Stunted legs. His head too big for his spindly shoulders. His strange waxy-pale moon-shaped face, almond eyes beautiful in shadowed sockets, small wet mouth perpetually sucking inward. As if to keep the bad words, words of filth and damnation, safely inside.

The sign of Satan coiled on his underjaw began to fade. Like his adolescent skin eruptions. Blood drawn gradually back into tissue, capillaries.

Not a demon-child but a pure good anxious loving child someone betrayed by squeezing him from her womb before he was ready.

Not a demon-child but for years he rode wild thunderous razor-hooved black stallions by night and by day. Furious galloping on sidewalks, in asphalt playgrounds. Through the school corridors trampling all in his way. Furious tearing hooves, froth-flecked nostrils, bared teeth. God's wrath, the black stallion rearing, whinnying. *I destroy all in my path. Beware!*

Not a demon-child but he'd torched the school, rows of stores, woodframe houses in the neighborhood. How many times the smelly bed where Mama and Da hid from him. And no one knew.

This January morning bright and windy and he's staring at the face floating in a mirror. Dirty mirror in a public lavatory, Trailways Bus Station. Where at last the demon has been released. For it is the NewYear. The shifting of the Earth's axis. For to be away from what is familiar, like walking on a sharp-slanted floor, allows *something other* in. Or the *something other* has been inside you all along and until now you do not know.

In his right eyeball a speck of dirt? dust? blood?

Scared, he knows right away. Knows even before he sees: sign of Satan. In the yellowish-white of his eyeball. Not the coiled little snake but the five-sided star: *pentagram.*

He knows, he's been warned. Five-sided star: *pentagram.*

It's there, in his eye. Tries to rub it out with his fist.

Backs away terrified and gagging and he's running out of the fluorescent-bright lavatory and through the bus station where eyes trail after him curious, bemused, pitying, annoyed. He's a familiar sight here though no one knows his name. Runs home, about three miles. His mother knows there's trouble, has he lied about taking his medicine? hiding the pill under his tongue? Yes but God knows you can't oversee every minute with one like him. Yes but your love wears thin like the lead backing of a cheap mirror corroding the glass. Yes but you have prayed, you have prayed and prayed and cursed the words echoing not upward to God but downward as in an empty well.

Twenty-six years old, shaved head glinting blue. Luminous shining eyes women in the street call beautiful. In the neighborhood he's known by his first name. Sweet guy but strange, excitable. A habit of twitching his shoulders like he's shrugging free of somebody's grip.

Fast as you run somebody runs faster!

In the house that's a semi-detached rowhouse on Mill Street he's not listening to his angry mother asking why is he home so early, has a job in a building supply yard so why isn't he there? Pushes past the old woman and into the bathroom, shuts the door and there in the mirror oh God it's there: the five-sided star, *pentagram*. Sign of Satan. Embedded deep in his right eyeball, just below the dilated iris.

No! No! God help!

Goes wild, rubs with both fists, pokes with fingers. He's weeping, shouting. Beats at himself, fists and nails. His sister now pounding on the door what is it? what's wrong? and Mama's voice loud and frightened. It's *happened*, he thinks. His first clear thought. *Happened*. Like a stone sinking so calm. Because hasn't he always known the prayers did no good, on your knees bowing your head inviting Jesus into your heart does no good. The sign of the demon would return, absorbed into his blood but must one day re-emerge.

Pushes past the women and in the kitchen paws through the drawer scattering cutlery that falls to the floor, bounces and clatters and there's the big carving knife in his hand, his hand shuts about it like fate. Pushes past the women now in reverse where they've followed him into the kitchen, knocks his one-hundred-eighty-pound older sister aside with his elbow as lightly as he lifts bags of gravel, armloads of bricks. Hasn't he prayed Our Father to be a machine many times. A machine does not feel, a machine does not think. A machine does not hurt. A machine does not starve for love. A machine does not starve for what it does not know to name: salvation.

Back then inside the bathroom, slamming the door against the screaming women, and locking it. Gibbering to himself, *Away Satan! Away Satan! God help!* With a hand strangely steely as if practiced wielding the point of the knife, boldly inserting and twisting into the accursed eyeball. And no pain – only a burning

cleansing roaring sensation as of a blast of fire. Out pops the
eyeball, and out the sign of Satan. But connected by tissue,
nerves. It's elastic so he's pulling, fingers now slippery-excited
with blood. He's sawing with the sharp blade of the steak knife.
Cuts the eyeball free, like Mama squeezing baby out of her
belly into this pig trough of sin and filth, and no turning back
till Jesus calls you home.

He drops the eyeball into the toilet, flushes the toilet fast.

Before Satan can intervene.

One of those antiquated toilets where water swirls about the
stained bowl, wheezes and yammers to itself, sighs, grumbles,
finally swallows like it's doing you a favor. And the sign of the
demon is gone.

One eye socket empty and fresh-bleeding he's on his knees
praying Thank you *God! thank you God!* weeping as angels in
radiant garments with faces of blinding brightness reach down
to embrace him not minding his red-slippery mask of a face.
Now he's one of them himself, now he will float into the sky
where, some wind-blustery January morning, you'll see him,
or a face like his, in a furious cloud.

Alabaster

Caitlín R. Kiernan

*Caitlín Kiernan created the character of Dancy Flammarion for
her second novel,* Threshold *(1998). She also wrote several
short stories about Dancy, of which this is one. Dark Horse
comics recently began a series of comics featuring the albino girl
who wanders the South killing monsters that only she can see.
Dancy believes herself to be guided by an angel. Ascertaining the
veracity of someone experiencing angelophany – angelic manifestation to a human through one or more of the five senses – is
difficult. In ancient Judeo-Christian belief, angelophanies were
often extraordinary visionary experiences involving brilliant light,
fire, lightning, thunder and even earthquakes. Sometimes angels
appeared as fellow humans and were not immediately recognized
as heavenly beings. Like Dancy's, these angelophanies were
usually personal and rarely witnessed by others.*

The albino girl, whose name is Dancy Flammarion, has walked
a long way since the fire in Bainbridge five nights ago. It rained
all morning long, and the blue-gray clouds are still hanging
sullen and low above the pines, obscuring the wide south
Georgia sky. But she's grateful for the clouds, for anything that
hides her from the blistering June sun. She's already thanked
both St George and St Anthony the Abbott for sending her the
clouds, because her grandmother taught her they were the

patron saints of people suffering from skin diseases. Her
grandmother taught her lots of things. The damp air smells
like pine straw and the fat white toadstools growing along the
side of the highway. Dancy knows not to eat those, not ever, no
matter how hungry she gets. Her grandmother taught her
about toadstools, too.

She stops, shifting the weight of her heavy old duffel bag
from one shoulder to the other, the duffel bag and the black
umbrella tied to it with hemp twine, and looks back the way
she's just come. Sometimes it's hard to tell if the voices she
hears are only inside her head or if they're coming from somewhere else. The highway glistens dark and wet and rough, like
a cottonmouth moccasin that's just crawled out of the water.
But there's no one and nothing back there that she can see, no
one who might have spoken her name, so Dancy turns around
and starts walking again.

It's what you don't *see that's almost always the worst,* her grandmother told her once. *It's what you don't see will drag you down
one day, if you ain't careful.*

Dancy glances over her shoulder, and the angel is standing
in the center of the highway, straddling the broken yellow
dividing line. Its tattered muslin and silk robes are even blacker
than the wet asphalt, and they flutter and flap in a fierce and
holy wind that touches nothing else. The angel's four ebony
wings are spread wide, and it holds a burning sword high
above its four shimmering kaleidoscope faces, both skeletal
hands gripped tightly around the weapon's silver hilt.

"I was starting to think maybe I'd lost you," Dancy says and
turns to face the angel. She can hear the wind that swirls always
about it, like hearing a freight train when you're only half way
across a trestle and there's no way to get off the tracks before
it catches up with you, nowhere to go unless you want to fall,
and that sound drowns out or silences the noises coming from
the woods at the edge of the road.

And there's another sound, too, a rumble like thunder, but
she knows that it isn't thunder.

"If I went any slower," she replies, "I'd just about be standing still."

The thunder sound again, and the roar of the angel's scalding wind, and Dancy squints into the blinding light that's begun to leak from its eight sapphire eyes.

"No, angel," she says quietly. "I ain't forgot about you. I ain't forgotten about any of it."

The angel shrieks and swings its burning sword in a long, slow arc, leaving behind bits of fire and ember, ash and cinders, and now the air smells more like burning pitch and charred flesh than it smells like pine trees and summer rain and poisonous toadstools.

"Oh, I think you can probably keep up," she says, and turns her back on the Seraph.

And then there's only the dead, violated emptiness and the terrible silence that the angel always leaves behind when it goes. Very slowly, by hesitant degrees, all the murmuring forest noises return, and Dancy walks just a little faster than before; she's relieved when the high pines finally fall away on either side of the road and the land opens up, changing once more to farms and wild prairie. Pastures and cows, barbed-wire fences and a small service station maybe a hundred yards or so further down the highway, and Dancy wishes she had the money for a Coke. A Coke would be good, syrupy sweet and ice cold and bubbling on her tongue. But at least they won't charge her to use the toilet, and she can wash up a little and piss without having to worry about squatting in poison oak.

She doesn't look back at the woods again, the trees standing straight and tall on either side of the highway. That part of her life is over, lived and past and done with, one small stretch of road she only needed to walk once, and, besides, she knows the angel won't come to her again for days.

After the rain and the Seraph's whirlwind, the afternoon is still and cool, and her boots seem very loud on the wet pavement. It only takes her a few more minutes to reach the service station, where an old man is sitting on a plastic milk crate beneath a corrugated tin awning. He waves to her, and Dancy waves back at him, then she tugs at the green canvas strap on her duffel bag because her shoulder's gone to sleep again.

There's a big plywood billboard beside the road, but it's not nearly so tall as the faded Texaco sign – that round placard dangling from a lamppost, a perfect black circle to contain its five-pointed red pentacle, that witch's symbol to keep out some great evil. Dancy already knows all about pentagrams, so she turns her attention to the billboard instead; it reads live panther-deadly maneater in sloppy whitewash lettering.

She leaves the highway, skirting the edges of a wide orange-brown mud hole where the Texaco's parking lot and driveway begins, crunching across the white-gray limestone gravel strewn around the gasoline pumps. The old man is standing up now, digging about in a pocket of his overalls.

"How ya doin' there, sport?" he asks her, and his hand reappears with half a roll of wintergreen Certs.

"I'm fine," she says, not smiling because her shoulder hurts too much. "You got a bathroom I can use?"

"You gonna buy somethin'?" he asks and pops one of the Certs into his mouth. His teeth are stained yellow-brown, like turtle bones that have been lying for years at the bottom of a cypress spring.

"I don't have any money," she tells him.

"Hell," he says and sits back down on the plastic milk crate. "Well, I don't guess that makes no difference. The privy's right inside. But you better damn flush when you're done, you hear me? And don't you get piss on the seat."

Dancy nods her head, then stares at him until the old man leans back and blinks at her.

"You want somethin' else?"

"Do you really have a live panther?" she asks him, and the man arches both his eyebrows and grins, showing off his yellow-brown, tobacco-stained smile again.

"That's what the sign says, ain't it? Or cain't you read?"

"I can read," Dancy Flammarion replies and looks down at the toes of her boots. "I wouldn't have known to ask if I couldn't read."

"Then why'd you ask such a fool question for? You think I'm gonna put up a big ol' sign sayin' I got a live panther if I ain't?"

"Does it cost money to see it?"

"You better believe it does. I'll let you use the jake free of charge, 'cause it wouldn't be Christian to do otherwise, but a gander at that cat's gonna set you back three bucks, cold, hard cash."

"I don't have three dollars."

"Then I guess you ain't gonna be seein' my panther," the old man says, and he grins and offers her a Certs. She takes the candy from him and sets her duffel bag down on the gravel between them.

"How'd you get him?"

The old man rubs at the coarse salt-and-pepper stubble on his chin and slips what's left of the roll of Certs into the bib pocket of his overalls.

"You some kind of runaway or somethin'? You got people out lookin' for you, sport? You a druggie?"

"Is he in a cage?" she asks, matching his questions with a question of her own.

"He's a she," the old man grunts. "'Course she's in a cage. What you *think* someone's gonna do with a panther? Keep it in a damned burlap sack?"

"No," she says. "How'd you say you caught him?"

"I didn't."

"Did someone else catch him for you?"

"It *ain't* no him. It's a *she*."

Dancy looks up at the old man and rolls the quickly shrinking piece of candy from one side of her mouth to the other and back again.

"You're some kinda albino, ain't you," the old man says, and he leans a little closer. He smells like sweat and Beech-Nut chewing tobacco, old cars and fried food.

"Yeah," she says and nods her head.

"Yep. I thought so. I used to have some rabbits had eyes like yours."

"Did you keep them in cages too?"

"You keep rabbits in hutches, sport."

"What's the difference?"

The old man glares at her a moment and then sighs and jabs his thumb at the screen door. "The shitter's inside," he grumbles. "Right past the Pepsi cooler. And don't you forget to flush."

"Where do you keep him?" Dancy asks, looking past the old man at the closed screen door and the shadows waiting on the other side.

"That ain't exactly none of your business, not unless you got the three bucks, and you done told me you don't."

"I've seen some things," she says. "I've seen black bears, out in the swamps. I've seen gators, too, and once I saw a big ol' bobcat, but I've never seen a panther before. Is it the same thing as a cougar?"

"You gonna stand there talkin' all damn day long? I thought you needed to take a leak?"

Dancy shrugs her narrow shoulders and then looks away from the screen door, staring north and east down the long road to the place it finally vanishes, the point where the cloudy sky and the pastures collide.

"If any police show up askin' if I seen you, don't expect me to lie about it," the old man says. "You sure look like a runaway to me. No tellin' what kind of trouble you might be in."

"Thank you for the candy," she says and points at her duffel bag. "Is it okay if I leave that out here while I use your toilet? It's heavy."

"Don't make no difference to me," the man says. "But don't you forget to flush, you understand me?"

"Sure thing," Dancy says. "I understand," and she steps past him, climbs the four squeaky wooden steps up to the screen door and lets it bang shut. Inside, the musty air stinks of motor oil and dust, dirty rags and cigarette smoke, and the only light comes from the door and the flyspecked windows. The walls and floor are bare pine boards gone dark as rotten teeth, and a huge taxidermied bass hangs above the cash register. There are three short rows of canned goods, candy bars in brightly colored paper wrappers, oil and windshield wipers and transmission fluid, snack foods and mousetraps, bottles of Bayer aspirin and cherry-flavored Maalox. There's a wall of hardware and fishing tackle. She finds the tiny restroom right where he said she would, and Dancy latches the door behind her.

The restroom is illuminated by a single, naked incandescent bulb hanging from the ceiling. Dancy squints up at it, raises her left hand for an eclipse, and then glances at her reflection in the smudgy mirror above a sink stained by decades of iron water. She isn't sure how long it's been since she's seen herself like that; not since sometime before Bainbridge, so more than a week at least. Her white hair is still wet from the rain, wet and tangled like a drowned thing. A drowned rabbit that spent its whole short life trapped in a cage called a hutch, maybe, and she lowers her hand so the stark light spills down on her again.

The albino girl in the mirror lowers her hand, too, and stares back at Dancy with eyes that seem a lot older than Dancy's sixteen years. Eyes that might have been her grandmother's, if they were brown, or her mother's, if they were the easy green of magnolia leaves.

"You should wash your face," the albino girl in the mirror says. "You look like some sort of hobo."

"I didn't know it was so dirty," Dancy replies, embarrassed at her own raggedness, and almost adds, *I thought the rain would have washed it clean*, but then she thinks better of it.

There's a stingy violet-brown sliver of soap on the sink, but when she turns on the hot water, the knob marked "h", she remembers how badly she has to pee and turns the water off again. She loosens her belt, and the pearl-handled straight razor tucked into the waistband of her jeans almost falls out onto the floor. She catches it and slips it into her back pocket. The razor, like the duffel bag, was her grandfather's, and he carried both of them when he fought the Nazis in Italy and France. Dancy didn't take many things out of her grandmother's cabin in

Shrove Wood before she burned it, and the bodies inside, to the ground. But she took the straight razor, because the old man had shaved with it every morning, and it helped her remember him.

After she pees, Dancy wipes off the seat with a big wad of toilet paper, even though there's not a drop of urine on it anywhere. She drops the wad into the porcelain bowl, flushes, and the water swirls round and round like the hot wind that always swirls about her angel.

"You look like hell," the albino girl in the mirror says and frowns.

"I'm just tired, that's all. I didn't sleep very well last night," which is the truth. She slept a few hours in the back seat of an abandoned car that someone had stolen, stripped, and left in the woods, and her dreams were filled with images of the things she'd seen and done in Bainbridge and Shrove Wood, the angel and the things that want her dead and damned, the past and the present and the slippery, hungry future.

Dancy turns the hot water on again and uses the yellowish sliver of soap to wash her hands, her arms, her grimy face and neck. The soap smells like soap, but it also smells very faintly of black-eyed Susans and clover and sunshine, and she doesn't remember ever having smelled that sort of soap before. When she's done, she dries with brown paper towels from a chrome dispenser mounted on the wall. All that hot water's steamed up the mirror, and she uses another paper towel to wipe it clear again.

The albino girl is still there, watching Dancy from the other side.

"That's better," the girl in the mirror says. "Don't you think so?"

"It feels better," Dancy says, "if that's what you mean. And I like the way that soap smells."

"You know, I think you're running out of time," the girl in the mirror tells her, smoothing her hair with her wet hands, just like Dancy's doing. "I don't even think you're going to have to worry about Waycross, or Sinethella and her hound, or the nine crazy ladies in their big house in Savannah, not the way things are going."

"I don't even know what you're talking about. Who's Sinethella?"

The mirror girl looks skeptical and furrows her brow. "It hasn't even told you about—"

"He tells me what I need to know, when I need to know it. He tells me—"

"Just enough to keep you moving, and not one word more, because it knows the big picture would shut you down, send you running off back to the swamp with your tail tucked between your legs."

"I don't have a tail," Dancy says, wishing the albino girl in the mirror, the girl who isn't her reflection after all, would shut up and go away.

"You might as well, as far as the Seraphim are concerned. To them, you're nothing but a trained monkey, an ugly little freak of evolution they can swindle into wiping their Heavenly asses for them."

"Is this another test?" Dancy asks the mirror, and she imagines balling up her fist and punching the glass as hard as she can, imagines the blood and pain, the glittering shards and the silvery sound they would make falling into the rust-stained sink.

"Christ, you can be a tiresome little cunt," the girl in the mirror sighs, and now her face is changing, years rolling through her rose-colored eyes like waves against a sandy shore, waves to diminish her grain by grain and draw deep lines in her pale skin. And, in only a moment more, the girl in the mirror is a grown woman – thirty, thirty-five, forty – looking backwards at the lost child she was, or Dancy's only looking ahead to the lost woman she'll become, if she lives that long. Or maybe it works both ways, Dancy thinks, and she reaches out, expecting their fingers to brush, but there's only the cold, impenetrable surface of the looking glass and her own sixteen-year-old face gazing back at her again.

"Just a trick," Dancy whispers, even though she doesn't really believe it. "The angel said there would be lots of tricks."

The girl in the mirror says nothing more or less than Dancy says, and does nothing that she doesn't do, and Dancy Flammarion turns her back on the sink, and whatever it might, or might not, mean. She makes sure her jeans are zipped, and tightens her belt again, and unlocks the restroom door.

Dancy's holding a red and white can of Campbell's chicken and stars soup, the label enough to make her mouth water, and she thinks briefly about trying to steal it before she sets it back on the shelf. She glances towards the screen door leading out to the cloudy day and the old man and the front of the Texaco station. There's a shiny black pickup truck idling by the pumps, and the old man is talking to the driver. No one who's looking for her, just someone who's stopped to buy gas or a pack of cigarettes, someone the old man knows, or maybe he talks like that to everyone who stops. Maybe he offers everyone a wintergreen Certs and tells them to be sure and flush.

"He's a son of a bitch," she hears the old man say. "When the Good Lord was handin' out assholes, that cocksucker went back for seconds."

The driver of the black truck laughs, laughs the way that fat men and very small demons laugh, and Dancy looks at the can of soup again.

"Son of a whore wanted his money back," the old man says. "I told him sure thing, just as soon as ol' Gabriel starts playin' taps."

The man from the black truck laughs again, and Dancy's empty stomach rumbles.

And then she looks the other way, towards the rear of the store. There's another screen door back there that she didn't notice before she went into the restroom, a door with a wooden plaque hung above it, but she has to get closer to read all the words painted on it. "Hyenas will howl in their fortified towers And jackals in their luxurious palaces," the plaque declares in fancy calligraphic letters like the ones on the cover of her grandmother's old Bible. *Her fateful time also will soon come And her days will not be prolonged.* Isaiah 13.19–22.

"I'm doing my part," she whispers, reaching for the brass door handle, smelling the musky wild animal smell getting in through the screen wire. "Now you better keep him busy long enough for me to finish this, you hear?"

The angel doesn't answer her, but then it rarely ever does, so she doesn't take the silence one way or another.

The door creaks very loudly, like the hinges have never once seen so much as a single drop of oil, the hinges and the long spring that's there to snap the door closed again. Dancy steps over the threshold, eases the noisy door shut behind her, and now she's standing on a small back porch cluttered with an assortment of crates and cardboard boxes and greasy, rusting pieces of machinery that she doesn't recognize.

And before she even sees the cage, before she sees what's waiting *in* the cage, Dancy Flammarion is out on the highway again, the air filled with that thunder that isn't thunder, and the Seraph shrieks and slices the storm-damp air with its sword of fire and molten steel.

The scorching light pouring from the angel's purple-blue eyes almost blinds her, and she turns her head away.

In His right hand he held seven stars, and out of His mouth came a sharp double-edged sword. His face was like the sun shining in all its brilliance —

On the porch behind the Texaco station, Dancy reaches for her knife, the big carving knife she used in Bainbridge, something else salvaged from the cabin in Shrove Wood. But her knife is still tucked safely inside the duffel bag, and her bag's out front with the old man.

And then she sees the cage, big enough to hold at least five panthers, a great confining box of thick steel bars and seam welds and black iron bolts. But the only thing inside is a naked woman huddled in the dirt and filthy hay covering the floor of the cage. Her long auburn hair hangs about her narrow face in knots and matted coils, and her skin is so streaked with shit and mud and grime that Dancy can't be sure if she's black or white or some other color altogether. The woman looks up, her eyes so deep and dark and filled with pain, and when she speaks Dancy thinks that it's surely the most broken and desperate voice she's ever heard from simple human lips.

"Help me," the woman pleads. "You *have* to help me. He's insane."

Dancy slowly descends the four steps to the weathered square of concrete laid between the porch and the cage and stands only five or six feet back from the bars. "That old man locked you up in there?" she asks, and there are tears streaming from the woman's brown eyes, eyes the same rich brown as chocolate. She nods her head and reaches through the bars for Dancy.

I don't have my knife, she thinks, half praying to anything that's listening, and Dancy imagines the angel's fiery sword sweeping down to divide her careless soul from her flesh, to burn her so completely that there'll be nothing left to send to Hell.

"He's crazy," the woman says. "He's going to *kill* me. Whoever you are, you *have* to help me."

"He said there was a live panther back here," Dancy tells her and looks over her shoulder at the back door of the little store, wondering if the old man is still busy talking to the guy in the pickup truck about the cocksucker who went back for seconds.

"I just told you. He's insane. He'll say anything. *Please.*"

"He put you in that cage? Why'd he do that? Why didn't he just kill you?"

"You're not *listening* to me!" the woman hisses and bares her teeth; her voice has changed, has grown as angry and impatient as it was desperate and broken only a few seconds before. "We don't have much *time*. He'll figure out you're back here and come after you."

Dancy looks at the heavy Yale padlock holding the cage door shut, and then she looks back at the woman. "I don't have the key," she says. "How am I supposed to open that, if I don't have the key?"

The woman's dark eyes glimmer and flash, and Dancy real-izes that they're not the same color they were before, the deep and chocolate brown replaced suddenly by amber shot through with gleaming splinters of red. She retreats one step, then another, putting that much more distance between herself and the naked woman in the cage.

"I *know* who you are, Dancy Flammarion. I know what you did in Bainbridge. I know about the angel." And the woman's voice has changed again, too. This is the voice of an animal that has learned to talk, or a human being who's forgetting. "I know you've been sent here to save me."

"Who told you that?" Dancy asks, and she kicks at a loose bit of concrete, pretending that she isn't afraid. "I was just looking for the panther, that's all."

"We don't have *time* for this shit," the woman growls and seizes the iron bars in both hands, and now Dancy can see the long black claws where her fingernails used to be. The naked woman, who isn't really a woman at all, slams herself against the bars so hard that the whole cage shakes and the padlock rattles loudly.

"Now open this fucking cage!"

"Don't you talk to me like that," Dancy says; her face feels hot and flushed, and her heart's beating so fast she thinks maybe it means to explode. "I don't care what you are, I don't like to be talked to that way."

The thing in the cage presses its face to the bars, and its thick lips curl back to show Dancy eyeteeth that have grown long and sharp, the teeth of something that hunts for its supper, something that might even send a panther packing. Its amber eyes blaze and spark, and Dancy tries not to imagine the soul burning beneath its skin, inside that skull, a soul so hot it will wither her own if she doesn't look away.

"What? You think you're some kind of holy fucking *saint*," it snarls and then makes a sound that isn't precisely laughter. "Is that it? You think you're something so goddamn pure that strong language is gonna make your ears bleed?"

"I think maybe it's a good thing, you being in that cage," Dancy replies, almost whispering now.

And the thing locked in the iron cage roars, half the cheated, bottomless fury in the whole world bound up in that roar, and then it slams itself against the bars again. Its bones have begun to twist and pop, rearranging themselves inside its shifting skin. Its hands have become a big cat's paws, sickle talons sheathed in velvet, and its spine buckles and stretches and grows a long tail that ends in a tuft of black fur.

And Dancy turns to run, because she doesn't have her knife, because somehow she wasn't ready for this, no matter what she saw in Bainbridge or Shrove Wood, no matter if maybe those things were more terrible; maybe the angel was wrong about this one. She turns to run, running for the first time, and she'll worry about the angel later, but the old man is right there to stop her. He holds her firmly by the shoulders and grins down at her with his tobacco-stained teeth.

"Where you goin', sport? I thought you *wanted* to see my panther?"

"Let go of me. I told you I ain't got three dollars."

"Hey, that's right. You did say that. So that makes this sort of like stealin', don't it? That means you *owe* me somethin'," and he spins her roughly around so she's facing the cage again. The thing inside has changed so much that there's hardly any trace of the cowering, filthy woman left; it paces restlessly, expectantly, from one side of the cage to the other, its burning, ravenous eyes never leaving Dancy for very long. And she can still hear its animal voice inside her head.

You were supposed to save me, it lies. *You were supposed to set me free.*

"Big ol' cat like that one there," the old man says and spits a stream of Beech-Nut onto the concrete, "she'll just about eat a fella out of house and home. And seein' as how you owe me that three bucks—"

"Do you even know what you've got in that cage, old man? You got any idea?"

"Near enough to know she ain't none too picky in her eatin' habits."

"You don't hold a thing like that with steel and locks," Dancy says, matching the monster's gaze because she knows this has gone so far that it'll be worse for her if she looks away.

"Oh, don't you fret about locks. I might not be old Mr Merlin at the goddamn Round Table, but I can cast a binding good enough. Now, tell me somethin', Dancy," the old man says and shoves her nearer the cage. "How far d'you think you'd get after that mess you made down in Bainbridge? You think they were gonna just let you stroll away, pretty as you please?"

And she reaches for her grandfather's straight razor, tucked into the back pocket of her jeans, not her knife but it's plenty enough to deal with this old wizard.

"You think there's not gonna be a price to pay?" he asks, watching the thing in the cage, and he doesn't even notice until it's too late and she's folded the razor open. The blade catches the dull, cloud-filtered sun and shines it back at her.

"Whole lot of good folks out there want you dead, sport. Lots of folks, they want you fuckin' *crucified*. It's only a matter of time before some ol' boy puts you down for what you done."

But then she slips free of his big, callused hands, and before the old man can say another word, she's slashed him twice across the face, laying open his wrinkled forehead all the way to the bone and slicing a three-inch gash beneath his chin that just misses his carotid artery. The old man yelps in pain and surprise and grabs for her, but Dancy steps quickly to one side and shoves him stumbling towards the cage. He trips and goes down hard on his knees; the wet crunch of shattered bone is loud, and the thing that isn't a woman or a panther stops pacing and lunges towards the bars and the old man.

"Yeah, that may be so," Dancy says, breathless, blood spattered across her face and T-shirt and dripping from the razor to the cracked gray concrete. "But *you* won't be the one to do it."

And then the thing is on him, dragging the old man up against side of the cage, its sickle claws to part his clothes and flesh like a warm fork passing through butter, but he only screams until it wriggles its short muzzle between the bars and bites through the top of his skull. The old man's body shudders once and is still. And then the thing looks up at her, more blood spilling from its jaws, flecks of brain and gore caught in its long whiskers.

"Well?" it growls at her. "You gonna do what they sent you here to do, or you just gonna stand there all damn day with your mouth hanging open?"

Dancy nods her head once, wanting to tell it that there's no way she could have ever opened the cage door, even if she had the key, even if the angel hadn't told her to kill them both.

"Then you best stop gawking and get to work."

And Dancy wipes the bloody razor on her jeans, then folds it shut, and she runs back up the steps to the cluttered porch and the noisy screen door and the shadows waiting for her inside the little store.

It doesn't take her very long to find what she's looking for among the dusty shelves and pegboard wall displays – a cardboard box of Diamond kitchen matches and a one-gallon gasoline can. She takes out a handful of the wooden matches and puts them in her pocket, tears away the strip of sandpaper on the side of the box, and puts that in her pocket as well. Then Dancy gets a paper bag from behind the cash register and also takes some of the Campbell's chicken and stars soup and a handful of Zero bars, some Slim Jims and a cold bottle of Coca-Cola. While she's bagging the food, she hears thunder, and at first she thinks that it's the angel, the angel come back around to check up on her, to be sure she's doing it right. But then there's lightning and the *tat-tat-tat* of rain starting to fall on the tin roof, so she knows it's only another thunderstorm. She rolls the top of the paper bag down tight and tells herself it's not stealing, not really, that she's not taking much and nothing that she doesn't need, so whatever it is, it isn't stealing.

Over the staccato patter of the rain against the roof, she can hear the noises the cat thing in its cage is making as it tears the old man apart. She thinks about looking for a key to the cage, no matter what the angel has said. The old man might have it hidden in the register, or somewhere in the clutter behind the counter, or in an old snuff tin somewhere. She might get lucky and find it, if it's even there to be found, if she spends the rest of the afternoon searching the Texaco station. Or she might not. And anyway, there would still be the binding spell, and she wouldn't know where to begin with that.

"It's just another monster," Dancy says, as though saying the words aloud might make it easier for her to believe them. And she remembers her mother reading to her from the Bible about King Darius and Daniel and the angel God sent down to shut the mouths of the lions in the pit. Would it even be grateful, the thing in the cage, or would it try to kill her for setting it free? And would her angel shut its mouth, or would it let the thing eat her the way it's eating the old man? Would that be her punishment for disobeying the angel's instructions?

Then there's another thunderclap, louder than the first, loud enough to rattle the windows, and this time the lightning follows almost right on top of it, no seconds in between to be counted, no distance to calculate, and Dancy takes her brown paper bag and the matches and the gas can and goes out to the pumps. The screen door slams shut behind her, and she finds her duffel bag right where she left it with the old man, beneath the corrugated tin awning. The rain's not coming down so hard as she thought, but she has a feeling it's just getting started. She opens the duffel and tucks the paper bag inside with her clothes and the carving knife, then Dancy shoulders the heavy duffel again and steps out from beneath the cover of the awning.

The rain feels good, the soothing tears of Heaven to wash her clean again, and she goes to the pump marked regular, switches it on, and fills the gasoline can to overflowing. Then she lays the nozzle down on the ground at her feet, and the fuel gushes eagerly out across the gravel and the mud and cement. Dancy takes a few steps back, then stands there in the rain and watches the wide puddle that quickly forms around the pumps. She wrinkles her nose at the fumes, and glances up at the low purple-black clouds sailing past overhead. The rain speckles her upturned face; it's cold, but not unpleasantly so.

"Is this really what you want from me?" she asks the clouds, whatever might be up there staring down at her. "Is this really what happens next?" There's no answer, because the angel doesn't ever repeat itself.

Dancy picks up the gas can, and there's a moment when she's afraid that it might be too heavy now, that the weight of the duffel bag and the full can together might be too much for her to manage. But then she shifts the duffel to one side, ignoring the pain as the thick canvas strap cuts into her right shoulder, and the can doesn't seem so heavy after all. She splashes a stream of gasoline that leads from the pumps, across the highway and then down the road for another hundred yards, before she stops and sets down the almost empty can.

This is what I do, she thinks, taking one of the matches and the rough strip of cardboard from her pocket. Just like our cabin, just like that old church in Bainbridge, this is what I do next.

She strikes the match and drops it onto the blacktop, and the gasoline catches fire immediately, a yellow-orange beast, undaunted by the summer rain, blooming to life to race hungrily back the way she's come. Dancy gets off the highway as quickly as she can and crouches low in a shallow, bramble- and trash-filled ditch at the side of the road. She squeezes her eyes shut and covers her ears, trying not to think about the thing in the iron cage, or the naked woman it pretended to be, or the old man who would have fed her to the monster, trying not to think of anything but the angel and all the promises it's made.

That there will someday be an end to this, the horrors and the blood, the doubt and pain, the cleansing fires and the killing.

That she is strong, and one day soon she will be in Paradise with her grandmother and grandfather and her mother, and even though they will know all the terrible things she's had to do for the angel, they'll still love her, anyway.

And then she feels the sudden rush of air pushed out before the blast, and Dancy makes herself as small as she can, curling fetal into the grass and prickling blackberries, and the ancient, unfeeling earth, indifferent to the affairs of men and monsters, gods and angels, trembles beneath her.

Sanji's Demon

Richard Parks

Richard Parks has written a series of stories about Lord Yamada, a minor aristocrat in Heian Japan (794–1185) who makes his living as a "nobleman's proxy": basically a private investigator who handles situations, mostly of a paranormal nature, that his social betters either can't handle or would be too embarrassed to try. Here, he encounters a type of Japanese demon, the oni. *Although there are different types of* oni, *some far more benign than others – sometimes they are even portrayed as lovable and cuddly – they are primarily thought of as described by Parks: hideous, savage, gigantic supernatural creatures with the ability to shape-shift and a tendency to devour humans. Masks and other portrayals usually depict them with two horns and huge mouths sporting multiple fangs or tusks.* Oni *are often found nowadays in anime, manga and film.*

Kenji the reprobate priest was in a strange mood, even by Kenji's standards. "I've traveled a great deal, Yamada-san, but I think Echizen may be one of the most charming places I've ever seen."

It was the middle of the afternoon. Kenji and I traveled on foot along the Hokuriku Road on our way to find a demon-queller near the village of Takefu. I happily conceded that

Echizen had its charm. It was early fall and the leaves were starting to turn; the breeze was pleasantly warm still but with a hint of chill. Even so, Echizen's leaves and mountains and wooded hillsides were not much different than those to the west or north and, like them, after sunset would be stirring with creatures both unpleasant and dangerous. I shrugged. "It's nice enough."

Kenji sighed. "Nice? Lady Shikibu herself lived here for a year. The poets Nakatomi no Yakamori and Ōtomo no Yakamochi were exiled here. They were two of the greatest poets of our grandfathers' time! I can see how this place could inspire them."

I scratched my chin. "Kenji, a great many courtiers get exiled at one time or another, and every single one of them is a poet, by necessity. It stands to reason that *some* of them would be good at it. As for inspiration, Nakatomi's love was still in Kyoto while he was trapped *here*, so of course he wrote brilliant poetry full of regret and longing. Honestly, what's gotten into you?"

Kenji just sighed. "I could ask the same of you, Yamada-san. You're in an exceptionally sour mood, and for you that is saying a great deal."

I started to answer harshly, but that impulse just proved to me that Kenji was right. At first I thought it was simply because I'd given up saké for the duration of my assignment, and that sacrifice always darkened my outlook, but there had to be more to the matter. My hand kept creeping to my sword hilt as if I wanted to strike someone, and I didn't particularly care who that someone might be. The idea of losing control, even for an instant, and what I might *do* in that instant, both terrified and infuriated me.

"You know me, Kenji-san. I'm not the easiest person to be near, but I'm neither impulsive nor arbitrary," I said finally. "There must be a reason. Why am I so angry?"

Kenji rubbed the graying stubble on top of what should have been a properly shaven head, except that, in his case, it almost never was. "How can I know, if you do not? Have I done something to offend you?"

"No more than usual," I said, because it was so. "Though I will say that you're a bit more insufferably cheerful than usual . . ." A new thought stopped me. "Kenji-san, you're carrying demon-wards and sutras with you, are you not?"

He patted his travel bundle, which he wore looped around his neck. "Of course. You were a little vague as to the nature of your client's need, so I brought everything I could think of."

"Say rather that my client was discreet. Do me a favor – put your bundle down."

Kenji frowned but did as I asked. He took one step away from his priestly supplies and his frown deepened. "Oh. I feel it now."

My hand went back to the hilt of my *tachi*, but not out of anger this time. "Demon aura?"

"I think so. With my wards and the holy writs so close, I was oblivious. You've been sensing it for a while, no doubt. Which perhaps explains your mood."

"Perhaps. How close?"

Kenji closed his eyes for a few moments, then scowled and went riffling through his bundle. "Very close."

My sword was clear of its scabbard before we both heard something crashing through the undergrowth uphill of the road, something very large and in a hurry. Kenji scrabbled to find a ward, but it was too late. The *oni* broke through the undergrowth beside the road and charged straight at us. It was just taller than a man, with pointed talons and long yellow teeth, but I barely had time to note its appearance before it was upon us and my blade was in motion.

I took one quick step to the side and brought my sword across and up as the thing, unable to check its momentum, hurtled past me. I got one clear look at its face before its head separated from its shoulders and went rolling off down the ravine on the other side of the road. It was a foolish thought, but for that moment, I wished I had stayed my hand. In an instant it was all over. The creature's body took two steps without its head and then slammed onto the road, skidding to a stop at the verge, its hot, dark blood pooling in the dust.

"Well done, sir."

A burly young man stood just above us on the hillside. He wore the plain brown clothing of a *yamabushi*, but unlike a mountain monk, he wore his black hair long and confined it with a red headband. He carried a short sword and leaned on a gnarled club bound with iron. He was breathing heavily as if after a run, but he was not completely winded. He bowed. "Forgive me for putting you in harm's way. The creature was faster than I judged. I am Sago no Daiki."

Kenji and I bowed in turn. "I was fairly certain of your identity before you spoke, Master Daiki. I am Yamada no Goji. This gentleman is the priest, Kenji. Kenji, Sago no Daiki is our client."

The young man smiled. "Ah! I was expecting you. I'm also happy to see that your reputation is well deserved, Lord Goji. Again, I must say 'well done'."

I pulled a *tegami* from my pouch and began to wipe the demon's blood from my sword. "My thanks, but I think the credit for this particular demon-slaying incident belongs more to you than to me, Daiki-san."

Kenji eyed the creature's body. "With all due respect to Master Daiki, why do you say so? This was a very powerful devil, and I don't think even my strongest ward could have blocked its attack completely, off-guard as I was. Yet you took it down with one blow!"

I put my sword away. "The creature wasn't attacking, Kenji-san. I doubt it even realized we were here until it was too late."

Kenji almost sputtered. "Not attacking? Then, pray, what *was* the beast doing?"

I nodded toward Master Daiki. "Fleeing in terror."

The letter I had received the previous week from Master Daiki had, frankly, astonished me. The Sago clan had been demon-quellers of great renown for 400 years, starting with the clan's founder, Sanji the Demon Slayer. The clan's fame had reached far beyond Echizen, their ancestral province. Yet here was the heir of that noble tradition, Sago no Daiki, asking me for help with, of all things, a demon. The promised reward had been only part of my inducement for agreeing to see him; the remainder was simple fascination. While I was confident enough in my skills, I had no idea what I could possibly do that Master Daiki could not, and I was curious to find out.

Daiki paused in the road only long enough to retrieve the devil's head, then escorted us to his clan's compound north of Takefu. He made no more than polite conversation on the way. I took my cue from him and reluctantly asked none of the questions I was impatient to ask.

While the Sago clan compound was certainly nothing like the grand mansions and gardens one could find in the Imperial Compound, it compared favorably with many other dwellings in the Capital. The gate and green tile-roofed wall were in good repair, and the main living and servants' quarters were spacious and connected by fine covered walkways in proper *shinden* style. Master Daiki was clearly studying me as I in turn studied my surroundings.

"What you see here is not a home, but the gratitude of generations of people who were protected by my family," he said, sounding almost embarrassed. "I am but the caretaker until the next heirs of the Sago clan are ready to take on my burden. Speaking of which . . ."

"Chi-chi-san!"

Daiki laid his club and his trophy aside just in time. The words jumbled together almost like the children themselves. Two little boys and a girl, none more than five years old, came scampering down the steps and into their father's – or so I surmised – arms. They were followed closely by a distressed young woman dressed as a servant.

She bowed low. "Forgive me, Master Daiki, but when they heard you were home, it was impossible to contain them."

Daiki looked stern, or perhaps as stern as one *could* look with an armful of laughing progeny. I felt a pang of envy just then, which was not an emotion I experienced often, but I did not bother denying it to myself. A proper home of my own, a wife and family . . . these were things I once thought that I, too, would one day possess. Knowing that such a thing could not be so, and knowing the reasons, did not quite remove the desire.

"You're not at fault, Aniko. No one can contain a son or daughter of the Sago clan if they do not *wish* to be contained. Still . . ." He set the children down again and lined them up in proper order. "It was wrong of you to run away from Aniko and wrong also to ignore our guests. Where are your manners?"

The children managed to restrain their giggles long enough to bow formally in my and Kenji's general direction. Now that they were standing somewhat still, it was easier to sort one from another. The two boys were the oldest, perhaps five and four, with the girl no more than three or so. If this had been the Capital, Daiki's wife and any children would either have resided in a separate household or remained in the care of the wife's family, but here in the provinces such arrangements were less common. Daiki kept his family close to him and obviously preferred it that way.

"Lady Takara is away on a pilgrimage, fortunately," he said. "So she does not yet know of our misfortune."

It was the first time Master Daiki had touched on the matter that had brought us here, however obliquely. He sent the children off under Aniko's care, after first instructing her to see that refreshment was prepared and our lodgings made ready. When we were alone again, he merely said, "Gentlemen, if you would follow me?"

Daiki led us through the front garden and around to the rear of the main house. There the compound continued for about a bowshot until the walls ended at the base of a stone outcrop, where sat what appeared to be a large shrine. Kenji was not the most proper of monks, to put it mildly, but to his credit he sensed the demon spoor before I did.

"The place fairly reeks, Yamada-san," he whispered.

Another few moments and I had it, too – an acrid, musty scent which I can only describe as equal parts animal, decay, sweat and fear. Though what I thought of as a scent was probably the product of a higher sense, rendered, perhaps, in terms

·nore easily amenable to human interpretation. The "scent" was as much sensation as smell, much like I had felt in a different way the demon's rage and fear earlier that day on the road.

"Yuichi should be here," Master Daiki said, looking around. He sounded puzzled.

"Who is Yuichi?" I asked.

"He's been in the service of the Sago clan since before I was born. He oversees our gardens and the grounds and especially the family shrine. He was away visiting relatives, but I was told he had returned."

"And he's usually found near the shrine?"

Daiki smiled. "As well one could say that the shore is found near the ocean. The man is scrupulously attentive to his duties."

Still, there was no sign of anyone near the shrine. The grounds were deserted except for two guards, bowmen wearing the Sago *mon*, who could be seen patrolling along the outer walls.

"The compound is under guard at all times?" I asked.

"Yes, Lord Yamada. One doesn't answer my clan's calling without making enemies, demonic and otherwise. Besides, there are always one or two bandit clans active in the area, despite Governor Ishikawa's and my own best efforts. It's wise to be cautious."

"Indeed."

We proceeded to the shrine building and went inside, and we immediately understood where the demon-aura was coming from. One look and I revised my perception of the building from "shrine" to "trophy hall". The building was long and relatively narrow, ending against the rock face at the north end of the compound. The walls were lined with the skulls of demons: some very old by the look of them, others gleaming white as if they had just returned from the rendering vat. There were greater and lesser demons, monsters, and a few creatures I could not identify and frankly had no wish to.

Master Daiki paused. "Yuichi?"

An old man with thinning white hair and stooped shoulders

was adjusting a skull that hung crooked on the wall. When he heard Daiki's voice, he immediately turned and bowed low.

"Greetings, Master Daiki," he said. "I am pleased to see that you have returned safely."

"And I am astonished, Yuichi-san, to see that you have entered the shrine. I know how you feel about this place."

The old man bowed lower. "With so little life left to me, I did not wish to spend what remained as a coward. Besides, my assistant is ill and there was work to do."

Daiki practically beamed. "Well said. These are my guests, Lord Yamada no Goji and the priest Kenji."

"I am honored."

I frowned. "Yuichi-san, am I to understand that you don't normally enter the shrine itself?"

"Demons frighten me," the old man said, and he bowed again. "Even dead ones. I have always been ashamed of this failing."

"More like common sense," Master Daiki said. "Come with us. Lord Yamada may have more questions for you."

We continued down the length of the building, Yuichi following a few paces behind, while Master Daiki spoke.

"You have heard something of my ancestor, Sago no Sanji?" he asked.

Kenji grunted. "There are few who deal with spirits and monsters who have not. The founder of your clan, he was a minor provincial official who slew a particularly troublesome monster and was awarded the title 'Demon Queller' by the Emperor Temmu himself. Since that time his descendants have carried on this proud tradition."

Daiki bowed slightly. "I have done my best, as did my father and those who came before him. But it all started with Sago no Sanji, who kept the preserved body of the demon he slew as a trophy. It was to house this precious heirloom that this shrine was constructed. As you see, our clan has added to the collection over the centuries."

"It is not a pleasant place," I said frankly, "but I imagine the very knowledge of its existence gives pause to all but the most vicious and determined monsters."

"That is my hope as well," Master Daiki said, "though the presence of the first demon, as I said, was the reason the shrine was established. Which brings us to the crux of my problem."

There was little light near the north end of the shrine, and the poor illumination didn't add to the cheeriness of the place. We were fairly close before we saw what was there. Or rather, what wasn't there.

A square hollow had been carved into the face of the rock, twice as tall as a man and about half that in width. In that alcove sat a sort of raised dais, and on that was what appeared to be a stool with a low back. It was empty.

Now I understood. Master Daiki's problem wasn't a demon, but rather the lack of one.

"The demon's corpse . . . ?" Kenji began, and Master Daiki finished.

". . . has been stolen."

Despite the day's events, sleep did not come easily nor did it last especially long. Dawn was barely evident before I used Kenji's snoring as my excuse to stop lying where I was and rise. From our guest quarters I could hear very faint voices as if the servants were already up and about preparing the morning meal and getting the household ready for the day. I visited the privy and then took the opportunity to walk around the compound.

There were guards about as before, though a different shift from the previous night. I could not fault their attention; it was quite evident that they took their duties seriously. Yet somehow a thief – or more likely several – had managed to slip into the compound unseen and make off with the corpse of a seven-foot tall demon. Granted, the desiccated trophy could not have weighed as much as the demon did in life, but it would have still been too large and clumsy for even a strong man to handle alone, never mind the problem of getting it over the wall or through one of the gates without being detected. And who would wish to steal a dead demon in the first place?

Again I went over everything I knew of the matter: Yuichi had been visiting family, so he had been away when the theft apparently occurred. His assistant was ill and under the priests' care at Mt Hino Shrine, so as best I could tell no one had been in the trophy building for a few days. It was quite possible the demon corpse was missing for some time before anyone noticed. I idly wondered if the Lady Takara had seen anything unusual, since the theft may have happened at about the time she was preparing to leave for her pilgrimage to Hino Temple. I made a mental note to speak to her as soon as she had returned from her pilgrimage and then went in search of breakfast.

After some rice and fish, I was feeling a little more restored. Master Daiki had just sent the children off with their nurse Aniko when one of the *bushi* on watch entered the room and presented Master Daiki with a letter. He had not read more than a moment or two when he went pale, then bolted upright. "Tell Tarou and Ichigo to meet me at the front gate, armed and ready to travel."

"My lord, they are asleep—"

"Then wake them! Now!"

The guard was gone in an instant. Master Daiki turned to us. "This letter is from the Chief Priest at Mt Hino Shrine. My lady's party was attacked by bandits before she reached the temple. Her escort was slain . . . every one."

"Buddha be merciful," Kenji said, rising only a heartbeat slower than I did. "Is there word of your lady?"

"She's alive, but her condition . . . I don't know."

"We will go with you, of course," I said. "The matter of the theft can wait."

"Thank you. I normally travel on foot, but we're in a hurry. I must go to the stables first."

Kenji and I paused only long enough to gather up my sword and Kenji's supplies before we joined Master Daiki at the main gate. The two *bushi* arrived only a few moments after us. They were looking a bit disheveled, but they were armed, one with a spear and the other a sword and bow, and both men were clearly ready to go. Servants brought out five horses from the clan stables and Master Daiki vaulted into the saddle of the lead mount.

"If you fall behind, find me there," was all he said, and he was gone. All the way to Mt Hino we saw little of the man save the rear of his horse.

The shrine to the gods of Mt Hino was one of the oldest in the province. The mountain itself was impressive, but we had no time to appreciate it properly. Attendants saw to our horses, and a young priest led the two guards and myself to where Lady Takara was being tended. Kenji stayed behind.

"Forgive me, Lord Yamada, but I'm not always welcome in such places. Perhaps I had best wait here."

As a Buddhist, Kenji might be seen as competition by the servants of the gods. While many shrine priests would not object to his presence, as many more just might. Since we had no leisure to test his reception at the shrine, I agreed.

A junior priest led us to one of the outbuildings of the shrine set aside for travelers. The two guards took up positions outside, and I went in to find Lady Takara propped up by cushions, attended by an old priest and a relieved-looking Daiki. Custom demanded that the lady be veiled, and so a translucent curtain had been arranged in front of her bedding, but it was a mere formality and barely obstructed our view. It was my first look at Master Daiki's wife. She had a sweet face and long, black hair, but her eyes were red and puffy. She had clearly been weeping uncontrollably for some time and every now and then would break out sobbing anew.

The old priest whispered something in Master Daiki's ear, and he frowned, nodded, and then turned to me. "May I ask you to wait outside for a moment, Lord Yamada? My lady wishes to speak to me in private."

"Of course."

I bowed and withdrew, and the old priest followed me out as well. "Lord Yamada? My name is Jurou. I'm the senior priest at Mt Hino Shrine."

I bowed. "I value the meeting, if not the circumstances. You were here when Lady Takara was found?"

He nodded. "One of our junior priests came to the scene after the bandits were gone. Her guards and attendants were all slain, I'm afraid, and Lady Takara was hysterical. She told the boy that Yamaguchi no Mikio's bandit clan had attacked them in great force, but she didn't say much else. She was close to collapse, as one might imagine. She is better today but still in a very delicate state, as you saw."

"Indeed. Do you think that your priest's sudden presence might have startled her assailants into fleeing? If so, she is extremely fortunate."

The old man looked uneasy. "It's possible, I suppose."

"But you don't think so?"

"My chief concern now is Lady Takara's well-being."

"I share that. Even so, you must admit that these circumstances are a bit strange. Men who would slaughter both a lady's guards and her female servants would not hesitate to kill their mistress as well."

"I don't know how to answer you, Lord Yamada. She told me that a bandit was coming for her, waving his sword, when Mikio himself called the man back. I admit that is strange and I don't pretend to understand it. I know only that the bandits took everything except for Lady Takara's life, for which we must be grateful, even as we grieve for those who did not survive."

"Forgive me. I also count Lady Takara fortunate; it is just my nature to try to understand why. Do you know where the bodies have been taken?"

"To Hino Temple, which is further east along the mountain road."

That made sense. A dead body was a serious ritual impurity for a shrine, but the Buddhist temples often specialized in funerals.

"I know that Master Daiki appreciates all that you have done."

"The gods are merciful," the old priest said, and then he bowed and withdrew. I went outside to the shrine's *torii* gate to find Kenji.

"Are you familiar with Hino Temple?" I asked.

"Only that it exists. I've never been there," Kenji said.

"Then this will be your first visit. If you gentlemen care to accompany me, we'll be going there now." So quiet was Master Daiki's approach that even I had not heard him. He had a strange look in his eye. I had questions, but one look at the man's face and I knew they had best wait.

We recovered our horses and mounted, save for the *bushi* named Ichigo, who was left behind to keep watch over Lady Takara. We set off down the road again, though at a more reasonable pace this time, which was fortunate, as I did not think Master Daiki's horse was fit for another gallop.

The other guard fell behind slightly to protect our flank. As we rode, I kept a close eye on Master Daiki. After a mile or so, the quiet fury I had read in him before gave way to a deep sadness. It was only then that I dared to speak again.

"Was your lady able to describe the persons who attacked her party?"

"Vividly. Their leader is someone known to me, and with my lady's description of him, there can be no doubt. I did not think him fool enough to commit such an outrage upon my family, but no matter. The shrine has sent messengers on my behalf to Governor Ishikawa, and we will deal with him in due course. For now I have more pressing business at Hino Temple."

"It was to Hino Temple that your lady intended to go on pilgrimage, wasn't it?"

"Yes." Master Daiki fairly spit out the word.

"There is more to this matter of the ambush. You know there is."

His expression went as cold as ice but did not last. He finally sighed. "Lord Yamada, I am ashamed to tell you."

"You have suffered grievous losses, but your lady has survived. Some men might not count that so heavily in the balance, but you are different. Tell me what your lady said to you, if you can. I would not ask if I did not think it important."

"I do not know what you suspect, Lord Yamada. It's certainly nothing that would have occurred to me . . ." His voice trailed off. "Lady Takara herself is the one who took Sanji's demon."

We could hear the chants from the funeral rites as we approached the building in the temple compound set aside for the purpose. Master Daiki and Kenji accompanied me. I was reluctant to let Master Daiki out of my sight since, unless I completely misread the man, he wanted nothing more than to burn the entire temple to the ground. Considering the story his lady wife had related it to him, I couldn't say that I blamed him.

According to her account, Lady Takara had received a visitor, a monk from Hino Temple on his way home from the Capital. He had warned her of the imminent return of the spirit of the demon slain long ago by Sago no Sanji, that the signs and portents pointed to the destruction of her family unless she headed the spirit off by bringing the demon's corpse to Hino Temple, where – for a suitable donation – the priests could properly ward it against the vengeful spirit's return.

Master Daiki had been away hunting the demon that brought him to Kenji and myself on the Hokuriku Road, so the next morning she had taken it upon herself to have the two guards on duty bundle the corpse and place it in an oxcart along with several bolts of fine cloth as an offering to the temple. No one knew save herself, her personal attendants and the two guards. All were dead now except the lady herself.

"Do you really think the temple was in league with the bandits?" Kenji asked.

"I do," Master Daiki said.

I had to admit that this wouldn't be the first time such a thing had occurred, but there was a flaw in the reasoning. "They must share the blame in any case, if they are the reason Lady Takara was on the road. Yet, even assuming the monk was from Hino-ji, why attack the procession? The offering was theirs to begin with."

Daiki looked grim. "Sanji's demon was what they really wanted. And this way no one could prove that they were involved . . . until I get my hands on that worthless Mikio. I'll wring it out of him!"

"Why would the temple want the corpse in the first place?" I asked.

"To shame my family and weaken our position. It's no secret that relations between the Sago Clan and Hino Temple have not always been the best. They see our activities as an incursion into matters best handled by the Temple. Meaning that the rewards and prestige should come to them, not us. If it were not for my family's honor, I would let them have the risk of it as well. See how well the abbot sings that song after a demon pulls his head off!"

Kenji might have been a disreputable Buddhist at best, but he was a loyal one. "Your pardon, my lord," he said dryly, "but some followers of the Eightfold Way do know a thing or two about demons."

I held up a hand. "That may be true, but it's not relevant to the matter at hand. And, Master Daiki, I'd consider it a personal favor if you'd let me speak to the abbot before you 'accidentally' drop a club on him."

"As you wish." The man practically growled the words.

We received word that the abbot was detained but would greet us shortly. I wanted to use that time to attend to an unpleasant but necessary duty. We entered the hall where the monks were chanting sutras. The bodies had been laid out on four biers in the center of the hall. They had already been washed as was the custom. Kenji spoke a word to the monks on duty, and they ceased their chants and withdrew, though not without a few scowls in my direction.

"Master Daiki, you knew these people. What follows may be a bit indelicate. You may not wish to see it."

"There is little I have not seen, Lord Yamada," he said, but the anguish on his face was plain. I resolved to do what I needed to do as quickly as possible.

One by one I went to each bier and pulled aside the white funeral robes covering the body, and one by one the story they told was the same. Both the men and women had been killed in the same fashion – several powerful sword blows. One poor girl, probably no more than fifteen, had been cut nearly in half. Brute force was evident but no art. Any competent swordsman would have done the job with one stroke each and no wasted effort. What had happened to Lady Takara's attendants was sheer butchery by comparison. I covered the last body.

"Curious," I said. "Even if taken by surprise, the two *bushi* should have given a better account of themselves. It's clear that whoever attacked them did not really understand swordsman-ship."

"Bandits are noted for viciousness, not for skill," Master Daiki pointed out. "It's possible the guards were simply over-whelmed."

"Judging from the number of sword-cuts and the lack of consistency in angle of attack, I'd say you were right."

"Something's bothering you, though," Kenji said.

"Many things are bothering me at the moment," I said. I did not mention that the least of them was the sheer *enthusiasm* of the attack. Bandits were often deemed vicious by the simple necessities of their chosen profession, and there was no deny-ing that some even took pleasure in that viciousness. Yet I couldn't get past the feeling that whoever had done this had enjoyed it to a degree beyond anything I had ever seen before or ever hoped to see again.

We had just emerged from the funeral hall when the abbot approached. He was an old man, frail, discreetly supported by two young monks on either side.

"Forgive my tardiness, Master Daiki. At my age one cannot move very quickly."

Daiki gave a perfunctory bow. "Abbot Hideo, this is Lord Yamada and his associate Kenji-san. They are acting on my behalf."

Hideo raised an eyebrow. "Indeed? We only just learned of your wife's unfortunate encounter."

Master Daiki's smile was all teeth. "Indeed?"

I thought it prudent to interrupt. "Sir, before Lady Takara undertook her pilgrimage, she was reported to have received a visitor from your temple. With your permission, we would like to speak to this person."

"I am afraid that is not possible," he said.

Daiki would not keep silent. "Abbot Hideo, I *will* discover the people who attacked my lady and killed several treasured members of our household. I will do it with or without your cooperation."

The old man looked grim. "I have no intention of interfering. I, too, would like this matter resolved. Members of my temple travel the Hokuriku Road often, as well as pilgrims to and from here. It is in both our interests to ensure their safety."

"Then why may we not speak to your priest?" I asked.

"You misunderstand me," the abbot said. "I didn't mean that I wouldn't allow it. I meant that it was impossible that Lady Takara received a visitor from this temple. Hino-ji was in a period of ritual seclusion that only ended yesterday. No one has been allowed to enter or leave this temple for the past two weeks."

Daiki was obviously skeptical, so the abbot grudgingly allowed us to fully search the temple and grounds. There were many offerings in their storehouse, as one would expect, but no sign of the cloth that Lady Takara had taken from the Sago Clan storeroom nor, of course, Sanji's demon. Daiki equally as grudgingly admitted that he didn't have enough proof to raze the temple. I wouldn't have called it a reconciliation, but at least matters between the Sago Clan and Hino Temple were no worse than they had been.

Master Daiki scowled. "I was so certain we'd find proof of Hino Temple's guilt in this. Yet I still find it hard to believe that the bandits acted alone. Why court their own destruction?"

"Court? Ask rather why they guaranteed their destruction by leaving a witness. I am pleased beyond measure that Lady Takara lived, yet also puzzled."

Master Daiki scowled. "Lord Yamada, surely you're not suggesting that Lady Takara is complicit in this? Other than removing the trophy from our shrine, I mean."

"Hardly. But as I said, I am puzzled."

Just then a young man arrived, a mounted messenger

bearing the *mon* of the provincial governor. The messenger presented Master Daiki with a letter and then rode with us to await any reply.

"Ah! A detachment of *bushi* from the governor's own forces will join us tomorrow. Fifty in number, and that's more than enough. Perhaps tomorrow all our questions will be answered."

"Perhaps," I said, though my thoughts were elsewhere. "Supposedly the person, whoever it was who spoke to Lady Takara, came by in the afternoon? Who would have been on guard then?"

He frowned. "That would have been . . . Tarou and Ichigo."

"The same Tarou riding with us now?"

"Yes. Why?"

"Probably nothing. But there is some small matter he might be able to assist me with. Excuse me."

I dropped back until I was riding beside Tarou. He was perhaps thirty years old and of a blunt but cheerful disposition. "My lord?"

"You and Ichigo were on duty the afternoon that Lady Takara received her visitor, yes?"

"So I am told," he said.

I frowned. "So you were told? Can you explain that, please? Any visitors would have to pass by the gate, yes? One of you would have seen him."

Tarou looked extremely uncomfortable. "If Lady Takara said she had a visitor, then of course she did."

I smiled a grim smile. "You're avoiding the question, Tarou-san, and I have to say you're not very good at that. No one is blaming you for what happened, but I do need to know about that visitor."

Tarou admitted defeat. "I am at a loss, Lord Yamada. I spoke to Aniko that very evening, and she told me that Lady Takara received a visitor, a young monk. I don't understand how that can be. No one came to the compound that day. I remember clearly – the gate was never opened."

"You're certain?"

He looked miserable. "I am. Which means that someone

must have slipped over the wall unseen. We failed our duties
and placed Lady Takara in danger. This is our fault."

"That may or may not be the case, but I would not repeat
that story to anyone else. Let it be our secret for now.'

I rode back to the front of the column. "Master Daiki, will
you have need of this messenger today?"

"Today? No. I won't report to His Excellency until after
we've cleaned out that bandit viper's nest."

"Then, with your indulgence, I will borrow him."

I was doubtful that Daiki would be able to find the bandit's
hideout in any reasonable time, but I had underestimated the
esteem in which the Sago Clan was held. He merely had to let
it be known that Yamaguchi no Mikio's bandits were the ones
who attacked Lady Takara, and information from the country-
side suddenly became available in abundance. There were a
few false leads, as one would expect, but the others all pointed
to an isolated farming compound west of Takefu. Now Kenji
and I watched with Daiki opposite the dilapidated south gate
as his men took up positions around that compound. Once
they were in place, Daiki would give the word to attack.

He never got the chance.

Almost immediately there were shouts and the sound of
steel meeting steel from the hillside on the north side of the
compound. Daiki swore and picked up his club.

"They've been warned!"

He set out across the meadow in a dead run with Kenji,
myself, and five or six of the governor's *bushi* not far behind. He
barely hesitated at the gate, taking his massive demon-queller's
club in both hands and smashing it into the gate as soon as he
reached it. Whatever strength the timbers had once contained
had clearly fled years ago. The gate shattered into splinters
hardly big enough for kindling, and Daiki was through.

I wasn't sure what we'd find in the compound, but the
answer proved to be hardly anything at all. Two women in
peasant clothes hugged each other in terror as they tried to
hide behind a well, but there was no sign of anyone else.

"Take everyone alive!" Daiki shouted to the warriors behind us. "I want prisoners, not bodies!"

The only sounds of fighting were from the hillside beyond the north gate. Two *bushi* remained behind to search for anyone else hiding and to guard the women, but the rest of us sped out the north gate. By the time we reached the fighting, it was over.

The captain of the hillside detachment bowed to Daiki. "I'm sorry, my lord, but they didn't give us much choice. They were determined to escape."

Daiki ignored that. "Where is he?"

I didn't have to ask whom he meant, but it seemed that Daiki, in this one regard, was not going to get his wish. The *bushi* produced two flea-bitten, scruffy men. Both were bruised and bloody but alive. Two more were not. One of them was Yamaguchi no Mikio. Daiki kicked the body so that it rolled face up and studied the dead man's features.

"*Che* . . . It would seem the bandit has escaped me after all."

Whatever Daiki had thought to do with Mikio, killing him would perhaps have been the least of it. But that was a moot point now. By the time the prisoners were bound and the rest of the soldiers recalled, the *bushi* left behind had completed their search of the compound.

"We found this in the storeroom and more besides," the man said, showing us several bolts of cloth. "Do you recognize any of them?"

Daiki barely glanced at them. "Lady Takara wove that cloth herself. I'd know it anywhere. What about Sanji's demon?"

The *bushi* was a hard-bitten man who looked as if he also had faced down a demon or two in his time, but he was almost pale now. "My lord, it's not here."

"It has to be here! I'll find it if we have to take every building apart plank by plank!"

In the end, that was exactly what Daiki and his men did. But when the dilapidated compound was reduced to piles of rotting wood, Sanji's demon was still nowhere to be found.

*　　*　　*

We didn't get much from the prisoners. Yes, they were thieves. No, they had not attacked Lady Takara. Yes, there were the spoils of thievery in their storeroom; no sense denying the obvious. No, they had no idea how the cloth from Lady Takara's temple offering had come into their hands. Daiki finally grew frustrated and ordered them all bound on a line. As we rode back to the Sago compound with the prisoners led on a rope and surrounded by guards, I pondered what little we had learned. It seemed to me that it might be far more than a first glance might reveal.

"Why lie about the temple offering and the demon and then tell the truth about all else?" I mused. "The penalty for banditry is death, as is the penalty for murder. They can't be beheaded twice."

"Because they knew that I would not be so merciful as the governor," Daiki growled. "I know they've hidden Sanji's trophy somewhere, and they will tell me where. I will find the truth."

"That is my intention as well. I just do not believe that the truth you're looking for is to be had from these wretches."

"Why not?" Daiki asked.

"Because, my lord, I think they've already told us the truth."

Now even Kenji was staring at me. "Yamada-san, what do you mean?"

"Simple: Yamaguchi no Mikio and his followers did not attack Lady Takara. They couldn't have."

"Lord Yamada, are you saying the Lady Takara, my wife, lied to me?"

Now Daiki was glaring, and I knew his anger was more than ready to erupt in any direction, including my own. I proceeded carefully.

"On the contrary – it is the truth of her words that speaks on behalf of Yamaguchi and his followers. She stated that Mikio himself prevented his man from killing her during the raid. Why would he do that? What bandit is foolish enough to slaughter so many and let a witness to that slaughter live? More, make a *special effort* to let that witness live? Does that make any sense to you?"

"No," he said reluctantly. "It does not. Unless . . ."

I finished. "Unless the entire point was to leave a witness. Whoever attacked your wife wanted it known that Yamaguchi no Mikio was to blame."

"Whoever?" Kenji asked.

"Which brings me back to my first point," I said. "You saw that 'bandit stronghold', Master Daiki, just as I did. Yamaguchi had four men, at most, and they were a sorry lot. Nor was there bedding or supplies at the compound to indicate any more. Lady Takara's party was attacked by at least a dozen, probably more. I saw the results of their work and would swear to that on my life. It is simply impossible that Yamaguchi is the culprit."

I could see the doubt creeping into Daiki's face, but he shook it away. "Nonsense! How else could they have obtained that cloth?"

"That question is more than fair, and at the moment I cannot answer it. But, with your indulgence, I may yet do so."

"Very well," Daiki said, "but I will warn you ahead of time that I am short on temper at the moment and not terribly fond of riddles in the best circumstances."

Kenji leaned over. "I think Master Daiki is just about ready to turn his club on you. I hope you know what you're doing."

I smiled. "So do I. But I will need your help as well. I require a talisman of truth. Surely there is something of the sort in that bag of yours."

Kenji frowned. "As in to compel the truth? I have something that will serve the purpose."

"Later. Before the truth can be compelled, first it must be revealed."

As I hoped, the governor's messenger was waiting for me when we reached the Sago Clan compound, and I took him aside to hear his report. Afterwards I nodded and turned to Daiki. "I need to speak to Yuichi again. Will you and Kenji accompany me?"

He frowned. "If you wish."

I turned to the messenger. "Your name?"

"Nobu, my lord."

"Nobu-san, follow us, please."

I had two weapons, a sword and a short dagger. I chose the dagger and kept its hilt close to hand. We went behind the compound and approached the Sago family shrine. "Yuichi-san? I need a word with you."

The old man poked his head around the door to shrine. "Ah! Master Daiki. I am so pleased to see you returned safely. What news?"

"The bandits have been caught, though their leader was slain. I'm afraid we did not recover our heirloom."

"A pity," he said as he emerged from the shrine, wiping the dust from his hands with a small cloth and awaiting our approach. "No doubt you will find it yet."

"No doubt," I said. I took one long step and trapped the old man's arms with my left arm while I pressed the dagger blade against his throat. His body was as taut as a bowstring in my grip.

Daiki raised his club. "Lord Yamada, what is the meaning of this outrage?"

"If I am wrong," I said through clenched teeth. "I will apologize with all sincerity. Nobu-san, will you tell Master Daiki what you just told me?"

Daiki scowled at the man. "Well?"

"L-Lord Yamada charged me to enquire of Ishiyama no Yuichi's family when they had last seen him."

"And their answer?"

"He has not returned home in over a month, my lord. They are becoming concerned."

Daiki's gaze narrowed. "Yuichi, what does this mean?"

The old man just glared, and continued to struggle. I nodded at the priest. "Now, Kenji-san."

Kenji produced a slip of mulberry paper with exquisite calligraphy flowing down its length. He raised a single hand in a blessing gesture and slapped the paper onto Yuichi's forehead. "Diamond Sutra. Let illusion be dispelled."

The old man's form *shimmered* in my grasp, like a mountain peak glimpsed through summer haze. Another instant and I did not hold an old man at all, but rather an *oni*. He was perhaps a head taller than myself, with red skin, gleaming tusks and horns, and black hair as coarse and thick as a horse's mane. He continued to struggle, and it was all I could do to hold him.

"When we think of shape-shifters, we think of foxes and *tanuki*, but demons have the knack as well, when they care to use it," I said.

Master Daiki's hands gripped his club so tightly that I could hear the wood creaking. "In my own home! Lord Yamada, how did you know?"

"I wasn't certain until Nobu returned, but it was the only answer that made any sense. We know that Lady Takara received a visitor, both she and Aniko confirmed that. Yet Tarou told me that no one entered your compound that day. If the visitor had come from Hino-ji as you believed, he would have come in the front gate. Since no one did, the only reasonable conclusion was that the visitor *was already here*."

Kenji frowned. "But how did you know it was Yuichi, rather than one of the guards? Tarou, for instance?"

I shifted my grip, slightly. The demon felt as heavy as stone.

"The same way I knew that our shape-shifter wasn't Lady Takara or Aniko. Demon-aura, Kenji. They can disguise their form, but their aura is one thing they cannot disguise."

Kenji smiled. "Ah! Any one of us would have noticed that, including Master Daiki. And Lady Takara—"

"—was being tended in Mt Hino Shrine. The priests there are neither fools nor incompetents. If Lady Takara had been a demon in disguise they would have spotted the deception immediately. Yuichi, on the other hand . . . Master Daiki, did you not find it strange that Yuichi-san's lifelong fear of demons should suddenly disappear to the point that he not only no longer avoided your family shrine but hardly ever seemed to leave it?"

"The demon scent," Daiki said grimly.

"Precisely. There, he was one among many, and so none of us noticed a thing. Clever, really." I glanced at my glaring prisoner. "I think it is time you told us where the heirloom you stole is hidden. Kenji-san?"

The priest stepped forward again, this time with a different talisman. "Lotus Sutra. Truth." He slapped the second talisman beside the first, though now he almost had to stand on tiptoe to reach the demon's forehead

"Why did you cozen Lady Takara?"

"So the silly woman would remove the trophy from the compound for us, of course. The wards on this place are such that I could not do it alone." The demon's voice was like rocks grating together in an avalanche.

"I knew you weren't working by yourself. Where is the real Yuichi?"

"In the privy. I must have shat the rest of him by now," said the demon, grinning.

Master Daiki growled and raised his club, but Kenji put a hand on his arm. "Not yet, my lord."

"Your confederates assumed the forms of Mikio's band for the attack, and one of you placed the cloth in Mikio's storeroom to assure their guilt. It was easily done, wasn't it?"

"Very easily done," said the demon. "Much like this."

He broke free. I would have sworn that I had him under control, but he produced a surge of strength I hadn't realized he possessed, and the force of it threw me back against the shrine wall, knocking the wind out of me. Everything went black for a moment and, when my vision cleared, there was much confusion and shouting. Kenji kneeled beside me.

"Lord Yamada, the demon has scaled the wall and escaped. Perhaps a binding talisman would have been more in order?"

I groaned and rubbed the back of my head. A knot was already rising. "You might have let me know that you had such a thing . . . Where is Master Daiki?"

"Right here." The man stood before me, leaning on his massive club.

I struggled to rise and made it on the second try. "My lord, there's no time to waste! If you are ever to recover your family's heirloom . . ."

He grinned. "Lord Yamada, I am grateful for your assistance in clearing up this matter, but you forget: if there's anything I *do* know, it's how to track a demon."

Once Daiki was on the trail, it was impossible to keep up with him. We had been forced to leave our horses behind on the thickly wooded hillsides the demon had fled through. I took command of the remaining *bushi*, and we followed Sago no Daiki as quickly as we could, kept on course by following the crashing sound he made as he hurtled through the undergrowth. I was beginning to understand what had so terrified that first demon that day on the Hokuriku Road.

I glanced up the hillside and knew we had found what we were searching for. No less than a small fortress had been carved into a flat niche on the hillside. It was made of stone and mossy logs, difficult to see unless one looked, as I had, directly at it. I paused long enough to let the straggling *bushi* catch up and then arranged them in a rough skirmish line. I had no sooner placed them in some semblance of order when I heard the crash of wood on wood from the hillside and realized it was Sago no Daiki breaking in the gate.

Kenji was still catching his breath. "Why . . . why didn't he wait for us? Does he mean to take on the whole demon band on his own?"

"That's exactly what he intends to do. Let's go!"

The defenders had been alerted by Daiki's noisy entrance. There were demon archers on the wall in a grotesque parody of *bushi* bowmen. Two of our number were struck and went down. I grimaced as another barbed shaft grazed my shoulder before our own archers cleared the top of the wall with their own volley. In a heartbeat we were through the gate, our swords drawn.

Dead and dying *oni* were lying in the courtyard. I spotted Daiki in the middle of a circle of demons. He had been struck

twice by arrows, once in the left thigh and again in the shoulder, but the wounds seemed little more than an inconvenience.
He howled like a wolf as he swung his great club here and
there, batting down any demons who tried to close the circle.
Before they could rush him properly, he charged and took out
two of the smaller demons with one blow as he crashed through
their line.

"To Master Daiki!" I shouted, and a dozen warriors rushed
to his side. The rest of our force scattered through the inner
courtyard, battling the demons in groups of two or three.

It was impossible to judge the demons' number accurately,
but I counted at least two dozen, not including the ones already
on the ground. They were all armed like men: some with bows,
others with spears and rusty, nicked swords. For demons, it
amounted to a level of organization and discipline that I hadn't
believed the creatures capable of achieving. I didn't have time
to consider my admiration before an *oni* charged me and I
killed it with a slash across the throat. Another struck at Kenji,
and we killed it together with sword and staff.

"Lord Yamada! Find that demon! We'll deal with this."

I heard Daiki's shout from across the battlefield and knew
which demon he meant. One or two of the outbuildings within
the fortress were already burning, which explained his urgency.
The largest building not yet engulfed in flames had the mark
of a storehouse. I ran toward it, Kenji following close. When I
got nearer, I knew I'd judged correctly. The door was massively
thick but slightly ajar, as if someone had just gone in or out.

"Keep watch here. If you need help, shout," I said.

"Depend on it," Kenji said cheerfully.

A lit lantern hung on a peg just inside the doorway. I took it
and held it up. At first I saw only what one might expect to see
in any storeroom: casks of rice and saké, even bolts of rough
fabric and racks of weapons. I knew beyond questioning that
we had met the chieftain of the demons, disguised as the
unfortunate Yuichi, and that this demon was much more intelligent than the usual sort. What I had seen within the demon's
fortress and now in this storeroom bore that out. Whatever he

intended, this demon obviously had plans for his followers other than mere survival. So involved was I in examining the more mundane contents that I almost missed the silhouette at the end of the building, the very distinctive silhouette of a demon.

I raised my sword, but it did not move. I took one slow step forward and then another. I noticed that I was not seeing the red glow of its eyes in the lamplight, as I would rightly expect. I took another step and I realized that its eye sockets were hollow.

This is it.

Sanji's demon sat on a rough seat of hewn timber, much like it would have sat in its place of honor in the Sago family shrine. Even with the demon seated I could tell that it had been about seven feet tall in life, with dull yellow tusks and black coarse hair, though much of that hair had fallen out of its dried scalp over the years. It had obviously been an object of veneration for some time. Rather than the crude loincloth or rough clothing that demons normally wore, this one had been dressed in fine robes, though clearly the robes were very old. The cloth was ripped in several places now, practically in tatters, apparently due to its rough handling during the theft.

Sanji's demon resembled others I had seen before, but there were some differences. Rather than tusks in both top and bottom jaws there were tusks in its upper jaw only, and they appeared more like a tiger's fangs than tusks. I took a closer look, and the lamplight reflected on something like a design on its skin, now visible in a tear in its old robes.

A tattoo?

I leaned closer. Not a tattoo. Stitches. Very skillfully done. I examined the corpse and found others. I examined the teeth again, closer this time. I hadn't gotten far when I heard Kenji's shout.

"Lord Yamada, if you would be so kind . . .?"

I dropped the lantern. I raised my sword and rushed to the doorway.

Two of the larger demons were approaching Kenji. "Take the left, Kenji-san," I said, and took up position on his right side.

The rightmost demon roared, but in pain, not rage. It dropped its sword and reached around as if trying to swat a bee. Then it fell to its knees, an arrow protruding from its back, before toppling face first into the dirt. While its companion was distracted, Kenji crushed its skull with one sharp blow from his priest's staff.

"With all the talismans and whatnot worked into that staff, you hardly needed—" I didn't finish. The blow from above caught me completely by surprise, and I slammed to the ground as something large and reeking of demon-aura fell on me. Only then did I curse myself for not checking the roof of the storehouse.

I had dropped my sword. I tried to grasp my dagger but a taloned foot pinned my arm. I recognized the demon chieftain from the compound.

"You," he growled. "You ruined everything!"

He stabbed down at me with a long dagger, and it was only Kenji's staff, thrust between me and the demon, that blocked him. In its rage the creature swatted the priest's staff aside as if it were a twig. I struggled, but I was trapped, and the demon's second blow had already begun.

Then there was a loud swoosh, as if someone had thrown a tree trunk at us, and then a very loud and wet thud. The demon flew off me as if it had sprouted wings. I heard it slam into the storehouse door and then silence.

Sago no Daiki leaned on his club, panting. Young and strong though he was, he was clearly near his limit. Both his arrow wounds were bleeding now, and his clothes were torn and mired in blood, both demons' blood and his own.

"That's twice I've been overpowered," I said, as Kenji helped me to stand. "I think I'm getting too old for such things."

Kenji just shook his head. "And yet you live still. Luck favors you, Lord Yamada," he said.

"If this is favor, then the Gods of Fortune have a twisted sense of humor," I muttered.

Daiki tried to catch his breath and didn't completely succeed. "Is . . . is it here? Did you find it?"

"It's here, Master Daiki." I looked behind me. The flames were already emerging from the eaves of the storeroom. "In there."

He cursed and stumbled to the door, which the demon's body was still blocking. He yanked its arm, and the demon's corpse fell several feet away from the building in a crumpled, bloody heap. Daiki grabbed the iron ring bolted to the door, but the impact of the demon chieftain's body had wedged the door against the frame and it would not budge. He tried to raise his club again to smash his way through, but he was so weakened that the club fell out of his hands.

"Lord Yamada, Kenji-san . . . help me!"

We did try, all of us together, but in the end we could do nothing but watch the storehouse burn.

Later as we took stock, it was clear that most of the demons had been killed; a few had escaped but not very many. Our losses were heavy enough as well: five dead and as many again hurt, including Daiki. Kenji got busy binding up wounds and offering prayers to the dead. I cleaned my sword but otherwise tried not to move any more than I could help. There was little that I claimed as mine that was not battered, bruised or aching.

Daiki sat down on an empty cask by the demon chieftain's body. He was still a little shaky, but thanks to Kenji's expert care the arrows had been removed and the wounds were no longer bleeding. We would likely both live, though we might not be proud of that fact for a few days.

"I feel I've let my ancestor down," he said. "It was our family's greatest treasure. It's gone."

"Your family's greatest treasure is your reputation and honor. Both of which you have defended here today. The loss of Sanji's demon is unfortunate, but that is all."

He sighed. "Yet there is this empty place in our shrine now. I will always be reminded of my failure."

"Then perhaps it is time for a new heirloom." I nodded at the stiffening body of the demon chieftain. "You can start with that troublesome fellow. I think it would be in your descendants' best interests to remember him and what he almost accomplished. In case they ever feel the urge to underestimate their enemies."

Daiki smiled then, faintly. "Perhaps you are right . . . who's that there?"

A rather odd procession was making its way up the trail and through the shattered gates of the demon fortress. Abbot Hideo, in a palanquin borne by two young monks and flanked by two others, was being escorted in by the *bushi* we'd assigned to guard the path.

I didn't let Daiki see me smile. *At last, the final lines of this poem are written.*

The abbot surveyed the carnage in obvious bewilderment. Daiki bowed. "My lord abbot. You're a bit off the pilgrim trail, are you not?"

"Well, I . . . what's happened here?"

"This was a demon stronghold," I said. "With the aid of the governor, Master Daiki has dealt with it in appropriate fashion. May we ask what brings you to this place?"

The abbot then told at least part of the truth. I'm not sure if he meant to or if it was just impossible to think of a plausible lie with such little warning. "Well . . . I received a messenger who said that he had information embarrassing to the Sago Clan. Naturally, I played along to discover who the miscreant was."

"Naturally," I said. "Then it was doubly fortunate for you that Master Daiki got here first, else you would have walked right into this demons' nest. In addition to saving my own life today, he saved yours as well."

"Well then," the abbot said, looking uncomfortable. "Umm . . . thank you?"

"You're welcome," Daiki said, then he turned to me. "You think the demon messenger meant the fact that my heirloom was stolen out from under my very nose? Did the chieftain need someone to gloat to, and chose Abbot Hideo?"

I smiled. "Yes, my lord. I'm sure that's what the demon meant."

★   ★   ★

Kenji managed to hold his tongue for the several days it took us to recover and begin our journey back to the Capital along the Hokuriku Road.

"Such a pity," he said, "that the demons burned the storehouse before we could recover Master Daiki's property."

"Such a pity," I agreed.

He went on. "Though I am curious as to how it was managed. You were in there for several moments. The others didn't see, but I did. The fire," he said pointedly, "began on the inside."

I nodded. "The demons didn't set the fire, Kenji-san. I did."

Kenji's mouth opened, then slowly closed again. For a moment or two he just stared at me as we walked. "You know," he said finally, "I didn't really expect you to admit it."

"I am not responsible for your expectations, Kenji-san," I said.

"But why? Why did you destroy Sanji's demon?"

"There was no demon. It was a fake."

Kenji just blinked. "You are joking."

"I am quite serious. A first-class fake, I grant you. Very skillfully done by a master artisan. Only a close examination would reveal the deception, but Sanji's demon was no more than a clever arrangement of boar's tusks, leather and dyed horsehair."

"No wonder he wanted it back so badly," Kenji said thoughtfully.

"To the contrary – Master Daiki wanted it back because it was his family's sacred treasure," I said.

Kenji frowned. "You mean he doesn't know?"

"Of course he doesn't know. It's only when the heirloom's clothing is removed that the stitching becomes visible, and no one had touched those robes for centuries. I doubt the demon chieftain himself knew until after the theft. Before that, it was just a clever ruse to embarrass the Sago family. After he discovered the deception, well, Sanji's demon potentially became so much more. That's why the demon chieftain didn't abandon his deception once the theft was accomplished. He had to wait for the Sago family's utter destruction, and witness his triumph firsthand. As demons go, this one had pride."

Kenji understood then. "If this information had become known—"

"It would have been the end of the Sago clan as demon-quellers. That's why Abbot Hideo had been summoned to the mountain fortress. I have no doubt the *oni* chieftain intended to turn the fake over to the abbot and let the monks of Hino Temple do his dirty work for him."

"You still haven't answered my question. Why did you destroy the fake demon?"

I shrugged. "To protect my patron, of course. What other reason could there be?"

"Anyone else might believe that, Yamada-san," Kenji said. "I know you too well."

"You met Master Daiki," I said. "You saw what he was and what his family has accomplished. Perhaps his ancestor was not the demon-slayer that he was reputed to be. Perhaps the real demon fell to a god of disease or simply left for a new place to terrorize. Perhaps Sanji, like his demon, was a fake and a fraud. But the clan he founded most definitely is not. That is what I chose to protect."

"A lie," Kenji said.

"No, the truth," I demurred.

"That's a contradiction, Lord Yamada."

I shook my head. "Facts are whatever facts may be," I said. "But truth? That is something we humans create, Kenji-san, and it belongs to us."

Kenji just sighed. "Buddha be merciful."

I nodded in agreement. "Someone needs to be."

Oh Glorious Sight

Tanya Huff

Angels are often associated with light. The prophet Muhammad is said to have stated: "The angels were created from light . . ." According to Jewish and Christian traditions, Lucifer, whose name means "light bearer", radiated glorious light before he rebelled against God. In Tanya Huff's touching story, the Fir Chlis *are referred to as the souls of fallen angels God caught before they reached earthly realms.* Na Fir-Chlis *is a term still used in the Orkney Islands for the northern lights or aurora borealis. In Gaelic* na *is the definite article.* Fir *is the plural of* fair – *meaning a person or one.* Chlis *means nimble or lively. So Na Fir-Chlis would literally translate as "the nimble ones" or "the lively ones" – appropriate for light that seems to dance in the sky. "The Merry Dancers", another name for the aurora mentioned by Huff, is also common in the Orkneys. "Merry" is a mispronunciation of* mirrie *which means "shimmering". "Shimmering Dancers" is a most suitable description of the northern lights – and probably for angels.*

Will Hennet, first mate on *The Matthew* stood at the rail and watched her master cross the dock, talking with great animation to the man by his side.

"So the Frenchman goes with you?"

"Aye."

"He a sailor, then?"

"He tells me he's sailed."

"And that man, the Italian?"

"Master Cabot's barber."

The river-pilot spat into the harbor scoring a direct hit on the floating corpse of a rat, his opinion of traveling with barbers clear. "Good to have clean cheeks when the sirens call you over the edge of the world."

"So they say." Only a sailor who'd never left the confines of the Bristol Channel could still believe the world was flat, but Hennet had no intention of arguing with a man whose expert guidance they needed if they were to reach the anchorage at King's Road on this tide.

"Seems like Master Cabot's taking his time to board."

That, Hennet could agree with wholeheartedly.

"By God's grace, this time tomorrow we'll be on the open sea."

Gaylor Roubaix laughed at the excitement in his friend's voice. "And this time a month hence, we'll be in Cathay sleeping in the arms of sloe-eyed maidens."

"*What* kind of maidens?"

"You aren't the only one to have read the stories of Marco Polo; it isn't my fault if you only remember silk and spice. Slow down," he added with a laugh. "It's unseemly for the master of the ship to run across the docks."

"Slow down?" Zoane Cabatto – now John Cabot by grace of the letters patent granted by the English king – threw open his arms. "How? When the wind brings me the scent of far off lands and I hear . . ." His voice trailed off and he stopped so suddenly, Roubaix had gone another six steps before he realized he was alone.

"Zoane!"

"*Ascoltare*. Listen." Head down, he charged around a stack of baled wool.

Before Roubaix – who'd heard nothing at all – could follow, angry shouting in both Italian and English rose over the ambient noise of the docks. The shouting stopped, suddenly punctuated by a splash, and the mariner reappeared.

"A dockside tough was beating a child," he said by way of explanation. "I put a stop to it."

Roubaix sighed and closed the distance between them. "Why? It was none of your concern."

"Perhaps, but I leave three sons in God's grace until we return and it seemed a bad omen to let it continue." He stepped forward and paused again at Roubaix's expression. "What is it?"

In answer, the other man pointed.

Cabot turned.

The boy was small, a little older than a child but undernourished by poverty. Dark hair, matted into filthy clumps, had recently been dusted with ash, purple and green bruises gave the grime on the thin arms some color, and the recent winter, colder than any in living memory, had frozen a toe off one bare foot. An old cut, reopened on his cheek, bled sluggishly.

His eyes were a brilliant blue, a startling color in the thin face, and quickly shuttered as he dropped his gaze to the toes of Cabot's boots.

"Go on, boy, you're safe now!"

Roubaix snorted. "Safe until the man who was beating him is out of the water, then he'll take his anger at you out on the boy."

Beginning to regret his impulsive action, Cabot spread his hands. "What can I do?"

"Take him with us."

"Are you mad?"

"There is a saying, the further from shore, the further from God. We go a long way from shore, a little charity might convince God to stay longer." Roubaix's shrug held layers of meaning. "Or you can leave him to die. Your choice."

Cabot looked across the docks to the alleys and tenements of dockside, dark in spite of early morning sunlight that danced across the harbor swells and murmured, "Your father was right, Gaylor, you should have been a priest." After a long moment, he turned his attention back to the boy. "What is your name?" he asked, switching to accented English.

"Tam." His voice sounded rusty, unused.

"I am John Cabot, master of *The Matthew*."

The brilliant blue gaze flicked to the harbor and back with a question.

"*Sí*. That ship. We sail today for the new world. If you wish, you sail with us."

He hadn't expected to be noticed. He'd followed only because the man had been kind to him and he'd wanted to hold the feeling a little longer. When the man turned, he nearly bolted. When he was actually spoken to, his heart began beating so hard he could hardly hear his own answer.

And now this.

He knew, for he'd been told it time and time again, that ships were not crewed by such as he, that sailors had legitimate sons to find a place for, that there'd never be a place for some sailor's get off a tuppenny whore.

"Well, boy? Do you come?"

He swallowed hard, and nodded.

"Is Master Cabot actually bringing that boy on board?"

"Seems to be," Hennet answered grimly.

"A Frenchman, a barber and a piece of dockside trash." The river-pilot spat again. "He'll sail you off the edge of the world, you mark my words."

"Mister Hennet, are we ready to sail?"

"Aye sir." Hennet stepped forward to meet Cabot at the top of the gangplank, the river-pilot by his side. "This is Jack Pyatt. He'll be seeing us safe to King's Road."

"Mister Pyatt." Cabot clapped the man's outstretched hand in both of his in the English style. "I thank you for lending us your skill this day."

"Lending?" The pilot's prominent brows went up. "I'm paid well for this, Master Cabot."

"Yes, of course." Dropping the man's hand, Cabot started toward the fo'c'sle. "If you are ready, the tide does not wait. Mister Hennet, cast off."

"Zoane . . ."

Brows up, Cabot turned. "Oh yes, the boy. Mister Hennet, this is Tam. Make him a sailor. Happy now?" he asked Roubaix pointedly in French.

"Totally," Roubaix replied. "And when you have done making him a sailor," he murmured in English to Hennet as he passed, "you may make a silk purse from a sow's ear."

"Aye sir."

He wanted to follow Master Cabot but the sudden realization that a dozen pairs of eyes had him locked in their sight, froze him in place. It wasn't good, it wasn't safe to be the center of attention.

Hennet saw the worship in the strange blue eyes replaced by fear, saw the bony shoulders hunch in on themselves to make a smaller target and looked around to find the source. It took him a moment to realize that nothing more than the curiosity of the crew had evoked such terror.

"Right then!" Fists on his hips, he turned in place. "You heard the master!"

"We're to make him a sailor, then?" Rennie McAlonie called out before anyone could move.

"You're to cast off the lines, you poxy Scots bastard."

"Aye, that's what I thought."

"And you . . ." The boy cringed and Hennet softened his voice to a growl. "For now, stay out of the way."

He didn't know where out of the way was. After he'd been cursed at twice and cuffed once, the big man the master called Hennet shoved him down beside the chicken coop and told him to stay put. He could see a bit of Master Cabot's leg so he hugged his knees to his chest and chewed on a stalk of wilted greens he'd taken from an indignant hen.

★   ★   ★

The tenders rowed *The Matthew* down the channel and left her at King's Road, riding at anchor with half a dozen other ships waiting for an east wind to fill the sail.

"Where's the boy?"

"Now that's a right good question, Mister Hennet." Rennie pulled the ratline tight and tested his knot. "Off somewhere dark and safe's my guess."

The mate snorted. "We've ballast enough. Master Cabot wants him taught."

"It'd be like teachin' one of the wee folk. He's here, but he's no a part of us. It's like the only other livin' thing he sees is Master Cabot."

"It's right like havin' a stray dog around," offered another of the crew, "the kind what runs off with his tail 'tween his legs when ya tries ta make friends."

Hennet glanced toward the shore. "If he's to be put off it has to be soon, before the wind changes. I'll speak with Master Cabot."

"Come now, it's only been three days." Rope wrapped around his fist, Rennie turned to face the mate. "This is right strange to him. Give the poor scrawny thing a chance."

"You think you can win him?"

"Aye, I do."

The boy's eyes were the same color as the piece of Venetian glass he'd brought back for his mother from his first voyage. Wondering why he remembered that now, Hennet nodded. "All right. You've got one more day."

Master Cabot wanted him to be a sailor and he tried, he truly did. But he couldn't be a sailor hiding in dark corners and he couldn't tell when it was safe to come out and he didn't know any other way to live.

He felt safest after sunset when no one moved around much and it was easier to disappear. Back pressed up against the aftcastle wall, as close to Master Cabot as possible, he settled into a triangle of deep shadow and cupped his hand protectively over the biscuits he'd tied into the tattered edge of his shirt. So far, there'd been food twice a day, but who knew how long it would keep coming.

Shivering a little, for the nights were still cold, he closed his eyes.

And opened them again.

What was that sound?

"Ren, look there."

Rennie, who'd replaced the shepherd's pipe with a leather mug of beer, peered over the edge of the mug. Eyes that gleamed as brilliant a blue by moon as by sun, stared back at him.

"He crept up while you was playin'," John Jack murmured, leaning in to his ear. "Play sumptin else."

Without looking aside, Rennie set down the last of his beer, put the pipe between his lips and blew a bit of a jig. Every note drew the boy closer. When he blew the last swirl of notes, the boy was an arm's reach away. He could feel the others holding their breath, could feel the weight of the boy's strange eyes. It was like something out of a story had crept out of the shadows. Moving slowly, he held out the pipe.

"Rennie . . .!"

"Shut up. Go on, boy."

Thin fingers closed around the offered end and tentatively pulled it from Rennie's grasp.

He stroked the wood, amazed such sounds could come out of something so plain, then he put it in his mouth the way he'd seen the red-haired man do.

The first noise was breathy, unsure. The second had an unexpected purity of tone.

"Cover and uncover the holes; it makes the tune." Rennie wiggled his fingers, grinned as the boy wiggled his in imitation, and smacked John Jack as he did the same.

Tam covered each hole in turn, listening. Brows drawn in, he began to put the sounds together.

Toes that hadn't tapped to Rennie's jig, moved of their own accord.

When he ran out of sounds and stopped playing, he nearly bolted at the roar of approval that rose up from the men, but he couldn't take the pipe away and he wouldn't leave it behind.

Rennie tapped his front teeth with a fingernail. "You've played before?" he asked at last.

Tam shook his head.

"You played what I played, just from hearing?"

He nodded.

"Do you want to keep the pipe?"

He nodded again, fingers white around the wooden shaft, afraid to breathe in case he shattered.

"If you stay out where you can be seen, be a part of the crew, you can keep it."

"Rennie!"

"Shut up, John Jack, I've another. And—" he jabbed a finger at the boy "—you let us teach you to be a sailor."

Recoiling from the finger, Tam froze. He looked around at the semicircle of men then down at the pipe. The music made it safe to come out so as long as he had the pipe he was safe. Master Cabot wanted him to be a sailor. When he lifted his head, he saw that the red-haired man still watched him. He nodded a third time.

By the fifth day of waiting, the shrouds and ratlines were done and the crew had been reduced to bitching about the delay, everyone of them aware it could last for weeks.

"Hey, you!"

Tam jerked around and nearly fell over as he leapt back from John Jack looming over him.

"You bin up ta crow's nest yet?"

He shook his head.

"Well, get yer arse up there then."

It was higher than it looked and he'd have quit halfway but Master Cabot was standing in his usual place on the fo'c'sle not watching, but there, so he ignored the trembling in his arms and legs and kept going, finally falling over the rail and collapsing on the small round of planking.

After he got his breath back, he sat up and peered through the slats.

He could see to the ends of the earth, but no one could see him. He didn't have words to describe how it made him feel.

Breezes danced around the nest that couldn't be felt down on the deck. They chased each other through the rigging, playing a tune against the ropes.

Tam pulled out his pipe and played the tune back at them.

The breezes blew harder.

"Did you send him up there, McAlonie?"

"No, Mister Hennet, I did not." Head craned back, Rennie grinned. "But still, it's best he does the climb first when we're ridin' steady."

"True." Denying the temptation to stare aloft at nothing, the mate frowned. "That doesn't make the nest his own private minstrel's gallery though. Get him down."

"He's not hurtin' aught and it's right nice to be serenaded like."

"MISTER HENNET!" The master's bellow turned all heads.

"I don't think Master Cabot agrees," Hennet pointed out dryly.

The breezes tried to trip him up by changing direction. Fingers flying, Tam followed.

Although the Frenchman seemed to be enjoying the music, Master Cabot did not. Lips pressed into a thin line, Hennet climbed onto the fo'c'sle.

He barely had his feet under him when Master Cabot pointed toward the nest and opened his mouth.

Another voice filled the space.

"East wind rising, sir!"

Tam's song rose triumphantly from the top of the ship.

★   ★   ★

"Get him down now, McAlonie!" Hennet bellowed as he raced aft.

"Aye sir!" But Rennie spent another moment listening to the song, and a moment more watching the way the rigging moved in the wind.

Once out of the channel and sailing hard toward the Irish coast, the crew waited expectantly for Tam to show the first signs of seasickness but, with the pipe tied tight in his shirt, the dockside brat clambered up and down the pitching decks like he'd never left land.

Fortunately, Master Cabot's Genoese barber provided amusement enough.

"Merciful Father, why must I wait so for the touch of your Grace on this, your most wretched of children?"

Tam didn't understand the words but he understood the emotion – the man had thrown his guts into the sea both before and after the declaration. Legs crossed, back against the aftcastle wall, he frowned thoughtfully. The shivering little man looked miserable.

"Seasickness won't kill ya," yelled down one of the mast hands, "but you'll be wishing it did."

Tam understood that too. There'd been many times in his life when he'd wished he were dead.

He played to make the barber feel better. He never intended to make him cry.

"What do you mean, you could see Genoa as the boy played?"

The barber feathered the razor along Cabot's jaw. "What I said, patron. The boy played, I saw Genoa. I was sick no more."

"From his twiddling?"

"Yes."

"That is ridiculous. You got your sea legs, nothing more."

"As you say, patron."

"What happened to your head, boy?"

Braced against the rolling of the ship, Tam touched his bare scalp and risked a shrug. "Shaved."

Hennet turned to a snickering John Jack for further explanation.

"Barber did it ta thank him, I reckon. Can't understand his jabbering."

"It's an improvement," the mate allowed. "Or will be when those sores heal."

"That the new world?" "Don't be daft, boy, 'tis Ireland. We'll be puttin' in to top the water casks."

"We can sail no closer to the wind than we are." Cabot glared up at an overcast sky and then into the shallow bell of the lateen sail. "It has been blowing from the west since we left Ireland! Columbus had an east wind, but me, I am mocked by God."

Roubaix spread his hands, then grabbed for a rope as the bow dipped unexpectedly deep into a trough. "Columbus sailed in the south."

"*Stupido*! Tell me something I don't know!" Spinning on one heel, balance perfected by years at sea, Cabot stomped across to the ladder and slid down into the waist.

Exchanging a glance with the bow watch that needed no common language, Roubaix followed. At the bottom of the ladder, he nearly tripped over a bare leg. The direction of the sprawl and the heartbroken look still directed at Cabot's back told as much of the story as necessary.

"He is not angry at you, Tam." The intensity of joy that replaced the hurt in the boy's stare gave him pause. He doubted Zoane had any idea how much his dockside brat adored him. "He only pushes you because he cannot push the winds around to where he needs them. Do you understand?"

Tam nodded. It was enough to understand that he'd done nothing wrong in the master's sight.

"What's he playing?" Hennet muttered, joining Rennie and John Jack at the bow. "There's no tune to it."

"I figure that depends on who's listenin'," Rennie answered with a grin. He jerked his head toward where Tam was leaning over the rail. "Have a look Mister Hennet."

Brows drawn in, Hennet leaned over by the boy and looked down at the sea.

Seven sleek, gray bodies rode the bow wave.

"He's playing for the dolphins," he said, straightening, and turning back toward the two men.

"Aye. And you can't ask for better luck."

The mate sighed. Arms folded, he squinted into the wind. "We could use a bit of luck."

"Master Cabot still in a foul mood, is he?"

"Better than he be in a mood for fowl," John Jack cackled. Two days before, a line squall had snapped the mainstay sail halberd belaying pin and dropped the full weight of the sail across the chicken coop. The surviving hens had been so hysterical they'd all been killed, cooked, and eaten.

A little surprised John Jack had brains enough for such a play on words, Hennet granted him a snort before answering Rennie. "If the winds don't change . . ."

There was no need to finish.

Tam had stopped playing at the sound of the master's name and now, pipe tightly clutched, he crossed to Hennet's side. "We needs . . ." he began then froze when the mate turned toward him.

"We need what?"

He shot a panicked glance at Rennie who nodded encouragingly. He licked salt off his lips and tried again. "We needs ta go north."

"We need to go west, boy."

His heart beat so violently he could feel his ribs shake. Pushing the pipe against his belly to keep from throwing his guts, Tam shook his head. "No. North."

Impressed – in spite of the contradiction – by obvious fear overcome, Hennet snorted again. "And who tells you that, boy?"

Tam pointed over the side.

"The dolphins?" When Tam nodded, Hennet turned on the two crewmen, about to demand which of them had been filling the boy's head with nonsense. The look on Rennie's face stopped him. "What?"

"I fished the Iceland banks, Mister Hennet, outa the islands with me da' when I were a boy. Current runs west from there and far enough north, the blow's east, north-east."

"You told the boy?"

"Swear to you, not a word."

The three men stared at Tam and then, at a sound from the sea, at each other. The dolphins were laughing.

"North." Cabot glanced down at his charts, shook his head, and was smiling when he looked up again at the mate. "Good work."

Hennet drew in a long breath and let it out slowly. He didn't like taking credit for another's idea but he liked even less the thought of telling the ship's master they were changing course because Tam had played pipes for a pod of dolphins. "Thank you, sir."

"Make the course change."

"Aye, sir." As he turned on his heel to leave the room, he didn't like the way the Frenchman was looking at him.

"He was hiding something, Zoane."

"What?"

"I don't know." Smiling a little at his own suspicion, Roubaix shook his head. "But I'll wager it has to do with the boy. There's something about those eyes."

Cabot paused at the cabin door, astrolabe in hand. "Whose eyes?"

"The boy's."

"What boy?"

"Tam." When no comprehension dawned, he sighed. "The dockside boy you saved from a beating and brought with us ...What latitude are we at, Zoane?"

Face brightening Cabot pointed to the map. "Roughly

forty-eight degrees. Give me a moment to take a reading and I can be more exact. Why?"

"Not important. You'd better go before you lose the sun." Alone in the room, he rubbed his chin and stared down at the charts. "If he were drawn here, you'd remember him, wouldn't you?"

"S'cold."

"We're still north, ain't we; though the current's run us more south than we was." John Jack handed the boy a second mug of beer. "Careful, yer hands'll be sticky."

He'd spent the afternoon tarring the mast to keep the wood from rotting where the yard had rubbed and had almost enjoyed the messy job. Holding both mugs carefully as warned, he joined Rennie at the south rail.

"Ta, lad."

They leaned quietly beside each other for a moment, staring out at a sea so flat and black the stars looked like they continued above and below without a break.

"You done good work today," Rennie said at last, wiping his beard with his free hand. He could feel Tam's pleasure and he smiled. "I'll make you a sailor yet." When he saw the boy turn from the corner of one eye, he turned as well, following his line of sight, squinting up onto the darkness on the fo'c'sle. There could be no mistaking the silhouette of the master. "Give it up, boy," he sighed. "The likes of him don't see the likes of us unless we gets in their way."

Shoulders slumped, Tam turned all the way around, and froze. A moment later, he was racing across the waist and throwing himself against the north rail.

Curious, Rennie followed. "I don't know what he's seen, do I?" he snarled at a question. "I've not asked him yet." He didn't have to ask – the boy's entire body pointed up at the flash of green light in the sky. "'Tis the *Fir Chlis*, the souls of fallen angels God caught before they reached earthly realms. Call 'em also the Merry Dancers – though they ain't dancing much this time of year."

When Tam scrambled up a ratline without either speaking or taking his eyes from the sky, Rennie snorted and returned to the beer barrel. John Jack had just lifted the jug when the first note sounded.

The pipe had been his before it was Tam's, but Rennie'd never heard it make that sound. Beer poured unheeded over his wrist as he turned to the north.

The light in the sky was joined by another.

For every note, another light.

When a vast sweep of sky had been lit, the notes began to join each other in a tune.

"I'll be buggered," John Jack breathed. "He's playin' fer the Dancers."

Rennie nodded. "Fast dance brings bad weather, boy!" he called. "Slow dance for fair!"

The tune slowed, the dance with it.

The lights dipped down, touched their reflections in the water and whirled away.

"I ain't never seen them so close."

"I ain't never seen them so . . ." Although he couldn't think of the right word, Rennie saw it reflected in the awe on every uplifted face. It was like . . . like watching angels dance.

The sails gleamed green and blue and orange and red.

All at once, the music stopped, cut off in mid-note. The dancers lingered for a heartbeat then the sky was dark again, the stars dimmer than they'd been before.

Blinking away the after-images, Rennie ran to the north rail only to find another man there before him. As there had been no mistaking the master's silhouette, so there was no mistaking the master.

Tam lay stunned on the deck, yanked down from the ratlines.

Cabot bent and picked up the pipe. Chest heaving, he lifted his fist, the pipe clenched within it, into the air. "I will not have this witchcraft on my ship!"

"Master Cabot . . ."

He whirled around and jabbed a finger of his free hand toward the mate. "*Tacere!* Did you know of this?!"

Hennet raised both hands but did not back away. "He's just a boy."

"And damned!" Drawing back his upraised arm, he flung the pipe as hard as he could into the night, turned to glare down at Tam . . . "Play one more note and you will follow it!" . . . and in the same motion strode off and into his cabin.

Hennet barely managed to stop John Jack's charge.

In the silence that followed, Roubaix stepped forward, looked down at Tam cradled in Rennie's arms, then went after Cabot.

"Let me go," John Jack growled.

Hennet started, as though he hadn't even realized he still held the man's shoulders. He opened his hands and knelt by Rennie's side. "How's the boy."

"Did you ever hear the sound of a heart breaking, Mister Hennet?" The Scot's eyes were wet as he shifted the limp weight in his arms. "I heard it tonight and I pray to God I never hear such a sound again."

Cabot was bent over the charts when Roubaix came into the cabin. The slam of the door jerked him upright and around.

"You are a fool, Zoane!"

"Watch your tongue," Cabot growled. "I am still master here."

Roubaix shook his head, too angry to be cautious. "Master of what?" he demanded. "Timber and canvas and hemp! You ignore the hearts of your men!"

"I save them from damnation. Such witchery will condemn their souls."

"It was not witchcraft!"

"Then what?" Cabot demanded, eyes narrowed, his fingers clenched into fists by his side.

"I don't know." Roubaix drew in a deep breath and released it slowly. "I do know this," he said quietly, "there is no evil in that boy in spite of a life that should have destroyed him. And, although the loss of his pipe dealt him a blow, that it was by your hand, the hand of the man who took him from darkness, who he adores and only ever wants to please, that was the greater blow."

"I cannot believe that."

Roubaix stared across the cabin for a long moment, watched the lamp swing once, twice, a third time painting shadows across the other man's face. "Then I am sorry for you," he said at last.

He would have retreated again to dark corners but he couldn't find them anymore, he'd been too long away. Instead, he wrapped shadows tightly around him, thick enough to hide the memory of the master's face.

"He spoke yet?"

"No." Arms folded, Rennie stared across at the slight figure who sat slumped at the base of the aftcastle wall.

"Ain't like he ever said much," John Jack sighed. "You give 'im yer other pipe?"

"I tried yesterday. He won't take it."

They watched Cabot's barber emerge from below and wrap a blanket around the boy murmuring softly in Italian the whole while.

John Jack snorted. "I'd not be sittin' in Master Cabot's chair when that one has a razor in his hand, though I reckon he hasn't brains to know his danger."

"I don't want to hear any more of that talk."

Both men whirled around to see Hennet standing an arm's length away.

"And if ya stopped sneakin' up on folk, ya wouldn't," John Jack sputtered around a coughing fit.

Hennet ignored him. "There's fog coming in and bow watch saw icebergs in the distance. I want you two up the lines, port and starboard."

"Ain't never been near bergs when we couldn't drop anchor and wait 'til we could see."

"Nothing to drop anchor on," the mate reminded them. "Not out here. Now go, before it gets any worse."

It got much worse.

Hennet dropped all the canvas he could and still keep *The Matthew* turned into the swell, but they were doing better than two knots when the fog closed in. It crawled over the deck, soaking everything in its path, dripping from the lashes of silent men peering desperately into the night. They couldn't see, but over the groans of rope and canvas and timber, they could hear waves breaking against the ice.

No one saw the berg that lightly kissed the port side.

The ship shuddered, rolled starboard, and they were by.

"That were too buggerin' close."

Terror wrapped them closer than the fog.

"I hear another! To port!"

"Are you daft? Listen! Ice dead ahead!"

"Be silent! All of you." Cabot's command sank into the fog. "How long to dawn, Mister Hennet?"

Hennet turned to follow the chill and unseen passage of a mountain of ice. "Too long, sir."

"We must have light!"

The first note from the crow's nest backlit the fog with brilliant blue.

Cabot moved to edge of the fo'c'sle and glared down into the waist. "Get him down from there, Mister Hennet."

Hennet folded his arms. "No, sir. I won't."

The second note streaked the fog with green.

"I gave you an order!"

"Aye, sir."

"Follow it!"

"No, sir."

"You!" Cabot pointed up at a crewman straddling the yard. "Get him down."

John Jack snorted. "Won't."

The third note was golden and at its edge, a sliver of night sky.

"Then I'll do it myself!" But when he reached for a line, Roubaix was there before him.

"Leave him alone, Zoane."

"It is witchcraft!"

"No." He switched to English so everyone would understand. "You asked for light, he does this for you."

The dance moved slow and stately across the sky.

Cabot looked around, saw nothing but closed and angry
faces. "He sends you to Hell!"

"Better than sending us to the bottom," Rennie told him.
"Slow dance brings fair weather. He's piping away the fog."

Tam stopped when he could see the path through glittering
green-white palaces of ice. He leaned over, tossed the pipe
gently, and watched it drop into Rennie's outstretched hands.
Then he stepped up onto the rail, and scanned the upturned
faces for the master's. When he found it, he took a deep breath
and jumped out as hard as he was able.

No one spoke. No one so much as shouted a protest or moaned
a denial.

The small body arced out, further than should have been
possible, then disappeared in the darkness . . .

The silence lingered.

"You killed him." Hennet stepped toward Cabot, hands
forming fists at his side. "You said if he played another note,
he'd follow his pipe. And he did. And you killed him."

Still blinded by the brilliant blue of the boy's eyes, Cabot
stepped back. "No . . ."

John Jack dropped down out of the lines. "Yes."

"No." As all heads turned toward him, Rennie palmed salt
off his cheeks. "He didn't hit the water."

"Impossible . . ."

"Did you hear a splash? Anything?" He swept a burning
gaze over the rest of the crew. "Did any of you? No one called
man overboard, no one even ran to the rails to look for a body.
There is no body. He didn't hit the water. Look."

Slowly, as though on one line, all eyes turned to the north
where a brilliant blue wisp of light danced between heaven and
earth.

"Fallen angels. He fell a little further than the rest is all; now he's back with his own."

Then the light went out, and all the sounds of a ship at sea rushed in to fill the silence.

"Mister Hennet, iceberg off the port bow!"

Hennet leapt to the port rail and leaned out. "Helmsman, two degrees starboard! All hands to the mainsail!"

As *The Matthew* began to turn to safety, Roubaix took Cabot's arm and moved him unprotesting out of the way of the crew.

"Gaylor," he whispered. "Do you believe?"

Roubaix looked up at the sky and then down at his friend. "You are a skilled and well-traveled mariner, Zoane Cabatto, and an unparalleled cartographer but sometimes you forget that there are things in life you cannot map and wonders you will not find on any chart."

The Matthew took thirty-five days to travel from Bristol to the new land Cabot named Bona Vista, Glorious Sight. It took only fifteen days for her to travel back home again and, for every one of those days, the sky was a more brilliant blue than any man on-board had ever seen and the wind played almost familiar tunes in the rigging.

Angel

Pat Cadigan

The angelic being in Pat Cadigan's story lives in a universe that does not know good or evil, only less or more. Although "he" can speak, he and his human companion communicate tele-pathically. The idea of angels who can speak, but communicate through silence can be found in the writings of the great medie-val Jewish philosopher and Torah scholar Maimonides. He called them chashmalim *because "they are sometimes silent* [**chash**im] *and sometimes they speak* [me**mal**elim]*". These angels rank slightly above midlevel in the angelic hierarchy and help convey human prayer by donning our thoughts as one would clothing, then passing them on to the next rank of angel until the prayer reaches God.*

Stand with me a while, Angel, I said, and Angel said he'd do that. Angel was good to me that way, good to have with you on a cold night and nowhere to go. We stood on the street corner together and watched the cars going by and the people and all. The streets were lit up like Christmas, street lights, store lights, marquees over the all-night movie houses and bookstores blinking and flashing; shank of the evening in east midtown. Angel was getting used to things here and getting used to how I did nights. Standing outside, because what else are you going to do. He was *my* Angel now, had been since that other cold night when I'd been going home, because where are you going to go, and I'd found him, and took him with me. It's good to have someone to take with you, someone to look after. Angel knew that. He started looking after me, too.

Like now. We were standing there a while and I was looking around at nothing and everything, the cars cruising past, some of them stopping now and again for the hookers posing by the curb, and then I saw it, out of the corner of my eye. Stuff coming out of the Angel, shiny like sparks but flowing like liquid. Silver fireworks. I turned and looked all the way at him and it was gone. And he turned and gave a little grin like he was embarrassed I'd seen. Nobody else saw it, though; not the short guy who paused next to the Angel before crossing the street against the light, not the skinny hype looking to sell the boom box he was carrying on his shoulder, not the homeboy strutting past us with both his girlfriends on his arms, nobody but me.

The Angel said, *Hungry?*

Sure, I said. I'm hungry.

Angel looked past me. Okay, he said. I looked, too, and here they came, three leather boys, visor caps, belts, boots, key rings. On the cruise together. Scary stuff, even though you know it's not looking for you.

I said, Them? *Them?*

Angel didn't answer. One went by, then the second, and the Angel stopped the third by taking hold of his arm.

Hi.

The guy nodded. His head was shaved; I could see a little gray-black stubble under his cap. No eyebrows, disinterested eyes. The eyes were because of the Angel.

I could use a little money, the Angel said. My friend and I are hungry.

The guy put his hand in his pocket and wiggled out some bills, offering them to the Angel. The Angel selected a twenty and closed the guy's hand around the rest.

This will be enough, thank you.

The guy put his money away and waited.

I hope you have a good night, said the Angel.

The guy nodded and walked on, going across the street to where his two friends were waiting on the next corner. Nobody found anything weird about it.

Angel was grinning at me. Sometimes he was *the* Angel, when he was doing something, sometimes he was Angel, when he was just with me. Now he was Angel again. We went up the street to the luncheonette and got a seat by the front window so we could still watch the street while we ate.

Cheeseburger and fries, I said without bothering to look at the plastic-covered menus lying on top of the napkin holder. The Angel nodded.

Thought so, he said. I'll have the same, then.

The waitress came over with a little tiny pad to take our order. I cleared my throat. It seemed like I hadn't used my voice in a hundred years. "Two cheeseburgers and two fries," I said, "and two cups of—" I looked up at her and froze. She had no face. Like, *nothing*, blank from hairline to chin, soft little dents where the eyes and nose and mouth would have been. Under the table, the Angel kicked me, but gentle.

"And two cups of coffee," I said.

She didn't say anything – how could she? – as she wrote down the order and then walked away again. All shaken up, I looked at the Angel, but he was calm like always.

She's a new arrival, Angel told me and leaned back in his chair. Not enough time to grow a face.

But how can she breathe? I said.

Through her pores. She doesn't need much air yet.

Yah, but what about – like, I mean, don't other people notice that she's got nothing there?

No. It's not such an extraordinary condition. The only reason you notice is because you're with me. Certain things have rubbed off on you. But no one else notices. When they look at her, they see whatever face they expect someone like her to have. And eventually, she'll have it.

But you have a face, I said. You've always had a face.

I'm different, said the Angel.

You sure are, I thought, looking at him. Angel had a

beautiful face. That wasn't why I took him home that night, just because he had a beautiful face – I left all that behind a long time ago – but it was there, his beauty. The way you think of a man being beautiful, good clean lines, deep-set eyes, ageless. About the only way you could describe him – look away and you'd forget everything except that he was beautiful. But he did have a face. He *did*.

Angel shifted in the chair – these were like somebody's old kitchen chairs, you couldn't get too comfortable in them – and shook his head, because he knew I was thinking troubled thoughts. Sometimes you could think something and it wouldn't be troubled and later you'd think the same thing and it would be troubled. The Angel didn't like me to be troubled about him.

Do you have a cigarette? he asked.

I think so.

I patted my jacket and came up with most of a pack that I handed over to him. The Angel lit up and amused us both by having the smoke come out his ears and trickle out of his eyes like ghostly tears. I felt my own eyes watering for his; I wiped them and there was that stuff again, but from me now. I was crying silver fireworks. I flicked them on the table and watched them puff out and vanish.

Does this mean I'm getting to *be* you, now? I asked.

Angel shook his head. Smoke wafted out of his hair. Just things rubbing off on you. Because we've been together and you're – susceptible. But they're different for you.

Then the waitress brought our food and we went on to another sequence, as the Angel would say. She still had no face but I guess she could see well enough because she put all the plates down just where you'd think they were supposed to go and left the tiny little check in the middle of the table.

Is she . . . I mean, did you know her, from where you . . .

Angel, gave his head a brief little shake. No. She's from somewhere else. Not one of my . . . people. He pushed the cheeseburger and fries in front of him over to my side of the table. That was the way it was done; I did all the eating and somehow it worked out.

I picked up my cheeseburger and I was bringing it up to my mouth when my eyes got all funny and I saw it coming up like a whole series of cheeseburgers, whoom-whoom-whoom, trick photography, only for real. I closed my eyes and jammed the cheeseburger into my mouth, holding it there, waiting for all the other cheeseburgers to catch up with it.

You'll be okay, said the Angel. Steady, now.

I said with my mouth full, That was . . . that was *weird*. Will I ever get used to this?

I doubt it. But I'll do what I can to help you.

Yah, well, the Angel would know. Stuff rubbing off on me, he could feel it better than I could. He was the one it was rubbing off from.

I had put away my cheeseburger and half of Angel's and was working on the French fries for both of us when I noticed he was looking out the window with this hard, tight expression on his face.

Something? I asked him.

Keep eating, he said.

I kept eating, but I kept watching, too. The Angel was staring at a big blue car parked at the curb right outside the diner. It was silvery blue, one of those lots-of-money models and there was a woman kind of leaning across from the driver's side to look out the passenger window. She was beautiful in that lots-of-money way, tawny hair swept back from her face, and even from here I could see she had turquoise eyes. Really beautiful woman. I almost felt like crying. I mean, Jeez, how did people get that way and me too harmless to live.

But the Angel wasn't one bit glad to see her. I knew he didn't want me to say anything, but I couldn't help it.

Who is she?

Keep eating, Angel said. We need the protein, what little there is.

I ate and watched the woman and the Angel watch each other and it was getting very . . . I don't know, very *something* between them, even through the glass. Then a cop car pulled up next to her and I knew they were telling her to move it along. She moved it along.

Angel sagged against the back of his chair and lit another cigarette, smoking it in the regular, unremarkable way.

What are we going to do tonight? I asked the Angel as we left the restaurant.

Keep out of harm's way, Angel said, which was a new answer. Most nights we spent just kind of going around soaking everything up. The Angel soaked it up, mostly. I got some of it along with him, but not the same way he did. It was different for him. Sometimes he would use me like a kind of filter. Other times he took it direct. There'd been the big car accident one night, right at my usual corner, a big old Buick running a red light smack into somebody's nice Lincoln. The Angel had had to take it direct because I couldn't handle that kind of stuff. I didn't know how the Angel could take it, but he could. It carried him for days afterwards, too. I only had to eat for myself.

It's the intensity, little friend, he'd told me, as though that were supposed to explain it.

It's the intensity, not whether it's good or bad. The universe doesn't know good or bad, only less or more. Most of you have a bad time reconciling this. *You* have a bad time with it, little friend, but you get through better than other people. Maybe because of the way you are. You got squeezed out of a lot, you haven't had much of a chance at life. You're as much an exile as I am, only in your own land.

That may have been true, but at least I belonged here, so that part was easier for me. But I didn't say that to the Angel. I think he liked to think he could do as well or better than me at living – I mean, I couldn't just look at some leather boy and get him to cough up a twenty-dollar bill. Cough up a fist in the face, or worse, was more like it.

Tonight, though, he wasn't doing so good, and it was that woman in the car. She'd thrown him out of step, kind of.

Don't think about her, the Angel said, just out of nowhere. Don't think about her any more.

Okay, I said, feeling creepy because it was creepy when the Angel got a glimpse of my head. And then, of course, I couldn't think about anything else hardly.

Do you want to go home? I asked him.

No. I can't stay in now. We'll do the best we can tonight, but I'll have to be very careful about the tricks. They take so much out of me, and if we're keeping out of harm's way, I might not be able to make up for a lot of it.

It's okay, I said. I ate. I don't need anything else tonight, you don't have to do any more.

Angel got that look on his face, the one where I knew he wanted to give me things, like feelings I couldn't have any more. Generous, the Angel was. But I didn't need those feelings, not like other people seem to. For a while, it was like the Angel didn't understand that, but he let me be.

Little friend, he said, and almost touched me. The Angel didn't touch a lot. I could touch him and that would be okay, but if he touched somebody, he couldn't help *doing* something to them, like the trade that had given us the money. That had been deliberate. If the trade had touched the Angel first, it would have been different, nothing would have happened unless the Angel touched him back. All touch meant something to the Angel that I didn't understand. There was touching without touching, too. Like things rubbing off on me. And sometimes, when I did touch the Angel, I'd get the feeling that it was maybe more his idea than mine, but I didn't mind that. How many people are going their whole lives never being able to touch an Angel?

We walked together and all around us the street was really coming to life. It was getting colder, too. I tried to make my jacket cover more. The Angel wasn't feeling it. Most of the time hot and cold didn't mean much to him. We saw the three rough trade guys again. The one Angel had gotten the money from was getting into a car. The other two watched it drive away and then walked on. I looked over at the Angel.

Because we took his twenty, I said.

Even if we hadn't, Angel said.

So we went along, the Angel and me, and I could feel how different it was tonight than it was all the other nights we'd walked or stood together. The Angel was kind of pulled back into himself and seemed to be keeping a check on me, pushing us closer together. I was getting more of those fireworks out of the corners of my eyes, but when I'd turn my head to look, they'd vanish. It reminded me of the night I'd found the Angel standing on my corner all by himself in pain. The Angel told me later that was real talent, knowing he was in pain. I never thought of myself as any too talented, but the way everyone else had been just ignoring him, I guess I must have had something to see him after all.

The Angel stopped us several feet down from an all-night bookstore. Don't look, he said. Watch the traffic or stare at your feet, but don't look or it won't happen.

There wasn't anything to see right then, but I didn't look anyway. That was the way it was sometimes, the Angel telling me it made a difference whether I was watching something or not, something about the other people being conscious of me being conscious of them. I didn't understand, but I knew Angel was usually right. So I was watching traffic when the guy came out of the bookstore and got his head punched.

I could almost see it out of the corner of my eye. A lot of movement, arms and legs flying and grunty noises. Other people stopped to look but I kept my eyes on the traffic, some of which was slowing up so they could check out the fight. Next to me, the Angel was stiff all over. Taking it in, what he called the expenditure of emotional kinetic energy. No right, no wrong, little friend, he'd told me. Just energy, like the rest of the universe.

So he took it in and I *felt* him taking it in, and while I was feeling it, a kind of silver fog started creeping around my eyeballs and I was in two places at once. I was watching the traffic and I was in the Angel watching the fight and feeling him charge up like a big battery.

It felt like nothing I'd ever felt before. These two guys slugging it out – well, one guy doing all the slugging and the other skittering around, trying to get out from under the fists and having his head punched but good, and the Angel drinking it like he was sipping at an empty cup and somehow getting it to have something in it after all. Deep inside him, whatever made the Angel go was getting a little stronger.

I kind of swung back and forth between him and me, or swayed might be more like it was. I wondered about it, because the Angel wasn't touching me. I really was getting to *be* him, I thought; Angel picked that up and put the thought away to answer later. It was like I was traveling by the fog, being one of us and then the other, for a long time, it seemed, and then after a while I was more me than him again, and some of the fog cleared away.

And there was that car, pointed the other way this time, and the woman was climbing out of it with this big weird smile on her face, as though she'd won something. She waved at the Angel to come to her.

Bang went the connection between us dead and the Angel shot past me, running away from the car. I went after him. I caught a glimpse of her jumping back into the car and yanking at the gear shift.

Angel wasn't much of a runner. Something funny about his knees. We'd gone maybe a hundred feet when he started wobbling and I could hear him pant. He cut across a Park and Lock that was dark and mostly empty. It was back-to-back with some kind of private parking lot and the fences for each one tried to mark off the same narrow strip of lumpy pavement. They were easy to climb but Angel was too panicked. He just *went* through them before he even thought about it; I knew that because if he'd been thinking, he'd have wanted to save what he'd just charged up with for when he really needed it bad enough.

I had to haul myself over the fences in the usual way, and when he heard me rattling on the saggy chainlink, he stopped and looked back.

Go, I told him. Don't wait on me!

He shook his head sadly. Little friend, I'm a fool. I could stand to learn from you a little more.

Don't stand, run! I got over the fences and caught up with him. Let's go! I yanked his sleeve as I slogged past and he followed at a clumsy trot.

Have to hide somewhere, he said, camouflage ourselves with people.

I shook my head, thinking we could just run maybe four more blocks and we'd be at the freeway overpass. Below it were the butt-ends of old roads closed off when the freeway had been built. You could hide there the rest of your life and no one would find you. But Angel made me turn right and go down a block to this rundown crack-in-the-wall called Stan's Jigger. I'd never been in there – I'd never made it a practice to go into bars – but the Angel was pushing too hard to argue.

Inside it was smelly and dark and not too happy. The Angel and I went down to the end of the bar and stood under a blood-red light while he searched his pockets for money.

Enough for one drink apiece, he said.

I don't want anything.

You can have soda or something.

The Angel ordered from the bartender, who was suspicious. This was a place for regulars and nobody else, and certainly nobody else like me or the Angel. The Angel knew that even stronger than I did but he just stood and pretended to sip his drink without looking at me. He was all pulled into himself and I was hovering around the edges. I knew he was still pretty panicked and trying to figure out what he could do next. As close as I was, if he had to get real far away, he was going to have a problem and so was I. He'd have to tow me along with him and that wasn't the most practical thing to do.

Maybe he was sorry now he'd let me take him home. But he'd been so weak then, and now with all the filtering and stuff I'd done for him, he couldn't just cut me off without a lot of pain.

I was trying to figure out what I could do for him now when the bartender came back and gave us a look that meant order or get out, and he'd have liked it better if we got out. So would everyone else there. The few other people standing at the bar weren't looking at us, but they knew right where we were, like a sore spot. It wasn't hard to figure out what they thought about us, either, maybe because of me or because of the Angel's beautiful face.

We got to leave, I said to the Angel, but he had it in his head this was good camouflage. There wasn't enough money for two more drinks so he smiled at the bartender and slid his hand across the bar and put it on top of the bartender's. It was tricky doing it this way; bartenders and waitresses took more persuading because it wasn't normal for them just to give you something.

The bartender looked at the Angel with his eyes half closed. He seemed to be thinking it over. But the Angel had just blown a lot going through the fence instead of climbing over it and the fear was scuttling his concentration and I just knew that it wouldn't work. And maybe my knowing that didn't help, either.

The bartender's free hand dipped down below the bar and came up with a small club. "Faggot!" he roared and caught Angel just over the ear. Angel slammed into me and we both crashed to the floor. Plenty of emotional kinetic energy in here, I thought dimly as the guys standing at the bar fell on us, and then I didn't think anything more as I curled up into a ball under their fists and boots.

We were lucky they didn't much feel like killing anyone. Angel went out the door first and they tossed me out on top of him. As soon as I landed on him, I knew we were both in trouble; something was broken inside him. So much for keeping out of harm's way. I rolled off him and lay on the pavement, staring at the sky and trying to catch my breath. There was blood in my mouth and my nose, and my back was on fire.

Angel? I said, after a bit.

He didn't answer. I felt my mind get kind of all loose and runny, like my brains were leaking out my ears. I thought about the trade we'd taken the money from and how I'd been scared of him and his friends and how silly that had been. But then, I was too harmless to live.

The stars were raining silver fireworks down on me. It didn't help.

Angel? I said again.

I rolled over onto my side to reach for him, and there she was. The car was parked at the curb and she had Angel under the armpits, dragging him toward the open passenger door. I couldn't tell if he was conscious or not and that scared me. I sat up.

She paused, still holding the Angel. We looked into each other's eyes, and I started to understand.

"Help me get him into the car," she said at last. Her voice sounded hard and flat and unnatural. "Then you can get in, too. In the back seat."

I was in no shape to take her out. It couldn't have been better for her if she'd set it up herself. I got up, the pain flaring in me so bad that I almost fell down again, and took the Angel's ankles. His ankles were so delicate, almost like a woman's, like *hers*. I didn't really help much, except to guide his feet in as she sat him on the seat and strapped him in with the shoulder harness. I got in the back as she ran around to the other side of the car, her steps all real light and peppy, like she'd found a million dollars lying there on the sidewalk.

We were out on the freeway before the Angel stirred in the shoulder harness. His head lolled from side to side on the back of the seat. I reached up and touched his hair lightly, hoping she couldn't see me do it.

Where are you taking me, the Angel said.

"For a ride," said the woman. "For the moment."

Why does she talk out loud like that? I asked the Angel.

Because she knows it bothers me.

"You know I can focus my thoughts better if I say things out loud," she said. "I'm not like one of your little pushovers." She glanced at me in the rear-view mirror. "Just what have you gotten yourself into since you left, darling? Is that a boy or a girl?"

I pretended I didn't care about what she said or that I was

too harmless to live or any of that stuff, but the way she said it, she meant it to sting.

Friends can be either, Angel said. It doesn't matter which. Where are you taking us?

Now it was *us*. In spite of everything, I almost could have smiled.

"Us? You mean, you and me? Or are you really referring to your little pet back there?"

My friend and I are together. You and I are *not*.

The way the Angel said it made me think he meant more than not together; like he'd been with her once the way he was with me now. The Angel let me know I was right. Silver fireworks started flowing slowly off his head down the back of the seat and I knew there was something wrong about it. There was too much all at once.

"Why can't you talk out loud to me, darling?" the woman said with fakey-sounding petulance. "Just say a few words and make me happy. You have a lovely voice when you use it."

That was true, but the Angel never spoke out loud unless he couldn't get out of it, like when he'd ordered from the bartender. Which had probably helped the bartender decide about what he thought we were, but it was useless to think about that.

"All right," said Angel, and I knew the strain was awful for him. "I've said a few words. Are you happy?" He sagged in the shoulder harness.

"Ecstatic. But it won't make me let you go. I'll drop your pet at the nearest hospital and then we'll go home." She glanced at the Angel as she drove. "I've missed you so much. I can't stand it without you, without you making things happen. Doing your little miracles. You knew I'd get addicted to it, all the things you could do to people. And then you just took off, I didn't know what had happened to you. And it *hurt*." Her voice turned kind of pitiful, like a little kid's. "I was in real *pain*. You must have been, too. Weren't you? Well, *weren't you?*"

Yes, the Angel said. I was in pain, too.

I remembered him standing on my corner, where I'd hung out all that time by myself until he came. Standing there in pain. I didn't know why or from what then, I just took him home, and after a little while, the pain went away. When he decided we were together, I guess.

The silvery flow over the back of the car seat thickened. I cupped my hands under it and it was like my brain was lighting up with pictures. I saw the Angel before he was my Angel, in this really nice house, the woman's house, and how she'd take him places, restaurants or stores or parties, thinking at him real hard so that he was all filled up with her and had to do what she wanted him to. Steal sometimes; other times, weird stuff, making people do silly things like suddenly start singing or taking their clothes off. That was mostly at the parties, though she made a waiter she didn't like burn himself with a pot of coffee. She'd get men, too, through the Angel, and they'd think it was the greatest idea in the world to go to bed with her. Then she'd make the Angel show her the others, the ones that had been sent here the way he had for crimes nobody could have understood, like the waitress with no face. She'd look at them, sometimes try to do things to them to make them uncomfortable or unhappy. But mostly she'd just stare.

It wasn't like that in the very beginning, the Angel said weakly and I knew he was ashamed.

It's okay, I told him. People can be nice at first, I know that. Then they find out about you.

The woman laughed. "You two are so sweet and pathetic. Like a couple of little children. I guess that's what you were looking for, wasn't it, darling? Except children can be cruel, too, can't they? So you got this . . . *creature* for yourself." She looked at me in the rear-view mirror again as she slowed down a little, and for a moment I was afraid she'd seen what I was doing with the silvery stuff that was still pouring out of the Angel. It was starting to slow now. There wasn't much time left. I wanted to scream, but the Angel was calming me for what was coming next. "What happened to you, anyway?"

Tell her, said the Angel. To stall for time, I knew, keep her occupied.

I was born funny, I said. I had both sexes.

"A hermaphrodite!" she exclaimed with real delight.

She loves freaks, the Angel said, but she didn't pay any attention.

There was an operation, but things went wrong. They kept trying to fix it as I got older but my body didn't have the right kind of chemistry or something. My parents were ashamed. I left after a while.

"You poor thing," she said, not meaning anything like that. "You were *just* what darling, here, needed, weren't you? Just a little nothing, no demands, no desires. For anything." Her voice got all hard. "They could probably fix you up now, you know."

I don't want it. I left all that behind a long time ago, I don't need it.

"*Just* the sort of little pet that would be perfect for you," she said to the Angel. "Sorry I have to tear you away. But I can't get along without you now. Life is so boring. And empty. And . . ." She sounded puzzled. "And like there's nothing more to live for since you left me."

That's not me, said the Angel. That's you.

"No, it's a lot of you, and you know it. You know you're addictive to human beings, you knew that when you came here – when they sent you here. Hey, you, *pet*, do you know what his crime was, why they sent him to this little backwater penal colony of a planet?"

Yeah, I know, I said. I really didn't, but I wasn't going to tell her that.

"What do you think about *that*, little pet neuter?" she said gleefully, hitting the accelerator pedal and speeding up. "What do you think of the crime of refusing to mate?"

The Angel made a sort of an out-loud groan and lunged at the steering wheel. The car swerved wildly and I fell backwards, the silver stuff from the Angel going all over me. I tried to keep scooping it into my mouth the way I'd been doing, but it was flying all over the place now. I heard the crunch as the tires left the road and went onto the shoulder. Something struck the side of the car, probably the guard rail, and made it fishtail, throwing me down on the floor. Up front the woman was screaming and cursing and the Angel wasn't making a sound, but, in my head, I could hear him sort of keening. Whatever happened, this would be it. The Angel had told me all that time ago, after I'd taken him home, that they didn't last long after they got here, the exiles from his world and other worlds. Things tended to *happen* to them, even if they latched on to someone like me or the woman. They'd be in accidents or the people here would kill them. Like antibodies in a human body rejecting something or fighting a disease. At least I belonged here, but it looked like I was going to die in a car accident with the Angel and the woman both. I didn't care.

The car swerved back onto the highway for a few seconds and then pitched to the right again. Suddenly there was nothing under us and then we thumped down on something, not road but dirt or grass or something, bombing madly up and down. I pulled myself up on the back of the seat just in time to see the sign coming at us at an angle. The corner of it started to go through the windshield on the woman's side and then all I saw for a long time was the biggest display of silver fireworks ever.

It was hard to be gentle with him. Every move hurt but I didn't want to leave him sitting in the car next to her, even if she was dead. Being in the back seat had kept most of the glass from flying into me but I was still shaking some out of my hair and the impact hadn't done much for my back.

I laid the Angel out on the lumpy grass a little ways from the car and looked around. We were maybe a hundred yards from the highway, near a road that ran parallel to it. It was dark but I could still read the sign that had come through the windshield and split the woman's head in half. It said, CONSTRUCTION AHEAD, REDUCE SPEED. Far off on the other road, I could see a flashing yellow light and at first I was afraid it was the police or something but it stayed where it was and I realized that must be the construction.

"Friend," whispered the Angel, startling me. He'd never spoken aloud to me, not directly.

Don't talk, I said, bending over him, trying to figure out some way I could touch him, just for comfort. There wasn't anything else I could do now.

"I have to," he said, still whispering. "It's almost all gone. Did you get it?"

Mostly, I said. Not all.

"I meant for you to have it."

I know.

"I don't know that it will really do you any good." His breath kind of bubbled in his throat. I could see something wet and shiny on his mouth but it wasn't silver fireworks. "But it's yours. You can do as you like with it. Live on it the way I did. Get what you need when you need it. But you can live as a human, too. Eat. Work. However, whatever."

I'm not human, I said. I'm not any more human than you, even if I do belong here.

"Yes, you are, little friend. I haven't made you any less human," he said, and coughed some. "I'm not sorry I wouldn't mate. I couldn't mate with my own. It was too . . . I don't know, too little of me, too much of them, something. I couldn't bond, it would have been nothing but emptiness. The Great Sin, to be unable to give, because the universe knows only less or more and I insisted that it would be good or bad. So they sent me here. But in the end, you know, they got their way, little friend." I felt his hand on me for a moment before it fell away. "I did it after all. Even if it wasn't with my own."

The bubbling in his throat stopped. I sat next to him for a while in the dark. Finally I felt it, the Angel stuff. It was kind of fluttery-churny, like too much coffee on an empty stomach. I closed my eyes and lay down on the grass, shivering. Maybe some of it was shock but I don't think so. The silver fireworks started, in my head this time, and with them came a lot of pictures I couldn't understand. Stuff about the Angel and where he'd come from and the way they mated. It was a lot like how we'd been together, the Angel and me. They looked a lot like us but there were a lot of differences, too, things I couldn't make out. I couldn't make out how they'd sent him here, either – by *light*, in, like, little bundles or something. It didn't make any sense to me, but I guessed an Angel could be light. Silver fireworks.

I must have passed out, because when I opened my eyes, it felt like I'd been laying there a long time. It was still dark, though. I sat up and reached for the Angel, thinking I ought to hide his body.

He was gone. There was just a sort of wet sandy stuff where he'd been.

I looked at the car and her. All that was still there. Somebody was going to see it soon. I didn't want to be around for that.

Everything still hurt but I managed to get to the other road and start walking back toward the city. It was like I could feel it now, the way the Angel must have, as though it were vibrating like a drum or ringing like a bell with all kinds of stuff, people laughing and crying and loving and hating and being afraid and everything else that happens to people. The stuff that the Angel took in, energy, that I could take in now if I wanted.

And I knew that taking it in that way, it would be bigger than anything all those people had, bigger than anything I could have had if things hadn't gone wrong with me all those years ago.

I wasn't so sure I wanted it. Like the Angel, refusing to mate back where he'd come from. He wouldn't there, and I couldn't here. Except now I could do something else.

I wasn't so sure I wanted it. But I didn't think I'd be able to stop it, either, any more than I could stop my heart from beating. Maybe it wasn't really such a good thing or a right thing. But it was like the Angel said: the universe doesn't know good or bad, only less or more.

Yeah. I heard *that*.

I thought about the waitress with no face. I could find them all now, all the ones from the other places, other worlds that sent them away for some kind of alien crimes nobody would have understood. I could find them all. They threw away their outcasts, I'd tell them, but here, we kept ours. And here's how. Here's how you live in a universe that only knows less or more.

I kept walking toward the city.

The Man Who Stole the Moon

Tanith Lee

Tanith Lee's stories of the Flat Earth are based in a mythology of her own brilliant devising. Above her Earth is the rather uninteresting Upperearth, where indifferent gods do little more than think and sleep. Below are two realms: Underearth – ruled by Azhrarn, Prince of Demons — and Innerearth, where Uhlume, Lord Death, keeps dead spirits for a thousand years. Obviously, in our context we are most interested in Azhrarn and the demons he rules. The Vazdru are beautiful demons similar to their prince; they can transform themselves into animals. The rather dreamy (and equally beautiful) Eshva serve them. The Drin are ugly, dwarfish craftsmen. All three types of demons tend towards making mischief amongst the humans of Earth. In "The Man Who Stole the Moon" we meet both Yulba, a Drin who expects an unnamed but no doubt questionable reward in exchange for assisting a trickster thief, and the Prince of Demons himself.

Several tales are told concerning the Moon of the Flat Earth. Some say that this Moon, perhaps, was a hollow globe, within which lay lands and seas, having even their own cool Sun. However, there are other stories.

One evening, Jaqir the accomplished thief rose from a bed of love and said to his mistress, "Alas, sweetheart, we must now part forever." Jaqir's mistress looked at him in surprise and shook out her bright hair. "You are mistaken. My husband, the old merchant, is miles off again, buying silk and other stuff, and besides suspects nothing. And I am well satisfied with you."

"Dear heart," said Jaqir, as he dressed his handsome self swiftly, "neither of these things is the stumbling block to our romance. It is only this. I have grown tired of you."

"Tired of me!" cried the lady, springing from the bed.

"Yes, though indeed you are toothsome in all respects. I am inconstant and easily bored. You must forgive me."

"Forgive you!" screamed the lady, picking up a handy vase.

Jaqir ducked the vase and swung nimbly out of the high window, an action to which he was quite accustomed, from his trade. "Although a deceiver in my work, honesty in my private life is always my preferred method," he added, as he dropped quickly down through the vine to the street below. Once there he was gone in a flash, and just in time to miss the jar of piddle the lady that moment upended from the window.

However, three of the king's guard, next second passing beneath, were not so fortunate.

"A curse upon all bladders," they howled, wringing out their cloaks and hair. Then, looking up, they beheld the now no-longer mistress of Jaqir, and asked her loudly what she meant by it.

"Pardon me, splendid sirs," said she. "The befoulment was not intended for you, but for that devilish thief, Jaqir, who even now runs through that alley there toward a hiding place he keeps in the House of the Thin Door."

At the mention of Jaqir, who was both celebrated and notorious in that city, the soldiers forgot their inconvenience, and gave instant chase. Never before had any been able to lay hands on Jaqir, who, it was said, could steal the egg from beneath a sleeping pigeon. Now, thanks to the enragement of his discarded lover, the guard knew not only of Jaqir's proximity, but his destination. Presently then they came up with him by the House of the Thin Door.

"Is it he?"

"So it is, for I have heard, when not in disguise, he dresses like a lord, like this one, and, like this one, his hair is black as a panther's fur."

At this they strode up to Jaqir and surrounded him.

"Good evening, my friends," said Jaqir. "You are fine fellows, despite your smell."

"That smell is not our own, but the product of a night-jar emptied on us. And the one who did this also told us where to find the thief Jaqir."

"Fate has been kind to you. I will not therefore detain you further."

"No, it is you who shall be detained."

"*I?*" asked Jaqir modestly.

But within the hour he discovered himself in chains in the king's dungeons.

"Ah, Jaqir," said he to himself, "a life of crime has taught you nothing. For have the gods not always rewarded your dishonesty – and now you are chastised for being truthful."

Although of course the indifferent, useless gods had nothing to do with any of it.

A month or so later, the king got to hear that Jaqir the Prince of Thieves languished in the prison, awaiting trial.

"I will see to it," said the king. "Bring him before me."

So Jaqir was brought before the king. But, despite being in jail, being also what he was, Jaqir had somehow stolen a gold piece from one jailor and gifted it to another, and so arrived in the king's sight certainly in chains, but additionally bathed, barbered and anointed, dressed in finery, and with a cup of wine in his hand.

Seeing this, the king laughed. He was a young king and not without a sense of the humorous. In addition, he knew that Jaqir, while he had stolen from everyone he might, had never harmed a hair of their heads, while his skills of disguise and escape were much admired by any he had not annoyed.

"Now then, Prince of Thieves, may a mere king invite you to sit? Shall I strike off your chains?" added the king.

"Your majesty," said one of the king's advisers, "pray do not unchain him, or he will be away over the roofs. Look, he has already stolen two of my gold rings – and see, many others have lost items."

This was a fact. All up and down the palace hall, those who had gathered to see Jaqir on trial were exclaiming over pieces of jewelry suddenly missing. And one lady had even lost her little dog, which abruptly, and with a smile, Jaqir let out of an inner compartment in his shirt, though it seemed quite sorry to leave him.

"Then I shall not unchain you," said the king. "Restore at once all you have filched."

Jaqir rose, shook himself somewhat, and an abundance of gold and gems cascaded from his person.

"Regrettably, lord king, I could not resist the chance to display my skills."

"Rather you should deny your skills. For you have been employed in my city seven years, and lived like the prince you call yourself. But the punishment for such things is death."

Jaqir's face fell, then he shrugged. He said, "I see you are a greater thief, sir, than I. For I only presume to rob men of their goods. You are bold enough to burgle me of my life."

At that the court made a noise, but the king grew silent and thoughtful.

Eventually he said, "I note you will debate the matter. But I do not believe you can excuse your acts."

"There you are wrong. If I were a beggar calling for charity on the street you would not think me guilty of anything but ill luck or indigence. Or, if I were a seller of figs you would not even notice me as I took the coins of men in exchange for my wares."

"Come," said the king. "You neither beg nor sell. You thieve."

"A beggar," said Jaqir, "takes men's money and other alms, and gives nothing in return but a blessing. Please believe me, I heap blessings on the heads of all I rob, and thank them in my prayers for their charity. Had I begged it, I might, it is true, not have received so great a portion. How much nobler and blessed are they then, that they have given over to me the more generous amount? Nor do they give up their coins for nothing.

"For what they buy of me, when it is *I* who steal from them, is a dramatic tale to tell. And indeed, lord king, have you never heard any boast of how they were robbed by me?"

The king frowned, for now and then he had heard this very thing, some rich noble or other reciting the story of how he had been despoiled of this or that treasure by the nimble Jaqir, the only thief able to take it. And once or twice, there were women, too, who said, "When I woke, I found my rings were gone, but on my pillow lay a crimson rose. Oh, would he had stayed a while to steal some other prize."

"I am not," declared Jaqir, "a common thief. I purloin from none who cannot afford the loss. I deduct nothing that has genuine sentimental or talismanic weight. I harm none. Besides, I am an artist in what I do. I come and go like a shadow, and vanish like the dawn into the day. You will have been told, I can abstract the egg of a pigeon from beneath the sleeping bird and never wake it."

The king frowned deeply. He said, "Yet with all this vaunted knack, you did not, till today, leave my dungeons."

Jaqir bowed. "That was because, lord king, I did not wish to miss my chance of meeting you."

"Truly? I think rather it was the bolts and bars and keys, the numerous guards – who granted you wine, but not an open door. You seem a touch pale."

"Who can tell?" idly answered pale Jaqir.

But the king only said, "I will go apart and think about all this." And so he did, but the court lingered, looking at Jaqir, and some of the ladies and young men came and spoke to him, but trying always not to get near enough to be robbed. Yet even so, now and then, he would courteously hand them back an emerald or amethyst he had removed from their persons.

Meanwhile the king walked up and down a private chamber where, on pedestals of marble, jewel-colored parrots sat watching him.

"He is clever," said the king, "handsome, well mannered and decorative. One likes him at once, despite his nefarious career. Why cast such a man out of the state of life? We have callous villains and nonentities enough. Must every shining star be snuffed?"

Then a scarlet parrot spoke to him.

"O king, if you do not have Jaqir executed, they will say you are partial, and not worthy to be trusted with the office of judge."

"Yes," said the king, "this I know."

At this another parrot, whose feathers shone like a pale-blue sky, also spoke out. "But if you kill him, O king, men may rather say you were jealous of him. And no king must envy any man."

"This is also apt," said the king, pacing about.

Then a parrot spoke, which was greener than jade. "O king, is Jaqir not a thief? Does he not brag of it? Set him then a test of thieving, and make this test as impossible as may be. And say to him, 'If you can do this, then indeed your skill is that of a poet, an artist, a warrior, a prince. But if you fail you must die.'"

Then the king laughed again. "Well said. But what test?"

At that a small gray parrot flew from its pedestal and, standing on his shoulder, spoke in the king's ear with a jet-black beak. The king said, "O wisest of all my counselors."

In the palace hall Jaqir sat among the grouped courtiers, being pleasant and easy with them in his chains, like a king. But then the king entered and spoke as follows:

"Now, Jaqir, you may have heard, in my private rooms four angels live, that have taken another form. With these four I have discussed your case.

"And here is the verdict. I shall set you now a task that, should you succeed at it, must make you a hero and a legend among men – which happy state you will live to enjoy, since also I will pardon all your previous crimes.

"Such shall be your fame then, that hardly need you try to take anything by stealth. A million doors shall be thrown wide for you, and men will load you with riches, so astonishing will your name have become."

Jaqir had donned a look of flattering attention.

"The task then. You claim yourself a paragon among thieves. You must steal that which is itself a paragon. And as you say you have never taken anything which may be really missed, on this occasion I say you will have to thieve something all mankind shall miss and mourn."

The court stood waiting on the king's words. Jaqir stood waiting, perforce.

And all about, as at such times it must (still must), the world stood waiting, hushing the tongues of sea and wind, the whispers of forests and sands, the thunder of a thousand voiceless things.

"Jaqir, Prince of Thieves, for your life, fly up and steal the Moon from the sky. The task being what it is, I give you a year to do it."

Nine magicians bound Jaqir. He felt the chains they put on him as he had scarcely felt the other chains of iron, thinking optimistically as he had been, that he would soon be out of them.

But the new chains emerged from a haze of iridescent smokes and a rumble of incantations, and had forms like whips and lions, thorns and bears. Meeting his flesh, they disappeared, but he felt them sink in, painless knives, and fasten on his bones and brain and mind.

"You may go where you wish and do what you will and suffer nothing. But if you should attempt, in any way, to abscond, then you will feel the talons and the fangs of that which has bound you, wrapped gnawing inside your body. And should you persist in your evasion, these restraints shall accordingly devour you from within. Run where you choose, seek what help you may, you will die in horrible agony, and soon. Only when you return to the king, your task accomplished fully, and clearly proven, will these strictures lapse – but that at once. Success, success alone, spells your freedom."

So then Jaqir was let go, and it was true enough, honesty being the keynote to his tale so far, that he had no trouble, and could travel about as he wanted. Nor did any idea enter his mind concerning escape. Of all he was or was not, Jaqir was seldom a fool. And he had, in the matter of his arrest, surely spent sufficient foolishness to last a lifetime.

Since he was *not* a fool, Jaqir, from the moment the king had put the bargain to him, had been puzzling how he might do what was demanded.

In the past, many difficult enterprises had come Jaqir's way, and he had solved the problem of each. But it is to be remembered, on none of these had his very existence depended. Nor had it been so strange. One thing must be said, too, the world being no longer as then it was – Jaqir did not at any point contest the notion on the grounds that it was either absurd or unconscionable. Plainly sorcery existed, was everywhere about, and seldom doubted. Plainly the Moon, every night gaudily on show, might be accessible, even to men, for there were legends of such goings on. Thus Jaqir never said to himself, *What madness have I been saddled with?* Only: *How can I effect this extraordinary deed?*

So he went up and down in the city, and later through the landscape beyond, walking mostly, to aid his concentration. Sometimes he would spend the night at an inn, or in some rich house he had never professionally bothered but which had heard of him. And occasionally men did know of him to recognize him, and some knew what had been laid upon him. And unfortunately, the nicest of them would tend to a similar, irritating act. Which was, as the Moon habitually rose in the east, to mock or rant at him. "Aiee, Jaqir. Have you not stolen her *yet*?"

Because the Earth was then flat, the Moon journeyed over and around it, dipping, after moonset, into the restorative seas of chaos that lay beneath the basement of the world. Nor was the Moon of the Flat Earth so very big in circumference (although the size of the Moon varied, influenced by who told – or tells – the tales).

"What is the Moon?" pondered Jaqir at a wayside tavern, sipping sherbet.

"Of what is the Moon *made*?" murmured Jaqir, courting sleep, for novelty, in an olive grove.

"Is it heavy or light? What makes it, or she, glow so vividly? Is it a she?"

"How," muttered Jaqir, striding at evening between fields of silver barley, "am I to get hold of the damnable thing?"

Just then the Moon willfully and unkindly rose again, unstolen, over the fields. Jaqir presently lay down on his back among the barley stalks, gazing up at her as she lifted herself higher and higher. Until at length she reached the apex of heaven, where she seemed for a while to stand still, like one white lily on a stem of stars.

"Oh Moon of my despair," said Jaqir softly, "I fear I shall not master this riddle. I would do better to spend my last year of life – of which I find only nine months remain! – in pleasure, and forget the hopeless task."

At that moment Jaqir heard the stalks rustling a short way off and, sitting up, he saw through the darkness how two figures wandered between the barley. They were a young man and a girl and, from their conduct, lovers in search of a secret bed. With a rueful nod at the ironies of Fate, Jaqir got up and meant to go quietly away. But just then he heard the maiden say, "Not here, the barley is trampled – we must lie where the stalks are thicker, or we may be heard."

"Heard?" asked the youth. "There is no one about."

"Not up in the fields," replied the girl, "but down *below* the fields the demons may be listening in the Underearth."

"Ho," said the youth (another fool), "I do not believe in demons."

"Hush! They exist and are powerful. They love the world by night, as they must avoid the daylight, and like moonlit nights especially, for they are enamored of the Moon, and have made ships and horses with wings in order to reach it. And they say, besides, the nasty magician, Paztak, who lives only a mile along the road from this very place, is nightly visited by the demon Drin, who serve him in return for disgusting rewards."

By now the lovers were a distance off, and only Jaqir's sharp ears had picked up the ends of their talk after which there was silence, save for the sound of moonlight dripping on the barley. But Jaqir went back to the road. His face had become quite purposeful, and perhaps even the Moon, since she watched everything so intently, saw that too.

Now Paztak the magician did indeed live nearby, in his high, brazen tower, shielded by a thicket of tall and not ordinary laurels. Hearing a noise of breakage among these, Paztak undid a window and peered down at Jaqir, who stood below with drawn knife.

"What are you at, unruly felon?" snapped Paztak.

"Defending myself, wise sir, as your bushes bite."

"Then leave them alone. My name is Paztak the Unsociable. Be off, or I shall conjure worse things – to attack you."

"Merciful mage, my life is in the balance. I seek your help, and must loiter till you give it."

The mage clapped his hands, and three yellow, slavering dogs leaped from thin air and also tried to tear Jaqir into bite-size pieces. But, avoiding them, Jaqir sprang at the tower and, since he was clever at such athletics, began climbing up it.

"Wretch!" howled Paztak. And then Jaqir found a creature, part wolverine and part snake, had roped the tower and was striving to wind him as well in its coils. But Jaqir slid free, kicked shut its clashing jaws, and vaulted over its head onto Paztak's windowsill.

"Consider me desperate rather than impolite."

"I consider you *elsewhere*," remarked Paztak with a new and ominous calm.

Next instant Jaqir found himself in a whirlwind, which turned him over and over, and cast him down at last in the depths of a forest.

"So much for the mage," said Jaqir, wiping snake-wolverine, dog and laurel saliva from his boots. "And so much for me, I have had, in my life, an unfair quantity of good luck, and evidently it is all used up."

"Now, now," said a voice from the darkness, "let me get a proper look at you, and see if it is."

And from the shadows shouldered out a dwarf of such incredible hideousness that he might be seen to possess a kind of beauty.

Staring in awe at him then, from his appearance, and the fabulous jewelry with which he was adorned, Jaqir knew him for a Drin.

"Now, now," repeated the Drin, whose coal-black, luxuriant hair swept the forest floor. And he struck a light by the simple means of running his talonous nails – which were painted indigo – along the trunk of a tree.

Holding up his now-flaming hand, the Drin inspected Jaqir, gave a leer and smacked his lips. "Handsome fellow," said the Drin. "What will you offer me if I assist you?"

Jaqir knew a little of the Drin, the lowest caste of demon-kind, who were metalsmiths and artisans of impossible and supernatural ability. He knew, too, as the girl had said, that the Drin required, in exchange for any service to mortals, recompense frequently of a censorable nature. Nor did this Drin seem an exception to the rule.

"Estimable sir," said Jaqir, "did you suppose I needed assistance?"

"I have no doubt of it," said the Drin. "Sometimes I visit the old pest Paztak, and was just now idling in his garden, in chat with a most fascinating woodlouse, when I heard your entreaties, and soon beheld you hurled into this wood. Thinking you more interesting than the mage, I followed. And here I am. What would you have?"

"What would *you* have?" asked Jaqir uneasily.

"Nothing you are not equipped to give."

"Well," said Jaqir resignedly, "we will leave that for the moment. Let *me* first see if you are as cunning as the stones say." And Jaqir thought, pragmatically, After all, what is a little foul and horrible dreadfulness, if it will save me death?

Then he told the Drin of the king's edict, and how he, Jaqir the thief, must thieve the Moon.

When he had done speaking, the Drin fell to the ground and rolled amid the fern, laughing, and honking like a goose, in the most repellent manner.

"You cannot do it," assumed Jaqir.

The Drin arose, and shook out his collar and loin-guard of rubies.

"Know me. I am Yulba, pride of my race, revered even among our demonic high castes of Eshva and Vazdru. Yulba, that the matchless lord, Azhrarn the Beautiful, has petted seven hundred times during his walkings up and down in the Underearth."

"You are to be envied," said Jaqir prudently. He had heard, too, as who had not who had ever heard tales about the demons, of the Prince of Demons, Azhrarn. "But that does not mean you are able to assist me."

"Pish," said the Drin. "It is a fact, no mortal thing, not even the birds of the air, might fly so high as the Moon, let alone any *man* essay it. But I am Yulba. What cannot Yulba do?"

Three nights Jaqir waited in the forest for Yulba to return. On the third night Yulba appeared out of the trunk of a cedar tree, and after him he hauled a loose, glimmering, almost-silky bundle, that clanked and clacketed as it came.

"Thus," said the Drin, and threw it down.

"What is that?"

"Have you no eyes? A carpet I have created, with the help of some elegant spinners of the eight-legged sort, but reinforced with metals fashioned by myself. Everything as delicate as the wings of bees, strong as the scales of dragons. Imbued by me with spells and vapors of the Underearth, as it is," bragged the Drin, "the carpet is sorcerous, and will naturally fly. Even as far as the gardens of the stars, from where, though a puny mortal, you may then inspect your quarry, the Moon."

Jaqir, himself an arch-boaster, regarded Yulba narrowly. But then, Jaqir thought, a boaster might also boast truthfully, as he had himself. So as Yulba undid the carpet and spread it out, Jaqir walked on there. The next second Yulba also bounded aboard. At which the carpet, with no effort, rose straight up between the trees of the forest and into the sky of night.

"Now what do you say?" prompted the Drin.

All the demon race were susceptible to flattery. Jaqir spoke many winning sentences of praise, all the while being careful to keep the breadth of the carpet between them.

Up and up the carpet flew. It was indeed very lovely, all woven of blue metals and red metals, and threaded by silk, and here and there set with countless tiny diamonds that spangled like the stars themselves.

But Jaqir was mostly absorbed by the view of the Earth he now had. Far below, itself like a carpet, unrolled the dark forest and then the silvery fields, cut by a river-like black mirror. And as they flew higher yet, Jaqir came to see the distant city of the king, like a flower garden of pale lights and, further again, lay mountains, and the edges of another country. "How small," mused Jaqir, "has been my life. It occurs to me the gods could never understand men's joy or tribulation, for from the height of their dwelling, how tiny we are to them, less than ants."

"Ants have their own recommendations," answered Yulba.

But the Moon was already standing high in the eastern heaven, still round in appearance, and sheerest white as only white could be.

No command needed be given the carpet. Obviously Yulba had already primed it to its destination. It now veered and soared, straight as an arrow, toward the Moon and, as it did so, Jaqir felt the tinsel roots of the lowest stars brush over his forehead.

And what was the Moon of the Flat Earth, that it might be approached and flown about on a magic carpet? It was, as has been said, maybe a globe containing other lands, but also it was said to be not a globe at all, but, like the Earth itself, a flat disk, yet placed sidelong in the sky, and presenting always a circular wheel of face to the world. And that this globe or disk altered its shape was due to the passage of its own internal sun, now lighting a quarter or a half or a whole of it – or, to the interference of some invisible body coming between it and some other (invisible) light, or to the fact that the Moon was simply a skittish shape-changer, making itself now round, and now a sliver like the paring of a nail.

As they drew ever nearer, Jaqir learned one thing, which in the many stories is a constant – that heat came from the Moon. But (in Jaqir's story) it was an appealing heat, quite welcome in the chilly upper sky. Above, the stars hung, some of them quite close, and they were of all types of shape and shade, all brilliant, but some blindingly so. Of the closer ones, their sparkling roots trailed as if floating in a pond, nourished on some unknown substance. While below, the world seemed only an enormous smudge.

The Drin himself, black eyes glassy, was plainly enraptured by the Moon. Jaqir was caught between wonder and speculation.

Soon enough, the vast luminescence enveloped them, and the heat of the Moon was now like that of a summer morning. Jaqir estimated that the disk might be only the size of a large city, so in his story, that is the size of the Moon.

But Jaqir, as the carpet began obediently to circle round the lunar orb, gazed at it with a proper burglar's care. Soon he could make out details of the surface, which was like nothing so much as an impeccable plate of white porcelain, yet here and there cratered, perhaps by the infrequent fall of a star. And these craters had a dim blue ghostly sheen, like that of a blue beryl.

When the carpet swooped yet nearer in, Jaqir next saw that the plate of the moon had actually a sort of landscape, for there were kinds of smooth, low, blanched hills, and here and there something which might be a carven watercourse, though without any water in it. And there were also strewn boulders, and other stones, which must be prodigious in girth, but they were all like the rarest pearls.

Jaqir was seized by a desire to touch the surface of the hot, white Moon.

He voiced this.

Yulba scowled, disturbed in his rapturous trance.

"Oh ignorant man, even my inspired carpet may go no closer, or the magnetic pull of the Moon will tug, and we crash down there."

As he spoke, they passed slowly around the globe, and began moving across the *back* of the Moon, which, until that minute, few mortals had ever seen.

This side lay in a deep violet shadow, turned from the Earth, and tilted upward somewhat at the vault of the sky. It was cooler here, and Jaqir fancied he could hear a strange sound, like harps playing softly, but nothing was to be seen. His hands itched to have something away.

"Peerless Yulba, in order to make a plan of assault, I shall need to get, for reference, some keepsake of the Moon."

"You ask too much," grumbled Yulba.

"Can you not do it? But you are *Yulba*," smarmed Jaqir, "lord among Drin, favorite of the Prince of Demons. What is there Yulba *cannot* do? And, I thought we were to be friends . . ."

Yulba cast a look at Jaqir, then the Drin frowned at the Moon with such appalling ugliness, Jaqir turned his head.

"I have a certain immense power over stones," said the Drin, "seeing my kind work with them. If I can call you a stone from the Moon, what is it worth?"

Jaqir, who was not above the art of lying either, lied imaginatively at some length, until Yulba lumbered across the carpet and seemed about to demonstrate affection. "*Not* however," declared Jaqir, "any of this, until my task is completed. Do you expect me to be able to concentrate on such events, when my life still hangs by a thread?"

Yulba withdrew once more to the carpet's border. He began a horrible whistling, which set on edge not only Jaqir's teeth but every bone in his body. Nevertheless, in a while, a single pebble, only about the size of an apricot, came flying up and struck Yulba in the eye.

"See – I am blinded!" screeched Yulba, thrashing on the carpet, but he was not. Nor would he then give up the pebble. But soon enough, as their transport – which by now was apparently tiring – sank away from the Moon, Jaqir rolled a moment against the Drin, as if losing his balance.

Thereafter the moon-pebble was in Jaqir's pocket.

What a time they had been on their travels. Even as the carpet flopped, wearily and bumpily now, toward the Earth, a blossoming of rose pink appeared in the east.

This pretty sight, of course, greatly upset Yulba, for demons feared the Sun, and with good reason, it could burn them to ashes.

"Down, down, make haste accursed fleabag of a carpet!" ranted he, and so they rapidly fell, and next landed with a splashy thump in a swamp, from which green monkeys and red parakeets erupted at their arrival.

"I shall return at dusk. Remember what I have risked for you!" growled Yulba.

"It is graven on my brain."

Then the Drin vanished into the ground, taking with him the carpet. The Sun rose, and the amazing Moon, now once more far away, faded and set like a dying lamp.

By midday, Jaqir had forced a path from the swamp. He sat beneath a mango tree and ate some of the ripe fruit, and stared at the moon-pebble.

It shone, even in the daylight, like a milky flame. "You are more wonderful than anything I have ever thieved. But still I do not see how I can rob the sky of that other jewel, the Moon."

Then he considered, for one rash moment, running away. And the safeguarding bonds of the king's magicians twanged around his skeleton.

Jaqir desisted, and lay back to sleep.

In sleep, a troop of tormenters paraded.

The cast-off mistress who had betrayed him slapped his face with a wet fish. Yulba strutted, seeming hopeful. Next came men who cried, "Of what worth is this stupid Jaqir, who has claimed he can steal an egg from beneath a sleeping bird."

Affronted in his slumber, Jaqir truthfully replied that he had done that very thing. But the mockers were gone.

In the dream then Jaqir sat up, and looked once more at the shining pebble lying in his hand.

"Although I might steal a million eggs from beneath a million birds, what use to try for this? I am doomed and shall give in."

Just then something fluttered from the mango tree, which was also there in the dream. It was a small gray parrot. Flying down, it settled directly upon the opalescent stone in Jaqir's palm and put out its light.

"Well, my fine bird, this is no egg for you to hatch."

The parrot spoke. "Think, Jaqir, what you see, and what you say."

Jaqir thought. "Is it possible?"

And at that he woke a second time.

The Sun was high above, and over and over across it and the sky, birds flew about, distinct as black writing on the blue.

"No bird of the air can fly so high as the Moon," said Jaqir. He added, "But the Drin have a mythic knack with magical artifacts and clockworks."

Later, the Sun lowered itself and went down. Yulba came bouncing from the ground, coyly clad in extra rubies, with a garland of lotuses in his hair.

"Now, now," commenced Yulba, lurching forward.

Sternly spoke Jaqir, "I am not yet at liberty, as you are aware. However, I have a scheme. And knowing your unassailable wisdom and authority, only you, the mighty Yulba, best and first among Drin, can manage it."

In Underearth it was an exquisite dusk. It was always dusk there, or a form of dusk. As clear as day in the upper world, it was said, yet more radiantly somber. Sunless, naturally, for the reasons given above.

Druhim Vanashta, the peerless city of demonkind, stretched in a noose of shimmering nonsolar brilliance, out of which pierced, like needles, chiseled towers of burnished steel and polished corundum, domes of faceted crystal. While about the gem-paved streets and sable parks strolled or paced or strode or lingered the demons. Night-black of hair and eye, snow-frozen-white of complexion, the high-caste Vazdru and their mystic servants, the Eshva. All of whom were so painfully beautiful, it amounted to an insult.

Presently, along an avenue, there passed Azhrarn, Prince of Demons, riding a black horse, whose mane and tail were hyacinth blue. And if the beauty of the Eshva and Vazdru amounted to an insult, that of Azhrarn was like the stroke of death.

He seemed himself idle enough, Azhrarn. He seemed too musing on something as he slowly rode, oblivious, it appeared, to those who bowed to the pavement at his approach, whose eyes had spilled, at sight of him, looks of adoration. They were all in love with Azhrarn.

A voice spoke from nowhere at all.

"Azhrarn, Lord Wickedness, you gave up the world, but the world does not give up you. Oh Azhrarn, Master of Night, what are the Drin doing by their turgid lake, hammering and hammering?"

Azhrarn had reined in the demon horse. He glanced leisurely about.

Minutes elapsed. He too spoke, and his vocality was like the rest of him.

"The Drin do hammer at things. That is how the Drin pass most of eternity."

"Yet how," said the voice, "do *you* pass eternity, Lord Wickedness?"

"Who speaks to me?" softly said Azhrarn.

The voice replied, "Perhaps merely yourself, the part of you that you discard, the part of you which yearns after the world."

"Oh," said Azhrarn. "The world."

The voice did not pronounce another syllable, but along an adjacent wall a slight mark appeared, rather like a scorch.

Azhrarn rode on. The avenue ended at a park, where willows of liquid amber let down their watery resinous hair, to a mercury pool. Black peacocks with seeing eyes of turquoise and emerald in their tails, turned their heads and all their feathers to gaze at him.

From between the trees came three Eshva, who obeised themselves.

"What," said Azhrarn, "are the Drin making by their lake?"

The Eshva sighed voluptuously. The sighs said (for the Eshva never used ordinary speech), "The Drin are making metal birds."

"Why?" said Azhrarn.

The Eshva grew downcast; they did not know. Melancholy enfolded them among the tall black grasses of the lawn, and then one of the Vazdru princes came walking through the garden.

"Yes?" said Azhrarn.

"My Prince, there is a Drin who was to fashion for me a ring, which he has neglected," said the Vazdru. "He is at some labor for a human man he is partial to. They are *all* at this labor."

Azhrarn, interested, was, for a moment, more truly revealed. The garden waxed dangerously brighter, the mercury in the pool boiled. The amber hardened and the peacocks shut every one of their 450 eyes.

"Yes?" Azhrarn murmured again.

"The Drin, who is called Yulba, has lied to them all. He has told them you yourself, my matchless lord, require a million clockwork birds that can fly as high as the Earth's Moon. Because of *this*, they work ceaselessly. This Yulba is a nuisance. When he is found out, they will savage him, then bury him in some cavern, walling it up with rocks, leaving him there a million years for his million birds. And so I shall not receive my ring."

Azhrarn smiled. Cut by the smile, as if by the slice of a sword, leaves scattered from the trees. It was suddenly autumn in the garden. When autumn stopped, Azhrarn had gone away.

Chang-thrang went the Drin hammers by the lake outside Druhim Vanashta. *Whirr* and *pling* went the uncanny mechanisms of half-formed sorcerous birds of cinnabar, bronze and iron. Already-finished sorcerous birds hopped and flapped about the lakeshore, frightening the beetles and snakes. Mechanical birds flew over in curious formations, like demented swallows, darkening the Underearth's gleaming day-dusk, now and then letting fall droppings of a peculiar sort.

Eshva came and went, drifting on Vazdru errands. Speechless enquiries wafted to the Drin caves: Where is the necklace of rain vowed for the Princess Vasht? Where is the singing book reserved for the Prince Hazrond?

"We are busy elsewhere at Azhrarn's order," chirped the Drin.

They were all dwarfs, all hideous, and each one lethal, ridiculous and a genius. Yulba strode among them, criticizing their work, so now and then there was also a fight for the flying omnipresent birds to unburden their bowels upon.

How had Yulba fooled the Drin? He was no more Azhrarn's favorite than any of them. All the Drin boasted as Yulba had. Perhaps it was only this: turning his shoulder to the world of mankind, Azhrarn had forced the jilted world to pursue him underground. In ways both graphic and insidious, the rejected one permeated Underearth. Are you tired of me? moaned the world to Azhrarn. Do you hate me? Do I bore you? See how inventive I am. See how I can still ensnare you fast.

But Azhrarn did not go to the noisy lake. He did not summon Yulba. And Yulba, puffed with his own cleverness, obsessively eager to hold Jaqir to his bargain, had forgotten all accounts have a reckoning. *Chung-clungk* went the hammers. *Brakk* went the thick heads of the Drin, banged together by critical, unwise Yulba.

Then at last the noise ended.

The hammering and clamoring were over.

Of the few Vazdru who had come to stare at the birds, less than a few remarked that the birds had vanished.

The Drin were noted skulking about their normal toil again, constructing wondrous jewelry and toys for the upper demons. If they waited breathlessly for Azhrarn to compliment them on their bird-work, they did so in vain. But such omissions had happened in the past, the never-ceasing past-present-future of Underearth.

Just as they might have pictured him, Azhrarn stood in a high window of Druhim Vanashta, looking at his city of needles and crystals.

Perhaps it was seven mortal days after the voice had spoken to him.

Perhaps three months.

He heard a sound within his mind. It was not from his city, nor was it unreal. Nor actual. Presently he sought a magical glass that would show him the neglected world.

How ferocious the stars, how huge and cruelly glittering, like daggers.

How they exalted, unrivaled now.

★   ★   ★

The young king went one by one to all the windows of his palace. Like Azhrarn miles below (although he did not know it), the young king looked a long while at his city. But mostly he looked up into the awful sky.

Thirty-three nights had come and gone, without the rising of the Moon.

In the king's city there had been at first shouts of bewildered amazement.

Then prayers. Then, a silence fell which was as loud as screaming.

If the world had lost the Sun, the world would have perished and died. But losing the Moon, it was as if the soul of this world had been put out.

Oh those black nights, blacker than blackness, those yowling spikes of stars dancing in their vitriolic glory – which gave so little light.

What murders and rapes and worser crimes were committed under cover of such a dark? As if a similar darkness had been called up from the mental guts of mankind, like subservient to like. While earth-over, priests offered to the gods, who never noticed.

The courtiers who had applauded, amused, the judgement of the witty young king now shrank from him. He moved alone through the excessively lamped and benighted palace, wondering if he was now notorious through all the world for his thoughtless error. And so wondering, he entered the room where, on their marble pedestals, perched his angels.

"What have you done?" said the king.

Not a feather stirred. Not an eye winked.

"By the gods – may they forgive me – what? What did you make *me* do?"

"*You* are king," said the scarlet parrot. "It is your word, not ours, which is law."

And the blue parrot said, "We are parrots, why name us angels? We have been taught to speak, that is all. What do you expect?"

And the jade parrot said, "I forget now what it was you asked of us." And put its head under its wing.

Then the king turned to the gray parrot. "What do you have to say? It was your final advice which drove me to demand the Moon be stolen – as if I thought any man might do it."

"King," said the gray parrot, "it was your sport to call four parrots 'angels'. Your sport to offer a man an impossible task as the alternative to certain death. You have lived as if living is a silly game. But you are mortal, and a king."

"You shame me," said the king.

"We are, of course," said the gray parrot, "truly angels, disguised. To shame men is part of our duty."

"What must I do?"

The gray parrot said, "Go down, for Jaqir, Thief of Thieves, has returned to your gate. And he is followed by his shadow."

"Are not all men so followed?" asked the king perplexedly.

The parrot did not speak again.

Let it be said, Jaqir, who now entered the palace, between the glaring, staring guards of the king, was himself in terrible awe at what he had achieved. Ever since succeeding at his task, he had not left off trembling inwardly. However, outwardly he was all smiles, and in his best attire.

"See, the wretch's garments are as fine as a lord's. His rings are gold. Even his shadow looks well dressed! And this miscreant it is who has stolen the Moon and ruined the world with blackest night."

The king stood waiting, with the court about him.

Jaqir bowed low. But that was all he did, after which *he* stood waiting, meeting the king's eyes with his own.

"Well," said the king. "It seems you have done what was asked of you."

"So it does seem," said Jaqir calmly.

"Was it then easy?"

"As easy," said Jaqir, "as stealing an egg."

"But," said the king. He paused, and a shudder ran over the hall, a shuddering of men and women, and also of the flames in all the countless lamps.

"*But?*" pressed haughty Jaqir.

"It might be said by some, that the Moon – which is surely

not an egg – has disappeared, and another that you may have removed it. After all," said the king stonily, "if one assumes the Moon may be pilfered at all, how am I to be certain the robber is yourself? Maybe others are capable of it. Or, too, a natural disaster has simply overcome the orb, a coincidence most convenient for you."

"Sir," said Jaqir, "were you not the king, I would answer you in other words that I do. But king you are. And I have proof."

And then Jaqir took out from his embroidered shirt the moon-pebble, which even in the light of the lamps blazed with a perfect whiteness. And so like the Moon it was for radiance that many at once shed tears of nostalgia on seeing it. While at Jaqir's left shoulder, his night-black shadow seemed for an instant also to flicker with fire.

As for the king, now he trembled too. But like Jaqir, he did not show it.

"Then," said the king, "be pardoned of your crimes. You have surmounted the test, and are directly loosed from those psychic bonds my magicians set on you, therefore entirely physically at liberty, and besides, a legendary hero. One last thing . . ."

"Yes?" asked Jaqir.

"Where have you put it?"

"What?" said Jaqir, rather stupidly.

"That which you stole."

"It was not a part of our bargain to tell you this. You have seen by the proof of this stone I have got the Moon. Behold, the sky is black."

The king said quietly, "You do not mean to keep it."

"Generally I do keep what I take."

"I will give you great wealth, Jaqir, which I think anyway you do not need, for they say you are as rich as I. Also, I will give you a title to rival my own. You can have what you wish. Now swear you will return the Moon to the sky."

Jaqir lowered his eyes. "I must consider this."

"Look," they whispered, the court of the king, "even his shadow listens to him."

Jaqir, too, felt his shadow listening at his shoulder.

He turned, and found the shadow had eyes.

Then the shadow spoke, more quietly than the king, and not one in the hall did not hear it. While every flame in every lamp spun like a coin, died, revived and continued burning upside down.

"King, you are a fool. Jaqir, you are another fool. And who and what am I?"

Times had changed. There are always stories, but they are not always memorized. Only the king, and Jaqir the thief, had the understanding to plummet to their knees. And they cried as one, "*Azhrarn!*"

"Walk upon the terrace with me," said Azhrarn. "We will admire the beauty of the leaden night."

The king and Jaqir found that they got up, and went on to the terrace, and no one else stirred, not even hand or eye.

Around the terrace stood some guards like statues. At the terrace's center stood a chariot that seemed constructed of black and silver lava, and drawn by similarly laval dragons.

"Here is our conveyance," said Azhrarn, charmingly. "Get in."

In they got, the king and the thief. Azhrarn also sprang up, and took and shook the reins of the dragons, and these great ebony lizards hissed and shook out in turn their wings, which clapped against the black night and seemed to strike off bits from it. Then the chariot dove up into the air, shaking off the Earth entire, and green sparks streamed from the chariot wheels.

Neither the king nor Jaqir had stamina – or idiocy – enough to question Azhrarn. They waited meekly as two children in the chariot's back, gaping now at Azhrarn's black eagle wings of cloak, that every so often buffeted them, almost breaking their ribs, or at the world falling down and down below like something dropped.

But then, high in the wild, tipsy-making upper air, Jaqir did speak, if not to Azhrarn.

"King, I tricked you. I did not steal the Moon."

"Who then stole it?"

"No one."

"A riddle."

At which they saw Azhrarn had partly turned. They glimpsed his profile, and a single eye that seemed more like the night than the night itself was.

And they shut their mouths.

On raced the dragons.

Below raced the world.

Then everything came to a halt. Combing the sky with claws and wheels, dragons and chariot stood static on the dark.

Azhrarn let go the jeweled reins.

All around spangled the stars. These now appeared less certain of themselves. The brighter ones had dimmed their glow, the lesser hid behind the vapors of night. Otherwise, everywhere lay blackness, only that.

In the long, musician's fingers of the Prince of Demons was a silver pipe, shaped like some sort of slender bone. Azhrarn blew upon the pipe.

There was no sound, yet something seemed to pass through the skulls of the king and of Jaqir, as if a barbed thread had been pulled through from ear to ear. The king swooned – he was only a king. Jaqir rubbed his temples and stayed upright – he was a professional of the working classes.

And so it was Jaqir who saw, in reverse, that which he had already seen happen the other way about.

He beheld a black cloud rising (where before it had settled) and behind the cloud suddenly something incandescent blinked and dazzled. He beheld how the cloud, breaking free of these blinks of palest fire (where before it had obscured said fire), ceased to be one entity, and became instead one million separate flying pieces. He saw, as he had seen before when first they burst up from the ground in front of him, and rushed into the sky, that these were a million curious birds. They had feathers of cinnabar and bronze, sinews of brass; they had clockworks of iron and steel.

Between the insane crowded battering of their wings, Jaqir watched the Moon reappear, where previously (scanning the

night, as he stood by Yulba in a meadow) he had watched the
Moon *put out*, all the birds flew down against her, covering and
smothering her. Unbroken by their landing on her surface,
they had roosted there, drawn to and liking the warmth, as
Yulba had directed them with his sorcery.

But now Azhrarn had negated Yulba's powers – which were
little enough among demons. The mechanical birds swarmed
round and round the chariot, aggravating the dragons somewhat. The birds had no eyes, Jaqir noticed. They gave off great
heat where the Moon had toasted their metals. Jaqir looked at
them as if for the first, hated them, and grew deeply embarrassed.

Yet the Moon – oh, the Moon. Uncovered and alight, how
brilliantly it or she blazed now. Had she ever been so bright?
Had her sojourn in darkness done her good?

End to end, she poured her flame over the Earth below. Not
a mountain that did not have its spire of silver, not a river its
highlight of diamond.

The seas lashed and struggled with joy, leaping to catch her
snows upon the crests of waves and dancing dolphin. And in
the windows of mankind, the lamps were doused, and like the
waves, men leaned upward to wash their faces in the Moon.

Then gradually, a murmur, a thunder, a roar, a gushing sigh
rose swirling from the depths of the Flat Earth, as if at last the
world had stopped holding its breath.

"What did you promise Yulba," asked Azhrarn of Jaqir, mild
as a killing frost, "in exchange for this slight act?"

"The traditional favor," muttered Jaqir.

"Did he receive payment?"

"I prevaricated. Not yet, lord Prince."

"You are spared then. Part of his punishment shall be
permanently to avoid your company. But what punishment for
you, thief? And what punishment for your king?"

Jaqir did not speak. Nor did the king, though he had recovered his senses.

Both men were educated in the tales, the king more so. Both
men turned ashen, and the king accordingly more ashen.

Then Azhrarn addressed the clockwork birds in one of the demon tongues, and they were immediately gone. And only the white banner of the moonlight was there across the night.

Now Azhrarn, by some called also Lord of Liars, was not perhaps above lying in his own heart. It seems so. Yet maybe tonight he looked upon the Moon, and saw in the Moon's own heart, the woman that once he had loved, the woman who had been named for the Moon. Because of her, and all that had followed, Azhrarn had turned his back upon the world – or attempted to turn it.

And even so here he was, high in the vault of the world's heaven, drenched in earthly moonshine, contemplating the chastisement of mortal creatures whose lives, to his immortal life, were like the green sparks which had flashed and withered on the chariot wheels.

The chariot plunged. The atmosphere scalded at the speed of its descent. It touched the skin of the Earth more slightly than a cobweb. The mortal king and the mortal thief found themselves rolling away downhill, toward fields of barley and a river. The chariot, too, was gone. Although in their ears as they rolled, equal in their rolling as never before, and soon never to be again, king and thief heard Azhrarn's extraordinary voice, which said, "Your punishment you have already. You are human. I cannot improve upon that."

Thus, the Moon shone in the skies of night, interrupted only by an infrequent cloud. The king resumed his throne. The four angels – who were or were not parrots – or only meddlers – sat on their perches waiting to give advice, or to avoid giving it. And Jaqir – Jaqir went away to another city.

Here, under a different name, he lived on his extreme wealth, in a fine house with gardens. Until one day he was robbed of all his gold (and even of the moon-pebble) by a talented thief. "Is it the gods who exact their price at last, or Another, who dwells further down?" But by then Jaqir was older, for mortal lives moved and move swiftly. He had lost his taste for his work by then. So he returned to the king's city, and to the door of the merchant's wife who had been his mistress.

"I am sorry for what I said to you," said Jaqir. "I am sorry for what I did to you," said she. The traveling merchant had recently departed on another, more prolonged journey, to make himself, reincarnation-wise, a new life after death. Meanwhile, though the legend of a moon-thief remained, men had by then forgotten Jaqir. So he married the lady and they existed not unhappily, which shows their flexible natures.

But miles below, Yulba did not fare so well. For Azhrarn had returned to the Underearth on the night of the Moon's rescue, and said to him, "Bad little Drin. Here are your million birds. Since you are so proud of them, be one of them." And in this way Azhrarn demonstrated that the world no longer mattered to him a jot, only his own kind mattered enough that he would make their lives Hell-under-Earth. Or, so it would seem.

But Yulba had changed to a clockwork bird, number one million and one.

Eyeless, still able to see, flapping over the melanic vistas of the demon country, blotting up the luminous twilight, cawing, clicking, letting fall droppings, yearning for the warmth of the Moon, yearning to be a Drin again, yearning for Azhrarn, and for Jaqir – who by that hour had already passed himself from the world, for demon time was not the time of mortals.

As for the story, that of Jaqir and Yulba and the Moon, it had become as it had and has become, or *un*-become. And who knows but that, in another little while, it will be forgotten, as most things are. Even the Moon is no longer *that* Moon, nor the Earth, nor the sky. The centuries fly, eternity is endless.

The Big Sky

Charles de Lint

Charles de Lint offers a modern, not traditionally religious take on guardian angels with the "watchers" in "The Big Sky". The concept of special spirits protecting individuals or groups is probably as old as humanity. Judaic belief includes angels as heavenly guides and intercessors. Muslims also have guardian angels. But guardian angels linked to individual souls from birth to death to protect, inspire and aid in salvation are associated most closely with Christianity, particularly with Catholicism. Although not an article of faith, it is a firm tradition of the Church. As St Jerome wrote in the fourth century, "How great the dignity of the soul, since each one has from his birth an angel commissioned to guard it."

"We need Death to be a friend. It is best to have a friend as a traveling companion when you have so far to go together."
—attributed to Jean Cocteau

1

She was sitting in John's living room when he got home from the recording studio that night, comfortably ensconced on the sofa, legs stretched out, ankles crossed, a book propped open on her lap which she was pretending to read. The fact that all the lights in the house had been off until he turned them on didn't seem to faze her in the least. She continued her pretense, as though she could see equally well in the light or dark and it made no difference to her whether the lights were on or off. At least she had the book turned right side up, John noted.

"How did you get in?" he asked her.

She didn't seem to present any sort of a threat – beyond having gotten into his locked house, of course – so he was more concerned with how she'd been able to enter than for his own personal safety. At the sound of his voice, she looked up in surprise. She laid the book down on her lap, finger inserted between the pages to hold her place.

"You can see me?" she said.

"Jesus."

John shook his head. She certainly wasn't shy. He set his fiddle case down by the door. After dropping his jacket down on top of it, he went into the living room and sat down in the chair across the coffee table from her.

"What do you think?" he went on. "Of course I can see you."

"But you're not supposed to be able to see me – unless it's time and that doesn't seem right. I mean, really. I'd know, if anybody, whether or not it was time."

She frowned, gaze fixed on him, but she didn't really appear to be studying him. It was more as though she were looking into some unimaginably far and unseen distance. Her eyes focused suddenly and he shifted uncomfortably under the weight of her attention.

"Oh, I see what happened," she said. "I'm so sorry."

John leaned forward, resting his hands on his knees. "Let's try this again. Who are you?"

"I'm your watcher. Everybody has one."

"My watcher."

She nodded. "We watch over you until your time has come, then if you can't find your own way, we take you on. They call us the little deaths, but I've never much cared for the sound of that, do you?"

John sighed. He settled back in his chair to study his unwanted guest. She was no one he knew, though she could easily have fit in with his crowd. He put her at about twenty-something, a slender five foot two with pixie features made more fey by the crop of short blond hair that stuck up from her head with all the unruliness of a badly mowed lawn. She wore black combat boots; khaki trousers, baggy, with two or three pockets running up either leg; a white T-shirt that hugged her thin chest like a second skin. She had little in the way of jewelry – a small silver ring in her left nostril and another in the lobe of her left ear – and no make-up.

"Do you have a name?" he tried.

"Everybody's got a name."

John waited a few heartbeats. "And yours is?" he asked when no reply was forthcoming.

"I don't think I should tell you."

"Why not?"

"Well, once you give someone your name, it's like opening the door to all sorts of possibilities, isn't it? Any sort of relationship could develop from that, and it's just not a good idea for us to have an intimate relationship with our charges."

"I can assure you," John told her. "We're in no danger of having a relationship – intimate or otherwise."

"Oh," she said. She didn't look disappointed so much as annoyed. "Dakota," she added.

"I'm sorry?"

"You wanted to know my name."

John nodded. "That's right. I . . . oh, I get it. Your name's Dakota?"

"Bingo."

"And you've been . . . watching me?"

"Well, not just you. Except for when we're starting out, we look out after any number of people."

"I see," John said. "And how many people do you watch?"

She shrugged. "Oh, dozens."

That figured, John thought. It was the story of his life. He couldn't even get the undivided attention of a loony.

She swung her boots to the floor and set the book she was holding on the coffee table between them.

"Well, I guess we should get going," she said.

She stood up and gave him an expectant look, but John remained where he was sitting.

"It's a long way to the gates," she told him.

He didn't have a clue as to what she was talking about, but he was sure of one thing.

"I'm not going anywhere with you," he said.

"But you have to."

"Says who?"

She frowned at him. "You just do. It's obvious that you won't be able to find your way by yourself, and if you stay here you're just going to start feeling more and more alienated and confused."

"Let me worry about that," John said.

"Look," she said. "We've gotten off on the wrong foot – my fault, I'm sure. I had no idea it was time for you to go already. I'd just come by to check on you before heading off to another appointment."

"Somebody else that you're *watching*?"

"Exactly," she replied, missing, or more probably ignoring the sarcastic tone of his voice. "There's no way around this, you know. You need my help to get to the gates."

"What gates?"

She sighed. "You're really in denial about all of this, aren't you?"

"You were right about one thing," John told her. "I am feeling confused, but it's only about what you're doing here and how you got in."

"I don't have time for this."

"Me, neither. So maybe you should go."

That earned him another frown.

"Fine," she said. "But don't wait too long to call me. If you change too much, I won't be able to find you and nobody else can help you."

"Because you're my personal watcher."

"No wonder you don't have many friends," she said. "You're really not a very nice person, are you?"

"I'm only like this with people who break into my house."

"But I didn't . . . oh, never mind. Just remember my name and don't wait too long to call me."

"Not that I'd want to," John said, "but I don't even have your number."

"Just call my name and I'll come," she said. "If it's not too late. Like I said, I might not be able to recognize you if you wait too long."

Though he was trying to take this all in his stride, John couldn't help but start to feel a little creeped out at the way she was going on. He'd never realized that crazy people could seem so normal except for what they were saying, of course.

"Goodbye," he said.

She bit back whatever it was that she was going to say and gave him a brusque nod. For one moment, he half expected her to walk through a wall – the evening had taken that strange a turn – but she merely crossed the living room and let herself out the front door. John waited for a few moments, then rose and set the deadbolt. He walked through the house, checking the windows and back door, before finally going upstairs to his bedroom.

He thought he might have trouble getting to sleep – the woman's presence had raised far more questions than it had answered – but he was so tired from twelve straight hours in the studio that it was more a question of could he get all his clothes off and crawl under the blankets before he faded right out. He had one strange moment: when he turned off the light, he made the mistake of looking directly at the bulb. His uninvited guest's features hung in the darkness along with a hundred dancing spots of light before he was able to blink them away. But the moment didn't last long, and he was soon asleep.

2

He didn't realize that he'd forgotten to set his alarm last night until he woke up and gave the clock a bleary look. Eleven fifteen. Christ, he was late.

He got up, shaved, and took a quick shower. You'd think someone would have called him from the studio, he thought as he started to get dressed. He was doing session work on Darlene Flatt's first album, and the recording had turned into a race to get the album finished before her money ran out. He had two solos up first thing this morning, and he couldn't understand why no one had called to see where he was.

There was no time for breakfast – he didn't have much of an appetite at the moment anyway. He'd grab some coffee and a bagel at the deli around the corner from the studio. He tugged on his jeans, then carried his boots out into the living room and phoned the studio while he put them on. All he got was ringing at the other end.

"Come on," he muttered. "Somebody pick it up."

How could there be nobody there to answer?

It was as he was cradling the receiver that he saw the book lying on the coffee table, reminding him of last night's strange encounter. He picked the book up and looked at it, turning it over in his hands. There was something different about it this morning. Something wrong. And then he realized what it was. The color dust wrapper had gone monochrome. The book and . . . His gaze settled on his hand and he dropped the book in shock. He stared at his hand, turning it front to back, then looked wildly around the living room.

Oh, Jesus. Everything was black and white.

He'd been so bleary when he woke up that he hadn't noticed that the world had gone monochrome on him overnight. He'd had a vague impression of gloominess when he got up, but he hadn't really thought about it. He'd simply put it down to it being a particularly overcast day. But this . . . this.

It was impossible.

His gaze was drawn to the window. The light coming in was

devoid of color where it touched his furniture and walls, but outside . . . He walked slowly to the window and stared at his lawn, the street beyond it, the houses across the way. Everything was the way it was supposed to be. The day was cloudless, the colors so vivid, the sunlight so bright it hurt his eyes. The richness of all that color and light burned his retinas.

He stood there until tears formed in his eyes and he had to turn away. He covered his eyes with his hands until the pain faded. When he took his palms away, his hands were still leached of color. The living room was a thousand monochrome shades of black and white. Numbly, he walked to his front door and flung it open. The blast of color overloaded the sensory membranes of his eyes. He knelt down where he'd tossed his jacket last night and scrabbled about in its pockets until he found a pair of shades.

The sunglasses helped when he turned back to the open door. It still hurt to look at all that color, but the pain was much less than it had been. He shuffled out onto his porch, down the steps. He looked at what he could see of himself. Hands and arms. His legs. All monochrome. He was like a black and white cut-out that someone had stuck onto a colored background.

I'm dreaming, he thought.

He could feel the start of a panic attack. It was like the slight nervousness that sometimes came when he stepped on stage – the kind that came when he was backing up someone he'd never played with before, only increased a hundredfold. Sweat beaded on his temples and under his arms. It made his shirt clammy and stick to his back. His hands began to shake so much that he had to hug himself to make them stop.

He was dreaming, or he'd gone insane.

Movement caught his eye down the street and he recognized one of his neighbors. He stumbled in the man's direction.

"Bob!" he called. "Bob, you've got to help me."

The man never even looked in his direction. John stepped directly in front of him on the sidewalk and Bob walked right into him, knocking him down. But Bob hadn't felt a thing, John realized. Hadn't seen him, hadn't felt the impact, was just walking on down the street as if John had simply ceased to exist for him.

John fled back into the house. He slammed the door, locked it. He pulled the curtains in the living room and started to pace, from the fireplace to the hallway, back again, back and forth, back and forth. At one point he caught sight of the book he'd dropped earlier. Slowly, he walked over, to where it lay and picked it up. He remembered last night's visitor again. Her voice returned to him.

If you change too much . . .

This was all her fault, he thought.

He threw the book down and shouted her name.

"Yes?"

Her voice came from directly behind him and he started violently.

"Jesus," he said. "You could've given me a heart attack."

"It's a little late for that."

She was wearing the same clothes she'd worn last night except today there was a leather bomber jacket on over her T-shirt and she wore a hat that was something like a derby except the brim was wider. There was one other difference. Like himself, like the rest of his house, she'd been leached of all color.

"What did you do to me?" he demanded.

She reached out and took his hand to lead him over to the sofa. He tried to pull free from her grip, but she was stronger than she looked.

"Sit down," she said. "And I'll try to explain."

Her voice was soothing and calm, the way one would talk to an upset child – or a madman. John was feeling a little bit like both at the moment, helpless as a child and out of his mind. But the lulling quality of her voice and the gentle manner of her touch helped still the wild drumming of his pulse.

"Look," he said. "I don't know what you've done to me – I don't know how you've done this to me or why – but I just want to get back to normal, okay? If I made you mad last night, I'm sorry, but you've got to understand. It was pretty weird to find you in my house the way I did."

"I know," she said. "I didn't realize you could see me, or I would have handled it differently myself. But you took me by surprise."

"I took *you* by surprise?"

"What do you remember about last night?" she asked.

"I came home and found you in my living room."

"No, before that."

"I was at High Lonesome Sounds, working on Darlene's album."

She nodded. "And what happened between when you left the studio and came home?"

"I . . . I don't remember."

"You were hit by a car," she said. "A drunk driver."

"No way," John said, shaking his head. "I'd remember something like that."

She took his hand. "You died instantly, John Narraway."

"I . . . I . . ."

He didn't want to believe her, but her words settled inside him with a finality that could only be the truth.

"It's not something that anyone could have foreseen," she went on. "You were supposed to live a lot longer – that's why I was so surprised that you could see me. It's never happened to me like that before."

John had stopped listening to her after she'd said, "You were supposed to live a lot longer." He clung to that phrase, hope rushing through him.

"So it was a mistake," he said.

Dakota nodded.

"So what happens now?" he asked.

"I'll take you to the gates."

"No, wait a minute. You just said it was a mistake. Can't you go back to whoever's in charge and explain that?"

"If there's anyone in charge," she said, "I've never met or heard of them."

"But—"

"I understand your confusion and your fear. Really I do. It comes from the suddenness of your death and my not being there to help you adjust. That's the whole reason I exist – to help people like you who are unwilling or too confused to go on by themselves. I wasn't ready to go myself when my time came."

"Well, I'm not ready, either."

Dakota shook her head. "It's not the same thing. I wasn't ready to go because when I saw how much some people need help to reach the gates, I knew I had to stay and help them. It was like a calling. You just aren't willing to accept what happened to you."

"Well, Christ. Who would?"

"Most people. I've seen how their faces light up when they step through the gates. You can't imagine the joy in their eyes."

"Have you been through yourself?" John asked.

"No. But I've had glimpses of what lies beyond. You know how sometimes the sky just seems to be so big it goes on forever?"

John nodded.

"You stand there and look up," she went on, "and the stars seem so close you feel as though you could just reach up and touch them, but at the same time the sky itself is enormous and has no end. It's like that, except that you can feel your heart swelling inside you, big enough to fill the whole of that sky."

"If what's waiting beyond these gates is so wonderful," John wanted to know, "why haven't you gone through?"

"One day I will. I think about it more and more all the time. But what I'm doing now is important and I'm needed. There are never enough of us."

"Maybe I'll become a watcher instead – like you."

"It's not something one takes on lightly," Dakota said. "You can't just stop when you get tired of doing it. You have to see through all of your responsibilities first, make sure that all of your charges have gone on, that none are left behind to fend for themselves. You share the joys of your charges, but you share their sorrows, too. And the whole time you know them, you're aware of their death. You watch them plan, you watch their lives and the tangle of their relationships grow more complex as they grow older, but the whole time you're aware of their end."

"I could do that," John said.

Dakota shook her head. "You have always been sparing with your kindnesses. It's why your circle of friends is so small. You're not a bad person, John Narraway, but I don't think you have the generosity of spirit it requires to be a watcher."

The calm certainty with which she delivered her judgement irritated John.

"How would you know?" he said.

She gave him a sad smile. "Because I've been watching you ever since you were born."

"What? Every second of my life?"

"No. That comes only at first. It takes time to read a soul, to unravel the tangle of possibilities and learn when the time of death is due. After that it's a matter of checking in from time to time to make sure that the assessment one made still holds true."

John thought about the minutes that made up the greater portion of everyone's life and slowly shook his head. And what if you picked a person who was really dull? Everybody had slow periods in their lives, but some people's whole lives were one numbed shuffle from birth to death. And since you knew the whole time when the person was going to die . . . God, it'd be like spending your whole life in a doctor's waiting room. Boring and depressing.

"You don't get tired of it?" he asked.

"Not tired. A little sad, sometimes."

"Because everybody's got to die."

She shook her head. "No, because I see so much unhappiness and there's nothing I can do about it. Most of my charges never see me – they make their own way to the gates and beyond. I'm just there as a kind of insurance for those who can't do it by themselves, and I'm only with them for such a little while. I miss talking to people on a regular basis. Sometimes I see some of the other watchers, but we're all so busy."

"It sounds horrible."

She shrugged. "I never think of it that way. I just think of those who need help and the looks on their faces when they step through the gates." She fell silent for a moment, then gave him a smile. "We should go now. I've got other commitments."

"What if I refuse to go? What happens then?"

"No one can force you, if that's what you mean."

John held up his hand. He looked around himself.

Okay, it was weird, but he could live with it, couldn't he? Anything'd be better than to be dead – even a half-life . . .

"I know what you're thinking," she said. "And no, it's not because I'm reading your mind, because I can't."

"So what's going to happen to me?"

"I take it you're already experiencing some discomfort?"

John nodded. "I see everything in black and white, but only in the house. Outside, nothing's changed."

"That will grow more pronounced," she told him. "Eventually, you won't be able to see color at all. You might lose the clarity of your vision as well so that everything will seem to be a blur. Your other senses will become less effective as well."

"But—"

"And you won't be able to interact with the world you've left behind. In time, the only people you'll be able to see are others like yourself – those too willful or disturbed to have gone on. They don't exactly make the best of companions, John Narraway, but then, by that point, you'll be so much like them, I don't suppose it will matter."

"But what about all the stories of ghosts and hauntings and the like?"

"Do you have a particularly strong bond with a certain place or person?" she asked. "Someone or something you couldn't possibly live without?"

John had to admit that he didn't, but he could tell that she already knew that.

"But I'll still be alive," he said, knowing even as he said the words that they made no real sense.

"If you want to call it that."

"Don't you miss life?"

Dakota shook her head. "I only miss happiness. Or maybe I should say, I miss the idea of happiness because I never had it when I was alive."

"What happened to you?" John wanted to know.

She gave him a long sad look. "I'm sorry, John Narraway, but I have to go. I will listen for you. Call me when you change your mind. Just don't wait too long—"

"Or you won't be able to recognize me. I know. You already told me that."

"Yes," she said. "I did."

This time she didn't use the door. One moment she was sitting with him on the sofa and the next she had faded away like Carroll's Cheshire cat except with her it was her eyes that lingered the longest, those sad dark eyes that told him he was making a mistake, those eyes to which he refused to listen.

3

He didn't move from the sofa after Dakota left. While the sunlight drifted across the living room, turning his surroundings into a series of shifting chiaroscuro images, he simply sat there, his mind empty more often than it was chasing thoughts. He was sure he hadn't been immobile for more than a few hours, but when he finally stood up and walked to the window, it was early morning, the sun just rising. He'd lost a whole night and a day. Maybe more. He still had no appetite, but now he doubted that he ever would again. He didn't seem to need sleep, either. But it scared him that he could lose such a big chunk of time like that.

He turned back to the living room and switched on the television set to make sure that all he'd lost had been the one day. All he got on the screen was snow. White noise hissed from the speaker grille. Fine, he thought, remembering how he'd been unable to put a call through to the recording studio yesterday morning. So now the TV wouldn't work for him. So he couldn't interact with the everyday mechanics of the world anymore. Well, there were other ways to find out what he needed to know.

He picked up his fiddle case out of habit, put on his jacket and left the house. He didn't need his shades once he got outside, but that was only because his whole street was now delineated in shades of black and white. He could see the color start up at the far ends of the block on either side. The sky was overcast above him, but it blued the further away from his house it got.

This sucked, he thought. But not so much that he was ready to call Dakota back.

He started downtown, putting on his sunglasses once he left the monochromic zone immediately surrounding his house. Walking proved to be more of a chore than he'd anticipated. He couldn't relax his attention for a moment or someone would walk into him. He always felt the impact while they continued on their way, as unaware of the encounter as his neighbor Bob had been.

He stopped at the first newsstand he came upon and found the day's date. Wednesday, he read on the masthead of the *Newford Star*. November tenth. He'd only lost a day. A day of what, though? He could remember nothing of the experience. Maybe that was what sleep would be like for him in this state – simply turning himself off the way fiction described vampires at their rest. He had to laugh at the thought. The undead. He was one of the undead now, though he certainly had no craving for blood.

He stopped laughing abruptly, suddenly aware of the hysterical quality that had crept into the sound. It wasn't that funny. He pressed up close against a building to keep out of the way of passing pedestrians and tried to quell the panic he could feel welling up inside his chest. Christ, it wasn't funny at all.

After a while he felt calm enough to go on. He had no particular destination in mind, but when he realized he was in the general vicinity of High Lonesome Sounds, he decided to stop by the studio. He kept waiting for some shock of recognition at every corner he came to, something that would whisper, this is where you died . . . This is where the one part of your life ended and the new part began. But the street corners all looked the same, and he arrived at the recording studio without sensing that one had ever had more importance in his life than the next.

He had no difficulty gaining entrance to the studio. At least doors still worked for him. He wondered what his use of them looked like to others, doors opening and closing, seemingly of their own accord. He climbed the stairs to the second-floor loft where the recording studio was situated and slipped into the control booth where he found Darlene and Tom Norton listening to a rough mix of one of the cuts from Darlene's album. Norton owned the studio and often served as both producer and sound engineer to the artists using his facilities. He turned as John quietly closed the door behind him, but he looked right through John.

"It still needs a lead break," Norton said, returning his attention to Darlene.

"I know it does. But I don't want another fiddle. I want to leave John's backing tracks just as they are. It doesn't seem right to have somebody else play his break."

Thank you, Darlene, John thought.

He'd known Darlene Flatt for years, played backup with her on and off through the past decade and a half as she sang out her heart in far too many honky-tonks and bars. Her real name was Darlene Johnston, but by this point in her career everyone knew her by her stage name. Dolly Parton had always been her idol and when Darlene stepped on stage with her platinum wig and over-the-top rhinestone outfits, the resemblance between the two was uncanny. But Darlene had a deeper voice, and now that she'd finally lost the wigs and stage gear, John thought she had a better shot at the big time. There was a long tradition of covering other people's material in country music, but as far as John was concerned, nothing got tired more quickly than a tribute act.

She didn't look great today. There was a gaunt look about her features, hollows under her eyes. Someone mourned him, John realized.

"Why don't we have Greg play the break on his dobro?" Darlene said. She sounded so tired, as though all she wanted to do was get through this.

"That could work," Norton said.

John stopped listening to them, his attention taken by the rough mix that was still playing in the control booth. It was terrible. All the instruments sounded tinny and flat, there was no bass to speak of, and Darlene's voice seemed to be mixed so far back you felt you had to lean forward to be able to hear it. He winced, listening to his own fiddle playing.

"You've got a lot more problems here than what instrument to use on the break," he said.

But of course they couldn't hear him. As far as he could tell, they liked what they were hearing which seemed particularly odd, considering how long they'd both been in the business. What did they hear that he couldn't? But then he remembered what his mysterious visitor had told him. How his sight would continue to deteriorate. How . . .

Your other senses will become less effective as well.

John thought back to the walk from his house to the studio. He hadn't really been thinking of it at the time, but now that he did he realized that the normal sounds of the city had been muted. Everything. The traffic, the voices of passers-by, the construction site he'd passed a couple of blocks away from the studio. When he concentrated on Darlene and Norton's conversation again, listening to the tonal quality of their voices rather than what they were saying, he heard a hollow echo that hadn't registered before.

He backed away from them and fumbled his way out into the sitting room on the other side of the door. There he took his fiddle out of his case. Tuning the instrument was horrible. Playing it was worse. There was nothing there anymore. No resonance. No depth. Only the same hollow echoing quality that he'd heard in Darlene and Norton's voices.

Slowly he laid his fiddle back into its case, loosened the frog on his bow and set it down on top of the instrument. When he finally made his way back down the stairs and out into the street, he left the fiddle behind. Outside, the street seemed overcast, its colors not yet leached away, but definitely faded. He looked up into a cloudless sky. He crossed the street and plucked a pretzel from the cart of a street vendor, took a bite even though he had no appetite. It tasted like sawdust and ashes. A bus pulled up at the curb where he was standing, let out a clutch of passengers, then pulled away again, leaving behind a cloud of noxious fumes. He could barely smell them.

It's just a phase, he told himself. He was simply adjusting to his new existence. All he had to do was get through it and things would get back to normal. They couldn't stay like this.

He kept telling himself that as he made his way back home, but he wasn't sure he believed it. He was dead, after all – that was the part of the equation that was impossible to ignore. Dakota had warned him that this was going to happen. But he wasn't ready to believe her, either. He just couldn't accept that the way things were for him now would be permanent.

4

He was right. Things didn't stay the same. They got worse. His senses continued to deteriorate. The familiar world faded away from around him until he found himself in a gray-toned city that he didn't always recognize. He stepped out of his house one day and couldn't find his way back. The air was oppressive, the sky seemed to press down on him. And there were no people. No living people. Only the other undead. They huddled in doorways and alleys, drifted through the empty buildings. They wouldn't look at him, and he found himself turning his face away as well. They had nothing they could share with each other, only their despair, and of that they each had enough of their own.

He took to wandering aimlessly through the deserted streets, the high points of his day coming when he recognized the corner of a building, a stretch of street, that gargoyle peering down from an utterly unfamiliar building. He wasn't sure if he was in a different city, or if he was losing his memory of the one he knew. After a while, it didn't seem to matter.

The blank periods came more and more often. Like the other undead, he would suddenly open his eyes to find himself curled up in a nest of newspapers and trash in some doorway, or huddled in the rotting hulk of a sofa in an abandoned building. And finally he couldn't take it anymore.

He stood in the middle of an empty street and lifted his face to gray skies that only seemed to be kept aloft by the roofs of the buildings.

"Dakota!" he cried. "Dakota!"

But he was far too late, and she didn't come.

Don't wait too long to call me, she'd told him. *If you change too much, I won't be able to find you and nobody else can help you.*

He had no one to blame but himself. It was as she'd said. He'd changed too much and now, even if she could hear him, she wouldn't recognize him. He wasn't sure he'd even recognize himself. Still, he called her name again, called for her until the hollow echo that was his voice grew raw and weak. Finally, he slumped there in the middle of the road, shoulders sagging, chin on his chest, and stared at the pavement.

"The name you were calling," a voice said. "Did it belong to one of those watchers?"

John looked up at the man who'd approached him so silently. He was a nondescript individual, the kind of man he'd have passed by on the street when he was alive and never looked at twice. Medium height, medium build. His only really distinguishing feature was the fervent glitter in his eyes.

"A watcher," John repeated, nodding in response to the man's question. "That's what she called herself."

"Damn 'em all to hell, I say," the man told him. He spat on the pavement. " 'Cept that'd put 'em on these same streets and Franklin T. Clark don't ever want to look into one of their stinkin' faces again – not unless I've got my hands around one of their necks. I'd teach 'em what it's like to be dead."

"I think they're dead, too," John said.

"That's what they'd like you to believe. But tell me this: if they're dead, how come they're not here like us? How come they get to hold on to a piece of life like we can't?"

"Because . . . because they're helping people."

Clark spat again. "Interferin's more like it." The dark light in his eyes seemed to deepen as he fixed his gaze on John. "Why were you calling her name?"

"I can't take this anymore."

"An' you think it's gonna be better where they want to take us?"

"How can it be worse?"

"They can take away who you are," Clark said. "They can try, but they'll never get Franklin T. Clark I'll tell you that. They can kill me, they can dump me in this stinkin' place, but I'd rather rot here in hell than let 'em change me."

"Change you how?" John wanted to know.

"You go through those gates of theirs an' you end up part of a stew. Everythin' that makes you who you are, it gets stole away, mixed up with everybody else. You become a kind of fuel – that's all. Just fuel."

"Fuel for what?"

"For 'em to make more of us. There's no goddamn sense to it. It's just what they do."

"How do you know this?" John asked.

Clark shook his head. "You got to ask, you're not worth the time I'm wastin' on you."

He gave John a withering look, as though John was something he'd stepped on that got stuck to the bottom of his shoe. And then he walked away.

John tracked the man's progress as he shuffled off down the street. When Clark was finally out of sight, he lifted his head again to stare up into the oppressive sky that hung so close his face.

"Dakota," he whispered.

But she still didn't come.

5

The day he found the infant wailing in a heap of trash behind what had once been a restaurant made John wonder if there wasn't some merit in Clark's anger toward the watchers. The baby was a girl and she was no more than a few days old. She couldn't possibly have made the decision that had left her in this place – not by any stretch of the imagination. A swelling echo of Clark's rage rose up in him as he lifted the infant from the trash. He swaddled her in rags and cradled the tiny form in his arms.

"What am I going to do with you?" he asked.

The baby stopped crying, but she made no reply. How could she? She was so small, so helpless. Looking down at her, John knew what he had to do. Maybe Clark was right and the watchers were monsters, although he found that hard to reconcile with his memories of Dakota's empathy and sadness. But Clark was wrong about what lay beyond the gates. He had to be. It couldn't be worse than this place.

He set off then, still wandering aimlessly, but now he had a destination in mind, now he had something to look for. He wasn't doing it for himself, though he knew he'd step through those gates when they stood in front of him. He was doing it for the baby.

"I'm going to call you Dolly," he told the infant. "Darlene would've like that. What do you think?"

He chucked the infant under her chin. Her only response was to stare up at him.

6

John figured he had it easier than most people who suddenly had an infant come into their lives. Dolly didn't need to eat and she didn't cry unless he set her down. She was only happy in his arms. She didn't soil the rags he'd wrapped her in. Sometimes she slept, but there was nothing restful about it. She'd be lying in his arms one minute, the next it was as though someone had thrown a switch and she'd been turned off. He'd been frantic the first time it happened, panicking until he realized that she was only experiencing what passed for sleep in this place.

He didn't let himself enter that blank state. The idea had crept into his mind as he wandered the streets with Dolly that to do so, to let himself turn off the way he and all the other undead did, would make it all that much more difficult for him to complete his task. The longer he denied himself, the more seductive the lure of that strange sleep became, but he stuck to his resolve. After a time, he was rewarded for maintaining his purposefulness. His vision sharpened; the world still appeared monochromatic, but at least it was all back in focus. He grew more clear-headed. He began to recognize more and more parts of the city. But the gates remained as elusive as Dakota had proved to be since the last time he'd seen her.

One day he came upon Clark again. He wasn't sure how long it had been since the last time he'd seen the man – a few weeks? A few months? It was difficult to tell time in the city as it had become because the light never changed. There was no day, no night, no comforting progression from one into the other. There was only the city, held in eternal twilight.

Clark was furious when he saw the infant in John's arms. He ranted and swore at John, threatened to beat him for interfering in what he saw as the child's right of choice. John stood his ground, holding Dolly.

"What are you so afraid of?" he asked when Clark paused to take a breath.

Clark stared at him, a look of growing horror spreading across his features until he turned and fled without replying. He hadn't needed to reply. John knew what Clark was afraid of. It was the same fear that kept them all in this desolate city: death. Dying. They were all afraid. They were all trapped here by that fear. Except for John. He was still trapped like the others; the difference was that he was no longer afraid.

But if a fear of death was no longer to be found in his personal lexicon, despair remained. Time passed. Weeks, months. But he was no closer to finding those fabled gates than he'd been when he first found Dolly and took up the search. He walked through a city that grew more and more familiar. He recognized his own borough, his own street, his own house. He walked slowly up his walk and looked in through the window, but he didn't go in. He was too afraid of succumbing to the growing need to sit somewhere and close his eyes. It would be so easy to go inside, to stretch out on the couch, to let himself fall into the welcoming dark.

Instead he turned away, his path now leading toward the building that housed High Lonesome Sounds. He found it without any trouble, walked up its eerily silent stairwell, boots echoing with a hollow sound, a sound full of dust and broken hopes. At the top of the stairs, he turned to his right and stepped into the recording studio's lounge. The room was empty, except for an open fiddle case in the middle of the floor, an instrument lying in it, a bow lying across the fiddle, horsehairs loose.

He shifted Dolly from the one arm to the crook of the other. Kneeling down, he slipped the bow into its holder in the lid of the case and shut the lid. He stared at the closed case for a long moment. He had no words to describe how much he'd missed it, how incomplete he'd felt without it. Sitting more comfortably on the floor, he fashioned a sling out of his jacket so that he could carry Dolly snuggled up against his chest and leave his arms free.

When he left the studio, he carried the fiddle case with him. He went down the stairs, out onto the street. There were no cars, no pedestrians. Nothing had changed. He was still trapped in that reflection of the city he'd known when he was alive, the deserted streets and abandoned buildings peopled only by the undead. But something felt different. It wasn't just that he seemed more himself, more the way he'd been when he was still alive, carrying his fiddle once more. It was as though retrieving the instrument had put a sense of expectation in the air. The dismal gray streets, overhung by a brooding sky, were suddenly pregnant with possibilities.

He heard the footsteps before he saw the man: a tall, rangy individual, arriving from a side street at a brisk walk. Faded blue jeans, black sweatshirt with matching baseball cap. Flat-heeled cowboy boots. What set him apart from the undead was the purposeful set to his features. His gaze was turned outward, rather than inward.

"Hello!" John called after the stranger as the man began to cross the street. "Have you got a minute?"

The stranger paused in mid-step. He regarded John with surprise but waited for him to cross the street and join him. John introduced himself and put out his hand. The man hesitated for a moment, then took John's hand.

"Bernard Gair," the man said in response. "Pleased, I'm sure." His look of surprise had shifted into one of vague puzzlement. "Have we met before . . .?"

John shook his head. "No, but I do know one of your colleagues. She calls herself Dakota."

"The name doesn't ring a bell. But then there are so many of us – though never enough to do the job."

"That's what she told me. Look, I know how busy you must be so I won't keep you any longer. I just wanted to ask you if you could direct me to . . ."

John's voice trailed off as he realized he wasn't being listened to. Gair peered more closely at him.

"You're one of the lost, aren't you?" Gair said. "I'm surprised I can even see you. You're usually so . . . insubstantial. But there's something different about you."

"I'm looking for the gates," John told him.

"The gates."

Something in the way he repeated the words made John afraid that Gair wouldn't help him.

"It's not for me," he said quickly. "It's for her."

With each step he took, the sounds she made grew more piteous.

He stood directly before the archway, bathed in its golden light. Through the pulsing glow, he could see the big sky Dakota had described. It went on forever. He could feel his heart swell to fill it. All he wanted to do was step through, to be done with the lies of the flesh, the lies that had told him, this one life was all, the lies that had tricked him into being trapped in the city of the undead.

But there was the infant to consider, and he couldn't abandon her. Couldn't abandon her, but he couldn't explain it to her, that there was nothing to fear, that it was only light and an enormous sky. And peace. There were no words to capture the wonder that pulsed through his veins, that blossomed in his heart, swelled until his chest was full and he knew the light must be pouring out of his eyes and mouth.

Now he understood Dakota's sorrow. It would be heart-breaking to know what waited for those who turned their backs on this glory. It had nothing to do with gods or religions. There was no hierarchy of belief entailed. No one was denied admittance. It was simply the place one stepped through so that the journey could continue.

John cradled the sobbing infant, jigging her gently against his chest. He stared into the light. He stared into the endless sky.

"Dakota," he called softly.

"Hello, John Narraway."

He turned to find her standing beside him, her own solemn gaze drinking in the light that pulsed in the big sky between the gates and flowed over them. She smiled at him.

"I didn't think I'd see you again," she said. "And certainly not in this place. You did well to find it."

"I had help. One of your colleagues showed me the way."

"There's nothing wrong with accepting help sometimes."

"I know that now," John said. "I also understand how hard it is to offer help and have it refused."

Dakota stepped closer and drew the infant from the sling at John's chest.

"It is hard," she agreed, cradling Dolly. Her eyes still held the reflected light that came from between the gates, but they were sad once more as she studied the weeping infant. She sighed, adding, "But it's not something that can be forced."

John nodded. There was something about Dakota's voice, about the way she looked that distracted him, but he couldn't quite put his finger on it.

"I will take care of the little one," Dakota said. "There's no need for you to remain here."

"What will you do with her?"

"Whatever she wants."

"But she's so young."

The sadness deepened in Dakota's eyes. "I know."

There was so much empathy in her voice, in the way she held the infant, in her gaze. And then John realized, what was different about her. Her voice wasn't hollow, it held resonance. She wasn't monochrome, but touched with color. There was only a hint, at first, like an old tinted photograph, but it was like looking at a rainbow for John. As it grew stronger, he drank in the wonder of it. He wished she would speak again, just so that he could cherish the texture of her voice, but she remained silent, her solemn gaze held by the infant in her arms.

"I find it hardest when they're so young," she finally said, looking up at him. "They don't communicate in words, so it's impossible to ease their fears."

But words weren't the only way to communicate, John thought. He crouched down to lay his fiddle case on the ground, took out his bow, and tightened the hair. He ran his thumb across the fiddle's strings to check the tuning, marveling anew at the richness of sound. He thought perhaps he'd missed that the most.

"What are you doing?" Dakota asked him.

John shook his head. It wasn't that he didn't want to explain it to her, but that he couldn't. Instead he slipped the fiddle under his chin, drew the bow across the strings, and used music to express what words couldn't. He turned to the gates, drank in the light and the immense wonder of the sky, and distilled it into a simple melody, an air of grace and beauty. Warm generous notes spilled from the sound holes of his instrument, grew stronger and more resonant in the light of the gates, gained such presence that they could almost be seen, touched and held with more than the ear.

The infant in Dakota's arms fell silent and listened. She turned innocent eyes toward the gates and reached out for them. John slowly brought the melody to an end. He laid down his fiddle and bow and took the infant from Dakota, walked with her toward the light. When he was directly under the arch, the light seemed to flare and suddenly the weight was gone from his arms. He heard a joyous cry, but could see nothing for the light. His felt a beating in his chest as though he were alive once more, pulse drumming. He wanted to follow Dolly into the light more than he'd ever wanted anything before in his life, but he slowly turned his back on the light and stepped back onto the boulevard.

"John Narraway," Dakota said. "What are you doing?"

"I can't go through," he said. "Not yet. I have to help the others – like you do."

"But—"

"It's not because I don't want to go through anymore," John said. "It's . . ."

He didn't know how to explain it and not even fiddle music would help him now. All he could think of was the despair that had clung to him in the city of the undead, the same despair that possessed all those lost souls he'd left there, wandering forever through its deserted streets, huddling in its abandoned buildings, defying themselves the light. He knew that, like Dakota and Gair, he had to try to prevent others from making the same mistake. He knew it wouldn't be easy, he knew there would be times when it would be heartbreaking, but he could see no other course.

"I just want to help," he said. "I have to help. You told me before that there aren't enough of you and the fellow that brought me here said the same thing."

Dakota gave him a long considering look before she finally smiled. "You know," she said, "I think you do have the generosity of heart now."

John put away the fiddle. When he stood up, Dakota took his hand and they began to walk back down the boulevard, away from the gates.

"I'm going to miss that light," John said.

Dakota squeezed his hand. "Don't be silly," she said. "The light has always been inside us."

John glanced back. From this distance, the light was like a heat mirage again, shimmering between the pillars of the gates, but he could still feel its glow, see the flare of its wonder and the sky beyond it that went on forever. Something of it echoed in his chest, and he knew Dakota was right.

"We carry it with us wherever we go," he said.

"Learn to play that on your fiddle, John Narraway," she said.

John returned her smile. "I will," he promised. "I surely will."

Elegy for a Demon Lover

Sarah Monette

Whether a supernatural being who entices humans into their realm, an incubus or succubus, a mysterious seducer who damns the beloved's soul, or simply a dangerous human whose love ultimately destroys – the motif of the demon lover is an ancient one. Mortals who encounter such demons are sure to suffer. But the virginal Kyle Murchison Booth in Sarah Monette's story is not exactly a typical human himself. As demonstrated in other Booth stories, he is not only an eccentric, socially awkward museum archivist who frequently finds himself in the midst of the most unsettling supernatural experiences and strange necromantic mysteries, he's also the last of a most unusual family. The result is poignant tale with an atypical outcome for such a theme.

I first saw him at the corner of Atwood and Haye.

It was dusk; I was on my way home from the museum, standing at the crosswalk waiting for the light to change. Even now, I do not know what made me look up. I only know that I did look, and I saw him. He was standing on the opposite corner, a tall, slender figure in a gray overcoat. His hair was a shock of gold over his pale face, and even at that distance I could see the brilliance of his blue eyes. I looked away at once.

The light changed. I stepped down into the street. I had no intention whatsoever of looking at him again, but as I neared the middle of the street, my eyes rose of their own accord. He was perhaps five feet away, and he was staring at me. He walked like a conqueror, like a lion. He could not have been more than twenty-two or twenty-three. His eyes were not merely vivid blue, they were intense, blazing, as if they were lit from within, as if this young man was burning with a flame that no one else could feel. His mouth was twisted in a mocking smile. He had known that I would look. I looked away at once, my face reddening, and then we were past each other.

I went home. I locked the door behind me and then circled the apartment, nervously checking the windows, the door to my postage-stamp balcony. But when I asked myself, I did not know what I was nervous of. It is a wonder I did not burn myself badly as I made dinner, for all the time I was listening, although I did not know for what. I ate without tasting anything, and as I washed the dishes my mind was so far away that I was washing the same saucepan for the third time before I noticed what I was doing. And all the time I was listening without knowing what I listened for and fearing when I did not know what there was to fear.

I did not attempt to go to bed that night. I picked a book at random from the shelves and stayed reading by the fire. Eventually, I did sleep, although I only realized it when I woke, my head thick and my neck stiff, to the knowledge that I had been dreaming of his blue eyes and beautiful, arrogant face. I looked at the book, lying open on my lap like a dead bird, and discovered that I had spent the dark hours staring at the pages of Wells-Burton's *Demonologica* without taking in a single letter of its dry, disturbing text.

It was four in the morning. I put the *Demonologica* back on the shelf, showered, shaved, and changed my clothes. I met no one on my way to the Parrington, and I did not see the blond man, not even in the darkest shadows where my nerves insisted he must be standing, watching me. I was so overwrought by the time I reached the museum that it took me three tries to open the door and two to lock it again when I was safely inside. I do not know why or how I knew that the blond man would not find me inside the museum, but I did know it; the knowledge was at once reassuring and disappointing.

I was distracted all day, without quite knowing why, unable to concentrate on anything. The people I talked to in the course of my duties looked at me strangely. Mr Lucent asked if I was ill, and I did not quite know how to answer him. I did not feel ill, but I did not feel normal; from the look on his face, I knew that the febrile shimmer I sensed in my blood must somehow be showing through.

As I knew he would be, the young man was waiting for me on the steps of the museum when I came out at sundown. It was he, indisputably, the man who had stared at me in the crosswalk the day before, the man whose face had haunted my thin dreams. He was leaning against one of the great stone sphinxes that flanked the portico and smoking a narrow, foreign cigarette. There was no scent of smoke, although I could see it wreathing his head, only the sweet, strong scent of viburnum. His blue eyes were full of fire and darkness.

I knew that I should walk past him, go down the stairs and into the city, to a theater or a restaurant or even the house of my former guardians. I knew that, but I could not do it. I stayed where I was, as if I had been turned to stone, a new column for the portico, ugly and graceless.

He dropped his cigarette and ground it out with his left foot. He looked at me, his eyebrows raised in enquiry. "Are you Lot's wife, that you can only stare at me and not speak? What is your name?" His voice was warm and rich and smooth, like the scent of viburnum that surrounded him. He had a trace of an accent, though I could not place it.

I opened my mouth; the hinges of my jaw seemed corroded with rust. "Kyle Murchison Booth." My voice was deeper than his, husky and rasping, like the caw of a crow.

"Kyle," he said and smiled. I stood transfixed; no one had ever smiled at me like that in my life. "My name is Ivo Balthasar, and I hope you do not intend to stand here all night."

★   ★   ★

We went out to dinner. Ivo said he was a stranger to the city, but I knew most of the restaurants near the Parrington, and I took him to the best of them, a bistro run by a fat, cheerful Parisian. We talked through dinner; Ivo did not seem annoyed by my stammering inarticulateness, and he listened to what I told him without the faintest hint of boredom or impatience. When at one point I apologized for talking too much, he said, "Don't be silly. I think your problem is that you don't talk enough." I found myself telling him things I had never told anyone else, things about my parents, about the Siddonses, about prep school and college, even about my friend Blaine, who was dead. Ivo sat and listened, the look in his blue eyes enrapt, and I knew, though I could hardly believe it, that he was not bored or uninterested, that to him I mattered as I had never mattered to anyone in my life.

We walked back to my apartment through the dark, deserted streets, Ivo making me laugh with the story of a strange thing that had happened to him in Cairo. He seemed to have traveled everywhere, despite his youth; I had never been further than two hundred miles from the house in which I had been born, and I could have listened to his stories of London and Berlin, Johannesburg and Moscow and Beijing, for the rest of my life.

He came upstairs with me when we reached my building; I unlocked my door and stepped inside, then looked back at him.

He was standing in the hallway, watching me. "Well, Kyle, aren't you going to invite me in?"

A blush scalded my cheekbones; his smile told me he had noticed. "Please . . ." I said, "come in."

"Thank you," he murmured and stepped past me into the apartment.

Catlike, he insisted on exploring every nook and cranny, the kitchen, living room, bedroom, bathroom, study, even the closets and the narrow stair that twisted up to the attic. He admired the prints on the walls, the rugs on the floor. I stood in the living room, once I had hung up our overcoats, and waited for him to come back to me, aware of something fluttering in the pit of my stomach like a bird. Eventually he returned, his blue eyes sparkling.

"This is very nice, Kyle," he said, "but it seems so cold."

"Cold?"

He came up to me, tilting his head back slightly to look me in the eyes; he was tall, but I was taller, as I was taller than almost everyone, all knees and elbows and clumsiness. "Have you ever loved anyone in these rooms?"

I could not meet his eyes. "I . . . I don't know what you mean."

"No?" His tone was gently teasing, and I knew he could see the blush that made my skin feel as if it were burning. He raised his hand; his nails were like a woman's, long and sharp and slightly hooked. I flinched from his touch.

"Kyle," he said. The scent of viburnum was very strong. "Do you think I intend to hurt you?"

"I don't . . . I don't know what you want."

He laughed, and although his laugh was as beautiful as his voice, something in it disturbed me, some hint of a wolf's howl, or of the cry of a loon. Then he was speaking again; I could not help but listen. "And here I thought I had been as transparent as glass, Kyle." He touched my face; I could feel the heat of his fingers, and this time I did not flinch away, although I was trembling. "I want to make love to you. Will you let me?"

I did not know how to answer him; I could not imagine words either to reject or accept. As if I were reaching out to put my fingers into flame, I looked up into his face. There was no mockery there, no sign that this was some huge and elaborate joke at my expense. He was waiting for my answer, the hard lines of his face softened, his blue eyes containing nothing but warmth and something that almost seemed to be anxiety.

I said a stupid, senseless non sequitur: "No one calls me Kyle."

But Ivo did not snort with laughter, or sigh with impatience; he did not turn and walk back out into the darkness. He said, "Then I think it's high time someone did." His smile was sweet and warm, like the lifting of a burden. "Kyle. Come to me." I felt the hardness of his nails at the back of my neck as he gently pulled my head down so that his mouth could meet mine. His lips were soft, his teeth wickedly sharp behind them.

After a moment he released me, moving back a little so he could look me in the eyes. "Kyle, are you a virgin?"

Of course I was. I had never before met anyone who would look twice at me. My heart was clamoring in my chest as if I had been running, and I looked away from him.

"Beloved," Ivo said, "there is no shame, only an undiscovered country to explore. Come." His hands slid down gently to where my hands hung stiff and icy at my sides. The heat of his flesh was like fire. He took my hands and stepped slowly backwards, leading me step by halting step into the bedroom.

My life became bifurcated. From eight to five I was the museum's Mr Booth, following the rounds of my duties as I always had, and I did not think of Ivo at all, except to remember to keep my cuffs carefully buttoned, so that the long welts left by his nails would not be noticed. And even that caution was queerly divorced from Ivo himself; it was simply something I knew I had to be careful about, without knowing or caring why.

At five, I went home and became Ivo's Kyle. I do not know what Ivo did while I was at work; he was always there, waiting, when I returned. The apartment became filled with the scent of viburnum and the darker scent of sex. I trusted Ivo as blindly as a child; he taught me pleasure and pain and the shadowed places in-between. It ceased to matter that I was ten years or more older than he; his knowledge and experience were more than I could have gathered in three lifetimes. I asked him no questions about himself; he told me stories of his travels but nothing more personal. There was only the slender beauty of his body, the flawless marble whiteness of his skin, the pleasures which he taught me to give as well as receive.

I had always been an insomniac; now I slept only when I had to, both of us loath to lose the beauties we could share. Moreover, when I did sleep, my dreams were bad and ugly. I dreamed of humiliation and shame and guilt; words like *monstrosity* and *abomination* shouted themselves through my dreaming mind, and when I woke, my eyes would be raw with unshed tears.

After one such dream – I had lost all track of the calendar, so I do not know how long Ivo had been there, how long I had known him – I rolled over, away from the moonlight streaming between the slats of the Venetian blinds. My eyes opened as my head came down on the pillow again, and I startled back so violently I nearly fell off the bed.

Ivo was lying there, perfectly still, his face as serene as a statue's, his eyes open, fixed, and brilliant with moonlight. He looked as if he had been lying there for hours, just watching me sleep.

"Ivo?"

His face did not change, but he said, "Kyle?" his voice as warm and caressing as ever.

"Are you . . . that is . . ." I could not articulate what was bothering me, and so fell silent. I did not know why he frightened me, lying there so still and quiet, except that he did not seem to be blinking. I realized that though I had seen Ivo close his eyes, I had never noticed him blink.

"Is all well with you, beloved? Another bad dream?" He did not move, and I could not, lying there, our faces inches apart, staring.

"Yes," I said. I did not lie to Ivo, although I would have to anyone else. I was staring, transfixed, at the opalescent brilliance of his eyes in the moonlight.

He moved then, one hand reaching forward to caress my hip. "Do you wish to sleep again?"

All at once, out of my fear and the memories of my dreams, I blurted, "Ivo, are you all right?"

"Of course," he said, his lips curving in a smile, although still he did not blink. "I am here with you, Kyle. How could I be otherwise?" His hand moved, and my breath caught in my throat.

I forgot my questions, forgot my fear. But as we moved closer together, the moonlight still lighting his eyes like lamps,

I saw something I had never seen before, although I could not count the hours I had spent staring into Ivo's eyes: his pupils were vertically slit, like a cat's.

I could not think about Ivo. I discovered this only slowly, out of a nagging, angering sense that there was something I was missing, some blind spot in my mind. At the museum my thoughts would slide away from him, and I would only remember two or three hours later that I had been trying to put together the things I had observed. And then it would be another two or three hours before I remembered remembering that. At home, when Ivo was there, I could not think at all, mesmerized by his brilliant eyes, the scent of viburnum that surrounded him, the burning warmth of his skin. It was as if I had been divided in two. One part of me knew about Ivo; the other part was capable of rational thought. I could not bring the two together.

But I was more and more aware that something was wrong. In the washroom at the museum, when I rolled up my cuffs to wash my hands, I would look at the angry welts on my forearms, and I would not know how I had come by them. At home, it was part of my life that Ivo was always watching me, unblinking, the slits of his pupils expanding and contracting as a cat's do when it considers whether or not to pounce on its prey. And although I still wanted his touch, wanted the kaleidoscopic passion that only he could give me, at the same time I was coming to fear his hands, their heat and sharpness, as I feared his mouth and the roughness of his tongue.

Then, one night, Ivo burned me. It was not anything he meant to do – that, I still believe – merely that he caught my wrist, and I screamed at his touch.

He jerked his hand away, his eyes wide. "Kyle?"

I was staring at my left wrist, at the already blistering imprint, terribly distinct, of his fingers: the index, middle and ring fingers clutching across the back of my arm, the little finger stretching down toward my elbow, the mark of his thumb resting across the vulnerable blue veins on the inside of my wrist.

I looked up at him. I had never seen fear on Ivo's face, and I hated the way it made him look. He said, his voice barely a whisper, "Oh, Kyle, I am so sorry. Oh, my beloved, I never meant to hurt you. Here, come with me. I know what to do."

I let him lead me to the bathroom, let him wash the burn with cold water – his hands now barely warmer than mine – let him smear it with some ointment that he got out of his over-coat, a crumpled tin tube without a label. He wrapped my arm then, carefully, lovingly, in strips torn from an old shirt of mine. I was aware, all the while, of his eyes returning again and again to my face, of the anxiety he could not conceal. Finally, when he was done, he released me and stepped back, his gaze fixed on my face with such a naked look of pleading that I could not meet his eyes.

The pain had cleared my head; at least for this moment, I could both be with Ivo and think about him. I said, "What are you?"

"Kyle, beloved, please." He tried to smile. "I love you. Isn't that enough?"

"What are you, Ivo?"

I saw then that he would not answer me. Before he could choose his lie, I turned and walked past him, out of the bath-room, through the bedroom, out into the living room, buttoning my shirt with stiff, trembling fingers as I went.

"Kyle?" He followed me. I realized that I could hear the click of his toenails on the parquet floor, like a dog's. "Kyle? Where are you going? What are you doing?"

I found my shoes, my coat, my keys. "I need to think," I said, without turning back to look at him, and I left.

I walked for hours through the empty, night-haggard streets of the city. I neither noticed nor cared where I went, and if I had happened to fall in the river, I would have been glad of it. Perhaps because it was night, I found that I could remember Ivo, could piece together isolated, stranded thoughts that I had been having and forgetting for weeks: his eyes; his nails and teeth; the fact that I had never seen him either blink or sleep; the scent of viburnum that always surrounded him; the heat that he could only imperfectly control; the way he watched me, as if I were the only thing in the world that existed; the way I had become – I flinched from the word, but I knew it for truth – addicted to him. I remembered that after the first time I had seen him, my hands had dragged down the *Demonologica* from my shelves. And I knew.

Had I, I wondered, ever not known?

I stopped at last, in one of the city's many small parks; I sat on a bench and wept as I had not wept since I had been caned at the age of thirteen for mourning my mother. It felt as if, not only my heart, but my mind and soul and spirit were broken, lying in shattered pieces around my untied shoes. For a long time it did not seem to me as if I would ever find the strength or the courage to leave this bench, and it did not seem that there would be any point in any action I could take after I stood up. There was no point in anything.

But I knew what had to be done. I had read Wells-Burton and everything he had to say on the subject of incubi. The fact that I would rather have ripped my own heart out of my chest and left it for the crows was not relevant. I reached down with fingers that felt like dry twigs and tied my shoes; then I stood up and walked home.

Ivo was waiting in the living room. He had been crying; his eyes looked raw and hollow. "Kyle!" he said, coming toward me. "Kyle, you came—"

"You aren't here, Ivo," I said, hanging up my coat. "You never have been."

He stopped where he was, his hands still outstretched, his eyes widening with horror. "Kyle, what are you talking about? Kyle, don't you—"

"I know what you are, Ivo. *You aren't here.*"

I walked through into the bedroom. He trailed after me. "Kyle, please, what are you saying? You know I love you. You know I'd do anything for you."

"You aren't here," I said again. It was almost four o'clock. I took off my clothes, put on the pajamas I had not worn since I had invited Ivo into my apartment and my life. I dragged the covers back and lay down on the bed, on my back, as stiff and comfortless as a medieval Christ. I stared at the ceiling. I could hear Ivo crying, but he did not come near me.

We stayed that way until seven o'clock, when I got up. I showered, shaved, dressed. My burns were already healing, thanks to Ivo's ointment, but I could see that the scars were going to remain with me for the rest of my life, as sharp and pitiless as a morgue photograph.

Ivo followed me from room to room, weeping. His control had slipped further during the night; his eyes were inhuman, without whites, the unearthly blue of marsh fire. His hair looked less like hair now, more like an animal's rich pelt. He did not try to speak to me, but I left without making any move toward the kitchen. I could buy something to eat later, if I had to, though I could not imagine being hungry.

As I was opening the door, I said again, "You aren't here, Ivo."

In the museum, in the daylight, I did not remember him. I did not know why I felt so ill and strained, why, on my lunch break, I slipped down to the basement and wept for half an hour, huddled for comfort against a bad Roman copy of a Greek nude. I did not remember him until I opened my door to the scent of viburnum.

"Kyle, please, I'll do anything you want, I'll be anything you need me to be. I don't care what it is, if it's wicked or depraved or perverted, *please*, I'll do it, I'll do anything, just don't do this to me. Kyle, please."

He was not as solid as he had been; I could see the wall through him, and his voice was faint. Only his eyes were still vivid, still fully present, and the terror and wretchedness and need in them tore at me like cruel teeth. For he did love me; to him I was the world. The fact that his love would infallibly kill me, leeching my essence away to feed his, as his previous lovers had fed him, was no desire of his. And when he had killed me, he would go on to his next hapless victim, his prey, whom he would love and destroy just as he loved and was destroying me.

"You aren't here, Ivo," I said.

He was weaker. Light hurt him now. I turned on the lights in every room in the apartment, pretending that I could not hear his cries of pain, driving him eventually into the bedroom closet, where he huddled like a beaten child, sobbing, only half visible against my suits. I stayed in the living room that night, sitting with Wells-Burton's *Demonologica* by the fire, as I had sat on that other night, the night after he had chosen me, staring at the engraving that illustrated the chapter on incubi and succubi: a smiling youth with the teeth of a beast.

By morning, the scent of viburnum was fainter. I made myself ready for the day. When I looked in the mirror to shave, I could see him reflected behind me, a smear of gold, a smudge of blue against the white wall. I knew that if I concentrated I would be able to hear him, that by now all he would be able to say was my name. I did not try to hear him; I was trying with all my might to forget him, to bring that daylight oblivion into the night kingdom where once Ivo had ruled.

When I left, I said again, "You aren't here, Ivo," and this time I could feel the silence that answered my words, as if what I had said were true. When I returned that night, I could not smell viburnum.

That was effectively the end of it. There were still nights when I would wake in the middle of the night to the faint sweetness of viburnum, a feeling that there was almost weight on the mattress next to me, and I would have to get up, stumbling through the rooms of my apartment to turn on the lights. But as time passed those nights came further and further apart, and within six months they had ceased entirely. Ivo was truly gone, and now I cannot remember, even in the darkness, exactly what he looked like or how his voice sounded. Even in dreams, I cannot see him clearly, and although I know that is for the best, I know I do not want him back, yet I still miss him. I will always miss him – although I know that soon I will forget him entirely – for he was the only one I have ever known who loved me for what I am.

And the Angels Sing

Kate Wilhelm

*Kate Wilhelm's story poses an interesting question: As a member
of the media, what do you do when you find an otherworldly
creature in need? Written slightly before the internet and mobile
phones with photo and video capabilities were common,
Wilhelm's story is still an evocative contemplation of the question. As for today's Fifth Estate – which includes, for better or
worse, plenty of amateur reportage – a quick online search will
deliver videos of "real" angels and demons on YouTube with
millions of viewers.*

Eddie never left the office until one or even two in the morning
on Sundays, Tuesdays and Thursdays. The *North Coast News*
came out three times a week, and it seemed to him that no one
could publish a paper unless someone in charge was on hand
until the press run. He knew that the publisher, Stuart Winkle,
didn't particularly care, as long as the advertising was in place,
but it wasn't right, Eddie thought. What if something came up,
something went wrong? Even out here at the end of the world
there could be a late-breaking story that required someone to
write it, to see that it got placed. Actually, Eddie's hopes for
that event, high six years ago, had diminished to the point of
needing conscious effort to recall. In fact, he liked to see his
editorials before he packed it in.

This night, Thursday, he read his own words and then bellowed, "Where is she?" *She* was Ruthie Jenson, and *she* had spelled *frequency* with one *e* and an *a*. Eddie stormed through the deserted outer office, looking for her, and caught her at the door just as she was wrapping her vampire cloak about her thin shoulders. She was thin, her hair was cut too short, too close to her head, and she was too frightened of him. And, he thought with bitterness, she was crazy, or she would not wait around three nights a week for him to catch her at the door and give her hell.

"Why don't you use the goddamn dictionary? Why do you correct my copy? I told you I'd wring your neck if you touched my copy again!"

She made a whimpering noise and looked past him in terror, down the hallway, into the office.

"I . . . I'm sorry. I didn't mean . . ." Fast as quicksilver then, she fled out into the storm that was still howling. He hoped the goddamn wind would carry her to Australia or beyond.

The wind screamed as it poured through the outer office, scattering a few papers, setting alight a-dance on a chain. Eddie slammed the door against it and surveyed the space around him, detesting every inch of it at the moment. Three desks, the fluttering papers that Mrs Rondale would heave out because anything on the floor got heaved out. Except dirt; she seemed never to see quite all of it. Next door the presses were running; people were doing things, but the staff that put the paper together had left now. Ruthie was always next to last to go, and then Eddie. He kicked a chair on his way back to his own cubicle, clutching the ink-wet paper in his hand, well aware that the ink was smearing onto skin.

He knew that the door to the pressroom had opened and softly closed again. In there they would be saying Fat Eddie was in a rage. He knew they called him Fat Eddie, or even worse, behind his back, and he knew that no one on Earth cared if the *North Coast News* was a mess except him. He sat at his desk, scowling at the editorial – one of his better ones, he thought – and the word *frequancy* leaped off the page at him;

nothing else registered. What he had written was "At this time of year the storms bear down onshore with such regularity, such frequency, that it's as if the sea and air are engaged in the final battle." It got better, but he put it aside and listened to the wind. All evening he had listened to reports from up and down the coast, expecting storm damage, light outages, wrecks, something. At midnight he had decided it was just another Pacific storm and had wrapped up the paper. Just the usual: Highway 101 under water here and there, a tree down here and there, a head-on, no deaths . . .

The wind screamed and let up, caught its breath and screamed again. Like a kid having a tantrum. And up and down the coast the people were like parents who had seen too many kids having too many tantrums. Ignore it until it goes away and then get on about your business, that was their attitude. Eddie was from Indianapolis, where a storm with eighty-mile-per-hour winds made news. Six years on the coast had not changed that. A storm like this, by God, should make news!

Still scowling, he pulled on his own raincoat, a great black waterproof garment that covered him to the floor. He added his black, wide-brimmed hat and was ready for the weather. He knew that behind his back they called him Mountain Man, when they weren't calling him Fat Eddie. He secretly thought that he looked more like The Shadow than not.

He drove to Connally's Tavern and had a couple of drinks, sitting alone in glum silence, and then offered to drive Truman Cox home when the bar closed at two.

The town of Lewisburg was south of Astoria, north of Cannon Beach, population nine hundred and eighty-four. And at two in the morning they were all sleeping, the town blacked out by rain. There were the flickering night-lights at the drugstore, and the lights from the newspaper building, and two traffic lights, although no other traffic moved. Rain pelted the windshield and made a river through Main Street, cascaded down the side streets on the left, came pouring off the mountain on the right. Eddie made the turn onto Third and hit the brakes hard when a figure darted across the street.

"Jesus!" he grunted as the car skidded, then caught and righted itself. "Who was that?"

Truman was peering out into the darkness, nodding. The figure had vanished down the alley behind Sal's Restaurant. "Bet it was the Boland girl, the younger one. Not Norma. Following her sister's footsteps."

His tone was not condemnatory, even though everyone knew exactly where those footsteps would lead the kid.

"She sure earned whatever she got tonight," Eddie said with a grunt and pulled up into the driveway of Truman's house. "See you around."

"Yep. Probably will. Thanks for the lift." He gathered himself together and made a dash for his porch.

But he would be soaked anyway, Eddie knew. All it took was a second out in this driving rain. That poor, stupid kid, he thought again as he backed out of the drive, retraced his trail for a block or two, and headed toward his own little house. On impulse he turned back and went down Second Street to see if the kid was still scurrying around; at least he could offer her a lift home. He knew where the Bolands lived, the two sisters, their mother, all in the trade now, apparently. But God, he thought, the little one couldn't be more than twelve.

The numbered streets were parallel to the coastline; the cross streets had become wind tunnels that rocked his car every time he came to one. Second Street was empty, black. He breathed a sigh of relief. He hadn't wanted to get involved anyway, in any manner, and now he could go on home, listen to music for an hour or two, have a drink or two, a sandwich, and get some sleep. If the wind ever let up. He slept very poorly when the wind blew this hard. What he most likely would do was finish the book he was reading, possibly start another one. The wind was good for another four or five hours. Thinking this way, he made another turn or two and then saw the kid again, this time sprawled on the side of the road.

If he had not already seen her once, if he had not been thinking about her, about her sister and mother, if he had been driving faster than five miles an hour, probably he would have

missed her. She lay just off the road, face down. As soon as he
stopped and got out of the car, the rain hit his face, streamed
from his glasses, blinding him almost. He got his hands on the
child and hauled her to the car, yanked open the back door
and deposited her inside. Only then he got a glimpse of her
face. Not the Boland girl. No one he had ever seen before. And
as light as a shadow. He hurried around to the driver's side and
got in, but he could no longer see her now from the front seat.
Just the lumpish black raincoat that gleamed with water and
covered her entirely. He wiped his face, cleaned his glasses,
and twisted in the seat; he couldn't reach her, and she did not
respond to his voice.

He cursed bitterly and considered his next move. She could
be dead, or dying. Through the rain-streaked windshield the
town appeared uninhabited. It didn't even have a police station,
a clinic, or a hospital. The nearest doctor was ten or twelve
miles away, and in this weather . . . Finally he started the engine
and headed for home. He would call the state police from
there, he decided. Let them come and collect her. He drove up
Hammer Hill to his house and parked in the driveway at the
walk that led to the front door. He would open the door first,
he had decided, then come back and get the kid; either way he
would get soaked, but there was little he could do about that.
He moved fairly fast for a large man, but his fastest was not
good enough to keep the rain off his face again. If it would
come straight down, the way God meant rain to fall, he
thought, fumbling with the key in the lock, he would he able to
see something. He got the door open, flicked on the light
switch, and went back to the car to collect the girl. She was as
limp as before and seemed to weigh nothing at all. The slicker
she wore was hard to grasp, and he did not want her head to
loll about for her to brain herself on the porch rail or the door
frame, but she was not easy to carry, and he grunted although
her weight was insignificant. Finally he got her inside, and
kicked the door shut.

Then he took off his hat that had been useless, and his
glasses that had blinded him with running water, and the

raincoat that was leaving a trail of water with every step. He backed off the Navajo rug and out to the kitchen to put the wet coat on a chair, let it drip on the linoleum. He grabbed a handful of paper toweling and wiped his glasses, then returned to the bedroom.

He reached down to remove the kid's raincoat and jerked his hand away again. "Jesus Christ!" he whispered and backed away from her. He heard himself saying it again, and then again, and stopped. He had backed up to the wall, was pressed hard against it. Even from there he could see her clearly. Her face was smooth, without eyebrows, without eyelashes, her nose too small, her lips too narrow, hardly lips at all. What he had thought was a coat was part of her. It started on her head, where hair should have been, went down the sides of her head where ears should have been, down her narrow shoulders, the backs of her arms that seemed too long and thin, almost boneless.

She was on her side, one long leg stretched out, the other doubled up under her. Where there should have been genitalia, there was too much skin, folds of skin.

Eddie felt his stomach spasm; a shudder passed over him. Before, he had wanted to shake her, wake her up, ask questions; now he thought that if she opened her eyes, he might pass out. And he was shivering with cold. Moving very cautiously, making no noise, he edged his way around the room to the door, then out, back to the kitchen where he pulled a bottle of bourbon from a cabinet and poured half a glass that he drank as fast as he could. He stared at his hand. It was shaking.

Very quietly he took off his sodden shoes and placed them at the back door, next to his waterproof boots that he invariably forgot to wear. As soundlessly as possible he crept to the bedroom door and looked at her again. She had moved, was now drawn up in a huddle as if she was as cold as he was. He took a deep breath and began to inch around the wall of the room toward the closet, where he pulled out his slippers with one foot and eased them on, and then tugged on a blanket on a shelf. He had to let his breath out; it sounded explosive to his ears. The girl shuddered and made herself into a tighter ball. He moved toward her slowly, ready to turn and run, and finally was close enough to lay the blanket over her. She was shivering hard. He backed away from her again and this time went to the living room, leaving the door open so that he could see her, just in case. He turned up the thermostat, retrieved his glass from the kitchen, and went to the door again and again to peer inside. He should call the state police, he knew, and made no motion toward the phone. A doctor? He nearly laughed. He wished he had a camera. If they took her away, and they would, there would be nothing to show, nothing to prove she had existed. He thought of her picture on the front page of the *North Coast News* and snorted. The *National Enquirer*? This time he muttered a curse. But she was news. She certainly was news.

Mary Beth, he decided. He had to call someone with a camera, someone who could write a decent story. He dialed Mary Beth, got her answering machine, and hung up, dialed it again. At the fifth call her voice came on. "Who the hell is this, and do you know that it's three in the fucking morning?"

"Eddie Delacort. Mary Beth, get up, get over here, my place, and bring your camera."

"Fat Eddie? What the hell—"

"Right now, and bring plenty of film." He hung up.

A few seconds later his phone rang; he took it off the hook and laid it down on the table. While he waited for Mary Beth, he surveyed the room. The house was small, with two bedrooms, one that he used for an office, on the far side of the living room. In the living room there were two easy chairs covered with fine, dark green leather, no couch, a couple of tables and many bookshelves, all filled. A long cabinet held his sound equipment, a stereo, hundreds of albums. Everything was neat, arranged for a large man to move about easily, nothing extraneous anywhere. Underfoot was another Navajo rug. He knew the back door was securely locked; the bedroom windows were closed, screens in place. Through the living room was the only way the kid on his bed could get out, and he knew she would not get past him if she woke up and tried to make a run. He nodded, then moved his two easy chairs so that they faced the bedroom; he pulled an end table and made his way to the bedroom, where he dumped her on the bed between them, got another glass, and brought the bottle of bourbon. He sat down to wait for Mary Beth, brooding over the girl in his bed. From time to time the blanket shook hard; a slight movement that was nearly constant suggested that she had not yet warmed up. His other blanket was under her, and he had no intention of touching her again in order to get to it.

Mary Beth arrived as furious as he had expected. She was his age, about forty, graying, with suspicious blue eyes and no make-up. He had never seen her with lipstick on, or jewelry of any kind except for a watch, or in a skirt or dress. That night she was in jeans and a sweatshirt and a bright red hooded rain-coat that brought the rainstorm inside as she entered, cursing him. He noted with satisfaction that she had her camera gear. She cursed him expertly as she yanked off her raincoat and was still calling him names when he finally put his hand over her mouth and took her by the shoulder, propelled her toward the bedroom door.

"Shut up and look," he muttered. She was stronger than he had realized and now twisted out of his grasp and swung a fist at him. Then she faced the bedroom. She looked, then turned back to him red-faced and sputtering. "You . . . you got me out . . . a floozy in your bed. . . . So you really do know what that thing you've got is used for! And you want pictures! Jesus God!"

"Shut up!"

This time she did. She peered at his face for a second, turned and looked again, took a step forward, then another. He knew her reaction was to his expression, not the lump on the bed. Nothing of that girl was visible, just the unquiet blanket and a bit of darkness that was not hair but should have been. He stayed at Mary Beth's side, and his caution was communicated to her; she was as quiet now as he was.

At the bed he reached out and gently pulled back the blanket. One of her hands clutched it spasmodically. The hand had four apparently boneless fingers, long and tapered, very pale. Mary Beth exhaled too long, and neither of them moved for what seemed minutes. Finally she reached out and touched the darkness at the girl's shoulder, touched her arm, then her face. Abruptly she pulled back her hand. The girl on the bed was shivering harder than ever, in a tighter ball that hid the many folds of skin at her groin.

"It's cold," Mary Beth whispered.

"Yeah." He put the blanket back over the girl.

Mary Beth went to the other side of the bed, squeezed between it and the wall and carefully pulled the bedspread and blanket free, and put them over the girl also. Eddie took Mary Beth's arm, and they backed out of the bedroom. She sank into one of the chairs he had arranged and automatically held out her hand for the drink he was pouring.

"My God," Mary Beth said softly after taking a large swallow, "what is it? Where did it come from?"

He told her as much as he knew, and they regarded the sleeping figure. He thought the shivering had subsided, but maybe she was just too weak to move so many covers.

"You keep saying it's a she," Mary Beth said. "You know that thing isn't human, don't you?"

Reluctantly he described the rest of the girl, and this time Mary Beth finished her drink. She glanced at her camera bag but made no motion toward it yet. "It's our story," she said. "We can't let them have it until we're ready. Okay?"

"Yeah. There's a lot to consider before we do anything."

Silently they considered. He refilled their glasses, and they sat watching the sleeping creature on his bed. When the lump flattened out a bit, Mary Beth went in and lifted the covers and examined her, but she did not touch her again. She returned to her chair very pale and sipped bourbon. Outside the wind moaned, but the howling had subsided, and the rain was no longer a driving presence against the front of the house, the side that faced the sea.

From time to time one or the other made a brief suggestion.
"Not radio," Eddie said.

"Right," Mary Beth said. She was a stringer for NPR.

"Not newsprint," she said later.

Eddie was a stringer for AP. He nodded.

"It could be dangerous when it wakes up," she said.

"I know. Six rows of alligator teeth, or poison fangs, or mind
rays."

She giggled. "Maybe right now there's a hidden camera
taking in all this. Remember that old TV show?"

"Maybe they sent her to test us, our reaction to them."

Mary Beth sat up straight "My God, more of them?"

"No species can have only one member," he said very seriously. "A counterproductive trait." He realized that he was
quite drunk. "Coffee," he said and pulled himself out of the
chair, made his way unsteadily to the kitchen.

When he had the coffee ready, and tuna sandwiches, and
sliced onions and tomatoes, he found Mary Beth leaning
against the bedroom door, contemplating the girl.

"Maybe it's dying," she said in a low voice. "We can't just let
it die, Eddie."

"We won't," he said. "Let's eat something. It's almost
daylight."

She followed him to the kitchen and looked around it. "I've
never been in your house before. You realize that? All the years
I've known you, I've never been invited here before."

"Five years," he said.

"That's what I mean. All those years. It's a nice house. It
looks like your house should look, you know?"

He glanced around the kitchen. Just a kitchen – stove, refrigerator, table, counters. There were books on the counter and
piled on the table. He pushed the pile to one side and put
down plates. Mary Beth lifted one and turned it over. Russet-
colored, gracefully shaped pottery from North Carolina,
signed by Sara. She nodded, as if in confirmation. "You picked
out every single item individually, didn't you?"

"Sure. I have to live with the stuff."

"What are you doing here, Eddie? Why here?"

"The end of the world, you mean? I like it."

"Well, I want the hell out. You've been out and chose to be here. I choose to be out. That thing on your bed will get me out."

From the University of Indiana to a small paper in Evanston, on to Philadelphia, New York. He felt he had been out plenty, and now he simply wanted a place where people lived in individual houses and chose the pottery they drank their coffee from. Six years ago he had left New York, on vacation, he had said, and he had come to the end of the world and stayed.

"Why haven't you gone already?" he asked Mary Beth.

She smiled her crooked smile. "I was married, you know that? To a fisherman. That's what girls on the coast do – marry fishermen or lumbermen or policemen. Me, Miss Original No-Talent herself. Married, playing house forever. He's out there somewhere. Went out one day and never came home again. So I got a job with the paper, this and that. Only one thing could be worse than staying here at the end of the world, and that's being in the world broke. Not my style."

She finished her sandwich and coffee and now seemed too restless to sit still. She went to the window over the sink and gazed out. The light was gray. "You don't belong here any more than I do. What happened? Some woman tell you to get lost? Couldn't get the job you wanted? Some young slim punk worm in front of you? You're dodging just like me."

All the above, he thought silently, and said, "Look, I've been thinking. I can't go to the office without raising suspicion, in case anyone's looking for her, I mean. I haven't been in the office before one or two in the afternoon for more than five years. But you can. See if anything's come over the wires, if there's a search on, if there was a wreck of any sort. You know. If the FBI's nosing around, or the military. Anything at all." Mary Beth rejoined him at the table and poured more coffee, her restlessness gone, an intent look on her face. Her business face, he thought.

"Okay. First some pictures, though. And we'll have to have a story about my car. It's been out front all night," she added crisply. "So, if anyone brings it up, I'll have to say I keep you company now and then. Okay?"

He nodded and thought without bitterness that that would give them a laugh at Connally's Tavern. That reminded him of Truman Cox. "They'll get around to him eventually, and he might remember seeing her. Of course, he assumed it was the Boland girl. But they'll know we saw someone."

Mary Beth shrugged. "So you saw the Boland girl and got to thinking about her and her trade and gave me a call. No problem."

He looked at her curiously. "You really don't care if they start that scuttlebutt around town about you and me?"

"Eddie," she said almost too sweetly, "I'd admit to fucking a pig if it would get me the hell out of here. I'll go on home for a shower, and by then maybe it'll be time to get on my horse and go to the office. But first some pictures."

At the bedroom door he asked in a hushed voice, "Can you get them without using the flash? That might send her into shock or something."

She gave him a dark look. "Will you for Christ's sake stop calling it a *her*!" She scowled at the figure on the bed. "Let's bring in a lamp, at least. You know I have to uncover it."

He knew. He brought in a floor lamp, turned on the bedside light, and watched Mary Beth go to work. She was a good photographer, and in this instance she had an immobile subject; she could use time exposures. She took a roll of film and started a second one, then drew back. The girl on the bed was shivering hard again, drawing up her legs, curling into a tight ball.

"Okay. I'll finish in daylight, maybe when she's awake."

Mary Beth was right, Eddie had to admit; the creature was not a girl, not even a female probably. She was elongated, without any angles anywhere, no elbows or sharp knees or jutting hip bones. Just a smooth long body without breasts, without a navel, without genitalia. And with that dark growth that started high on her head and went down the backs of her arms, covered her back entirely. Like a mantle, he thought, and was repelled by the idea. Her skin was not human, either. It was pale with yellow rather than pink undertones. She obviously was very cold; the yellow was fading to a grayish hue. Tentatively he touched her arm. It felt wrong, not yielding the way human flesh covered with skin should yield. It felt like cool silk over something firmer than human flesh.

Mary Beth replaced the covers, and they backed from the room as the creature shivered. "Jesus," Mary Beth whispered. "You'd think it would have warmed up by now. This place is like an oven, and all those covers." A shudder passed through her.

In the living room again, Mary Beth began to fiddle with her camera. She took out the second roll of film and held both rolls in indecision. "If anyone's nosing around, and if they learn that you might have seen it, and that we've been together, they might snitch my film. Where's a good place to stash it?"

He took the film rolls and she shook her head. "Don't tell me. Just keep it safe." She looked at her watch. "I won't be back until ten or later. I'll find out what I can, make a couple of calls. Keep an eye on it. See you later."

He watched her pull on her red raincoat and went to the porch with her, where he stood until she was in her car and out of sight. Daylight had come; the rain had ended, although the sky was still overcast and low. The fir trees in his front yard glistened and shook off water with the slightest breeze. The wind had turned into no more than that, a slight breeze. The air was not very cold, and it felt good after the heat inside. It smelled good, of leaf mold and sea and earth and fish and fir trees . . . He took several deep breaths and then went back in. The house really was like an oven, he thought, momentarily refreshed by the cool morning and now once again feeling logy. Why didn't she warm up? He stood in the doorway to the bedroom and looked at the huddled figure. Why didn't she warm up?

He thought of victims of hypothermia; the first step, he had read, was to get their temperature back up to normal, any way possible. Hot water bottle? He didn't own one. Hot bath? He stood over the girl and shook his head slightly. Water might be toxic to her. And that was the problem; she was an alien with unknown needs, unknown dangers. And she was freezing.

With reluctance he touched her arm, still cool in spite of all the covering over her. Like a hothouse plant, he thought then, brought into a frigid climate, destined to die of cold. Moving slowly, with even greater reluctance than before, he began to pull off his trousers, his shirt, and when he was down to under-shirt and shorts, he gently shifted the sleeping girl and lay down beside her, drew her to the warmth of his body.

The house temperature by then was close to eighty-five, much too warm for a man with all the fat that Eddie had on his body; she felt good next to him, cooling, even soothing. For a time she made no response to his presence, but gradually her shivering lessened, and she seemed to change subtly, lose her rigidity; her legs curved to make contact with his legs; her torso shifted, relaxed, flowed into the shape of his body; one of her arms moved over his chest, her hand at his shoulder, her other arm bent and fitted itself against him. Her cool cheek pressed against the pillows of flesh over his ribs. Carefully he wrapped his arms about her and drew her closer. He dozed, came awake with a start, dozed again. At nine he woke up completely and began to disengage himself. She made a soft sound, like a child in protest, and he stroked her arm and whis-pered nonsense. At last he was untangled from her arms and legs and stood up and pulled on his clothes again. The next time he looked at the girl, her eyes were open, and he felt entranced momentarily. Large, round, golden eyes, like pools of molten gold, unblinking, inhuman. He took a step away from her.

"Can you talk?"

There was no response. Her eyes closed again and she drew the covers high up onto her face, buried her head in them.

Wearily Eddie went to the kitchen and poured coffee. It was hot and tasted like tar. He emptied the coffee maker and started a fresh brew. Soon Mary Beth would return and they would make the plans that had gone nowhere during the night. He felt more tired than he could remember and thought ruefully of what it was really like to be forty-two and a hundred pounds overweight and miss a night's sleep.

"You look like hell," Mary Beth said in greeting at ten. She looked fine, excited, a flush on her cheeks, her eyes sparkling. "Is it okay? Has it moved? Come awake yet?" She charged past him and stood in the doorway to the bedroom. "Good. I got hold of Homer Carpenter, over in Portland. He's coming over with a video camera around two or three. I didn't tell him what we have, but I had to tell him something to get him over. I said we have a coelacanth."

Eddie stared at her. "He's coming over for that? I don't believe it."

She left the doorway and swept past him on her way to the kitchen. "Okay, he doesn't believe me, but he knows it's something big, something hot, or I wouldn't have called him. He knows me that well, anyway."

Eddie thought about it for a second or two, then shrugged. "What else did you find out?"

Mary Beth got coffee and held the cup in both hands, surveying him over the top of it. "Boy oh boy, Eddie! I don't know who knows what, or what it is they know, but there's a hunt on. They're saying some guys escaped from the pen over at Salem, but that's bull. Roadblocks and everything. I don't think they're telling anyone anything yet. The poor cops out there don't know what the hell they're supposed to be looking for, just anything suspicious, until the proper authorities get here."

"Here? They know she's here?"

"Not *here* here. But somewhere on the coast. They're closing in from north and south. And that's why Homer decided to get his ass over here, too."

Eddie remembered the stories that had appeared on the wire services over the past few weeks about an erratic comet that was being tracked. Stuart Winkle, the publisher and editor in chief, had chosen not to print them, but Eddie had seen them. And more recently the story about a possible burnout in space of a Soviet capsule. Nothing to worry about, no radiation, but there might be bright lights in the skies, the stories had said. Right, he thought.

Mary Beth was at the bedroom door again, sipping her coffee. "I'll owe you for this, Eddie. No way can I pay for what you're giving me." He made a growly noise, and she turned to regard him, suddenly very serious.

"Maybe there is something," she said softly. "A little piece of the truth. You know you're not the most popular man in town, Eddie. You're always doing little things for people, and yet, do they like you for it, Eddie? Do they?"

"Let's not do any psychoanalysis right now," he said coldly. "Later."

She shook her head. "Later I won't be around. Remember?" Her voice took on a mocking tone. "Why do you suppose you don't get treated better? Why no one comes to visit? Or invites you to the clambakes, except for office parties, anyway? It's all those little things you keep doing, Eddie. Overdoing maybe. And you won't let anyone pay you back for anything. You turn everyone into a poor relation, Eddie, and they begin to resent it."

Abruptly he laughed. For a minute he had been afraid of her, what she might reveal about him. "Right," he said. "Tell that to Ruthie Jenson."

Mary Beth shrugged: "You give poor little Ruthie exactly what she craves – mistreatment. She takes it home and nurtures it. And then she feels guilty. The Boland kid you intended to rescue. You would have had her, her sister and their mother all feeling guilty. Truman Cox. How many free drinks you let him give you, Eddie? Not even one, I bet. Stuart Winkle? You run his paper for him. You ever use that key to his cabin? He really wants you to use it, Eddie. A token repayment. George Allmann. Harriet Davies . . . it's a long list, Eddie, the people you've done little things for. The people who go through life owing you, feeling guilty about not liking you, not sure why they don't. I was on that list, too, Eddie, but not now. I just paid you in full."

"Okay," he said heavily. "Now that we've cleared up the mystery about me, what about her?" He pointed past Mary Beth at the girl on his bed.

"It, Eddie. It. First the video, and make some copies, get them into a safe place, and then announce. How does that sound?"

He shrugged. "Whatever you want."

She grinned her crooked smile and shook her head, at him. "Forget it, Eddie. I'm paid up for years to come. Look, I've got to get back to the office. I'll keep my eyes on the wires, anything coming in, and as soon as Homer shows, we'll be back. Are you okay? Can you hold out for the next few hours?"

"Yeah, I'm okay." He watched her pull on her coat and walked to the porch with her. Before she left, he said, "One thing, Mary Beth. Did it even occur to you that some people like to help out? No ulterior motive or anything, but a little human regard for others?"

She laughed. "I'll give it some thought, Eddie. And you give some thought to having perfected a method to make sure people leave you alone, keep their distance. Okay? See you later."

He stood on the porch, taking deep breaths. The air was mild; maybe the sun would come out later on. Right now the world smelled good, scoured clean, fresh. No other house was visible. He had let the trees and shrubbery grow wild, screening everything from view, it was like being the last man on Earth, he thought suddenly. The heavy growth even screened out the noise from the little town. If he listened intently, he could make out engine sounds, but no voices, no one else's music that he usually detested, no one else's cries or laughter.

Mary Beth never had been ugly, he thought then. She was good-looking in her own way even now, going on middle age. She must have been a real looker as a younger woman. Besides, he thought, if anyone ever mocked her, called her names, she would slug the guy. That would be her way. And he had found his way, he added, then turned brusquely and went inside and locked the door after him.

He took a kitchen chair to the bedroom and sat down by her. She was shivering again. He reached over to pull the covers more tightly about her, then stopped his motion and stared. The black mantle thing did not cover her head as completely as it had before. He was sure it now started further back. And more of her cheeks was exposed. Slowly he drew away the cover and then turned her over. The mantle was looser, with folds where it had been taut before. She reacted violently to being uncovered, shuddering long spasmlike movements.

He replaced the cover.

"What the hell are you?' he whispered. "What's happening to you?"

He rubbed his eyes hard and sat down, regarding her with a frown. "You know what's going to happen, don't you? They'll take you somewhere and study you, try to make you talk, if you can, find out where you're from, what you want, where there are others . . . They might hurt you. Even kill you."

He thought again of the great golden pools that were her eyes, of how her skin felt like silk over a firm substance, of the insubstantiality of her body, the lightness when he carried her.

"What do you want here?" he whispered. "Why did you come?"

After a few minutes of silent watching, he got up and found his dry shoes in the closet and pulled them on. He put on a plaid shirt that was very warm, and then he wrapped the sleeping girl in the blanket and carried her to his car and placed her on the back seat. He went back inside for another blanket and put that over her, too.

He drove up his street, avoiding the town, using a back road that wound higher and higher up the mountain. Stuart Winkle's cabin, he thought. An open invitation to use it any time he wanted. He drove carefully, taking the curves slowly, not wanting to jar her, to roll her off the back seat. The woods pressed in closer when he left the road for a log road. From time to time he could see the ocean, then he turned and lost it again. The road clung to the steep mountainside, climbing, always climbing;

there was no other traffic on it. The loggers had finished with this area; this was state land, untouchable, for now anyway. He stopped at one of the places where the ocean spread out below him and watched the waves rolling in forever and ever, unchanging, unknowable. Then he drove on. The cabin was high on the mountain. Up here the trees were mature growth, mammoth and silent, with deep shadows beneath them, little understory growth in the dense shade. The cabin was redwood, rough, heated with a wood stove, no running water, no electricity. There was oil for a lamp, and plenty of dry wood stacked under a shed, and a store of food that Stuart had said he should consider his own. There were twin beds in the single bedroom and a couch that opened to a double bed in the living room. Those two rooms and the kitchen made up the cabin.

He carried the girl inside and put her on one of the beds; she was entirely enclosed in blankets like a cocoon. Hurriedly he made a fire in the stove and brought in a good supply of logs. Like a hothouse orchid, he thought; she needed plenty of heat. After the cabin started to heat up, he took off his outer clothing and lay down beside her, the way he had done before, and as before, she conformed to his body, melted into him, absorbed his warmth. Sometimes he dozed, then he lay quietly thinking of his childhood, of the heat that descended on Indiana like a physical substance, of the tornadoes that sometimes came, murderous funnels that sucked life away, shredded everything. He dozed and dreamed and awakened and dreamed in that state also.

He got up to feed the fire and tossed in the film Mary Beth had given him to guard. He got a drink of water at the pump in the kitchen and lay down by her again. His fatigue increased, but pleasurably. His weariness was without pain, a floating sensation that was between sleep and wakefulness. Sometimes he talked quietly to her, but not much, and what he said he forgot as soon as the words formed. It was better to lie without sound, without motion. Now and then she shook convulsively and then subsided again. Twilight came, darkness, then twilight again. Several times he aroused enough to build up the fire.

When it was daylight once more, he got up, reeling as if drunken; he pulled on his clothes and went to the kitchen to make instant coffee. He sensed her presence behind him. She was standing up, nearly as tall as he was, but incredibly insubstantial, not thin, but as slender as a straw. Her golden eyes were wide open. He could not read the expression on her face.

"Can you eat anything?" he asked. "Drink water?"

She looked at him. The black mantle was gone from her head; he could not see it anywhere on her as she faced him. The strange folds of skin at her groin, the boneless appearance of her body, the lack of hair, breasts, the very color of her skin looked right now not alien, not repellent. The skin was like cool silk, he knew. He also knew this was not a woman, not a she, but something that should not be here, a creature, an it.

"Can you speak? Can you understand me at all?"

Her expression was as unreadable as that of a wild creature, a forest animal, aware, intelligent, unknowable.

Helplessly he said, "Please, if you can understand me, nod. Like this." He showed her, and in a moment she nodded. "And like this for no," he said. She mimicked him again.

"Do you understand that people are looking for you?"

She nodded slowly. Then very deliberately she turned around, and instead of the black mantle that had grown on her head, down her back, there was an iridescence, a rainbow of pastel colors that shimmered and gleamed. Eddie sucked in his breath as the new growth moved, opened slightly more.

There wasn't enough room in the cabin for her to open the wings all the way. She stretched them from wall to wall. They looked like gauze, filmy, filled with light that was alive. Not realizing he was moving, Eddie was drawn to one of the wings, reached out to touch it. It was as hard as steel and cool. She turned her golden liquid eyes to him and drew her wings in again.

"We'll go someplace where it's warm," Eddie said hoarsely; "I'll hide you. I'll smuggle you somehow. They can't have you!"

She walked through the living room to the door and studied the handle for a moment. As she reached for it, he lumbered after her, lunged toward her, but already she was opening the door, slipping out.

"Stop! You'll freeze. You'll die!"

In the clearing of the forest, with sunlight slanting through the giant trees, she spun around, lifted her face upward, and then opened her wings all the way. As effortlessly as a butterfly, or a bird, she drew herself up into the air, her wings flashing light, now gleaming, now appearing to vanish as the light reflected one way and another.

"Stop!" Eddie cried again. "Please! Oh, God, stop! Come back!"

She rose higher and looked down at him with her golden eyes. Suddenly the air seemed to tremble with sound, trills and arpeggios and flutings. Her mouth did not open as the sounds increased until Eddie fell to his knees and clapped his hands over his ears, moaning. When he looked again, she was still rising, shining, invisible, shining again. Then she was gone. Eddie pitched forward into the thick layer of fir needles and forest humus and lay still. He felt a tugging on his arm and heard Mary Beth's furious curses but as if from a great distance. He moaned and tried to go to sleep again. She would not let him.

"You goddamn bastard! You filthy son of a bitch! You let it go! Didn't you? You turned it loose!"

He tried to push her hands away.

"You scum! Get up! You hear me? Don't think for a minute, Buster, that I'll let you die out here! That's too good for you, you lousy tub of lard. Get up!"

Against his will he was crawling, then stumbling, leaning on her, being steadied by her. She kept cursing all the way back inside the cabin, until he was on the couch, and she stood over him, arms akimbo, glaring at him.

"Why? Just tell me why. For God's sake, tell me, Eddie, why?" Then she screamed at him, "Don't you dare pass out on me again. Open those damn eyes and keep them open!"

She savaged him and nagged him, made him drink whiskey that she had brought along, then made him drink coffee. She got him to his feet and made him walk around the cabin a little, let him sit down again, drink again. She did not let him go to sleep, or even lie down, and the night passed.

A fine rain had started to fall by dawn. Eddie felt as if he had been away a long time, to a very distant place that had left few memories. He listened to the soft rain and at first thought he was in his own small house, but then he realized he was in a strange cabin and that Mary Beth was there, asleep in a chair. He regarded her curiously and shook his head, trying to clear it. His movement brought her sharply awake.

"Eddie, are you awake?"

"I think so. Where is this place?"

"Don't you remember?"

He started to say no, checked himself, and suddenly he was remembering. He stood up and looked about almost wildly.

"It's gone, Eddie. It went away and left you to die. You would have died out there if I hadn't come, Eddie. Do you understand what I'm saying?"

He sat down again and lowered his head into his hands. He knew she was telling the truth.

"It's going to be light soon," she said. "I'll make us something to eat, and then we'll go back to town. I'll drive you. We'll come back in a day or so to pick up your car." She stood up and groaned. "My God, I feel like I've been wrestling bears all night. I hurt all over."

She passed close enough to put her hand on his shoulder briefly. "What the hell, Eddie. Just what the hell."

In a minute he got up also and went to the bedroom, looked at the bed where he had lain with her all through the night. He approached it slowly and saw the remains of the mantle. When he tried to pick it up, it crumbled to dust in his hand.

The Goat Cutter

Jay Lake

Jay Lake's chilling story uses the association of goats and flies with the devil and demons. The equation of flies with the demonic is easily traced to the New Testament. Beelzebub (literally "lord of flies") is identified as the "prince of demons" in Matthew, Mark and Luke. The goat connection is not as direct: the Greek god Pan was half man, half goat; pastoral, but bestial, he was also a fertility god. Pan and his band of goat-men satyrs were a randy lot and overt sexuality was not a positive with the early Church. Moreover, St Jerome (c. 347–420) interpreted the Hebrew se'irim, "hairy ones" (derived from sa'ir, or "goat") in Isaiah's description of the ruins of Babylon to mean "satyr". Leviticus 17:7 refers to the practice of sacrificing to the se'irim (variously translated into English as "devils", "demons", "he-goats", "goat idols", etc.). Pan's cloven hooves, horns, hairiness, and prominent phallus were eventually turned into demonic symbolism by artists seeking a way to portray Satan.

The Devil lives in Houston by the ship channel in a high-rise apartment fifty-seven stories up. They say he's got cowhide sofas and a pinball machine and a telescope in there that can see past the oil refineries and across Pasadena all the way to the Pope in Rome and on to where them Arabs pray to that big black stone.

He can see anyone anywhere from his place in the Houston sky, and he can see inside their hearts.

But I know it's all a lie. Except about the hearts, of course. Cause I know the Devil lives in an old school bus in the woods outside of Dale, Texas. He don't need no telescope to see inside your heart, on account of he's already there.

This I know.

Central Texas gets mighty hot come summer. The air rolls in heavy off the Gulf, carries itself over two hundred miles of cow shit and sorghum fields and settles heavy on all our heads. The katydids buzz in the woods like electric fans with bad bearings, and even the skeeters get too tired to bite most days. You can smell the dry coming off the Johnson grass and out of the bar ditches.

Me and my best friend Pootie, we liked to run through the woods, climbing bob wire and following pipelines. Trees is smaller there, easier to slip between. You gotta watch out in deer season, though. Idiots come out from Austin or San Antone to their leases, get blind drunk and shoot every blessed thing that moves. Rest of the time, there's nothing but you and them turkey vultures. Course, you can't steal beer coolers from turkey vultures.

The Devil, he gets on pretty good with them turkey vultures.

So me and Pootie was running the woods one afternoon somewhere in the middle of summer. We was out of school, waiting to be sophomores in the fall, fixing to amount to something. Pootie was bigger than me, but I already got tongue off Martha Dempsey. Just a week or so ago back of the church hall, I even scored a little titty squeeze inside her shirt. It was over her bra, but that counts for something. I knew I was coming up good.

Pootie swears he saw Rachel MacIntire's nipples, but she's his cousin. I reckoned he just peeked through the bathroom window of his aunt's trailer house, which ain't no different from me watching Momma get out of the shower. It don't count. If there was anything to it, he'd a sucked on 'em, and I'd of never heard the end of *that*. Course I wouldn't say no to my cousin Linda if she offered to show me a little something in the shower.

Yeah, that year we was big boys, the summer was hot, and we was always hungry and horny.

Then we met the Devil.

Me and Pootie crossed the bob wire fence near the old bus wallow on county road 61, where they finally built that little bridge over the draw. Doug Bob Aaronson had that place along the south side of 61, spent his time roasting goats, drinking tequila and shooting people's dogs.

Doug Bob was okay, if you didn't bring a dog. Three years back, once we turned ten, he let me and Pootie drink his beer with him. He liked to liquor up, strip down to his underwear and get his ass real warm from the fire in his smoker. We was just a guy and two kids in their shorts drinking in the woods. I'm pretty sure Momma and Uncle Reuben would of had hard words, so I never told.

We kind of hoped now that we was going to be sophomores, he'd crack some of that Sauza Conmemorativo Anejo for us.

Doug Bob's place was all grown over, wild rose and stretch vine and beggar's lice everywhere, and every spring a huge-ass wisteria wrapped his old cedar house with lavender flowers and thin whips of wood. There was trees everywhere around in the brush, mesquite and hackberry and live oak and juniper and a few twisty old pecans. Doug Bob knew all the plants and trees, and taught 'em to us sometimes when he was less than half drunk. He kept chickens around the place and a mangy duck that waddled away funny whenever he got to looking at it.

We come crashing through the woods one day that summer, hot, hungry, horny and full of fight. Pootie'd told me about Rachel's nipples, how they was set in big pink circles and stuck out like little red thumbs. I told him I'd seen that picture in *Hustler* same as him. If'n he was gonna lie, lie from a magazine I hadn't stole us from the Triple E Grocery.

Doug Bob's cedar house was bigger than three double-wides. It set at the back of a little clearing by the creek that ran down from the bus wallow. He lived there, fifty feet from a rusted old school bus that he wouldn't never set foot inside. Only time I asked him about that bus, he cracked me upside the head so hard I saw double for days and had to tell Uncle Reuben I fell off my bike.

That would of been a better lie if I'd of recollected that my bike'd been stolen three weeks gone. Uncle Reuben didn't beat me much worse than normal, and we prayed extra long over the Bible that night for forgiveness.

Doug Bob was pretty nice. He about never hit me, and he kept his underpants on when I was around.

That old smoker was laid over sidewise on the ground, where it didn't belong. Generally, Doug Bob kept better care of it than anything except an open bottle of tequila. He had cut the smoker from a gigantic water heater, so big me and Pootie could of slept in it. Actually, we did a couple of times, but you can't never get ash out of your hair after.

And Pootie snored worse than Uncle Reuben.

Doug Bob roasted his goats in that smoker, and he was mighty particular about his goats. He always killed his goats hisself. They didn't usually belong to him, but he did his own killing. Said it made him a better man. I thought it mostly made him a better mess. The meat plant over in Lockhart could of done twice the job in half the time, with no bath in the creek afterward.

Course, when you're sweaty and hot and full of piss and vinegar, there's nothing like a splash around down in the creek with some beer and one of them big cakes of smelly purple horse soap me and Pootie stole out of barns for Doug Bob. Getting rubbed down with that stuff kind of stings, but it's a good sting.

Times like that, I knew Doug Bob liked me just for myself. We'd all smile and laugh and horse around and get drunk. Nobody got hit, nobody got hurt, everybody went home happy.

★   ★   ★

Doug Bob always had one of these goats, and it was always a buck. Sometimes a white Saanen, or maybe a creamy La Mancha or a brown Nubian looked like a chubby deer with them barred goat eyes staring straight into your heart. They was always clean, no socks nor blazes nor points, just one color all over. Doug Bob called them *unblemished*.

And Doug Bob always killed these goats on the north side of the smoker. He had laid some rocks down there, to make a clear spot for when it was muddy from winter rain or whatever. He'd cut their throats with his jagged knife that was older than sin, and sprinkle the blood all around the smoker.

He never let me touch that knife.

Doug Bob, he had this old gray knife without no handle, just rags wrapped up around the end. The blade had a funny shape like it got beat up inside a thresher or something, as happened to Momma's sister Cissy the year I was born. Her face had that funny shape until Uncle Reuben found her hanging in the pole barn one morning with her dress up over her head.

They puttied her up for the viewing at the funeral home, but I recall Aunt Cissy best with those big dents in her cheek and jaw and the one brown eye gone all white like milk in coffee.

Doug Bob's knife, that I always thought of as Cissy's knife, it was kind of wompered and shaped all wrong, like a corn leaf the bugs been at. He'd take that knife and saw the head right off his goat.

I never could figure how Doug Bob kept that edge on.

He'd flay that goat, and strip some fatback off the inside of the hide, and put the head and the fat right on the smoker where the fire was going, wet chips of mesquite over a good hot bed of coals.

Then he'd drag the carcass down to creek, to our swimming hole, and sometimes me and Pootie could help with this part. We'd wash out the gut sac and clean off the heart and lungs and liver. Doug Bob always scrubbed the legs specially well with that purple horse soap. We'd generally get a good lot of blood in the water. If it hadn't rained in a while, like most summers, the water'd be sticky for hours afterward.

Doug Bob would take the carcass and the sweetbreads – that's what he called the guts, sweetbreads. I figured they looked more like spongy purple and red bruises than bread, kind of like dog food fresh outta the can. And there wasn't nothing sweet about them.

Sweetbreads taste better than dog food, though. We ate dog food in the winter sometimes, ate it cold if Uncle Reuben didn't have work and Momma'd been lazy. That was when I most missed my summers in the woods with Pootie, calling in on Doug Bob.

Doug Bob would drag these goat parts back up to the smoker, where he'd take the head and the fat off the fire. He'd always give me and Pootie some of that fat, to keep us away from the head meat, I guess. Doug Bob would put the carcass and the sweetbreads on the fire and spit his high-proof tequila all over them. If they didn't catch straight away from that, he'd light 'em with a Bic.

We'd watch them burn, quiet and respectful like church on account of that's what Doug Bob believed. He always said God told him to keep things orderly, somewhere in the beginning of Leviticus.

Then he'd close the lid and let the meat cook. He didn't never clean up the blood around the smoker, although he would catch some to write Bible verses on the sides of that old school bus with.

The Devil lives in San Francisco in a big apartment on Telegraph Hill. Way up there with all that brass and them potted ferns and naked women with leashes on, he's got a telescope that can see across the bay, even in the fog. They say he can see all the way to China and Asia, with little brown people and big red demon gods, and stare inside their hearts

The Devil, he can see inside everybody's heart, just about.

It's a lie, except that part about the hearts. There's only one place in God's wide world where the Devil can't see.

*   ★   ★

Me and Pootie, we found that smoker laying over on its side,
which we ain't never seen. There was a broken tequila bottle
next to it, which ain't much like Doug Bob neither.

Well, we commenced to running back and forth, calling out
"Doug Bob!" and "Mr Aaronson!" and stuff. That was dumb
cause if he was around and listening, he'd of heard us giggling
and arguing by the time we'd crossed his fence line.

I guess we both knew that, 'cause pretty quick we fell quiet
and starting looking around. I felt like I was on TV or something, and there was a bad thing fixing to happen next. Them
saloon doors were flapping in my mind and I started wishing
mightily for a commercial.

That old bus of Doug Bob's, it was a long bus, like them revival
preachers use to bring their people into town. I always thought
going to Glory when you died meant getting on one of them
long buses painted white and gold, with Bible verses on the
side and a choir clapping and singing in the back and some
guy in a powder-blue suit and hair like a raccoon pelt kissing
you on the cheek and slapping you on the forehead.

Well, I been kissed more than I want to, and I don't know
nobody with a suit, no matter the color, and there ain't no
choir ever going to sing me to my rest now, except if maybe
they're playing bob wire harps and beating time on burnt
skulls. But Doug Bob's bus, it sat there flat on the dirt with the
wiry bones of tires wrapped over dented black hubs grown
with morning glory, all yellow with the rusted old metal showing through, with the windows painted black from the inside
and crossed over with duct tape. It had a little vestibule Doug
Bob'd built over the double doors out of wood from an old
church in Rosanky. The entrance to that vestibule was crossed
over with duct tape just like the windows. It was bus number
seven, whatever place it had come from.

And bus number seven was covered with them Bible verses
written in goat's blood, over and over each other to where
there was just red-brown smears on the cracked windshield
and across the hood and down the sides, scrambled scribbling

that looked like Aunt Cissy's drool on the lunch table at Wal-Mart. And they made about as much sense.

I even seen Doug Bob on the roof of that bus a few times, smearing bloody words with his fingers like a message to the turkey vultures, or maybe all the way to God above looking down from His air-conditioned heaven.

So I figured, the smoker's tipped, the tequila's broke, and here's my long bus bound for glory with Bible verses on the side, and the only choir is the katydids buzzing in the trees and me and Pootie breathing hard. I saw the door of the wooden vestibule on the bus, that Doug Bob never would touch, was busted open, like it had been kicked out from the inside. The duct tape just flapped loose from the door frame.

I stared all around that bus, and there was a new verse on the side, right under the driver's window. It was painted fresh, still shiny and red. It said, "Of the tribe of Reuben were sealed twelve thousand."

"Pootie."

"Huh?" He was gasping pretty hard. I couldn't take my eyes off the bus, which looked as if it was gonna rise up from the dirt and rumble down the road to salvation any moment, but I knew Pootie had that wild look where his eyes get almost all white and his nose starts to bleed. I could tell from his breathing.

Smelled like he wet his pants, too.

"Pootie," I said again, "there ain't no fire, and there ain't no fresh goat been killed. Where'd the blood come from for that there Bible verse?"

"Reckon he talking 'bout your uncle?" Pootie's voice was duller than Momma at Christmas.

Pootie was an idiot. Uncle Reuben never had no twelve thousand in his life. If he ever did, he'd of gone to Mexico and to hell with me and Momma. "Pootie," I tried again, "where'd the blood come from?"

I knew, but I didn't want to be the one to say it.

Pootie panted for a little while longer. I finally tore my eyes off that old bus, which was shimmering like summer heat, to see Pootie bent over with his hands on his knees and his head hanging down. "It ain't his handwritin' neither," Pootie sobbed.

We both knew Doug Bob was dead.

Something was splashing around down by the creek. "Aw, shit," I said. "Doug Bob was . . . is our friend. We gotta go look."

It ain't but a few steps to the bank. We could see a man down there, bending over with his bare ass toward us. He was washing something big and pale. It weren't no goat.

Me and Pootie, we stopped at the top of the bank, and the stranger stood up and turned around. I about shit my pants.

He had muscles like a movie star, and a gold tan all the way down, like he'd never wore clothes. The hair on his chest and his short-and-curlies was blond, and he was hung good. What near to made me puke was that angel's body had a goat head. Only it weren't no goat head you ever saw in your life.

It was like a big heavy ram's head, except it had *antlers* coming up off the top, a twelve-point spread off a prize buck, and baby's eyes – big, blue and round in the middle. Not goat's eyes at all. That fur kind of tapered off into golden skin at the neck.

And those blue eyes blazed at me like ice on fire.

The tall, golden thing pointed to a body in the creek. He'd been washing the legs with purple soap. "Help me with this. I think you know how it needs to be done." His voice was windy and creaky, like he hadn't talked to no one for a real long time.

The body was Doug Bob, with his big gut and saggy butt, and a bloody stump of a neck.

"You son of a bitch!" I ran down the bank, screaming and swinging my arms for the biggest punch I could throw. I don't know, maybe I tripped over a root or stumbled at the water's edge, but that golden thing moved like summer lightning just as I slipped off my balance.

Last thing I saw was the butt end of Doug Bob's ragged old knife coming at me in his fist. I heard Pootie crying my name when my head went all red and painful.

* * *

The Devil lives in your neighborhood, yours and mine. He lives in every house in every town, and he has a telescope that looks out the bathroom mirror and up from the drains in the kitchen and out of the still water at the bottom of the toilet bowl. He can see inside of everyone's heart through their eyes and down their mouth and up their asshole.

It's true, I know it is.

The hope I hold secret deep inside my heart is that there's one place on God's green earth the Devil can't see.

I was naked, my dick curled small and sticky to my thigh like it does after I've been looking through the bathroom window. A tight little trail of cum itched my skin. My ass was on dirt, and I could feel ants crawling up the crack. I opened my mouth to say, "Fine," and a fly buzzed out from the inside. There was another one in the left side of my nose that seemed ready to stay a spell.

I didn't really want to open my eyes. I knew where I was. My back was against hot metal. It felt sticky. I was leaning against Doug Bob's bus and part of that new Bible verse about Uncle Reuben under the driver's window had run and got Doug Bob's heart blood all down my back. I could smell mesquite smoke, cooked meat, shit, blood and the old oily metal of the bus.

But in all my senses, in the feel of the rusted metal, in the warmth of the ground, in the stickiness of the blood, in the sting of the ant bites, in the touch of the fly crawling around inside my nose, in the stink of Doug Bob's rotten little yard, there was something missing. It was an absence, a space, like when you get a tooth busted out in a fight and notice it for not being there.

I was surrounded by absence, cold in the summer heat. My heart felt real slow. I still didn't want to open my eyes.

"You know," said that windy, creaky voice, sounding even more hollow and thin than before, "if they would just repent of their murders, their sorceries, their fornication and their thefts, this would be a lot harder."

The voice was sticky, like the blood on my back, and cold,

coming from the middle of whatever was missing around me.
I opened my eyes and squinted into the afternoon sun.

Doug Bob's face smiled at me. Leastwise it tried to. Up
close I could tell a whole lot of it was burnt off, with griddle
marks where his head had lain a while on the smoker. Blackened bone showed through across the cheeks. Doug Bob's
head was duct-taped to the neck of that glorious, golden body,
greasy black hair falling down those perfect shoulders. The
head kept trying to lop over as he moved, like it was stuck on
all wompered. His face was puffy and burnt up, weirder than
Doug Bob mostly ever looked.

The smoker must of been working again.

The golden thing with Doug Bob's head had Pootie spread out
naked next to the smoker. I couldn't tell if he was dead, but
sure he wasn't moving. Doug Bob's legs hung over the side of
the smoker, right where he'd always put the goat legs. Cissy's
crazy knife was in that golden right hand, hanging loose like
Uncle Reuben holds his when he's fixing to fight someone.

"I don't understand . . ." I tried to talk, but burped up a little
bit of vomit and another fly to finish my sentence. The inside
of my nose stung with the smell, and the fly in there didn't
seem to like it much neither. "You stole Doug Bob's head."

"You see, my son, I have been set free from my confine-
ment. My time is at hand." Doug Bob's face wrinkled into a
smile, as some of his burnt lip scaled away. I wondered how
much of Doug Bob was still down in the creek. "But even I
cannot walk the streets with my proud horns."

His voice got sweeter, stronger, as he talked. I stared up at
him, blinking in the sunlight.

"Rise up and join me. We have much work to do, preparations
for my triumph. As the first to bow to my glory you shall rank
high among my new disciples, and gain your innermost desire."

Uncle Reuben taught me long ago how this sweet bullshit
always ends. The old Doug Bob liked me. Maybe even loved
me a little. He was always kind to me, which this golden Doug
Bob ain't never gonna be.

It must be nice to be loved a lot.

I staggered to my feet, farting ants, using the ridges in the sheet metal of the bus for support. It was hot as hell, and even the katydids had gone quiet. Except for the turkey vultures circling low over me, I felt like I was alone in a giant dirt coffin with a huge blue lid over my head. I felt expanded, swollen in the heat like a dead coyote by the side of the road.

The thing wearing Doug Bob's head narrowed his eyes at me. There was a faint crinkling sound as the lids creased and broke.

"Get over here, *now*." His voice had the menace of a Sunday morning twister headed for a church, the power of a wall of water in the arroyo where kids played.

I walked toward the Devil, feet stepping without my effort.

There's a place I can go, inside, when Uncle Reuben's pushing into me, or he's using the metal end of the belt, or Momma's screaming through the thin walls of our trailer the way he can make her do. It's like ice cream without the cone, like cotton candy without the stick. It's like how I imagine Rachel MacIntire's nipples, sweet and total, like my eyes and heart are in my lips and the world has gone dark around me.

It's the place where I love myself, deep inside my heart.

I went there and listened to the little shuffling of my pulse in my ears.

My feet walked on without me, but I couldn't tell.

Cissy's knife spoke to me. The Devil must of put it in my hand.

"We come again to Moriah," it whispered in my heart. It had a voice like its metal blade, cold from the ground and old as time.

"What do you want?" I asked. I must of spoke out loud, because Doug Bob's burned mouth was twisting in screaming rage as he stabbed his golden finger down toward Pootie, naked at my feet next to the smoker. All I could hear was my pulse, and the voice of the knife.

Deep inside my heart, the knife whispered again. "Do not lay a hand on the boy."

The golden voice from Doug Bob's face was distant thunder in my ears. I felt his irritation, rage, frustration building where I had felt that cold absence.

I tried again. "I don't understand."

Doug Bob's head bounced up and down, the duct tape coming loose. I saw pink ropy strings working to bind the burned head to his golden neck. He cocked back a fist, fixing to strike me a hard blow.

I felt the knife straining across the years toward me. "You have a choice. The Enemy promises anything and everything for your help. I can give you nothing but the hope of an orderly world. You choose what happens now, and after."

I reckoned the Devil would run the world about like Uncle Reuben might. Doug Bob was already dead, and Pootie was next, and there wasn't nobody else like them in my life, no matter what the Devil promised. I figured there was enough hurt to go around already and I knew how to take it into me.

Another one of Uncle Reuben's lessons.

"Where you want this killing done?" I asked.

The golden thunder in my ears paused for a moment, the tide of rage lapped back from the empty place where Doug Bob wasn't. The fist dropped down.

"Right here, right now," whispered the knife. "Or it will be too late. Seven is being opened."

I stepped out of my inside place to find my eyes still open and Doug Bob's blackened face inches from my nose. His teeth were burnt and cracked, and his breath reeked of flies and red meat. I smiled, opened my mouth to speak, but instead of words I swung Cissy's knife right through the duct tape at the throat of Doug Bob's head.

He looked surprised.

Doug Bob's head flew off, bounced into the bushes. The golden body swayed, still on its two feet. I looked down at Pootie, the old knife cold in my hands.

Then I heard buzzing, like thunder made of wires.

★　　★　　★

I don't know if you ever ate a fly, accidental or not. They go down fighting, kind of tickle the throat, you get a funny feeling for a second, and then it's all gone. Not very filling, neither.

These flies came pouring out of the ragged neck of that golden body. They were big, the size of horseflies. All at once they were everywhere, and they came right at me. They came pushing at my eyes and my nose and my ears and flying right into my mouth, crawling down my throat. It was like stuffing yourself with raisins till you choke, except these raisins crawled and buzzed and bit at me.

The worst was they got all over me, crowding into my butt crack and pushing on my asshole and wrapping around my balls like Uncle Reuben's fingers right before he squeezed tight. My skin rippled, as if them flies crawled through my flesh.

I jumped around, screaming and slapping at my skin. My gut heaved, but my throat was full of flies and it all met in a knot at the back of my mouth. I rolled to the ground, choking on the rippling mess I couldn't spit out nor swallow back down. Through the flies I saw Doug Bob's golden body falling in on itself, like a balloon that's been popped. Then the choking took me off.

I lied about the telescope. I don't need one.

Right after, while I was still mostly myself, I sent Pootie away with that old knife to find one of Doug Bob's kin. They needed that knife, to make their sacrifices that would keep me shut away. I made Pootie seal me inside the bus with Doug Bob's duct tape before he left.

The bus is hot and dark, but I don't really mind. There's just me and the flies and a hot metal floor with rubber mats and huge stacks of old Bibles and hymnals that make it hard for me to move around.

It's okay, though, because I can watch the whole world from in here.

I hate the flies, but they're the only company I can keep. The taste grows on me.

I know Pootie must of found someone to give that old knife to. I try the doors sometimes, but they hold firm. Somewhere one of Doug Bob's brothers or uncles or cousins cuts goats the old way. Someday I'll find him. I can see every heart except one, but there are too many to easily tell one from another.

There's only one place under God's golden sun the Devil can't see into, and that's his own heart.

I still have my quiet place. That's where I hold my hope, and that's where I go when I get too close to the goat cutter.

Spirit Guides

Kristine Kathryn Rusch

Despite what various historical markers state and the protagonist of Kris Rusch's "Spirit Guides" thinks, historians still disagree on the original name of the "City of Angels". On 2 August 1769, Father Juan Crespí, a Franciscan priest accompanying the first European land expedition through California, described a "beautiful river" in his journal. He dubbed the river Nuestra Señora de los Ángeles de la Porciúncula. [The second of August was a feast day celebrated at the tiny Italian chapel where St Francis of Assisi lived and founded the Franciscan order. Located on a porziuncola *(Italian for a "very small portion of land"), a fresco of the Virgin Mary surrounded by angels was painted on the wall behind its altar – thus the chapel's name: St Mary of the Angels at the Little Portion. In 1781, a settlement was established on the river. According to the first map of the area (1785) the village was named El Pueblo de la Reina de los Ángeles: "The Town of the Queen of the Angels". The more unwieldy attribution El Pueblo de Nuestra Señora Reina de los Ángeles sobre el Río Porciúncula (or "The Town of Our Lady the Queen of Angels on the River of the Little Portion") and variants were, most likely, a later Franciscan historian's effort to firmly acknowledge a connection to his order. The Porciuncula River is now called the Los Angeles River.*

★　　★　　★

Los Angeles. City of the Angels.

Kincaid walked down Hollywood Boulevard, his feet stepping on gum-coated stars. Cars whooshed past him, horns honking, tourists gawking. The line outside Graumann's Chinese clutched purses against their sides, held windbreakers tightly over their arms. A hooker leaned against the barred display window of the corner drugstore, her make-up so thick it looked like a mask in the hot sun.

The shooting had left him shaken. The crazy had opened up inside a nearby Burger Joint, slaughtering four customers and three teenaged kids behind the counter before three men, passing on the street, rushed inside and grabbed him. Half a dozen shots had gone wild, leaving fist-sized holes in the drywall, shattering picture frames, and making one perfect circle in the center of the cardboard model for a bacon-double cheeseburger.

He'd arrived two minutes too late, hearing the call on his police scanner on his way home, but unable to maneuver in traffic. Christ, some of those people who wouldn't let him pass might have had relatives in that Burger Joint. Still and all, he had arrived first to find the killer trussed up in a chair, the men hovering around him, women clutching sobbing children, blood and bodies mixing with French fries on the unswept floor.

A little girl, no more than three, had grabbed his sleeve and pointed at one of the bodies, long slender male and young, wearing a '49ers T-shirt, ripped jeans and Adidas, face a bloody mass of tissue, and said, "Make him better," in a whisper that broke Kincaid's heart. He cuffed the suspect, roped off the area, took names of witnesses before the backup arrived. Three squads, fresh-faced uniformed officers, followed by the SWAT team, nearly five minutes too late, the forensic team and the ambulances not far behind.

Kincaid had lit a cigarette with shaking fingers and said, "All yours," before taking off into the sun-drenched crowded streets.

He stopped outside the Roosevelt, and peered into the plate glass. His own tennis shoes were stained red, and a long brown streak of drying blood marked his Levis. The cigarette had burned to a coal between his nicotine-stained fingers, and he tossed it, stamping it out on the star of a celebrity whose name he didn't recognize.

Inside stood potted palms and faded glamour. Pictures of motion picture stars long dead lined the second-floor balcony. Within the last ten years, the hotel's management had restored the Roosevelt to its twenties glory, when it had been the site for the first-ever Academy Award celebration. When he first came to LA, he spent a lot of time in the hotel, imagining the low-cut dresses, the clink of champagne flutes, the scattered applause as the nominees were announced. Searching for a kind of beauty that existed only in celluloid, a product of light and shadows and nothing more.

El Pueblo de Nuestra Señora la Reina de los Angeles de Porciúncula.

The City of Our Lady, Queen of the Angels of Porciuncula.

He knew nothing of the Angels of Porciuncula, did not know why Felipe de Neve in 1781 named the city after them. He suspected it was some kind of prophecy, but he didn't know.

They had been fallen angels.

Of that he was sure.

He sighed, wiped the sweat from his forehead with a grimy hand, then returned to his car, knowing that home and sleep would elude him for one more night.

Lean and spare, Kincaid survived on cigarettes, coffee, chocolate and bourbon. Sometime in the last five years, he had allowed the LAPD to hire him, although he had no formal training. After a few odd run-ins and one overnight jail stay before it became clear that Kincaid wasn't anywhere near the crime scene, Kincaid had met Davis, his boss. Davis had the flat gaze of a man who had seen too much, and he knew, from the records and the evidence before him, that Kincaid was too precious to lose. He made Kincaid a plain clothes detective and never assigned him a partner.

Kincaid never told anyone what he did. Most of the cops he worked with never knew. All they cared about was that when Kincaid was on the job, suspects were found, cases were closed, and files were sealed. He worked quietly and he got results.

They didn't need him on this one. The perp was caught at the scene. All he had to do was write his report, then go home, toss the tennies in the trash, soak the Levi's, and wait for another day.

But it wasn't that easy. He sat in his car, an olive green 1988 Olds with a fading pine-shaped air freshener hanging from the rear-view mirror, long after his colleagues had left. His hands were still shaking, his nostrils still coated with the scent of blood and burgers, his ears dogged with the faint sobs of a pimply faced boy rocking over the body of a fallen co-worker. The images would stick, along with all of the others. His brain was reaching overload. Had been for a long time. But that little girl's voice, the plea in her tone, had been more than he could bear.

For twenty years, he had tried to escape, always ending up in a new town, with new problems. Shootings in Oklahoma parking lots, bombings in Upstate New York, murders in restaurants and shopping malls and suburban family pickups. The violence surrounded him, and he was trapped.

Surely this time, they would let him get away.

A hooker knocked on the window of his car. He thought he could smell the sweat and perfume through the rolled-up glass. Her cleavage was mottled, her cheap elastic top revealing the top edge of brown nipple.

He shook his head, then turned the ignition and grabbed the gearshift on the column to take the car out of park. The Olds roared to life, and with it came the adrenaline rush, hormones tinged with panic. He pulled out of the parking space, past the hooker, down Hollywood Boulevard toward the first freeway intersection he could find.

Kincaid would disappear from the LAPD as mysteriously as he had arrived. He stopped long enough to pick up his clothes, his credit cards and a hand-painted coffee mug a teen-aged girl in Galveston had given him twenty years before, when she mistakenly thought he had saved her life.

He merged into the continuous LA rush-hour traffic for the last time, radio off, clutching the wheel in white-knuckled tightness. He would go to Big Bear, up in the mountains, where there were no people, no crimes, nothing except himself and the wilderness.

He drove away from the angels.

Or so he hoped.

Kincaid drove until he realized he was on the road to Las Vegas. He pulled the Olds over, put on his hazards and bowed his head, unwilling to go any further. But he knew, even if he didn't drive there, he would wake up in Vegas, his car in the lot outside. It had happened before.

He didn't remember taking the wrong turn, but he wasn't supposed to remember. They were just telling him that his work wasn't done, the work they had forced him to do ever since he was a young boy.

With a quick, vicious movement, he got out of the Olds and shook his fist at the star-filled desert sky. "I can't take it anymore, do you hear me?"

But no shape flew across the moon, no angel wings brushed his cheek, no reply filled his heart. He could turn around, but the roads he drove would only lead him back to Los Angeles, back to people, back to murders in which little girls stood in pools of blood. He knew what Los Angeles was like. Maybe they would allow him a few days rest in Vegas.

Las Vegas, the fertile plains, originally founded in the late 1700s like LA, only the settlement didn't become permanent until 1905 when the first lots were sold (and nearly flooded out five years later). He thought maybe the city's youth and brash-ness would be a tonic, but even as he drove into town, he felt the blood beneath the surface. Despair and hopelessness had come to every place in America. Only here it mingled with the cajing-jing of slot machines and the smell of money.

He wanted to stay in the MGM Grand, but the Olds wouldn't drive through the lot. He settled on a cheap tumble-down hotel on the far side of the strip, complete with chenille bedspreads and rattling window air conditioners that dripped water on the thin brown indoor-outdoor carpet. There he slept in the protective dark of the blackout curtains, and dreamed:

Angels floated above him, wings so long the tips brushed his face. As he watched, they tucked their wings around them-selves and plummeted, eagle-like, to the ground below, banking when the concrete of a major superhighway rose in front of them. He was on the bed, watching, helpless, knowing that each time the long white tail feathers touched the earth, violence erupted somewhere it had never been before.

He started awake, coughing the deep racking cough of a three-pack-a-day man. His tongue was thick and tasted of bad coffee and nicotine. He reached for the end table, clicking on the brown glass bubble lamp, then grabbed his lighter and a cigarette from the pack resting on top of the cut-glass ashtray. His hands were still shaking and the room was quiet except for his labored breathing. Only in the silence did he realize that his dream had been accompanied by the sound of the pimply faced boy, sobbing.

It happened just before dawn. A woman's scream, outside, cut off in mid-thrum, followed by a sickening thud and footsteps. He had known it would happen the minute the car had refused to enter the Grand's parking lot. And he had to respond, whether it was his choice or not.

Kincaid paused long enough to pull on his pants, checking to make sure his wallet was in the back pocket. Then he grabbed his key and let himself out of the room.

His window overlooked the pool, a liver-shaped thing built of blue tile in the late fifties. The management left the terrace lights on all night, and Kincaid used those to guide him across the interior courtyard. In the half-light, he saw another shape running toward the pool, a pear-shaped man dressed in the too-tight uniform of a national rent-a-cop service. The air smelled of chlorine and the desert heat was still heavy despite the early morning hour. Leaves and dead bugs floated in the water, and the surrounding patio furniture was so dirty it took a moment for Kincaid to realize it was supposed to be white.

The rent-a-cop had already arrived on the scene, his pasty skin turning green as he looked down. Kincaid came up behind him, stopped, and stared.

The body was crumpled behind the removable diving board. One look at her bloodstained face, swollen and braised neck, her chipped and broken fingernails and he knew.

All of it.

"I'd better call this in," the rent-a-cop said, and Kincaid shook his head, knowing that if he were alone with the body, he would end up spending the next few days in a Las Vegas lock-up.

"No, let me." He went back to his room, packed his meager possessions and set them by the door. Then he called 911 and reported the murder, slipping on a shirt before going back outside.

The rent-a-cop was wiping his mouth with the back of his hand. The air smelled of vomit. Kincaid said nothing. Together they waited for the Nevada authorities to show: a skinny plain clothes detective whose eyes were red-rimmed from lack of sleep and his female partner, busty and official in regulation blue.

While the partner radioed in, the rent-a-cop told his version: that he had been making his rounds and heard a couple arguing poolside. He was watching from the window when the man backhanded the woman, and then took off through the casino. The woman didn't get up, and the cop decided to check on her instead of chasing the guy. Kincaid had shown up a minute or two later from his room in the hotel.

The plain clothes man turned his flat gaze on Kincaid. Kincaid flashed his LAPD badge, then told the plain clothes man that the killer's name was Luther Hardy, that he'd killed her because her anger was the last straw in a day that had seen him lose most of their $10,000 savings on the Mirage's roulette table. Even as the men spoke, Hardy was sitting at the only open craps table in Circus Circus, betting $25 chips on the come line.

Then Kincaid waited for the disbelief, but the plain clothes man nodded, thanked him, rounded up the female partner and headed toward Circus Circus, leaving Kincaid, not the rent-a-cop, to guard the scene. Kincaid rubbed his nose with his thumb and forefinger, trying to stop a building headache, feeling the rent-a-cop's scrutiny. Kincaid could always pick them, the ones who had seen everything, the ones who had learned through hard experience and crazy knocks to check any lead that came their way. Like Davis. Only Kincaid was new to this plain clothes man, so there would be a hundred questions when they returned.

Questions Kincaid was too tired to answer.

He told the rent-a-cop his room number, then staggered back, picked up his things and checked out, figuring he would be halfway to Phoenix before they discovered he was gone for good. They would call LAPD, and Davis would realize that Kincaid had finally left, and would probably light a candle for him later that evening because he would know that Kincaid's singular talent was still controlling his life.

Like a hick tourist, Kincaid stopped on the Hoover Dam. At 8 a.m., he stood on the miraculous concrete structure, staring at the raging blue of the Colorado below. An angel fluttered past him, then wrapped its wings around its torso and dove like a gull after prey. It disappeared in the glare of the sunlight against the water, and he strained, hoping and fearing he'd catch a glimpse as the angel rose, dripping from the water.

The glimpses had haunted him since he was thirteen. He'd been in St Patrick's Cathedral with his mother, and one of the stained glass angels left her window, floated through the air, and kissed him before alighting on the pulpit to tickle the visiting priest during Mass. The priest hadn't noticed the feathers brush his face and neck, but he had died the next day in a mugging outside the subway station at 63rd and Lexington.

Kincaid hadn't seen the mugging, but his train had arrived only a few seconds after the priest died.

Years later, Kincaid finally thought to wonder why he hadn't died from the angel's kiss. And, although he still didn't have the answer, he knew that his second sight came from that morning. All he needed to do was look at a body to know who had driven the spirit from it, and why. The snapshots remained in his mind in all their horror, surrounded by faces frozen in agony, each shot a sharp moment of pain that pierced a hole in his increasingly fragile soul.

As a young man, he believed he could stop the pain, that he had been given the gift so that he could end the horrors. He would ride out, like St George, and defeat the dragon that had terrified the village. But these terrors were as old as time itself, and instead of stopping them, Kincaid could only observe them, and report what his inner eye had seen. He had thought, as he grew older, that using his skills to imprison the perpetrators would help, but the deaths continued, more each year, and the little girl in the Burger Joint had provided the final straw.

Make him better.

Kincaid didn't have that kind of magic.

The angel flew out of the wide crevice, past the canyon walls, its tail feathers dripping just as Kincaid had feared. Somewhere within a two hundred mile radius, someone would die violently because an angel had brushed the earth. Kincaid hunched himself against the bright morning, then turned and walked along the rock-strewn highway to his car. When he got inside, he kept the radio off so that the news of the atrocity would not hit him when it happened.

But the silence wouldn't keep him ignorant forever. He would turn on the TV in a hotel, or pass a row of newspapers outside a restaurant, and the information would present itself to him, as clearly and brightly as it always had, as if it were his responsibility, subject to his control.

The car led him into Phoenix. From the freeway, the city was a row of concrete lanes, marred by machine-painted lines. From the side streets, it had well-manicured lawns and tidy houses, too many strip restaurants and the ubiquitous mall. He was having a chimichanga in a neighborhood Garcia's when he watched the local news and realized that he might not hear of an atrocity after all. He finished the meat and left before the national news aired.

He was still in Phoenix at midnight, and had not yet found a hotel. He didn't want to sleep, didn't want to be led to the next place where someone would die. He was sitting alone at a small table in a high-class strip joint, sipping bourbon that actually had a smooth bite instead of the cheap stuff he normally got. The strippers were legion, all young, with tits high and firm and asses to match. Some had long lean legs and others were all torso. But none approached him, as if a sign were flashing above him warning the women away. He drank until he could feel it – he didn't know how many drinks that was anymore – and was startled that no one noticed him getting tight.

Even drunk, he couldn't relax, couldn't laugh. Enjoyment had leached out of him, decades ago.

When the angel appeared in front of him, he thought it was another stripper, taller than most, wrapped in gossamer wings. Then it unfolded the wings and extended them, gently, as if it were doing a slow-motion fan dance, and he realized that its face had no features, and its body was fat and nippleless like a butterfly.

He raised his glass to it. "You gonna kiss me again?" His thoughts had seemed clear, but the words came out slurred.

The angel said nothing – it probably couldn't speak since it had no mouth. It merely took the drink from him, and set the glass on the table. Then it grabbed his hand, pulled him to his feet, and led him from the room like a recalcitrant child. He vaguely wondered how he looked, stumbling alone through the maze of people, his right arm outstretched.

When the fresh air hit him, the bourbon backed up in his throat like bile. He staggered away from the beefy valets behind the potted cactus, and threw up, the angel standing beside him, still as a statue. After a moment, he stood up and wiped his mouth with the crumpled handkerchief he kept folded in his back pocket. He still felt drunk, but not as bloated.

Then the angel scooped him in its arms. Its body was soft and cold as if it contained no life at all. It cradled him like a baby, and they flew up until the city became a blaze of lights.

The wind ruffled his hair and woke him even more. He felt strangely calm, and he attributed that to the alcohol. Just as he was getting used to the oddness, the angel wrapped its wings around them and plummeted toward the ground.

They were moving so fast, he could feel the force of the air like a slap in his face. He was screaming – he could feel it, ripping at his throat – but he could hear nothing. They hurtled over the interstate. The cars were the size of ants before the angel extended its wings to ease their landing.

The angel tilted them upright, and they touched down in an empty glass-strewn parking lot that led to an insurance office whose door was surrounded by yellow police tape. He recognized the site from the local newscast he had caught in Garcia's: ever since eight that morning, the insurance office had been the location of a hostage situation. A husband had decided to terrorize his wife who worked inside and, although shots had been fired, no one had been injured.

He stared at the building, felt the terror radiate from its walls as if it were a furnace. The insurance company was an old one: the gold lettering on the hand-painted window was chipped, and inside, he could barely make out the shape of an overturned chair. He turned to ask the angel why it had brought him there, when he realized it was gone.

Kincaid stood in the parking lot for a moment, one hand wrapped around his stomach, the other holding his throbbing head. They had flown for miles. He still had his wallet, but had no idea where he was or how he would find a payphone.

And he didn't know what the angel had wanted from him.

He sighed and walked across the parking lot. The broken glass crunched beneath his shoes. His mouth was dry. The police tape looked too yellow in the glare of the street light. He stood on the stoop and peered inside, half hearing the voices from earlier in the day, the shouts from the police bullhorn, the low tense voice of the wife, the terse clipped tones of her

husband. About noon the husband had gone outside to smoke
a cigarette – his wife hated smoke – and had shot a stray dog
to warn off the policeman who had been sneaking up behind
him.

Kincaid could smell the death. He followed his nose to the
side of the building. There, among the gravel and the spindly
flowerless rose bushes, lay the dog on its side. It was scrawny
and its coat was mottled. Its tongue protruded just a bit from
its open mouth. Its glassy eyes seemed to follow Kincaid, and
he wondered how the news had missed this, the sympathy
story amidst all the horror.

The stations in LA would have covered it.

Poor dog. A stray in life, unremembered in death. Just
standing over it, he could see the last moments – the enticing
smell of food from the police cars suddenly mingled with the
scent of human fear, the glittery eyes of the male human and
then pain, sharp, deep and complete.

Kincaid crouched beside it. In all his years, he had never
touched a dead thing, never felt the cold lifeless body, never
totally understood how a body could live and then not live
within the same instant. In the past he had left the dead for
someone else to clean up, but here no one would. The dog
would rot in this site of trauma and near-human tragedy, and
no one would take the care to bury the dead.

Perhaps that was why the angel brought him, to show him
that there had been carnage after all.

He didn't know how to bury it. All he had were his hands.
But he touched the soft soil of the rose garden, his wrist brushing the dog's tail as he did so. The dog coughed and struggled
to sit up.

Kincaid backed away so quickly he nearly fell. The dog
choked, then coughed again, spraying blood all over the
bushes, the gravel and the concrete. It looked at him with a
mixture of fear and pain.

"Jesus," Kincaid muttered.

He pushed himself forward, then grabbed the dog's shoulders. Its labored breathing eased and its tail thumped slightly

against the ground. Something clattered against the pavement, and he saw the bullet, rolling away. The dog stood, whimpered, licked his hand, and then trotted off to fill its empty stomach.

Kincaid sat down in the glass and gravel, staring at his blood-covered hands.

Phoenix.

A creature of myth that rose from its own ashes to live again.

He had been such a fool.

All those years. All those lives.

Such a fool.

He looked up at the star-filled desert sky. The angel that had brought him hovered over him like a teacher waiting to see if the student understood the lecture. He couldn't relive his life, but maybe, just maybe, he could help one little girl who had spoken with the voice of angels.

Make him better.

"Take me back to Los Angeles," he said to the angel. "To the people who died yesterday."

And in a heartbeat, he was back in the Burger Joint. The killer, an overweight acne-scarred man with empty eyes, was tied to a chair near the window, a group of men milling nervously around him, the gun leaning against the wall behind them. All the children were crying, their parents pressing the tiny faces against shoulders, trying to block the sight. The air smelled of burgers and fresh blood.

A little girl, no more than three, grabbed Kincaid's sleeve and pointed at one of the bodies, long slender male and young wearing a '49ers T-shirt, ripped jeans and Adidas, face a bloody mass of tissue, and said, "Make him better," in a whisper that broke Kincaid's heart.

Kincaid crouched, hands shaking, wishing desperately for a cigarette, and grabbed the body by the arm. Air whistled from the lungs, and the blood bubbled in the remains of the face. As Kincaid watched, the face returned, the blood disappeared and a young man was staring at him with fear-filled eyes.

"You all right, friend?" Kincaid asked.

The man nodded – and the little girl flung herself in his arms.

"Jesus," someone said behind him.

Kincaid shook his head. "It's amazing how bad injuries can look when someone's covered with blood."

He didn't wait for the response, just went to the next body and the next, his need for a cigarette decreasing with touch, the blood drying as if it had never been. When he got behind the counter, he gently pushed aside the pimply faced boy sobbing over the dead co-worker, and then he paused.

If he reversed this one, they would have nothing to indict the killer on.

The boy's breath hitched as he watched Kincaid. Kincaid turned and looked over his shoulder at the killer tied to the chair near the entrance. Holes the size of fists marred the drywall and made one perfect circle in the center of the card-board model for a bacon-double cheeseburger. It would be enough.

He grabbed the body's shoulders, feeling the grease of the uniform beneath his fingers. The spirit slid back in as if it had never left, and the wounds sealed themselves as they would on a videotape run backwards.

All those years. All those wasted years.

"How did you do that?" the pimply faced boy asked, his face shiny with tears.

"He was only stunned," Kincaid said.

When he was done, he went outside to find the backup team interviewing witnesses, the ambulances just arriving, five minutes too late.

"All yours," he said, before taking off into the sun-drenched crowded streets.

Now he had to keep moving. No jobs with police depart-ments, no comfortable apartments. He had to stay one step ahead of a victim's shock, one step ahead of the press who would someday catch wind of his ability. He couldn't let them corner him, because the power was not his to control.

He was still trapped.

He stopped outside the Roosevelt, lit a cigarette, and peered into the plate glass. His own tennis shoes were stained red, and a long brown streak of drying blood marked his Levi's. The cigarette had burned to a coal between his nicotine-stained fingers before he had a chance to take a drag, and he tossed it, stamping it out on the star of a celebrity whose name he didn't recognize.

All those years and he never knew. The kiss made some kind of cosmic sense. Even Satan, the head of the fallen angels, was once beloved of God. Even Satan must have felt remorse at the pain he caused. He would never be accepted back into the fold, but he might use his powers to repair some of the pain he caused. Only he wouldn't be able to alone, for each time he touched the earth, he would cause another death. What better to do, then, but to give healing power to a child, who would learn and grow into the role.

Kincaid's hands were still shaking. The blood had crusted beneath his fingernails.

"I never asked for this!" he shouted, and people didn't even turn as they passed on the street. Shouting crazies were common in Hollywood. He held his hands to the sky. "I never asked for this!"

Above him, angels flew like eagles, soaring and dipping and diving, never coming close enough to endanger the Earth. Their featureless faces radiated a kind of joy. And, although he would never admit it, he felt that joy too.

Although he would not slay the dragon, he wouldn't have to live with its carnage either. Finally, at last, he could make some kind of difference. He let his hands fall to his side, and wondered if the Roosevelt would shirk at letting him wash the blood off inside. He was about to ask when a stray dog pushed its muzzle against his thigh.

"Ah, hell," he said, looking down and recognizing the mottled fur, the wary yet trusting eyes. He glanced up, saw one angel hovering. A gift then, for finally understanding. He touched the dog on the back of its neck, and led it to the Olds. The dog jumped inside as if it knew the car. Kincaid sat for a moment, resting his shaking hands against the steering column.

A hooker knocked on the window. He thought he could smell the sweat and perfume through the rolled-up glass. Her cleavage was mottled, her cheap elastic top revealing the top edge of brown nipple.

He shook his head, then turned the ignition and grabbed the gearshift on the column to take the car out of park. The dog barked once, and he grinned at it, before driving home to get his things. This time he wouldn't try Big Bear. This time he would go wherever the spirit led him.

Demons, Your Body, and You

Genevieve Valentine

Modern paranormal romance and urban fantasy often depict love and sexual activity with demons or angels. In these alternate fictional worlds, supernatural creatures and powers are part of a world that, otherwise, closely resembles our own. The romantic beings with whom humans get involved have little resemblance to traditional asexual angels or sexual (if not endearing) demons, but are fun twists on past lore and convention. Genevieve Valentine, however, takes a different look at the consequences of a teenage romance with a hot (pun intended) demon. Her story and its young protagonists entertain while introducing some very real social issues and commentary. Unlike many provocative novels of paranormal desire, this story provokes thought.

Between sophomore and junior years was the summer my parents sent me to the urban day camp, and Katie got impregnated by the demon.

My parents told me the day I came home, so that I would know why she might not be coming back to school.

Finally I managed, "How is she?"

"Feeling pretty badly about what she did, I imagine," said my dad, like that had better be the case or else.

"Can I see her?"

"Sure," said my dad. "But let's wait a while, hey? You have a lot on your mind with school coming up."

My mom nodded. "Now do you see why we sent you to that day camp?"

Only if she got pregnant on a school day while I was at a museum, I thought.

The way my parents had sounded, Katie would never have the disrespect to show her face after what had happened, but when I went out to the bus stop on the first day of school, there she was.

Katie and I weren't close. We were just proximity friends; three houses down. (For Winter Ball freshmen year her mom had driven there and my dad had driven back, and we knew each other just well enough to be happy because my dad was less likely to take photos and her mom was less likely to shout the pickup time out the car window in front of everyone.)

I don't know what I had expected Katie to look like now – maybe that she'd have the little horns coming out of her forehead or something. But she looked the same as last year, except for the circles under her eyes, and since we weren't really friends I didn't know what to say.

Finally I said helpfully, "You don't look pregnant."

She frowned, shrugged. "It might not be as accelerated as they tell you. Usually it takes, like, six months for a demon to gestate, and since it's half-human, nobody knows."

"Are you feeling okay?"

"I guess," she said. "My dad's talking to this coven. They're going to try to summon him."

I tried to imagine the magnitude of my embarrassment if my dad was tracking down some demon I had gone all the way with. "Are you okay?"

For a second Katie's eyes welled up; then she looked down the street, gripping the straps of her book bag in both hands.

"We're going to miss opening bell," she said.

*   *   *

By the end of lunch on the first day of school, this was what
everyone knew:

– Katie was disgusting. ("How could she let that happen?
What was she *thinking*?")

– It was probably rape. ("Sure you can drink like a rock star
if you want, but look what it gets you.")

– There was no way it was rape. ("Do you know how much
sex you have to have with a demon before he can get you pregnant? Forget it. That is a two-person pregnancy.")

– The demon was hot. ("Like, *so* hot. You would have ripped
his pants off, don't even fool yourself. I'm proud of her for
getting it when she could. Too bad that ship sails as soon as
your ankles blow up.")

– She had stopped coming to church. ("Just as well. What if
she bursts into flames or something?")

– She was looking swollen. ("I mean, she already has two
chins. Poor thing.")

What actually happened was, Katie sat all lunch period at
one of the loser tables near the assembly stage, the tables that
only had three chairs, and didn't say a word.

Ms Parker began our first health studies class with a speech
about abstinence.

She started reading from a binder labeled YOUR BODY AND
YOU, but after a little while she got carried away and went off-
book, looking very seriously at everyone in the room, one at a
time, except Katie.

"It's imperative that you use self-control," she said, pointing
at a projection of two teens holding hands. "Sexual feelings are
perfectly normal, but you are simply too immature to handle
the consequences. Your teenage years are no time to be thinking about getting some sex."

Next to me, Cody Reese snickered.

"There's just no way for you, at this age, to be ready for all the
possible consequences once you've given in to sex," Ms Parker
said. "This is the best reason to practice abstinence *now*, before
your hormones run away with you. Forewarned is forearmed."

There was a pause as the class made an effort not to look at Katie.

"You have to be careful," Ms Parker said, dropping her fist into her palm for emphasis. "Sex is a big commitment, and you never know what can go wrong. For example," she said, both eyebrows up, "you can get pregnant the very first time you have sex."

Cody went a little pale.

"For example," Ms Parker said, "you can get pregnant even if you use a condom. Condoms break."

"And demon sperm eats right through a condom," Katie said. "For example."

The whole class turned to look at her.

"Forewarned is forearmed," she said.

Katie's dad stopped by to ask Dad to help with the coven that was coming over.

"We don't want you to worry," Mr Banks said to my mom and me. "I mean, in case it looks unorthodox. Things will be fine."

Behind him, three women in business casual were walking up his driveway.

"Of course," said my mom, all sympathetic. "Good luck with the summoning."

When they had gone we went back to the dinner table, and my mom said a lot of things like, "I hope it works out for the best," and, "It must be so hard for them," that were all Adult Code for, "Thank God my daughter's not knocked up."

If you looked out the window to Katie's house, there were little flickers of light in the family room.

When my dad came home I was already in bed, and I crept down the hallway until I could hear what was going on downstairs.

"The summoning got so bad Tom and I had to hold her down," my dad was saying, "but not a damn thing happened. If you ask me, that coven's overcharging. Bunch of nonsense effects, and she's still as pregnant as ever."

"Well, that's what happens," said my mom, like it was all exactly what she figured if you brought some cut-rate coven into the house.

Even though the teachers had been told not to mention it, we heard a lot about fertilization and demons in the next couple of months.

I don't know if it was because they were trying to prepare us for Katie's pregnancy somehow, or they wanted to punish Katie for getting pregnant. I guess it was the kind of thing you couldn't stop thinking about, and it was just weirder to see it coming from the grown-ups.

("This week, let's take a look at some of the religious history of the demon people," said Mr Harris, the history teacher, and he gave Katie a look so disappointed that even Cody made a face.)

Other kids talked about Katie all the time, which was kind of awful but at least it was more honest than what the teachers were doing.

I kept hearing the report that the demon had been hot. No one had seen him, but it seemed to be the consensus, and Katie hadn't contradicted it.

Sumati said that it didn't matter how hot he was if he had gotten Katie pregnant and then just left her. She had a point, but he was a demon, so what did Katie expect?

(Everyone knew demons didn't stick around. I guess. People seemed to know a lot about demons that I had never known, all of a sudden.)

We studied the mitosis of demon cells, and the history of human–demon relations, and the importance of self-control when it came to sex, until even I started feeling ashamed when I walked into school in the morning.

Katie must have lodged a complaint after the human/demon Punnett square worksheet in bio, because the assignment was reissued with sweet peas like usual.

But Cody was her lab partner, and he told everyone at our lunch table that Katie had done the demon Punnett anyway and just stared at the outcome.

"Turns out horns are a dominant trait," he said, "and her kid's chances do not look good."

The doctor Katie had been seeing told her after ten weeks that he felt unsafe handling a fetus that would soon burst out of her stomach and devour her immortal soul in its ungodly crawl forth from her womb, so she texted me and asked me for a ride to Planned Parenthood.

When we got there, there were people in church T-shirts waving signs with fetuses on them, screaming and chanting.

"That's my church," Katie said when she saw them.

"Oh, shit," I said.

Katie sat in the car for a long time before she took a deep breath, opened the door and got out.

The crowd looked over at us and started the screaming again, louder, but as they saw Katie, one by one, everybody stopped chanting.

There was a long, confused silence.

Even after Katie started forward (with me following her, trying to look intimidating), the crowd didn't pick up the chanting again; they were looking at one another, baffled about what exactly to tell her to do.

By the time she opened the clinic door, two people in the crowd were arguing.

"But it's a DEMON."

"It's still God's creature!"

"By definition, that's not true," Katie called over her shoulder, and then we were inside.

The receptionist asked Katie if she wanted me to go in with her. She looked at me.

"Sure," I said. I'd never seen a demon baby.

(Turns out it looks like a rolled-up shrimpy smudge, with tiny horns.)

She might have teared up a little during the sonogram. I looked really intently at the posters on the wall until we were alone.

"You going to keep it?" I asked, as she was getting dressed again.

"I don't know," she said. "What if I call the vengeful demon hordes down on me or something because I did the wrong thing one way or the other? I don't know how all this goes."

"The summoning didn't work?"

Katie shook her head. "They're going to try again next week. Not like it matters, anyway. Bringing him back won't make me less pregnant."

"Maybe it could," I said. Demons could do a lot of things; they could probably absorb fetuses or whatever.

But Katie gave me a look, and I realized she meant that, even if the baby disappeared, the fact that she had gotten pregnant never would.

For the first time I thought how weird that was, and how sad it was.

Just for a second, I wondered why she'd slept with the demon; as far as I knew, no one had ever actually asked her. Then I looked over at her, and she seemed so alone that I didn't really wonder anymore.

"I went to day camp over the summer," I said.

She frowned. "That's . . . cool."

"It was awful," I said, "but I completely fell in love with this guy named Patrick."

She zipped up her hoodie and looked at me.

"I mean, seriously," I said. "It was the worst. You can't imagine how hard it was just to try not to stare at him all the time. I looked like a complete asshole. I will literally never recover."

After a second, Katie said, "Yeah," in that tone people use when they've decided to really be your friend.

On the way out, the people from her church had taken a vote or something, because they chanted, "All babies are God's babies!" and "God loves demons, too!" until we were peeling away.

I spent seven weeks at that urban day camp going to historical landmarks and hitting museums and, once, going out to a farm.

Every minute of it was awful, and it was double awful because of Patrick, who had messy hair that he was always pushing back from his forehead.

(Once I got away from the day camp I realized how stupid a thing this was, but when you're a hostage on a school bus five days a week during your summer vacation, you get Stockholm syndrome.)

He had a crush on Linda Rich, but he thought I was okay, so sometimes we'd sit together on the bus and I would play it really cool and try not to think about the backs of my arms sticking to the seat.

I must have played it really cool, because he shared a joint with me the morning before we got on the bus for the field trip to the City Museum, so by the time I got there I was a little high.

A little high was plenty – I took one look at that huge slinky slide and knew I'd snap my wrist in half if I even tried – but Patrick went up all the slides and found the ball pit and crawled around in the plane fuselage, better than he did anything sober, which I guess tells you some people are just cut out to be high.

When I went up to the roof for air, I saw the bus.

It was on a corner of the building; the back half was planted on the roof, but the front half of the bus just stuck out into the air, and it was open if you wanted to go in it, but you had to trust that the welding or whatever was going to hold you up. Otherwise you were going down eight stories in half a bus.

I sort of wanted to do it. I trusted buses more than slinkys, and I wanted to see what the city looked like when you were high, just in case it was different.

(I hate heights. I must have been pretty high to forget how much I hate heights.)

I made it into the back half of the bus, and I started for the front like a normal person who trusts welding. But with the next step I was afraid, and then I was more afraid, and then I swore I heard the bus pulling free until it was just a huge seesaw with me in the middle.

(I didn't have any weapons on hand except a rolled-up magazine, but still, I'd fight them if they came.)

But the only thing that happened was the nurse coming out to tell me that Katie was resting after her procedure, and it would be a couple of hours, if I wanted to come back later.

"I'm good here," I said, and picked up a three-month-old copy of *People*.

Katie looked a little pale, and on the way back she was glancing out the window a lot.

"Do you feel like they're coming?" I asked.

She shook her head. "I don't think so," she said.

She sounded like she was about to cry, and after a second I realized what she must be thinking about.

"I'm sorry he never came back," I said.

I was quiet after that, and she rested her fingertips on the window and breathed carefully in and out, like her ribs hurt.

After a long time she said, "I've been looking at some colleges."

"That's awesome," I said.

The next day, Ms Parker gave us a lesson on the terrors of abortion.

"It's dangerous," she said, ticking off points on her fingers. "As with any medical procedure, it has an uncertain outcome."

"Just like pregnancy," said Katie.

Ms Parker kept going. "And it has documented psychological side effects. Depression, shame, guilt."

"I wonder why," I said.

"Seriously," said Cody from next to me, the first time he'd said anything in sex ed. class all year, and he and Katie and I smiled at each other for a second, like Musketeers.

During enrollment in the spring, Katie signed up for a bunch of AP classes.

There was some confusion about it amongst the teachers, like getting pregnant had lowered her IQ, but of course she tested into them all.

"Well," said my mother when she heard, and glanced down the table at me, like maybe I would be more dedicated to my schoolwork if only I'd had a pregnancy scare to motivate me.

The weekend before spring break I took Katie to the City Museum, and we climbed into the bus.

"This is already more fun than doing it high," I said.

"Problem child," she said.

There's a picture I took of her, and even though it's a little blurry because I took it from halfway back in the bus, you can still see it's Katie at the wheel, grinning, driving out into the sky.

The Monsters of Heaven

Nathan Ballingrud

*Winner of the Shirley Jackson Award, Nathan Ballingrud's
story reminds one of a verse from Dylan Thomas's "Poem on
His Birthday":*

> And freely he goes lost
> In the unknown, famous light of great
> And fabulous, dear God.
> Dark is a way and light is a place,
> Heaven that never was
> Nor will be ever is always true,
> And, in that brambled void,
> Plenty as blackberries in the woods
> The dead grow for His joy.

*Heaven, after all, might be a dark place, and comfort not neces-
sarily without pain . . .*

"Who invented the human heart, I wonder? Tell me,
then show me the place where he was hanged."
                                    – Lawrence Durrell, *Justine*

For a long time, Brian imagined reunions with his son. In the
early days, these fantasies were defined by spectacular violence.

He would find the man who stole him and open his head with a claw hammer. The more blood he spilled, the further removed he became from his own guilt. The location would often change: a roach-haunted tenement building; an abandoned warehouse along the Tchoupitoulas wharf; a prefab bungalow with an American flag out front and a two-door hatchback parked in the driveway.

Sometimes the man lived alone, sometimes he had his own family. On these latter occasions, Brian would cast himself as a moral executioner, spraying the walls with the kidnapper's blood but sparing his wife and child – freeing them, he imagined, from his tyranny. No matter the scenario, Toby was always there, always intact; Brian would feel his face pressed into his shoulders as he carried him away, feel the heat of his tears bleed into his shirt. *You're safe now,* he would say. *Daddy's got you. Daddy's here.*

After some months passed, he deferred the heroics to the police. This marked his first concession to reality. He spent his time beached in the living room, drinking more, working less, until the owner of the auto shop told him to take time off, a lot of time off, as much as he needed. Brian barely noticed. He waited for the red and blue disco lights of a police cruiser to illuminate the darkness outside, to give some shape and measure to the night. He waited for the phone to ring with a glad summons to the station. He played out scenarios, tried on different outcomes, guessed at his own reactions. He gained weight and lost time.

Sometimes he would get out of bed in the middle of the night, careful not to wake his wife, and get into the car. He would drive at dangerous speeds through the city, staring into the empty sockets of unlighted windows. He would get out of the car and stand in front of some of these houses, looking and listening for signs. Often, the police were called. When the officers realized who he was, they were usually as courteous as they were adamant. He'd wonder if it had been the kidnapper who called the police. He would imagine returning to those houses with a gun.

★   ★   ★

This was in the early days of what became known as the Lamentation. At this stage, most people did not know anything unusual was happening. What they heard, if they heard anything, was larded with rumor and embellishment. Fogs of gossip in the barrooms and churches. This was before the bloodshed. Before their pleas to Christ clotted in their throats.

Amy never told Brian that she blamed him. She elected, rather, to avoid the topic of the actual abduction, and any question of her husband's negligence. Once the police abandoned them as suspects, the matter of their own involvement ceased to be a subject of discussion. Brian was unconsciously grateful, because it allowed him to focus instead on the maintenance of grief. Silence spread between them like a glacier. In a few months, entire days passed with nothing said between them.

It was on such a night that Amy rolled up against him and kissed the back of his neck. It froze Brian, filling him with a blast of terror and bewilderment; he felt the guilt move inside of him, huge but seemingly distant, like a whale passing beneath a boat. Her lips felt hot against his skin, sending warm waves rolling from his neck and shoulders all the way down to his legs, as though she had injected something lovely into him. She grew more ardent, nipping him with her teeth, breaking through his reservations. He turned and kissed her. He experienced a leaping arc of energy, a terrifying, violent impulse; he threw his weight onto her and crushed his mouth into hers, scraping his teeth against hers. But there immediately followed a cascade of unwelcome thought: Toby whimpering somewhere in the dark, waiting for his father to save him; Amy, dressed in her bedclothes in the middle of the day, staring like a corpse into the sunlight coming through the windows; the playground, and the receding line of kindergarteners. When she reached under the sheets she found him limp and unready. He opened his mouth to apologize but she shoved her tongue into it, her hand working at him with a rough urgency, as though more depended on this than he knew. Later he would learn that it did. Her teeth sliced his lip and blood eeled into his mouth. She was pulling at him too hard, and it was starting to hurt. He wrenched himself away.

"Jesus," he said, wiping his lip. The blood felt like an oil slick in the back of his throat.

She turned her back to him and put her face into the pillow. For a moment he thought she was crying. But only for a moment.

"Honey," he said. "Hey." He put his fingers on her shoulder; she rolled it away from him.

"Go to sleep," she said.

He stared at the landscape of her naked back, pale in the street light leaking through the blinds, feeling furious and ruined.

The next morning, when he came into the kitchen, Amy was already up. Coffee was made, filling the room with a fine toasted smell, and she was leaning against the counter with a cup in her hand, wearing her pink terrycloth robe. Her dark hair was still wet from the shower. She smiled and said, "Good morning."

"Hey," he said, feeling for a sense of her mood.

Dodger, Toby's dog, cast him a devastated glance from his customary place beneath the kitchen table. Amy had wanted to get rid of him – she couldn't bear the sight of him anymore, she'd said – but Brian wouldn't allow it. When Toby comes back, he reasoned, he'll wonder why we did it. What awful thing guided us. So Dodger remained, and his slumping, sorrowful presence tore into them both like a hungry animal.

"Hey, boy," Brian said, and rubbed his neck with his toe.

"I'm going out today," Amy said.

"Okay. Where to?"

She shrugged. "I don't know. The hardware store. Maybe a nursery. I want to find myself a project."

Brian looked at her. The sunlight made a corona around her body. This new resolve, coupled with her overture of the night before, struck him as a positive sign. "Okay," he said.

He seated himself at the table. The newspaper had been

placed there for him, still bound by a rubber band. He snapped it off and unfurled the front page. Already he felt the gravitational pull of the Jack Daniel's in the cabinet, but when Amy leaned over his shoulder and placed a coffee cup in front of him, he managed to resist the whiskey's call with an ease that surprised and gratified him. He ran his hand up her forearm, pushing back the soft pink sleeve, and he kissed the inside of her wrist. He felt a wild and incomprehensible hope. He breathed in the clean, scented smell of her. She stayed there for a moment, and then gently pulled away.

They remained that way in silence for some time – maybe fifteen minutes or more – until Brian found something in the paper he wanted to share with her. Something being described as "angelic" – "apparently not quite a human man", as the writer put it – had been found down by the Gulf Coast, in Morgan City; it had been shedding a faint light from under two feet of water; whatever it was had died shortly after being taken into custody, under confusing circumstances. He turned in his chair to speak, a word already gathering on his tongue, and he caught her staring at him. She wore a cadaverous, empty look, as though she had seen the worst thing in the world and died in the act. It occurred to him that she had been looking at him that way for whole minutes. He turned back to the table, his insides sliding, and stared at the suddenly indecipherable glyphs of the newspaper. After a moment he felt her hand on the back of his neck, rubbing him gently. She left the kitchen without a word.

This is how it happened:

They were taking Dodger for a walk. Toby liked to hold the leash – he was four years old, and gravely occupied with establishing his independence – and more often than not Brian would sort of half-trot behind them, one hand held indecisively aloft should Dodger suddenly decide to break into a run, dragging his boy behind him like a string of tin cans. He probably bit off more profanities during those walks than he ever did changing a tire. He carried, as was their custom on

Mondays, a blanket and a picnic lunch. He would lie back in the sun while Toby and the dog played, and enjoy not being hunched over an engine block. At some point they would have lunch. Brian believed these afternoons of easy camaraderie would be remembered by them both for years to come. They'd done it a hundred times.

A hundred times.

On that day a kindergarten class arrived shortly after they did. Toby ran up to his father and wrapped his arms around his neck, frightened by the sudden bright surge of humanity; the kids were a loud, brawling tumult, crashing over the swings and monkey bars in a gabbling surf. Brian pried Toby's arms free and pointed at them.

"Look, screwball, they're just kids. See? They're just like you. Go on and play. Have some fun."

Dodger galloped out to greet them and was received as a hero, with joyful cries and grasping fingers. Toby observed this gambit for his dog's affections and at last decided to intervene. He ran toward them, shouting, "That's my dog! That's my dog!" Brian watched him go, made eye contact with the teacher and nodded hello. She smiled at him – he remembered thinking she was kind of cute, wondering how old she was – and she returned her attention to her kids, gamboling like lunatics all over the park. Brian reclined on the blanket and watched the clouds skim the atmosphere, listened to the sound of children. It was a hot, windless day.

He didn't realize he had dozed until the kindergarteners had been rounded up and were halfway down the block, taking their noise with them. The silence stirred him.

He sat up abruptly and looked around. The playground was empty. "Toby? Hey, Toby?"

Dodger stood out in the middle of the road, his leash spooled at his feet. He watched Brian eagerly, offered a tentative wag.

"Where's Toby?" he asked the dog, and climbed to his feet. He felt a sudden sickening lurch in his gut. He turned in a quick circle, a half-smile on his face, utterly sure that this was an impossible situation, that children didn't disappear in broad daylight while their parents were *right fucking there*. So he was still here. Of course he was still here. Dodger trotted up to him and sat down at his feet, waiting for him to produce the boy, as though he were a hidden tennis ball.

"Toby?"

The park was empty. He jogged after the receding line of kids. "Hey. *Hey!* Is my son with you? *Where's my son?*"

One morning, about a week after the experience in the kitchen, Brian was awakened by the phone. Every time this happened he felt a thrill of hope, though by now it had become muted, even dreadful in its predictability. He hauled himself up from the couch, nearly overturning a bottle of Jack Daniel's stationed on the floor. He crossed the living room and picked up the phone.

"Yes?" he said.

"Let me talk to Amy." It was not a voice he recognized. A male voice, with a thick rural accent. It was the kind of voice that inspired immediate prejudice: the voice of an idiot; of a man without any right to make demands of him.

"Who is this?"

"Just let me talk to Amy."

"How about you go fuck yourself."

There was a pause as the man on the phone seemed to assess the obstacle. Then he said, with a trace of amusement in his voice, "Are you Brian?"

"That's right."

"Look, dude. Go get your wife. Put her on the phone. Do it now, and I won't have to come down there and break your fucking face."

Brian slammed down the receiver. Feeling suddenly light-headed, he put his hand on the wall to steady himself, to reassure himself that it was still solid, and that he was still real. From somewhere outside, through an open window, came the distant sound of children shouting.

★　★　★

It was obvious that Amy was sleeping with another man. When confronted with the call, she did not admit to anything, but made no special effort to explain it away, either. His name was Tommy, she said. She'd met him once when she was out. He sounded rough, but he wasn't a bad guy. She chose not to elaborate, and Brian, to his amazement, found a kind of forlorn comfort in his wife's affair. He'd lost his son; why not lose it all?

On television the news was filling with the creatures, more of which were being discovered all the time. The press had taken to calling them angels. Some were being found alive, though all of them appeared to have suffered from some violent experience.

At least one family had become notorious by refusing to let anyone see the angel they'd found, or even let it out of their home. They boarded their windows and warned away visitors with a shotgun.

Brian was stationed on the couch, staring at the television with the sound turned down to barely a murmur. He listened to the familiar muted clatter from the medicine cabinet as Amy applied her make-up in the bathroom. A news program was on, and a hand-held camera followed a street reporter into someone's house. The J. D. bottle was empty at his feet, and the knowledge that he had no more in the house smoldered in him.

Amy emerged from the kitchen with her purse slung over her arm and made her way to the door. "I'm going out," she said.

"Where?"

She paused, one hand on the doorknob. She wavered there, in her careful make-up and her push-up bra. He tried to remember the last time he'd seen her look like this and failed dismally. Something inside her seemed to collapse – a force of will, perhaps, or a habit of deception. Maybe she was just too tired to invent another lie.

"I'm going to see Tommy," she said.

"The redneck."

"Sure. The redneck, if that's how you want it."

"Does it matter how I want it?"

She paused. "No," she said. "I guess not."

"Well well. The truth. Look out."

She left the door, walked into the living room. Brian felt a sudden trepidation; this is not what he imagined would happen. He wanted to get a few weak barbs in before she walked out, that was all. He did not actually want to talk.

She sat on the rocking chair across from the couch. Beside her, on the television, the camera focused on an obese man wearing overalls smiling triumphantly and holding aloft an angel's severed head.

Amy shut it off.

"Do you want to know about him?" she said.

"Let's see. He's stupid and violent. He called my home and threatened me. He's sleeping with my wife. What else is there to know?"

She appraised him for a moment, weighing consequences. "There's a little more to know," she said. "For example, he's very kind to me. He thinks I'm beautiful." He must have made some sort of sound then, because she said, "I know it must be very hard for you to believe, but some men still find me attractive. And that's important to me, Brian. Can you understand that?"

He turned away from her, shielding his eyes with a hand, although without the TV on there was very little light in the room. Each breath was laced with pain.

"When I go to see him, he talks to me. Actually talks. I know he might not be very smart, according to your standards, but you'd be surprised how much he and I have to talk about. You'd be surprised how much more there is to life – to my life – than your car magazines, and your TV, and your bottles of booze."

"Stop it," he said.

"He's also a very considerate lover. He paces himself. For my sake. For me. Did you *ever* do that, Brian? In all the times we made love?"

He felt tears crawling down his face. Christ. When did that start?

"I can forget things when I sleep with him. I can forget about . . . I can forget about everything. He lets me do that."

"You cold bitch," he rasped.

"You passive little shit," she bit back, with a venom that surprised him. "You let it happen, do you know that? You let it all happen. Every awful thing."

She stood abruptly and walked out the door, slamming it behind her. The force of it rattled the windows. After a while – he had no idea how long – he picked up the remote and turned the TV back on. A girl pointed to moving clouds on a map.

Eventually Dodger came by and curled up at his feet. Brian slid off the couch and lay down beside him, hugging him close. Dodger smelled the way dogs do, musky and of the earth, and he sighed with the abiding patience of his kind.

Violence filled his dreams. In them he rent bodies, spilled blood, painted the walls using severed limbs as gruesome brushes. In them he went back to the park and ate the children while the teacher looked on. Once he awoke after these dreams with blood filling his mouth; he realized he had chewed his tongue during the night. It was raw and painful for days afterward. A rage was building inside him and he could not find an outlet for it. One night Amy told him she thought she was falling in love with Tommy. He only nodded stupidly and watched her walk out the door again. That same night he kicked Dodger out of the house. He just opened the door to the night and told him to go. When he wouldn't – trying instead to slink around his legs and go back inside – he planted his foot on the dog's chest and physically pushed him back outside, sliding him backwards on his butt. "*Go find him!*" he yelled. "*Go find him! Go and find him!*" He shut the door and listened to Dodger whimper and scratch at it for nearly an hour. At some point he gave up and Brian fell asleep. When he awoke it was raining. He opened the door and called for him. The rain swallowed his voice.

"Oh no," he said quietly, his voice a whimper. "Come back! I'm sorry! Please, I'm so sorry!"

When Dodger did eventually return, wet and miserable, Brian hugged him tight, buried his face in his fur, and wept for joy.

Brian liked to do his drinking alone. When he drank in public, especially at his old bar, people tried to talk to him. They saw his presence as an invitation to share sympathy, or a request for a friendly ear. It got to be too much. But tonight he made his way back there, endured the stares and the weird silence, took the beers sent his way, although he wanted none of it. What he wanted tonight was Fire Engine, and she didn't disappoint.

Everybody knew Fire Engine, of course; if she thought you didn't know her, she'd introduce herself to you post haste. One hand on your shoulder, the other on your thigh. Where her hands went after that depended on a quick negotiation. She was a redhead with an easy personality, and was popular with the regular clientele, including the ones that would never buy her services. She claimed to be twenty-eight but looked closer to forty. At some unfortunate juncture in her life she had contrived to lose most of her front teeth, either to decay or to someone's balled fist; either way common wisdom held she gave the best blowjob in downtown New Orleans.

Brian used to be amused by that kind of talk. Although he'd never had an interest in her he'd certainly enjoyed listening to her sales pitch; she'd become a sort of bar pet, and the unself-conscious way she went about her life was both endearing and appalling. Her lack of teeth was too perfect, and too ridiculous. Now, however, the information had acquired a new kind of value to him. He pressed his gaze onto her until she finally felt it and looked back. She smiled coquettishly, with gruesome effect. He told the bartender to send her a drink.

"You sure? She ain't gonna leave you alone all night."

"Fuck yeah, I'm sure."

All night didn't concern him. What concerned him were the next ten minutes, which was what he figured ten dollars would buy him. After the necessary negotiations and bullshit they left the bar together, trailing catcalls; she took his hand and led him around back, into the alley.

The smell of rotting garbage came at him like an attack, like a pillowcase thrown over his head. She steered him into the alley's dark mouth, with its grime-smeared pavement and furtive skittering sounds, and its dumpster so stuffed with straining garbage bags that it looked like some fearsome monster choking on its dinner. "Now you know I'm a lady," she said, "but sometimes you just got to make do with what's available."

That she could laugh at herself this way touched Brian, and he felt a wash of sympathy for her. He considered what it would be like to run away with her, to rescue her from the wet pull of her life, to save her.

She unzipped his pants and pulled his dick out. "There we go, honey, that's what I'm talking about. Ain't you something."

After a couple of minutes she released him and stood up. He tucked himself back in and zipped his pants, afraid to make eye contact with her.

"Maybe you just had too much to drink," she said.

"Yeah."

"It ain't nothing."

"I know it isn't," he said harshly.

When she made no move to leave, he said, "Will you just get the fuck away from me? Please?"

Her voice lost its sympathy. "Honey, I still got to get paid."

He opened his wallet and fished out a ten dollar bill. She plucked it from his fingers and walked out of the alley, back toward the bar. "Don't get all bent out of shape about it," she called. "Shit happens, you know?"

He slid down the wall until his ass hit the ground. He brought his hand to his mouth and choked out a sob, his eyes squeezed shut. He banged his head once against the brick wall behind him and then thought better of it. Down here the stench was a steaming blanket, almost soothing in its awfulness. He felt like he deserved to be there, that it was right that he should sleep in shit and grime. He listened to the gentle ticking of the roaches in the dark. He wondered if Toby was in a place like this.

Something glinted further down the alley.

He strained to see it. It was too bright to be merely a reflection.

It moved.

"Son of a," he said, and pushed himself to his feet.

It lay mostly hidden; it had pulled some stray garbage bags atop itself in an effort to remain concealed, but its dim luminescence worked against it. Brian loped over to it, wrenched the bags away; its clawed hands clutched at them and tore them open, spilling a clatter of beer and liquor bottles all over the ground. They caromed with hollow music through the alley, coming at last to silent rest, until all Brian could hear was the thin, high-pitched noise the creature made through the tiny O-shaped orifice he supposed passed for a mouth. Its eyes were black little stones. The creature – angel, he thought, they're calling these things angels – was tall and thin, abundantly male, and it shed a thin light that illuminated exactly nothing around it. If you put some clothes on it, Brian thought, hide its face, gave it some gloves, it might pass for a human.

Exposed, it held up a long-fingered hand, as if to ward him off. It had clearly been hurt: its legs looked badly broken, and it breathed in short, shallow gasps. A dark bruise spread like a mold over the right side of its chest.

"Look at you, huh? You're all messed up." He felt a strange glee as he said this; he could not justify the feeling and quickly buried it. "Yeah, yeah, somebody worked you over pretty good."

It managed to roll onto its belly and it scrabbled along the pavement in a pathetic attempt at escape. It loosed that thin, reedy cry. Calling for help? Begging for its life?

The sight of it trying to flee from him catalyzed some deep predatory impulse, and he pressed his foot onto the angel's ankle, holding it easily in place. "No you don't." He hooked the thing beneath its shoulders and lifted it from the ground; it was astonishingly light. It mewled weakly at him. "Shut up, I'm trying to help you." He adjusted it in his arms so that he held it like a lover, or a fainted woman. He carried it back to his car, listening for the sound of the barroom door opening behind him, of laughter or a challenge chasing him down the sidewalk. But the door stayed shut. He walked in silence.

Amy was awake when he got home, silhouetted in the doorway. Brian pulled the angel from the passenger seat, cradled it against his chest. He watched her face alter subtly, watched as some dark hope crawled across it like an insect, and he squashed it before it could do any real harm.

"It's not him," he said. "It's something else."

She stood away from the door and let him come in.

Dodger, who had been dozing in the hallway, lurched to his feet with a sliding and skittering of claws and growled fiercely at it, his lips curled away from his teeth.

"Get away, you," Brian said. He eased past him, bearing his load down the hall.

He laid it in Toby's bed. Together he and Amy stood over it, watching as it stared back at them with dark flat eyes, its body twisting away from them as if it could fold itself into another place altogether. Its fingers plucked at the train-spangled bedsheets, wrapping them around its nakedness. Amy leaned over and helped to tuck the sheets around it.

"He's hurt," she said.

"I know. I guess a lot of them are found that way."

"Should we call somebody?"

"You want camera crews in here? Fuck no."

"Well. He's really hurt. We need to do something."

"Yeah. I don't know. We can at least clean him up I guess."

Amy sat on the mattress beside it; it stared at her with its expressionless face. Brian couldn't tell if there were thoughts passing behind those eyes, or just a series of brute reflex arcs. After a moment it reached out with one long dark fingernail and brushed her arm. She jumped as though shocked.

"Jesus! Be careful," said Brian.

"What if it's him?"

"What?" It took him a moment to understand her. "Oh my God. Amy. It's not him, okay? It's *not him*."

"But what if it is?"

"It's *not*. We've seen them on the news, okay? It's a . . . it's a *thing*."

"You shouldn't call it an 'it'."

"How do I know what the fuck to call it?"

She touched her fingers to its cheek. It pressed its face into them, making some small sound.

"Why did you leave me?" she said. "You were everything I had."

Brian swooned beneath a tide of vertigo. Something was moving inside him, something too large to stay where it was. "It's an angel," he said. "Nothing more. Just an angel. It's probably going to die on us, since that's what they seem to do." He put his hand against the wall until the dizziness passed. It was replaced by a low, percolating anger. "Instead of thinking of it as Toby, why don't you ask it where Toby *is*. Why don't you make it explain to us why it happened."

She looked at him. "It happened because you let it," she said.

Dodger asked to be let outside. Brian opened the door for him to let him run around the front yard. There was a leash law here, but Dodger was well known by the neighbors and generally tolerated. He walked out of the house with considerably less than his usual enthusiasm. He lifted his leg desultorily against a shrub, then walked down to the road and followed the sidewalk further into the neighborhood. He did not come back.

Over the next few days it put its hooks into them, and drew them in tight. They found it difficult to leave it alone. Its flesh seemed to pump out some kind of soporific, like an invisible spoor, and it was better than the booze – better than anything they'd previously known. Its pull seemed to grow stronger as the days passed. For Amy, especially. She stopped going out, and for all practical purposes moved into Toby's room with it. When Brian joined her in there, she seemed to barely tolerate his presence. If he sat beside it she watched him with naked trepidation, as though she feared he might damage it somehow.

It was not, he realized, an unfounded fear. Something inside him became turbulent in its presence, something he couldn't identify but which sparked flashes of violent thought, of the kind he had not had since just after Toby vanished. This feeling came in sharp relief to the easy lethargy the angel normally inspired, and he was reminded of a time when he was younger, sniffing heroin laced with cocaine. So he did not object to Amy's efforts at excluding him.

Finally, though, her vigilance slipped. He went into the bathroom and found her sleeping on the toilet, her robe hiked up around her waist, her head resting against the sink. He left her there and crept into the angel's room.

It was awake, and its eyes tracked him as he crossed the room and sat beside it on the bed. Its breath wheezed lightly as it drew air through its puckered mouth. Its body was still bruised and bent, though it did seem to be improving.

Brian touched its chest where the bruise seemed to be diminishing. Why does it bruise? he wondered. Why does it bleed the same way I do? Shouldn't it be made of something better? Also, it didn't have wings. Not even vestigial ones. Why were they called angels? Because of how they made people feel? It looked more like an alien than a divine being. It has a cock, for Christ's sake. What's that all about? Do angels fuck?

He leaned over it, so his face was inches away, almost touching its nose. He stared into its black, irisless eyes, searching for some sign of intelligence, some evidence of intent or emotion. From this distance he could smell its breath; he drew it into his own lungs, and it warmed him like a shot of whiskey. The angel lifted its head and pressed its face into his. Brian jerked back and felt something brush his elbow. He looked behind him and discovered the angel had an erection.

He lurched out of bed, tripping over himself as he rushed to the door, dashed through it and slammed it shut. His blood sang. It rose in him like the sea and filled him with tumultuous music. He dropped to his knees and vomited all over the carpet.

Later, he stepped into its doorway, watching Amy trace her hands down its face. Through the window he could see that night was gathering in little pockets outside, lifting itself toward the sky. At the sight of the angel his heart jumped in his chest as though it had come unmoored. "Amy, I have to talk to you," he said. He had some difficulty making his voice sound calm.

She didn't look at him. "I know it's not really him," she said. "Not really."

"No."

"But don't you think he is, kind of? In a way?"

"No."

She laid her head on the pillow beside it, staring into its face. Brian was left looking at the back of her head, the unwashed hair, tangled and brittle. He remembered cupping the back of her head in his hand, its weight and its warmth. He remembered her body.

"Amy. Where does he live?"

"Who."

"Tommy. Where does he live?"

She turned and looked at him, a little crease of worry on her brow. "Why do you want to know?"

"Just tell me. Please."

"Brian, don't."

He slammed his fist into the wall, startling himself. He screamed at her. "*Tell me where he lives! God damn it!*"

Tommy opened the door of his shotgun house, clad only in boxer shorts, and Brian greeted him with a blow to the face. Tommy staggered back into his house, due more to surprise than the force of the punch; his foot slipped on a throw rug and he crashed to the floor. The small house reverberated with the impact. Brian had a moment to take in Tommy's hard physique and imagine his wife's hands moving over it. He stepped forward and kicked him in the groin.

Tommy grunted and seemed to absorb it. He rolled over and pushed himself quickly to his feet. Tommy's fist swung at him and he had time to experience a quick flaring terror before his head exploded with pain. He found himself on his knees, staring at the dust collecting in the crevices of the hardwood floor. Somewhere in the background a television chattered urgently.

A kick to the ribs sent Brian down again. Tommy straddled him, grabbed a fistful of hair, and slammed Brian's face into the floor several times. Brian felt something in his face break and blood poured onto the floor. He wanted to cry but it was impossible, he couldn't get enough air. I'm going to die, he thought. He felt himself hauled up and thrown against a wall. Darkness crowded his vision; he began to lose his purchase on events.

Someone was yelling at him. There was a face in front of him, skin peeled back from its teeth in a smile or a grimace of rage. It looked like something from hell.

He awoke to the feel of cold grass, cold night air. The right side of his face burned like a signal flare; his left eye refused to open. It hurt to breathe. He pushed himself to his elbows and spit blood from his mouth; it immediately filled again. Something wrong in there. He rolled onto his back and lay there for a while, waiting for the pain to subside to a tolerable level. The night was high and dark. At one point he felt sure that he was rising from the ground, that something up there was pulling him into its empty hollows.

Somehow he managed the drive home. He remembered nothing of it except occasional stabs of pain as opposing headlights washed across his windshield; he would later consider his safe arrival a kind of miracle. He pulled into the driveway and

honked the horn a few times until Amy came out and found
him there. She looked at him with horror, and with something
else.

"Oh, baby. What did you do. What did you do."

She steered him toward the angel's room. He stopped himself
in the doorway, his heart pounding again, and he tried to catch
his breath. It occurred to him, on a dim level, that his nose was
broken. She tugged at his hand, but he resisted. Her face was
limned by moonlight, streaming through the window like some
mystical tide, and by the faint luminescence of the angel tucked
into their son's bed. She'd grown heavy over the years, and the
past year had taken a harsh toll: the flesh on her face sagged,
and was scored by grief. And yet he was stunned by her beauty.

Had she always looked like this?

"Come on," she said. "Please."

The left side of his face pulsed with hard beats of pain; it
sang like a war drum. His working eye settled on the thing in
the bed: its flat black eyes, its wickedly curved talons. Amy sat
beside it and put her hand on its chest. It arched its back,
seeming to coil beneath her.

"Come lay down," she said. "He's here for us. He's come
home for us."

Brian took a step into Toby's room, and then another. He
knew she was wrong; that the angel was not home, that it had
wandered here from somewhere far away.

Is heaven a dark place?

The angel extended a hand, its talons flexing. The sheets
over its belly stirred as Brian drew closer. Amy took her
husband's hands, easing him onto the bed. He gripped her
shoulders, squeezing them too tightly. "I'm sorry," he said
suddenly, surprising himself. "I'm sorry! I'm sorry!" Once he
began he couldn't stop. He said it over and over again, so many
times it just became a sound, a sobbing plaint, and Amy
pressed her hand against his mouth, entwined her fingers into
his hair, saying, "Shhhh, shhhhh," and finally she silenced him
with a kiss. As they embraced each other the angel played its

hands over their faces and their shoulders, its strange reedy breath and its narcotic musk drawing them down to it. They caressed each other, and they caressed the angel, and when they touched their lips to its skin the taste of it shot spikes of joy through their bodies. Brian felt her teeth on his neck and he bit into the angel, the sudden dark spurt of blood filling his mouth, the soft pale flesh tearing easily, sliding down his throat. He kissed his wife furiously and when she tasted the blood she nearly tore his tongue out; he pushed her face toward the angel's body, and watched the blood blossom from beneath her. The angel's eyes were frozen, staring at the ceiling; it extended a shaking hand toward a wall decorated with a Spider-Man poster, its fingers twisted and bent.

They ate until they were full.

That night, heavy with the sludge of bliss, Brian and Amy made love again for the first time in nearly a year. It was wordless and slow, a synchronicity of pressures and tender familiarities. They were like rare creatures of a dying species, amazed by the sight of each other.

Brian drifts in and out of sleep. He has what will be the last dream about his son. It is morning in this dream, by the side of a small country road. It must have rained during the night, because the world shines with a wet glow. Droplets of water cling, dazzling, to the muzzle of a dog as it rests beside the road, unmenaced by traffic, languorous and dull-witted in the rising heat. It might even be Dodger. His snout is heavy with blood. Some distance away from him Toby rests on the street, a small pile of bones and torn flesh, glittering with dew, catching and throwing sunlight like a scattered pile of rubies and diamonds.

By the time he wakes, he has already forgotten it.

Come to Me

Sam Cameron

What if airport security checks were really searching for the supernaturally sinister as well as harm from human sources? And a reminder: "If men were angels, no government would be necessary. If angels were to govern men, neither external nor internal controls on government would be necessary. In framing a government which is to be administered by men over men, the great difficulty lies in this: you must first enable the government to control the governed; and in the next place oblige it to control itself. A dependence on the people is, no doubt, the primary control on the government; but experience has taught mankind the necessity of auxiliary precautions." – James Madison, The Federalist No. 51, *6 February 1788*

In other news today, the Transportation Security Agency is under public fire for the treatment of an elderly, wheelchair-bound grandmother with leukemia. The 92-year-old woman was flying to a family reunion in Boston when she was subjected to a TSA pat down, scanned with a portable back-scatter unit, and then forced to remove her adult diaper. So far, the official government response is that the treatment of the elderly woman was "appropriate" and "within federal guidelines." – NBC 4, Columbus

Elsa knew from sad experience that most hotel gyms weren't worth the time it took to swipe a card key. Usually she exercised alone in her room. With the furniture arranged just right, she could mambo left and grapevine right without bashing into anything. Exercising alone was lonely, but it wasn't as if she was looking to make friends. She was in the business of constant travel. She had one small suitcase, very efficiently packed, and spent much of her time in the clouds.

But the very nice thing about this hotel at the Columbus airport was that it had an indoor swimming pool, and she'd bought a bathing suit in an overpriced shop two airports ago. Fifteen minutes after checking in on a gray Tuesday afternoon, she was sticking her toes into the blue-green water and taking the plunge.

Warm, but not as warm as bathwater. Chlorinated, but not so much that her eyes stung. The maximum depth was only three and a half feet. It was designed for recreation, not lap swimming. The area was empty except for herself, the water, some fake palm trees, and white deckchairs. Elsa swam east to west, then north to south – maybe twenty-five yards total. She figured she could get a mile done in thirty-six circuits.

She had just passed the quarter-mile mark when the glass door opened and a woman in a white bathrobe came in. Her long dark hair was very curly, and her heart-shaped face open and friendly. Elsa met her gaze, nodded politely. The woman smiled back with dimples that made Elsa dead jealous – she'd never had dimples, herself. Just acne-prone skin and a tendency to sunburn.

The other guest slid out of her bathrobe. Underneath was a very nice green bikini clinging to a very nice body – tall but shapely, not so skinny that you'd want to sit her down and force-feed her a plate of pasta. Elsa could think of more enjoyable things to do with her, frankly. Which reminded her she hadn't had a date in seven months, and that she had to work tonight, and wouldn't it be better to just get her swimming done? She didn't hook up with strangers in hotels.

"Is it cold?" the woman asked. "It's usually cold."

Elsa shook her head.

The woman stood at the top of the steps and stuck one perfectly manicured foot in. Purple toenail polish. Long leg, smooth and muscled – a runner, maybe.

"I'm a wimp when it comes to cold," the woman confided, wagging her foot. "I think I was supposed to have been born in the tropics. Near those fruity drinks with umbrellas in them. And those thatch buildings you drink the fruity drinks under. What are they called?"

Elsa stopped swimming. "Tiki huts?"

"Tiki huts," the woman said, and those dimples showed themselves again. "I'm a big fan of fruity drinks, tiki huts, and sunsets. All of which are sadly far away from Columbus, Ohio."

"We are at an airport," Elsa pointed out. "You could get on a plane."

"I've heard of these things called vacations, but they don't exist in my world." The woman stepped down and let the water rise up to her knees, then her firm, smooth thighs; perhaps five or six feet away from Elsa now. She wore no jewelry, and only a little make-up to accent her dark brown eyes. "What about you? Don't tell me Columbus is your idea of a relaxing retreat."

Elsa was torn between chatting and continuing her swim. She glanced at the clock hanging over the complimentary towels. Her crew wouldn't pick her up until midnight. There was time for chatting and maybe even dinner, and was that hope flaring in her chest? A little romance? No, probably just heartburn from swallowing chlorine.

"I'm not on vacation," she said. "Just passing through."

"Then you're lucky." The woman stuck out her hand. "I'm Lisa-Marie. Like Elvis's daughter."

"I'm Elsa, like the British actress."

Lisa-Marie's face brightened. "Elsa Lancaster! She was in *Mary Poppins*."

"Most people wouldn't know that," Elsa said, amused.

"Most people don't have a five-year-old niece who watches it at least once a day, even when you beg her not to, because how many times can one person endure 'Chim-Chim-Cheree' without going crazy?"

"That's a rhetorical question, isn't it?" Elsa asked.

"Absolutely." Lisa-Marie showed her dimples again. "I have no intention of subjecting you to Dick Van Dyke or any faux Cockney accents. But as a long-time resident of Columbus, I feel terrible for anyone stuck eating hotel food when there's a great Italian restaurant nearby. How do you feel about fettuccini?"

Now it was Elsa's turn to smile. "Love it."

Near midnight, an unmarked black utility van pulled into the hotel parking lot. Andrew popped the side door for Elsa and she climbed in. He was sucking on the straw of an empty Frappucino cup and had cinnamon frosting on his chin.

"We stopped for breakfast," he said, burping. "Late-night snack. Whatever."

"Saved you one," said Christopher, from the driver's seat. He always drove, because he liked being behind the wheel. As opposed to flying, which he hated. Andrew always teased him about that: a guy who hated to fly, and his job was to fly around and fix things.

Elsa said, "I had dinner. A real dinner. With vegetables. You've heard of them?"

Andrew burped. "Filled with radioactive fallout from that Japanese reactor. It's spread all over the world by now, carried by the winds. Seeps into the earth. You're much healthier with artificial food substances."

Christopher checked his rear-view mirrors, though traffic was non-existent at this hour. "You look different. Did these vegetables happen to come with some extra-friendly companionship?"

"None of your business," Elsa replied.

"You scored!" Andrew grabbed the last cinnamon roll. "We're proud of you."

"Shut up," she suggested. "I didn't score anything. Ships that pass in the night. I'm never going to see her again."

Which was a shame, really, because Lisa-Marie was bright and funny and they'd had a fabulous dinner. She lived with her parents, grandmother, sister, and two nieces because her job with the Legal Aid Society didn't pay much. One of her former clients was a night manager at Elsa's hotel, and whenever she needed to escape the noise at home, he let her crash in one of the empty rooms. Lisa-Marie was a good flirt, but Elsa was accomplished at dodging. The dinner had ended with no promises, no exchange of phone numbers, but Lisa-Marie had sounded very sincere when she said, "Next time you're in Columbus, you should call me."

It had been the nicest dinner Elsa had experienced in quite some time, and if the memory of Lisa-Marie's bright eyes and pretty face still gave her a warm little glow, there was no harm in that.

While Christopher circled the airport, Elsa pulled on a brown jumpsuit that smelled like laundry detergent. The airport IDs were still warm from the laminator. The service parking lot was empty except for some cleaning vans and three airport security cars. Their local TSA contact was a big, unhappy-looking woman named Dorothy Armstrong.

"I wish you guys could do this earlier," she said. "I've got to be back here at 6 a.m."

Elsa sympathized, but all she said was, "Not our rules, ma'am."

"Less chance of nosy tourists," Andrew added, eyeing the empty food kiosks.

Midnight was actually early for them. Elsa preferred 2 or 3 a.m., but scheduling this job had already been hard – Christopher was due to fly to Memphis for a cleaning there, and Andrew had to travel out to San Francisco to train some new technicians. Their jobs paid well, but the travel was grueling; at the lower levels, employee turnover was high.

Port Columbus International Airport had three security checkpoints for passengers. They headed directly for Concourse A, which had already shut down for the night. Four screening lanes, typical formation, with four traditional scanners and two enormous backscatter units. The machine that had alerted was a model AXB-78-09-DZ, one of the best, but sometimes a little temperamental. Christopher powered it up, Elsa plugged her laptop into the control panel, and Andrew unpacked the containment unit.

Dorothy Armstrong was still complaining. "I don't under-stand why a software update can't be done remotely. I mean, does it really take three people?"

"It's very complicated machinery," Elsa said. "It'll take about an hour if it goes well. You don't have to stick around, if there's something you'd rather be doing."

"I'd rather be sleeping," Dorothy Armstrong said. "I'll be in my office, how's that?"

Elsa nodded. "Sounds good."

It was a relief when she left. Not that Elsa couldn't handle curiosity and questions, but the process went faster without distractions. She popped on her goggles and started scanning the AXB's memory. Thousands of images flickered by, naked or nearly so – the vacationing grandmothers and grandfathers of America, the harried moms and impatient husbands and frazzled business travelers, the teenagers who'd forgotten to unpack their MP3 players. The images captured pacemakers, artificial hips, metal pins in bones, and other surgical remnants. Sometimes she saw people who'd had transgender surgery. Or people wearing sex toys. The screening was more invasive than most people knew, and always uncomfortable for Elsa.

The Class B image popped up. The passenger was a tall woman with nipple rings. Her body was shaded white against the black background. Elsa inverted the image. Black on white now, which highlighted the second image right behind her – a large, gray shape with two ominous wings, like a two-foot-wide bat.

"That's a biggie," Elsa said. She pulled off the goggles and toggled the view for Andrew and Christopher.

"Pretty girl," Christopher said.

Andrew glanced up while he screwed a transfer cable into the port under Elsa's right hand. "Sweet demon."

"Only you could call a soul-sucking destructive force of the universe 'sweet'," Christopher complained.

Elsa glanced around. It was just the three of them, and no one could possibly be eavesdropping. But loose lips sank ships, or so her father liked to say.

Gleefully Andrew said, "You're violating your security clearance."

"Tell the mice in the wall," Christopher said. "How long's she been in storage?"

"The demon is not a 'her'," Elsa said. "Don't be sexist. Seventeen hours."

"Okay. Should be lulled into a nice sleep by now. Send her down."

The AXB hummed. The containment unit, which was the size of a large upright vacuum cleaner (and did a similar job, Elsa often thought), beeped as it began to work. Elsa switched to a view of the interior of the storage unit just as the winged creature began to fade. This was the best part of Elsa's job. Knowing the technology that perplexed and aggravated so many travelers was, in fact, performing its job exceptionally well. Keeping the plane safe and other passengers from infection, and preventing innocent people from who-knew-what disaster down the road.

The demon went into storage in just under twenty minutes. It took another fifteen for Elsa to match up the passenger record with a report for the Department of Homeland Security and file the necessary paperwork. It wasn't the woman's fault that she'd been a carrier, but her home environment would have to be scrutinized. Agents would break in during the day while she was at work and scan the place. Had to be done; the woman would probably never even know she'd been investigated.

Fifteen minutes after the report went in, Elsa and her team departed the terminal. Christopher and Andrew would take the containment unit to the nearest storage facility for indefinite safekeeping.

She thought about that sometimes: locked up forever, no chance of reprieve. Not exactly in keeping with the American justice system or any concept of human rights. But demons weren't Americans or human.

Tonight it was more satisfying to think about Lisa-Marie, and wonder if she was sleeping well, and imagine what she was sleeping in. Silk pajamas, maybe. Or a lacy gown, tight in all the right places. Maybe Lisa-Marie spent time that night thinking about her, too, because when Elsa woke, there was a note and email address attached to the receipt under her door.

Elsa took the email address with her to Boston, and then to Tampa, and then back up to Syracuse. But she didn't email Lisa-Marie. Dinner had been nice, but she never expected to see her again.

More complaints were voiced today about the TSA after a five-year-old girl was separated from her parents for a backscatter X-ray. This video shows the girl growing upset and crying while her parents voiced their objections. A TSA spokesman today said that all passengers, regardless of age and size, are required to comply with government regulations for national security. – WCVB, Boston MA.

Orlando was a tricky airport for extractions. An abundance of international and delayed flights meant a lot of late-night arrivals and departures at over one hundred and twenty gates. Even late at night, people were milling around – janitors, maintenance workers, security guards, stranded passengers in plastic chairs. This particular checkpoint still had two lanes open when Elsa's crew arrived. The conditions were not optimal. But the Class A had already been trapped for twenty-six hours, and the specs called for thirty hours tops, so here they were, Elsa and Christopher and Sam, who was a last-minute fill in. Elsa didn't like Sam. He was cocky and rushed through jobs. She preferred Andrew, but he was stuck overnight in Houston with indigestion.

Their TSA contact was a short, stocky guy in rumpled white shirt, garish orange tie and pants that needed to be hemmed. His name was Robert Henderson Clark and he talked a lot.

"These machines need more maintenance than my car, and that's saying a lot," he complained. "When taxpayers bitch about their money being wasted, I know what they mean. I should buy stock in the manufacturer. Or your company. You guys are the only ones who service them, right? Big monopoly?"

"I don't know much about the back-end," Elsa said vaguely.

Clark kept talking. "I hear that half of Congress owns stock in these machines. Easy for them, right? They all fly private jets and don't have to listen to the complaints I get."

"Hmm," Elsa said.

The image playback stopped at the scan of a woman about Elsa's size. The woman was wearing a clunky necklace and had a tampon inserted in her vagina. The Class A behind her had an extra-wide wingspan, but what was extraordinary, really, was the fist-sized head with hooded ears. Elsa hardly ever saw heads on demons.

She checked the size of the demon in the machine's storage bank and tried not to blanch. "Christopher, can you verify this?"

He sidled up to her while Clark continued his financial and investment speculations.

"That's a bigger allocation than usual," he said.

"Let me see," Sam said, bouncing over like an enthusiastic puppy. "Wow."

"Wow what?" Clark asked. "Is the machine really broken?"

"It's not broken," Elsa said, with a pointed look at Christopher.

"Let's take a look at your other AXB," he said, and steered the annoying man away.

Elsa double-checked the cables and triple-checked the storage unit, but Sam's work seemed okay. She initiated the transfer and watched as the demon slowly disappeared. She wondered what havoc it had wreaked in the tampon lady's life, or what it might have done if it had been left to board the plane. No one could officially say it, of course, but it was widely believed that the Brazilian jet that had recently gone down over the Atlantic had been due to a Class A. The sooner this demon was locked up, the better. At twenty-five per cent the download began to slow. At forty per cent, she realized the creature was fighting the transfer.

"Sam, you're going to need power from the backup unit."

He was at her side instantly. "What? Nah. This one can handle it."

"If the download slows too much, we'll have a breach," she said.

Sam shook his head. "It won't. See, it's holding steady—"

The AXB began to shriek. Elsa tried an emergency abort, which should have sucked the demon right back up the pipeline into the backscatter machine. Instead, the storage unit jumped a foot into the air and emitted a spray of sparks. The terminal lights all flickered, and the warning sound turned into a whooping alarm.

"Oh, shit," said Christopher as he dashed back.

"That shouldn't have happened!" Sam protested.

Everyone was turning to stare at her. Elsa ignored them. Although normal vision was useless, she instinctively glanced upwards. Where had it gone? Whirling over their heads, unseen and menacing? Racing down toward the gates to attach itself to a sleepy kid, a flight attendant, a pilot?

Damn it, they were going to have re-screen everyone who had passed through recently and was still at a gate.

And screen themselves.

And file a half-dozen reports.

It was the first Class A she'd ever let escape.

She didn't get back to her hotel until nearly dawn. The front desk clerk let her extend her reservation. Elsa crashed hard on her pillows, waking near noon to a series of upset voicemails from her bosses in Philadelphia. Leftover pizza in the minifridge filled her growling stomach. After three conference calls and two aspirin, she changed into her bathing suit and went down to the outdoor pool. The weather was sunny and warm, and six or seven other guests were also swimming. Elsa ignored them. She wasn't in the mood to talk to anyone.

A friendly voice said, "Hey! It's Elsa Lancaster."

Elsa turned in surprise. Lisa-Marie was stretched out on a beige lounge chair. She was wearing the same green bikini she'd been wearing in Columbus four months before and looked just as fabulously pretty. She lifted up her oversized sunglasses and gave Elsa a grin.

"Small world," Lisa-Marie said.

Elsa felt off-balance. In both a good way – the day suddenly seemed a lot less crappy – but in a suspicious way as well. How small was the world, really?

"What brings you here?" Elsa asked cautiously.

Lisa-Marie waved her right hand toward the horizon. "Mom and Dad had a hankering for Disney World. I thought I booked us into a hotel over in Kissimmee, but I guess I clicked the wrong button. At least there's a shuttle bus. I had to leave them there, or one more trip through 'It's a Small World' would have made me commit hari-kiri."

Elsa relaxed. "I don't do theme parks."

"Smart woman," Lisa-Marie replied. "So what do you do when you have a day off in Orlando?"

"What makes you think I have a day off?" Elsa asked.

"Because check-out was hours ago, and you're in the pool, and you said you don't do theme parks." Lisa-Marie leaned forward, filling out her bikini top even more. Suntan lotion glistened on her skin. "Don't you want to spend a few hours playing tourist with me?"

Elsa had nothing to do until the Class A showed up again at the airport or she got her next assignment. She had the feeling that Philadelphia would punish her a little for this, maybe keep her cooling her heels for another day or two.

"I'd love to play with you," she replied.

They lounged by the pool, went for ice cream at Downtown Disney, and then walked around the lake and shops there while canned music played in the perfectly trimmed flowerbeds.

Every now and then Lisa-Marie's parents called from the Magic Kingdom with updates on how much fun they'd just had in the Haunted Mansion or *Pirates of the Caribbean* ride, and Lisa-Marie would roll her eyes and grin. Elsa's own folks never left suburban Chicago. Certainly they wouldn't be walking around a theme park all day.

"They probably rented electric wheelchairs," Lisa-Marie mused. "Last time, Dad slammed right into a Mickey Mouse who was signing autographs."

They had a seafood dinner at a restaurant built to look like a steamboat, and afterward drank hot chocolate at a small table in the Godiva shop. Shoppers streamed in and out of the Disney Store next door. Elsa was feeling a bit like Snow White herself. She'd immensely enjoyed the day, and the way Lisa-Marie smiled at her, and her sense of humor about just about everything. But it couldn't last. Like coaches turning back into pumpkins, Elsa had to return to her normal life.

Knowledge of that couldn't keep her from wanting to lean across the table and kiss Lisa-Marie. Just once for memory's sake, to see if those lips tasted as sweet as they looked.

They talked and talked and talked. Once their cups were empty Lisa-Marie said, "Be right back," and dashed off to the bathroom. Her phone buzzed as soon as she was out of sight. Elsa thought Lisa-Marie's parents would worry if she didn't pick up, so she scooped up the smartphone. But there was no call. Instead, it was a message and her own name was the subject line. That was odd. After further investigation she realized her name was attached to several messages, and documents were attached as well.

Her hotel itinerary for here in Orlando

Her hotel itinerary for her last job, back in Atlanta.

Her hotel itinerary for the job before that, in Roanoke.

Shivers went down her back and left her feeling ice cold. Quickly Elsa dropped the phone, left the shop, and walked toward the nearest exit. She felt like she was thinking perfectly clearly, but also like she was moving through unseen bales of thick cotton. Dimly she heard Lisa-Marie calling after her.

"Elsa, wait!" Lisa-Marie was calling out. "I can explain!"

A long line of yellow cabs was idling in the parking lot. Elsa slid into the back seat of the first one and muttered her hotel's name. The driver, an elderly man with a shiny bald head, was pulling out when the other passenger door opened and Lisa-Marie climbed in.

"Hey!" protested the driver.

Elsa ordered, "Get out."

"I can explain," Lisa-Marie said breathlessly. "Everything. I'm not some stalker following you around the country."

"That's exactly what you are," Elsa retorted.

The driver was eyeing both of them in the rear-view mirror. "Keep going?"

"No," Elsa said.

"Yes," Lisa-Marie told him. "Elsa, I know you're upset. But it's not what you think—"

"That you have my hotel reservations on your phone?" Elsa said, glaring at her. "That today wasn't a coincidence? That your parents probably aren't even at the park, are they? Who's been calling you?"

Lisa-Marie grimaced. "My secretary."

The cabbie turned, but the Cirque de Soleil show was letting out and the lane was jammed with cabs and vans. Exasperated, Elsa reached for the door handle.

Quickly Lisa-Marie said, "I'm a lawyer working on a class action suit against the Department of Homeland Security and their routine violations of civil rights, especially electronic privacy issues and unreasonable searches. Your company is the only one that services backscatter machines and we need technical information. My firm asked me to contact you, to see if you could help us."

"Help you?" Elsa demanded. Anger boiled up in her head and heart. "Why? Do I look like someone who wants to be unemployed? I have a security clearance—"

Too late she shut her mouth.

Lisa-Marie asked, "Why does a technician need a security clearance? Why is it that the TSA went ahead and implemented this technology, as unproven and dangerous as it might be? At first we thought: back-room politics. Pork spending. Everyone knows that a real terrorist these days wouldn't go through security – there's a half-dozen easier ways, from the food service people to the plane cleaners. So there's got to be some other reason for all this security theater, all this ridiculous pretense we can prepare for everything. Some reason why millions of passengers a year have to take off their shoes, why little kids get frisked, and why the TSA constantly lies about what the technology is or does. And you know what it is, don't you?"

"I don't know anything," Elsa said, squeezing the bridge of her nose. "Other than the fact that you lied to me and tricked me and made me think—well, that doesn't matter, because it wasn't true."

Lisa-Marie touched Elsa's leg. The expression on her face seemed almost as distraught as Elsa felt. "It was true. I'm not that good an actress. As much as I care about my job, I care about you, too. Do you know that they're starting to identify possible cancer clusters around TSA agents? Tell me you wear a dosimeter to measure radiation."

"I'm not worried about radiation," Elsa retorted. "I'm worried about lawyers who try to use me so they can win some frivolous lawsuit!"

"It's not frivolous!" Lisa-Marie insisted. "Backscatter and other screening machines could pose more dangers to the public than we've ever seen. I was supposed to ask you about your job, but I couldn't. I didn't want to ruin what we've got started here. Tell me you don't feel the same way."

The taxi inched forward. They were still stuck in the damned parking lot, and might be for an hour. The cabbie was watching them in the rear-view mirror with unabashed interest. Elsa glared at him until he dropped his gaze and started fiddling with his meter.

"I don't feel anything," Elsa said. "How could I?"

She tossed a ten dollar bill over the divider and slid out of the cab. Lisa-Marie followed, but it was easy to lose her in the crowd pouring from the theater. Elsa kept moving and kept her gaze down. She seemed surrounded by lovers walking hand in hand, laughing and kissing, all these happy people, while she suffered the hollow, queasy feeling of being humiliated.

When her phone rang with a text message she nearly threw it in the lake, but the number was Christopher's. The Class A had been caught again at the Orlando airport. Where should he pick her up?

Elsa squared her shoulders, wiped her face dry and went back to work.

A Freedom of Information lawsuit filed today against the Department of Homeland Transportation alleges that images of thousands of people entering federal courthouse have been saved and stored without consent or awareness. The backscatter technology involved is the same used in airport screening lanes. A separate lawsuit alleges that the zones around these machines can expose the population to radiation that exceeds the "general public dose limit". – WJCT, Jacksonville FL.

Norfolk. Hartford. Manchester. Albany. Elsa figured that Lisa-Marie had tracked her so easily because she preferred one particular hotel chain, so she started mixing up her choices. She kept away from any that had swimming pools. Her back started to ache from so many hours in airplane seats, and her clothes began to get depressingly tight, so she doubled the workouts she did in her room. In Boston she tripped over an ottoman while doing lunges and had to use crutches for three days.

Elsa knew she should have reported Lisa-Marie to DHS but she didn't really want to call down that kind of scrutiny on her. Once the government started keeping files, it kept on collecting information. Better to just forget the whole thing. Elsa didn't answer emails or calls from people she didn't know, she ate alone in her room each night, and she went to bed resolutely not thinking about long dark hair, a heart-shaped face and lovely dimples.

The last part would have been easier if she didn't turn on the news one night to see Lisa-Marie on TV, being interviewed about electronic privacy. She looked smart and professional in a black business suit, her eyes hidden behind glasses. Like Superman masquerading as Clark Kent, Elsa thought uncomfortably. Fighting for what seemed like civil rights, but only because she didn't know what danger America really was in.

"More people need to realize what information is being collected without their knowledge," Lisa-Marie was saying. "We need to understand more about these machines."

Elsa turned off the TV.

An AXB machine in Newark alerted with a Class A. Christopher picked her up at a Holiday Inn parking lot with a new technician named Alice. "Andrew's out on disability," Christopher said tightly when Elsa asked about him.

"What for?" Elsa asked.

Christopher turned the van toward the terminal. "Stomach cancer."

"It's not job-related," Elsa said, though she wasn't sure if she was asking a question or not.

Christopher said, "Probably not."

"We're not exposed to enough," Elsa insisted. "You know the specs."

"I know what they tell us," he replied.

Alice popped her head up from the back seat of the van. She was short and dark-haired, with a pixie cut and purple eyeshadow. "Are we there yet? This is my first big one."

Elsa sat back in her seat. Christopher said nothing.

The B1 security checkpoint was closed by the time they arrived. Their TSA contact was a big ex-football player named Tyrone Graham who sat in a plastic chair, arms folded, and glared at them for making him work overtime. Elsa ignored him. She had a hard time locating the Class A image. She realized that someone on the local staff had been moving around images in direct violation of protocol – storing groups of them in a local folder instead of keeping everything in one place.

She opened a sub-folder. Over a hundred images had been saved there. Woman, all of them, their faces blurred but their curvy bodies in clear view. Another folder had children, all of them standing with their arms raised over their heads in the same way as the adults.

"Ew," Alice said. "Someone's a creep, huh? I thought operators weren't supposed to set up their little peep shows."

"They're not supposed to." Elsa angrily deleted the folders. She would report the incident, but didn't know if anything would come of it. Philadelphia was good at collecting information and not very good at passing it down. Meanwhile whoever had been hoarding images would just start all over again, with plenty of material passing by every day.

She tried to focus on the task in front of her. When the Class A image popped up, it was attached to the image of an overweight man with a prosthetic knee. Like that long-ago one in Columbus, this demon had a head perched above the spread-open wings. The head was round and small, tilted slightly as if quizzically looking at the scanner. Some kind of circle hung around it, like a ring around Saturn.

"What is that?" Christopher asked curiously.

"I don't know," Elsa said. Her heart thumped faster in her chest and her palms turned sweaty.

Alice snapped her chewing gum. "Looks like a halo. Pretty funny."

Elsa met Christopher's gaze. If you believed in demons, then why not their opposites? For a moment he looked like he wanted to say something, but then his gaze slid across the empty security lanes to their TSA guy.

"Let's do it and get out of here," he said.

Elsa couldn't help herself. "What if some of them are protecting people, not hurting them? What if everything we've been told is wrong?"

"It's not," Christopher said tightly. "It's not, because then you would lose your job. Do you understand me? You would lose your job and your income, and anything more would violate your security clearance, and how do you feel about a home visit from federal agents with guns? Because I, myself, would not like that at all."

Alice snapped her chewing gum again.

Elsa's fingers trembled as she started the download. She watched the creature slowly fade down the pipeline, its head tilted thoughtfully, its halo and wings disappearing into nothingness.

Later that night, Elsa herself disappeared.

"I didn't know," she said, standing in the drenching rain outside of Lisa-Marie's front door. "I didn't know any of it."

Lisa-Marie was dressed only in a white bathrobe. It was just after dawn. Her hair was messy and her face creased from the pillow. "You're soaked. Come in."

Elsa shook her head. She didn't deserve to be warm and dry yet. "I want to help find out what's really going on. I want people to know the truth and what the government is doing. But I don't know how, and I don't know who to trust. What do you do when you don't even know if you're standing on solid ground anymore?"

Thunder rolled in the sky over their heads. The rain came down harder, but Elsa was beyond feeling cold.

"You come to someone who cares about you." Lisa-Marie stepped out into the rain with her arms open and Elsa buried her head against her shoulder. "You come to me, and we'll find out the truth together."

One Saturday Night, with Angel

Peter M. Ball

The word apocalypse *originally meant "revelation": the disclosure of something previously hidden. In the Christian New Testament, the Revelation of John (in Greek:* Apocalypsis Ioannou*), describes the ultimate triumph of good over evil and, consequently, the world. Apocalypse is commonly used today to connote total devastation or the end of the world as we know it. Angels play many roles in John's Apocalypse, but the most prominent capacity is to bring judgement to those on Earth. The angels in Peter M. Ball's story are not biblical, but they do bring judgement.*

If you ask Mike, the problem with the angels is they smell like laundry powder. They have that real caustic, back-of-the-throat kind of smell that burns itself in. Mike is sick of having that smell in his throat 24-7, and he wants it gone.

There's an angel on the roof of the Nite Owl when Mike comes in for the late shift. He thinks it's the same angel that's been following him for six days, but all the angels look the same. The angel is nude, covering its gaunt body with black wings and gauze bandages around its hands and feet. Mike's stuck in the puke-yellow Nite Owl uniform that makes everyone look sick.

Conventional wisdom says six days of seeing the same angel increases your chances of a purging. Mike tries not to worry about it. He's got a graveyard shift, ten 'til morning, the one he traded with Skull last week before the angel showed up. Skull says he's playing a gig with his death-metal band tonight and that's why he can't work. Mike doesn't buy that for a second. No one plays death-metal after midnight on a Saturday anymore, not unless they've got a death wish.

Not that Mike cares; he likes the nightshift. He waves to the angel.

"Hey," Mike says. The angel crouches down, mute shadow against the sky, wings spread out so they eliminate a broad swathe of stars. People say you're supposed to avoid talking to angels but Mike figures it isn't going to hurt. It's been six days after all, it's not like anything he does in the next couple of hours will make a difference.

They use fluorescent lights in the Nite Owl. Mike's eyes are raw after a week of being followed by an angel and its smell so the fluorescents make his eyes water. The entire building creaks every time the angel on the roof moves. Mike takes Patty's spot behind the counter and changes the radio station on the stereo.

"You look tired," Patty says. She's too young for this job and prone to stating the obvious.

"Whatever," Mike says. "Have a good night, yeah?"

The angel makes people nervous, so the first hour is dead in the water. Nothing happens until Elvis shows up at midnight. Not the real Elvis, he's still dead, just an Elvis whose parents happened to be big fans of the King. Elvis disappears into the fridges at the back of the store, stocking up on the staples that will take him through 'til morning. His next stop is the magazine aisle. Elvis paws through the racks and picks up a *Playboy*. He considers it for a few seconds and looks up at the ceiling, then shakes his head and puts it back. The other side of the aisle is filled with foil-wrapped chocolates. Elvis grabs a fistful of Violet Crumbles and dumps them on the counter.

"Hey," Elvis says.

"Hey," Mike says. He yawns and rubs his eyes. Elvis shuffles from foot to foot. The sliding doors open and a small group of club-girls wanders through fresh off the bus and hungry for hot dogs. Four girls in the group, and one of them is hot, all bare midriff and long legs.

"You got an angel on the roof," Elvis says. He's maybe twenty-six and soft, belly bulging beneath his loose-fitting Sex Pistols T. Elvis doesn't want his parents to think he shares their music tastes, and he wants to hide his gut. He has the kind of belly you want to poke.

Mike starts ringing up the Cokes and the chocolate. The angel on the roof shifts its weight again, just a little, and the entire building creaks. One of the girls squeals, the club-girls always squeal, and the floor is full of dropped onions and hot dog buns. The other girls giggle. Mike finishes ringing up the last Crumble bar.

"That's twelve seventy," he tells Elvis. They look at the mess on the floor by the hot dog bar. Mike says, "Yeah, I might have noticed the angel."

Elvis fishes in his pockets. Then he stops.

"I wanted a pack of cigarettes," he says. "Sorry. Winnie Blues."

Mike turns around and picks up a pack. One of the girls has put a hot dog in the microwave. The smell of melting cheddar starts fighting back against the angel smell. Mike rings up the cigarettes and tosses them into a plastic bag with the Coke. Elvis has noticed the club-girls now. He's gawking at the hot one.

"How long do you reckon it will hang around?" Elvis says. "The angel, I mean."

Mike shakes his head.

"They're usually here for a couple of hours, at least," he says. "This one's mine though; it's been following me for days."

"Man, that sucks," Elvis says. "Why the hell did you come to work?"

Mike yawns. "What else are you going to do? Repent? You know how the winged bastards work."

Elvis grins like he does, but he doesn't. All he's got are theories, just like Mike. Just like everyone else. It's stupid, if you ask Mike; all those purges and no one knows a damn thing for sure. All they've got are theories.

The angel smell is getting worse. The first of the club-girls makes it to the counter. She's carrying two hot dogs, a liter-bottle of Coke and a purse held open so she can dig for her wallet. It's the hot one. Elvis swallows, really loud and noticeable. Mike rolls his eyes.

"Hey," the girl says. She's a looker, but her voice is a little nasal. Mike doesn't mind that too much when they've got good legs. He probably shouldn't be thinking that on a day like today, but he does.

"Hey," Mike says. Elvis stands there, running fingers through his lank hair. The girl flicks him a quick look and a nervous smile.

"Hey," Elvis says. "Did you see the angel on the roof? He's a beauty, yeah?"

"Sure," the girl says. "I guess. I didn't pay much attention."

She pulls a pack of Life Savers from the stand by the counter and adds them to her pile.

"I don't really believe in angels," she says.

Mike rings up the Life Savers and her hot dog. Elvis blinks a couple of times. The girl starts dredging the bottom of her purse for spare change. It's a silver purse, metallic and shiny. It hurts Mike's eyes.

"You're kidding, right?" Elvis says. "About not believing in angels? I mean, they're right there."

"No," the girl says. "There's something there, but I don't have to believe it's an angel."

Elvis looks at Mike. Mike focuses on the cash register. It beeps obligingly as he scans the bottle of Coke.

"So, what, are you – stupid?" Elvis says. "What about the purging?"

The girl shrugs.

"Haven't got me yet," she says. She pushes a fistful of change across the counter and picks up her hot dog. She gives

Mike a wink. Mike doesn't want any trouble with a crazy woman, not even a hot one.

"Why?" Mike says.

"Why what?"

"Why don't you believe in angels?" Mike says.

The hot girl flashes Mike a smile, just a quick one. She loops the purse on her forearm and picks up the Life Savers and the Coke.

"Bumper stickers," she says. Elvis shakes his head. The girl waves to her friends in the aisles and points outside.

"Have a nice night," Mike says, and the girl walks outside and flops onto the bench beside the bus stop. She's just inside the light that spills out from the sliding doors of the Nite Owl. She puts her Coke on the concrete and starts eating the hot dog. Elvis stares at her through the glass door.

"Wow," he says.

"Yeah," Mike says.

"She was hot," Elvis says.

"Yeah," Mike says. The other club-girls finish up at the microwave. Elvis has the good sense to shut the hell up while they pay for their food. When they go outside they cluster around the bus stop. There is eating and laughing. Someone points at the angel. They're all wearing big, chunky, dangly earrings.

"What do you reckon her name is?" Elvis says.

"Candice," Mike says. "She seems like the type."

"You think?" Elvis says. "I dunno. I was thinking something a little more traditional. Mary-Anne? Annabelle? Something Anne-ish."

"What about Anne?" Mike says.

"No," Elvis says. He fishes one of the Coke cans out of his bag and opens it. The fizz sparks the air for a few seconds. "She's Anne-ish, but she's not an Anne."

Mike watches the girl through the window. She's a redhead, but he doubts the color is natural.

"No, I guess not," he says.

The angel on the roof shifts its weight again, and this time it flaps its wings. Mike and Elvis hold their breath, listening to the soft *whap-whap-whap* of the black feathers. It's too slow for the angel to be taking off, so they start breathing again. Outside, the girls are caught in the thick breeze of the angel's wings. The girl who is probably-not-an-Anne is smoothing her bottle green skirt. The other girls struggle to fix their mussed hair.

"I reckon she's probably a philosophy student," Elvis says, "one of those brainy, existential types in disguise. That's why she doesn't believe in angels."

"Philosophy's dead, remember?" Mike says. He tries not to sound bitter, but it doesn't work. He wishes someone would dim the fucking florescent lights. He wishes the angels smelled like something nicer, like fresh bread or lavender.

"Not altogether dead," Elvis says. "I saw this thing on *Today Tonight* about these rogue classes that still exist, reading Nietzsche and Sartre in secret. Probably a little Camus on the side."

"You think?" Mike says. He's never liked Nietzsche readers, even before the angels. He starts tapping his fingers on the counter, drumming out the chorus to some Adam Ant song on the radio. He checks his watch. Seven hours to go. He can take a break at three. The caustic angel-smell gets stronger, thick and heavy like the angel has started sweating. Mike blinks back tears as the smell works its way towards the back of his throat. He contemplates getting a bottle of water out of the fridge.

"I reckon she's probably a hairdresser," Mike says. "She's got the look."

"You think?" Elvis says. He swills the last few drops of Coke out of the can.

"It's the hair," Mike says. "She's got one of those flick-things going at the end. No one has those at this time of night, not unless they know what they're doing during the set up."

Elvis rubs his chin and watches the girl who's probably-not-an-Anne.

"I dunno," he says. "She might just have some really good product. They sell product that good."

Elvis pats his pockets, looking for a lighter. One of the girls outside makes a joke and not-Anne laughs. Her laughter is high and tinkly, like tapping a wine glass.

"I dunno," Elvis says. "A hairdresser. You really reckon?"

"I reckon," Mike says. He yawns without bothering to cover his mouth. The girls have lost interest in their hot dogs by now, but that's okay. No one can really eat an entire Nite Owl hot dog. Not even when they're drunk. It's a sign of sanity.

"So do you reckon the angel-thing would have worked?" Elvis says. "As a pickup, I mean. If she'd believed in angels."

"No," Mike says.

"No?"

"There's nowhere to go," Mike says. "What do you say after that? Hope we're safe here? Ever seen them purge? When was the last time you went for an absolution?"

"We could talk about the Arrival," Elvis says. "What we were doing, where we were; all that kind of stuff?"

"Downer," Mike says. "Remember the first purge? You really want to start comparing notes, working out who lost who?"

"We could talk about what constitutes a sin," Elvis says. "I mean, that's supposed to be flirty, right? If you can get them talking about something naughty? Anything that gets them thinking in the right direction?"

Mike shakes his head. It's too late to be putting up with Elvis.

"I don't think it works that way," Mike says. "And she wouldn't have done you regardless. She's hot."

"And I'm not?"

Mike rolls his eyes and Elvis grins. An angel would have purged Elvis years ago if the world was a fair place.

"It used to be easier," Elvis says. "Fuck it. It used to be so much easier."

"Yeah," Mike says. "I guess it did."

The laundry powder angel-smell rolls through the Nite Owl, so strong that both of them have tears in their eyes. They both gag and cough, trying not to breathe. The angel starts to move again. This time the wings are thumping hard and fast, the angel is taking to the air. The entire store creaks. Mike puts both hands on the counter, holding himself steady.

"Shit," Elvis says. "Look at that."

He points a finger through the glass door, towards the bus stop and the club-girls and the angel shadow that falls over them as wings block out the street lights. The bandaged feet drop down through the frame of the glass doors, cracking the concrete as the angel settles onto the ground. It spreads its black feather wings. It points at the girl who is probably-not-an-Anne. Mike checks his watch, twelve thirty-two. Technically right, but somehow it seems like cheating. Sundays don't really start until you wake up and the church bells are ringing.

"Shit," Elvis says. "She was hot."

The club-girls are screaming. One of them is begging, but not not-Anne. She's just whimpering quietly, tears on her cheeks. The angel hugs her close and the wings start flapping. Lazy flaps, just enough to slowly get back to the roof. There are still a couple of hours 'til dawn, and that means the angel's got to wait. The building creaks again and a little dust falls from the ceiling.

"Told you," Elvis says. "Philosophy student."

He pops the top of his second can of Coke and unwraps a Violet Crumble. Mike closes his eyes and pretends he can't hear not-Anne whimpering on the roof. He pretends that flutter in his stomach isn't relief. Not-Anne's friends are buzzing outside, all bleating cries and desperate mobile calls. Like the cops give a damn when divine retribution is involved.

The angel will be carrying not-Anne into the sunrise and no one will do a goddamn thing. That's how purging works. The angel carries you away and no one knows what happens after that, but Mike's willing to bet it's not good. The angels look sad when they're carrying people away, and that's never a good sign.

Six hours and forty-two minutes until Mike can go home. Another three hours and twelve minutes until he gets his break. The angel is back on the roof with the hot girl held in his arms, waiting for the sunrise so he can take off and no one will see not-Anne again. Elvis finishes his Violet Crumble and pulls the plastic wrapper off his pack of Winfields.

"Outside," Mike says.

"Come on," Elvis says. He has a cigarette between his lips and a lighter in his hand.

"Seriously," Mike says. "Out."

He jerks his thumb towards the sliding door and the hysterical girls. He wishes he could go out and smoke with Elvis. The angel smell in the Nite Owl is so thick Mike wants to spit it out, again and again and again.

Lammas Night

Chelsea Quinn Yarbro

Although very little can be solidly confirmed about Count Alessandro di Cagliostro, it is highly likely he was Giuseppe Balsamo (2 June 1743–26 August 1795). A skilled forger and gifted con artist, Cagliostro claimed he possessed occult powers. And, as Chelsea Quinn Yarbro once pointed out, he was "one of the most famous, most sloppy of the eighteenth century self-proclaimed magi". He could not even get his calendar right: the events portrayed in this story take place on Beltane Eve not Lammas. Beltane – the solar opposite of All Hallow's Eve/ Samhain – celebrates fertility and the advent of the season of growth on 1 May. Lammas takes place on 1 August in the northern hemisphere. But, as Yarbro discovered, Cagliostro once claimed in a letter that Lammas was in April. The author was happy to accurately convey this example of his typically slipshod mysticism while granting him the possibility of some true dark powers.

Inside the circle that held the pentagram the air shimmered and, in the dark, cold room, Giuseppe felt he was staring into great distances.

The shimmer broadened, and now it was time to speak the final summons. Giuseppe cleared his throat and took a firmer grip on the sword he carried, though he knew it was useless against the forces he called. "*Io te commando* . . ." he began in his Sicilian-accented Italian. "I command thee. I, Count Alessandro Cagliostro . . ." There was a sudden popping sound, like the breaking of glass or a burst keg and the air was still once more.

Giuseppe flung down his sword in disgust. He should have known better. He could not use any but his real name, and although his title was self-awarded and therefore, he felt, certainly as valid as the unpretentious name his parents had given him, he knew that the demon would not respond to anything but plain Giuseppe Balsamo.

Of course he couldn't do that. No one in Paris knew he was not a nobleman, and he could not admit it now, particularly with the threat of prosecution for fraud hanging over him. He had already had trouble in England. He could not afford to fail here in France. He had promised to raise a demon, and he would have to do it.

The demon would not come to any name but his baptismal one.

Giuseppe sank onto the cold floor, the stones pressing uncompromisingly against his naked buttocks. The sweat, which had run off him so freely, grew clammy and smelled sour. He touched the old ceremonial sword he had picked up in Egypt six years before. The old sorcerer had guaranteed that sword, and Giuseppe knew now that the mad old man had not spoken idly.

One of the candles set at the point of the pentagram guttered and the hot wax ran through the edge of the chalked circle. In spite of himself, Giuseppe flinched. If the demon had still been there, the circle would not have bound it any longer. If that had occurred when the ceremony was under way, no one would have been safe. A shudder gripped him that had little to do with the cold.

In three days it would be Lammas Night, and it would be then that the jaded aristocrats expected him to give them the thrill of seeing a demon. Cynically Giuseppe considered handing out mirrors and taking his chances in a coach with a team of fast horses. But he could not risk it. There was too much at stake. For one thing he needed money. For another there were few places he could run. England was out of the question – he did not want to be sent to prison for fraud. He had to be very cautious if he returned home to Sicily, for the Inquisition took a dim view of self-confessed devil-raisers. Spain was even worse, for the Holy Office was stronger there than elsewhere. Germany would not welcome him, besides the question of debt. He could flee to the New World, but that took money unless he wanted to be stranded in New Orleans without contacts or possibilities. He could go east, but what little he had seen of the Ottoman Empire convinced him that it would be safer with an unbound demon than he would be in Istanbul.

Reluctantly he pulled himself to his feet. He was in a lot of trouble, and he would have to deal with it immediately. There really were no alternatives.

The salon glowed in the light of four hundred candles in six huge crystal chandeliers. One wall was mirrored and it reflected back the brilliant light and the grand ladies and gentlemen who crowded about the long gambling tables. The rustle of fine stiff silks combined with the susurrus of talk and the clink of glasses of wine and piles of gold louis.

Giuseppe stood on the threshold of this splendid room, a sudden sinking feeling making him pause and tug at the three cascades of Mechlin lace at his throat. He covered this nervousness with a finicky movement as he adjusted the pearl-and-sapphire stickpin that nestled there. He congratulated himself mentally on that stickpin. Even the English duchess had admired it and had never suspected it was a fake.

"Count?" said a lackey at his shoulder.

"Yes?" Giuseppe asked. He assumed his most charming manner. He knew how important the good opinion of servants could be. If he found later that he needed help to flee, servants would be of more use to him than anyone else.

"DeVre has asked for you." The lackey assumed his wooden expression again. "He is in the second salon, sir. With Martillion and Cries."

Giuseppe nodded reluctantly. "I will be with them directly. Thank you for the message." Assuming his best manner he strolled into the salon, happily acknowledging the greetings of the glittering people as he went toward the second salon.

"Count," called Countess Beatrisse du Lac Saint Denis. She held out a rounded white arm dripping with diamonds below the fall of lace at her elbow.

Giuseppe stopped and bent to kiss her hand. "Countess," he murmured and gave her a wide, warm smile. His expressive large eyes rested on her face, full of unspoken promise. He was surprised at how unruffled he was, how little his fear affected his behavior.

"I vow I shall be with your party on Lammas Night," the countess said archly. In her tall wig, diamonds sparkled like the sea foam, and the confection was crowned with a model of a full-rigged ship.

Giuseppe smoothed the gold Milanese brocade of his coat. "It may be dangerous, Countess. I would hate to see anyone as lovely as you at the mercy of a demon."

Countess Beatrisse laughed, but Giuseppe saw a strange light in her face. "You are too late, my dear Count. I have been at the mercy of my husband for seven years. Your demon cannot frighten me."

As his inner chill deepened, Giuseppe kissed her hand and passed on. He had assumed, obviously wrongly, that his special service would be secret, that only a few would know of it or attend. He glanced around as he walked into the second salon, and heard a brief hiatus in the sound of conversation. It boded ill. He nodded in answer to the wave of DeVre, and made his way through the crowd to the buffet table where DeVre, Martillion and Cries waited, their elegant, vicious faces showing their eagerness.

"Ah, Cagliostro," DeVre said as Giuseppe came up to him. "We are all agog with anticipation. Tell me how your preparations are going." He smiled to disguise the order.

"I have begun my calculations. But I must warn you, we cannot have more than thirteen at the service." He reached automatically for a glass of wine as a lackey bowed at his arm.

"Of course, of course," said DeVre at his most soothing, which Giuseppe knew meant nothing.

Desperately, he tried again. "You have not seen a demon before." He remembered what the Countess du Lac Saint Denis had said a moment before. Perhaps she was right, and these were the faces of demons.

But Gries was talking, his saturnine face masklike in the scintillating light. "It's all very well for you to build up this meeting, Cagliostro. Theatrics are part of it, are they not? But you cannot expect us to keep this secret. Not in Paris. *Nom du nom*, it is not possible." He half turned to wave at Madame du Randarte, who hesitated before acknowledging his greeting. "There's a rare piece for you," he said to Martillion when he turned back. "She's vain, though; doesn't want her breasts bitten."

Giuseppe nodded uncomfortably. He did not like the venality of these men, and he now regretted his boast as a binder of demons. Somewhat startled, he realized he had finished the wine. As he put down the glass he reminded himself that he would need a clear head for what he had to do here.

"Not drinking, count?" Martillion asked, one ironic brow raised. He almost sneered as he took another glass and drank eagerly.

"I cannot. I am preparing for the ceremony, you will recall." He saw a certain flicker in Martillion's eyes and took full advantage. "As I have said, this is a dangerous matter, and only those of us who have been initiated into the rites may undertake this ordeal. But there are conditions. I must meet those conditions if the ceremony is to go successfully."

Although the three laughed, Giuseppe had the satisfaction of knowing that this time they were uneasy, and that he had frightened them. He pressed on, speaking more forcefully now. "I have come because you did not specify the form you would want the demon to appear in. As you may know, demons can be charged to present themselves in guises other than their own."

"More chicanery," Gries scoffed.

"If you wish to think so . . ." Giuseppe pulled himself up to his full, if modest height. "So that you will have the choice," he went on, "I will tell you that I may conjure the demon to appear as a monster, although that is the greatest danger, and I am not certain this is wise."

Martillion tittered uneasily. "Oh, I have no fear of monsters," he said as he took another glass of wine.

Giuseppe set his jaw. "Monsters can occasionally break the protective circle, and then nothing I, or anyone else save an uncorrupted priest, can do will save you."

"Mountebank," Gries said.

"There are other forms." Giuseppe colored his voice, made it warmer, more flattering. "Perhaps you would prefer a youth with supple limbs, or a beautiful woma . . . ?" He let the suggestion hang, and saw the response in their faces.

"A beautiful woman?" DeVre mused. "A fiend from hell?"

"All women are fiends from hell." Gries laughed cynically.

Keeping hold of his calm, Giuseppe said, "You must tell me which you want." He had an idea now, a way that he could save himself. It was a greater gamble than he wanted to take, but that choice was out of his hands. He would have to risk being denounced or flee France with yet another charge of fraud hanging over him.

"If the demon were a beautiful woman," Martillion said reflectively, staring into the red heart of his wine, "could we use her?"

"There will be another woman at the ceremony for that purpose, and you may choose among yourselves for that. But you lose your immortal soul if you have commerce with the demon."

"It's already lost, if the Church is to be believed." Gries looked hungrily around the room, his quizzing glass held up

"You could lose your manhood as well," Giuseppe said with asperity. "What the demon has touched it will not give back."

For a moment the cynical men were silent. Then Martillion laughed. "Still, to see a demon as a woman . . . It might be more to our purposes than to see a monster." He glanced at the others and saw the assent in their eyes. "A woman, then, Cagliostro. Beautiful. Nude?"

"It would not be wise," Giuseppe said after pretending to think. "The flames of hell make strange garments." He made an enigmatic gesture. "I will do what I can."

"What time on Lammas Night?" Gries asked, his eyes growing bleary from the wine.

For a moment Giuseppe pondered the time, weighing theatricality with the forces he would fool. "Arrive on the stroke of nine, for we must prepare you for the ceremony at midnight. And I warn you," he said, his manner growing grander, "that you must be prompt. I cannot admit anyone after nine is struck, no matter who asks for admission. I trust you will make this plain to the others."

Martillion sketched a bow. "Of course, Cagliostro."

His bow was returned with formal flourish, and then Giuseppe turned and strode from the inner salon. As he passed the gambling table, he turned to Beatrisse de Lac Saint Denis. "Madame," he said in a lowered tone, "that information you requested, concerning an amulet?" He knew this was a dreadful chance, and he waited in fright for her answer.

Fleetingly her face showed surprise, then she said, "Yes? Have you decided on a price?"

Giuseppe let his breath out, relieved. "Yes, Madame, I have. If you would be kind enough to wait on me in the morning? Say, at ten?"

There was speculation and a touch of fear in her eyes. "I will be there, Count. At ten." She turned back to the table and did not look at Giuseppe again.

It was shortly after ten when the elegant town coach pulled up outside the home of Count Alessandro Cagliostro, and the steps were let down for a beautifully dressed and heavily veiled woman. A maid followed her into the house.

Giuseppe himself met her in the foyer, extending his hands to her, and bowed punctiliously. "I am honored, Countess," he said, then added softly, "If you seek to keep your visit here secret, it would have been wiser to hire a coach. Your arms are blazoned on the doors of that one."

She shrugged. "As long as the spies of my husband's household follow me, I do not want to put them to any special effort. Besides, he knows that I come here. It was he who insisted on the veil." With these words she drew the veil aside and made a travesty of a smile. "Where is this amulet you spoke of?"

Giuseppe was prepared. He held out a strangely cut jewel on a chain. "It is efficacious in matters of the heart and children. But you must take special care of it. Allow me to take you to my experiment room and demonstrate how you are to wear it, and what you must do with it when you do not wear it." He turned to the maid who waited inside the door. "Accompany us, please. I do not want to cast the countess into disfavor with her husband."

The maid started forward, then hung back. She had heard much about Count Cagliostro, but none of it said he was lascivious. She bowed her head. "I will remain here, sir."

It was the answer that Giuseppe had hoped for. "As you wish. We should not be more than half an hour." He offered his arm to the Countess du Lac Saint Denis. "Come with me, if you please," he said, and led her into the west wing of the house.

When they were safely out of earshot, Beatrisse du Lac Saint Denis said, "What is this about, Count? You bewildered me last night. I did not know what to think, and this, with the jewel, confuses me even more."

He handed her the jewel. "Take it with you, in any case."

"Is it an amulet?"

"Yes," he said. "It is to bring you your heart's desire."

The devastation in her face upset him. "That cannot be, Count. But it is a kindness for you to offer." She took the jewel and absent-mindedly put it around her neck.

Giuseppe nodded. "You have heard of what is planned for Lammas Night?"

"My husband speaks of little else," she said more bitterly than she knew. "DeVre's set are expecting wonders of you. They are in an ugly mood."

In spite of himself Giuseppe shuddered. "I gathered that. And it is a pity that I will have to disappoint them."

Her brows rose. "You daren't," she said, lowering her voice as if she feared an eavesdropper. "You must not. They will not allow that."

"Yes, I realize this."

Impulsively she put her hand on his arm. "Is it that you cannot? Or that you will not?"

Giuseppe grimaced. "Some of both, Countess. I can summon certain demons, but I will not bring them to do the bidding of those men. You understand why, Madame. I need not tell you why."

"But you must." She turned her lovely, haunted face toward him. The light from the tall windows at the end of the gallery made her fine unpowdered curls glow bright chestnut. The jewels at her throat were alive with their garnet fire, and the silk of her billowing skirt glowed with light. "I know what these men can be. None knows better than I. They permit no one to cross them, and if they suspect fraud, they will show no mercy to you. You will be imprisoned, either by Louis' courts or by the Church. There is no way to escape them, Alessandro," she used his name in a sudden rush of intimacy. "They are too many and too strong."

Giuseppe took her hand and kissed it. "Madame, I believe you. And that is why I have taken you into my confidence. I know something of your marriage, and I have wondered if perhaps you would like to be revenged on Jean Gabriel Louis Martillion, Count du Lac Saint Denis?" He thought of the count's younger brother, and realized that Martillion's vice was small beside the count's.

Her hands closed convulsively on his. "You cannot know how dearly I would treasure revenge, even one little revenge."

With a profound nod, Giuseppe said, "If you are willing to take a risk I am sure that you may have it. There is a saying in

Italy that revenge is a dish best served cold. It will take cold blood to do what I suggest."

Beatrisse du Lac Saint Denis turned away. "My blood was frozen long ago, Count. What do you want of me?"

Giuseppe smiled, and felt relief run through him. "When I summon the demon, it will be you."

She turned to him again. "What? How can you . . . ?"

"That is my concern," he said, raising her hand to his lips. He found it easier to deal with women who trusted his confidential manner and charm than with those who were attracted by his handsomeness. He was pleased to see excitement kindle in the countess's amber eyes. "You must listen to me, and I will outline what I have done. And if you are afraid, remember that you will be heavily disguised by the lights and by the strange garments you wear. And," he added as he saw her falter, "I will paint your face as they do for the theatre. No one will suspect that Beatrisse Countess du Lac Saint Denis is the embodiment of a demon."

She looked bewildered. "But if this is as you say, how will I be revenged?"

"That, Madame, is where the risk occurs."

It was Lammas Night. The springtime moon rode low in the sky over Paris, and rode the echoes of church bells as they tolled the hour of eight. The streets were already quiet, for when darkness descended it was not wise to be found out of doors.

The sedan chair that arrived at the servants' entrance to the home of Count Alessandro Cagliostro was run-down, and the two chairmen who carried it were not the sort most aristocrats would put their trust in. They collected their fee from the plainly dressed young woman who had hired them and watched her go into the dark passage by the kitchens. They assumed she was to be part of the celebration that would occur later. Cagliostro's summoning of a demon had given most of Paris food for speculation, and the chairmen were glad to have their own tidbit to add to the chatter. Servant girls at demon raisings were something of a surprise.

★   ★   ★

They would have been more surprised yet had they known that the kitchen door was opened by Cagliostro himself, and that he bowed over the disguised countess's hand as formally as if she had been in all her court finery.

"Is it ready?" she whispered, somewhat taken aback by his strange white robe with the silver embroidery on it.

"Yes, just as I described it to you. But come quickly, Madame. There is not much time and I want you to practice the trick just once before I dress you."

She hung back. "You are certain that the candles will be out when I appear? I do not want anyone to see the trapdoor."

"No one will see it," he assured her as he opened the hidden door into a secret passage that led to his own austere quarters located over the room where the materialization would take place.

The garment, when he showed it to her, delighted her, though it was shockingly indecent. She touched the flamelike tongues of sheer silk that moved with every draught. Giuseppe pointed out the mechanism of the dress and she laughed at the simplicity of it. "Even if they suspect trickery," she said as she fitted the garment over her, "they would not think of this. They will look for tricks of the theatre, of strange engines." She started across the room, and stopped, suddenly modest, as the silk fell back to reveal the length of her thigh.

"No, no, Madame," Giuseppe assured her. "No demon would behave so. And in a moment I will paint your legs with red, and paste jewels on them. You must not notice your manner of dress." He pointed to the mirror near his worktable. "See? this is not Beatrisse du Lac Saint Denis, this is some hellish vision."

The thought seemed to strike her, for she rose on her toes and turned gracefully so that the silk drifted about her. "This way, Count?"

Remembering the hungry faces of the men coming that night, Giuseppe said, "It is lovely, Countess, but do not make it too beautiful. A demon may lure, but only to hell."

She nodded, then followed him into the withdrawing room. It had been cleared of furniture, and there, by the light of three candles, he showed her what she would do. "Do not let the darkness or the incense frighten you. It will be no different than the way we have done it now. I will always stand just here, and you will know by the candles by the door and by the mantel when you are in the right position. I will not fail you, Countess."

"Nor I you," she promised him, her long hands clenched . . .

DeVre did not like the fit of his robe, and complained bitterly that it was not seemly for him to be wearing such outlandish things.

"That is up to you," Giuseppe said coldly. "But if you are not protected, I cannot save you from the demon."

Martillion chuckled unpleasantly and looked toward his older brother, the Count du Lac Saint Denis. "It's a masquerade," he said lazily.

This was much too close to the truth, and Giuseppe did what he could to turn their minds from the idea. "Of course it is a masquerade, gentlemen. Hell is clothing its own in flesh." He gave Gries a robe and warned him not to drink any more.

Henri Valdonne studied the others, thinking himself above all this. His position as the aristocratic head of shippers who traded in China gave him a certain world-wise reputation. He did not comply with Cagliostro's orders immediately, but made a show of inspecting the garment. "I have heard that such garments must be without seam," he challenged as he pulled off his brocaded waistcoat.

"In some rites this is so. But we are not concerned with virgins tonight, Chevalier. Only when a virgin is sacrificed must the robes be of seamless cloth." And seeing the faces of the nine men and four women around him, Giuseppe was deeply grateful that he was not subjecting a virgin to any such as these.

When all were dressed in their robes, Giuseppe led the way to the rear withdrawing room. None of the halls were lit and there were no servants in the house. Giuseppe moved quickly and was pleased that the others went clumsily in their unfamiliar robes and unlighted passages.

The pentagram and circle were already on the floor. The sword, chalice, wand, wafers and salt stood at each point of the pentagram outside the circle. Giuseppe went quickly to the bay of heavily curtained windows and made a show as if to adjust the curtains against prying eyes. He saw that the concealed levers were set and ready. He turned back to the others who stood, uncertainly glancing about them in the dim light. He put his foot over a spring that worked the concealed bellows.

"Kneel!" he told them, and his generally pleasant voice was stern as a field commander. "Go to the pentagram and kneel."

He watched while the white-robed figures sorted themselves out. In a moment they were ready, and had begun to whisper among themselves.

"You must be silent!" Giuseppe pulled a diamond medallion from around his neck and hung it in front of the nearest branch of candles. A flick of his finger set it to swinging. "We call on the Forces of Darkness," he intoned, garbling the invocation so that he would not inadvertently summon an unexpected Power. "We suppliants call the Forces of Darkness on this, Lammas Night, when they have sway in the darkness."

Martillion tittered and his hands strayed toward the chalk marks.

"Do not touch that!" Giuseppe's voice cut like a knife. "That is all that will protect you from the fires of hell. If any one of you break it, none are safe."

There was a pause and Martillion drew back. The others moved back, too.

"We summon you," Giuseppe went on, "in the Glory of your Power." He moved toward the circle and reached first for the chalice. "Here we call you with the call of blood." He elevated the chalice. Then, like a priest, he went from one kneeling figure to another, tilting the red-colored liquid into their waiting mouths. He did not tell them that what they drank was salted mead in which he had steeped Persian hashish. The color was nothing more than dye, but Giuseppe could see the concealed revulsion on the faces of his ill lot of initiates. Good.

If they were revolted, they would not be too critical of the taste of what they drank, and the salt was enough to make most of them believe.

Returning to the window bay, he said, "I summon you, demons of the pit, I call on one of your number. I tell you that there is work for you here, that the souls wait for you. I, Alessandro Cagliostro, call you. I call you."

The figures waited, but nothing happened. Giuseppe came forward again, and picked up the wand. With this he tapped all the others on the forehead, and when that was done, he drew blood from their fingertips with his sword. When that was over, he took the wafers, and marking each with the print of a cloven hoof, he passed these to each of his celebrants. They were a paste made with poppy syrup, and they took strong effect.

Sure now that the thirteen before him were muzzy in thought, he began the call again. He touched a loose board with his foot and hidden bells rang. A wind from nowhere chilled the room as the concealed bellows began to work, and extinguished one branch of candles. Then Giuseppe pulled one of the hidden levers and the room was plunged into darkness.

A moan came from the group, and in the next instant the niches with their candles had revolved back as the false hearthstone returned to its proper place, and in the circle stood a blazing female demon, alive with fire and with smoke in her hair.

Giuseppe almost smiled as he saw his acolytes draw back from this apparition. He waited until the whole effect had sunk in, and then he cried out: "Demon! I, Alessandro Cagliostro, charge you. Identify these who kneel before you. Tell us the names of those who kneel. Tell us the secrets of their souls. What are the abominations that will condemn them to perdition on the Day of Wrath?"

There was a pause, and then Beatrisse du Lac Saint Denis began to recite the vices and crimes of those gathered before her, calling up every lewd boast of her husband, every shoddy bit of gossip she had heard, every detail that had caused her shame and embarrassment. The list was a long one, and it frightened the thirteen kneeling around the pentagram.

Gradually the room grew darker as Giuseppe once more pulled the lever controlling the candle niches. One of the initiates was breathing hard and Giuseppe knew he would have to give the count a composing drug before he let him leave the house.

At last the long catalogue of debauchery was over. Again the bells rang and the room went dark. In the returning light the figure of the demon was seen shimmering before them. Giuseppe forced the bellows into greater breath.

Giuseppe clapped his hands three times. "Depart! Depart! Depart!" he commanded. Suddenly the air was very still.

And the demon shriveled, became a single flame, and then disappeared entirely in the center of the circle.

"Are they gone?" Beatrisse du Lac Saint Denis asked when Giuseppe came into his quarters a little more than an hour later.

"They are gone." He held out his hand. In it lay a wired dress of red silk which trailed a long thin thread. "Perhaps you might want this, Countess."

She touched it, a secret smile on her face. Then, with a decisive nod of her head, "No. There is always the slim chance that my husband might find it. That must not happen." She paused. "I pulled the thread when the bellows stopped."

"I think you will find that your husband is not well. When he left his pulse was very rapid and he had a look about his eyes that was not good."

"Did he?" she asked, disinterested. "I left the bath water, as you said. It is quite red. The servants may see it."

"The powder removed it all from your skin?" he asked. He knew his servants would never see the reddened water.

"Yes." She pulled her maid's dress about her more tightly. "Do you think he will ever suspect?"

Giuseppe laughed outright. "Madame, after they had drunk wine tainted with hashish and eaten wafers of poppy, you could have come in there in your most famous toilette, and if I had told them you were a demon, they would have believed it."

She nodded. "A bellows and a wired dress. How simple to make a demon."

"You are troubled, Countess?" Giuseppe took her hand solicitously.

"It is just that I do not know when you will betray me," she said after a moment.

"I might say the same of you," he said easily. "Come, this is our secret. You know what I did to make the demon, and I know the demon is you. If you cannot trust me out of faith, remember that we both have a hold on the other."

The countess nodded once more. "I must return home," she said.

Giuseppe stood aside. "I have ordered a hack for you, Madame. It will take you home, if not in fashion, at least in victory."

At that she smiled. "I saw his face, you know, as I told him all the dreadful things he had done. His eyes were like an animal in a trap. He could not move." She went to the door. "I will always remember his eyes, Cagliostro. It will give me strength."

"You have the amulet as well, Countess. It is for your heart's desire."

"Surely you do not expect me to believe that?" she asked incredulously. "When you are nothing more than a charlatan?"

When the door closed behind the countess, Giuseppe Balsamo, known to the world as Count Alessandro Cagliostro, went into his withdrawing room to remove the chalk marks from the floor. And to remove the holy water and Host that had protected that venal gathering from the perils of Lammas Night.

Pinion

Stellan Thorne

The angel in Stellan Thorne's story breaks human law, and a
tough, if vulnerable, veteran cop arrests it. Angels do have a
biblical connection with the law – angels played a part in giving
Moses the Ten Commandments. In the Old Testament,
(Deuteronomy 33.2, NIV) this is not clear. One assumes the
"holy ones" are angels: "He said: 'The Lord . . . came with
myriads of holy ones from the south, from his mountain slopes.'"
But in the New Testament, it is specifically angels who help
deliver the laws of God: "you who received the law as delivered
by angels and did not keep it". (Acts 7.38, NIV).

The witness was beautiful, in a way that was almost hard to
look at. His face was abstract and fashionable, all eyes and
angles, with a luminous innocence too perfect to be entirely
sincere.

Detective Greyling wondered idly how that face would look
with a fat lip. Like a magazine cover, probably, a model fresh
off a photo shoot. Saturday night fight fashion. A little trickle
of blood down one corner of his mouth, like smudged lipstick.

"Cigarette?" Greyling asked.

"Please."

He leaned over the table to offer a light – sparks off a grind-
ing wheel, cheap plastic sticky in his hands.

"I don't usually smoke."

Not cigarettes, at least, Greyling thought. He lit up his own; the two cherries pointed away from each other like strabismic eyes, glowing in the gloom.

"I guess I'm a still a bit shaky." The witness smiled, quick and charming, the kind of smile that knows it is currency. The exchange rate was low here, in Greyling's territory – he hated charm, hated its tawdry uses – but he nodded.

"We just need your statement," he said. The tape recorder was spinning slowly.

"I've told the officer at the front desk everything already." Just a little schoolboy wheedling in his tone, a little note of oh-do-I-*have*-to?

Greyling smiled. It was not charming. "This is for the official record. Please." He gestured at the tape recorder.

The witness cleared his throat, with an actor's skill, and began. "I was robbed by an angel last night."

Nobody had wanted the case. "He's high or he's a liar," the desk sergeant had said. "Angels don't rob people." On the first two points Greyling agreed; he wasn't sure on the last. In the end, he'd ended up with the case. Better that than hear some rookie piss and moan when it landed in their lap.

He went around the neighborhood with a rough sketch, and saw faces shutter with suspicion. They had seen the suspect, he was sure of that, but they kept their silence.

He thought of returning later, when he was off duty. Sidle up sideways to his questions, in dive bars and on street corners. He thought better of it almost instantly. He'd never been good even at that half-undercover kind of work – that had been Mayer's thing, Mayer with his blankly handsome looks. Greyling's face, once seen, was hard to forget. In any case, he seemed to always wear an invisible uniform; he spoke and smelled like a cop.

He ducked into a corner store. The pack of cigarettes tucked in his inside pocket was empty already; this was looking like a two-pack day. He laid his money down on the counter; the clerk held it up to the light before giving him his smokes.

He took out the sketch and brandished it at the clerk. "You wouldn't happen to have seen—"

"No habla ing-less," he said, in a flat Midwestern accent, and grinned.

With slow clarity, Greyling saw himself grabbing the clerk by his collar, dragging him across the counter, breaking his nose. There was no joy in the fantasy; it was like a worn film reel, looping methodically inside his head. He turned away, crumpling the sketch in his hand.

Then he saw it through the window: a flash of nacreous white. A winged figure. It was standing not fifteen yards away, on the other side of the street. Watching him.

He was out the door in a moment. "Hey!" He started towards it, taking swift strides. "Hey, stop right there!"

It froze for a moment, wings outstretched. They looked terribly fragile, a delicate latticework of feathers. Then it ran, and Greyling took off after. It ducked under a fire escape, tucking its wings in close. A few steps away, beyond the building, Greyling could see the blue of empty sky.

With lungs like bellows, the great engine of his heart clanking, Greyling ran. A few more feet and they'd be out from under the fire escape – those wings would pump once, twice, and his suspect would be gone. He lunged, all the world contracting. He hadn't moved this fast in years.

He landed hard but upright, and the angel was beneath him. He kneeled down on the curving joint of a wing. Great muscles strained up underneath him. That fine fragility was a con. One hand came down on the angel's head – its hair was duckling-soft – and tangled hard, jerking upward. "You're not going anywhere." His breathing was labored, paunch and nicotine conspiring. "You have the right—"

A massive wing-heave nearly lifted him – nearly sent him sprawling. For a moment he rode the angel like a broncobuster. His heart was wild with pain, chest burning. Then, victory: it sagged beneath him, breathing slowly.

He cuffed together long lovely wrists, then bent back one wing at a painful angle. The angel cried out with a voice like a tuning fork. "Try to use these," Greyling said, "and you'll get a bullet through them; that's a promise. You're under arrest."

The angel was locked in the back of Greyling's car, and he had just got off the radio – he wished, for the first time in months, for a partner, any partner, even a whining rookie. Just someone else to make the calls while he was trying to catch his breath.

He looked in the rear-view mirror at the suspect. The angel was gray and white; a layer of city grime had settled lightly on its essential cleanness. The wings, massive in the back seat, quivered like wind-caught sheets.

"I am a messenger of the most holy," the angel said. There was no arrogance in its voice, just a calm surety.

Greyling lit a cigarette. He couldn't think of driving just yet. "You're a thief."

Wings shrugged, like a cat raising its hackles. The angel's eyes were colorless in the mirror, like water or wind. "I don't understand."

"The man you robbed – you don't remember that?"

"Robbed?"

They looked alike, a little, Greyling thought, the angel and the victim. That same invincible prettiness, so hard to sully. "You threatened him, took his guitar and his wallet."

"Yes. I was protecting him."

Greyling snorted. "Oh yeah? From what, playing bad music?"

The angel was silent.

"So, what, are you his *guardian* angel or something?"

"Yes."

A low anger rose, like an ulcer. It figures; the charming boy got an angel all his own. To protect him. His fingers tightened on the steering wheel. "Well, he turned you in. So I'm taking you in."

He started the car. It took several tries, fingers fumbling with the key. Wings blocked the window and the mirror; he

stuck his head out the window and carefully maneuvered onto
the streets.

"Jason Greyling," the angel said, "will you not let me go?"

He grimaced. "That's 'Detective Greyling' to you. And I
strongly advise you use your right to remain silent."

"I have done what is right."

Again that calm surety – the tone of the innocent or the
insane. Greyling supposed the angel fell somewhere in
between.

"Will you not let me go?"

"Shut up," he said.

He was still shaking, he noticed. His heart would not calm.
He sucked at the cigarette dangling hands-free between his
lips; the ash fell in his lap.

He missed Mayer with sudden fierceness. He would have
handled this better, his old partner. Mayer was never shaken,
not by anything – Greyling only had the armor of his cynicism,
imperfect protection against miraculous things.

A feather brushed his neck, so lightly. The tip of a wing slid
in between the cross-hatched metal partitioning back seat
from front. He flinched away, at first, then pounded the cage
– it left diamond-shaped imprints on his hand.

"Your heart is known in Heaven," the angel said. "And all
that you are."

Blackmail, Greyling thought vaguely. His hand ached; his
lungs ached. Maybe he should consider retiring.

The traffic was impenetrable before them, loud with horns
and smoke. Again there came the soft brush of a feather,
against his cheek this time. He swallowed, Adam's apple shifting painfully in his throat. Charm. "You'll want to stop that,"
he said, voice level, "or you'll end up stuffing a pillow."

The angel dropped its wing. In the mirror, eyes shone like
light on waves.

The angel made bail – Greyling never found out how – and
vanished. The paperwork was useless: there was no name, no
address, only an elegant sigil the angel had consented to scrawl

as its signature, before being processed as a John Doe and put in an empty cell. Marching past the holding tank, Greyling had heard the howls and hoots of the day's catch, seen fingers reaching out grubby-greedy for the frail-looking wings.

The victim called a few days later. Greyling never spoke to him, but there was a message left on his desk: the stolen things had been returned, anonymously. The case was closed, no need to look further, except he was still finding feathers on the back seat of his car a week later.

And other places. They drifted into his path. Once into his coffee: a small tuft floating on its oily black surface. He fished it out and looked skyward, where there was nothing but clouds and wires.

He lulled himself to sleep at home with windows cracked, just enough to let the sounds in, and when he woke he found feathers clinging to the windowsills. Pigeons, he told himself. He took one between his fingers, turning it. The shaft was pearly white; the barbs shimmered like silver. Pigeons. Like hell.

He didn't catch the angel watching him until after a week of night shifts. Coming home in the light, that's what did it – hard to miss that stretch of wings, perched like a gargoyle on a cornice across the street. It looked fresh from the sky, sun-washed and brilliant.

Greyling shut the curtains with a hard tug. If he – if *it* came here, landed on his narrow balcony, he'd have every right to shoot it. He still had his old .38 revolver, kept it oiled and loaded.

There was a rustling – wings scraping his windowsill. No time to get his old .38. His new service revolver would have to do. Wings mounted over his fireplace.

What happens to men that kill angels?

Instead of shooting, he opened the curtains, opened the window. The angel came in.

"You've been following me," Greyling said.

"Will you take me into custody?"

It almost sounded like a joke; Greyling smiled. "Why are you here?"

The angel reached for him, long perfect fingers outstretched. Greyling sidestepped the possibility of touch.

"Please."

"What the hell do I have that you could want?"

The angel shook long downy hair. "I have to show you. Please."

"Show me what?"

"There is something gone wrong. Jason Greyling, will you not let me show you?"

Every word sounded like a prayer from that mouth, sweet as a bell. If he had to be *charmed*, at least it took this creature. He stepped forward, mouth gone dry.

"You have to see."

The angel's wings were massive around him, and silver-edged, wavering between their form and their function. Here, where he could touch them, they were as strong as a swan's wing; they could break limbs. Where angels lived, they were as strong as the laws of physics.

Between those wings the world shook, and he saw: the whole of his life, like a sphere in his hand. Where it began, and where it ended. How on a perfect summer day, with laughter and the scent of frying onions in the air, he thought, It will never be better than this, how he went to the roof with his old .38 cradled in his hands and took a last long look at the sky, waiting for wings.

He stepped out of the white parabola. "And you don't come."

The angel's perfect mouth turned down, a sculpture of despair. "You were never further away from me."

Greyling laughed. "It's your fault, isn't it? That's why you're here. How did it end without you? Sixty, seventy, with my liver shot? Huh? Or in a cheap home. And that would have been *better*?"

"You have to live."

"For how long?"

"For your lifetime."

Angels' wingtips sliced through time; their colorless eyes

saw the whole of things. A stolen guitar, a feather in a cup of coffee: what consequences things had. And even angels made mistakes. He had become a ragged edge, a loose thread; he smiled. He wasn't being fair, not at all. But then, what was?

"Then you'll have to keep watching me."

He took a desk job; it was that, or get used to a new partner. He could have, he supposed, but didn't want to. Didn't want to settle for second best. So he made a home behind his big metal slab, stamping paperwork. It didn't matter. He was too tired for ambition.

A week after the angel left – two wingbeats, and into the air, from the railing of his balcony – he went to visit Mayer's grave. He liked it: simple, another tombstone in a neat row under the shade of an ash tree. He didn't stay long; he went home, went on with his life.

Some days he finds feathers floating around him, like a memory of snow, and smiles.

Maybe one day, when it's summer and the sky is blue-gorgeous and shaky with heat, he'll go up to the roof. And he'll wait for wings.

Only Kids Are Afraid of the Dark

George R. R. Martin

A pair of nefarious adventurers stir up the supernatural evil of Saagael, Prince of Demons and Lord of Darkness, and eternal darkness soon rules the world. Never fear, a mystic avenger will save the world . . . and the virgin sacrifice tied to the altar. What compilation of demonic stories would be complete without a bit of devilishly sensational fiction? George R. R. Martin wrote this story while still a teenager; adapted to comic form for fanzine Star-Studded Comics #10, *"Only Kids Are Afraid of the Dark" made Martin's name in comic fandom. The author later went on to other claims to fame, but even as a kid, he could curdle your blood.*

> *Through the silent, shifting shadows*
> *Grotesque forms go drifting by;*
> *Phantom shapes prowl o'er the darkness;*
> *Great winged hellions stalk the sky.*
> *In the ghostly, ghastly grayness*
> *Soul-less horrors make their home.*
> *Know they well this land of evil –*
> *Corlos is the world they roam.*
> — found in a Central European cavern,
> once the temple of a dark sect; author unknown

Darkness. Everywhere there was darkness. Grim, foreboding, omnipresent; it hung over the plain like a great stifling mantle. No moonlight sifted down; no stars shone from above; only night, sinister and eternal, and the swirling, choking gray mists that shifted and stirred with every movement. Something screeched in the distance, but its form could not be seen. The mists and the shadows cloaked all.

But no. One object was visible. In the middle of the plain, rising to challenge the grim black mountains in the distance, a smooth, needle-like tower thrust up into the dead sky. Miles it rose up to where the crackling crimson lightnings played eternally on the polished black rock. A dull scarlet light gleamed from the lone tower window, one single isle in a sea of night.

In the swirling mists below, things stirred uneasily, and the rustles of strange movements and scramblings broke the deathly silence. The unholy denizens of Corlos were uneasy, for when the light shone in the tower, it meant that its owner was at home. And even demons can know fear.

High in the summit of the black tower, a grim entity looked out of the single window at the yawning darkness of the plains and cursed them solemnly. Raging, the being turned from the swirling mist of the eternal night toward the well-lighted interior of its citadel. A whimper broke the silence. Chained helplessly to the marble wall, a hideous shape twisted in vain against its bonds. The entity was displeased. Raising one hand, it unleashed a bolt of black power toward the straining horror on the wall.

A shriek of agony cut the endless night, and the bonds went limp. The chained demon was gone. No sound disturbed the solitude of the tower or its grim occupant. The entity rested on a great batlike throne carved from some glowing black rock. It stared across the room and out the window, at the half-seen somethings churning through the dark clouds.

At last the being cried aloud, and its shout echoed and re-echoed down the miles and miles of the sinister tower. Even in the black pit of the dungeons far below it was heard, and the demons imprisoned there shuddered in expectation of even greater agony, for the cry was the epitome of rage.

A bolt of black power shot from an upraised fist into the night. Something screamed outside, and an unseen shape fell writhing from the skies. The entity snarled.

"Feeble sport. There is better to be had in the realm of mortals, where once I reigned, and where I would roam once more, to hunt again for human souls! When will the commandment be fulfilled, and the sacrifice be made that will release me from this eternal exile?"

Thunder rumbled through the darkness. Crimson lightnings played among the black mountains. And the denizens of Corlos cringed in fear. Saagael, Prince of Demons, Lord of Corlos, King of the Netherworld, was angry and restless once more. And when the Lord of Darkness was displeased, his subjects were sent scrambling in terror through the mists.

For long ages the great temple had lain hidden by sand and jungle, alone and deserted. The dust of centuries had gathered on its floor, and the silence of eons brooded in the grim, dark recesses. Dark and evil it was, so generations of natives declared it taboo, and it stood alone through the ages.

But now, after timeless solitude, the great black doors carved with their hideous and forgotten symbols creaked open once more. Footsteps stirred the dust of three thousand years, and echoes disturbed the silence of the dark places. Slowly, nervously, with cautious glances into the darkness, two men sneaked into the ancient temple.

They were dirty men, unwashed and unshaven, and their faces were masks of greed and brutality. Their clothes were in rags, and they each carried long, keen knives next to their empty, useless revolvers. They were hunted men, coming to the temple with blood on their hands and fear in their hearts.

The larger of the two, the tall, lean one called Jasper, surveyed the dark, empty temple with a cold and cynical eye. It was a grim place, even by his standards. Darkness prevailed everywhere, in spite of the burning jungle sun outside, for the few windows there were had been stained a deep purple hue through which little light could pass. The rest was stone, a grim ebony stone carved centuries ago. There were strange, hideous murals on the walls, and the air was dank and stale with the smell of death. Of the furnishings, all had long decayed into dust save the huge black altar at the far end of the room. Once there had been stairs leading to a higher level, but they were gone now, rotted into nothingness.

Jasper unslung his knapsack from his back and turned to his short, fat companion. "Guess this is it, Willie," he said, his voice a low guttural rumble. "Here's where we spend the night."

Willie's eyes moved nervously in their sockets, and his tongue flicked over dry lips. "I don't like it," he said. "This place gives me th' creeps. It's too dark and spooky. And lookit them things on the walls." He pointed toward one of the more bizarre of the murals.

Jasper laughed, a snarling, bitter, cruel laugh from deep in his throat. "We got to stay some place, and the natives will kill us if they find us out in the open. They know we've got those sacred rubies of theirs. C'mon, Willie, there's nothing wrong with this joint, and the natives are scared to come near it. So it's a little dark . . . big deal. Only kids are afraid of the dark."

"Yeah, I . . . I guess yer right," Willie said hesitantly. Removing his knapsack, he squatted down in the dust next to Jasper and began removing the makings of a meal. Jasper went back out into the jungle and returned minutes later, his arms laden with wood. A small fire was started, and the two squatted in silence and hastily consumed their small meal. Afterward they sat around the fire and spoke in whispers of what they would do in civilization with the sudden wealth they had come upon.

Time passed, slowly but inexorably. Outside, the sun sank behind the mountains in the west. Night came to the jungle.

The temple's interior was even more foreboding by night. The creeping darkness that spread from the walls put a dampener on conversation. Yawning, Jasper spread his sleeping bag out on the dust-covered floor and stretched out. He looked up at Willie. "I'm gonna call it a day," he said. "How about you?"

Willie nodded. "Yeah," he said. "Guess so." He hesitated. "But not on the floor. All that dust . . . could be bugs . . . spiders, mebbe. Nightcrawlers. I ain't gonna be bit all night in my sleep."

Jasper frowned. "Where, then? Ain't no furniture left in the place."

Willie's hard dark eyes traveled around the room, searching. "There," he exclaimed. "That thing looks wide enough to hold me. And the bugs won't be able to get at me up there."

Jasper shrugged. "Suit yourself," he said. He turned over and soon was asleep. Willie waddled over to the great carven rock, spread his sleeping bag open on it, and clambered up noisily. He stretched out and closed his eyes, shuddering as he beheld the carving on the ceiling. Within minutes his stout frame was heaving regularly, and he was snoring.

Across the length of the dark room Jasper stirred, sat up, and peered through the gloom at his sleeping companion. Thoughts were running feverishly through his head. The natives were hot on their trail, and one man could move much faster than two, especially if the second was a fat, slow cow like Willie. And then there were the rubies gleaming wealth, greater than any he had ever dreamed of. They could be his, all his.

Silently Jasper rose, and crept wolflike through the blackness toward Willie. His hand went to his waist, and extracted a slim, gleaming knife. Reaching the dais, he stood a moment and looked down on his comrade. Willie heaved and tossed in his sleep. The thought of those gleaming red rubies in Willie's knapsack ran again through Jasper's brain. The blade flashed up, then down.

The fat one groaned once, briefly, and blood was spilled on the ancient sacrificial altar.

Outside, lightning flashed from a clear sky, and thunder rumbled ominously over the hills. The darkness inside the temple seemed to deepen, and a low, howling noise filled the room. Probably the wind whistling through the ancient steeple, thought Jasper, as he fumbled for the jewels in Willie's knapsack. But it was strange how the wind seemed to be whispering a word, lowly and beckoningly. "Saagael," it seemed to call softly. "Saaaaagael . . ."

The noise grew, from a whisper to a shout to a roar, until it filled the ancient temple. Jasper looked around in annoyance. He could not understand what was going on. Above the altar, a large crack appeared, and beyond it mist swirled and things moved. Darkness flowed from the crack, darkness blacker and denser and colder than anything Jasper had ever witnessed. Swirling, shifting, it gathered itself into a pocket of absolute black in one corner of the room. It seemed to grow, to change shape, to harden, and to coalesce.

And quickly it was gone. In its place stood something vaguely humanoid; a large, powerful frame clad in garments of a soft, dark grey. It wore a belt and a cape, leathery things made from the hide of some unholy creature never before seen on earth. A hood of the cape covered its head, and underneath it only blackness stared out, marked by two pits of final night darker and deeper than the rest. A great batlike clasp of some dark, glowing rock fastened the cape in place.

Jasper's voice was a whisper. "W-w-who are you?"

A low, hollow, haunting laughter filled the recesses of the temple and spread out through the night. "I? I am War, and Plague, and Blood. I am Death, and Darkness, and Fear." The laughter again. "I am Saagael, Prince of Demons, Lord of Darkness, King of Corlos, unquestioned Sovereign of the Netherworld. I am Saagael, he whom your ancestors called the Soul-Destroyer. And you have called me."

Jasper's eyes were wide with fear, and the rubies, forgotten, lay in the dust. The apparition had raised a hand, and blackness and night gathered around it. Evil power coursed through the air. Then, for Jasper, there was only darkness, final and eternal.

Halfway around the world, a spectral figure in gold and green stiffened suddenly in mid-flight, its body growing tense and alert. Across the death-white features spread a look of intense concern, as the fathomless phantom-mind once again became in tune with the very essence of its being. Doctor Weird recognized the strange sensations; they were telling him of the presence of a supernatural evil somewhere on the earth. All he had to do was to follow the eerie emanations drawing him like a magnet to the source of the abominable activities.

With the speed of thought, the spectral figure flashed away toward the east, led swiftly and unwaveringly to the source of evil; mountains, valleys, rivers, woodlands zipped under him with eye-blurring speed. Great seacoast cities appeared on the horizon, their skyscrapers leaning on the heavens. Then they, too, vanished behind him, and angry, rolling waves moved below. In a wink a continent had been spanned; in another an ocean was crossed. Earthly limits of speed and matter are of no consequence to a spirit; and suddenly it was night.

Thick, clutching jungles appeared below the Golden Ghost, their foliage all the more sinister by night. There was a patch of desert, a great roaring river, more desert. Then the jungle again. Human settlements popped up and vanished in the blink of an eye. The night parted in front of the streaking figure.

Doctor Weird stopped. Huge and ominous, the ancient temple appeared suddenly in front of him, its great walls hiding grim and evil secrets. He approached cautiously. There was an aura of intense evil here, and the darkness clung to the temple thicker and denser than to the jungle around it.

Slowly and warily the Astral Avenger approached a huge black wall. His substance seemed to waver and fade as he passed effortlessly through it into the blackened inside.

Doctor Weird shuddered as he beheld the interior of that dread sanctum; it was horribly familiar to him now. The dark, hideous murals, the row on row of felted, ebony benches, and the huge statue that stared down from above the altar marked this unclean place as a temple of a long-forgotten sect; those who had worshipped one of the black deities that lurk Beyond. The earth had been cleaner when the last such had died out.

And yet . . . Doctor Weird paused and pondered. Everywhere, everything looked new and unused and – a sense of horror gripped him – there was fresh blood on the sacrificial altar! Could it be that the cult had been revived? That the dwellers in the shadows were worshipped again?

There was a slight noise from a recess near the altar. Instantly, Doctor Weird whirled and searched for its source. Something barely moved in the darkness; and in a flash the Golden Ghost was upon it.

It was a man or what remained of one. Tall, lean and muscular, it lay unmoving on the floor and stared from unseeing eyes. A heartbeat, and lungs inhaled, but there was no other motion. No will stirred this creature; no instincts prompted it. It lay still and silent, eyes focused vacantly on the ceiling; a discarded, empty shell.

It was a thing without a mind or a soul.

Anger and horror raged through the breast of the Astral Avenger as he whirled, searching the shadows for the thing of evil whose presence now overwhelmed him. Never had he encountered such an engulfing aura of raw, stark wickedness.

"All right!" he shouted. "I know you are here somewhere. I sense your evil presence. Show yourself . . . if you dare!"

A hollow, haunting laughter issued from the great dark walls and echoed through the hall. "And who might *you* be?"

But Doctor Weird did not move. His spectral eyes swept the length and breadth of the temple, searching for the source of the eerie laughter.

And again it came, deep, booming and full of malevolence. "But what does it matter? Rash mortal, you presume to challenge forces you cannot begin to comprehend! Yet, I shall fulfill your request – I shall reveal myself!" The laughter grew louder. "You shall soon rue your foolhardy words!"

From above, where polished ebony steps wound upward into the highest reaches of the black temple's tower and steeple, a viscous, fluid, living darkness seemed to ooze down the winding staircase. Like a great cloud of absolute black from the nightmare of a madman it descended until, halfway down, it solidified and took shape. The thing that stood on the stairs was vaguely manlike, but the resemblance only made it even more horrible. Its laughter filled the temple again. "Doth my visage please you, mortal? Why do you not answer? Can it be you know – fear?"

The answer rang back instantly, loud, clear, and defiant. "Never, dark one! You call me mortal and expect me to tremble at the sight of you. But you are wrong, for I am as eternal as you. I, who have battled werewolves, vampires and sorcerers in the past have no qualms about subduing a demon of your ilk!" With this, Doctor Weird shot forward toward the grotesque apparition on the stairs.

Underneath the dark hood, the two great pits of blackness blazed scarlet for an instant, and the laughter began again, wilder than ever. "So then, spirit, you would fight a demon? Very well! You shall have a demon! We will see who survives!" The dark shape gestured impatiently with its hand.

Doctor Weird had gotten halfway to the staircase when the crack above the altar suddenly opened in front of him and something huge and evil blocked his path. It stood well over twice his height, its mouth a mass of gleaming fangs, the eyes two baleful pinpoints of red. There was a musty odor of death in the air surrounding the monstrous entity.

Barely pausing long enough to size up the situation, the Golden Ghost lashed out at the hideous newcomer, fist burying itself in the cold, clammy flesh. In spite of himself, Doctor Weird shuddered. The flesh of the monster was like soft, yet superstrong dough; foul and filthy, so repulsive as to make the skin crawl.

The being shrugged off the blow. Demoniac talons raked painfully and with stunning force across the shoulder of the Mystic Marauder, leaving a trail of agony in their wake. With sudden alarm, Doctor Weird realized that this was no creature of the ordinary realm, against which he was invulnerable; this horror was of the netherworld, and was as fully capable of inflicting pain upon him as he was on it.

A great arm flashed out, catching him across the chest and sending him staggering backward. Gibbering and drooling horribly, the demon leaped after him, its great clawed hands reaching. Doctor Weird was caught squarely, thrown off balance, and slammed backward onto the cold stone floor. The thing landed on top of him. Gleaming yellow fangs flashed for his throat.

In desperation, Doctor Weird swung his left arm around and up into the face of the demon as it descended upon him. Spectral muscles strained, and his right fist connected with brutal force, smashing into the horrid visage like a pile driver. The thing gave a sickening squeal of pain, rolled to the side, and scrambled to its feet. In an instant the Golden Ghost had regained his footing.

Eyes blazing hungrily at him, the demon rushed the Super Spirit once again, arms spread wide to grab him. Neatly side-stepping the charge and ducking under the outstretched arms, Doctor Weird took to the air as the creature's speed carried it past him. The demon stopped and whirled quickly, and the airborne wraith smashed into him feet first. The thing roared in anger as it toppled and lay flat. With all of the force he could muster, Doctor Weird brought the heel of his boot down squarely onto the demon's neck.

Like a watermelon hit by a battering ram, the monster's head bulged, then smashed under the impact. Thick dark blood formed a great pool on the stone floor, and the hulklike demon did not stir. Doctor Weird staggered to one side in exhaustion.

Devilish laughter rang about him, snapping him instantly to attention. "Very good, spirit! You have entertained me! You *have* overcome a demon!" Scarlet flashed again under the hood of the thing on the stairway. "But I, you see, am no ordinary demon. I am Saagael, the Demon Prince, the Lord of Darkness! That subject of mine you disposed of with such difficulty is as nothing against my power!"

Saagael raised a hand and gestured at the fallen demon. "You have shown me your might, so I will tell you of mine. That shell you found was my work, for I am he they called the Soul-Destroyer, and it is long since I have exercised my power. That mortal shall know no afterlife, no bliss or damnation, no

Immortality. He is gone, as if he had never been, completely non-existent. I have eradicated his soul, and that is a fate far worse than death."

The Golden Ghost stared up at him unbelievingly, and a cold chill went through him. "You mean . . ."

The voice of the Demon Prince was raised in triumph. "Yes! I perceive you know what I mean. So think, and now tremble! You are but a spirit, a discorporate entity. I cannot affect the physical shell of one of mortal birth, but you, a spirit, I could destroy utterly. But it will amuse me to have you stand by helpless and fearful while I enslave your world, so I shall spare you for now. Stand, and behold the fate of the planet where I reigned once, before history began, and now shall reign again!"

The Lord of Darkness gestured expansively, and all light in the temple vanished. A thick darkness prevailed everywhere, and a vision slowly took shape before the awestruck eyes of Doctor Weird.

He saw men turn against other men in anger and hatred. He witnessed wars and holocaust and blood. Death, grinning and horrible, was everywhere. The world was bathed in chaos and destruction. And then, in the aftermath, he beheld flood and fire and plague, and famine upon the land. Fear and superstition reached new heights. There was a vision of churches being torn down, and of crosses burning against the night sky. Awesome statues were raised in their stead, bearing the hideous likeness of the Demon Prince. Everywhere men bowed before the great dark altars, and gave their daughters to the priests of Saagael. And, lo, the creatures of the night burst forth again in new strength, walking the earth and lusting for blood. Locked doors were no protection. The servants of Saagael ruled supreme on earth, and their dark lord hunted for men's souls. The gates of Corlos were opened, and a great shadow descended over the land. Not in a thousand generations would it be lifted.

As suddenly as it had come the vision was gone, and there was only the thick blackness and the hideous ringing laughter, more cruel now, coming from everywhere and nowhere, echo-ing and re-echoing in the confines of the huge temple. "Go now, spirit, before I tire of you. I have preparations to make abroad, and I do not wish to find you in my temple when I return. Hark you this – it is morning now, yet all is still dark outside. From this day forth, night shall be eternal on earth!"

The darkness cleared and Doctor Weird could see again. He stood alone in the empty temple. Saagael was gone, as were the remains of the vanquished demon. Only he and the thing that had once been a man called Jasper remained amongst the silence, and the darkness, and the dust.

They came from all over, from the hot nearby jungles, from the burning desert beyond, from the great cities of Europe, from the frigid north of Asia. They were the hard ones, the brutal ones, the cruel ones, those who had long waited the coming of one like the Demon Prince and welcomed him now. They were students of the occult; they had studied those black arts and ancient scrolls that sane men do not believe in, and they knew the dark secrets others spoke of in whispers. Saagael was no mystery to them, for their lore went back to the dim forgotten eras before history had begun when the Lord of Darkness had held dominion over the earth.

And now, from all the corners of the globe, they flocked to his temple and bowed before his statue. Even a dark god needs priests and they were eager to strain in his service in return for forbidden knowledge. When the long night had come over the earth, and the Demon Prince had roamed abroad and feasted, they knew their hour had arrived. So the unclean ones, the dark ones, the evil ones, jammed the great temple even as in the days of yore and formed again the dreaded Sect of Saagael. There they sang their songs of worship, and read their black tomes, and waited for the coming of their lord, for Saagael was still abroad. It was long since he had hunted men's souls, and his hunger was insatiable.

But his servants grew impatient, and so they made for to summon him back. Torches lit the black hall, and hundreds sat moaning a hymn of praise. They read aloud from the unholy texts, as they had not dared to do for many a year, and they sang his name. "Saagael," the call went up and echoed in the depths of the temple. "Saagael," it beckoned, louder and louder, until the hall rang with it. "Saagael," it demanded, a roar now, shrieking out into the night and filling the land and the air with the awful call.

A young girl was strapped to the sacrificial altar, straining and tugging at her bonds, a look of horror in her wide staring eyes. Now the chief of priests, a huge monster of a man with a brutal red slash for a mouth and two dark, piglike eyes, approached her. A long, gleaming, silver knife was in his hand, flashing with reflected torchlight.

He halted and raised his eyes to the huge, towering image of the Demon Prince that loomed above the altar. "Saagael," he intoned, his voice a deep, eerie whisper that chilled the blood. "Prince of Demons, Lord of Darkness, Monarch of the Netherworld, we summon thee. Soul-Destroyer, we, your followers, call. Hear us and appear. Accept our offer of the soul and spirit of this maiden!"

He lowered his eyes. The blade lifted slowly, began to descend. A hush came over the assemblage. The blade flashed silver. The girl screamed.

Then something caught the sleeve of the priest's robe, bent his arm back with a wrench, and snapped it. A spectral figure glowed in front of the altar, and the night paled in the illumination of the green and gold interloper. Pale white fingers grasped the knife as it fell from the hand of the priest. Wordlessly, they lifted the slim blade and drove it down into the heart of the huge man. Blood flowed, a gasp shocked the silence, and the body fell to the floor.

As the intruder turned and calmly slit the bonds of the now-fainted girl, everywhere cries of rage and fear went up among the people, followed by cries of "Sacrilege," and "Saagael, protect us!"

Then, as if a heavy cloud had drifted overhead, a great darkness came over the hall and, one by one, the torches winked out. Utter blackness flowed through the air, shimmered, and took shape. A cry of relief and triumph went up from the mortals present.

Scarlet fires flamed under the blackness inside the hood. "You have gone too far, spirit," boomed the voice of the Demon Prince. "You attack the mortals who wisely choose to serve me, and for that you shall pay with your very soul!" The dark aura that surrounded the Lord of Corlos grew in strength, and pushed back the light that emanated from the muscular figure in green and gold.

"Shall I?" Doctor Weird replied. "I think not. You have witnessed but a small part of my power – I have more I have never shown you! You were born of darkness and death and blood, Saagael. You stand for all that is evil and foul-made-flesh. But I was created by the Will of Powers that dwarf you, that could destroy you with but a mere thought. I stand in defiance of you, those like you, and the vermin that serve you!"

The light that surrounded the Golden Ghost blazed once more and filled the hall like a small sun, driving the inky blackness of the Demon Prince before it. It was as if, suddenly, the Lord of Corlos had felt his first twinge of doubt. But he rallied himself and, without deigning the use of further talk, raised a gloved hand. To it flowed the powers of darkness and death and fear. Then a massive bolt of black pulsating power streaked through the air, evil and unclean. Straight it flew, and fast.

The Golden Ghost stood his ground, hands on hips. The bolt struck him squarely, and light and darkness flashed for a moment. Then the light went out, and the figure fell quickly and soundlessly.

A horrible, mocking laughter filled the room, and Saagael turned to his worshippers. "Thus perish those who would defy the dark power, those who would oppose the will of . . ." He stopped. There was a look of total, awesome fear on the faces of his disciples, as they stared at something behind him. The Demon Prince whirled.

The golden figure was rising to his feet. The light blazed forth once more, and momentary fear smote the Lord of Corlos.

But again he overcame his doubt, and again an awesome bolt of black power shot through the air, smashing into the advancing Doctor Weird. Again the Astral Avenger keeled over. An instant later, as Saagael watched in mounting horror, the figure rose once more. Silently, wordlessly, it strode toward him.

Panicking, Saagael smashed down the figure a third time. A third time it rose. A gurgle of horror went up from the crowd. The Golden Ghost advanced again toward the Demon Prince. Raising a glowing arm, at last he spoke. "Too bad, Saagael. I have withstood the best you could throw at me, and I still live. But now, Dark One, you shall feel my power!"

"N-NOOOOoooo," a hideous shriek went through the hall. The figure of the Lord of Darkness shuddered, paled, and melted away into a great black cloud. The crack opened again above the ebony altar. Beyond it mists swirled, and things moved in an eternal night. The black cloud expanded, flowed to the crack, and was gone. An instant later the crack vanished.

Doctor Weird turned to the mortals who filled the room, the shocked and broken servants of Saagael. A howl of fear went up and they fled screaming from the temple. Then the figure turned to the altar, shuddered, and fell. Something fluttered in the air above it, streaked across the room, and vanished into the shadows.

An instant later, a second Astral Avenger strode from the dark recesses, walked to the altar, and bent over the first. A spectral hand wiped a layer of white make-up from the fallen figure's face. An eerie voice broke the silence. "He called you a shell, an empty thing, and he was right. By reverting to my ectoplasmic form and hiding my physical self in the shadows, I was able to wear you like a suit of clothing. He could not affect your corporeal body, so I left you just before his bolts struck, and got back in afterward. And it worked. Even he could be fooled, and frightened."

Outside the sun was coming up in the east. In the interior of the grim sanctum, ebony benches and carved stairways rotted, decayed swiftly, and gave way to piles of dust. One thing, now, remained.

Doctor Weird rose and approached the black altar. Mighty hands gripped the great legs of the statue of Saagael, and rippling muscles strained. The statue toppled, and shattered. It fell, broken and smashed, near the empty hulk of the thing called Jasper, clad in a green and gold costume.

Doctor Weird surveyed the scene with an ironic smile flicking over his dead-white features. "Even after he had destroyed your mind and soul, it was a man who brought about the downfall of the Lord of Darkness."

He lifted his eyes to the girl on the altar, now beginning to stir from the terror that had taken her consciousness. He approached her and said, "Do not be afraid of me. I will take you home now."

It was day outside. The shadow had lifted. The eternal night was over.

Murder Mysteries

Neil Gaiman

A classic murder mystery and a fantasy about the nature of God, angels, and the universe (with a bit of horror thrown in), Neil Gaiman's enthralling "Murder Mysteries" features seven named angels, of whom only Carasel is a made-up name. Lucifer is the best known. Mentioned only once in the Hebrew Bible, as hêl l or heylel, "shining one, morning star", Christians later came to use lucifer, *the Latin word for "morning star" as a proper name to designate Satan before his fall. Raguel is mentioned in the Book of Enoch, a Jewish holy work not part of the biblical canon, as one of seven archangels. His name means "friend of God" and he is referred to as the archangel of justice, fairness and harmony. Phanuel is mentioned by Enoch as one of four voices heard praising God and "is set over the repentance unto hope of those who inherit eternal life". His name means "the face of God". Azazel ("who God strengthens") is mentioned in Leviticus, but in a context that may mean a place, a demon, or a scapegoat. Enoch portrays Azazel as responsible for instructing humans on how to make weapons and cosmetics, for which he was cast out of Heaven. Zephkiel, more properly Tzaphqiel, comes from Kabbalistic tradition, and is associated with understanding and compassion. Saraquael's name has many variants, the most common seems to be Sariel. Although there is differing lore, Sariel is usually seen as a benevolent angel of death.*

★   ★   ★

The Fourth Angel says:

> Of this order I am made one,
> From Mankind to guard this place
> That through their Guilt they have foregone
> For they have forfeited His Grace;
> Therefore all this must they shun
> Or else my Sword they shall embrace
> And myself will be their Foe
> To flame them in the Face.

– Chester Mystery Cycle:
The Creation and Adam and Eve, 1461

This is true.

Ten years ago, give or take a year, I found myself on an enforced stopover in Los Angeles, a long way from home. It was December, and the California weather was warm and pleasant. England, however, was in the grip of fogs and snowstorms, and no planes were landing there. Each day I'd phone the airport, and each day I'd be told to wait another day.

This had gone on for almost a week.

I was barely out of my teens. Looking around today at the parts of my life left over from those days, I feel uncomfortable, as if I've received a gift, unasked, from another person: a house, a wife, children, a vocation. Nothing to do with me, I could say, innocently. If it's true that every seven years each cell in your body dies and is replaced, then I have truly inherited my life from a dead man; and the misdeeds of those times have been forgiven, and are buried with his bones.

I was in Los Angeles. Yes.

On the sixth day, I received a message from an old sort-of-girlfriend from Seattle: she was in LA, too, and she had heard I was around on the friends-of-friends network. Would I come over?

I left a message on her machine. Sure.

That evening: a small, blonde woman approached me as I came out of the place I was staying. It was already dark.

She stared at me, as if she was trying to match me to a description, and then, hesitantly, she said my name.

"That's me. Are you Tink's friend?"

"Yeah. Car's out back. C'mon. She's really looking forward to seeing you."

The woman's car was one of the huge old boatlike jobs you only ever seem to see in California. It smelled of cracked and flaking leather upholstery. We drove out from wherever we were to wherever we were going.

Los Angeles was at that time a complete mystery to me; and I cannot say I understand it much better now. I understand London, and New York, and Paris: you can walk around them, get a sense of what's where in just a morning of wandering, maybe catch the subway. But Los Angeles is about cars. Back then I didn't drive at all; even today I will not drive in America. Memories of LA for me are linked by rides in other people's cars with no sense there of the shape of the city, of the relationships between the people and the place. The regularity of the roads, the repetition of structure and form mean that when I try to remember it as an entity, all I have is the boundless profusion of tiny lights I saw from the hill of Griffith Park one night, on my first trip to the city. It was one of the most beautiful things I had ever seen, from that distance.

"See that building?" said my blonde driver, Tink's friend. It was a redbrick art deco house, charming and quite ugly.

"Yes."

"Built in the thirties," she said, with respect and pride.

I said something polite, trying to comprehend a city inside which fifty years could be considered a long time.

"Tink's real excited. When she heard you were in town. She was so excited."

"I'm looking forward to seeing her again."

Tink's real name was Tinkerbell Richmond. No lie.

She was staying with friends in a small apartment clump, somewhere an hour's drive from downtown LA.

What you need to know about Tink: she was ten years older

than me, in her early thirties; she had glossy black hair and red, puzzled lips, and very white skin, like Snow White in the fairy stories; the first time I met her I thought she was the most beautiful woman in the world.

Tink had been married for a while at some point in her life and had a five-year-old daughter called Susan. I had never met Susan – when Tink had been in England, Susan had been staying on in Seattle with her father.

People named Tinkerbell name their daughters Susan.

Memory is the great deceiver. Perhaps there are some individuals whose memories act like tape recordings, daily records of their lives complete in every detail, but I am not one of them. My memory is a patchwork of occurrences, of discontinuous events roughly sewn together: the parts I remember, I remember precisely, whilst other sections seem to have vanished completely.

I do not remember arriving at Tink's house, nor where her flatmate went.

What I remember next is sitting in Tink's lounge with the lights low, the two of us next to each other, on her sofa.

We made small talk. It had been perhaps a year since we had seen one another. But a twenty-one-year-old boy has little to say to a thirty-two-year-old woman, and soon, having nothing in common, I pulled her to me.

She snuggled close with a kind of sigh, and presented her lips to be kissed. In the half-light her lips were black. We kissed for a little on the couch, and I stroked her breasts through her blouse and then she said:

"We can't fuck. I'm on my period."

"Fine."

"I can give you a blowjob, if you'd like."

I nodded assent, and she unzipped my jeans, and lowered her head to my lap.

After I had come, she got up and ran into the kitchen. I heard her spitting into the sink, and the sound of runnling water: I remember wondering why she did it, if she hated the taste that much.

Then she returned and we sat next to each other on the couch.

"Susan's upstairs, asleep," said Tink. "She's all I live for. Would you like to see her?"

"I don't mind."

We went upstairs. Tink led me into a darkened bedroom. There were child-scrawl pictures all over the walls – wax-crayoned drawings of winged fairies and little palaces – and a small fair-haired girl was asleep in the bed.

"She's very beautiful," said Tink, and kissed me. Her lips were still slightly sticky. "She takes after her father."

We went downstairs. We had nothing else to say, nothing else to do. Tink turned on the main light. For the first time, I noticed tiny crow's feet at the corners of her eyes, incongruous on her perfect Barbie doll face.

"I love you," she said.

"Thank you."

"Would you like a ride back?"

"If you don't mind leaving Susan alone . . .?"

She shrugged, and I pulled her to me for the last time.

At night Los Angles is all lights. And shadows.

A blank, here, in my mind. I simply don't remember what happened next. She must have driven me back to the place where I was staying – how else would I have gotten there? I do not even remember kissing her goodbye. Perhaps I simply waited on the sidewalk and watched her drive away.

Perhaps.

I do know, however, that once I reached the place I was staying, I just stood there, unable to go inside, to wash, and then to sleep, unwilling to do anything else.

I was not hungry. I did not want alcohol. I did not want to read or talk. I was scared of walking too far in case I became lost, bedeviled by the repeating motifs of Los Angeles, spun around and sucked in so I could never find my way home again. Central Los Angeles sometimes seems to me to be nothing more than a pattern, like a set of repeating blocks: a gas station, a few homes, a mini-mall (doughnuts, photo developers,

Laundromats, fast foods), and repeat until hypnotized and the tiny changes in the mini-malls and the houses only serve to reinforce the structure.

I thought of Tink's lips. Then I fumbled in a pocket of my jacket and pulled out a packet of cigarettes.

I lit one, inhaled, blew blue smoke into the warm night air.

There was a stunted palm tree growing outside the place I was staying, and I resolved to walk for a way, keeping the tree in sight, to smoke my cigarette, perhaps even to think; but I felt too drained to think. I felt very sexless, and very alone.

A block or so down the road there was a bench, and when I reached it I sat down. I threw the stub of the cigarette onto the pavement, hard, and watched it shower orange sparks.

Someone said, "I'll buy a cigarette off you, pal. Here."

A hand in front of my face, holding a quarter. I looked up.

He did not look old, although I would not have been prepared to say how old he was. Late thirties, perhaps. Mid-forties. He wore a long, shabby coat, colorless under the yellow street lamps, and his eyes were dark.

"Here. A quarter. That's a good price."

I shook my head, pulled out the packet of Marlboros, offered him one. "Keep your money. It's free. Have it."

He took the cigarette. I passed him a book of matches (it advertised a telephone sex line; I remember that), and he lit the cigarette. He offered me the matches back, and I shook my head. "Keep them. I always wind up accumulating books of matches in America."

"Uh-huh." He sat next to me and smoked his cigarette. When he had smoked it halfway down, he tapped the lighted end off on the concrete, stubbed out the glow, and placed the butt of the cigarette behind his ear

"I don't smoke much," he said. "Seems a pity to waste it, though."

A car careened down the road, veering from one side to the other. There were four young men in the car; the two in the front were both pulling at the wheel and laughing. The windows were wound down, and I could hear their laughter, and the two in the back seat (*"Gaary you asshole! What the fuck are you onnn, mannnn?"*) and the pulsing beat of a rock song. Not a song I recognized. The car looped around a corner, out of sight.

Soon the sounds were gone, too.

"I owe you," said the man on the bench.

"Sorry?"

"I owe you something. For the cigarette. And the matches. You wouldn't take the money. I owe you."

I shrugged, embarrassed. "Really, it's just a cigarette. I figure, if I give people cigarettes, then if ever I'm out, maybe people will give me cigarettes." I laughed, to show I didn't really mean it, although I did. "Don't worry about it."

"Mm. You want to hear a story? True story? Stories always used to be good payment. These days—" he shrugged "—not so much."

I sat back on the bench, and the night was warm, and I looked at my watch: it was almost one in the morning. In England, a freezing new day would already have begun: a workday would be starting for those who could beat the snow and get into work; another handful of old people, and those without homes, would have died in the night from the cold.

"Sure," I said to the man. "Sure. Tell me a story."

He coughed, grinned white teeth – a flash in the darkness – and he began.

"First thing I remember was the Word. And the Word was God. Sometimes, when I get *really* down, I remember the sound of the Word in my head, shaping me, forming me, giving me life.

"The Word gave me a body, gave me eyes. And I opened my eyes, and I saw the light of the Silver City.

"I was in a room – a silver room – and there wasn't anything in it except me. In front of me was a window that went from floor to ceiling, open to the sky, and through the window I could see the spires of the City, and at the edge of the City, the Dark.

"I don't know how long I waited there. I wasn't impatient or anything, though. I remember that. It was like I was waiting until I was called; and I knew that some time I would be called. And if I had to wait until the end of everything and never be called, why, that was fine, too. But I'd be called, I was certain of that. And then I'd know my name and my function.

"Through the window I could see silver spires, and in many of the other spires were windows; and in the windows I could see others like me. That was how I knew what I looked like.

"You wouldn't think it of me, seeing me now, but I was beautiful. I've come down in the world a way since then.

"I was taller then, and I had wings.

"They were huge and powerful wings, with feathers the color of mother-of-pearl. They came out from just between my shoulder blades. They were so good. My wings.

"Sometimes I'd see others like me, the ones who'd left their rooms, who were already fulfilling their duties. I'd watch them soar through the sky from spire to spire, performing errands I could barely imagine.

"The sky above the City was a wonderful thing. It was always light, although lit by no sun – lit, perhaps, by the City itself; but the quality of light was forever changing. Now pewter-colored light, then brass, then a gentle gold, or a soft and quiet amethyst . . ."

The man stopped talking. He looked at me, his head on one side. There was a glitter in his eyes that scared me. "You know what amethyst is? A kind of purple stone?"

I nodded . . .

My crotch felt uncomfortable.

It occurred to me then that the man might not be mad; I found this far more disquieting than the alternative.

The man began talking once more. "I don't know how long it was that I waited in my room. But time didn't mean anything. Not back then. We had all the time in the world.

"The next thing that happened to me, was when the Angel Lucifer came to my cell. He was taller than me, and his wings were imposing, his plumage perfect. He had skin the color of sea mist, and curly silver hair, and these wonderful gray eyes . . .

"I say he, but you should understand that none of us had any sex, to speak of." He gestured toward his lap. "Smooth and empty. Nothing there. You know.

"Lucifer shone. I mean it – he glowed from inside. All angels do. They're lit up from within, and in my cell the Angel Lucifer burned like a lightning storm.

"He looked at me. And he named me.

"'You are Raguel,' he said. 'The Vengeance of the Lord.'

"I bowed my head, because I knew it was true. That was my name. That was my function.

"'There has been a . . . a wrong thing,' he, said. 'The first of its kind. You are needed.'

"He turned and pushed himself into space, and I followed him, flew behind him across the Silver City to the outskirts, where the City stops and the Darkness begins; and it was there, under a vast silver spire, that we descended to the street, and I saw the dead angel.

"The body lay, crumpled and broken, on the silver sidewalk. Its wings were crushed underneath it and a few loose feathers had already blown into the silver gutter.

"The body was almost dark. Now and again a light would flash inside it, an occasional flicker of cold fire in the chest, or in the eyes, or in the sexless groin, as the last of the glow of life left it forever.

"Blood pooled in rubies on its chest and stained its white wing feathers crimson. It was very beautiful, even in death.

"It would have broken your heart.

"Lucifer spoke to me then. 'You must find who was responsible for this, and how; and take the Vengeance of the Name on whosoever caused this thing to happen.'

"He really didn't have to say anything. I knew that already. The hunt, and the retribution: it was what I was created for, in the Beginning; it was what I was.

"'I have work to attend to,' said the Angel Lucifer.

"He flapped his wings once, hard, and rose upward; the gust of wind sent the dead angel's loose feathers blowing across the street.

"I leaned down to examine the body. All luminescence had by now left it. It was a dark thing, a parody of an angel. It had a perfect, sexless face, framed by silver hair. One of the eyelids was open, revealing a placid gray eye; the other was closed. There were no nipples on the chest and only smoothness between the legs.

"I lifted the body up.

"The back of the angel was a mess. The wings were broken and twisted, the back of the head staved in; there was a floppiness to the corpse that made me think its spine had been broken as well. The back of the angel was all blood.

"The only blood on its front was in the chest area. I probed it with my forefinger, and it entered the body without difficulty.

"He fell, I thought. And he was dead before he fell.

"And I looked up at the windows that ranked the street. I stared across the Silver City. You did this, I thought. I will find you, whoever you are. And I will take the Lord's vengeance upon you."

The man took the cigarette stub from behind his ear, lit it with a match. Briefly I smelled the ashtray smell of a dead cigarette, acrid and harsh; then he pulled down to the unburnt tobacco, exhaled blue smoke into the night air.

"The angel who had first discovered the body was called Phanuel.

"I spoke to him in the Hall of Being. That was the spire beside which the dead angel lay. In the Hall hung the . . . the blueprints, maybe, for what was going to be . . . all this." He gestured with the hand that held the stubby cigarette, pointing to the night sky and the parked cars and the world. "You know. The universe.

"Phanuel was the senior designer; working under him were a multitude of angels laboring on the details of the Creation. I watched him from the floor of the Hall. He hung in the air below the Plan, and angels flew down to him, waiting politely in turn as they asked him questions, checked things with him, invited comment on their work. Eventually he left them and descended to the floor.

"'You are Raguel,' he said. His voice was high and fussy. 'What need have you of me?'

"'You found the body?'

"'Poor Carasel? Indeed I did. I was leaving the Hall – there are a number of concepts we are currently constructing, and I wished to ponder one of them, *Regret* by name. I was planning to get a little distance from the City – to fly above it, I mean, not to go into the Dark outside, I wouldn't do that, although there has been some loose talk amongst . . . but, yes. I was going to rise and contemplate.

"'I left the Hall, and . . .' he broke off. He was small, for an angel. His light was muted, but his eyes were vivid and bright. I mean really bright. 'Poor Carasel. How could he *do* that to himself? How?'

"'You think his destruction was self-inflicted?'

"He seemed puzzled – surprised that there could be any other explanation. 'But of course. Carasel was working under me, developing a number of concepts that shall be intrinsic to the universe when its Name shall be Spoken. His group did a remarkable job on some of the real basics – *Dimension* was one, and *Sleep* another. There were others.

"'Wonderful work. Some of his suggestions regarding the use of individual viewpoints to define dimensions were truly ingenious.

"'Anyway. He had begun work on a new project. It's one of the really major ones – the ones that I would usually handle, or possibly even Zephkiel.' He glanced upward. 'But Carasel had done such sterling work. And his last project was so remarkable. Something apparently quite trivial that he and Saraquael elevated into . . .' He shrugged. 'But that is unimportant. It was *this* project that forced him into non-being. But none of us could ever have foreseen . . .'

"'What was his current project?'

"Phanuel stared at me. 'I'm not sure I ought to tell you. All the new concepts are considered sensitive until we get them into the final form in which they will be Spoken.'

"I felt myself transforming. I am not sure how I can explain it to you, but suddenly I wasn't me – I was something larger. I was transfigured: I was my function.

"Phanuel was unable to meet my gaze.

"'I am Raguel, who is the Vengeance of the Lord,' I told him. 'I serve the Name directly. It is my mission to discover the nature of this deed, and to take the Name's vengeance on those responsible. My questions are to be answered.'

"The little angel trembled, and he spoke fast.

"'Carasel and his partner were researching *Death*. Cessation of life. An end to physical, animated existence. They were putting it all together. But Carasel always went too far into his work – we had a terrible time with him when he was designing *Agitation*. That was when he was working on Emotions . . .'

"'You think Carasel died to . . . to research the phenomenon?'

"'Or because it intrigued him. Or because he followed his research just too far. Yes.' Phanuel flexed his fingers, stared at me with those brightly shining eyes. 'I trust that you will repeat none of this to any unauthorized persons, Raguel.'

"'What did you do when you found the body?'

"'I came out of the Hall, as I said, and there was Carasel on the sidewalk, staring up. I asked him what he was doing, and he did not reply. Then I noticed the inner fluid, and that Carasel seemed unable, rather than unwilling, to talk to me.

"'I was scared. I did not know what to do.

"'The Angel Lucifer came up behind me. He asked me if there was some kind of problem. I told him. I showed him the body. And then . . . then his Aspect came upon him, and he communed, with the Name. He burned so bright.

"'Then he said he had to fetch the one whose function embraced events like this, and he left – to seek you, I imagine.

"'As Carasel's death was now being dealt with, and his fate was no real concern of mine, I returned to work, having gained a new – and, I suspect, quite valuable – perspective on the mechanics of Regret.

"'I am considering taking *Death* away from the Carasel and

Saraquael partnership. I may reassign it to Zephkiel, my senior partner, if he is willing to take it on. He excels on contemplative projects.'

"By now there was a line of angels waiting to talk to Phanuel. I felt I had almost all I was going to get from him.

"'Who did Carasel work with? Who would have been the last to see him alive?'

"'You could talk to Saraquael, I suppose – he was his partner, after all. Now, if you'll excuse me . . .'

"He returned to his swarm of aides: advising, correcting, suggesting, forbidding."

The man paused.

The street was quiet now; I remember the low whisper of his voice, the buzz of a cricket somewhere. A small animal – a cat perhaps, or something more exotic, a raccoon, or even a jackal – darted from shadow to shadow among the parked cars on the opposite side of the street.

"Saraquael was in the highest of the mezzanine galleries that ringed the Hall of Being. As I said, the universe was in the middle of the Hall, and it glinted and sparkled and shone. Went up quite a way, too . . ."

"The universe you mention, it was, what, a diagram?" I asked, interrupting for the first time.

"Not really. Kind of. Sorta. It was a blueprint; but it was full-sized, and it hung in the Hall, and all these angels went around and fiddled with it all the time. Doing stuff with *Gravity* and *Music* and *Klar* and whatever. It wasn't really the universe, not yet. It would be, when it was finished and it was time for it to be properly Named."

"But . . ." I grasped for words to express my confusion. The man interrupted me.

"Don't worry about it. Think of it as a model if that makes it easier for you. Or a map. Or a – what's the word? *Prototype*. Yeah. A Model-T Ford universe." He grinned. "You got to understand, a lot of the stuff I'm telling you, I'm translating already; putting it in a form you can understand. Otherwise I couldn't tell the story at all. You want to hear it?"

"Yes." I didn't care if it was true or not; it was a story I needed to hear all the way through to the end.

"Good. So shut up and listen.

"So I met Saraquael in the topmost gallery. There was no one else about – just him, and some papers, and some small, glowing models.

"'I've come about Carasel,' I told him.

"He looked at me. 'Carasel isn't here at this time,' he said. 'I expect him to return shortly.'

"I shook my head. 'Carasel won't be coming back. He's stopped existing as a spiritual entity,' I said.

"His light paled, and his eyes opened very wide. 'He's dead?'

"'That's what I said. Do you have any ideas about how it happened?'

"'I . . . this is so sudden. I mean, he'd been talking about . . . but I had no idea that he would . . .'

"'Take it slowly.'

"Saraquael nodded.

"He stood up and walked to the window. There was no view of the Silver City from his window – just a reflected glow from the City and the sky behind us, hanging in the air, and beyond that the Dark. The wind from the Dark gently caressed Saraquael's hair as he spoke. I stared at his back.

"'Carasel is . . . no, was. That's right, isn't it? *Was*. He was always so involved. And so creative. But it was never enough for him. He always wanted to understand everything – to experience what he was working on. He was never content to just create it – to understand it intellectually. He wanted *all* of it.

"'That wasn't a problem before, when we were working on properties of matter. But when we began to design some of the Named emotions . . . he got too involved with his work.

"'And our latest project was *Death*. It's one of the hard ones – one of the big ones, too, I suspect. Possibly it may even become the attribute that's going to define the Creation for the Created: if not for *Death*, they'd be content to simply exist, but with Death, well, their lives will have meaning – a boundary beyond which the living cannot cross . . .'

"'So you think he killed himself?'

"'I know he did,' said Saraquael.

"I walked to the window and looked out. Far below, a *long* way, I could see a tiny white dot. That was Carasel's body. I'd have to arrange for someone to take care of it. I wondered what we would do with it; but there would be someone who would know, whose function was the removal of unwanted things. It was not my function. I knew that.

"'How?'

"He shrugged. 'I know. Recently he'd begun asking questions – questions about Death. How we could know whether or not it was right to make this thing, to set the rules, if we were not going to experience it ourselves. He kept talking about it.'

"'Didn't you wonder about this?'

"Saraquael turned, for the first time, to look at me.

"'No. That is our function – to discuss, to improvise, to aid the Creation and the Created. We sort it out now, so that when it all Begins, it'll run like clockwork. Right now we're working on *Death*. So obviously that's what we look at. The physical aspect; the emotional aspect; the philosophical aspect.

"'And the *patterns*. Carasel had the notion that what we do here in the Hall of Being creates patterns. That there are structures and shapes appropriate to beings and events that, once begun, must continue until they reach their end. For us, perhaps, as well as for them. Conceivably he felt this was one of his patterns.'

"'Did you know Carasel well?'

"'As well as any of us know each other. We saw each other here; we worked side by side. At certain times I would retire to my cell across the City. Sometimes he would do the same.'

"'Tell me about Phanuel.'

"His mouth crooked into a smile. 'He's officious. Doesn't do much – farms everything out and takes all the credit.' He lowered his voice, although there was no other soul in the gallery. 'To hear him talk, you'd think that *Love* was all his own work. But, to his credit, he does make sure the work gets done. Zephkiel's the real thinker of the two senior designers, but he doesn't come here. He stays back in his cell in the City and contemplates; resolves problems from a distance. If you need to speak to Zephkiel, you go to Phanuel, and Phanuel relays your questions to Zephkiel . . .'

"I cut him short. 'How about Lucifer? Tell me about him.'

"'Lucifer? The Captain of the Host? He doesn't work here . . . He has visited the Hall a couple of times, though – inspecting the Creation. They say he reports directly to the Name. I have never spoken to him.'

"'Did he know Carasel?'

"'I doubt it. As I said, he has only been here twice. I have seen him on other occasions, though. Through here.' He flicked a wingtip, indicating the world outside the window. 'In flight.'

"'Where to?'

"Saraquael seemed to be about to say something, then he changed his mind. 'I don't know.'

"I looked out of the window at the Darkness outside the Silver City. 'I may want to talk with you some more later,' I told Saraquael.

"'Very good.' I turned to go. 'Sir? Do you know if they will be assigning me another partner? For *Death*?'

"'No,' I told him. 'I'm afraid I don't.'

"In the center of the Silver City was a park – a place of recreation and rest. I found the Angel Lucifer there, beside a river. He was just standing, watching the water flow.

"'Lucifer?'

"He inclined his head. 'Raguel. Are you making progress?'

"'I don't know. Maybe. I need to ask you a few questions. Do you mind?'

"'Not at all.'

"'How did you come upon the body?'

"'I didn't. Not exactly. I saw Phanuel standing in the street. He looked distressed. I enquired whether there was some-thing wrong, and he showed me the dead angel. And I fetched you.'

"'I see.'

"He leaned down, let one hand enter the cold water of the river. The water splashed and rolled around it. 'Is that all?'

"'Not quite. What were you doing in that part of the city?'

"'I don't see what business that is of yours.'

"'It is my business, Lucifer. What were you doing there?'

"'I was . . . walking. I do that sometimes. Just walk and think. And try to understand.' He shrugged.

"'You walk on the edge of the City?'

"A beat, then 'Yes.'

"'That's all I want to know. For now.'

"'Who else have you talked to?'

"'Carasel's boss and his partner. They both feel that he killed himself – ended his own life.'

"'Who else are you going to talk to?'

"I looked up. The spires of the City of the Angels towered above us. 'Maybe everyone.'

"'All of them?'

"'If I need to. It's my function. I cannot rest until I understand what happened, and until the Vengeance of the Name has been taken on whosoever was responsible. But I'll tell you something I do know.'

"'What would that be?' Drops of water fell like diamonds from the Angel Lucifer's perfect fingers.

"'Carasel did not kill himself.'

"'How do you know that?'

"'I am Vengeance. If Carasel had died by his own hand,' I explained to the Captain of the Heavenly Host, 'there would have been no call for me. Would there?'

"He did not reply.

"I flew upward into the light of the eternal morning.

"You got another cigarette on you?"

I fumbled out the red and white packet, handed him a cigarette.

"Obliged.

"Zephkiel's cell was larger than mine. It wasn't a place for waiting. It was a place to live, and work, and be. It was lined with books, and scrolls, and papers, and there were images and representations on the walls: pictures. I'd never seen a picture before.

"In the center of the room was a large chair, and Zephkiel sat there, his eyes closed, his head back.

"As I approached him, he opened his eyes. They burned no brighter than the eyes of any of the other angels I had seen, but somehow they seemed to have seen more. It was something about the way he looked. I'm not sure I can explain it. And he had no wings.

"'Welcome, Raguel,' he said. He sounded tired.

"'You are Zephkiel?' I don't know why I asked him that. I mean, I knew who people were. It's part of my function, I guess. Recognition. I know who *you* are.

"'Indeed. You are staring, Raguel. I have no wings, it is true, but then my function does not call for me to leave this cell. I remain here, and I ponder. Phanuel reports back to me, brings me the new things for my opinion. He brings me the problems, and I think about them, and occasionally I make myself useful by making some small suggestions. That is my function. As yours is vengeance.'

"'Yes.'

"'You are here about the death of the Angel Carasel?'

"'Yes.'

"'I did not kill him.'

"When he said it, I knew it was true. 'Do you know who did?'

"'That is *your* function, is it not? To discover who killed the poor thing and to take the Vengeance of the Name upon him.'

"'Yes.'

"He nodded. 'What do you want to know?'

"I paused, reflecting on what I had heard that day. 'Do you know what Lucifer was doing in that part of the City before the body was found?'

"The old angel stared at me. 'I can hazard a guess.'

"'Yes?'

"'He was walking in the Dark.'

"I nodded. I had a shape in my mind now. Something I could almost grasp. I asked the last question: 'What can you tell me about *Love*?'

"And he told me. And I thought I had it all.

"I returned to the place where Carasel's body had been. The remains had been removed, the blood had been cleaned away, the stray feathers collected and disposed of. There was nothing on the silver sidewalk to indicate it had ever been there. But I knew where it had been.

"I ascended on my wings, flew upward until I neared the top of the spire of the Hall of Being. There was a window there, and I entered.

"Saraquael was working there, putting a wingless manne-quin into a small box. On one side of the box was a representation of a small brown creature with eight legs. On the other was a representation of a white blossom.

"'Saraquael?'

"'Hm? Oh, it's you. Hello. Look at this. If you were to die and to be, let us say, put into the earth in a box, which would you want laid on top of you – a spider, here, or a lily, here?'

"'The lily, I suppose.'

"'Yes, that's what I think, too. But *why*? I wish . . .' He raised a hand to his chin, stared down at the two models, put first one on top of the box, then the other, experimentally. 'There's so much to do, Raguel. So much to get right. And we only get one chance at it, you know. There'll just be one universe – we can't keep trying until we get it right. I wish I understood why all this was so important to Him . . .'

"'Do you know where Zephkiel's cell is?' I asked him.

"'Yes. I mean, I've never been there. But I know where it is.'

"'Good. Go there. He'll be expecting you. I will meet you there.'

"He shook his head. 'I have work to do. I can't just . . .'

"I felt my function come upon me. I looked down at him, and I said, 'You will be there. Go now.'

"He said nothing. He backed away from me toward the

window, staring at me; then he turned and flapped his wings, and I was alone.

"I walked to the central well of the Hall and let myself fall, tumbling down through the model of the universe: it glittered around me, unfamiliar colors and shapes seething and writhing without meaning.

"As I approached the bottom, I beat my wings, slowing my descent, and stepped lightly onto the silver floor. Phanuel stood between two angels who were both trying to claim his attention.

"'I don't care how aesthetically pleasing it would be,' he was explaining to one of them. 'We simply cannot put it in the center. Background radiation would prevent any possible life forms from even getting a foothold; and anyway, it's too unstable.'

"He turned to the other. 'Okay, let's see it. Hmm. So that's *Green*, is it? It's . . . not exactly how I'd imagined it, but . . . Mm. Leave it with me. I'll get back to you.' He took a paper from the angel, folded it over decisively.

"He turned to me. His manner was brusque, and dismissive. 'Yes?'

"'I need to talk to you.'

"'Mm? Well, make it quick. I have much to do. If this is about Carasel's death, I have told you all I know.'

"'It is about Carasel's death. But I will not speak to you now. Not here. Go to Zephkiel's cell: he is expecting you. I will meet you there.'

"He seemed about to say something, but he only nodded, walked toward the door.

"I turned to go when something occurred to me. I stopped the angel who had the *Green*. 'Tell me something.'

"'If I can, sir.'

"'That thing.' I pointed to the universe. 'What's it going to be *for*?'

"'For? Why, it is the universe.'

"'I know what it's called. But what purpose will it serve?'

"He frowned. 'It is part of the plan. The Name wishes it; He requires *such and such*, to *these* dimensions and having such and such properties and ingredients. It is our function to bring it into existence, according to His wishes. I am sure *He* knows its function, but He has not revealed it to me.' His tone was one of gentle rebuke.

"I nodded, and left that place.

"High above the City a phalanx of angels wheeled and circled and dove. Each held a flaming sword that trailed a streak of burning brightness behind it, dazzling the eye. They moved in unison through the salmon pink sky. They were very beautiful. It was – you know on summer evenings when you get whole flocks of birds performing their dances in the sky? Weaving and circling and clustering and breaking apart again, so just as you think you understand the pattern, you realize you don't, and you never will? It was like that, only better.

"Above me was the sky. Below me, the shining City. My home. And outside the City, the Dark.

"Lucifer hovered a little below the Host, watching their maneuvers.

"'Lucifer?'

"'Yes, Raguel? Have you discovered your malefactor?'

"'I think so. Will you accompany me to Zephkiel's cell? There are others waiting for us there, and I will explain everything.'

"He paused. Then, 'Certainly.'

"He raised his perfect face to the angels, now performing a slow revolution in the sky, each moving through the air keeping perfect pace with the next, none of them ever touching. 'Azazel!'

"An angel broke from the circle; the others adjusted almost imperceptibly to his disappearance, filling the space, so you could no longer see where he had been.

"'I have to leave. You are in command, Azazel. Keep them drilling. They still have much to perfect.'

"'Yes, sir.'

"Azazel hovered where Lucifer had been, staring up at the flock of angels, and Lucifer and I descended toward the City.

"'He's my second-in-command,' said Lucifer. 'Bright. Enthusiastic. Azazel would follow you anywhere.'

"'What are you training them for?'

"'War.'

"'With whom?'

"'How do you mean?'

"'Who are they going to fight? Who else is there?'

"He looked at me; his eyes were clear, and honest. 'I do not know. But He has Named us to be His army. So we will be perfect. For Him. The Name is infallible and all-just and all-wise, Raguel. It cannot be otherwise, no matter what—' He broke off and looked away.

"'You were going to say?'

"'It is of no importance.'

"'Ah.'

"We did not talk for the rest of the descent to Zephkiel's cell."

I looked at my watch; it was almost three. A chill breeze had begun to blow down the LA street, and I shivered. The man noticed, and he paused in his story. "You okay?" he asked.

"I'm fine. Please carry on. I'm fascinated."

He nodded.

"They were waiting for us in Zephkiel's cell: Phanuel, Saraquael and Zephkiel. Zephkiel was sitting in his chair. Lucifer took up a position beside the window.

"I walked to the center of the room, and I began.

"'I thank you all for coming here. You know who I am; you know my function. I am the Vengeance of the Name, the arm of the Lord. I am Raguel.

"'The Angel Carasel is dead. It was given to me to find out why he died, who killed him. This I have done. Now, the Angel Carasel was a designer in the Hall of Being. He was very good, or so I am told . . .

"'Lucifer. *Tell me* what you were doing before you came upon Phanuel, and the body.'

"'I have told you already. I was walking.'

"'Where were you walking?'

"'I do not see what business that is of yours.'

"'Tell me.'

"He paused. He was taller than any of us, tall, and proud. 'Very well. I was walking in the Dark. I have been walking in the Darkness for some time now. It helps me to gain a perspective on the City – being outside it. I see how fair it is, how perfect. There is nothing more enchanting than our home. Nothing more complete. Nowhere else that anyone would want to be.'

"'And what do you do in the Dark, Lucifer?'

"He stared at me. 'I walk. And . . . There are voices in the Dark. I listen to the voices. They promise me things, ask me questions, whisper and plead. And I ignore them. I steel myself and I gaze at the City. It is the only way I have of testing myself – putting myself to a kind of trial. I am the Captain of the Host; I am the first among the Angels, and I must prove myself.'

"I nodded. 'Why did you not tell me this before?'

"He looked down. 'Because I am the only angel who walks in the Dark. Because I do not want others to walk in the Dark: I am strong enough to challenge the voices to test myself. Others are not so strong. Others might stumble, or fall.'

"'Thank you, Lucifer. That is all, for now.' I turned to the next angel. 'Phanuel. How long have you been taking credit for Carasel's work?'

"His mouth opened, but no sound came out.

"'Well?'

"'I . . . I would not take credit for another's work.'

"'But you did take credit for *Love*?'

"He blinked. 'Yes. I did.'

"'Would you care to explain to us all what *Love* is?' I asked.

"He glanced around uncomfortably. 'It's a feeling of deep affection and attraction for another being, often combined with passion or desire – a need to be with another.' He spoke dryly, didactically, as if he were reciting a mathematical formula. 'The feeling that we have for the Name, for our Creator – that is *Love* . . . amongst other things. *Love* will be an impulse that will inspire and ruin in equal measure. We are . . .' He paused, then began once more. 'We are very proud of it.'

"He was mouthing the words. He no longer seemed to hold any hope that we would believe them.

"'Who did the majority of the work on *Love*? No, don't answer. Let me ask the others first. Zephkiel? When Phanuel passed the details on *Love* to you for approval, who did he tell you was responsible for it?'

"The wingless angel smiled gently. 'He told me it was his project.'

"'Thank you, sir. Now, Saraquael: whose was *Love*?'

"'Mine. Mine and Carasel's Perhaps more his than mine, but we worked on it together.'

"'You knew that Phanuel was claiming the credit for it? And you permitted this?'

"'He . . . he promised us that he would give us a good project of our own to follow. He promised that if we said nothing we would be given more big projects, and he was true to his word. He gave us *Death*.'

"I turned back to Phanuel. 'Well?'

"'It is true that I claimed that *Love* was mine.'

"'But it was Carasel's. And Saraquael's.'

"'Yes.'

"'Their last project – before *Death*?'

"'Yes.'

"'That is all.'

"I walked over to the window, looked at the silver spires, looked at the Dark. And I began to speak.

"'Carasel was a remarkable designer. If he had one failing, it was that he threw himself too deeply into his work.' I turned back to them. The Angel Saraquael was shivering, and lights were flickering beneath his skin. 'Saraquael? Who did Carasel love? Who was his lover?'

"He stared at the floor. Then he stared up, proudly, aggressively. And he smiled. 'I was.'

"'Do you want to tell me about it?'

"'No.' A shrug. 'But I suppose I must. Very well then.

"'We worked together. And when we began to work on *Love* . . . we became lovers. It was his idea. We would go back to his cell whenever we could snatch the time. There we touched each other, held each other, whispered endearments and protestations of eternal devotion. His welfare mattered more to me than my own. I existed for him. When I was alone, I would repeat his name to myself and think of nothing but him.

"'When I was with him . . .' He paused. He looked down. 'Nothing else mattered.'

"I walked to where Saraquael stood, lifted his chin with my hand, stared into his grey eyes. 'Then why did you kill him?'

"'Because he would no longer love me. When we started to work on *Death*, he . . . he lost interest. He was no longer mine. He belonged to *Death*. And if I could not have him, then his new lover was welcome to him. I could not bear his presence – I could not endure to have him near me and to know that he felt nothing for me. That was what hurt the most. I thought . . . I hoped . . . that if he was gone, then I would no longer care for him – that the pain would stop.

"'So I killed him. I stabbed him, and I threw his body from our window in the Hall of Being. But the pain has not stopped.' It was almost a wail.

"Saraquael reached up, removed my hand from his chin. 'Now what?'

"I felt my aspect begin to come upon me; felt my function possess me. I was no longer an individual – I was the Vengeance of the Lord.

"I moved close to Saraquael and embraced him. I pressed my lips to his, forced my tongue into his mouth. We kissed. He closed his eyes.

"I felt it well up within me then: a burning, a brightness. From the corner of my eyes, I could see Lucifer and Phanuel averting their faces from my light; I could feel Zephkiel's stare. And my light became brighter and brighter until it erupted – from my eyes, from my chest, from my fingers, from my lips: a white searing fire.

"The white flames consumed Saraquael slowly, and he clung to me as he burned.

"Soon there was nothing left of him. Nothing at all.

"I felt the flame leave me. I returned to myself once more.

"Phanuel was sobbing. Lucifer was pale. Zephkiel sat in his chair, quietly watching me.

"I turned to Phanuel and Lucifer. 'You have seen the Vengeance of the Lord,' I told them. 'Let it act as a warning to you both.'

"Phanuel nodded. 'It has. Oh, it has. I . . . I will be on my way, sir. I will return to my appointed post. If that is all right with you?'

"He stumbled to the window and plunged into the light, his wings beating furiously.

"Lucifer walked over to the place on the silver floor where Saraquael had once stood. He knelt, stared desperately at the floor as if he were trying to find some remnant of the angel I had destroyed, a fragment of ash, or bone, or charred feather, but there was nothing to find. Then he looked up at me.

"'That was not right,' he said. 'That was not just.' He was crying; wet tears ran down his face. Perhaps Saraquael was the first to love, but Lucifer was the first to shed tears. I will never forget that.

"I stared at him impassively. 'It was justice. He killed another. He was killed in his turn. You called me to my function, and I performed it.'

"'But . . . he *loved*. He should have been forgiven. He should have been helped. He should not have been destroyed like that. That was *wrong*.'

"'It was His will.'

"Lucifer stood. 'Then perhaps His will is unjust. Perhaps the voices in the Darkness speak truly, after all. How *can* this be right?'

"'It is right. It is His will. I merely performed my function.'

"He wiped away the tears with the back of his hand. 'No,' he said, flatly. He shook his head, slowly, from side to side. Then he said, 'I must think on this. I will go now.'

"He walked to the window, stepped into the sky, and he was gone.

"Zephkiel and I were alone in his cell. I went over to his chair. He nodded at me. 'You have performed your function well, Raguel. Shouldn't you return to your cell to wait until you are next needed?'"

The man on the bench turned toward me: his eyes sought mine. Until now it had seemed – for most of his narrative – that he was scarcely aware of me; he had stared ahead of himself, whispered his tale in little better than a monotone. Now it felt as if he had discovered me and that he spoke to me alone, rather than to the air, or the City of Los Angeles. And he said:

"I knew that he was right. But I *couldn't* have left then – not even if I had wanted to. My aspect had not entirely left me; my function was not completely fulfilled. And then it fell into place; I saw the whole picture. And, like Lucifer, I knelt. I touched my forehead to the silver floor. 'No, Lord,' I said. 'Not yet.'

"Zephkiel rose from his chair. 'Get up. It is not fitting for one angel to act in this way to another. It is not right. Get up!'

"I shook my head. 'Father, you are no angel,' I whispered.

"Zephkiel said nothing. For a moment, my heart misgave within me. I was afraid. 'Father, I was charged to discover who was responsible for Carasel's death. And I do know.'

"'You have taken your Vengeance, Raguel.'

"'*Your* Vengeance, Lord.'

"And then He sighed and sat down once more. 'Ah, little Raguel. The problem with creating things is that they perform so much better than one had ever planned. Shall I ask how you recognized me?'

"'I . . . I am not certain, Lord. You have no wings. You wait at the center of the City, supervising the Creation directly. When I destroyed Saraquael, You did not look away. You know too many things. You . . .' I paused and thought. 'No, I do not know how I know. As You say, You have created me well. But I only understood who You were, and the meaning of the drama we had enacted here for You, when I saw Lucifer leave.'

NEIL GAIMAN

"'What did you understand, child?'

"'Who killed Carasel. Or, at least, who was pulling the strings. For example, who arranged for Carasel and Saraquael to work together on *Love*, knowing Carasel's tendency, to involve himself too deeply in his work?'

"He was speaking to me gently, almost teasingly, as an adult would pretend to make conversation with a tiny child. 'Why should anyone have "pulled the strings", Raguel?'

"'Because nothing occurs without reason; and all the reasons are Yours. You set Saraquael up: yes, he killed Carasel. But he killed Carasel so that I could destroy *him*.'

"'And were you wrong to destroy him?'

"I looked into His old, old eyes. 'It was my function. But I do not think it was just. I think perhaps it was needed that I destroy Saraquael, in order to demonstrate to Lucifer the Injustice of the Lord.'

"He smiled, then. 'And whatever reason would I have for doing that?'

"'I . . . I do not know. I do not understand – no more than I understand why You created the Dark or the voices in the Darkness. But You did. You caused all this to occur.'

"He nodded. 'Yes. I did. Lucifer must brood on the unfairness of Saraquael's destruction. And that – amongst other things – will precipitate him into certain actions. Poor sweet Lucifer. His way will be the hardest of all my children; for there is a part he must play in the drama that is to come, and it is a grand role.'

"I remained kneeling in front of the Creator of All Things.

"'What will you do now, Raguel?' he asked me.

"'I must return to my cell. My function is now fulfilled. I have taken Vengeance, and I have revealed the perpetrator. That is enough. But . . . Lord?'

"'Yes, child.'

"'I feel dirty. I feel tarnished. I feel befouled. Perhaps it is true that all that happens is in accordance with Your will, and thus it is good. But sometimes You leave blood on Your instruments.'

"He nodded, as if He agreed with me. 'If you wish, Raguel, you may forget all this. All that has happened this day.' And then He said, 'However, you will not be able to speak of this to any other angel, whether you choose to remember it or not.'

"'I will remember it.'

"'It is your choice. But sometimes you will find it is easier by far not to remember. Forgetfulness can sometimes bring freedom, of a sort. Now, if you do not mind—' He reached down, took a file from a stack on the floor, opened it '—there is work I should be getting on with.'

"I stood up and walked to the window. I hoped He would call me back, explain every detail of His plan to me, somehow make it all better. But He said nothing, and I left His Presence without ever looking back."

The man was silent, then. And he remained silent – I couldn't even hear him breathing – for so long that I began to get nervous, thinking that perhaps he had fallen asleep or died.

Then he stood up.

"There you go, pal. That's your story. Do you think it was worth a couple of cigarettes and a book of matches?" He asked the question as if it was important to him, without irony.

"Yes," I told him. "Yes. It was. But what happened next? How did you . . . I mean, if . . ." I trailed off.

It was dark on the street now, at the edge of daybreak. One by one the street lamps had begun to flicker out, and he was silhouetted against the glow of the dawn sky. He thrust his hands into his pockets. "What happened? I left home, and I lost my way, and these days home's a long way back. Sometimes you do things you regret, but there's nothing you can do about them. Times change. Doors close behind you. You move on. You know?

"Eventually I wound up here. They used to say no one's ever originally from LA. True as Hell in my case."

And then, before I could understand what he was doing, he leaned down and kissed me, gently, on the cheek. His stubble was rough and prickly, but his breath was surprisingly sweet. He whispered into my ear: "I never fell. I don't care what they say. I'm still doing my job, as I see it."

My cheek burned where his lips had touched it.

He straightened up. "But I still want to go home."

The man walked away down the darkened street, and I sat on the bench and watched him go. I felt like he had taken something from me, although I could no longer remember what. And I felt like something had been left in its place – absolution, perhaps, or innocence, although of what, or from what, I could no longer say.

An image from somewhere: a scribbled drawing of two angels in flight above a perfect city; and over the image a child's perfect handprint, which stains the white paper blood-red. It came into my head unbidden, and I no longer know what it meant.

I stood up.

It was too dark to see the face of my watch, but I knew I would get no sleep that day. I walked back to the place I was staying, to the house by the stunted palm tree, to wash myself, and to wait. I thought about angels and about Tink; and I wondered whether love and death went hand in hand.

The next day the planes to England were flying again.

I felt strange – lack of sleep had forced me into that miserable state in which everything seems flat and of equal importance; when nothing matters, and in which reality seems scraped thin and threadbare. The taxi journey to the airport was a nightmare. I was hot, and tired, and testy. I wore a T-shirt in the LA heat, my coat was packed at the bottom of my luggage, where it had been for the entire stay.

The airplane was crowded, but I didn't care.

The stewardess walked down the aisle with a rack of newspapers: the *Herald Tribune*, *USA Today*, and the *LA Times*. I took a copy of the *Times*, but the words left my head as my eyes scanned over them. Nothing that I read remained with me. No. I lie: somewhere in the back of the paper was a report of a triple murder: two women and a small child. No names were given, and I do not know why the report should have registered as it did.

Soon I fell asleep. I dreamed about fucking Tink, while blood ran sluggishly from her closed eyes and lips. The blood was cold and viscous and clammy, and I awoke chilled by the plane's air conditioning, with an unpleasant taste in my mouth. My tongue and lips were dry. I looked out of the scratched oval window, stared down at the clouds, and it occurred to me then (not for the first time) that the clouds were in actuality another land, where everyone knew just what they were looking for and how to get back where they started from.

Staring down at the clouds is one of the things I have always liked best about flying. That, and the proximity one feels to one's death.

I wrapped myself in the thin aircraft blanket and slept some more, but if further dreams came then they made no impression upon me.

A blizzard blew up shortly after the plane landed in England, knocking out the airport's power supply. I was alone in an airport elevator at the time, and it went dark and jammed between floors. A dim emergency light flickered on. I pressed the crimson alarm button until the batteries ran down and it ceased to sound; then I shivered in my LA T-shirt in the corner of my little silver room. I watched my breath steam in the air, and I hugged myself for warmth.

There wasn't anything in there except me; but even so, I felt safe and secure. Soon someone would come and force open the doors. Eventually somebody would let me out; and I knew that I would soon be home.

About the Authors

Peter Atkins was born in Liverpool, England, and now lives in Los Angeles. He is the author of the novels *Morningstar, Big Thunder* and *Moontown* and the screenplays *Hellraiser II, Hellraiser III, Hellraiser IV, Wishmaster* and *Prisoners of the Sun*. His short fiction has appeared in such anthologies as *The Museum of Horrors, Dark Delicacies II* and *Hellbound Hearts,* and periodocals including *Weird Tales, The Magazine of Fantasy and Science Fiction, Postscripts* and *Cemetery Dance*. A collection of his short fiction, *Rumours of the Marvellous,* was shortlisted for the British Fantasy Society Award. He blogs at: peteratkins.blogspot.com.

Peter M. Ball's first published SF story appeared in *Dreaming Again* in 2007, and since then his short fiction has appeared in publications such as *Fantasy, Strange Horizons, Apex Magazine, Interfictions II, Shimmer* and *Years Best SF 15*. His faerie-noir novella, *Horn,* was published in 2009 by Twelfth Planet Press, followed by *Bleed* in 2010. He lives in Brisbane, Australia, and can be found online at www.petermball.com and on twitter @ petermball.

Nathan Ballingrud won the Shirley Jackson Award for "The Monsters of Heaven". He's published fiction in *Naked City: Tales of Urban Fantasy, Lovecraft Unbound, Teeth: Vampire*

Tales and *Inferno: New Tales of Terror*, among other venues, and has been reprinted in Year's Best anthologies several times. His first book, *North American Lake Monsters: Stories*, is due from Small Beer Press in 2013.

Clive Barker is a novelist, playwright, screenwriter, artist, director and producer. Following the publication of his earliest short stories as *The Books of Blood* in 1984, Barker went on to write numerous bestselling novels, including *The Great and Secret Show*, *Weaveworld*, *Imajica*, *The Thief of Always*, *Everville*, *Sacrament*, *Galilee* and *Coldheart Canyon*. The first book of a children's series, *Abarat*, was published in 2002 to critical acclaim, as were *Abarat: Days of Magic, Nights of War* (2004) and *Abarat: Absolute Midnight* (2011). He is currently working on the fourth of five volumes for the series. As a screenwriter, director and film producer, he is credited with the Hellraiser and Candyman franchises, as well as *Nightbreed*, *Lord of Illusions*, *Gods and Monsters*, *The Midnight Meat Train*, *Book of Blood* and *Dread*. An accomplished painter and visual artist, Barker has had exhibitions in New York and Los Angeles.

Thanks to classic works such as *The Last Unicorn*, *Tamsin* and *The Innkeeper's Song*, **Peter S. Beagle** is acknowledged as one of America's greatest fantasy authors. In addition to stories and novels, he has written numerous teleplays and screen-plays, including the animated versions of *The Lord of the Rings* and *The Last Unicorn*, plus the "Sarek" episode of *Star Trek: The Next Generation*. He is also a poet, lyricist and singer/songwriter. In 2007, Beagle won the Hugo and Nebula Awards for his original novelette, "Two Hearts". For more details on Peter's career and upcoming titles, see http://www.conlanpress.com and www.facebook.com/petersbeagle.

Pat Cadigan is the author of numerous acclaimed short stories and five novels. Her first novel, *Mindplayers*, was nominated for the Philip K. Dick Memorial Award, and her second and third novels – *Synners* and *Fools* – both won the Arthur C. Clarke

Award. Her collection, *Patterns*, was honoured with the Locus Award. Cadigan's work has also been nominated for both the Hugo and Nebula awards. The author lived in Kansas City for many years, but has resided in London, England since 1996.

Sam Cameron is the author of a young adult mystery series set in the Florida Keys that includes *Mystery of the Tempest*, a finalist for ForeWord Book of the Year. Other books in that series include *The Secret of Othello* and *The Missing Juliet*. Her work has appeared in several anthologies for GLBTQ audiences, including *Speaking Out*, *The Boys of Summer* and *Women of the Dark Streets*. Visit her at fisherkey.wordpress.com.

A born and bred New Yorker, **Suzy McKee Charnas** served in the Peace Corps as a teacher in Nigeria, taught high school, and wrote curriculum for a drug abuse treatment program. She married in 1969, and she and her husband went to live in New Mexico where she began writing science fiction and fantasy full time. Her books and stories have won her various awards over the years, and a play made from her best-known novel, *The Vampire Tapestry*, has been staged on both coasts. She lectures and teaches about fantasy, SF and fiction-writing whenever she gets a chance to. Her website is www.suzymckeecharnas.com.

Neil Gaiman is the *New York Times* bestselling author of novels *Neverwhere, Stardust, American Gods, Coraline, Anansi Boys, The Graveyard Book* and (with Terry Pratchett) *Good Omens*; the Sandman series of graphic novels; and the story collections *Smoke and Mirrors* and *Fragile Things*. He has won numerous literary awards including the Hugo, the Nebula, the World Fantasy, and the Stoker Awards, as well as the Newbery medal.

Tanya Huff lives in rural Ontario and loves country life. A prolific author, her work includes many short stories, five fantasy series and a science fiction series. One of these, her Blood Books series, featuring detective Vicki Nelson, was adapted for television under the title *Blood Ties* (writing the ninth episode allowed her to finally use her degree in Radio and Television Arts). Her most recent novel is *The Wild Ways*. When not writing, she practises her guitar and spends too much time online. Her blog is: andpuff.livejournal.com.

Caitlín R. Kiernan is the author of several novels, including the award-winning *Threshold*, *Daughter of Hounds*, *The Red Tree*, *The Drowning Girl* and, most recently (writing as Kathleen Tierney), *Blood Oranges*. Her short fiction has been collected in *Tales of Pain and Wonder*; *From Weird and Distant Shores*; *To Charles Fort, with Love*; *Alabaster*; *A is for Alien*; and *The Ammonite Violin & Others*. Her erotica has been collected in two volumes, *Frog Toes and Tentacles* and *Tales from the Woeful Platypus*. Subterranean Press published a retrospective of her early writing, *Two Worlds and In Between: The Best of Caitlín R. Kiernan (Volume One)* in 2011 and collection *Confessions of a Five-Chambered Heart* in 2012. She lives in Providence, Rhode Island with her partner, Kathryn.

Jay Lake lives in Portland, Oregon, where he works on numerous writing and editing projects. His most recent books in traditional print are *Kalimpura* from Tor Books, and *Love In the Time of Metal and Flesh* from Prime Books. His short fiction appears regularly in literary and genre markets worldwide. Jay is a winner of the John W. Campbell Award for Best New Writer, and a multiple nominee for the Hugo and World Fantasy Awards. Jay can be reached via his website at www.jlake.com or www.twitter.com/jay_lake.

Tanith Lee has written and published 78 novels, 13 collections and around 300 short stories, ranging through SF, Fantasy, Horror, YA, Contemporary, plus Gay/Lesbian and Detective fiction. She has also won, or been short-listed for, many awards. In 2009, she was made a Grand Master of Horror. She lives on the Sussex Weald close to the sea, with her husband, writer/artist John Kaiine, and under the iron paw of two tuxedo cats.

Charles de Lint is a full-time writer and musician who presently makes his home in Ottawa, Canada, with his wife MaryAnn Harris. His most recent books are *Under My Skin* (Razorbill Canada, 2012; Amazon.com for the rest of the world) and *Eyes Like Leaves* (Tachyon Press, 2012). His first album *Old Blue Truck* came out in early 2011. For more information about his work, visit his website at www.charlesdelint. com. He's also on Facebook, Twitter and MySpace.

Now a #1 *New York Times* bestselling author, **George R. R. Martin** sold his first story in 1971 and has been writing professionally ever since. He spent ten years in Hollywood as a writer-producer, working on *The Twilight Zone, Beauty and the Beast* and various feature films and television pilots that were never made. Martin also edited the Wild Cards series, fifteen novels written by teams of authors. In the mid-1990s he returned to prose, and began work on his epic fantasy series, A Song of Ice and Fire. In April 2011, HBO premiered its adaptation of the first of that series, *A Game of Thrones*, and he was named as one of *Time*'s most influential people of the year. *A Dance With Dragons*, the fifth A Song of Ice and Fire book, was published in 2011. He lives in Santa Fe, New Mexico, with his wife Parris.

Sarah Monette grew up in Oak Ridge, Tennessee, one of the three secret cities of the Manhattan Project, and now lives in a 106-year-old house in the Upper Midwest with a great many books, two cats, one grand piano and one husband. Her PhD diploma (English Literature, 2004) hangs in the kitchen. She has published six novels and more than forty short stories (some of each in collaboration with Elizabeth Bear). Some of her Kyle Murchison Booth stories have been collected in *The Bone Key*; some of other short fiction in *Somewhere Beneath Those Waves*. Her next novel, *The Goblin Emperor*, will come out from Tor under the pen name Katherine Addison. Visit her online at www.sarahmonette.com.

Joyce Carol Oates published her first book in 1963 and has since published over fifty novels, as well as many volumes of short stories, poetry and non-fiction. Her novel *them* (1969) won the National Book Award, and her novels *Black Water* (1992), *What I Lived For* (1994), and *Blonde* (2000) were nominated for the Pulitzer Prize. Oates is the Roger S. Berlind '52 Professor in the Humanities with the Program in Creative Writing at Princeton University, where she has taught since 1978. Among her many honours are the PEN Center USA Award for Lifetime Achievement, Mailer Prize for Lifetime Achievement, Howard T. Behrman Award for Distinguished Achievement in the Humanities, National Book Critics Circle Ivan Sandrof Lifetime Achievement Award, F. Scott Fitzgerald Award for Lifetime Achievement in American Literature, and Bram Stoker Award for Life Achievement.

Richard Parks's fiction has appeared in such diverse places as *Asimov's Science Fiction*, *Realms of Fantasy*, *Lady Churchill's Rosebud Wristlet*, *Beneath Ceaseless Skies*, *Weird Tales* and numerous anthologies, including *Year's Best Fantasy* and *Fantasy: The Best of the Year*. He's been a finalist for both the World Fantasy Award and the Mythopoeic Award. His second novel, *To Break the Demon Gate*, is due out from PS Publishing in 2013. A collection of his Lord Yamada stories, *Yamada Monogatari: Demon Hunter*, is also slated for publication in 2013 by Prime Books. You can find his blog at www.richard-parks.com.

Norman Partridge's fiction includes horror, suspense and the fantastic – "sometimes all in one story" according to Joe Lansdale. Partridge's novel *Dark Harvest* was chosen by *Publishers Weekly* as one of the best one hundred books of 2006, and two short-story collections were published in 2010 – *Lesser Demons* from Subterranean Press and *Johnny Halloween* from Cemetery Dance. Other work includes the Jack Baddalach mysteries *Saguaro Riptide* and *The Ten-Ounce Siesta*, plus *The Crow: Wicked Prayer*, which was adapted for film. His work has received multiple Bram Stoker awards. He can be found on the web at NormanPartridge.com and americanfrankenstein.blogspot.com.

Kristine Kathryn Rusch has written a lot of bestselling, award-winning fiction under a variety of names, including Kristine Grayson, Kris DeLake, Kris Nelscott and, of course, her own name. She's the former editor of *The Magazine of Fantasy & Science Fiction*. Her entire thirty-year backlist is slowly returning to print, courtesy of WMG Publishing. For more information on her work, go to www.kristinekathynrusch.com.

Lucius Shepard's short fiction has won the Nebula Award, the Hugo Award, International Horror Guild Award, National Magazine Award, Locus Award, Theodore Sturgeon Award and the World Fantasy Award. His most recent book is a short fiction collection, *The Dragon Griaule*. Forthcoming are two novels, tentatively titled *The Piercefields* and, for young adults, *The End of Life As We Know It*.

John Shirley is the author of more than thirty novels. The latest is *Everything is Broken*. His numerous short stories have been compiled into eight collections including *Black Butterflies: A Flock on the Darkside*, winner of the Bram Stoker Award, International Horror Guild Award, and named as one of the best one hundred books of the year by *Publishers Weekly* and, most recently, *In Extremis: The Most Extreme Short Stories of John Shirley*. He has written scripts for television and film, and is best known as co-writer of *The Crow*. As a musician, Shirley has fronted several bands over the years and written lyrics for Blue Öyster Cult and others. To learn more about John Shirley and his work, visit john-shirley.com.

Stellan Thorne is a transatlantic queer geek. He writes speculative fiction from his perch in Manchester, where he lives with his husband and two cats.

Genevieve Valentine's first novel, *Mechanique: A Tale of the Circus Tresaulti*, won the 2012 Crawford Award and was nominated for the Nebula. Her short fiction has appeared in *Clarkesworld, Strange Horizons, Journal of Mythic Arts, Fantasy Magazine, Lightspeed, Apex* and others, and the anthologies *Federations, The Living Dead 2, The Way of the Wizard, Running with the Pack, Teeth* and more. Her story "Light on the Water" was a 2009 World Fantasy Award nominee, and "Things to Know About Being Dead" was a 2012 Shirley Jackson Award nominee. Her non-fiction and reviews have been published by NPR.org, *Strange Horizons, Lightspeed, Weird Tales, Tor.com* and *Fantasy.* Valentine is a co-author of *Geek Wisdom* (Quirk Books). Her appetite for bad movies is insatiable, a tragedy she tracks at glvalentine.livejournal.com.

Over the span of her fifty-year career, **Kate Wilhelm**'s writing has spanned the genres of mystery, science fiction, speculative fiction, fantasy and magical realism; psychological suspense, mimetic, comic, and family sagas, a multimedia stage production, and radio plays. Her works have been adapted for television and movies in the United States, England and Germany. Wilhelm's novels and stories have been translated to more than a dozen languages. She has contributed to *Quark, Orbit, The Magazine of Fantasy & Science Fiction, Locus, Amazing Stories, Asimov's Science Fiction, Ellery Queen's Mystery Magazine, Fantastic, Omni, Alfred Hitchcock's Mystery Magazine, Redbook* and *Cosmopolitan.* Wilhelm and her husband, Damon Knight (1922–2002), also provided invaluable assistance to numerous other writers over the years as teachers and lecturers. Kate Wilhelm currently lives in Eugene, Oregon. In her spare time she likes to garden.

Gene Wolfe worked as an engineer before becoming editor of trade journal *Plant Engineering.* He retired to write full time in 1984. Long considered to be a premier fantasy author, he is the recipient of the World Fantasy Lifetime Achievement Award, as well as Nebula, World Fantasy, Campbell, Locus,

British Fantasy and British SF Awards. Wolfe has been inducted into the Science Fiction Hall of Fame. His short fiction has been collected over a dozen times, most recently in *The Best of Gene Wolfe* (2009). His latest novel is *Peace.* Both are from Tor.

Chelsea Quinn Yarbro is the first woman to be named a Living Legend by the International Horror Guild (2006). She was honored in 2009 as a Bram Stoker Lifetime Achievement by the Horror Writers association and, in 2003, was named as Grand Master of the World Horror Convention. She is the recipient of the Fine Foundation Award for Literary Achievement (1993) and (along with Fred Saberhagen) was awarded the Knightly Order of the Brasov Citadel by the Transylvanian Society of Dracula in 1997. A professional writer since 1968, Yarbro has worked in a wide variety of genres, from science fiction to westerns and from young adult adventure to historical horror. Yarbro is the author of over eighty books, more than seventy works of short fiction, and more than two dozen essays and reviews. Best-known for her Count Saint-Germain series, *Commedia della Morte* (2012) is its twenty-fifth book and twenty-third novel. Her website is chelseaquinnyarbro.net.

Acknowledgements

"Frumpy Little Beat Girl" by Peter Atkins © 2010 Peter Atkins. First publication: *Rolling Darkness Revue 2010* (Earthling Publications). Published by permission of the author.

"One Saturday Night, with Angel" by Peter M. Ball © 2010 Peter M. Ball. First publication: *Sprawl*, ed. Alison Kranostein (Twelfth Planet Press). Published by permission of the author.

"Monsters of Heaven" by Nathan Ballingrud © 2007 Nathan Ballingrud. First publication: *Inferno: New Tales of Terror and the Supernatural*, ed. Ellen Datlow (Tor). Published by permission of the author.

"Lost Souls" by Clive Barker ©1985 Clive Barker. First publication: *Time Out #800*, 19 December 1985–1 January 1986. Published by permission of the author.

"Uncle Chaim and Aunt Rifke and the Angel" by Peter S. Beagle © 2008 Avicenna Development Corporation. First publication: *Strange Roads* (DreamHaven Books). Published by permission of the author.

"Angel" by Pat Cadigan © 1987 Pat Cadigan. First Publication: *Isaac Asimov's Science Fiction Magazine,* May 1987. Published by permission of the author.

"Come to Me" by Sam Cameron © 2012 Sam Cameron. First published: *Women of the Dark Streets: Lesbian Paranormal,* eds. Radclyffe and Stacia Seaman (Bold Stroke Books). Published by permission of the author.

"Now I Lay Me Down to Sleep" by Suzy McKee Charnas © 1991 by Suzy McKee Charnas. First publication: *A Whisper of Blood,* ed. Ellen Datlow (William Morrow). Published by permission of the author.

"Murder Mysteries" by Neil Gaiman © 1992 Neil Gaiman. First publication: *Midnight Graffiti,* eds. Jessica Horsting and James Van Hise (Warner). Published by permission of the author.

"Oh Glorious Sight" by Tanya Huff © 2001 Tanya Huff. First publication: *Oceans of Magic,* ed. Martin H. Greenberg and Brian M. Thomsen (DAW Books). Published by permission of the author.

"Alabaster" by Caitlín R. Kiernan © 2005 Caitlín R. Kiernan. First publication: *Subterranean Press Newsletter,* April and May 2005 issues. Published by permission of the author.

"The Goat Cutter" by Jay Lake © 2004 Joseph E. Lake Jr. First publication: *Greetings From Lake Wu* (Wheatlands Press). Published by permission of the author.

"The Big Sky" by Charles de Lint © 1995 Charles de Lint. First publication: *Heaven Sent: 18 Glorious Tales of the Angels,* ed. Peter Crowther (DAW Books). Published by permission of the author.